Thunder Rolling
on the High Plains

Charley Reynolds and George Custer's
Journey to the Little Big Horn

An Original Story

Thunder Rolling on the High Plains

Charley Reynolds and George Custer's
Journey to the Little Big Horn

An Original Story

Lester Stanley Orestad

SANTA FE

Sunstone books may be purchased for educational, business, or sales promotional use.
For information please write: Special Markets Department, Sunstone Press,
P.O. Box 2321, Santa Fe, New Mexico 87504-2321.

Book and Cover design ▶ Vicki Ahl
Body typeface ▶ Times New Roman
Printed on acid free paper

Library of Congress Cataloging-in-Publication Data

Orestad, Lester Stanley.
  Thunder rolling on the high plains : Charley Reynolds and George Custer's journey to the
Little Big Horn, an original story / by Lester Stanley Orestad.
    p. cm.
  ISBN 978-0-86534-838-7 (softcover : alk. paper)
  1. Reynolds, Charley, 1844-1876--Fiction. 2. Custer, George A. (George Armstrong),
1839-1876--Fiction. 3. Little Bighorn, Battle of the, Mont., 1876--Fiction. I. Title. II. Title:
Charley Reynolds and George Custer's journey to the Little Big Horn.
  PS3615.R465T58 2011
  813'.6--dc22
                                        2011033426

WWW.SUNSTONEPRESS.COM
SUNSTONE PRESS / POST OFFICE BOX 2321 / SANTA FE, NM 87504-2321 /USA
(505) 988-4418 / ORDERS ONLY (800) 243-5644 / FAX (505) 988-1025

Preface

I was introduced to western stories almost from birth. When I was ten years old I read my first book on Custer's Last Stand inspiring my interest. For years I read most everything western I could get my hands on. I thoroughly enjoy both the Red Man and the White Man's side of the story. From David Crockett and Daniel Boone, to Geronimo and Cochise, Sitting Bull and Crazy Horse, Charley Reynolds and George Custer, and on to the many fascinating characters of the Little Big Horn my passion grew. I co-authored with my wife a duo music album, called *Big Horn River*. The album contains 20 songs about people, places and events, surrounding Custer, the 7th Cavalry and the Little Big Horn.

My first visit to the battlefield was 33 years ago. From the very start something seemed amiss. The story I was hearing did not seem to fit. I wondered what really happened. I began to see that the real story was yet to be told.

Almost every summer my wife and I made one or two trips to the Little Big Horn. There were times when I was at the field for several months. I attended many events of the historical associations, the Custer Battlefield and Museum Association and the Little Big Horn Association. I personally met descendents George Custer the III and IV, along with Charley Custer, whom to many, was a close image of George Custer had he grown old. Over the years I acquired many books and firsthand accounts. While on the set of *Son of the Morning Star*, I rode horse back over parts of the field. I have spent many, many years researching the fascinating characters of the Little Big Horn. In 1990 I discovered two linchpin landmarks that verify my conclusions.

Over the years my interest changed from one character to another. Although there are many interesting characters, both Indian and white, my special interest settled on Charley Reynolds. I have met Charley's grand-nephew and namesake, Charley Reynolds. I have also talked with Claude Reynolds, who was quite old at the time. Claude was the son of William, Charley's older brother.

Among many brave men who have ridden the western plains, a number of them are well-known in the country's history. Some are legends. Others are regarded as heroes. Men like Jim Bridger, Wild Bill Hickok, John (liver eatin') Johnston, William (Billy the Kid) Bonney, Jedediah Smith, Lewis and Clark among others. And there are those who remain in the background. Even though they are every bit as efficient and courageous, perhaps more of a brave man than most, they remain obscured from history. Yet, they are ordinary and unassuming, not seeking out the notoriety as others have.

Charley Reynolds was such a man. Amongst those daring men who rode the western plains, men who knew Charley Reynolds, men such as George Crook, William (Buffalo Bill) Cody, George Custer and Luther (Yellowstone) Kelly all had stated that

Charley Reynolds was one of the greatest plainsmen of them all. One writer judged him as the most excellent rifle shot in the entire west.

Well-educated for the times and raised in a good home, the adventurous Charley Reynolds favored exploring the plains instead of the so-called good life. From Buffalo hunting, to trapping wolves, to Army courier, to scouting and guiding Reynolds rode the Great Plains. He spent three years of his life in close association with George Armstrong Custer. When the 7th Horse Cavalry rode out of Fort Lincoln, Dakota Territory, Charley Reynolds was there with Custer as a guide and scout. Their friendship shaped a remarkable story between a flamboyant, energetic, controversial commander and a brave, unassuming scout. This is the story that I tell.

Let it be said that there were several hundred survivors of the Little Big Horn. Then why did George Custer and Charley Reynolds die? When all is said and done the answer that stands out is: They were abandoned, deserted.

Had Reno and Benteen carried out their orders, there would have been a battle at the Little Big Horn with many more survivors. Daniel Knipe, a sergeant who survived the Little Big Horn fight, had stated: *"…if Reno and Benteen had carried out their orders Custer and the five troops would not have met their sad fate."*

Not only that, just two years after the fight, after a full examination of the battlefield, General Nelson Miles conclusions verify the author's findings. This never-been-told story ends with a factual portrayal of Custer's actions.

1

*I*ndian eyes peer from the darkness of a high butte. The half-breed Sioux, Mitch Boyer, works his arms then rubs his shoulders for warmth. On a distant ridge, a lone lobo wolf howls. Its sound echoes eerily through the Wolf Mountains. The night drags on. Across the ridge, another wolf emits its haunting bay. Boyer anxiously paces. His ears catch the soft pat, pat of moccasin feet, and he stops to listen. Straining in the darkness, he gazes over at his Crow companions who tramp their feet restlessly. Boyer moves over closer to the Indian scouts. With a low voice, the breed calls the Crows over, "We smoke a while." The Crows kneel down in a low spot, concealing themselves behind some scrub cedar trees. Boyer rolls and lights a white man cigarette then sighs, his nostrils savoring the sweet grass smell. He cups the match, holding it out. Silently, the Crows stoop to light. The reflections of orange flame from the match, light up their eyes, revealing an impatient anticipation.

Several hundred feet below the butte, two men sleep on the ground. Charley Reynolds tosses and turns restlessly to a reoccurring dream. *A giant black bird, fearful and strange, soars above him. Its talons shoot arrows of fire. It dives closer, and then hovers. Its huge wings flutter vigorously, generating a thunderous noise. Reynolds laughs out loud, as it suddenly dawns on him, that the wings make the thunder echo through the hills.*

Swooping down, arrows of fire again shoot forth from its talons. Charley Reynolds jerks and quivers to avoid the fiery, feathered shafts. He hears the fear laden voice of an Indian Woman, "Old men talk, say Thunderbird angry, goes across prairie. Arrows of fire shoot the earth, Thunderbird big!" Frantically, Charley Reynolds shakes his head.

With a terrifying screech, the bird dives straight at him. Its long, sharp talons viciously spread. Charley raises his arms, shielding his face. Stiffening his legs and loud enough to wake up the dead, he yells out!

Nearby, Seventh Cavalry, Lieutenant Charles Varnum, sits up with a shout, "What! Wake up! Reynolds! Wake up! You must have seen your grandmother!"

Unnerved, Charley rises up, staring into the darkness. He wipes sweat from his face, and then slumps back down. Through eyes heavy from lack of sleep, Varnum gazes over at him, and then rests on his elbow. Soon, both men fall back asleep, Reynolds breathing easy.

Atop the high butte, Crow scout, Harry Moccasin, mouths his cigarette then drags long and hard. He puts the cigarette out with his fingers, making sure there is no spark to give away their presence. He quietly steps out from behind the cedars and pine trees. He looks out from the butte. Silently, he points to the western horizon. At long last, false dawn begins to unfold across Montana Territory.

White-man-runs-Him, excitedly waves his arm, pointing. Twelve miles away, scattered patches of light splinters over the hills. The breed Boyer turns, "Beyond hills flows the Greasy Grass River." Carefully, the keen eyed scouts observe the bench lands and valley beyond the river. In their constant warring against the Sioux, and hunting their life's blood, the buffalo they've spied from this lookout many times. Inherited warriors from birth, their well-trained eyes strain for signs.

Harry Moccasin glances at the seventeen-year-old scout, Curly, who remains silent. Moccasin then sites westward. He narrows an eye while he looks down his arm, "I see plenty smoke,"

White-man-runs-Him nods, then gestures, "Many white horses."

Boyer mutters a deep guttural sound and then motions Curly to follow him. They move to the trail leading down the hill. "We go below, awake large nose Soldier Chief."

Below the hill, Curly signs excitedly as he and Boyer approach the sleeping pair. "We all have found the Sioux," Boyer says, nudging the two men with his foot.

Curly nods and gestures while Boyer speaks in broken English, "Lieutenant! Arise! Arise! We see plenty smoke. Many Sioux across hills, Little Big Horn."

An eerie silence hangs heavy in the air. Even the wolves have stopped their mournful cries. After what seems like a long time, Reynolds quickly leans forward. Varnum sits up with a yawn, and then rubs his eyes. "Sun's not even up yet, Boyer."

Reynolds leaps to his feet. He yawns then stretches, "Lieutenant Varnum! Light comes early here!" Reynolds grabs his Sharps carbine and starts up the hill, "The Crows know this land. Most Indians I know are eagle eyed, Lieutenant."

"For Pete sakes, I rode over fifty miles yesterday, Reynolds!"

Boyer eyes the Seventh Horse Cavalry's Chief of Scouts, "Varnum, You miss trail sunset last."

"Lead the way, Boyer," Varnum glares, hooking his field glass strap over his neck. Then shouldering his carbine he follows.

Part way up the hill Reynolds stops abruptly, "Listen!" The others halt.

Varnum looks uneasy. "What is it, Reynolds?"

"I heard something."

The others listen for a moment, then Varnum moves ahead, "You're jumpy, Reynolds you're hearing things."

Gasping for breath for a moment, they stop at the top. Reynolds shakes his head. He swears he had heard a loud rumble—like thunder way off in the distance. Curly gives Reynolds a peculiar look and then follows Boyer.

Varnum then motions the men to spread out. Each picking a spot carefully, they begin to glass the broken land.

Charley Reynolds blinks his eyes. In the far western sky, narrow fingers of lightning coruscate to the earth. He cocks an ear as the low roll of distant thunder swells across the land. He turns to see if the others attested the phenomenon. They continue to gaze steady to the front. He wonders inquisitively, why they've heard nothing unusual? Is his mind playing tricks?

His Arapahoe sweetheart, Running-creek-Woman, flashes before him. Startled awake, in the middle of the night, a violent thunderstorm raged across the land of the Dakotas. Fiery bolts of lightning lit up the inside of their teepee. Again, he hears her trembling words, *"Old men talk, say Thunderbird angry, goes across prairie. Arrows of fire shoot the earth, Thunderbird big!"* In an audible undertone, Charley tries to make sense of her words, "Thunderbird angry. Arrows of fire. Thunderbird big. What does this mean, Thunder Bird big? What does this..."

"Tell the Crows I don't see any sign, Boyer," Varnum's expression snaps Reynolds out of reverie.

Rattled, Charley takes a quick glance at the lieutenant, and then as if Varnum's words were not uttered he returns to the task at hand. Raising his glasses, he looks across the hills.

Varnum gives Reynolds an odd look, and then glances at the breed.

"Beyond bluffs, see smoke beyond Greasy Grass!" The Crows point towards the river

"I wish you'd stop talking like an Indian, Boyer! I don't see signs of any Sioux."

"I am Indian, Lieutenant."

"You're only half."

"You send talk paper, General?"

After a while, Varnum finally nods, taking a writing pad and pencil from his pocket. Scribbling a note, he hurries off, shouting, over his shoulder, "I'll have one of the Arickaras ride back."

Charley watches him disappear down the hill. He then glasses the country while he listens to the Crows chatter. Behind him to the east, Charley gazes at the blood-red sun that suddenly erupts over the horizon, its splinters of light spreading across the Wolf Mountains and the hills and ridges to the west. He pulls his watch from his pocket, opening it. He looks at the time. It is nearly 5:00 a.m. The sun has been up well over a half hour, he believes. For a brief moment, he stares sadly at the inscription on the timepiece.

Four hours later, George Custer steps from the trail. His heavy breathing announces his arrival at the top. Another Crow and several Ree scouts come up behind. Custer removes his hat, wiping the sweat from his brow. He runs his fingers through his receding, strawberry blond hair. The energetic General strides his nearly six-foot 170-pound wiry frame over to the others. He brushes the dust from the fringes of his white deer skinned jacket. The General gazes over the land, long and hard. There is something about this man that catches the eye. He is a man with presence. With his full, bushy mustache and his white deerskin pants, that are tucked into black high-top boots with brass spurs, he looks every bit the plainsman that he is.

George Custer scrutinizes Boyer, then Varnum, "I have got mighty good eyes and I can see no Indians!"

"General Custer, that's two of us that don't see anything."

"Varnum, your eyes are blurred! Glued shut, like hide glue the women make."

"Da...darn you frog," Varnum had started to swear but quickly remembered Custer's aversion to his officers cussing. "I suppose Boyer, your eyes are any better!" Varnum grimaces.

"Heap, Sioux!" The older, wiser Half-yellow-Face, clenches the cigarette in his lips, and then nods several times. Puffs of smoke emit from his mouth and nose, as he utters a few grunts.

The wiry, energetic George Custer gazes out from the lookout, thoughtfully. During the Civil War he had reached the rank of Major General. Now, a Lieutenant Colonel, George Custer's Civil War rank merited the title. To most of the officers and men he was known as the General. He rubs his three-day stubble of whiskers, and then turns, "Lieutenant Varnum, the Rees brought your note—smoke ponies could be seen."

Varnum eyeballs each of the Crows. He then looks at Boyer. "The Crows claimed they could see smoke ponies, I could not distinguish anything."

"If you don't find more Indians in that valley than you ever saw together before you may hang me."

George Custer studies Mitch Boyer, long and hard. "It would do a damned sight of good to hang you wouldn't it?"

Varnum gives Custer a surprised look, "General Custer, I've never heard you cuss."

Charley Reynolds who stands off by himself, weighs the conversation, then mulls over his experience. His sixteen years on the plains—how quickly they seemed to have passed.

He considers that most of the officers and enlisted men had fought and trailed Indians since sixty-six. The 7th Horse had trailed the Sioux and Cheyenne, right near eighty-five miles from the Yellowstone River. A month or so before, these same Sioux and Cheyenne had repeatedly harassed Colonel Gibbon's Montana column on the north side of the Yellowstone. Gibbon's Chief of Scouts, Lieutenant Bradley and his Crow scouts, had spied these same Indians over a month ago. There was much speculation as to why Gibbon did not attack these same Indians. They had shot and killed several of Gibbon's soldiers that they caught out hunting. They had stolen Gibbon's horses. Time after time, they had shot at his soldiers and downright defied Gibbon to attack them.

Reynolds continues to mull over what has happened. He understands that in this country, looks can be deceiving. A weed, or tall grass on a rise of ground, can appear to be a tree. A man on a horse, on a distant ridge, can emerge to look like a giant.

Unless they are a huge group on a wide-open prairie, he understands that you can't see Indians from twelve miles away, only signs. Towards the river there are bluffs, hills and trees, which intervene. But the Crows had first spotted the smoke and horses at sunup before the wavy heat waves begin to fill the air.

The gruff words of his old mentor, Gabe Green, ring loud in his head, "White men need water. Indians need water. Horses and mules can only go so many days without." The creeks here are mostly all dry. What water there is turns out to be alkaline and undrinkable. The last water they had was before leaving the camp on the Rosebud. Anyone with half a lick of sense can figure out that once the Sioux trail turned west, those tracks they been following—lead right to the waters of the Little Big Horn River. There had been countless speculation by both the officers and the enlisted men as to which way the Indians would move. Would they travel upstream towards their favorite hunting grounds on Rotten Grass creek? Or would they head downstream towards the Big Horn River? What about Tullock's Creek?

"Lieutenant Varnum, get Reynolds over here," Custer says brusquely. "He's the best there is. Charley will know."

"He's right there, looking, Sir," Varnum motions to Charley, "Hey Reynolds."

Hurrying over, Charley leans his carbine against a scrub bush, and then glasses their front. He scans the bluffs and hills covered with sagebrush and stunted cedar and pine trees. Large patches of green grass here and there, huge boulders, dot the hills, intermingled with yellowish brown and reddish dirt patches. Beyond the hills is the Little Horn Valley. George Custer carefully notes his quiet scout, "What do you see, Reynolds?"

Charley mulls over Custer's words. He recalls early this morning, dead ahead to the west, an ominous smoke cloud hovering over the Little Big Horn Valley. After a while, Charley lowers his glasses, his soft voice penetrates the still morning air, and, "You'll find enough Indians in that valley to keep you fighting two or three days, Sir." Charley's words hang heavy in the air. There is a haunting silence.

Custer quietly fingers his long mustache, gazing from one to the other, and then eyeballing Reynolds.

Boyer breaks the spell. "We go middle night, hide. Morning come, see many Sioux. Start, shoot!"

"Well split my windpipe, Boyer. Why don't you talk like a White Man?" Varnum snaps, a little excited.

"I not White Man!"

"I've heard the talk your father was a Frenchman, a frog," Varnum fires.

The Crows chatter and break into quiet laughter. Charley Reynolds has caught their meaning and chuckles. Varnum inquisitively watches him.

Charley continues to chuckle, "The Crows say Frenchman is not a White man, he's a trader."

The others join in the sport, keeping their laughter restrained. General Custer discreetly snickers, "Captain French would surely enjoy this."

More laughter. Somehow it seems to ease the tension. Custer raises his hand. The others listen intently.

"Boyer's right, Lieutenant. I will keep the regiment hidden today. Morning come, we see many Sioux, start, shoot."

The Crows can understand some of the White man talk. They chortle at Custer's mimic of their talk. Half-yellow-Face chatters excitedly. Custer looks curiously at the Crow Indian, "What'd he say, Boyer?"

"The Crow leader, Half-yellow-Face, says we must attack now. He says the Sioux have seen our camp"

Varnum heaves a disgusted sigh, "Ah, buffalo dung, Boyer."

"The Lieutenant is afraid of the Sioux," Boyer stares at Varnum.

Custer rolls his eyes to and fro, glancing from Lieutenant Varnum to the breed. He's aware of Boyer's reputation. For many years, Boyer has traveled and rode this country. His knowledge of his adopted tribal brother's Crow land, now Sioux, is unexcelled—even down to the miles. The General mulls over Boyer's French heritage—his round dark eyes, his nose and strong chin. But his high cheekbones look Sioux. With the calfskin vest he wears, he looks Indian. "The Lieutenant has a strong heart. He has fought the Sioux before. I say our camp has not been discovered. I will keep the regiment concealed today, attack tomorrow," Custer snaps his riding quirt against his tall cavalry boots.

For a moment Boyer stares at Custer, then turns to the Crow scouts. Half-yellow-Face and Goes Ahead chatter in broken English. "Son Morn-ing Star. Bad plan. Sioux make big talk. Say Sioux must make war soldier."

"I wish the devil they'd speak English," Varnum shouts.

Half-yellow-Face mutters something in Crow. A little on edge Custer stammers. "Wh...what's that he says, Boyer?"

"The Crows Half-yellow-Face, say the Sioux have discovered the camp of the soldiers. Sioux will come, start heap shoot in hills. Plan bad."

Custer is steadfast. "I say again, we have not been seen! That camp has not seen us. I want to wait until dark and then we will place our army around the Sioux camp!"

Boyer rattles away speaking for Half-yellow-Face. "That plan is bad. It should not be carried out. We must attack at once. Those Indians will go straight for the camp. They will warn the village! The Sioux will attack! In this rough ground they will clean us out!"

The Crows again point excitedly. Boyer interprets, "Look beyond the bluffs. Big village. Look for the pony herd!"

"Only thing I see is two teepees! Over yonder there, past those white bluffs. They're in that large opening," Varnum responds.

Curly points beyond the hills and makes sign talk.

"Look for worms on the grass," Boyer interprets, "Like maggots on a rotting buffalo hide, all bunched together."

The others look at Reynolds, seemingly waiting for his respected opinion. Charley could read trail sign with the best of them, but the quiet scout silently looks

12

out. Catching his grave stare, they eyeball one another, sensing that Charley knows what is out there.

He sees the disappearing smoke cloud, the black mass of moving Sioux horses, and he's sure Custer can see the signs. From what he perceives about George Custer, he figures that he just wants to be sure, that's all.

Custer gives Reynolds the eye. Reynolds points, then un-straps his field glasses, reaching them out to Custer. The General gazes long and hard, finally he nods. He then examines high bluffs, maybe a mile away to their front. Charley watches. He can see the wheels turning. A fleeting thought runs through his mind—his days with the 7th Horse. He has spent the last three years in close association with the General. He understands his character. Very thoughtfully he nods as he watches Custer form a mental picture. Charley knows that he is planning his strategy.

The General removes a pair of glasses from a case hanging from his shoulder. "Lieutenant DeRudio was kind enough to lend his new glasses to me. Should see something with these, DeRudio says they're from Austria, the best," Custer smiles as he hands Reynolds back his glasses. He raises DeRudio's borrowed glasses to look, then lowers them. He turns to Reynolds and again nods, "I guess we'll get through them in one day, Lonesome Charley," The General gives a nervous smile, then turns and begins the descent to the bottom. Charley confidently cuts a smile and follows. Not a word is spoken, as the men reach the Ree Indians, who have stayed back to guard the horses.

Creaking saddle leather and the muffled sound of hoof beats breaks the morning stillness. Custer reins onto the path winding to the north. The trail wise horses avoid the sagebrush, stunted cedar and sparse pine trees. An eerie howl of a lone wolf causes the General to rein up. Suspiciously, he and his silent scout stare off into the hills. George Custer glances at the Crows, and then nods to Varnum, who leads off.

Custer motions Reynolds ahead and falls in behind. He contemplates his well-liked scout. He wonders, now that they are close to the Sioux, what is going through Charley's mind? In the land of the Dakotas, far and wide, Charley Reynolds was known as, "the greatest plainsman." For several years, he had supplied the forts along the Missouri River with fresh meat.

General George Crook had stated that Lonesome Charley Reynolds could get more meat with fewer bullets than any hunter or scout he had ever met.

Reynolds was not a big man. Strong and well built, he stood around five foot eight inches tall. Some called him, "Silent Charley" the Rees called him, "Lucky Man" and to the men of the romantic 7th United States Cavalry, some called him, "Chief Scout" to most of the men he was known as, "Lonesome Charley."

Sheltered Ravine, Wolf Mountains, Montana Territory, June 25, 1876, 10:00 a.m.

While Custer's party was at the high butte, the command had moved to a sheltered dry ravine just below the crest of the divide. Custer's party reins up at the campsite. All but Reynolds, dismount. Charley peels off, passing Lieutenant Cooke, Captains Tom Custer and Myles Keogh, rushing by. The officers nod to Charley, but their look is urgent. They hurriedly ride up to Custer and dismount.

Charley finds a likely place to rest. He dismounts, sits down and leans his back against a scrub pine tree. He is much surprised when General Custer walks away from his officers, then stops. Custer's grave look is deeply troubling. Custer stares at the hills for a moment before shouting to his Adjutant, "Lieutenant Cooke. Sound officer's call!"

"Aye, Sir," Lieutenant Cooke swings into the saddle, then spurring his charger forward, Cooke responds briskly. Charley watches as he stops abruptly to address the trumpeter.

Charley mulls over what has taken place the past couple of days. The Sioux and Cheyenne had left a broad path for the 7th to follow. The ground is chopped and torn apart by their trailing lodge poles. In places, the trail had broadened out to more than a quarter mile wide. All of the sign pointed to thousands of Indians and their ponies passing here. Of all the well-watered, good hunting and camping spots along the river, those Indians had set up their camp circles in the least expected place.

Not one of the commanding lieutenants had even considered that the Sioux would be in this most ominous place on the Little Big Horn.

Charley's gut feeling tells him that the 7th's expected junction with General Terry's column, is in serious peril. Surely, Charley thinks logically, the supporting Montana Column is headed straight for trouble. If the full warrior force strikes those five companies of the Seventh Infantry with only four companies of the Second Cavalry and a battery of three Gatling guns, some 377 odd soldiers, it will be a massacre. The Gatling guns might help but they were always troublesome. On Reno's scout they lagged behind, holding up the column. At times they proved to be downright dangerous to the men assigned to their detail. Only one thing will prevent that disaster in the making.

But Charley recalls Custer's words at the lookout, the 7th regiment would stay hidden the rest of the day. They would move in to attack the next day in the early morning.

On a distant ridge, a lone lobo wolf howls. As if in a raucous duet, the bugle sounds from the bivouac. Charley looks out into Montana's great ruggedness to contemplate. He knows what the men of the 7th Cavalry are about to face. He listens to the cries of the wolf, and the haunting notes from the bugle, echo across the Wolf Mountains. Over and over in his mind, his dream haunts him. *"Thunderbird angry, Thunderbird big."* What does this mean, Thunder Bird big? What does this mean? Maybe it's his painful left hand he reasons. It's been sore for days. But the surgeon,

Doctor Porter, has looked at it and John Burkman fixed some kind of southern poultice for it.

As the resonance fades and quiet comes to the hills, Lonesome Charley Reynolds readily slips back to his younger years.

2

Back Home Again Pardee Kansas December 1866

*T*he news of Charley's father, Dr. Reynolds' death catches him off guard. William tries to console his younger brother.

"Don't take it so hard, Charley. It was an accident. Father drowned while on a trip to Emporia for provisions. His wagon overturned on the Cottonwood River. There's nothing you could have done—whether you were here or not."

But Charley feels badly. "I should have stayed home and gone into practice like he wanted me to," his voice faltering. "At least I would have been here to help with the farm and things. Do you think I was a disappointment to him, Will?"

"You oughtn't to be talking that way. Father wasn't disappointed with any of his children. He knew we were all different. Get hold of yourself. No one's at fault."

By spring, Charley has come to terms with his emotions and begins taking an interest in Will's farm again. His sister-in-law has given birth to another child, and grass shoots in the pasture herald the new season.

Charley's mind wanders, as the horses chaff at the bit, struggling to pull the plow. He pays little attention as the horses stop on their own, looking back with a curious nicker. He finally notices his brother breaking a proud-looking, red-colored buckskin. Charley ties his reins to the plow handle and walks over.

"Well, which one of us is better, Charley? Are you going to let me do all the work, or are you going to show me how much your horsemanship has improved?"

Charley grabs the homemade rawhide hackamore and slips it over the saddled horse's nose. "He's a good-looking animal, Will," he remarks as the horse gives a hearty tug at the new restraint. "Powerful too! What's his name?"

"I haven't named him yet. I'm as bad as my wife. She hasn't named the baby either."

"Maybe she's waiting for you," Charley smiles.

"I have trouble remembering which names have been used and which haven't—what with all our stepsisters and stepbrothers and my own too. But we'll talk about that later. What do you think we should call this fellow?"

"Red," Charley gives a pleasing grin.

"Suits him all right, you like Big Red?"

Charley nods while he sizes up the horses' build. He's surely a likeable animal, well proportioned he thinks, as he gently rubs the soft sheen of his coat. Turning towards Will Charley grins. "He wears a pleasing color, Will. My favorite—claybank red."

"He and Rusty would make a good pair. I want you to have him, Charley."

Not sure what to say, Charley turns sheepishly away.

"Well," Will says, grabbing the mecate from Charley's hand, and slipping it over Red's bare neck. "If you're not going to ride him, I guess I'll have to show you how."

Will rides around, reining left and then right without difficulty. He hasn't the nerve to tell Charley that he's been training the horse for more than a month.

"Pretty fair, Will," Charley yells. "He's well behaved—got a heart too!"

"You know your horses, Charley. That's one thing we both inherited from our father. I know he was proud of us, even if we didn't follow in his profession."

Will urges the horse into a gallop. Suddenly a huge rattlesnake slithers across Red's path, coiling to strike. Charley's spine tingles at the unmistakable sound of the rattles. He loathes snakes as he fears them. Before he can react it is too late. Red screams, then bolts tossing William from the saddle. Charley grimaces at Will's sigh. His back hits the ground with a thud, his breath emits with a groan. "No!" Charley yells then sprints to help seeing that Will's foot is hung up in the stirrup.

"Whoa, boy. Easy fellow, whoa!" Red snorts, then whirls, flipping then dragging his brother, like a Sioux granddaughter doll that Charley had watched the young Indian girls play with. A sickening fear for his brother comes over him. Charley slows, he knows if he moves fast now it will panic Red. And who knows what the outcome will be? A memory instantly flashes to mind of a neighbor, who was killed, when dragged across the prairie by a panicky horse. If Red bolts across this vast prairie, there's no way on God's green earth he'll be able to stop him. "Easy, Red. Easy," Charley makes the kissing sound with his lips, "Whoa, boy. Whoa now."

Red slows, wild eyed and snorting. His eyes glued on Red, Charley moves too far. Breathing heavy, little beads of sweat form on his forehead, running into his eyes. The rattler—his tongue darting hither and thither is close enough to nail him. His monstrous head darts from side to side.

It is weird, Charley sees the snake, but he's only aware of the large rattles—the largest he's ever seen. Charley cringes as the beady eyes of the rattler hones in on him coiled to strike.

Out of the corner of his eye Charley sees William roll onto his stomach. Thank God his foot comes loose from the stirrup. Jumping up, Will yells. "Don't move! Hold still!"

"I hate them slimy creatures," grits Charley.

All at once, Red whirls screaming, bucking, screaming back and forth he runs, stomping the ground at the rattler. Uncoiling, the rattler crawls away through the grass. Charley hurries over to the closest thing he can find, an old forked branch.

Sprinting hard he approaches the riled snake with caution. After several attempts he pins the hissing coil to the ground. His aim is poor, leaving the head and neck free to strike.

Lightning fast the serpent strikes, barely missing. Feeling the branch is about to break, Charley yells. "Do something quick! This stick is about to…" He leaps back at another strike.

Will darts off to grab a nearby pitchfork, yelling, "Hold on, Charley!" Running back he stabs the monstrosity. At the same time, Charley's stick breaks in half. He sighs while he stares at his brother. They shudder at the terrifying rattles of the last dying quivers of the snake. Red stomps then snorts, William utters a relieved grin, "Darndest' thing I've ever seen! That horse hates snakes!"

"Likely because he has been raised wild," Charley chuckles. "Good boy, Red." He walks over to Red, who stomps his feet, still snorting.

"Hold on," Will says, spearing the snake then heaving it as far as he can with the pitchfork. Both Will and Charley suddenly break into bursts of relieved laughter while patting and praising Red.

"Should have seen the look on your face, Charley," Will laughs.

"Kinda looked scared yourself," Charley retorts. "I hate rattlesnakes."

Days later, Charley lifts his head as the fresh breezes of April catch his senses. He sniffs the wind. Will watches as Charley gazes longingly across the plains.

Several weeks later, at evening time, Will and his wife Jemima sit at the supper table. Charley approaches, seating himself. "I forgot to tell you that I have a namesake in Colorado."

"Oh do tell," Will says, wondering if his brother is going to reveal some scandalous tale involving the young Spanish girl in New Mexico.

"It's not what you're thinking, Will. The other Charley is a mule."

Jemima squeals. "A mule? Why that's an insult, Charley."

"Not at all, really. Gabe Green's mules are very special to him. He had to replace old Joe and named the new animal after me. I think it's an honor, in a way."

"Well, if that isn't the silliest thing I ever heard!" Jemima exclaims, joining with Will in a fit of laughter.

"I just don't think it's all that funny. I only mentioned it because I thought it was time you gave my nephew a name. He's almost two months old! I would be honored if you'd let me choose a name."

Will looks pleased and waits for his wife's response.

"Of course, Charley. Why, we could name him after you. Charles Alexander Reynolds."

"If you don't mind, I'd rather he didn't have my middle name. Do you like Charles Edwin?"

"That has a nice sound to it, Charley," Will remarks.

"I like it, Will," his wife agrees. "Let's send for Uncle Thomas to Baptize him right away before Charley leaves."

"That's a fine idea, dear. I'll ride up to Atchinson and fetch him in the morning."

"I'll go with you, Will," Charley says. "I was planning to leave in the morning but one day's delay won't make a lot of difference—especially on such an occasion."

While in Atchison, Charley waits on the street for Will. Two men approach. "Excuse me friend, I was told you are the famous hunter, Charles Reynolds."

Charley quietly smiles.

"My trader friend, Jeb Walmsley," the bearded Englishman in his forties steps forward, thrusting out his hand. Charley, with a look of curiosity, returns the shake. "Walmsley here is headed for Fort Dodge in Southwestern Kansas. He needs a guide. I hear tell that you're the best"

Charley politely replies, "I don't know, I was..."

Walmsley's friend urges, "Walmsley is a mite fine trader. He'd be much beholden to you. Besides, he's all alone."

Charley reluctantly agrees to travel with the egocentric salesman, "I was planning on riding West anyway."

"Then you'll do it," as the friend put it, "keep an eye on him." Walmsley's friend rattles on. "Uprisings among the Kiowa, Cheyenne and Arapaho tribes, brought on by recent railroad expansion, among other things, has raised concern for the safety of the White Man. It's unsafe for those who travel alone."

Reynolds and Walmsley argue at first over the route they should take, but after listening to Charley's reputation from some others in town, Walmsley is convinced that they should start out for the Republican River. While Charley is amused by the trader's pluck, his disregard for danger is unnerving, and he has to remind him constantly of the threat of Indian attack.

Nevertheless, the pair travel for more than a week without mishap, eventually reaching the Smoky Hill Trail near Fort Riley. From there, after replenishing supplies and taking on fresh rations, they head in a southerly direction, crossing the Solomon and Saline Rivers. Even Charley is surprised that they have not attracted the attention of the Indians, for Walmsley's wagon is surely the noisiest thing on wheels.

Fully laden with blankets, beads, foodstuffs from the east and other trade goods the pots and pans hanging on the outside, clang and rattle incessantly as they plod across the prairie. Surprisingly, another week passes without seeing a sign of man or beast. It is unusual indeed.

Suddenly, Charley reins to a stop. He spots telltale smoke several miles away. He remains steadfast while surveying the country. "Com'on, Rusty. Let's catch up with Walmsley," he spurs off at the gallop.

That evening while making camp near the Saline River, Reynolds trots up. Walmsley stares at the grass along the riverbank. It has been burned off.

"Must have been a thunderbolt, eh, Reynolds?"

"No," Charley replies quietly. "Cheyenne."

"Cheyenne my foot! Why ever would they light a bloody fire like that?"

"It keeps the buffalo from heading further north into Sioux Territory. When they find their food supply burned up they instinctively turn back."

"Really!" Walmsley grunts, pondering for a moment the probability of Charley's explanation. "I say, Reynolds, wherever did you collect all this Indian lore?"

"Oh, I read whenever I can. Traveled with an Osage Indian last summer too. He taught me many Indian customs. When I was eighteen I went into the mountains with an old trapper, Gabe Green." Rather then dwell on his own accomplishments, Charley changes the subject. "And you Jeb? Your friend in Atchinson says you've had many dealings with the Indians yourself."

Spurred on by an abundant supply of Scotch, Jeb Walmsley recants his adventures with the, "Red Man," in infinite detail. Charley thought he'd never stop talking. It was clear the man had the experience all right, but he evidently hadn't learned much from it.

The next morning, Reynolds hitches the horses and is ready to leave. He hasn't mentioned the smoke he saw yesterday. "We must travel cautiously, Jeb. We'll stay on the Smoky Hill Trail, no matter what. Stage stations are about fifteen miles apart. With the violent Indian attacks in the region, I'm sure the army is patrolling the route." Jeb scoffs then reins the wagon off. "Haaaya! Get up. Haaaya!"

Charley wipes the sweat from his brow and stares at the sun. "Must be getting close to noon," he mutters to himself as he checks his timepiece. He's not surprised. It is about noon. Suddenly, his attention is drawn to a familiar sound—the muffled sound of hoof beats clanging swords and tin cups, the distinct sound of rattling carbine stocks in their sockets. He is startled and wheels around, only to see: a large unit of cavalry approach from behind. The venerable General Hancock waves his hand, "Whoaaa!," as he stops to talk with the trader and his quiet partner.

"You and your men are doing a splendid job, Colonel," Walmsley says unaware of his misnomer. "Why we've been on the road more than a fortnight and haven't encountered a Red Man yet!"

General Hancock stares coldly into Jeb Walmsley's eyes. "There've been a number of raids around these parts. The Kiowa wiped out a whole family not more than a day's ride from here. Scalped them. Go take a look for yourself if you don't believe it!"

Charley stares at Hancock then Walsmley, as he recalls the smoke he had seen yesterday. His eyes miss little and he notices many of the officers ride thoroughbreds, and effectively changes the subject, "Your men have been afforded the finest horseflesh, General. I especially admire that good-looking animal over there."

"You mean Custer's horse?"

"That's Custer? George Armstrong Custer?"

"Yes. You know him?"

"No. But I've certainly heard about him. I was in the Tenth Kansas myself."

"What's your name, son?"

"Reynolds, Sir."

"Not Charley Reynolds, surely?"

"Yes, Sir."

"I've been hearing your name all over Kansas, son. I expected you to be at least ten feet tall and carrying a cannon for a rifle." He chuckles. "You're somewhat of a legend whether you know it or not."

Walmsley butts in. "That's the bloody Kings' truth, Colonel. Why Charles is the best rifle shot anywhere!"

The General sneers slightly at Walmsley then turns to Charley. "We could use a good man like you. How would you like to join up with my regiment?"

"Thank you, General. Maybe some other time. Walmsley here is counting on me to accompany him to Fort Dodge."

General Hancock notices that Charley has not taken his eyes off Custer's horse and beckons Custer to come forward. The striking young rider with the broad-brimmed hat trots toward them his strawberry-blond curls shining under his hat. He brushes the dust from his white deerskins as he approaches.

"Whoa, Custis!" commands the Colonel as he extends his hand to Charley. "George Custer. Yours?"

"Charles Reynolds. That's a fine-looking animal you're riding, Colonel."

"He's one of the best. You recognize a good horse when you see one."

"I recognize good breeding," Charley says, as he looks down the line of cavalry and infantry stretching a mile or more. "Biggest group of soldiers I've seen since the War. You must be on campaign, Colonel?"

General Hancock interrupts: "There's serious Indian trouble, Reynolds...clear to Pawnee Fork and even up on the Platte as far as Fort McPherson." He glances at Walmsley. "Those savages aren't much in the mood for trading. If I were you I'd hole up at Fort Harker."

Walmsley's words seem to flow even more freely, having emptied his flask. "Now, listen here, Colonel..."

"General!" barks Hancock impatiently.

Walmsley apparently doesn't make the connection. "I've been trading with the Red Man for two years and haven't had the slightest difficulty. I suggest you gentlemen go about your soldiering business and leave the trading to me."

"You best be heeding the General's advice," Custer speaks up.

"Hogwash!" exclaims the Englishman. "Those Indians wouldn't harm a fly."

Custer and Hancock look at each other in disgust. "Good day, Reynolds," says Hancock.

"Good day to you, Sir," Charley replies, saluting respectfully. As the two officers ride to the head of the cavalry, he can't help but notice Custer's horsemanship. "Sits a horse like few plainsmen I've ever seen," he remarks to a disinterested Walmsley.

The regiment finally disappears beyond the horizon, and an eerie silence hangs over the prairie as Reynolds and his traveling companion are left to continue their journey alone.

Charley looks around uneasy. "Walmsley. We ought to heed General Hancock's advice," he tries to convince Walmsley. "Hole up at For Harker."

"Bloody hog dung."

Charley sees that Jeb's inebriated stubbornness is impossible to penetrate and he reluctantly moves on.

The following evening, Charley squints into the last rays of sunshine. He is certain that they are being watched.

"You're so bloody fidgety Reynolds, you make me squirm. What's bothering you man?"

Charley begins to tend his horses, suddenly he notices something dripping from Walmsley's wagon. He approaches the puddle on the ground, dabbing his fingers in the liquid. The tell-tale smell gives away the Englishman's trade secret.

For the first time, Walmsley sees anger in Charley's eyes. "No wonder you've been boasting about how well you get along with the Indians! Whiskey is the worst possible thing you could give them. What in the devil's the matter with you, Walmsley?"

"I have no apologies, eh, Reynolds. As far as it concerns you, whatever Indians want, I'll get it for 'em." Charley sees no sense in arguing with the half drunk trader.

A full day passes and the pair utters not a word. Riding a quarter mile or so ahead, Charley's well-trained eye spots a dozen or more Indians riding in their direction. He quickly turns back toward the wagon to alert Walmsley.

"Not to worry, Reynolds. It's the Kiowas. They know who I am." He gives Charley a cock-eyed grin. "They'll be glad to see me."

"Not if you don't have any whiskey left...and by the looks of you, you probably drank the lion's share of it." All at once, Charley sees that the Indians have begun to charge toward them. But he has seen this Indian trick before. The warriors will charge straight at you on a horse killing gait, and if you're a stranger to their ways, most people will scatter like the wind. "Those aren't Kiowa you fool those are..."

There's no time to argue. Reynolds unties Red who's been following behind the wagon and slaps his flank. An arrow whistles nearby, followed immediately by another. Charley draws his carbine from the saddle. There are more warriors than he had first estimated. Walmsley suddenly screams in agony. He's been struck, not once but twice; the second deadly shaft has pierced his chest and lodged in his heart. Charley attempts to get close to the team, the wild-eyed horses bolt, tilting the wagon and unseating the dying man. He drops to the ground and is run over by the wagon.

Charley fires his carbine then empties all but one shot from his Navy revolver, holding the Indians at bay, giving him a chance to mount his horse. He realizes he is no match for the enraged Indians. Theorizing that they are more interested in the wagon's contents than himself however, he gambles that his fleet-footed buckskin will carry him to safety. At the mere touch of the spurs, Rusty lunges into a full gallop and flies across the plain. A few arrows threaten but the hunch pays off. All but one of the Indians let Reynolds go and begin tearing into Walmsley's cargo of firewater. The lone warrior rides hard after Red. Charley slows up and watches as the warrior grabs Red's neck rope and rides to join the others.

Charley quickly reins up. He leaps from the saddle laying his carbine on the ground. He quickly jerks the Remington from its scabbard. "Lay, Rusty! Lay!" He yells. He lifts Rusty's knee and fetlock. Obediently, Rusty's knees buckle and the well-trained buckskin drops to the ground. Charley lays the rifle over the saddle, Rusty braces himself but holds steady. Charley squeezes the trigger. The big Rolling Block .50 caliber, a gift from Will, barks. Flame and black powder belch from the muzzle.

Charley quickly reloads, "How could I miss," he mutters out loud. But there is a delayed action. At last the warrior quivers, pitches forward then drops straight to the ground on his head. Red runs loose. Charley yells! "Come on, Red!" and gives a whistle.

Charley swings into the saddle and spurs off. "Ha-yaaa!!" He yells! But Charley knows he's not out of trouble yet. He recognizes a familiar landmark—not far off is a wolfer's dugout that his Indian friend, Hard Rope, had pointed out to him on a previous journey. He leans forward and urges Rusty to hold the pace until they reach the shelter. The animal's powerful muscles respond, thrusting horse and rider ever faster across the hardened prairie.

The dugout is like a small fortress—a perfect hideaway! Charley hurriedly throws his gear into the dugout. He leaves the horse saddled. He leads Rusty closer to the river, leaving him loose, hidden in the brush and trees. He then sprints to the den, knowing that the horse won't stray far. Besides, if the Indians do come looking, Rusty will be sure to kick up a fuss and warn him. He is hoping Red has enough sense to find Rusty. He hopes so, but Red is still young.

He decides to stay hidden until dark. In the distance he can hear the Indians whooping and making an awful ruckus. Charley has seen the effects of alcohol on Indians before and knows what a dangerously unpredictable situation he's in. When they've had their fill—or the liquor runs out—they're likely to hunt him down.

Charley is sure that the cloudy sky is a gift from God and utters a short prayer. Finding himself in such a vulnerable position brings new meaning to his life. He thinks of all the things he hasn't yet accomplished; all the places he hasn't seen; all the people he hasn't met; and Ariana. He feels for the gold watch in his pocket.

Charley lights a candle and stares at the timepiece wondering if he'll ever see her again? Despite Walmsley's untimely death and no particular reason to go to Fort Dodge he decides if he gets out of this mess he'll continue westward.

He fingers the watch then pulls the bullet poke that Old Gabe Green gave him. He murmurs audibly, "You're a crude sumbuck, Gabe but I wish you were here now, I surely do." As Charley holds the poke, he remembers the days when Old Gabe was transforming a pilgrim into a mountain man.

They were moving up the Platte River headed for the, "beaver pond," as Gabe called it. Charley was just eighteen. He came across a dead, nearly naked Pawnee who was killed by Kiowa or Sioux. More than likely Sioux, Gabe figured. Except for his scant clothing, the corpse was painted vermilion. Nearly a dozen arrows protruded from various parts of the warrior. "Now yu know why there're called redskins, young'un."

"Sweet Jesus Gabe they didn't just kill him. It was like..." Charley never forgot how the Indian was hacked and carved and mutilated, like nothing he thought he could ever imagine. Trapper and pilgrim mounted their horses and continued going wherever it was they were headed. Gabe could no longer remember where it was. Charley finds now that he can smile at the memories.

Gabe had ridden alongside him. *"Pawnees n' Sioux's er meaner 'n a snake without rattlers. Degollados! He makes the sign for cutthroats. They'll castigate yuh up 'n' make a charm bag outta yer sack. Yuh get in a bad wrangle with Indians 'n' there ain't no way out—save two bullets."*

"What do you mean by castigate?" Charley asks. *"Yuh should know that, youngin'. Cut off yer male parts."*

"You meant to say castrate," Charley adds.

"Don't make no never yuh mind," Gabe tossed Charley the bullet poke. The poke had powder and two lead balls inside, enough for two shots. *"Kill the meanest cut-throated, red skinned Injun with the first bullet. Save the last bullet for yerself!"*

An unmistakable rattle brings Charley back to the dugout in the, "now." His neck hair rises. The cold damp sickness of panic begins spreading from his stomach. His eyes roll in the candle light—searching. There! At the edge of the light less than three feet away is a huge rattlesnake. Panic is bile in his throat. He fights off the panic. Then Reynolds regains control. Slowly, very slowly he reaches for his Colt. The snakes' eyes are honed in on Reynolds. Its tail quivers with subtle rattles of warning. Charley inches the barrel upwards. Trembling fingers grip the revolver while he thumbs back the hammer, slowly and quietly. As the booming report stirs dust the headless rattlesnake quivers in death. Coughing from the gun smoke and dust that has filled the dugout, he heaves the carcass outside.

His hands tremble as he reloads the empty chamber with a foil cartridge. He fumbles, putting a fresh cap on the nipple, still trembling he recalls the hammer slipping from his fingers. He had been holding down the trigger to silence the metallic clicking of the cocking hammer—and his thumb slipped. The pistol went off accidentally. He loathes them cussed rattlesnakes. And he's plain lucky his pistol was pointed in the right direction.

Charley cocks his ear to Rusty's faint wicker. He peers through the hole in the dugout. A half dozen mounted Indians are silently riding up. "That slimy rattlesnake, they heard my shot." The warrior who seems to be the leader of the others gestures in Charley's direction and mutters something. Charley pokes his rifle barrel out another small porthole in the fortress. The Remington vomits flame. He yanks the rifle back then empties his pistol in the Indians' direction. The well-liquored Indians are shocked to sobering reality. They wheel their horses around and hurriedly ride back to rejoin the rest of their war party at their camp.

Darkness finally blankets the prairie. Reynolds crawls from his shelter, he pauses and listens for any sign of the Indians. All is quiet. He grabs his gear and saddle carbine and makes his way along the river. He looks for his horse that has already detected his master's scent. Remarkably Red has found Rusty and the two of them snicker contentedly when Charley approaches.

Always on guard, Reynolds leads the horses for several miles along the riverbank before finally mounting and riding into the night. Using his compass and the stars as his guide Reynolds continues his journey by night resting by day.

3

*T*he early mountain man, though usually a tranquil rascal on his own, became quite the opposite when congregated with his peers. From time to time the men would gather in recognition of a profitable season, or even an Indian summer. They didn't always need a reason to celebrate. The, "Mountain man Jubilee" was a raucous occasion, its program not always in keeping with the laws of the land. It's not surprising that the revelers were refused accommodations in many parts. Citizens of such places as, Cabezon and Cripple Creek, drew their curtains and locked doors when the mountain men came to town. Taos, New Mexico was a regular haunt however, and trapper's and plainsmen alike were welcome there. The Spanish girls seemed to enjoy the excitement—the dancing, the singing and of course the liquor that seemed to flow freely, after furs and hides had been converted to gold and silver. On the other hand, Spanish men did not approve of their womenfolk commingling with the rough and rowdy outsiders; hence, the visits would often culminate in a round of fisticuffs. The result was usually injuries of varying severity and sometimes-even death.

Charles Reynolds did not fit the mold of a mountain man. Nevertheless, he could not in all honesty escape the title; after all, he had been earning a living trapping wolves and beavers, and hunting buffalo in the past. Without contemplating the consequences of their reunion, the young man returned to New Mexico to find the girl he loved.

Return to New Mexico Territory, November 1867

"Can't trap beaver 'n' wuffs lessen you been to Taos youngin'," Gabe Green's words echo so clearly in Charley's head he stops to see if the old man is riding alongside.

"I think we'll just head over Taos way, Red," Charley says to his horse. "Maybe you'll get a chance to meet Old Trapper Green after all."

The Taos pueblo is a remarkable sight and Reynolds reins in his horse to take a closer look. He can almost picture the brave Pueblo Indians defending their beautiful adobe palace, nestled in the pastel hills of the majestic Sangre de Cristo Range.

Riding further into the town itself, Charley spots a cantina. If he was going to find Gabe Green that would certainly be the place to start. He secures Rusty and Red to the hitching rail outside.

There's no mistake, this is mountain man territory. The walls are papered with newspaper clips of buffalo hunts, wild-looking men who'd, "earned their buckskins," and posters of others with the distinguishing black letters above their faces—WANTED!

Charley walks to the bar and orders a glass of whiskey. Its bitterness burns all the way down, causing memories of the Las Vegas fiesta to surface as if he was there.

He remembers that he and Ariana had been sitting silently for some time. They both were staring into the fire. Finally, she took his half-empty glass of wine and put it with hers on the floor.

He could feel his head spinning; and it seems like there is no escape like he's in a trap. It seems as if another person has entered his body and taken up the reins. From the corner of his eye he can see the fire. It is almost out now; only a small flame remains, flickering, flickering—

Charley remembers being awakened by an unfamiliar noise. The light on his face—it's not the firelight but the morning sun. He wonders if it was all a dream. He looks at the now-empty glasses on the floor; the sunlight beaming through the window onto the blackened coals of the fire. It seems like he must have been dreaming!

"That's good whiskey boy!" bellows the intoxicated man next to him. Unconsciously, Charley shoves the half-emptied glass aside. "I'll take it if you don't want it."

Startled to reality, Charley pushes the glass in front of his neighbor. "You ever heard of a fellow by the name Gabe Green?"

"I've heard of him. Is he owing you something?"

Charley feels the suspicion building and smiles to ease the tension. "No. We've been friends since sixty. I just wanted to thank him for something. I heard he named one of his mules after me."

"Well I wouldn't be bragging about that, son. But if you'll buy me another shot of that whiskey I'll tell you where to find your man."

Charley makes the mistake of buying the remainder of the bottle and gets little information for his investment.

"Know why we all wear long hair? It's to keep them cussed mosquitoes off my neck. That's why I don't ever get a haircut. Let that be a lesson to you son. The mosquitoes are going to get you if you don't do something before next summer." He chugs down the last three ounces. "I'm proud of my hair—proud I still got it, that is. Some of my friends aren't so lucky—give their top knot up to the Indians."

The stories go on for over an hour until Charley interrupts and puts the man back on track. "Gabriel Trapper Green is just fine," slurs the man. "The Ol' Hoss is still up on the Platte, "trappin' wuffs!" like always. Times he even acts like a wuff."

Sorry on the one hand, that Gabe hadn't been able to get to Taos for several years, but thankful on the other that he was still alive, "Farewell stranger. I'm obliged." Charley nods and takes leave of Taos.

When he rides into Las Vegas Reynolds heads directly for the dress shop where he had last seen Ariana. She is all he's been thinking about for the past several days. The clerk recognizes him and hurriedly gives him the directions to Ariana's new home in Santa Fe. He learns she is planning to wed that scoundrel Antonio. The store is empty; Charley senses he is unwelcome and leaves as requested.

He steps onto the dirt street. The plaza looks much the same; fond memories linger. He is anxious to ride on to Santa Fe but his horses are both exhausted, after being chased down Raton Pass by a band of Comanche warriors. Big Red has lost a shoe, so Charley leads him and Rusty to the livery stable and hires a man to feed and groom the weary animals. He rests for two days, then the threesome head out for Santa Fe.

Charley is amazed. What a difference three years makes. What once was a sleepy Spanish town is now a bustling city. Bull trains and mule trains leave for St Louis and Independence. The trains come and go with their loaded wagons and herds of mules. These big animals are quite valuable for the settler trains headed west from Missouri. Santa Fe has become an important trade center, attracting merchants to the southwest from all points of the compass.

Charley looks for a familiar landmark, finally recognizes the La Fonda Hotel. He rents a room and writes a brief note to Ariana, asking her to, "please," meet him the following day at their, "special place," near the Esteban Ranch. Charley's good fortune pays off—the desk clerk has a friend, who for a small fee, is willing to deliver the message. Charley then has a bath and shave and dons some clean duds.

Ariana waits anxiously in her buggy clutching the note from Charley. Every minute seems like an hour. Then dispelling her worst fears, he suddenly rides into view.

Big Red approaches at a full gallop and stops just short of the buggy's rear wheel. Their eyes meet, but no words are spoken. Charley dismounts and walks toward the buggy for a closer look. His legs are trembling.

"My, oh my, Ariana!" he exclaims finally. "You're much prettier than I remember."

Ariana smiles, her brown eyes sparkling brighter than ever before. "Thank you, Charley. I'm so happy to see you again."

Charley extends his arm, and helps the beautiful Spanish maiden climb down from the buggy. They embrace, just holding each other without speaking. The familiar scent of perfume in her hair starts Charley's heart beating.

"I still have the watch," he whispers in her ear. "If only you knew how many times I've wanted to come and find you. I finally gave in. I had to know if you were all right."

"I've worried about you since the day you left, Charley. I'm so glad you came." She wipes a tear from her cheek.

Charley takes a blanket from the buggy and puts his arm around her shoulder. They walk to the familiar little adobe shack.

"Burr-rr!" Ariana shudders. "It's cold in here."

"I'll light a fire. We'll be warm in no time."

Ariana wraps the blanket around her, watching Charley's every move and remembering their first visit here. He turns and smiles as he strikes the match. "Why are you smiling, Charles Reynolds?"

"Does this bring back memories?" he asks quietly.

"Yes. I remember it well," she smiles softly. "It was cold outside and we lit the fire to get warm. In the warmth of the fire we both fell asleep. We woke up to rush back to the ranch. My mother was so upset...she still mentions it whenever we have words. It seems so long ago, doesn't it?"

He walks over to her taking both of her hands and smiling into her eyes he answers, "Yes it does. Tell me what you've been doing. How are your father...and your mother?"

"Getting older but just fine. They still insist I marry Antonio," she says noticing Charley's immediate disappointment. "I don't know what to do about it." There is a long silence then..."But I'm so glad you're here. My heart was aching, crying and happy all at the same time when I read your note," she turns as a tear slides down her face. "I didn't expect to see you again. I always hoped to, but when I was really missing, you I would wonder...maybe you have a girl or a wife in the States by now and then I would get angry. It seems so long ago," she nods.

Charley looks at her confused. "What about us, Ariana? We were married. How can you marry another?"

"A priest did not marry us. My father says it is unlawful in the eyes of the Church. He says the paper we signed is useless." She hesitates while she straightens her dress. "But I'm so glad you're here."

Charley kisses her cheek. "I am not sure about what your father says. We should go away together—leave Las Vegas."

"Oh, Charley." She whispers.

Charley's stomach flips at the way she says his name. His thoughts turn to their meeting in Santa Fe—the wine, the fire, the touch of her. A flood of emotion runs through him and suddenly, the reality of her betrothal to Antonio comes to mind. He kisses her cheek. "We must go away—just you and I." She returns the kiss. The touch of her lips, so warm and moist sends shivers down the back of his neck.

"I've waited a long time for this moment, Charley. I was afraid it would never come. It seems forever since I've held you, kissed you."

Charley squeezes her tightly, "Many nights alone on the plains, especially when it was snowing and the wolves were howling at a full moon, I thought about you and our last time together in Santa Fe. Sometimes I'd stare at the stars for an hour, maybe longer looking at my watch and wondering about you, and what you were doing. Then I'd wake up the next morning and ask myself: What good is it? Why want for something I can't have?" Holding her, he wonders how things would be if Antonio was killed by Indians or in an accident?"

"I know, Charley," she says stroking his shoulder. "I've been dreaming about you too. I've tried to think of a way to come to you, but I couldn't. My mother doesn't like Antonio, but he has my father fooled and I don't know why." She pulls away. "I know it's cold out, Charley but let's go for a buggy ride."

"If that's what you want to do, I'll get another blanket."

The couple rides along in silence for some time, when Charley suddenly laughs aloud.

"What is so funny, Senor Reynolds?"

"I remember the first time we tried to dance."

"That was a long time ago," she laughs. "I was so happy showing you."

"Yeah until Antonio showed up. It seems like he's always ruining everything." Charley rolls his eyes upwards and nods his head. "I remember the very first time I laid eyes on you."

"Oh, Charley, tell me about it. What did you feel?"

"You remember. I was a soldier during the war. When my outfit first arrived at our station, Fort Union, we halted in Las Vegas. I was looking around, enjoying the new people the Spanish architecture and there you were standing in the crowd."

"You were looking at me, Charley."

"I couldn't take my eyes off you. You were the prettiest thing I'd ever seen. When we pulled out of town..."

She interrupts, "You were staring back at me."

"How do you know I was looking at you?"

"You were, Charles Reynolds. I was staring at you," she bursts into laughter.

The winter scene begins to disappear quickly as the sun starts its descent, leaving nothing but black silhouettes of jagged mountaintops and stately cactus.

"We'd better get back before dark, Charley. I don't like being alone on the desert at night."

"You weren't paying attention, Ariana. We're only a few feet from our hut. Look!" He laughs again and jumps down from the carriage, taking her hand and helping her to the ground.

Once inside the little house, Charley throws more wood on the fire and pulls a chair close for Ariana then begins rummaging through some wood boxes hanging on the wall.

"What are you looking for?" asks Ariana.

"I hoped I might find something to eat."

"Oh!" she exclaims with surprise. "I almost forgot. I brought something for us—something special. It's in the basket in the buggy."

Charley hurries outside to the buggy then returns and opens the basket. "What's this?" he says, smiling as he unwraps a bottle of Spanish wine.

"You know...that's the wine Evita served us in Santa Fe. But I forgot to bring the glasses."

"Don't worry, I've got one on my saddle. I'll take care of the horses while I'm outside."

After tending the horses, Charley returns with a large army-issue tin cup. "We'll have to drink from the same cup," he says with a grin.

Charley kneels on the rug beside her chair and gazes into her eyes. She pours some wine into the cup and returns a loving look. For the next several minutes they stare into the fire, sipping on the wine and savoring their love for each other. Charley begins to feel a little lightheaded as Ariana whispers in his ear and pours another cupful. He looks up at her lovely face—the light shimmering on her amber glow. She leans forward in the chair, and their lips meet, gently at first. She draws his head toward her and he hears her muffled voice.

"I've waited a long time for you," she whispers. Gently, he pulls her from the chair onto the hand woven rug. She sits beside him and he kisses her once again. She pulls the blanket around their shoulders, "It's November and not July." She giggles.

"I love you, Charley," she whispers. Then, caught up in a whirlwind of bittersweet memories, they are carried into a world all their own—far from Santa Fe; far from Don Luis and Sofia; and far from Antonio Delgado.

An early powder-snow warns of the long season ahead. Charley decides to winter in Santa Fe. It is not long, of course, before the Fernandez family learns of his plan. Don Luis is upset when he hears the news from an enraged Antonio Delgado, that Reynolds has been seeking work with a local freight company.

"There must be something we can do, Antonio...something to persuade this gringo to leave Santa Fe."

Delgado's devious nature shines. "Of course!" he shouts, his wicked grin, stretching as far as his thin jaw line will permit. "We'll put him to work ourselves. I'll tell Juan Carlos to hire him immediately. He'll never be out of our sight. I'll keep that gringo away from my Ariana if it's the last thing I do!"

Don Luis ponders Delgado's ploy. "Reynolds is not a foolish man, Antonio. Don't you think he will recognize your motive?"

Delgado fingers his mustache pointing menacingly under the tip of his nose. "I'll tell Juan Carlos to treat him like a friend, a confident. Yes, that's it! Make him believe Juan Carlos thinks you and I are devils. What do you think of that?"

"You are a cunning man, I suppose that's the best we can do, Antonio. I despise all this trickery and deceit. I wish Reynolds would just decide to leave and we'd be done with him. I shall talk to my wife this evening, and encourage her to start with the wedding plans, at once."

"Yes," agrees the sly one, "that is a good idea."

The men part with a handshake and Delgado hurries to tell Juan Carlos of his new role.

Sofia Fernandez is not at all happy that Charles Reynolds is in Santa Fe. She had planned a June wedding and moving the ceremony ahead was impractical. She had so wanted Ariana's grandmother to attend, but winter travel would not allow it. And the weather was unpredictable, too. She was planning an outdoor reception—a grand celebration with ribbons and piñatas, minstrels and a troupe of Brazilian dancers. She recalls telling her husband that Ariana's happiness does not seem important to him anymore, but he refuses to bend to her pleading.

Ariana begged her mother to cancel the wedding because she's in love with Charley, and it would not be fair to Antonio to have a wife who does not care whether he lives or dies. Besides, she reminded her mother, regardless of what father says Charley, and her are married.

They have spoken about this matter before, Sophia reminded her daughter, trying desperately to keep things in perspective. However, in her heart she wishes her daughter could be with the shy young man with the friendly smile, instead of Antonio Delgado, whom she likens to a weasel. She's never told Ariana. Despite several attempts to change her husband's mind Senora Fernandez eventually bows to his wishes and reschedules the wedding. Ariana is devastated.

Delgado's scheme is a success. Charley is grateful for the job; it's exactly what he had in mind. Juan Carlos first puts him to work loading and unloading wagons. The Esparza Freight Company has become a thriving entity in spite of continuing Indian raids. Charley demonstrates his abilities as a teamster and soon he's asked to drive the wagons. But Juan Carlos knows that Reynolds' talents are best suited for scouting, and eventually schedules him to escort the weekly runs to Albuquerque, Las Vegas and sometimes Fort Union, on the Santa Fe Trail.

Charley sees Ariana occasionally but Sofia is keeping her daughter at close rein. Hurried glances and veiled smiles are the highlights of these rare chance meetings. Ariana is otherwise miserable and her broody disposition is of great concern to her family, as well as to her suitor. She is so irritable around Delgado in fact, he decides to keep his distance for awhile. Now that Juan Carlos has Reynolds on the road and out of Ariana's sight, he's sure her mood will improve over time. Indeed he is correct.

Ariana's spin takes a remarkable turn, although not for the reason predicted by her fiancé. It is mid-January when she overhears her father and mother discussing a three-day business trip to Las Vegas. They will depart on Monday next; Antonio will accompany them. She immediately goes to the freight office and checks the timetable. Charley is scheduled to escort a caravan bound for Albuquerque on that day. The timing is perfect. She will take the stage, meet him there, and they'll make plans to run away to Colorado.

In Albuquerque Charley and Ariana are afforded only a brief rendezvous. Charley is excited at the thought of the two of them going away. They will leave at the first sign of spring, if not Colorado, then Kansas. Ariana tells Charley how they can keep in contact until then, with the help of her cousin.

"If you have a message for me put it behind the big rock in back of the Esparza freight shed; I'll do the same. It is Evita's job to deliver local dispatches for the company. She will check the rock every other day while she's at the office."

"That's quite a plan," remarks Charley, who is amused by the scheme. He looks at his watch. "It's time for me to go. I love you, Ariana."

The parting kiss is never the sweetest, but the young lovers are content with the promise of spring.

Delgado's plans for spring are much different however, and further developments serve only to speed up the nuptials. In an attempt to regain favor with the Esparza Company a discharged employee tells Juan Carlos of the tryst in Albuquerque. Delgado is furious and confronts Senor and Senora Fernandez in the plaza.

"We will have the wedding in March!" he screams. "At this time, your plans are not important!"

Sofia gets no support from Don Luis. The couple will be married in a quiet ceremony—no celebration, no friends and more importantly, no Charley Reynolds. Meanwhile, Delgado gets to work on yet another plan to keep his rival out of Santa Fe. Recalling a dishonest practice at Fort Union, whereby, the post trader is lining Colonel Smith's pockets, in return for higher profits at the commissary, he turns once more to Don Luis.

"Colonel Smith owes us a favor for remaining silent, Don Luis. I suggest it's time for repayment. Don't you agree?"

Senor Fernandez is feeling the weight of Delgado's constant badgering. "Do as you wish, Antonio. The Colonel is no friend of mine. He is a thief!"

"Well, I wouldn't go that far senor," the shocked Spaniard replies. "But I'm sure he can be persuaded to help us."

Colonel M. Nathan Smith, a friendly giant of a man responds agreeably and surprises Delgado with his ingenuity. He arranges immediately to have Reynolds accompany a special caravan of military supply wagons headed for Texas within the week. They will be gone for at least a month.

One cold afternoon while on duty with the Esparza Company, Charley receives the extra assignment upon his arrival at Fort Union. He is ordered to remain at the post. Why now? He had arranged to meet Ariana the following day in Las Vegas.

Unable to get a message to Evita he rides out with sorrow in his heart. After several days on patrol he begins to get suspicious. There are a dozen guards besides himself and little for him and Rusty to do but follow behind the wagons. A young private finally breaks the news.

"Must be someone wants you out of Santa Fe pretty bad, Reynolds. We don't need escorts on this route anymore—not since the War. I think you've been duped!"

It was true. That desperado Delgado had set him up!

Charley doesn't wait for a formal release from Colonel Smith. Since the campaign is nothing but a charade he sees no reason to stay with the caravan. He rides day and night, and upon his arrival at Santa Fe, goes directly to the freight shed and places a note behind the big rock hoping that Evita will soon find it.

It doesn't take long for Antonio to learn that Reynolds is back in town. One of his friends sees Charley near the Esparza office and runs to tell Delgado, who bursts into the street and confronts his rival face-to-face.

"There is no reason for you to stay in Santa Fe now," Delgado says sneering at Charley. "I suggest you leave. Tomorrow is not soon enough!"

A Delgado supporter taunts Reynolds in Spanish but Charley has learned enough of the language to understand that he's just been called a, "stinking pig." He feels a twinge of fury then turns to face Antonio. Strangely, mystically, he hears his father quoting from the Bible. *He that is slow to anger is better than a mighty man.* He begins to walk away.

"Ariana is mine, Reynolds. Mine!" screams Antonio. "Go back to Gringo land. Go hunt your wolves. You don't belong here. Comprende?"

Charley feels the blood rush to his face but he's not blushing this time. His reply is quiet, yet firm. "Frankly, Delgado, it's not your concern where I go or what I do."

The name-calling continues in the background. Charley doesn't understand all of it but, "slimy pig," and, "chicken liver," are both terms he's heard before. He takes another few steps but Delgado, brandishing a shiny silver dagger, runs from behind and darts into his path.

"I'm tired of hearing how well you handle a gun, Senor Reynolds. Let's see how you can fight with a knife."

Delgado's rambunctious friends have attracted a crowd. "Arriba! Arriba!" they cry as Charley notices the cold gray/brown eyes staring into his.

"Are you a coward, Charley Reynolds?" asks Delgado.

"Coward!" comes the echo from the sidelines. "Senor Reynolds ae un 'Coward'!"

Charley's anger begs for release. His response to the pent-up emotion, surprises even himself. "Your friend Delgado is the coward," he shouts to the onlookers. "If he were any kind of man at all—and I doubt any part of him is a man—he would let Senorita Fernandez take a man of her own choosing. I doubt she would want such a coward as this!"

A hush comes over the assemblage. Charley can't believe his own words. He scans the audience then looks again at Delgado. Antonio's expression has all the turbulence of a Blue Norther'. Suddenly, a half-drunk heckler enters the arena and starts kicking dirt up at Charley. "Ariana doesn't want to marry no gringo. Go home to your mother gringo...go home to that gringo whore!" He kicks more dirt.

Charley's life on the plains is reflected in his patience, his keen eye and his muscle—hard and strong, like a stout sinew-backed bow, capable of springing an arrow hundreds of yards toward a moving target. The bow is drawn fully taut and ready to release the shaft. Antonio feels the intensity of Charley's rage and raises his weapon. But like the strike of a rattlesnake, the butt of the big Sharps Carbine slams into Antonio's arm knocking the knife to the ground. The Spaniard retaliates with his fist. Charley ducks and the counterstroke from his rifle-barrel catches Delgado's chin, laying the flesh back against his cheek. As he falls Charley delivers a hard swift kick to the man's groin lifting him into the air momentarily, before he crashes face-first into the dirt. Reynolds feigns another blow with his boot as his wounded opponent crouches at his feet, clutching his crotch and pleading for mercy.

Just when Charley thinks the fight is over, another Spaniard, by the name of Mendoza, steps forward. Charley immediately recognizes the black flat-topped hat.

"You are finished in Santa Fe, Senor Reynolds. Antonio and Ariana are married now. Comprende? You might as well leave while you still can. If you don't..."

"If I don't what?" Charley replies angrier, now hurt. "If I don't what?" he demands, raising his rifle to eye-level. The crowd is still; there is not a sound, except the intimidating click as Charley cocks his Sharps.

"Why, you filthy swine," screeches Mendoza, reaching for the pistol tucked in his cummerbund. Realizing he may have pushed Reynolds too far, he steps back, but trips over his own spur.

When he finally frees the pistol, it is too late. The deafening blast shakes the earth beneath their feet. The shot sends dust flying everywhere and Mendoza goes down landing next to his companion. A blue-black cloud permeates the air as Charley reaches for another cartridge, slams the breech open and loads the 500-grain shell. Antonio, a clot of mud caked to the bloody wound on his face, is pleading, begging but Charley only hears the name-calling and the ugly remark about his mother. The big barrel closes in on Mendoza's face.

"I should kill you both," Charley manages to say, his teeth clenched so hard he couldn't spit if he wanted to.

Antonio jumps as the hammer is pulled back one more time. Mendoza feels the cold steel against his forehead; he whimpers uncontrollably. Reynolds pulls his carbine back and calmly squeezes the trigger. The slug misses Mendoza's head by less than an inch, ricochets off the dirt, and lodges in the wall of a nearby building. Only after the dust and smoke clears do the onlookers learn that Delgado and Mendoza are still alive. They watch in awe as the quiet man with the big gun turns his back and walks toward his horse.

"Senor Reynolds!" exclaims Don Luis when Charley appears at Casa Gonzales. "What a surprise!"

Reynolds is polite, though impatient. "I wish to ask permission to speak to your daughter, Senor."

"And may I ask what your business is, Senor?"

"It's a personal matter, Senor."

"My daughter has a husband now. I'm sure he would not approve."

"Then it is true," Charley says, a faltering note of defeat in his voice. "Delgado! You let your daughter marry that..."

The conversation is interrupted when a curious Ariana and her mother approach to see who the visitor is.

"Sofia! Ariana my daughter!" cries Fernandez nervously. "Senor Reynolds and I are discussing business. If you please."

"Perhaps I can help with this business," Sofia breaks in. She takes her husband aside and the couple quietly talk in Spanish.

Ariana and Charley exchange glances during the interlude, but nothing more. An air of suspicion and futility looms above them. Eventually, Sofia convinces Don Luis to allow the young man the courtesy of a few final words with their daughter. Ariana clasps Charley's hand in hers and leads him to a quiet corner of the courtyard. When she looks pleadingly at her parents, her mother smiles weakly and the couple disappear into the house.

"Is it true? Did you marry him? Why?" Charley asks all in one breath.

"I didn't want to marry Antonio. You know that, Charley. But my mother and father told me they would lose everything if I didn't. That's why they're living here in Santa Fe. Antonio already has taken the ranch for himself." She begins to cry.

"I should have said something before. I knew I should have told you. That Antonio is a snake! He has tricked your father, Ariana. He's nothing but a conniving snake!"

Ariana manages a smile. "My mother says he reminds her of a weasel. Tell me, what has Antonio done?"

"I can't prove anything, Ariana. It's too late anyway. Just forget it." Realizing that his reluctance to reveal Delgado's underhanded business deals is the reason Ariana is in such a mess. He turns to leave.

"Don't go, Charley," she sobs. "I'm so sorry. I love you. I'll never forget you."

"It's not your fault, Ariana," he says, turning back and drawing her toward him, whispering the comforting words over and over. He feels her familiar warmth, the sweet smell of her hair; then clinging to the moment, knowing it will have to last him a lifetime, he whispers sadly, "I'll always love you—always. There'll never be anyone else for me. Good-bye, Ariana." He kisses her lingeringly for the last time.

"Don't give up on me, Charley! Write to me!" Ariana sobs.

Putting spurs to Big Red, Charley Reynolds once more rides away to meet his other love—the Great Plains.

4

*I*n the 1860s the White Man's encroachment on Indian Territory had begun to take its toll. Slaughter of wild animals—particularly the bison—not only aggravated the Indians but rotting carcasses often fouled smaller rivers and streams, leaving settlers hopelessly stranded on hostile land without potable water. Many Whites and Indians alike died as a result.

Meanwhile, Washington's great round up of the Red Man began with the planning of reservations and more treaties—treaties that would later be broken or rewritten into oblivion. Kit Carson had corralled the Navaho in the West and as promised, General Hancock had burned out several Cheyenne villages at Pawnee Fork. The Indians were no match for Colonel Custer's 7th Cavalry that followed them in relentless pursuit as they retreated to the wilderness of the North Platte country.

For the courageous plainsmen and those other hunters who braved the rigors of the Western Territories, the hey-day was over, for the big fur companies had all but abolished the fur trade. The hearty individuals who stayed on were forced to hunt the buffalo for its valuable hide or trap muskrat and wolves, instead of beaver and fox. The emergence of the railroads further threatened their livelihoods as trade goods began to arrive in huge quantity from the East.

Despite Walmsley's death and several clashes with the Red Man himself, Charles Reynolds wondered who more deserved the title of savage. He reminisced about his travels with Hard Rope, the Osage Indian, and constantly observed the colorful Indians as he made his way across the plains. Defense against the White Man's trespass seemed impossible. He had watched Americans kill, not only the Red Man, but also their own brothers during the Civil War. And although the Sioux and Cheyenne were leaning toward a crude alliance, the various tribes often fought amongst themselves, too. It was a perplexing situation indeed!

On the move again, Colorado Territory, Late 1867

After several days' ride, stopping only to switch horses, Charley's reserve is spent. A little grove of pinion trees, on the knoll ahead, looks like a comfortable place to rest and he begs his weary horses to endure the final hundred yards up the trail.

"Get up, old boy," he urges gently, slapping Rusty's neck. "Come on, Red. You can do it!"

The sun slips behind the mountains and before Charley's makeshift lean-to is erected a giant snowflake lights on his shoulder. He shivers at the thought of a snow and stands his collar up around his neck. Another shiver hits him, a different kind of shiver.

"Hang it all!" he says aloud. "Everything I think about reminds me of that girl."

Rusty is startled by the outburst. A clump of half-chewed grass hangs from his mouth as he stares blankly at Charley.

"Eat your supper and mind your own business, Rusty!" he says, smiling at his own peculiar habit of talking to the animals. For the first time, since leaving Santa Fe, he feels an urge to eat. "See what you've done, old boy? You've made me hungry."

It doesn't' take long to find food. The ground squirrels are plentiful and Charley has his fill. For the moment at least, he convinced himself to stop thinking about Ariana, and begins to make plans for the upcoming hunt. He recalls the old man at Taos mentioning the abundance of wolves along the Big Sandy. There are lots to hunt along the Smoky Hill route, too. That commissary officer at Fort Wallace is always contracting for meat—Fort Hays too.

It's getting colder. The howl of a distant wolf echoes through the canyon below. Charley moves closer to the fire. Orange flame licks the wind as he hurls his blanket and wraps it tight around his shoulders. The fire sparks wildly for a few moments, spewing its fury to the heavens. He recalls his encounter with Delgado in the street at Santa Fe. He can still see the cowering Antonio with his hands between his legs. He smiles.

"Bet he thought that kick came all the way from Kansas!" The horses gawk as he laughs aloud.

Charley begins to feel weak, giddy from lack of sleep. As he gazes into the firelight flickering now, he begins to count the snowflakes falling. One then another—falling onto the burning log; melting, dissolving, vanishing forever. He sleeps till dawn.

Charley awakes to a clear morning sky and several inches of snow on the ground. He wrestles his way out of the twisted bedroll, rubs his hands briskly and takes a deep breath. The high-desert air is invigorating as he gathers some twigs to start a fire. After setting his tin cup of coffee near the warm blaze, he unwraps a slab of bacon from its brown paper. He cuts several slices and places them on a rock by the flame. Rusty and Red recognize the tantalizing aroma and begin pawing at the ground for something to eat. Charley is confident that Red will stay with Rusty, so he unties both animals and lets them graze in a valley not far from camp. He can watch them there.

"Eat hardy, boys," he says to the horses. "It might be slim pickins' up on the Platte."

Over a week passes before Charley reaches buffalo country. The north-south trails that the bison follow in their quest for food are many, although the number of animals seems to be less than before. Eventually, he sees the telltale dust clouds of the shaggy herd. It's mating time and the bulls are bellowing as they fight for the cows. "A bullin-n'-a-bellering," as Gabe Green used to call it. Charley watches as several wolves snap and snarl at an old bull they've managed to lure away from the herd. The buffalo wolves are not just ordinary wolves but bigger and more powerful than the others. Their huge teeth can crunch the bones of buffalo with their strong jaw muscles. Charley moves in for a closer look and startles the sneering gray canines. They growl at first and then slither away, only to return when Charley turns his back on their prey.

Sighting a ravine and a little knoll ahead, Charley begins to make plans to take one of the healthier animals. He turns his horses loose in the ravine and grabs his rifles. He still has his favorite Sharps and the Remington rifle. He climbs up onto the ridge for a better view. Once he glasses the animals, he realizes that there are two herds not just one. Luckily, he is downwind of the animals. With his Big Fifty Remington, balanced securely on a forked tree branch, Charley eases back the hammer and sights down the barrel.

Suddenly, as if spooked several of the beasts begin to move away, slowly at first, then all out. The ground rumbles and shakes as the stampede runs past Charley's position. Then, as if out of nowhere, come six Indian horsemen. Straining to peer through the dust, he recognizes, by their dress, that they are Sioux. A closer look through his glasses reveals a familiar necklace—just like the one worn by Little Bear, a fierce warrior whom Hard Rope, his Osage friend, had once identified at an Indian agency. Spellbound by the quickness and efficiency of the hunter, Charley lowers his rifle from its rest. With nothing but their buffalo hide pads cinched on with rawhide and rawhide thongs, looped through the mouths of their fleet buffalo ponies, their riding skills are unequaled.

The ponies possess skills of their own too. Charley watches in awe as they single out a big bull, moving alongside the animal so each rider has a perfect aim. With bow drawn full tilt, an arrow speeds into the flank of a stampeding beast, passing through its vital organs. Then, laboring for each step, the big animal goes down. Charley remembers Hard Rope's explanation of the nomadic hunters' nearly foolproof attack: riding up on the bison without getting trampled, shooting an arrow just behind the rib cage. That way the arrow penetrates the vital organs without striking their large ribs. The Indians then make a safe retreat. The process is repeated several times until the Indian leader signals that the hunt is over.

Soon the Indian women and children arrive to butcher the downed buffalo. They've killed a few bulls, as they use their tough hides for making war shields. But mostly, they desire the cows for their tender meat. After loading the meat onto pack horses and travois, they move off for their village. Charley feels sure that they are headed for a tribal feast, leaving him free to conduct his own hunt. There will be dancing for joy in the village tonight

Charley hurries out, setting his traps then conceals himself where he can keep watch on his traps. Charley has watched other wolfers use the deadly white poison, strychnine but he hates the stuff and will not use it. It is not long before a pack of hungry wolves descends upon the remains of the buffalo carcasses. Charley watches eagerly as the scavengers take their full. By next morning all four traps have been sprung.

For several days Charley follows the Indians as they chase the buffalo herds, moving a little further east each day. After killing two buffalo, he decides to head for the familiar Smoky Hill River and take the meat and wolf skins to Fort Wallace. Strangely, the Sioux are present along the Smoky Hill too and Charley fears for his safety. He had heard reports that land had been set-aside for them on the North Platte and their presence so far south leads him to believe that parleys with the tribes may have failed. Nevertheless, he loads up his belongings and rides in a northeasterly direction. He knows this country well, and once he passes Cheyenne Wells he'll ride north and catch the South Fork of the Smoky Hill following it to Fort Wallace.

Charley's fears are well founded. He is forced to hide in a ravine for several hours while fifty or more Indians move south. It's difficult to tell from a distance whether they're warriors or merely hunters, but no sense in arousing them. He decides to stay undercover during the day, traveling only at night. His caution pays off, for the Indians are too numerous to count after he passes Cheyenne Wells. After three days' travel he finally reaches Fort Wallace.

The hustle and bustle at Fort Wallace is a bit intimidating to the solitary hunter who is surprised by the numerous extra guards.

"Halt there, stranger. Identify yourself!"

"Charles Reynolds, Private."

"State your business, Mr. Reynolds!"

Charley points to his travois. "Professional huntsman."

After carefully looking over his travois and saddlebags, the guard escorts the weary hunter to the Sergeant-of-the-Guard. Charley attempts conversation.

"Say Private...I haven't seen so much activity since last year when I met General Hancock and colonel Custer on the move. What's all the excitement about?"

"Lot's of Bluecoats on the move, Mr. Reynolds. Big Indian trouble in these parts." He turns to the Sergeant-of-the-Guard, "This here's Mr. Reynolds—professional huntsman."

Reynolds nods. The Sergeant orders the guard to return to his post and then turns to Charley with a puzzled look.

"Something wide of the mark, Sir?" asks Charley.

"Naw, nothin' wrong. Did I hear you say Charles Reynolds?"

"Yes, Sir."

"And what is your business?"

"I do a lot of things but right now I've got some furs to trade at the trader's store and some meat for the commissary."

"That's it!" the Sergeant replies. "Now I know who you are. You're that buffalo hunter everyone has been talking about. From Kansas ain't you?"

"Yes, Sir. My family is still here in Kansas."

"I'm from Kansas myself—born here at least. I'm sure the commissary will be happy for the meat. We can use all we can get. We're expecting two hundred more soldiers to ride in any day. I'll take you to the commissary. Come on, Reynolds follow me!"

After weighing the meat and giving Charley his voucher, the curious Commissary Chief asks him about his travel plans.

"I'll likely head up the Geese River."

The interrogator looks frightened. "I don't think you ought to be going up there alone. I'd recommend you go see the Quartermaster. Maybe he'll hire you on to help here. It's a lot safer I tell you."

"Yeah he's right, Reynolds," agrees the overweight Quartermaster, Captain Walker. "Them Indians is ferocious! Why, they been scalping folks just for the fun of it. They're running wild up there on the Geese. They heard the railroad's coming and they're mad as hornets. We sure could use another guide here at Wallace. I'd be glad to hire you, if you'd stay."

After brief negotiation Reynolds signs his army contract and hands it to the beaming Quartermaster.

"By the way," the Commissary Chief breaks in, "I knew an outfit called the Reynolds Arkansas Brigade—any kin of yours?"

Charley shrugs his shoulders and the conversation ends when Captain Walker speaks up.

"Never mind, son. That's not important. Come on, I want you to meet another man I've just hired." He motions Charley to follow him over to the trader's store.

"But I'd like to take care of my horses," Charley protests. "They'll think I'm neglecting them."

The captain raises his eyebrows then tells his orderly to stable Rusty and Red. "You'll like this fellow, Reynolds. I think you two have a lot in common."

Standing impatiently with one foot perched on the walkway, is none other than William Cody. He extends his hand to the newcomer without speaking.

"Pleased to meet you, William," Charley says politely. "I have a brother named William. Should I call you William or Will?"

"How about Bill," Cody says with a slanted smile.

"Reynolds will be scouting with you from now on, Cody," announces a happy Captain Walker. "I'm sure you'll both earn that seventy-five dollars I give you every month."

"Not a heck of a lot of money to be risking our necks or our scalps for, is it, Reynolds?" Cody replies sarcastically, as he lifts his hat and fingers his hair.

To avoid offending the Quartermaster Charley merely shrugs at the comment. After all, seventy-five dollars can go a long way if a man doesn't waste it on gambling and drink or loose women. "As long as I live to spend it, I'm happy with it," he says at last.

"Well, looking at it that way," Cody continues thoughtfully, "I guess I shouldn't complain either. It's risky out there among those savages. I'm glad to have a partner, Reynolds. We can keep an eye out for each other—make sure we both come back with all our hair." The laughter echoes across the parade grounds as the trio continues the jovial conversation.

Buffalo Bill Cody, who had previously hunted buffalo for the railroad, accompanies Reynolds on several occasions during the next year hunting and scouting for the Army. But Charley's contract is a month-to-month agreement and although he appreciates Cody's expertise, he often travels alone to trap wolves. When news reaches Fort Wallace in November 1868, that the U.S 7th Cavalry has prevailed at the Battle of Washita, Reynolds declines the offer of a renewed contract. Now that Chief Black Kettle is dead and the fighting has died down, he explains to Captain Walker that it's safer for a man to hunt alone. The Quartermaster agrees that Charley's plan to hunt and trap along the Republican River is a good one. Besides, both Fort McPherson and Fort Kearney can use the meat. In return for the small bonus added to his final payment, Charley agrees to watch for Indian movements and to report any unusual activity to the post commander at Fort McPherson.

"Thank you. I'll do that, Captain," Charley promises. "I hope to see you again next year." With the customary quick wave of his arm, he disappears into the wintry landscape.

Riding at a brisk trot, Charley winces at the stinging North wind on his face and tilts his hat forward. Rusty and Red toss their heads at the same annoyance. Last week's windblown snow is frozen in scattered patches along the stark land and the threatening gray sky promises more of the same. After two days' ride he reaches the Republican River. The temperature has dropped noticeably and two to three inches of snow lines its banks. Charley starts to the east and soon spots a sheltered grove of cottonwood trees in the distance. In an attempt to ward off the Sioux, whom he has observed from time to time, he wades his horses in the river for a quarter mile or so, and waits until dark to make camp.

Charley decides to chance a small fire to warm his supper of meat and biscuits. He's certain he is alone—all alone. Now would be a good time to write a letter to Ariana. He wonders to himself what use is there for him to write, with her being married now, but maybe things have changed. From his possibles bag he takes his sheepherder's candle and tips the wick into the fire. The burning tallow flickers brightly against the shiny tin as he begins to write.

"*My Dearest Ariana...I am sitting beside my fire on the plains. It's the dead of winter and I can hear a wolf howling. It gives me a haunting feeling. The only other sound is the water in the river. The lamp I got from your father's herdsman is burning brightly, reflecting off the snow-covered riverbank It's a lonesome...*" Suddenly, the paper falls from his hand and he drifts off to sleep. He awakes several hours later annoyed that he had not doused the fire and the lamp. Only a small puddle of tallow remains in the bottom of the can.

In Indian country Charley usually does not sleep at his fire. In most cases, he's learned from Ol' Gabe, that you light a fire to eat then move a mile or so away and make a cold camp. Or you make sure the flame is hidden in a hole or behind thick brush. The Sioux do not attack at night so in Sioux country there is little bother, that is if you are up at before dawn and move camp.

Moving his camp every three days Charley spends most of his working hours under the light of the moon, trapping and skinning wolves then stretching their hides the way Trapper Green had taught him. He remembers Bill Cody's accounts of abundant game at Red Willow Creek and starts working his way northward. After a successful weeklong hunt he heads north across the bleak plains of the Nebraska Territory until he reaches the Platte River. It's a bitterly cold day in January 1869, when Reynolds finally arrives at Fort McPherson.

After collecting his voucher for his wares Charley spends the night and breakfasts with Colonel Egan.

The Colonel has a concerned look, "Now can't I change your mind? Where will you go anyway? It's the dead of winter—and a cold one at that!"

"I've heard that there was buffalo and antelope and beaver—game as far as the eye can see—up along the Missouri in Dakota Territory. I've had the urge for some time to travel out that way, Colonel."

The Colonel, deep in thought, bows his head and rubs the back of his neck. "You know, Reynolds, the Indian problem isn't over yet."

"What do you mean, Colonel?" Charley asks eagerly, hoping to get some new information about recent Indian movements.

"Well, Custer had quite a parley with one of the Sioux chiefs, Pawnee Killer. He counseled with both the Sioux and the Cheyenne leaders but none of the promises have been kept. Now, Santanta and his Kiowas are riled...and Little Raven has the Arapaho stirred up again. I think you should stay here for the winter for your own safety."

Charley looks closely at the Colonel. "I don't understand why the Army goes around making all these promises, never intending to keep them. Sometimes I feel badly for the Indians. I really think their leaders are trying to please the White Man. It's only a few young bucks that stray from the tribes now and then. If the politicians would let the Army have complete control we shouldn't have the problems we do."

"I'm not educated enough to discuss Indian politics, Reynolds. All I know, is that it's still not safe for a White Man to be roaming around on the plains alone." After a slight pause his blue eyes open wide and he grabs Charley's shoulder. "Have you heard of the Jack Marrow Ranch?" Charley shakes his head. "Don't know why I didn't think of it before. The ranch is only a few miles down the road. You could winter over there, then come Spring when the Army needs some dispatches carried to Fort Hays and Fort Larned, you can earn some extra money to make up for the loss over the winter."

The Colonel seems so genuinely considerate of Charley's well being that the young buffalo hunter decides to heed his advice. "That's a good idea, Colonel. Maybe I'll run into old Gabe Green. It wouldn't surprise me. I can just hear him yelling and shouting at his mules: "Hump, you arnery critters. Hump, Charley Boy! Haa-yaaa!""

Colonel Eagan laughs at Charley's surprising burst of excitement. "Charley Boy?" he asks quizzically.

For the first time in a long time Charley feels his face redden. "That's right. He named one of his mules after me. Please don't laugh."

Despite the disappointment of Green's failure to appear, the winter months prove to be much more lucrative than Reynolds had estimated. The game is plentiful and business at the Marrow Ranch is brisk. Mrs. Marrow's sister, a schoolteacher from Philadelphia, has an extensive library and Charley spends much of his time reading— particularly her books on botany and metallurgy.

Among the regular visitors at the ranch, is a half-breed mountain man by the name of, "Indian Joe," who has recently seen Gabe Green at Julesburg, over on the Geese River.

"Crusty old codger," remarks Joe. "I knowed him a long time. He still traps, wolfs...and cusses something awful."

Reynolds and Indian Joe spend a lot of time together during the cold winter months, each learning from the other's hunting experiences on the plains and in the mountains. In the spring of 1869, Colonel Eagan requests Charley to carry some dispatches to Fort Hays and Fort Larned. Charley asks Indian Joe to go with him but the half-breed prefers North Platte country and declines the offer. Charley completes his ride and once again strikes out on his own.

5

*J*ust as "gold fever" had spread through the mineral-rich mountains of California and Colorado during the early part of the Nineteenth Century "railroad fever" had begun sweeping across the so-called Great American Desert by the 1860s. More and more pioneers moved west and the demand for material goods was nearly insatiable. Many newcomers took up residence around the Army forts, in hopes that the coming of the railroad would transform their settlements into big cities. Some dreams came true but others did not. Adding to the other problems attributed to the new mode of transportation, towns began vigorous campaigns vying for political support in encouraging the railroad to come their way. Petty squabbles often turned into bloody battles. History had proven that railroad towns prosper and in the eyes of these townspeople smoke and cinders looked just as good as gold and silver.

The main by product of "railroad fever" was unrest—unrest among the new settlers, among the Indians and among the buffalo. Just as the Indian tribes were being divided, bison herds were split many times into smaller groups leaving them vulnerable to attack by man and beast alike.

The Army was having a difficult time too. George Armstrong Custer, who had orders to eradicate hostile Indian bands took it upon himself to avoid as much bloodshed as possible and worked with Indian leaders to attain his goal. While many Indians were content to stay on their reservations and receive their government annuities, some of the younger warriors were harder to tame. Defying even their own fathers they would leave the reservations in the dark of night and raid White settlements, often killing the men and always terrorizing women and children. It was frustrating for the elders who were trying to keep the peace. They seemed to have little control over their rebellious youngsters. It was equally frustrating for the men of the 7th Cavalry constantly having to rescue White families from their burned-out homes.

Charles Reynolds was aware of the White Man's progress and the Indians' resistance to it. It was an ongoing predicament and he longed for a resolution. For the next year or so, he wandered back and forth between the Republican and North Platte rivers, scouting for the Army and supplying the various forts with meat and furs as he went. He visited the Indian agencies and talked with the Indians whenever possible eager to learn their language and their customs. Some of the more inquisitive Sioux were curious about the lone hunter and greeted him with friendly smiles and expressive hand signs. While most Whites around the forts and agencies shunned the Red Man, Charley was always happy to communicate with them. Hard Rope had helped him understand Indian customs and he respected it.

Dakota Territory, the Late Sixties

Charley turns down the job of interpreter and guide at the Whetstone Agency deciding instead to fulfill his longtime dream and head up the Missouri River into Dakota Territory. He stops for supplies at Fort McPherson and then continues northeast across the Niobrara River and soon after, fording the Keya Paha and stopping at Fort Randall. It is spring and there is a feeling of newness all around. Rusty and Red are alert and full of energy as they cross the Makisi Ta-wakpa River. Charley likes the sound of the Indian name and recites it aloud several times trying to imitate Indian Joe's pronunciation. The term which refers to the White River means, "Smoking Earth River."

After spending a week near Fort Lookout and delivering fresh meat to that post, Charley rides on to the Brule Sioux Agency. He learns from a Brule chieftain that there is, "plenty game venison, Tatanka," on the, "Wakpa Shica," or the Bad River. The tip is a good one and Charley treats himself to a few days rest at the town of Pierre.

The Pierre Hotel is quiet and comfortable during the day and Charley revels in the luxury of a hot bath and fresh-smelling bed sheets. The gold watch glistens under the lamplight on the nightstand and he tries once more to write a letter to Ariana.

"My dear Ariana I am writing from Pierre Dakota Territory. I have arrived at last. How I wish you were here with me. I..."

The pen suddenly skips across the paper as a shot rings out from the saloon on the street below. Charley jumps up and hurries to the window. Another blast rips through the evening peace and two cowboys fall backwards from the saloon doors. The street is filled with curious onlookers, screaming and shouting and yet another shot is fired. Charley decides to investigate. He dresses and neatly folds the letter before leaving the room.

Once at street level Charley enjoys a full view of the ruckus. The source of the gunfire is unknown. Both cowboys unarmed and drunk are swinging their fists aimlessly as the crowd cheers them on. Eventually, the smaller of the two steadies himself against a hitching post and delivers a swift kick to the other's crotch. Just like Gabe's mules, Charley thinks to himself, as an agonizing moan denotes the end of the battle. The injured fighter falls to the ground in defeat; the winner staggers behind the saloon out of sight. Charley smiles as he recalls his victory over Antonio Delgado.

Charley stays in Pierre for three days. He has a new saddle made for Rusty and both horses get new reins and shoes. Hunting has been good and profits are high from the prime spring beaver he had traded at the general store. After resupplying his pack, he checks out of the hotel and heads deeper into Dakota Territory.

Charley is annoyed for not finishing the letter to Ariana, then reasons that she probably wouldn't get it even if he did send it. Taking the watch she had given him from his pocket, he reminisces for several minutes wondering how she is; hoping by now that her mother and father are aware of Delgado's deceit; wishing that Ariana would find a way out of her marriage to that skunk Antonio. He can still taste the

Spanish wine; still smell the perfume in her hair. But it's all so useless.

In the distance he can see the river the Indians call, "Good River"—Wakpa Washte. He marvels at the Sioux dialect—the way they carefully enunciate each syllable—as in Makisi Ta Wakpa.

"Maw-kee-see ta wawk-paw," he blurts out, causing Big Red to take an extra step. "Okay, old boy. I'll teach you a word too. How about Palanuta Wakpa? That's the Grand river Agency...and that's where we're headed." Charley laughs as Red's ears wiggle in response. He's a fine horse and Will would probably like to have him back.

Charley's thoughts turn to his brother and his family. His nephew Charles Edwin Reynolds will be three years come February. That's another letter he must write. Luckily he had remembered to get some more tallow for his lamp. No excuse this time!

The summer months are warm and dry and after draining his canteen on several occasions, Charley finally learns to ration his water carefully. He pities the suffering animals roaming day and night in search of rivers only to find dry creek beds. By allowing only the strongest members of the herd to drink and leaving the weak and old to the die under a scorching sun on the seething arid land, the bison population rations itself as efficiently as possible. This is not a friendly place.

It is fall of 1869, when Reynolds finally reaches the confluence of the Grand and Missouri rivers site of the Grand River Agency. The agent is amazed at the quality of meat on Charley's travois and signals the trader to come quickly and inspect the rest of the wares. The trader wastes no time in offering work to Charley. After a day's rest the weary hunter negotiates a contract with the trader, opting for less pay in return for more time to hunt on his own. Both parties seem pleased with the agreement.

Charley's reputation as a hunter, horseman and crack shot has caught the attention of White Man and Red Man alike and it doesn't take long for word to spread that he has actually arrived in Dakota Territory. From Yankton to the upper reaches of the Big Muddy...everyone wants to meet the White hunter they call Lonesome Charley.

At a Lakota (Sioux) village on the Dakota plains south of the Makisi Ta-Wakpa and west of the Missouri River, some warriors are discussing a lone white hunter they call Hunter-Who-Never-Goes-Out-For-Nothing.

"My friends, this is the hunting ground of our forefathers. Many moons, long time past they roamed this land. The people were the friends of the animals. The animals clothed us, sustained us and protected us." Iron Hawk, the wise one, pauses to look around at the others. "He take many Pte, Ta-tan-ka to Soldier Forts, soon there will be none for our people."

"Lakota must talk to this man they call Char-Lee," answers Two Dog. "He is brave...and carries a big gun."

"Many Wasichus have dogs," says Little Bear, "this Man Alone hunts with only two red horses."

"Hmm-mmn," Iron Hawk answers, rubbing his chin thoughtfully then holds up two fingers. "Two good horses! Iron Hawk would like to have the Red horse. Good."

Little Bear wonders if the man who had befriended him on the Geese River several years ago, was the same man. He remembers his horse had thrown him after being spooked by a Grizzly bear. He was afoot running for his life, the bear hot after him, when the White hunter had fired a shot, diverting the Grizzly's attention. The lone, young hunter caught Little Bear's horse and returned it to him. They spoke no words, but Little Bear was appreciative and had a good heart towards some of the Whites. "Little Bear not afraid of Man-Alone," he announces with confidence. "What is to fear of one Wasichus? What can he do to the Lakota? He is only one."

The warriors chatter excitedly until Iron Hawk interrupts them. "Our friend the Cheyenne say this Char-Lee is not big fool. I say Wasichus who hunt alone on Sioux land big fool!"

"What you say is good, Iron Hawk," replies Two Dog. "We must stop this Man-Alone-With-His-Two-Red-Horses before he takes all the Ta-tan-ka."

"I think it is not wise to harm this lone hunter," Iron Hawk says finally. "We must follow him. Maybe understand why the Wasichus slaughter Pte, Ta-tan-ka. Why the Wasichus want Sioux land. Why there are so many."

Little Bear speaks up. "Little Bear listen to White Man talk at Palanuta Wakpa. They say Man-Alone is called Lo-one-some Char-Lee... E-yo-ma-she-sha."

Iron Hawk chuckles and tells Little Bear he must have heard the name backwards. "Did you not hear Char-Lee Lo-onesome?" Opting for the transposed version he asks Little Bear to begin stalking Reynolds by sunrise the next day.

Charley is surprised when the small herd of buffalo he's been trailing suddenly begins to stampede for no apparent reason. Nevertheless, he spurs Red toward the running mass. It is Red's first time for this duty but Charley is confident the horse has learned from following Rusty in the past. Red seems willing at first, then leery. Charley urges him on gently, knowing the consequences, should the horse become spooked by the bison. Red balks again then bucks wildly. Charley slides from the saddle momentarily, as the skittish horse darts frantically amongst the buffalo.

On a distant hill, unknown to Reynolds, Little Bear is watching curiously as the skillful White hunter and his red horse maneuver into the herd to make the kill. He smiles to himself recalling the first time he hunted Pte, the buffalo. He was thrown from his pony and would have been trampled if it weren't for the long rawhide thong tied to his horse's neck.

Finally, after hearing his rider's reassuring commands, Red gets close enough and Charley fires the only shot needed to ground the big creature. Red is nervous and snorting violently. "Easy, Red. Calm down, boy. You did a good job. Easy, boy. Now, let's go get that meat." Before Charley dismounts he scans the horizon for any sign of danger. Although he senses the presence of an onlooker, none is in view.

Well hidden behind a ridge meanwhile, Little Bear is creeping up behind Rusty who is grazing in the ravine where Reynolds had left him. But the horse turns unexpectedly and sees the Indian. Charley hears Rusty neighing and calls out for him.

It is unusual behavior for Rusty; Charley is certain now that someone is watching him. Quickly he starts the hide with his knife and ties a rope to the neck hide then to his saddle, he uses Red to jerk the skin from the animal. He butchers the animal and starts his return journey to the agency.

Little Bear is sure that Rusty is the big horse he had seen on the Geese River. And after observing Little Bear at the Grand River Agency on two more occasions, Charley is convinced also that this is the same Indian he had seen on the North Platte. Once his contract with the trader at Grand River is fulfilled, he heads out for Fort Rice and Fort Stevenson. Both posts have sent word that they are short of venison, the favorite of the southern soldiers stationed there. Little Bear, on the other hand, vows to Iron Hawk that he will follow Char-Lee Lo-one-some, E-yo-ma-she-sha and talk to him when it seems safe to do so. For many sleeps he stays on Reynolds' trail back far enough so Charley doesn't detect him.

It is the twelfth sleep on the journey and Charley is roasting some fresh elk meat for supper. There is no moon and the sky is still cloudy after a steady day-long drizzle. His clothes are damp; the heat from the fire feels good. Staring into the flickering light he listens to a lone coyote sing its nocturnal lullaby. Charley catches himself drifting off, dreaming of Ariana and the warm fire in the adobe hut. All at once, a feeling of uneasiness consumes him. The coyote's scream is shrill now and another joins in a raucous duet. He jumps up to check the horses, peering into the darkness for a sign of an intruder. Finding none, he settles into his bedroll, removes his gold watch and gazes at it for several minutes, reminiscing of years past.

Charley is fully asleep when Rusty alerts him with a warning snort. In an instant, he pulls his rifle from between his knees and jumps to his feet. Standing alone by the fire is a Sioux warrior, his dark eyes twinkling in the glow from the remaining firelight.

"Sioux, friend," the Indian says quickly and loudly.

Charley at first is alarmed but even though still uneasy, he calms down a bit. Reynolds sees that the Indian's knife is sheathed and his bow and arrows are slung casually over his shoulder, hanging low near his waist. The Indian cautiously lays his blanket on the ground. He places his sheathed knife and his bow and arrows on the blanket to show that he means no harm. Reynolds slowly lowers his gun. It is the same Indian who was up on the Geese...the same one at the agency. Reynolds is absolutely certain this time. Little Bear raises his right hand palm forward, leaving the first two fingers extended in the friendship sign. Charley puts down his gun and mimics the sign.

Charley motions him to sit at his fire and he spreads a piece of canvas on the ground. Little Bear lowers himself to a cautious squat then sits quietly cross-legged. No words are spoken. His eyes calmly take in everything about Charley's camp.

Reynolds understands the Indian custom to offer tobacco. He always carries a plug for any kind of happening. Reynolds offers the plug to the Indian who removes a red stone pipe from its case. He cuts the tobacco up, mixing larb leaves with it then tamping it into the bowl. Reynolds hands him a branch. The Indian lights the branch in the coals of the fire then lights his pipe. He takes a couple of puffs blowing the smoke out. He then raises the pipe to the heavens then lowers it to the earth. He points the stem of the pipe towards the east and the west. He sits silently while he passes the pipe to Reynolds. Without speaking, Reynolds carefully imitates the Indians' actions then hands the pipe back.

Reynolds offers some meat to his curious visitor. Charley eats slowly, while the Indian hungrily gobbles the venison, wiping his mouth on his arm when he is done.

In the Lakota dialect, Little Bear tells Charley that he has come in friendship and wishes to talk. They stare at each other for some time, until Charley manages to make the Indian understand that he recognizes him from the Geese River. Little Bear begins to talk slowly and deliberately, using sign language and in the Sioux tongue:

Using his right thumb he points to his chest. "Day gone, sun gone. I Little Bear I watch Man-Alone-With-Two-Red-Horses for many sleeps," sweeping his extended hands then inclining his head to the right.

Charley can't hide an I-knew-it smile and urges Little Bear to tell more.

"I ride horse across prairie, see White man kill Pte," he continues posing menacingly with his two index fingers curling at the sides of his head to signify the horns of Pte, the buffalo. "My people Lakota worry...now we must ride horse many sleeps to find Pte. Lakota see many wagon trails, few pte."

Charley waits for a moment, trying to find enough Sioux words to express his thoughts. "I mean no harm to the Lakota," he says finally

"You Char-Lee," he says, belching so loud the echo startles his pony.

Reynolds assures his quest that he is indeed Char-Lee Lo-one-some, E-yo-ma-she-sha and that he once traveled with an Osage Indian named Hard Rope. Using his hands he describes the shaved head of the Osage tribe. Little Bear smiles knowingly.

After a while, Charley finally breaks a long silence and asks the Indian to tell him why he is called Little Bear. The Indian eagerly tells the story of a small black bear that had been his good friend when he was eight winter past or eight years old. Charley is amused and expresses his own love for all the wild animals.

"Why go kill Pte, Wapiti?" Little Bear asks.

"Like you and all the great hunters of the Sioux...I go, I shoot one Ta-tan-ka. I go, I shoot one elk. I hunt food for my people. Question, you understand?"

The blank look tells Charley that his visitor doesn't like the answer. Quickly he takes his tin cup and pours some coffee, adding a good measure of sugar before offering it to Little Bear.

"Washte," replies the Red Man with a grin, sweeping his hand over his heart. "Washte!" Charley understands the Sioux word meaning good and nods.

When Little Bear strikes the coffee pot with the empty cup, Charley refills it. He's not surprised when the Indian requests even more sugar. Hard Rope had been the same way—always taking enough of the sweet substance for three or four cups.

"The Corn Indians—call you Hunter-Who-Never-Goes-Out-For-Nothing,"

Little Bear says, urging Charley to tell him more about his hunting prowess.

"I go kill Ta-tan-ka and Wapiti yes—but only for food," Reynolds assures him.

"White Man go kill Ta-tan-ka, White Man kill white rump, the Shoshoni call Wapiti. White Man go kill, leave to die on prairie," replies the Indian with a tone of frustration.

Again, Reynolds states his case—more emphatically this time. He is relieved when Little Bear finally stands, a smile on his face. He takes a long piece of rawhide thong from his pony's neck and offers it to Charley. Then with hands clasped in front of him, left palm up, he gives Char-Lee Lo-one-some the Peace-Go sign and quietly disappears into the black night.

Realizing now that Little Bear must have been watching him all along, Charley makes a promise to himself to pay closer attention to his intuition—and to use the long rope next time he rides a green broke horse into a buffalo herd.

Charley travels up and down the Missouri stopping at all the posts and agencies along the way. The Standing Rock Agency just north of an old fort along the Missouri is a favorite haunt, as is Fort Rice, a stockade post overlooking the Big Muddy. Built in 1864, to serve the settling of Dakota Territory, it is here that most of the westward expeditions begin. Reynolds reputation as a professional huntsman and scout is well known and he is hired to guide a team of geologists on one occasion. Charley is fascinated by the scientists' work and when they return to Boston he is rewarded with a bound book, describing the rock formations found along the Missouri River. Although this new type of work appeals to him, it is rare and as a matter of survival, he is forced to take an assignment at Fort Stevenson.

In the early summer of 1871, Charley moves up to the Painted Woods area supplying meat to the, "New Fort Berthold," (Fort Stevenson) and several of the other smaller posts in the vicinity. If any place could be called home to this quiet, gentle man, it is here on the Great Plains of the Dakota Territory. He hungers to learn all there is to know about the land and investigates everything that Nature has laid before him, often resorting to his small but valuable collection of books for the answers to his never-ending list of questions. As each day passes, his expertise in the wilderness is honed near perfection.

Seventeen miles west of Fort Stevenson is the Berthold Agency, a popular gathering spot for Indians, trappers and wayward travelers. When Charley decides to contract with the agency he is persuaded to hire a half-breed Arickaree to help drive the wagon and do some of the other menial chores that Charley would rather not do. His mother had abandoned Peter, who never knew his French father, at an early age. He is a hard worker but proves to be overly superstitious, which tends to annoy Charley at times.

A fierce, hot wind persists for most of what the Indians called, Heat Moon or the month of July, but it does not stop Lonesome Charley from living up to the terms of his contract. Peter is amazed—envious in fact—of the White Man's uncanny hunting ability. But a particular curiosity to the half-breed is Charley's little black bottle of "scent" used to lure the elusive elk.

"Sure thing!" Charley says lightheartedly when Peter asks him about the bottle. "I sprinkle a little of this out on the flat where I can get a clean shot and the Wapiti come in herds. I just sit back behind the bushes and wait."

Unfortunately, Peter is not aware of what is really in the bottle and imagines it to be some sort of mystical potion. The following day, when they return to the Agency with eight elk, a gathering of one hundred or more Arickarees and Gros Ventres are there to meet them. Peter had told them of Charley's supernatural powers and they demand to have the, "magic medicine." One Gros Vertres chieftain threatens to have his scalp if Charley doesn't relinquish the bottle.

Reynolds' first thought is to be honest with the Indians but he knows that the consequences might be disastrous. Instead, he decides to deny the existence of the black bottle or any magic elixir. An Arickaree brave approaches the wagon team and holds a knife to the throat of the lead horse. But Charley's steely nerves and quick action persuade the Indians to back off. The Sharps .50 is a familiar sight and with the soft-spoken man's threat, that they'll all be sent to the Happy Hunting Grounds they finally withdraw, grumbling as they walk away.

With Fall approaching the lone hunter decides to head south. He has been thinking of his family often and how nice it would be to see his brother Will and his namesake little Charles Edwin. He loads up his possessions and makes his way to Fort Rice where he barters for free passage to Yankton on a steamer. He promises the captain that he will have fresh game for the passengers every time they stop to load wood. The cook, of course is, delighted.

While aboard the steamer Charley meets an assortment of travelers—a scientist, a journalist, several soldiers, two politicians from Washington and a number of emigrants anxious to get back home to the States. One day, he happens upon a discarded edition of the New York Times, in which appears a story of Russian royalty visiting the Americas. Charley is entertained by the tales of the flamboyant Duke Alexis, who has been complaining about all the pomp and ceremony afforded him by the American government. Evidently, the Duke has expressed a desire to see the, "real," America—the, "wild west," and "real," Indian savages and such. And most of all he wants to participate in a buffalo hunt.

When Charley reaches Yankton he purchases a more recent newspaper, hoping to read more about the Russian Duke. He is not disappointed; he learns that George Armstrong Custer has been asked to accompany the celebrity on a buffalo hunt at Red Willow Creek, Nebraska. Buffalo Bill Cody, who has made quite a name for himself, will be the guide.

Charley is excited. It is a chance of a lifetime. He folds the newspaper clippings neatly into an envelope and sends a short note, telling Will of his change of plans. He has applied for the job of scout on this, the most prestigious buffalo hunt of all.

The camp at Red Willow, in Charley's opinion, is a bit outlandish. A "tent city," is erected and the Duke's tent is not only floored but carpeted. Hand carved furniture, including his own bed from Russia and elaborate stoves transported by wagon from Chicago, are installed especially for the occasion. Indian dancers entertain the party as they sip fine liquors and dine on tasty venison and pheasant.

The hunt itself lasts five days. Charley loses count of the kill but thirty of the great beasts meet death during the first two hours. When it is all over, Charley is relieved to be back on his own again. He longs for the Dakota Territory. Again he cancels a trip home to Kansas, sending instead, a brief account of the hunt with Duke Alexis, together with another newspaper clip quoting the royal visitor's comments about his return stagecoach ride with Bill Cody. It reads:

"I would not have missed it for a large sum of money but rather than repeat it I would return to Russia via Alaska swim the Bering Strait and finish my journey on one of your Army mules."

The excitement of the big event dies quickly and Lonesome Charley Reynolds is hankering for the place that has become his home—the land of the Dakotas. He returns to Yankton where he once again boards a steamer to head up the wide Missouri. He is surprised to learn from the captain that word of his presence on the buffalo hunt with George Custer, Bill Cody and the Russian Duke has surfaced in the strangest of places.

"That story was on the front page of all the big city newspapers, Reynolds," Grant Marsh tells Charley. "But I'd rather hear it from someone who was there."

Charley describes all the details of the hunt to an amused Captain Marsh.

"Oh by the way, Reynolds," the Captain adds. "I almost forgot...I delivered a letter to Fort Rice for you...just last week. I hope it's still there."

"It's probably from my family. I'm not very good at writing letters. I'm sure they're wondering where I am. Thank you, Captain. I'll ride to Fort Rice right away."

The letter is postmarked St. Louis from Mildred.

Dear Charley—We read about your adventure with the Duke and are relieved to know that you are still alive. We have thought of you often over the many years and wondered where your travels had taken you. Oscar and I are celebrating our tenth wedding anniversary this year. Now that our two children are old enough we are making plans to go to Oregon come next spring. It's a promise I made to Oscar when I married him. Jeff and Jubal are grown men now and both have taken wives. They seem quite content to stay on the farm. If you get this letter please let us know how you are. We would like to see you once again before we go west.—Mildred and Oscar.

"It's been over ten years," Charley says out loud. Ten years since that Indian attack and he, along with Oscar, Mildred and the two boys, Jeff and Jubal, survived. "My how time flies."

Charley reins up to survey a dozen teepees not far from the river. Small herds of Indian Cayuses graze on the rich grasses. Meat dries on long skinny poles. He watches the Indian women move about at their daily labor.

Using large stone malls, the women drive wooden pegs through raw buffalo hides, staking them to the ground. On their knees, they scrape the flesh from the hides with their horn and bone scrapers. Mongrel dogs snap and snarl for any little tidbit of the fatty meat.

Charley is impressed. The women do the work in an Indian village. They erect the lodges or take them down. They do the cooking, tan the hides, do the beadwork, make moccasins and saddle the ponies, among other things.

He realizes that the entire life of the male is to hunt and supply the lodge with food, mainly wild game and skins and to take scalps from the enemy. The boys, from when they are babies, learn to ride and to guard the pony herd. And especially are the warriors trained to guard the camp and the women and children.

Reynolds leads his horses loaded with buffalo meat and hides, beaver and wolf pelts and traps. Thompson, a White Man, and Walks-on-Ice, his pleasant Arapaho woman, nod and wave a greeting.

Like many white men, trappers, traders, mountain men, Thompson has taken an Indian woman for his wife. To most whites he is called a squaw man. No one seems to know Thompson's first name, at least it is never used.

Thompson's band consists of mostly relatives, women, a few young men and several older men and some children. It is impossible for large numbers to congregate in one area for long periods, so small bands break off from the main village. Except for something strange, this is a typical, small Indian encampment.

Charley dismounts. He picks up a chunk of broken lodge pole four or five feet long before he enters the camp. Several Indian dogs slither and sneak up behind him, snapping and snarling, biting at his heels. The bold one has a distinct black and white ring around one eye. Hence, Charley calls him, Old Patch Eye. Charley watches slyly from the corner of his eye. Closer and closer they come. At the last instant, Charley wields the club and manages to whack one of the curs that yelps and runs off.

Thompson who has not been paying any heed to the dogs until now, yells out, "Get, you mangy lop-eared devil-eyed mutt. One of these days I'll cook yer' hair off jist like the Rapahoes' do when they cook up a gaggle of young pups!" The others scurry away.

Thompson motions Walks-on-Ice to help and the threesome begin to unload Charley's gear into one of the teepees. "Good bunch of pelts n' meat. No wonder the Rees call you, "Lucky Man."

Charley smiles. "Divide the meat with others, the older ones first. It was a worthy hunt."

Thompson chuckles. "You'n gits more meat with fewer bullets than any huntsman on the, Big Muddy. Hope yer' luck don't run out n' them fair locks of yours dangle from some Sioux 'er Cheyenne scalp pole."

Charley absentmindedly reaches up and rubs his fingers through his auburn hair. He chuckles.

Thompson chuckles along with Charley. "That Auburn hair of yers would surely decorate a Sioux scalp pole. Look right pretty alongside that red flannel that they tie on their shafts."

Thompson notices that Charley's look turns serious. "Naw! Yer hair is too short, Charley. Sioux like 'em long hair."

"Thompson, I've wondered about that red flannel for a long time. When I was eighteen I found a lance with the red flannel on it. My brother, William, said it was spooky. Get rid of it. That thing will haunt you the rest of your life."

"You knowed yer ownself, Charley injuns 'ur superstitious. I don't rightly know, I've seed some strange doings happen in this country. Some say it is what you b'leve." Thompson turns and yells at the curs, "Git you mangy..." While eyeing the dogs, he chatters on. "I'd venture a by golly if you b'leve strong enough, Charley, it will happen. You've seed as much or more." He turns to Charley while they walk to the fire. "Yuh' know, Charley, yuh risked your har a goin' ta injun country, I hardly knowest what fer?"

Charley looks away then, "I was eighteen when I told my father and my brother William that I wanted to be part of it. Be a Plainsman, see it all."

Thompson looks puzzled. "Part of what? See..."

Charley interrupts. "The West. I'd make my stash then settle down—I haven't seen it all. My Father always said, Finish what you start, Charles."

Walks-on-Ice who has been listening, speaks in Arapaho to Thompson.

Walks-on-Ice is from the Arapaho people to the south. She is attractive. In her womanly way, while living the free life on the plains, she has acquired much wisdom. She looks mostly Indian but there is something about her that hints that she has some white blood. Like most of the Plains Indian women, she takes pride in her dress. She wears knee high moccasins adorned with blue and red beadwork. Fancy silver ornaments enhance the sides.

She chatters away in Arapahoe. Thompson turns to Charley with a smile. "She says, yuh gots the heart of the buffalo, always on the move in search of the creeping buffalo grass. You are happy when there is danger."

Charley nods with a half smile. "Ask Walks-on-Ice to cook some buffalo." He rubs his stomach. "I am hungry."

After Thompson signs and chatters away in Arapaho, Walks-on-Ice motions for one of the other Indian women to come help her.

Reynold's eyes follow the young Indian woman as she walks over. He had paid no mind to the new woman before and he knew better than to ask too many questions.

She is taller and comely, more so than other Plains Indian women he has seen. Her stride is long and she moves with quickness about her.

While the two women prepare the buffalo, Charley seems curious and watches. The young woman wears a long deerskin dress, fancy beaded with fringes and elk teeth hanging in neat rows. Around her waist a belt holds an awl and a paint pouch. Both pouches are elaborately decorated with beads and dyed porcupine quills.

The two women smile and chatter away while they cut the meat into long strips. Charley doesn't understand the Arapahoe language but he understands their sign and he can sometimes glean the jest of what they talk about.

Charley looks at Thompson sharpening his knife, then he sees the women go to the river. The Indian woman's feet are dressed in the typical, just below the knee, moccasin leggings that are adorned with small brass buttons on the sides. Colorful purple and white and shades of blue beadwork mingle with the rich lavender dyed quillwork on the instep and up the sides. Charley can't help but notice that underneath her garments she is well proportioned. The way she walks reminds him of one of the cavalry's smooth gaited thoroughbred horses. She seemed to glide effortlessly across the prairie. Charley chuckles to himself, maybe she glides along because of her fancy moccasins. Whatever the case, he can see that she takes pride in her dress. He likes that.

Walks-on-Ice and her companion return from the river, each carrying a handful of green willow sticks. Her young companion seems to flow along like the gentle spring breezes of a hot afternoon. Charley watches her. It's been a long while since he's been with a woman.

His mind slips readily back to his time with Ariana. She was the only one that he had known but a bad case of in –laws and a scoundrel wrecked their marriage. Charley is snapped back to reality by several of the cur dogs fighting over a bone. He feels embarrassed and looks around sheepishly.

For some unknown reason he seems drawn to the Indian woman. And he wonders to himself, why? Maybe it was her hair. In the light her hair sheens an incomparable auburn color that blends into a lovely appearance. She must not be a full-bloodied Indian, he thinks to himself. He contemplates her heritage. Maybe she has some Russian or perhaps maybe Norseman ancestry.

He recalls his own English heritage and how his Grandfather had talked about the Vikings. He remembers an old trapper telling about Norsemen who had come many years ago and had married into the Cheyenne's that lived and hunted along the Missouri. Some of them he said were fair skinned and blue eyed.

Charley looks fascinated as the two women peel the bark off the green willow shoots. They then hold the sticks for a few minutes over the fire. After heating they skewer the rich red buffalo meat onto the sticks. They push the sticks into the ground near the fire to cook. His stomach growls reminding him that he is hungry.

He then remembers a chore that he has been putting off. Now would be a good time to do it. "Yell out when supper is ready," he tells Thompson. He lifts the flap and steps into his teepee.

Inside he sits downs and removes a pencil and paper from his belongings. He begins to write. He has just finished when he hears Thompson. "Come and get it, er I give it tuh the curs." Charley tucks the envelope away and goes outside.

He sits down across from Thompson who is already chewing a piece of the good smelling meat. Walks-on-Ice smiles at Charley and occupies herself at the fire. The young woman turns from the fire and hands Charley one of the meat-skewered sticks. Charley's shy nature compels him to look away but he makes himself turn back. He can't help but notice her look. She smiles at him. The way she grins out of the corner of her mouth, a cute little grin, that makes her whole face light up and makes his heart skip.

Thompson interrupts. "At the Sutler's Store there's talk."

Charley looks at Thompson. "Yeah."

"The railroad is gonna' push further west. The Army out of Fort Rice is gonna guard the survey."

Charley doesn't answer, he's preoccupied. Looking off he catches the Indian woman looking at him. He looks away, then pays her no attention. Running-creek-Woman and Walks-on-Ice chatter away in the Arapaho tongue.

"Chatterin' about something," Thompson says. He looks at Charley. "Yuh' know...the Army pays good. You could hire on, work for the Army, see the West n' lay up some money fer it."

Charley mulls it over then politely says. "I must tell you, Thompson. I am obliged that you and the others take care of my camp."

Thompson chuckles. "The pay could be better," Thompson smiles and they laugh. "I knowed yer appreciative, Charley n' that's all that matters. Besides, since Running-creek-Woman come to our camp we have more help."

Charley smiles about the name. "I am obliged, Thompson. You know that." Charley subtlety coughs. "The woman is called Running-creek-Woman? Kinda' pretty."

"Why, Charles, yuh surprise me. Hardly knew yuh to take interest in a woman."

"There is a lot you don't know about me, Thompson." Charley looks at Walks-on-Ice and signs good. "It's hard to beat buffalo loin cooked over an open fire. Tell the women that Tatanka," he uses the Sioux word for the buffalo bull, "is very good." Thompson nods in agreement and speaks to Walks-on-Ice and Running-Creek-Woman who return his nod along with a smile.

Charley looks at Thompson and his woman Walks-on-Ice. Their relationship is unlike many of the White-Man and Indian trappers who take an Indian woman just to keep them warm during the cold or to toil away doing hard work from dawn to dark.

"You have a good woman, Thompson. I have seen others who abuse their women. You treat her well. She is happy."

Thompson grins, "I'm obliged Charley. She is a good woman. The older men say, good woman in your lodge, good man in your lodge."

Charley stays for several days coming and going as he pleases. With the women's help he and Thompson flesh and stack beaver pelts. Charley loads cartridges, mends his gear, stopping only to eat. Around the campfire they eat, talk and laugh. He retires at night to his teepee. He has noticed, that often whatever he is doing, that on the sly, Running-creek-Woman watches him.

One morning Charley comes from his teepee. He has his bedroll and his rifles. While saddling up Red, Thompson walks over. Charley ties his belongings on the saddle then hands Thompson a letter. "Please mail this at the trader's store."

Thompson eyes the envelope.

Senorita Ariana Fernandez
c/o General Delivery
Santa Fe, New Mexico Territory

Thompson nods. Charley gives a quick wave. He leads Rusty from the camp then gallops along the river. Unknown to Charley, the young Indian maiden watches him.

June, the Month of the Fat Horses, passes and Reynolds is hired by the Quartermaster at Fort Rice as one of several scouts and guides for General Stanley's expedition to the Yellowstone River. He will receive 100 dollars a month pay. Charley acquires considerable knowledge of the land, escorting a team of surveyors for the Northern Pacific Railroad. In addition to scouting he also carries dispatches for the Army. His hunting experience in the land of the Sioux equips him well for this dangerous service. It is the Indian, Falling Leaf Moon, October when he finally accepts his pay, free to travel on his own again. Charley roams the wide expanse of the Dakota Territory until the Grass Moon, April, of the following year. But for now, Ariana his sweetheart, has been playing heavy on his mind and he contemplates returning to New Mexico.

6

*F*or the Northern Pacific Railroad, Dakota Territory represented both opportunity and uncertainty. Severe weather conditions—winter and summer—coupled with unpredictable Indian attacks, hampered surveying efforts to such a degree that railroad officials finally requested assistance from the United States Army.

Since the end of the Civil War and it's embryo in 1866, divisions of the 7th Cavalry had been assigned to various postwar campaigns in the South. One company was dispatched to South Carolina to monitor the Klu Klux Klan while another was sent to Tennessee. George Armstrong Custer—the colorful, "boy general," now a seasoned commander with an enviable list of credentials—had found a temporary home in Elizabeth Town, Kentucky. It was there that the 7th continues its policy of acquiring the finest thoroughbred horses, which ultimately became its trademark. Custer did not find Army life rewarding after the War, so he was understandably ecstatic when he received orders that the 7th Cavalry was to be reunited in Memphis. From there a large part of the regiment would be moved out by boat and rail to the northern plains of the Dakota Territory.

The rail cars are full of men of the spit and polished 7th U.S. Cavalry. Lieutenant Colonel George Armstrong Custer flamboyant and energetic talks with William Winer Cooke.

Cooke is a large man with mustache and huge pork chop whiskers, called Dundreries. He turns to the General, "Kentucky has been good but I'm sick n' tired of chasing those moonshiners."

"It's a difficult task. Especially when most of the men like drinking the stuff, Cookie," Custer smiles

"General, are you implying?"

Custer interrupts. "No, not at all Lieutenant."

"Thank you, Sir. It was too laid back in E-Town!" Cook says.

"Kentucky provided the 7th Horse with the finest thoroughbred horses of any cavalry outfit in the U.S. Army." Custer brags.

Cooke glances out the window for a moment. "You like having the best, Sir."

Custer nods. "That is why I've wired a Dakota scout."

Cooke is surprised. "The 7th Horse has several scouts that are trustworthy and of good character Sir."

"Indians raised so much trouble last year, the railroad survey was forced to turn back. The President says the railroad must push through. We need good men. This quiet man knows the country. He knows the Indians. He's roamed the plains for years, alone. He is of fine character. He is frank, steadfast, trustworthy, one of the greatest Plainsmen out there."

Cooke looks puzzled, "And just who might this gentleman be?"

"You will have the pleasure of his acquaintance soon." George Custer smiles.

When Charles Reynolds read the news of the impending arrival of, "the greatest horse cavalry in the world," he immediately rode to Yankton. He was eager to reacquaint himself with General Custer.

Yankton Dakota Territory, April, 1873

Lonesome Charley is caught up in the excitement. The mood of the townsfolk is festive, cheery and warm despite the cold whistle of a bitter prairie wind. Upon seeing his reflection in a shop window, Charley notices that his clothes are worn and dirty—hardly suitable for the mayor's ball. He chooses a complete new wardrobe, including a buffalo-hide coat, shiny black buttoned boots and a beaverskin hat just like the one Trapper Green wore. The shopkeeper's compliments add the finishing touch as the dapper gentleman steps confidently from the store.

Like a royal procession, the 7th Cavalry exits the long line of cars at the end of the Illinois-Central road about a mile from town. Soldiers, along with their horses and menagerie of other creatures—dogs, pigs and birds among them—spill onto the hard lifeless prairie. The two-week journey from Memphis has taken its toll. Many of the men, including the General himself, have fallen ill and are too weak to travel further. Custer orders camp be made immediately and finds shelter at a primitive cabin near the rail's end for his wife, Libbie, and their two servants.

Furiously snapping the regimental flags, a brisk wind warns of the oncoming storm. The temperature drops rapidly; sweeping, black clouds swallow the meek April sun and soon the snow is drifting in solid white waves to depths of three or four feet. Custer orders his men to leave camp in search of shelter in Yankton but a dozen or more are lost in the blizzard and return to the little shack dazed and severely frostbitten; some even requiring amputation of frozen fingers or toes. The pathetic noises of the animals outside, many near death, remind the cabin's occupants of their privilege. Above it all, Libbie Custer attempting to nurse her ailing husband, forces him to take the foul-tasting medicine prescribed by the Army's physician.

"Wretched stuff!" he protests. "If I drink anymore of that I'll surly die! I need some food, Libbie!"

After eating a small portion of steak and potatoes, warmed over the few remaining candles, the General regains enough strength to venture out into the waning hours of the storm. With his usual vigor in the face of adversity, he musters his cavalry with renewed spirit.

"The mayor of Yankton has invited the entire regiment to a ball at the hotel," Custer tells his adjutant. "The entire town will be there and every soldier is expected to attend in full dress uniform."

George Armstrong Custer never allows anything to keep him down for long.

Though prone to bouts of sniffles and wheezes, he recuperates quickly and expects nothing less of his men. Soon the 7th Cavalry is back on its feet and looking forward to the upcoming party.

It is the evening of the ball and Reynolds is pleased with his new clothes and haircut. He thanks the barber for his efforts and crosses the street to the hotel. If the spit-and-polish 7th Cavalrymen were suffering from ill health it is not evident now. Every button glistens and not a hair is out of place.

The gentleman scout declines the offer of a beverage and makes his way across the hotel ballroom where General and Mrs. Custer are talking with Lieutenant James Calhoun and his wife, Margaret, George's sister. His brother, Tom Custer is nearby.

The General acknowledges Reynolds as he approaches. "Well if it isn't Lonesome Charley Reynolds," he exclaims moving quickly to introduce first his wife then his sister and brother-in-law.

Lieutenant Cooke walks over. His giant frame dwarfs Charley's five foot eight stature. "Is this the scout, General?"

"That's him. Lieutenant Cooke, meet Charles Reynolds."

The giant and the small man shake hands. Cooke smiles. "I expected someone larger, I don't know why."

George Custer grins. "That's why gun powder comes in small kegs, Cookie." He eyes Charley. "Small keg, big explosion!"

They all laugh.

"I'm pleased to meet everyone," Charley responds politely. "What brings the famous 7th Cavalry to Dakota Territory?"

Custer looks surprised. "You never got my wire, Reynolds?"

"No, Sir. What wire? Never received anything."

"Never mind, now. You're here. Seems the Indians are not happy, Reynolds," Custer says. "That's why we're here. The Northern Pacific is determined to push west with the railroad and the Indians are just as determined to stop it."

Charley smiles and says, "I been hearing rumors since last year—ever since the Sioux harassed us so much on the survey that it was thought best to turn around."

Custer looks at Charley thoughtfully. "You were with the soldiers on the survey? I wasn't aware," he rubs his chin.

"Is this the same Reynolds who accompanied you on the buffalo hunt with the Duke, Autie?" asks Libbie Custer.

"Yes, dear. This is Lonesome Charley...one of the best..." Before correcting himself he glances apologetically at his wife. "Darned scouts I know."

"I was always in the background doing guard duty or scouting duty, Mrs. Custer."

Tom Custer overhears the name and breaks into the conversation. "Did you say Lonesome Charley, brother?"

A lively discussion follows the handshakes and other formalities and Charley begins to feel more at ease with the guests of honor. After dinner the ladies retire to their respective rooms to freshen up for the ball while the men congregate to hear General Custer's plans for containing the Indians in the Dakota Territory. Smiling waiters liberally dispense snifters of brandy and cigar smoke thickens the air in the smoking room.

"Here, Reynolds," says Tom Custer offering Charley a drink. "This is very fine brandy."

Charley shakes his head. "Not for me. Thank you, Tom."

"Reynolds knows the evils of strong drink, Tom." The elder brother says in a sarcastic tone. "Don't smoke either do you, Reynolds?"

"No, Sir!" is the simple reply.

"Tell me, Reynolds," Custer continues, "are you employed?"

"No, Sir. I work from time to time—more often during the summer months—mainly for the agencies and for Grant Marsh the riverboat captain. Of course, I trap now and then too. This is wide-open country. A man can do just about anything he wants to."

"The wire you never received, if you're not beholden to anyone we certainly could use a good scout on the upcoming Yellowstone Expedition. The Army would make it worth your while, I'm sure. Think about it, Reynolds and let me know. We'll be making camp tomorrow...just a day's ride north of town. We'll be there three to four weeks preparing for our journey up the Missouri."

Trying not to appear too eager Charley hesitates before his reply. "It would be an honor to ride with the 7th, Sir. I can be ready to leave tomorrow if you wish."

"Tomorrow it is then. I'll inform the Quartermaster you'll be there." Custer turns as a group of officers sing one of his favorite songs. "Come quick, Libbie."

"The hour was sad I left the maid A ling'ring farewell talking; Her sighs and tears my steps delay'd—I thought her heart was breaking. In hurried words her name I bless'd I breathed the vows that bind me And to my heart in anguish press'd The girl I left behind me."

Elizabeth Bacon Custer is comfortable in the saddle on her blooded thoroughbred. For many miles she has traveled like this alongside her husband over the barren Kansas, Nebraska and Texas plains. But never has she known a time when her General seemed so proud of his regiment. Turning back she can see two miles of mounted cavalry stretching in a long, winding line of white covered wagons, snaking across the untamed Dakota Territory. It is May 7th; the soldiers are healthy now and look immaculate, having been reviewed by the Governor and a number of other dignitaries before breaking camp earlier in the day.

"You have good reason to be proud of them, Autie," Libbie remarks to her husband.

"And you too, my dear. You ride as well as some of our officers."

"Oh, Autie. You shouldn't say such things. The officers will feel badly." She giggles and then points to an approaching rider. "Oh, look. I think it is Mr. Reynolds. He's terribly shy, isn't he? Why, he barely looked at me when you introduced us at the ball."

"I didn't notice, Libbie," he says directing his attention to Charley. "Good Afternoon, Reynolds."

Mrs. Custer echoes the greeting.

Charley tips his hat to Custer's wife. "Good afternoon, Mrs. Custer. General."

The General's wife replies: "No need to be so formal, Charley. Please call me Libbie."

Charley nods shyly. "Yes, ma'am," he says then turns to Custer. "General, I'm going to ride a few miles ahead. We'll have to cross a stream at some point. It narrows in a few places but with this late snow and the heavy spring rains the water is much higher than normal. You might have to build a bridge for the wagons."

"Good, Reynolds. The sooner we know, the sooner we can get started. But don't go alone. Take one of the other scouts with you and I'll have Captain Allison ride with you also."

"Yes, Sir. We should be back before sundown."

The following day, when it is clear that a bridge is needed for the wagons, Custer sends Captain McDougall and his company to begin building the makeshift crossing. Stripped down to their undergarments, the men wade gingerly into the chilly water, carrying ropes to the other side. While construction is underway, Reynolds and a few soldiers make use of their idle time, hunting for food. The soldiers have great fun trying to capture the hard-to-hit plover, the small plump bird that is so popular at the dinner table. They finally resort to shotguns. Meanwhile, Charley has no trouble finding a small herd of antelope. He downs eight of the creatures and has them loaded on the wagons before the bridge is complete.

After two weeks of steady progress the cavalry reaches Fort Sully. The General orders the troops to make camp where they'll wait for the steamer that was hired at Yankton to carry some of the heavier supplies and forage for the animals.

When the steamer finally arrives the soldiers are ferried across the Missouri and the five hundred mile journey to Fort Rice continues at a normal pace. The long trail of Bluecoats and white-topped wagons meanders alongside the big river for several weeks without incident. Charley Reynolds is surprised by Custer's seemingly endless supply of energy, riding sometimes beyond sunset then moving again before the next crack of dawn. On the other hand, it's not unusual for the General to bring the entire command to a halt in the middle of the day. "Nooning," the soldiers call it. When Custer reaches his point of exhaustion he simply dismounts spreads his lanky body on the ground and sleeps. His snoring evidently provides some comfort for his many dogs, for they often sleep alongside him and sometimes their furry forms are draped haphazardly over his torso. It's during these strange intermissions that Charley becomes acquainted with some of the others on the excursion; namely, one Captain

Edward Allison and of course, the lovely Libbie Custer. She always has a friendly smile for Charley and often writes in her diary about the very private scout.

Charley is equally amazed at Mrs. Custer's stamina as well as that of Mrs. Calhoun and the other wives. He marvels at their bravery, for few women would subject themselves to such an unappealing lifestyle.

"Hello, Charley," Libbie says, as Reynolds approaches. "I suppose you're looking for my Autie. He's sleeping but it's time he awoke."

Custer stirs at the sound of his wife's voice. "What is it, dear?" he asks stretching and squinting into the noonday sun. Suddenly he sees Charley. "Oh, it's you, Reynolds. Is there trouble?"

"No, Sir," Charley replies quietly.

The General, his energy fully restored jumps to his feet. "We best be moving onward then. I'll talk to you later, my dear," he says, smiling at his wife. "I have a few matters to discuss with Tom." He nods to his scout. "I'll be seeing you later, Reynolds."

They had not traveled far when Libbie rides up alongside Charley and alerts him to an odd-looking structure on the horizon. "Whatever is that, Charley?" she asks pointing westward into the afternoon sun.

Charley stares at the wavy patterns as the heat reflects from the golden landscape. In his head he hears the haunting Boom boom—boom-boom-boom of Indian drums. Gradually the wobbly uprights come into focus then the platform and the tight-wrapped bodies. A shiver travels the length of his spine as he recalls a similar scene.

Libbie feels Charley's discomfort. "What is it, Charley?"

"It's an Indian burial scaffold, Mrs. Custer. Nothing to be afraid of."

"I'm glad of that. What an eerie sight! Unlike the way the Indians bury their dead in Kansas. Why, there they lay them in trees."

Charley suddenly feels compelled to tell Libbie his experience of years ago and she listens intently.

"I was only eighteen, one morning my old mentor and I were plodding through the snow. Trapper Green discovered an Indian burial site. It made me shiver as I watched the low autumn sun reach across that bleak landscape, illuminating several burial scaffolds upon a barren hill. Long gray shadows stretched westward as we approached the eerie sanctuary."

"Sounds like something I'd be scared to death to see. Where were you, Charley?"

"In the mountains of Colorado. There were small beaded moccasins on one of the scaffolds, showing us that it was the body of a young woman which had been there only a few weeks."

Charley looks across at the burial scaffolds then looks at Libbie, who by her look, wants him to continue. "Sticking in the ground nearby, were several lances, red flannel strips fluttered in the breeze. I could feel the hair on my neck stand up. Ol' Gabe

Green dismounted, handed his reins to me and began dismantling the structure kicking it to the ground. I was shocked; I didn't know what he was going to do. As I watched, the body dropped silently into the snow. What on earth are you doing, Gabe? That's someone's grave! I said."

Libbie Custer looks awe struck, gasping.

"Ol' Gabe turned to me and said, She's been dead for weeks. She'll make good bait for the woofs. Get me a couple of traps, boy. I yelled. You can't do that, Gabe. That's a real person, not an animal. Isn't anything sacred to you?"

"Oh, my God, Charley. It must have been frightful," gasps Libbie.

"It was, then he stared at me. What the difference? She's dead ain't she? The woofs and buzzards will get her if I don't. Cussed buzzards. I don't want any part of this, Gabe Green, I yelled. I threw his reins to the ground and spurred my horse to ride on. But she's dead, youngin, old Gabe Green yells. What's the difference? Ol' Gabe glared until the crunch of my horse's hooves stopped and then there was silence. When I looked back, the red flannel fluttered with a whipping sound."

Charley's intuition tells him that Libbie understands his feelings. "I don't tell many people about it. Most men see nothing wrong with what Ol' Gabe did. I can still see those eerie red flannel strips hanging from the scaffold. My brother William said something about that red cloth being spooky. Now I understand what he meant."

Libbie looks thoughtful as she mulls over Charley's story. They ride on in silence for a while, then the lone scout drops back to check on the stragglers. Suddenly, Charley notices several soldiers ride up to the burial structures. They grab items and begin knocking them to the ground. Charley rides, "hell-bent-for-leather," and reins up sharply. "I wouldn't do that, boys!"

One of the soldiers stops and turns, "It's just Indian graves."

"To the Indian this is sacred ground."

General and Tom Custer ride up in a hurry. "Return to you companies, boys!" Custer snaps. The soldiers drop the items and leave, headed for their respective companies. Custer looks at the scaffold, then noticing how upset Charley is, he begins talking about other things. "After we get settled at our Post, we'll guard the surveyors."

Charley nods to Tom and the General. "Indians won't be friendly with us." Charley excuses himself and rides to the front.

Upon their arrival at Fort Rice, General Custer is informed that no accommodations are available for either Libbie or Margaret Calhoun. In fact, all women and civilians traveling with the 7th, are urged to carry on to Bismarck.

After a miserable mosquito-infested steamer trip to the little town of Bismarck, Libbie and Maggie are offered a more pleasant berth aboard the Northern Pacific Railroad's president's car. As the train makes its uninteresting journey to St. Paul, Mrs. Custer finds plenty of time to write in her diary, continuing to record the most recent adventure with her husband and the 7th.

Recalling the abundance of wild game and fowl along the way she turns to her sister-in-law, "Autie and Charley are a sight to see, aren't they, Maggie?"

"Both of them are superb horsemen," Maggie comments, "and crack shots too. They're very competitive."

"But Charley is so shy, he barely looks at me when I speak to him," Libbie continues. "Autie says that he's heard Charley has a sweetheart in New Mexico—Santa Fe, I believe."

"That's hard to imagine, Libbie. I can't see him gathering enough nerve to talk to a girl, much less become romantically involved."

"Oh, Maggie. You've heard about the strong, silent type haven't you? I like Charley very much. He's such a gentleman...always clean-shaven and so neatly dressed. And he did talk to me. He even told me one of his youthful experiences."

Maggie looks surprised. "He did?"

When the General sends word that he will be leaving on an expedition up the Yellowstone River, Elizabeth Custer and Margaret Calhoun decided to return to their home in Monroe, Michigan.

7

Was the White Man aware of his intrusive footprint as he made his way from East to West? If he was, he didn't care to admit it. "All in the name of progress," it was said.

As the railroad pushed deeper into the belly of the continent and pioneer settlements sprouted like prairie grass, it was soon clear to the Indians that they would have to fight for the right to remain on, "their," land. Much like the eagle, soaring high and free the Sioux had roamed the Land of the Dakota for many winters unencumbered, except for the necessities to prevail over the severest of Mother Nature's rigor. To them, the White Man's many contrivances were more of a nuisance than convenience. The "Wasichus"—a term describing that which is impossible to get rid of—continued to descend on them like locusts.

The story in Washington however, was viewed in a different light. While President Grant was convinced that the Indians would be much happier confined to their reservations, receiving their monthly allotments of beef, corn and such, he was under much pressure from the growing number of settlers, who wanted the Indian land for their own. Their persistence and, of course, that of the impatient railroad barons, resulted in one of the many expeditions into Dakota Territory.

On the Yellowstone River, August, 1873

It is a cloudy but warm day when Custer's regiment makes its way along the Yellowstone River. On the open prairie, pronghorn antelope stare curiously then dart off in a whirlwind of dust. Buffaloes roll and turn in their wallows while dusting themselves. Never far away, the always-present buffalo wolves keep their senses on guard for any stragglers, especially the young calves. Honking geese explode into flight from the river. Spooked elk flee. Wary mule deer bound away then stop to look back from a ridge top. Custer's hounds chase whatever is in sight.

Army life on the Yellowstone is as pleasurable as Army life gets. In Custer's own words he wrote; "Far famed—far distant—Yellowstone a new world a Wonderland." This is truly splendid country. The Great Wakan Tanka the Sioux words for The Great Spirit, has put his rich blessing on this productive land. The soldiers chatter with anticipation as their eyes shift here and there at the abundant wild life.

Tom Custer's soldiers, among them thirty-year-old Ignatz Stungwitz and Samuel Shade in his twenties, look eagerly at a refreshing pool as they pass by. At the noon rest the soldiers picket their horses to graze. They eat and make coffee. A dozen of Tom's soldiers, including Stungwitz and Shade, get together to talk. Led by the Corporal by ones and twos, they furtively lead their horses into the trees on the pretense of grazing them.

Reynolds has left the bivouac on a hunt for some fresh meat. He sees something that catches his eye. He looks through his field glass. Along the river he sees unsaddled horses. He sees weapons and clothes. He smiles while he watches Tom's soldiers roughhouse in the water.

Reynolds chuckles out loud as he lowers his field glass. He looks up to watch a large flock of honking geese flying overhead. They are a noisy bunch, he thinks to himself, then it dawns on him that something sounds strange. Intermingled with the honking geese it sounds like yelling. He's heard that sound before. He quickly looks around only to see; at least two-dozen whooping Sioux Indians galloping all out toward the naive soldiers.

At the river, Soldiers' horses raise a ruckus and pull on their picket ropes. Stungwitz rises up from the water. It is hard for him to distinguish honking geese from the whooping Indians. Taking a suspicion from his panicky horse Stungwitz hurries to the bank to look around. He sees the charging Indians.

Reynolds smile fades into a look of surprise. He quickly raises his carbine but their skittish horses have already alerted the soldiers. Even though the Sioux are closer to the soldiers and have a head start he spurs off to help. "Hyaaa! Com'on Red!"

At the river, Stungwitz shouts. "I'll be a-sow-gelding chicken plucker!"

Shade scrambles for a quick look. Corporal lunges for his revolver on the bank. Shade hastily looks at the others. "Might be they're friendly!"

"Could be they just want the horses!" shouts another.

"Let us give 'em the peace sign!" says one of the younger soldiers.

"Split my windpipe!" Corporal looks around with a dumfounded look.

The Sioux close in on the soldiers. The ground begins to shake. Hooves pound. Dirt flies. The soldiers move quickly to the bank, stumbling over each other in their haste to don their clothes.

Corporal reaches his pistol belt drawing his revolver. Apart from the corporal the other soldiers have foolishly placed their weapons with their saddles. Out of reach, on some logs nearby. Corporal fires a couple of shots but fails to slow the galloping Indians. He looks around distressed. "Leave 'em," shouts the Corporal. "There's no time!" He jerks the picket rope free grabs the mane of his skittish horse and swings onto its back.

The rest of the soldiers are reluctant to leave without their weapons and clothes. With a yell the Corporal tears out! The now panicky soldiers leap on their horses, stark naked and thunder off. Shade clutches the mane of his screaming horse. It bolts with an arrow sticking from its rump.

The incessant whooping from the Indians frightens the soldiers' horses into a wild race. Hooves pound. Dirt flies. Arrows thud. Flowing manes. Naked soldiers frantically hang on to their furiously running horses.

Stungwitz darts a look back and sees the toothy grins of the Indians. Corporal, naked except for his pistol belt, fires a couple of wild shots. Arrows whiz all around.

On seeing they are nearing the soldiers' camp, the Indians stop their pursuit. They whirl their horses around, racing back to gather the booty.

At the rest halt, the naked, embarrassed soldiers shield themselves with their horses as best they can. Others gather around. The onlookers are nearly in pain from laughing. Stungwitz attempts to cover himself with his horse's tail.

Doctor Porter laughs, "Ye gads! You boys are going to catch your death of pneumonia."

Stungwitz looks at the Corporal, "They were laughing at us!"

Corporal scowls, "You'd laugh too if it was them having their naked buttocks chased."

Tom walks up, laughing. "A heckova ride for your pale cheeks. Instead of the Indians calling you "pale-face," He eyes the Corporal. "They'll call you pale butt."

Stungwitz shields himself behind his horses' rump and tail. "Pale Butt's a tinker's dam better'n Benteen's beet-red nose 'n' rosy red buttocks or my name ain't..."

Captain Benteen roars with laughter. "Maybe we can talk Custer into making this a regular part of parade-ground drill."

Tom and George Custer heartily join the laughter. Reynolds rides up chuckling. "I tried to warn you but I couldn't ride I was laughing too hard."

Custer finally quits laughing long enough to have the adjutant send out a detachment to attempt to catch up with the Sioux. The Indians had quickly made off with the booty and the detachment returns to the moving command an hour later. Custer orders the errant Corporal and gang to stand extra duty. Adjutant Cooke assigns their company commanders to give them extra days of camp cooking and night guard duty.

The next day General Custer, who is intrigued by Lonesome Charley's knowledge of the plains, asks Reynolds to join him for a hunt. Custer would like to have the good fortune of taking a crack at the elusive elk that they've frequently seen along the river. Reynolds is honored by the invitation and leads the commander to a massive herd of elk that he had scouted out before. An enormous bull elk struts amongst the herd. Although there are several other bulls in the company of the herd this one stands out in particular.

Custer gleams, whispering, "He's mine, Reynolds." Custer's wildly barking dogs suddenly race ahead after the prey. Custer spurs Dandy and gallops after his dogs. The initial chase is hot and heavy and lasts for several miles. The dogs lose the scent, finally lagging behind. Charley stays back as Custer disappears into some breaks along the river followed by his two faithful dogs.

Reynolds watches then cuts across on an angle to head them off. On the way, Reynolds rides up on another herd of Wapiti, as the Shoshone call the elk, because of their large white rump. Without dismounting, he shoots a large bull. He quickly swings to the ground. Just as he bends over to bleed the dead animal he hears the brush crack.

The enormous bull trots out of the brush, crossing a small valley. Reynolds takes aim then decides not to shoot. He lowers his rifle. He could have easily shot the big animal but remembers Custer's words, "He's mine." Shortly thereafter Custer and dogs race by and disappear in to some trees.

Reynolds has finished gutting the animal when he hears Custer's shot. He speeds off arriving at the river in time to see the dogs thrashing around in the water with the huge animal. Custer quickly wades into the water then fires the fatal shot before the lashing hooves and horns can injure his dogs. Using ropes tied to the saddle, the horses drag the monster ashore. Custer gasps for breath then beams. "That is the biggest buck I've ever laid eyes on. Top that, Buffalo Hunter."

"Never!" replies the shy man. "Look at the size of it. It's as big as your horse. I have never seen such an elk."

"Yep! That's the king of the forest, Reynolds."

Custer is eager to get back to camp to show off his trophy. The animal is so large that a couple of wagons are brought. Poles are cut and placed under the animal. It takes eight soldiers to lift the contrivance. Then the elk is pulled and slid onto the wagon floor. On the way back they quarter and load Charley's prime bull aboard the other wagon. The soldiers are amazed at the size of Custer's magnificent beast and a special celebration ensues. Later that night, after the troops are bedded down, as is his custom, the General writes a letter to his wife.

Dear Libbie—I killed the King of the Forest today. Charley Reynolds says he has never seen an elk so large. The animal weighed eight hundred pounds. The taxidermist accompanying the expedition is going to mount it for me. I have grown to like Charley very much. He never ceases to amaze me. We shoot all the time. By far he is one of the surest shooting rifle shots I have ever seen on the plains. Next to my own expertise, of course.

Suddenly, he is interrupted by a sound outside the tent. It is Lonesome Charley. "Enter, Reynolds," he says offering a campstool to his visitor. "I was just writing a letter to Libbie telling her about my elk. Something on your mind, Reynolds? My compliments on our hunt. It was your know-how that made a success."

Reynolds nods, "I couldn't sleep, General. I was trying to remember if I've ever seen such a huge elk. There was one monarch in Colorado I remember well, and several others of course...some in Kansas, some in Nebraska."

"You sure have had your share of traveling." The General yawns. "It must be getting late. Do you have the time?"

Charley removes the gold watch from his pocket. "It's not late General. It's early." He answers Custer's puzzled looks. "It's after two a.m."

"I'm not surprised. I sometimes get carried away when I'm writing. That's a fine timepiece. Is it a family heirloom?"

"No, Sir," Charley says feeling the hint of a blush. "It's a gift from a girl I know."

"Must be a very special girl. Where is she now?"

"In Santa Fe. That's where I met her, when I was in the 10th Kansas Volunteers in New Mexico."

"You were in Santa Fe during the War...Fort Union?"

"Yes, Sir."

"Well I'll be...what's this girl's name?"

"Ariana."

"That's an unusual name...very pretty. It sounds Spanish."

"Her mother is Brazilian, her father is Spanish...and she is very pretty too."

"This Ariana must mean a lot to you. We'll be returning to Fort Lincoln in a month. You'll be free of your contract then. Why don't you take a ride to Santa Fe and go see her?"

"I'd like to, Sir, but it's too late."

"Too late? It's never too late, Reynolds. Why during the late War, Libbie came to me every chance she could. And I wanted her to. Even came and stayed not far from the fighting. Come hell, or high water nothing could keep us apart." He pauses. "That is, except these campaigns. Some of them that is, if I feel it is safe, I bring her along."

"It is in this case, Sir. She's married."

Custer is genuinely sorry and apologizes for being so insensitive. "It's getting late...I mean early, Reynolds. Reveille will be blowing before we know it. Better get some rest."

"Yes, General. I'll see you at breakfast." He thanks the General for his hospitality and returns to his tent.

At the sound of the bugle Reynolds has already left camp. He sets out to scout the trail ahead. He hasn't traveled far when he comes across fresh horse trace. He returns to the command at once.

"General, Sir, the Sioux have been through here already this morning."

"I've noticed some sign myself, Lonesome. There are no horses missing. I've already talked with the Officer-of-the-Guard."

Charley waits for the General to continue then politely offers his suggestion. "I've noticed the civilians traveling with us have been straying, Sir. We're in Indian country now and you know how fast they can strike."

"I shouldn't need reminding, Reynolds. I can still see those bare-butt soldiers being chased back to camp." He laughs heartily as he tucks an errant buckskin pant leg into his black high-topped cavalry boot.

"Those civilians you mentioned are Mr. John Baliran, a trader and Dr. John Honsinger. The good doctor is a veterinarian and a fine surgeon as well. Met the two of them back east in Kentucky."

"We wouldn't want to lose them then."

Custer recognizes Charley's subtle hint. "Of Course not!" he says with an official tone. "I'll take care of it right away, Reynolds. We can't have any stragglers. I'll tell my adjutant to spread the word. If you don't mind I'd like you to speak to Baliran and the Doctor. They're like most civilians—object to military orders but they'll likely pay heed to you."

Lonesome Charley rides back along the river's edge in search of the two civilians who are leading their horses to the water to drink. In some trees along the river Reynolds quietly searches for the men. He startles them. Baliran whirls. "Good God, Man! You scared the devil out of us."

"Fresh Indian sign, boys. The General says you should join the companies immediately."

Baliran and Honsinger exchange glances, nervously wiping their sweat. "Ain't seen no Injuns. You, John?" asks Baliran.

Honsinger attempts to hide his fear. "Indians wouldn't dare strike with the army so close at hand."

Reynolds is more forceful. "Just 'cause you don't see 'em, don't mean they ain't around. It's for your own safety, boys."

Baliran holds up an empty canvas water bag as Honsinger speaks up. "It's frightfully hot. Our horses are thirsty."

A few shots are heard in the direction of the command.

Baliran turns to look. "Soldiers shootin' at jack rabbits."

Reynolds shakes his head. "All right, boys. You've been told."

"The Indians wouldn't dare strike with the Army so close at hand," adds Dr. Honsinger. "We'll be careful, Mr. Reynolds. Thank you for your concern."

Reynolds spurs off towards the command. Honsinger and Baliran continue toward the river. They are startled by a noise and look around frightened. Cracking brush moves toward them. An elk suddenly bounds away. They sigh in relief.

Relief turns to white-eyed terror. Suddenly, a fierce ruckus erupts in the brush. Custer's hounds bay loudly and they hear the roar of a bear. A huge Grizzly stands up right in front of them. Honsinger and Baliran are too terrified to run. The Grizzly runs past them in the direction of the elk. The hounds are hot on its heels. Leaving the two terrified men standing agape.

Charley races his horse across the open prairie. He arrives in time to see a dozen painted feathered Sioux Indians riding slowly in front of Captain Tom Custer and two of the 7th Cavalries' companies A and C. Charley can see that the Indians act like a decoy. Tom pursues, the Indians ride off. Tom turns his men around.

Shadowed figures wait silently in the nearby trees. Charley hurries over. "Those Indians act mighty chary!"

Tom turns his companies and again pursues the Indians who again ride off slowly, glancing occasionally toward some trees. Off the Indians' look, Reynolds spots the figures in the trees and reins up. "Whoa up, Sir!" He shouts. Tom motions to halt.

Suddenly, out of the trees ride a hundred screaming, feathered Sioux warriors. Tom leads his men riding all out to the rear. The Indians are in hot pursuit. Tom suddenly yells out. "Prepare to fight on foot! Form a skirmish line! Trumpeter!" The bugle blows. Charley and the others dismount and form a skirmish line in the form of a three-sided triangle. Amongst the Sergeants' yells and war-whoops of the Sioux, the led horses are put in the middle. "Ready! Aim! Fire! Pour the lead to 'em, boys!" Tom yells!

Charley and the others lay down a heavy fire. The Indians turn around then retreat. Charley notices Baliran and Honsinger way behind the Indians leading their horses into some trees. He watches as several Indians ride towards them.

Tom Custer shouts! "Trumpeter. Sound the Charge!" Tom and the two companies mount up and charge after the retreating Indians. Charley splits off and races for the two civilians.

In the trees along the Yellowstone River, Rain-in-the-Face, a well-built Uncpapa Sioux, and several other Sioux Indians watch the two unharmed civilians. Honsinger screams as Rain-in-the-Face rides him down. The Sioux Indian strikes Honsinger's head with the stock of his rifle as he rides past. He then circles back drawing his war bow and drives an arrow into Honsinger. Leaving the feathered shaft sticking out the middle of his back. The iron tip passes clean through his body and through the water bag, gruesomely protruding from Honsinger's chest. He screams incessantly. Honsinger clutches the arrow and tries to pull it through. Unable to, he pitches face down onto the arrow. He emits some choking gurgles then lays still.

Baliran hides in some bushes and signals the peace sign. He stands up and slowly walks out. He opens his jacket to show that he is unarmed. All the time pleading, yelling, "How! Friend. No kill me. I am unarmed. No kill John! No kill Jo..." He screams in horror as Rain-in-the-Face shoots him and several other Sioux shoot arrows into his back. Rain quickly dismounts, grabs Baliran's money and starts to scalp him. He stops when he looks at the short hair. He then takes Honsinger's gold watch and puts the scalp knife to his head only to stop. Honsinger is bald too. Rain-in-the-Face is angry. He removes his stone hatchet and begins to pound Baliran's head.

In time to see Rain-in-the-Face pocket Honsinger's watch Charley surprises them. He shoots one of the Sioux warriors. Rain-in-the-Face quickly runs to his horse, leaps on him and the other Sioux race away. Charley spurs after them. It is a run and shoot. Hoof beats pound the ground along the Yellowstone as several other soldiers join in the chase. Charley drops another from his horse. The Indian hits face down, bounces, rolls over several times then lays still. The rest of the Sioux turn towards the river.

The Indians leap their fleet war-ponies into the river without hesitation. The current is swift but they swim safely to the other side. Charley reins up. Two of the soldiers fly past leaping their horses into the swift current. Charley shouts. "Whoa up, boys, water's too swift!"

One of the soldiers struggles. The other, both horse and rider struggles briefly then disappears under the water.

"Turn loose of the reins! Let him have his head!" Charley yells at the struggling soldiers. The first horse and rider reappear then go under and are not seen again.

Charley leaps his horse into the river and goes to the struggling soldier shouting, "Turn loose of your reins!" The soldier obeys and Charley's horse swims close. "Use your arm. Push his neck around."

The panicky soldier does what he is told. Charley helps lead the horse to shore. The soldier bails to the ground coughing and spitting water.

Another soldier cries out, "Murphy's gone, disappeared. He and his horse drowned! Them rotten dirty..."

Several more soldiers ride the bank searching for the soldier. A distraught private stares at the empty swirls. He yells to everyone and no one. "Murphy n' his horse is gone. Drown-ded." He fires his pistol wildly across the river. The others look around angry, ready to fire at anything that moves.

Reynolds looks sadly at the water. He wipes the water from his face. "Those Sioux and their ponies have been swimming since they were babies. I'm truly sorry about Murphy."

The others glare at the river's swirls. "I've got to go check those men." Charley quickly spurs off.

Back in the trees Charley rides up just as Tom Custer struggles to roll Honsinger over. The protruding arrowhead had pinned him to the ground. Honsinger's head is smashed but his right hand still clutches the arrow. His left hand is at his head and his eyes are open. Charley dismounts and closes the man's eyelids. Tom madly shouts, "Autie liked them, he'll be angry."

"I'm sorry, Tom. I had just warned them."

"Autie will be mad as all get out. He liked the doctor. Nothing we can do but bury them." He nods politely to Charley and turns to Sergeant Bobo. "Form a detail, Sergeant."

"Aye, Sir!"

Charley rides off to find the General. Word moves fast and by the time Charley finds Custer he's already been informed. Custer had been ahead with two companies scouting for the surveyors. The men are put into the wagons for later burial. They will be buried at night. They'll light fires over the graves and picket the horses over them. Making sure that no trace of the burials can be found. Otherwise the Indians would dig up the graves and desecrate them. After loading the bodies the 7th moves out. Most of these men are veterans of the Civil War and so even though death is sad and unnatural they've learned to live with it.

Charley rides alongside the General. "We lost two good soldiers, two fine civilians. Baliran was from Memphis; Honsinger was a fine man a good doctor. They were unarmed."

Charley is upset. "Easterners want the land. The Indian is being pushed to the limit."

Custer interrupts. "The government's policy towards the Indian needs to be changed. If I was ever to get in charge of Indian Affairs there will be some changes."

Charley looks surprised at Custer's answer.

"I'm a military man, you're a civilian. We don't make the policies. Politicians do, most are crooked. Our work is to guide and protect the survey. The Government needs to negotiate with the Indians."

Charley nods, "You are right, Sir. It's a situation we have no control over."

Custer adds, "Those Indians..."

"Pardon me, Sir. They were Uncpapa." Charley politely interrupts.

"Sitting Bull? Tatanka Iyotake was not there. I have a feeling he's around."

Custer looks at Charley amazed. "You know the Indian problem?"

"What do you mean, General?"

"On the Southern Plains, Santanta n' his Kiowas were riled. Little Raven had the Arapahos stirred up. The Sioux were warring. They had White captives. If ever there was a time to kill Indians it was then, but we didn't. I held a parley with the Sioux Chief, Pawnee Killer."

"I've heard the officers talk. They say you risked your life; you went right into their village alone and unarmed. Somehow I feel badly for the Indians."

Custer's eyes see red. "Politics! Those dunderheads that make the laws don't care or understand Indian ways. Easterners n' settlers moving west don't give a hoot neither! And the Army takes the blame."

Charley contemplates while the General and his scout ride along in silence.

An hour after the sun disappears in the western sky, Soldiers dig graves for two blanket-wrapped bodies. Benteen is mounted off to the side. "Four men dead n' where in the devil's nightmare was Custer? Off joy riding again."

Reynolds reins up. A lieutenant looks at Benteen. "General Custer was escorting the surveyors ahead."

"General, huh? My royal bee-hind."

The lieutenant starts to speak. "I don't think Custer could..."

Benteen interrupts. "I would have done things different."

Reynolds speaks up. "It's none of my affair, Captain but those men took it upon themselves to leave. They were warned—I warned 'em myself."

Benteen meets Reynolds' eyes then swallows and breaks eye contact. "Well," Benteen mutters, "I just do not care for the cut of the man. He's a blowhard n' a glory hound. He left Major Elliott."

Disgusted Benteen reins off. Reynolds shakes his head sadly and speaks after him. "You are dead wrong, Sir." Reynolds watches Benteen disappear into the darkness.

Reynolds and soldiers ride back and forth over the grave site to disguise the graves.

While camped on the Musselshell River, Reynolds is asked if he will carry some official dispatches to Fort Benton and other locations along the upper reaches of the Missouri near the Teton River. It is a dangerous assignment but Charley agrees. Meanwhile, Custer makes plans for the 7th Cavalry to return to Fort Rice.

Among other numerous civilians on the expedition are two adventuresome Englishmen Lewis William Molesworth and Henry Hugh Clifford Baron of Chudleigh. They are amazed at Reynolds' hunting abilities and are elated to learn that Charley's family originated in County Kent, England.

"Only a stone's throw from my home, old boy!" exclaims Molesworth. "Perhaps we are cousins?"

"I've often wondered how many of my relations had departed England for the colonies," adds the Baron. "I was told they were nothing but a bloody lot of black sheep. But never mind that, old chap. Lewis and I would like to do a little hunting— grizzlies and such. We could use the advice of an expert huntsman. Do you mind if we accompany you to Fort Benton?"

The men are mounted and ready to leave. Reynolds is flattered and happy to have the company of the two congenial sportsmen. Custer rides up and hands Charley a dispatch bag. "Here are the dispatches and mail for Fort Benton. General Stanley issued Special Order No. 35 that will provide you with transportation from Benton to Fort Rice. You'll receive 100 dollars for the trip. Keep a sharp eye for Indians. Wouldn't want anything to happen. There's a letter to Libbie in there." Custer smiles and bids farewell to the Englishmen.

"Thank you, Sir. I have these fine Englishmen to protect me," Charley smiles at Custer who grins and nods slyly.

"We feel quite safe with Charles, Ol' boy," Molesworth nods.

Clifford joins with a comment. "I say, Sir Charles's family is from County Kent."

"Only a stone's throw away from my home, Ol' boy!" Molesworth Chuckles.

"Show these chaps a jolly good time," Custer laughs, "Sir Charles."

Charley reins around. "I'll do that, Sir."

Charley and his group move across the dry country. He heads north avoiding the mountains and passes through Judith Gap. Charley leads them to, then watches as they each shoot a buffalo. They load up the meat and now Charley leads the group in a direction northwest.

Charley drops behind for a spell and watches some Sioux that follow at a distance. They finally arrive at Fort Benton on the upper Missouri. Charley delivers the dispatches and they head for the steamboat.

Charley's party loads aboard the boat with the buffalo meat for the Galley. Disembarking, Charley makes his way to the wheelhouse. He is elated to see his friend Grant Marsh and spends some time conversing with Marsh.

Suddenly, bullets ricochet off the deck. One of the deck hands is hit and drops to the deck. Charley runs for his rifle. He sees Indians onshore shooting from some bluffs. They then scramble for cover.

Charley reaches his rifle, which he always carries loaded. He lays the "Big Fifty" Rolling Block across the rail and fires. As if diving from a high cliff, an Indian warrior pitches forward off the steep bluffs. He lands sideways, making a tremendous splash. It is good that he was already dead or the force from striking the water on his side would probably have killed him. His lifeless body drifts downstream, blood begins to color the water.

Grant Marsh yells, "Pour the wood to her, boys! Pour it to her!" He blows the whistle hard. Smoke belches from the stack. The Indians' horses turn bug-eyed and frantic. They've never seen or heard anything like it. They snort, rear buck and wildly race off. Grant smiles, motions his assistant to take over then leaves the wheelhouse. "Men! Get Mahoney patched up. It's gettin' so a man can't travel the blasted river safe."

Charley reloads and keeps a cautious eye for other hidden Indians. Grant walks over to Charley. "Fine shot, Charley," he laughs. "Bet them cauyses never heard the likes of that whistle before. Them ponies won't quit running tell they drop."

Charley chuckles as he unconsciously fingers the poke hanging around his neck.

Grant stares at the poke. "Yer' charm bag, Charley?"

"From Gabe Green, best friend I ever had. Taught me more in a few months than most men will ever learn in a lifetime. There are two bullets in here. I can almost hear Ol' Gabe telling me, Youngin', If'n yer in tight wrangle n there's no way out, kill the meanest, cut-throated red skinned Injun with the first bullet. Save the last bullet for yerself!"

Grant looks mighty somber. "You serious, Charley? You wouldn't, would you?"

Charley has no answer, but smiles slightly.

8

Charley returns to Thompson's Indian camp. The camp has moved. Like most small bands their food source dictates where and when they move. Most follow the buffalo herds.

He is greeted by Thompson and Walks-on-Ice. Running-creek-Woman timidly smiles but Charley's not sure it was met for him. It has been several months and he had all but forgotten about the good-looking Indian woman.

Occasionally though, he had to admit, she would suddenly be there in his thoughts. He could see her sparkling brown eyes, her gorgeous auburn hair and her... her...what really affected him was her lips, the way she smiled. She had this cute little grin. But then he didn't know much about her and besides he feels he is still married to a woman.

Charley dismounts. In an instant the curs dart after him. Old Patch Eye in the lead. This time Charley uses a five foot braided piece of rawhide and swings at the dogs that snap and snarl. Their teeth click and their lips curl. They back off while still growling. He is aware that if one lets his guard down, in a flash they will nip your heels then dart away. He's never been able to whack Old Patch Eye. The dog is cunning and elusive. Charley turns around and steps backward into camp.

Thompson comes running, yelling. "Come winter time I'll cook yer' cussed hair off." He kicks his boot at the dogs. "You'll taste right fine skewered n' a cookin' on the fire! On anether thought I'll cook yer har off in boilin' water the rapaho' way!"

Charley drops his protective whip and Thompson and Walks-on-Ice walk over. "I'll make a feast fer all the injuns!" Thompson threatens a gesture at the curs then makes a wide sweep of his right arm.

Charley chuckles while they help him unpack a spare saddle, rifle and the rest of his gear, storing it inside his teepee. Thompson looks at Charley, thinking then nodding his head. He gathers that it will be a short stay for Charley.

A couple of days later Charley places cartridges in his prairie belt as he and Thompson walk to the horses.

"Where ya' headin this time, Charley?"

"I'll be gone for a while."

"Your pack will be safe here."

"I'm beholden, Thompson."

Charley saddles Red and packs his gear on Rusty. Walks-on-Ice comes over. She speaks to Thompson in Arapaho.

"Running-Creek-Woman smiles for the White-Hunter-Who-Never-Goes-Out-For-Nothing."

Charley has noticed her smile and occasional glance at him. "What does Walks-on-Ice say?"

Thompson grins then chuckles out loud. "She says her sister smiles at yuh."

"Smiles at me?" asks Charley. He looks puzzled and chuckles. Why, he doesn't know, maybe it's because he doesn't understand.

Thompson sarcastically exaggerates. "She says, Running-Creek-Woman smiles for The Mighty-White-Hunter-Who-Never-Goes-Out-For-Nothing." Thompson laughs slyly.

Reynolds is puzzled and barely chuckles. Thompson laughs. "Her people live tuh the South. Tis the rapaho way. When a woman smiles at you, she wants to be your woman, yer squaw."

Charley looks shocked. "Be my squaw?"

Thompson is serious. "Yer woman. Cook fer yuh...mend yer clothes. In White Man's lingo, marry you! She will even pack in the buffalo chips."

"Tell her, I have a woman." Charley laughs thinking it is some kind of a prank.

Again, Walks-on-Ice and Thompson chatter away in Arapaho. Charley isn't sure what is taking place and interrupts. "I know the way of the Sioux, the Crow and the Cheyenne. Never laid eyes on her sister."

Thompson nods at Charley and again speaks to his wife then turns back. "She says she's never seed yer woman...and it makes no matter, she has seen yuh."

Charley shakes his head in wonderment.

Walks-on-Ice gestures towards several Indian women who are gathered nearby. They look perplexed wondering what is going on. Charley looks at the women. Most, in the White Man's way of looking at things, are not so good looking. Running-creek-Woman, unaware of what is taking place, walks over and joins the women. She smiles shyly. The others giggle and chatter away.

Charley doesn't know how to get out of the situation and asks quietly. "Which one is she?"

Thompson walks over and leans near Charley speaking in half tones. "The ugly one. Yuh'd better hurry n' leave. I'll hold'em off. Don't matter if it costs me muh hair. Yer muh friend n' I'll go down a-shootin'.'"

Charley hurriedly mounts up and leads his spare horse from the camp. The women wave to him. Running-creek-Woman only looks.

Charley reins around and rides back. "Thompson! Tell whichever one it is that I have a woman." Charley rides off.

Thompson understands that the Indians have a much different way of asking a question. Whenever they want to know why or where they start with a question. When they want to know what or when they also start with a question. Walks-on-Ice knows quite a few White Man words and feels that Thompson makes a joke.

He speaks to Walks-on-Ice who asks her question. She holds her right hand shoulder height fingers and thumb spread and wiggles her wrist in a circular motion two or three times. "Question, he say?"

Thompson answers her. "He said he would talk when he returns."

Walks-on-Ice frowns and signs another question. "You tell friend. Running-creek-Woman sister?" Walks-on-Ice then sweeps her right arm placing her thumb into her chest indicating herself. "I only relative. Marriage for my people, only relative can say yes," she nods vigorously.

Thompson laughs heartily. He knows that Running-creek-Woman's closest relative can approve of her marriage. Walks-on-Ice is her only sister. Thompson continues to emit bursts of laughter while they watch Charley gallop away.

Constantly improving his rapport with the Red Man, Reynolds ventures into dangerous country where other White Men rarely set foot. The name Lonesome Char-Lee is familiar to the Gros Ventres, the Piegans, the Blood Blackfeet, and even the River Crow. They all wait for a chance to meet the brave lone hunter.

When Charley finally makes his way back down the Missouri, he learns that Custer had received orders while returning from the Yellowstone, to take the 7th to its new headquarters, Fort Abraham Lincoln. The General has taken leave to Monroe to bring his wife back to their spacious new home at the post. Upon receiving his pay, Charley returns to Bismarck where the steamer, "Josephine," is berthed. As usual, Captain Marsh is happy to see his friend once more and gives him passage on the steamer in return for bringing fresh game to the cook.

Retracing his steps of a year earlier, Reynolds once more finds himself at the Standing Rock Agency. He is surprised to see so many Lakota Indians, some in a drunken state, loitering around the agency, complaining bitterly about how badly they are treated by the White Man. When he goes to the trader's store to get supplies he is even more surprised to see his friend, Little Bear. The Indian gives Charley a half smile and asks where he has been hunting. Charley tells him about his adventures up near the Teton River then asks Little Bear if the hunting is good near the agency. Little Bear is honored that the great Char-Lee Lo-onesome would ask such a question of him. In the Sioux tongue he tells Charley about his own camp at the headwaters of the Cannonball River. Charley thanks his friend and gives him the peace-go sign.

The Long Night Moon, the White Man's December, has passed and it's the third sleep of the Snow Moon in January, when Little Bear picks up Reynolds' trail. He wraps his scarlet blanket tightly around his shoulders to keep out the cold night air, leaving his long black braids to hang stiffly down his back. A handsome beaded quiver complements the ermine and otter skin cover of his bow. When it appears safe to move on, the stealthy warrior gently nudges his coal-black stallion. The prized horse is his reward for scalping a Crow enemy during a raid in what the Sioux call, the White Rain Mountains. Unsurprisingly, the White Man calls them, the Big Horns.

Charley is sitting by his fire roasting some beavertail when he hears a faint splashing sound. He folds his collar down and tries to trace the origin of the noise. Maybe he's hearing things? There are times when the prairie noises play tricks on a man, especially in Indian country. It could be a beaver. Suddenly, there is a crunching of footsteps in the snow's icy crust along the river bank; then silence. Charley watches for signs of movement, straining his eyes to peer beyond the shadows in the snow. When he stands and turns to look behind him, he finally sees the horse and rider. The two men stare for several moments. Firelight twinkles in the gathering of snowflakes around the Indian's eyebrows and Charley is not sure that it's Little Bear. But Little Bear knows he has found his friend and offers the friendship sign. "How coula."

"And how do you do, to you, my friend." Charley offers a canvas for Little Bear to sit on. As before, Charley provides a piece of plug tobacco and the Indian's customary pipe smoking before eating and talking is repeated.

Charley sighs and welcomes the Indian with a portion of his supper. Reminiscent of before, his quest eats like he's half-starved so Charley hangs buffalo hump ribs over the fire to cook. When the beavertail is gone, the two men start in on the buffalo meat, eating in silence but watching each other constantly.

Finally Little Bear speaks. "Many moons ago, at the Geese River we talk. Your heart was good toward Lakota People, long grass time."

"My heart is still good toward the Lakota People," Charley replies.

"Question. Wasichus take our land? Question. They shoot pte only to kill?"

"I do not know the answer, Little Bear."

"White Man kills only to kill. White Man shoot buffalo, use the meat to kill the large wolf with their poison. Once the grey one is gone, buffalo all gone. The Lakotas, the Cheyenne, our friends soon will have no home for our children, our horse. The Wasichus keep coming and coming."

"The White Chiefs are meeting in Washington. Maybe they will make a new plan," Charley says, hoping the words will console his friend.

"Grandfather go to this place, Wash-ing-ton. Good Chiefs no," Little Bear replies in anger as he jumps to his feet. "Pentouchers with their talk paper," he continues shattering the brittle night air. "Lies! All lies!" The sad eyes and outstretched arms amplify his conclusion. "Empty words! Empty words!"

Charley tries to explain the White Man's point of view but the words seem to have little meaning—even to him. He shrugs his shoulders and makes the sign of the hand held coffee grinder. Little Bear nods. Charley pours some coffee.

"You different Char-Lee. Maybe your heart is still good toward the Lakota." He stops to wipe the grease from his chin. "You talk, White hunters who take many hides. Tell them—stop killing pte, tatanka! You friend, you talk, you tell Pentouchers we don't want their spotted cattle, they have bad smell, taste rotten. You talk, Char-Lee, then maybe our people can live together, no war."

"Many White Men are not hunters," Charley continues thoughtfully. "They are farmers...what the White Men call sod busters or honyonkers!"

Little Bear is amused at the sounds and tries unsuccessfully to imitate them. "Yon-honkers. Hoo-on Yooonkers. Hookers."

"Hooon-yoonk-ers," Charley speaks slowly. "Hon-yonk-ers!," He repeats, chuckling as the Indian tries over and over to pronounce the word. After several attempts at explaining that farmers are much like the Corn Indians, "What the Sioux call the corn Indians, the sugar and molasses Indians. The Gros Ventres, Mandans they dig the ground and plant squash, corn." He finally convinces Little Bear that most of the White Men are simply trying to feed their own families.

Seemingly satisfied with the explanation the Indian thanks Charley, "You friend, Char-Lee, I must warn you, warriors will come to your camp at daylight."

Charley doesn't try to understand the significance of the Indian's last comment thinking instead of the time. As a matter of habit he reaches into his pocket for the gold watch and holds its face toward the firelight. Little Bear's comical expression compels Charley to dangle the watch above the fire. After a moment or two, a cautiously outstretched arm reaches for the timepiece. Black eyes sparkle as Little Bear raises the watch to his ear. Then as if in a trance he throws it back at Reynolds. While Charley is trying to explain the meaning of time, Little Bear motions for the watch, again rubbing it, listening, shaking it, listening again. "The tick-tick counts time. It counts the sun and moon as it passes in the sky." Charley realizes it is futile for him to explain more.

Suddenly, a broad smile brushes the anxiety from Little Bear's handsome face. "White Man not wise enough to listen to the sun and the moon. He must keep his time in a box."

Charley is quite taken with the Indian's sense of humor and the two of them laugh aloud. Finally, Charley asks, "Question. You say two months ago? I meant to say moons?"

Little Bear is still smiling. "Two moon beyond." He bangs his coffee cup and Charley pours him another cup of coffee—with extra sugar, of course.

Little Bear again warns Charley. "Char-Lee...warriors will come at day break."

Reynolds bids farewell to the brave Lakota warrior and thanks him for the warning. He sleeps for three hours then loads up his horses and leaves the camp before dawn.

Two-dozen or more warriors descend upon the camp at daybreak. Charley's signature is nothing more than a few smoldering coals from last night's fire. Even his tracks have yielded to an early morning snowfall.

"My father say his medicine good," says one of the younger Indians who is surprised to find the camp empty.

"Char-Lee Lo-onesome like the white fox in winter," remarks the leader as they begin their ride back across the wintry plains.

9

*F*or reasons unexplained, unknown even to himself, Charles Reynolds had an urge to return to the Platte River country. In Charley's case it might be called just an educated gut feeling from a trail wise plainsman. Call it insight, luck, or whatever you want to call it. It was a good choice. Or, was it a bad choice?

It is cold when he reaches Fort McPherson. "I'll be darned, Reynolds!" exclaims the Quartermaster. "Even my best hunters don't bring meat like this. Most of them can't even find the tracks."

Charley smiles. "I don't know anyone who eats tracks do you?"

The Quartermaster laughs loudly. "There are a lot of hungry men around this post, Reynolds. They're liable to eat most anything—including tracks. That is, if we could learn the cook how to fix them. Say, you look like you could use a little drop of the creature. There's the sutler's store over yonder. Why don't you go? I'll see your horses are tended to and join you later with your voucher."

Charley grabs his rifle and thanks the lieutenant He listens to the crunch, crunch from the frozen snow as he walks towards the sutler's store. He notices several horses and mules tied near the barracks. The steam from their muzzles fills the air in little clouds.

Inside the store, Charley glances at a half dozen officers who are bending elbows at a table. They are half-lit and loud.

Several men clad in deerskins drink at another table. They wear fur hats. Buffalo skin botas cover their legs from the knees down to their thick fur moccasins. Long bowie knives hang at their belts. Charley recognizes the Mountain Man garb and nods to the men.

He warms himself for a moment by the small stove that spreads cheerful warmth across the room. In the dimly lit room another man, his back to the others, sits alone at a table in the far corner. His trappings lay on the table and a big rifle leans nearby. Charley glances at the bearded man as the man tips a brown jug to his lips and takes a healthy swallow.

Charley nods to the sutler and several other men who stand drinking at the crude bar. He leans his rifle while the man pours him a glass of brown jug whiskey.

"You could use a stiff belt." The sutler extends his hand. "Name's, Rube."

Charley shakes Rube's hand and politely answers. "Charley Reynolds, Sir."

Several men eye Charley when they hear his name. Rube looks at Charley thoughtfully, then wipes the bar.

The warming sensation of a shot of brown jug whiskey appeals to Charley but after the first swallow, he sips sparingly on the liquor and listens to the bar-room conversation.

Rube, who complains about the cold weather, eventually turns to Charley. "Colder'n a well diggers butt the middle of March! I've never seen it."

He is interrupted by loud profanities and laughter from the officers. Charley slowly sips his whiskey.

"You know, Lad. I used to hunt buffalo. Got too wild n' dangerous for me with the Indians n' all. It's a hard life n' a man don't live long hunting by himself."

"I've been doing all right," Charley comments in an unassuming tone.

"Oh, we hear you've been doing more than all right, Son. The talk is that you're by far the best—better than Bill Cody. That's something to well...to brag about! You know Buffalo Bill?"

"I know Bill Cody...spent some time with him and the 5th Cavalry out of Fort Wallace. He's a fine huntsman. No doubt!"

A captain who had been sitting at a table across the room walks over to the bar and stammers: "So you think you're better than Cody, huh?" For a moment, Charley is taken aback but only looks at the man.

The captain turns to Rube. "Tell this young whippersnapper how Cody got his name. Yeah! Tell us how Buffalo Bill got his name!"

Rube nervously wipes his rag across the bar. "Well, I heard that Cody got the name after killing thirty-six buffalo in one herd." Rube pauses then continues as the officer glares at him. "When he finished shootin' they say the buffalo were almost evenly spaced across the prairie."

The drunken captain shouts. "Now that's the man we call the best buffalo huntsman...Buffalo Bill Cody! This man is an impostor men. The best buffalo hunter... man what a laugh!" he slurs.

The obnoxious officer grabs a bottle, pours himself another drink, and continues to harass Charley. "Buffalo huntsman? Buffalo calves, maybe."

Finally Rube speaks up. "Hold your tongue, Captain. Lonesome Charley ain't botherin' you none. I say to you, mind your own business."

"Pardon me! Looo...ooon...some Char...rles!" The drunken captain attempts the howl of a wolf, but sounds more like the squeal of a pig.

"Lock yer jaw!" Rube yells. Charley still only looks.

"A man can smell you a comin'! You're nothin' but a flea-bitten, wolf trapper!" The officer shouts.

Rube pleads, "Captain, hold your tongue. I want no trouble."

The captain laughs and slaps his fist on the bar. "Better n' Bill Cody. I think not. You're nothin' but a two-bit wolf trapper! A stinking one at that!"

"Captain!" screams Rube, "You've had too much to drink. Hold your tongue!"

Finally, Charley turns to the captain and quietly says, "It's time you went to bed, Captain. Why don't you go sleep it off?"

The request is ignored and Charley, gentleman as always, lays a coin on the bar and then turns to Rube. "I'll be leaving, Rube." He turns to pick up his rifle.

"You stinking sonofa..." The captain shouts, lunging at Charley swinging his fists. Charley moves lighting fast then ducks, the blow glances off his forehead. He grabs the captain's arm and slams him against the bar.

The inebriated captain groans from the impact and attempts to grab onto the bar. Charley quickly kicks his feet out from under him. The captain falls hard, landing on top of the brass spittoon, spilling the metal container. Slop splashes all over the foot of the bar and onto the captain's head. The nasty smelling liquid drips off the bar and runs along the floor forming into a brown puddle. A hush comes over the room. The only noise is the spittoon as it slides across the floor. It seems like the sliding container rattles for a long time. All eyes watch as it finally clatters into the wall, bounces back, tips over then lays still.

The officer's angry voice shatters the quiet. "You stinkin', liver eatin', buffalo dung, lousy, so-called hunters-man!" Streaks of slimy brown spit and tobacco juice run into his eyes and down his face.

While the captain struggles to find his feet in the slime, his fellow officers rush Charley who backs up against the bar. An officer slams a blow that glances off Reynolds' head as he feints. Another lays a hard blow into Charley's stomach. He grunts slightly and swings back. Quick thoughts flash across Charley's mind. There are too many of them but he never has caused trouble. He's never run either. He sinks his fist into one of the men's guts, as the man sucks for air, Charley nails him straight on the jaw. One thing about fighting a bunch of men, he can swing at anybody. He doesn't have to worry about whom to hit.

Suddenly, a loud explosion ripples through the store. Officers and Mountain Men yell and cover their ears. A huge cloud lingers over the far corner table. The smell of black powder permeates the air.

"What in the month of March?" Rube yells.

"My ears!" Shouts a Mountain Man.

The echo of the explosion finally stops ringing. There is silence. Everyone looks around in surprise. "Who'n..."

A chair scrapes the floor from the far corner. All eyes turn. Near the table he stands alone.

In the smoke filled shadows of the far corner, through the powder smoke like a ghostly apparition, is the cloudy image of one impressive man. An animal sits on his head. It is a frightening appearance.

"What in tarnation? It's a ghost," shouts one of the drunken officers.

"Its the whiskey talk, you halfwit!" roars another.

The smoke begins to dissipate. Underneath a large beaveskin hat, black eyes peer out. A daunting figure, even at his age, the man is still the very essence of a Mountain Man.

Charley couldn't see it before but now, instantly, he recognizes the beaver hat. His eyes roll in shock. Charley looks at his long, lost friend and mentor, Gabriel Green.

He thought there was something familiar about that man. The way he took a swig from the bottle. But all those years he's been asking about Gabe he never found him. Maybe deep down inside himself he figured Gabe was dead. Maybe that's why he only paid casual attention. He should have known.

The other Mountain Men step away. It's not their fight but if needed they'll come running.

Gabe bellows. "Let's make this a fair fight boys, only two of ya' at a time."

"A ghost, we'll just see how tough." The officer catches Charley off guard and smacks Reynolds in the mouth.

"Yer' learnin', Boy!" Charley hears the illustrious words as Gabe shouts.

Charley's lip bleeds and now he is riled. His fist lashes out, the sound of knuckles and jawbone colliding, mingles with the groans of a man. The man pitches forward then falls onto the snuff covered floor.

Keeping himself away from the slippery floor Charley feints two left jabs then swings an overhand right, catching another man on the nose. Blood flows through the man's fingers as he clutches his face and staggers towards the door.

Another man from the table rushes over. Gabe kicks out; the man slides face down across the floor. Charley is instantly on him grabbing the man's legs. The man yells in pain as Charley puts him in Gabe's Indian death lock.

Rube grabs a club and runs around the bar. He pokes an officer in the guts, wields the club and shouts. "I'll split yer' fool head! Get you're drunken friends and get outta' here. The Colonel will hear of this!" The men stop as Rube yells.

One of the captain's friends helps him up from the floor, grabs a rag from the bar and begins to wipe the spit and tobacco juice from his face. The captain is enraged.

Gabe turns to Charley. "We best be leavin', Boy." He turns, grabs the bottle from the table and takes a big snort. He slams the bottle on the table and heads out the door. Charley grabs his rifle and follows.

The enraged captain still wipes the slop from his face. "You ain't no buffalo hunter, Reynolds," the drunken officer shouts through the doorway. "You only smell like a rotten buffalo—one that's been dead for thirty days!"

He laughs off another reprimand from the sutler, "You stinking coward! Come on back in here n'...." Impulsively he draws his pistol and fires at Charley the bullet ripping through the shoulder of Charley's jacket.

The quiet man whirls in his tracks. Gabe spins around cocking the hammer of his big rifle but Charley is hairsbreadth ahead. The roar from his rifle shatters the quiet of the parade grounds as ninety grains of black powder explodes from its barrel. The captain's pistol hits the floor and bounces out of the store onto the ground at Charley's feet. Amidst the yells and the powder smoke, Charley looks up and sees the officer's forearm dangling limply from his shoulder.

"My arm! God, my arm," the man shouts as his fellow officers run to help him. "Look what he did to my arm. Oh God, no!"

The nervous Rube yells to the captain, "Hush up now, Captain. Let's get him to the post surgeon, men. Quick! That arm is bad."

"Get the Officer of the Day," demands the wounded man. "I want to file charges against that stinking buffalo hunter. At once, I demand!" His eyes began to glaze over in shock as his fellow officers help him outside.

Charley is truly sorry. Rube tries to console him. "It wasn't yer' fault, Reynolds. You did everything you could to avoid the man."

A short distance from the sutler's store Gabe Green sees a Colonel and several officers talking. Gabe walks over. He gestures and waves his rifle. An officer walks away then shouts towards some soldiers. "Sergeant of the Guard, on the double quick!"

The 50-caliber lead slug had all but severed the captain's arm and the post surgeon reluctantly amputates the affected limb. Due to the serious nature of the injury the Officer of the Day decides to accept the captain's charges and a full hearing will take place. Charley is on detention and must stay on the grounds of Fort McPherson.

The talk around the Army post centers on the McPherson incident and, "deadly gunman," is added to the lone hunter's repertoire. Although the charges are dismissed and Colonel Eagan tries to make his detention as bearable as possible, Reynolds is very uncomfortable at Fort McPherson.

"I just know it would be better if I leave, Colonel," Charley says at breakfast. "I could have killed that captain; I was mad enough to do it. I have a feeling he's just waiting for me to let my guard down. He's holding a grudge and I can't blame him for that."

"Reynolds, that man has caused trouble before. He deserves what he got and he's lucky you didn't kill him. I know he would have got you with the next round if you hadn't defended yourself. But you don't have to worry about it now. You took off his shooting arm." He stops for a breath.

Charley stands, "I'm obliged to you, Colonel. I truly apologize." He gives his quick wave and walks out the door.

The next morning Charley walks to the Sutler's Store. It seems to him that it has warmed up quite a spell. He looks at the two mules tied near the store. They were here yesterday but he wasn't paying attention. He now recognizes Old Jake. Jake brays softly as Charley walks over and strokes his head, scratching below his ears. He reminds himself of Gabe's early lessons. Mules are kinda fussy around their ears and they can kick out fast.

"Old Jake, how ya' been old fellow? It's been a long time. Too long old boy, it's good to see ya'."

The other mule nibbles at Charley's arm. Charley turns his attention to the mule. "Well, well. You must be Charley Boy?" He rubs his ears. "I'm beholden' to finally get to meet my..."

Lightning fast the mule bites, brays and kicks out wildly. Charley leaps back just in time. He looks at the mule and laughs. "Spittin' image of yer master, Charley Boy!"

From inside, Gabe's voice carries out through the store door and across the frozen snow. "Git away from my mules 'er I'll blow yer brains out!"

Charley smiles and goes to the stable to his horses. He grabs a package wrapped in brown paper and some oats. He removes his beaver hat from his pack and puts it on.

Charley stops and gives Old Jake and Charley Boy a handful of oats. "You be fair to me, Charley Boy. Be like Old Jake. We have the same name."

The mule stops eating and lifts his head. Steam floats from his mouth as oats drop from his jaw. His large ears move to and fro, his eyes are on Charley. "You behave now, Charley," he says as he walks away. The mule nickers for more oats. Charley chuckles to himself.

Inside, Charley quietly walks to the bar where Gabe drinks a bottle of brown jug whiskey before him. Gabe doesn't look at Charley who stands quietly as Rube looks on.

Gabe suddenly slams his fist on the bar. Rube jumps in complete surprise. He drops the glass he holds. One hears the clatter and the sharp fragments scatter across the floor. Charley slams his fist on the bar. Gabe's eyes squint at him and he glares. After a while Gabe's expression changes. He stares at Charley's beaver hat then warmly says, "Charles Whatyacallit Reynolds."

"Hello, Old Friend."

They shake hands. Charley's not sure what Gabe will do being hugged by a man. In times past, anyone who got too near him, he was prone to a quick swat from his powerful hand. Charley quickly hugs Gabe then steps back.

Gabe yells at Rube. "Bring that Taos Lightnin," he turns to Charley. "You'll have a drink with me, youngin'."

Over his initial fright, Rube is in the spirit now. He slaps the bar, "One jug of the nastiest Taos Lightin' this side of Santa Fe." He slides the bottle down the crude bar.

Charley reaches out and grabs the bottle on the way by. He reads the label then hands it back to Rube shaking his head. "I don't know, Gabe." Gabe gives Charley that look. Charley has an instant change of mind. "Only for you, Gabe. Just one."

Rube fills the glasses. "Bottoms up, Son," yells Green. They salute and down them. Charley looks away coughing. Rube pours Gabe another, "and down the hatch," Gabe shouts.

Charley opens the brown package. "I had this in my pack, I want you to have it." Charley slides Gabe the package, "I usually eat it cooked."

Gabe is pleased. "Why, I declare, Youngin'." He pulls out his large knife and slices off a piece of the raw buffalo liver. He takes a bite and cuts a piece for Charley, holding it on the end of his knife.

Charley chews while Gabe cuts another piece holding it up for Rube. Rube balks shaking his head, makes a face and gestures. "Tried it before...not me!"

Gabe shoves it near Rube's face. "Try it! Eat that 'n that brown-skinned wife of yers' will love yuh tuh death." Gabe bellows in laughter. "She might smile 'n stop being a nag."

Charley turns his head and laughs. Rube reluctantly takes the liver from Gabe's knife. He nibbles on a small piece and spits it into the spittoon.

Gabe only looks. "Mighty fine, it's been a while."

Charley ponders then speaks out. "Even got some beaver tail, I remember it was your favorite."

Gabe roars with laughter. "Boy, what else did yuh bring?"

Charley smiles, Gabe regards Charley, serious like. "You ever get a hold of one 'uv 'em brown skins?"

Charley looks away. Gabe hits the bar then laughs. Rube jumps and pours him another.

"What's her name, Son?" asks Gabe quietly.

"How'd you know? Her name is Ariana."

"I wasn't born yesterday. I'll bet she's a pretty thing."

"She is."

"Yuh' goin' back?"

"It's crossed my mind."

"Let me tell you something, Youngin'," Gabe shakes his finger. "If 'n I learned anything, life is too short. You go back, Son."

Charley only looks at Gabe who rubs his arm.

"Maybe you should see the Post Surgeon about that arm."

Gabe shouts out, "Bunch of vet-a-narians, horse doctors. Don't ya' be a frettin' over me. I was on my own long before you came along." Gabe smiles and they have a good laugh.

"Been hearing your name everywhere I been, Son. You made quite a name fer' yerself, Lonesome Charley."

Charley smiles warmly. "You were a good teacher, Gabe."

Gabe gets that mischievous look and leans close to Charley. "Back in the thirties Mountain Men was trappin' the southern streams. I..." Gabe slips with his tongue. "One of the younger ones fell in love...with a girl who came from a rich family. She was in love with him too." He coughs and looks away. But Charley had noticed Gabe's eyes had begun to moisten.

Charley can see how Gabe is affected and quietly asks. "What happened, Ol' Hoss?"

"They made a plan to leave town. She stood on the street one afternoon a waitin' for him. He came ridin' through town and scooped her up onto his horse. His Mountain Man friends were waiting outside town and shot the hades out of the Mexicans chasing after her."

Thundering hooves, neighing horses and braying mules break the silence of the plains. At the gallop Gabriel Green rides Old Jake. Following close behind, runs Charley Boy. Next to Gabe, who wears a serious look and wears his large beaver hat, rides Lonesome Charley. Charley shakes his head and almost loses his large beaver skin hat. Rusty neighs from behind the pack. All are fully loaded and are headed south.

The two riders and their animals move fast. The land is now more desert like. Another four or five days and they will be there.

Santa Fe is a bustling city. Mule and horse caravans come and go. A dust covered Gabe Green and his companion trot down the street.

Bull whackers and muleskinners crack their whips and shout, "Missouri or bust!"

"Here we come Saint Louee!"

Attractive Senoritas wave at the riders. Gabe watches an attractive middle-aged senorita. She waves at him and Gabe reins up. Gabe looks at Charley then the senorita. He gets a sly grin. "You got two days, Youngin'."

Charley watches as Gabe rides over near the Mexican woman, dismounts and ties his two mules. He walks up to the woman and Charley sees them talking and gesturing. Finally she walks towards a Cantina. Gabe follows. He turns and smiles at Charley. Charley chuckles to himself and smiles back.

Reynolds rides to the La Fonda Hotel, scribbles a note and goes inside giving the note to the clerk. Charley then rides out of town.

The clerk immediately gets in touch with Antonio's friend.

The wisdom of Gabriel Green the Mountain Man has not diminished with age. If anything, he is much wiser. He has not survived all these years because of so called luck. He has always been a wary man. Gabe watches Antonio and a Mexican friend talk. The Mexican nods his head as Antonio gestures angrily. Gabe smiles to himself while he eyeballs the Mexican who gives a quick wave to Antonio then mounts up and rides out of town.

At the Esteban Ranch Antonio and his friend watch Ariana. They are a distance away but with the aid of field glasses they are able to see Ariana leave in her buggy.

Antonio's hateful look says it all when she stops at the Adobe Shack. They watch as she waits for Charley.

Ariana smiles and waves when Charley approaches the adobe cabin. Their eyes meet. Charley dismounts and walks over. "You're more beautiful than I remember."

Ariana's smile is one of pure delight. "Charley, I'm so happy to see you again."

Charley helps her down. They silently embrace.

Antonio gives a menacing scowl and tells his friend to stay and watch. He leaves in a fit of rage.

After a long while Charley is the first to speak. "You don't know how many times I've stopped myself from coming to find you."

Ariana looks concerned. She reaches up to wipe a tear. Charley grasps her arm and tenderly wipes the tears from her cheek. Then he holds her. After a few minutes he puts an arm around her and they walk to the Adobe Shack.

"It's cold in..."

Charley puts his fingers to his mouth, "Shhh...It's always cold in here. I'll soon have a fire going."

He hurries outside and returns with a blanket. He wraps the blanket around Ariana, "Gracious," she says. He stoops to kiss her cheek.

She watches while he gets the kindling and wood into the small rock fireplace. "Why are you smiling, Charles Reynolds?"

"I was just recalling the times we've met here, the memories? Regardless of what they say, we were married."

She looks at him warmly while nodding. "It seems so long ago. I'm so happy you're here. My heart was crying and joyful all at the same time when I read your note. It has been too long, Charley."

He kisses her cheek. She returns his kiss, her lips are so warm and soft. "I've waited so long for this moment, Charley. It seems like forever since I've held you, kissed you."

He hugs her tightly then pulls away to stoke the fire. He pulls a crude chair close to the fire for her.

"I almost forgot! I brought something for us—something special. It's in the basket." Charley hurries for the door. "Bring the box too," she says loudly.

He soon returns with a basket and the box, placing them on the table. The room is warm now and Ariana leaves the blanket on the chair, walking over. From the basket he unwraps a bottle of Spanish wine. He smiles and holds it up.

Ariana returns his smile as she opens the box. She removes a mist white hat. She grins joyfully as she places the hat on his head. "For you, Charley. The wine is the same we had in Santa Fe." She giggles as she runs her hands on the wide brim."Oh, Senor Reynolds! The hat fits you well." She caresses the pencil roll of the brim. She does a curtsy then shuffles her heels, laughing.

He removes the hat and admires it with a sheepish grin. "I'm obliged. It feels good."

"Do you like it? I like the pencil roll, it fits your character." She smiles, pleased with her choice. "I always knew you would come back. When I first saw the hat I just had to get it for you."

"It's perfect." He sits the hat on the box and opens the wine and pours them a glass. She walks over, picks up the hat and places it back on Charley's head with a smile. They touch glasses and sip the wine.

Charley gazes into her eyes. He sits his wine on the table and leans over to kiss her but the wide brim of the hat gets in the way.

She laughs while she reaches up, pushing the hat to the back of his head. "Now, you may kiss me, my Charley." He grabs her tightly and kisses her with a passion.

For several minutes they stand holding each other, staring into the fire sipping the wine and savoring their love.

Charley marvels to himself how beautiful she is in the firelight. He has spent many a night by his fire on the plains and could see her face, her image. The firelight glitters off her black hair. The amber glow of her skin as the light shines on her lovely face...she is so...

Ariana nudges him. "Oh, Charrr...ley." He looks at her embarrassed. '"You were lost in deep thought. Tell me what you were thinking."

He takes a sip of the wine. "I was thinking about how lovely you look in the firelight. The way the light shines off your hair. The color of your skin with the light glittering. I've seen you that way so many times on the plains that..."

She leans into him and their lips meet, barely touching, moist and warm. His lips continue to gently touch hers until she begs. "Kiss me, hard. Hold me, Charley." She draws his head towards her, whispering. "I've waited a long time for you. I love you, Charley," she whispers.

Hours later Charley wakes up. The fire has died down. Charley quickly jumps up and puts more wood on the fire, then lies beside her.

He leans on his elbow, facing Ariana. "You love your hunting, roaming the plains, the danger, don't you, Charley?"

He doesn't answer but looks at her thoughtfully.

"I've heard stories what the Comanches do to the Mexican people. The Sioux do the same. Aren't you afraid?"

"I have Indian friends. They are not what people think. They have been mistreated by the greedy politicians and the corrupt Indian ring."

"Don't you fear for your life? There's talk about the Sioux being riled."

Charley gives her a serious look. "There is something I want to tell you."

Ariana looks worried

Charley grins. "Don't be alarmed."

"Tell me."

"Well a long time ago, Mountain Men were trappin' the southern streams. One of the younger ones fell in love with a girl from a rich family. She was in love with him too. They made a plan go away together. She stood on the street one afternoon a waitin' for him. He came ridin' through town and scooped her up onto his horse.

"Would you do something like that, Charles Reynolds? It would be a big surprise for Antonio."

They laugh, then Charley turns serious. "Would you?"

Hooves pound, dust flies as onlookers gasp in surprise. Two riders race down the dirt covered street. Mexicans shout and streetwalkers hurry out of harm's way.

Ariana rides Rusty. A little behind her, Charley sporting his new hat, rides Red. The young lovers charge outside Santa Fe.

Charley takes a hurried glance behind. Riders are beginning to form coming their way. It looks like Antonio is in the front. Charley spurs up alongside Ariana and points behind. She looks back then shouts, "Antonio! I knew he would not let us leave without a fight."

Charley can't hear what she shouted but reads her lips. His feelings are the same. He looks around for Gabe.

Quick thoughts flash through Charley's mind. Where is Gabe? Where are the friends of the Mountain Man? Did he get waylaid in Santa Fe?

He motions Ariana faster and spurs Red into a dead gallop.

Suddenly, behind them they hear the echo of a loud shot. A single .65 caliber slug from Gabe's big rifle rips through the brain of Antonio's horse, dropping the horse instantly. Gabe Green steps from behind some rocks as Antonio's horse skids stone dead in front of the herd. Antonio flies through the air. He hits the dirt and slides face down for ten feet or so. He coughs, scrambles and crawls, all the time spitting dirt while trying to get out of the way. Horse screams mingle with Antonio's as three other Mexicans and their horses tumble over Antonio's dead mount. The dust is thick as horses and riders thrash and mix up in the dirt.

Horses leap up and limp away while the Mexicans rush to get out of the panicky horses way. Gabe's big .65 continues to wreak havoc while the Mexicans seek cover. Gabe's last glimpse of Antonio is his wild-eyed, scared rabbit look. Gabe turns quickly and gives a parting shot. He mounts Old Jake and shakes his fist, then follows after Charley and Ariana.

All day long the group holds a steady pace. Only for water and to give Ariana a brief rest, do they halt. When darkness is an hour away, Gabe motions Charley, and they pull up and make camp. Gabe has not been his typical boisterous self but smiles, even laughs out loud often.

Several times during the ride Charley noticed Gabe laughing to himself. And a couple of times at the water stops Gabe would burst out with laughter. Even Ariana looked at Gabe with a puzzled look. But she was glad Gabe was happy. He's probably happy that he stopped Antonio, she thinks.

The moon is already shedding light as Ariana collapses to the ground, she is spent. Charley grabs a couple of blankets and makes her as comfortable as possible. He then helps Gabe as they quickly unsaddle and tend the animals. They water the animals and fill their own canteens so they'll be ready for the morning ride.

Gabe chuckles as he hands Charley some biscuits and some Mexican cakes from his pack. "We're far 'nough ahead, we won't need to stand guard."

Charley nods then looks at the old man with a suspicious grin. "Gabe, I've never seen the likes of you." Gabe laughs out loud.

"You finally met your match, didn't you, Gabe?" Gabe laughs heartily as he prepares a place to lay his blanket. He stretches out on the ground and continues his frequent out bursts chuckling out loud.

Charley and Ariana talk in hushed tones as they munch on the biscuits and cakes.

"Why does your friend laugh all the time? You told me he was just the opposite."

Charley quietly chuckles. "It is just a prank between Gabe and I," then he bursts into laughter. She laughs along with Charley, even though she doesn't really understand what the prank is.

Gabe's loud snoring tells them that he is fast asleep.

Several days later, Charley mounted on Rusty, leads the group across the prairie. He reins to a halt when he spots a faint dust cloud ahead. He watches and listens as several magpies squawk and fly up. He cautiously moves forward. The birds cry out as they fly away. Charley turns when he hears Gabe's familiar bird whistle.

Charley motions for Ariana to stay where she is. Gabe waves at her and she dismounts standing beside Red.

Charley jerks his Sharps from the scabbard as Gabe rides alongside. Gabe's rifle rests across his saddle pommel. Charley removes his pistol from the holster, tucking the Army .44 into his belt, ready for quick action. He glasses ahead but sees nothing. He shakes his head at Gabe.

Gabe's wary eyes scan the sagebrush. In a gravely low tone he says. "Somethin' ain't right, Boy.Comanch' can hide most anywhere. Wouldn't think they would be this far north."

They cautiously ride forward. A jack rabbit scurries away, Rusty shies sideways. Charley gets Rusty under control and looks behind. He motions Ariana to get down, hoping she'll hide.

A long necked fast running bird darts past. Rusty is reluctant to move. Charley sees nothing but raises his rifle. His horse continues to act skittish. Old Jake brays softly, stomping his front hoof.

Gabe motions at Charley. "Ol' Jake 'n I got brushwhacked by a bunch of Comanch's. Came right up outta..."

Suddenly ahead of them hidden in the sagebrush and sand, rush a dozen Comanche warriors. They are painted and fierce looking devils. Their cries are terrifying to Ariana who crouches in horror.

Arrows fall near Charley and Gabe as Charley tries to get control of Rusty. He dismounts and holds the reins of his skittish horse. It is hard to aim with Rusty jerking and Charley turns him loose. He shoots one of the rushing warriors.

Gabe drops another then quickly dismounts.

Charley empties his pistol to keep the others at bay. The Comanches quickly take cover fanning out in the sagebrush.

They arch arrows into the air aiming especially for the horses. They know that an arrow sticking in the head of a man or the back of a horse causes sheer panic.

Rusty screams as an arrow drops with a thud sticking into his back quarters. Charley runs to Rusty and quickly jerks the arrow free. Thankful it didn't penetrate that deep.

Gabe yells. "Ya' gotta look where the arrows come from. Pick 'em off!"

Charley watches closely. He sees an arrow come from behind several clumps of sagebrush. He blasts into the brush and a yell comes from behind the hiding place.

Gabe gives Charley the thumbs up then for some unexplained reason looks behind. Maybe it's because he has been in these fights before. Gabe sees two Comanches going after Ariana.

Gabe quickly mounts and charges. The Comanches wheel on him. He kills one of them. The other arches his bow and lets an arrow go. The arrow strikes high on Gabe's chest knocking him off balance. His rifle drops into the dirt and Gabe reaches for the saddle horn then tumbles from the saddle. He utters a loud groan from the impact of the ground. The arrow breaks in two but leaves a long portion still in Gabe's chest.

Ariana screams. "Oh no, Gabe! No!" She rushes over to help him.

Charley is anxious as he sees the Comanche kick Gabe and grab Ariana. She struggles as the warrior drags her to his horse. He grabs her hair as she tries to resist and throws her onto his horse. He nimbly leaps on and rides off with Ariana screaming. "Chaar...leee!" she cries.

Charley quickly lays a heavy fire into the brush and kills two more Comanches. The others retreat away going for their horses.

Charley quickly mounts up and rushes over to Gabe.

Gabe groans, "Get her quick! He'll kill her!"

Charley races after Ariana. He can see her struggling to get free. He shouts and yells his own war whoop at the Comanche, who looks back to see Charley gaining on him.

The Comanche finally jerks Ariana by the hair and flings her to the ground. Ariana yells on impact and rolls over and over.

The warrior jerks the rawhide thong on his horse. The horse turns obediently and the Comanche charges. Hooves pound, muscles stretch, as the two riders ride, "hell bent for leather," towards each other.

The warrior pulls up sharply. He lets an arrow fly. Charley quickly slides side-saddle, the arrow swishes past his head.

The Indian grabs an eagle bone whistle that hangs around his neck. He kicks his mount into a charge blowing hard on the whistle. The whistle is loud and shrill intended to spook either man or horse.

Rusty and the Indian horse collide; both go down spilling their riders. The horses scramble to their feet.

At the same time, Charley and the Comanche move quickly to their feet. The warrior kicks Charley then reaches for his knife but finds it is not there. He gropes for the empty sheath. He looks surprised as he sees his knife on the ground. It had fallen out during the collision. He then nimbly mounts his horse. He blows the eagle bone whistle and attempts to ride Charley down.

Charley jumps aside. The warrior races away.

Charley quickly grabs the Remington, flips up the sight, lays it across Rusty's saddle and squeezes the trigger. It is a long shot and Charley feels he's missed. Finally the Comanche slumps forward then rolls off his horse to the ground.

Charley quickly rushes over to Ariana. "God! Are you hurt?"

She is scratched and bruised but nothing serious. "I will be fine. Where is Gabe?"

"Gabe took an arrow."

"Oh, Charley. He was helping me."

"Com'on."

He helps her into the saddle and they hurry back to Gabe.

"Gabe." Ariana shouts as they rein to a stop.

Charley dismounts as Gabe stands up. Charley quickly helps Ariana down and draws his knife.

"Are you hurt?" Ariana is anxious.

"Is it bad, Gabe?" Charley fires.

"I ain't never had an arrow stuck in me that was good." Gabe smiles.

"I'll have to cut some of that shaft off. We'll have to wait until it festers."

"Hope yer' better'n them horse doctors at McPherson."

Charley grabs a bottle of iodine from his pack and dabs some on the wound. Gabe yells. "Stuff burns!"

Charley smiles. "You didn't yell that loud when that arrow hit."

Gabe scowls.

"My father was a doctor remember?"

Gabe nods. Charley runs his knife around the shaft leaving a short stub.

Gabe growls. "Gotta' get movin'. We kilt a Comanch', they'll be back."

Charley looks serious at Gabe then nods in agreement. He sees Ariana's worried look. Charley helps Gabe into the saddle, then Ariana and they move along.

The sun is setting in the western sky as Charley begins to search for a camping spot. He has checked Gabe often but Gabe keeps saying he is all right. Charley decides on a sheltered pocket with some cover around. It is open on all sides for a hundred yards or so. It will be hard for anyone to ambush them here.

Ariana dismounts and falls to the ground. She sits on her butt and sighs. She is plumb tuckered out. Charley helps Gabe to the ground and immediately dabs iodine on the wound. Gabe complains that it burns and Charley chuckles to himself as he tends the wound on Rusty. He asks Ariana, "How are you doing?"

She gives him a worried look. "I'm just tired. I'll be okay. I'm worried about Gabe."

Charley glances over at Gabe. He's worried himself. He knows that on war arrows of the Indians, the head is lightly glued and the sinew thread wrapped around to hold the tip in place is barely wrapped. That way when the arrow is pulled out the head will stay, causing in most cases, a painful death. Before he left home Charley heard his father speak of Septicemia or blood poisoning, as it is called. He's not about to worry

Ariana but he's sure Gabe understands. Sometimes people survive. Gabe is a survivor. Charley has hope.

For several days they travel across the prairie. Charley and Ariana check Gabe often. Each day he gets worse. Charley finally reins up to make camp. He feels he is far enough away from the Comanches. Besides, Gabe needs rest and doctoring. They are hungry and the horses need rest.

Charley gets everything ready. Rusty and the mules are picketed and Gabe is somewhat comfortable. He begins to saddle up Red, who is the stronger of his horses. Rusty is still a mite sore from the arrow. Ariana walks over carrying a worried look.

"I've got to get us something to eat. Keep an eye on Gabe. I won't be far or gone too long."

Charley rides from the camp. He feels he can find some prairie chickens close by. After a mile or so Charley sees movement in the sagebrush. He's killed many a prairie chicken. The yellow sack on the male's head stands out. He sneaks quietly through the brush. He spots several, then a whole covey. He shoots the heads off two of the birds before the others fly away. He runs to pick them up.

He gathers the two chickens, quickly takes his knife, makes a slit across the belly and pulls the guts from the birds. He hurries to Red who is a short distance away.

Suddenly, he leaps back as a big rattlesnake slithers away, scaring the daylights out of him. He almost stepped right on top of it! One thing for sure, he hates snakes. He would rather fight a war party then deal with a slimy rattlesnake.

He looks around wide-eyed as he hears another rattle then another and another. Then more terrifying rattles seem to be everywhere. He holds dead still except for the movement of his eyes. His breathing comes in short gasps. He realizes that he is right in the middle of a bunch of rattlers heading for their lair.

He's heard that they are supposed to be non aggressive this time of year but he doesn't really believe that. He hates them crawlin' slimy creatures. He carefully moves his lips making the kiss sound for Red. Red trots over.

It is weird. Charley doesn't know why, but he recalls back in Kansas when his brother William got hung up in the stirrup and dragged. A big rattler almost got Charley but Red ran over snorting and bucking and kept Charley from getting bit.

Red snorts loudly on smelling the snakes. He instantly rears and bucks then stamps his front feet all the time screaming. He trots away then back stomping and wildly bucking. The shaking ground soon has the snakes slithering away.

Charley drops the two chickens, draws his pistol and empties it at the snakes. Blood and flesh are blown everywhere. From the corner of his eye Charley sees Red stomp near a sagebrush. Red snorts and lowers his head.

Charley shouts. "No, Red! No!" But it's too late.

Instantly, Red rears up with a scream. Shaking his head wildly. A large rattlesnake hangs from his lower jaw. The snake looks gruesome as it dangles from Red's skin and whips to and fro while Red wildly shakes his neck.

Charley runs, just as the fangs of the snake come loose, the rattler drops to the ground. Charley has never seen anything like this. The rattler's fangs must have got hung up in Red's skin.

He blasts the head of the rattler off with a quick shot from his rifle. Charley gingerly picks up the dead snake then grabs the chickens and hurries out of there. Red follows him. He lays the snake away from Red, who still snorts, lifting his head up and down like he is still trying to get rid of the rattler.

Charley checks the bite. "You all right, Ol' boy? Yuh' sure saved my skin. Will was right, you do hate snakes." Charley again examines Red's lower jaw. He has a worried look, "Sorry, boy. There's nothing I can do. I don't know what to do." Red watches Charley and moves his ears. Charley picks up his game and hurries back to camp, leading Red.

Ariana cooks the chickens over the fire while Charley broils the snake. He takes a piece to Gabe, who lays on the ground wrapped in a blanket. Charley nudges him with his boot. "Gotta eat something, Gabe." Charley looks away. "Red got bit by the rattler."

Gabe sits up and studies Red. He then takes a bite. "I'm gonna' enjoy eatin' this lizard." He looks up at Charley. "Some horses survive, others ain't so lucky. He's young n' tough, we'll watch n' see."

Charley looks over at Red, who stands one foot up, his head drooping. His jaw is swollen badly.

Ariana watches Charley's worried face.

Charley decides to stay in Camp and let both Gabe and Red rest. He and Ariana check Red and Gabe often. After several days Red's jaw is much better. Charley and Ariana rub Red while they talk.

Charley pats Red's flank. "You had me worried, Red, Ol' Boy." Red whickers softly.

Ariana gives Charley a serious look and says, "Gabe seems much worse. What can we do?"

Charley gives her an anxious stare then begins to saddle Rusty.

Gabe watches and motions Charley over.

"Take that girl 'n get! Them Injuns' will be comin'!"

"I'm not leaving you, Gabe!"

"I'm dead any way you look at it. Yuh save that girl!"

Charley shakes his head. Gabe draws his pistol pointing it at Charley. "Now git that girl 'n get movin'."

Rather then tempt Gabe, Charley feels there might be a better way. He reluctantly gets Ariana and rides from the camp. Ariana looks both frightened and worried. Charley tries to console her. "I know someone who might help."

Ariana sighs, exasperated. "Who? In this God forsaken land there's no medicine, no doctors! In Sante Fe we could find someone."

"Yearly, the Indians follow the rivers and the buffalo herds. Sometimes they will follow the same trails and rivers. My friend, Little Bear...hopefully his people are there." Charley spurs off with Ariana following.

Along a small stream Charley and his worried sweetheart watch an Indian village. Dogs bark, alerting the village of the intruders. Charley rides his horse in a circle.

The camp police run through the camp for their horses. Several talk in a huddle. It might be traders, who frequently trade their skins for beads, knifes and other trinkets. They see only two people mounted on horses. Charley rides in a circle while he raises his right arm, palm forward, several times.

One of the warriors comes forward. Little Bear recognizes the Red horses and signs that he is a friend. It is the Wasichus, the same one that he followed on the buffalo hunt. The wary eyes of the others watch as Little Bear rides from the camp.

"How! Coala." Charley raises his arm. Little Bear mimics then looks at Ariana, he nods in approval.

Charley explains with signs and the Lakota language that he wants Little Bear to keep his woman for him. Little Bear smiles, "Keep woman."

Charley waves and shakes his head. "My friend," he points to the south, "across prairie, his wound is bad from the Kwahadies' arrow. Big medicine, friend Medicine Lakota."

"Washte," In one fluid motion Little Bear's arm extends from his heart outward.

"It is good," Charley says then turns to Ariana. She looks fearful. "Trust me, Ariana. It will be all right. The Lakota women will take care of you. I will return as quickly as I can. Gabe needs their medicine." With a quick wave Charley wheels his horse and spurs off, leaving the dust flying.

Several Comanches surround the camp. Gabe lays dead still inside his blanket. The Indians have watched the camp for hours and have seen no movement. All they can see is the two mules on the picket.

Suddenly, they rush pell-mell into the camp. They stop dead in their tracks. All that is there is a smoldering fire and what appears to be a dead corpse underneath the blanket. They draw back in fear. They have entered the camp of the dead.

Charley is startled as he glasses the camp and sees the Indians. He feels he should have never left Gabe. He should have tried something different.

Abruptly, the distinct sound of Gabe's big rifle blasts across the prairie. "Com'on, Red." Charley rides hard for the camp. He draws his pistol and fires a couple of random shots. The Comanches look startled and hurry for their horses and ride off.

Charley is worried but he cautiously approaches the camp. "Gabe," he calls out.

"Yer' learnin', Boy." He's heard those words all too often, sometimes in disgust. But this time they sound encouraging.

Charley checks the dead Comanche and the lance on the ground near him. Blood drips from the dead warriors' chest. The scene quickly tells Charley that Gabe was pretending to sleep when they rushed the camp. He can picture Gabe tossing the blanket aside. But Gabe still does not look well.

Charley leads Ol' Jake. Gabe lays on a make shift litter on two poles suspended between the two mules. Charley decided to make the litter because Gabe's wound looks much worse. Had it not been for a couple of abandoned teepee poles that he stumbled on to he could not have accomplished his task. It has been a somewhat comfortable journey for Gabe. Better then him riding his mule.

Ariana runs from the village. With a sigh of relief she looks at Charley then grabs Gabe's hand. He lifts up his head. "Yer' bout the prettiest brown skin I ever did see." Ariana manages to crack a smile. "I must be some kinda royalty ridin' in a cussed contraption like this."

Ariana notices Charley's anxious look.

A cloud of steam blankets the air. A medicine man chants and dances around a sweat lodge. Little Bear and Charley stand at a distance observing the medicine man.

On a blanket draped over a log nearby, sits Ariana. She stares apprehensively at the lodge.

Little Bear gestures towards Ariana. "She is your woman?" Charley nods. Little Bear again motions towards the dark haired beauty. "Rainbow-on-shining-Water."

Charley smiles with a nod. The chant has stopped. Charley signs to Little Bear. The Indian walks over to the medicine man and they talk. The medicine man then goes off. Little Bear motions Charley over.

Charley opens the flap and waits for the steam to dissipate. He looks inside at Gabe. The sweat and water runs from Gabe's head. His beard, and what hair he has left, is wet and stringy.

"That blasted racket is about to kill me," Gabe growls.

"How ya doin', old friend?" Charley examines the festered wound.

"Ya' gotta' get that arrow out!"

Charley wasn't expecting Gabe's reaction and blurts out. "If that arrow-head stays?"

"What's the dif'ference? I'm gonna die anyhow."

Reluctantly, Charley crawls further inside, moving closer to Gabe. He grabs the short stub of the shaft protruding from Gabe's chest. He looks troubled as he stares at the stub. He's worried about blood poisoning. He doesn't want to admit it but Gabe is right. Infection has set in and he's got to get that arrow out of there. Charley figured if it festered like a sliver in a man's finger, it would come out.

Charley gives a hurried look at Gabe and then suddenly jerks the shaft. Gabe utters a deep sigh.

Charley stares at the headless stub.

"Don't fret, Son. Ol' Jake got kilt by a Comanch'! Better tuh die out here'n tuh drop dead in some smelly ol' town."

"You ain't gonna die, Gabe." Charley says hopefully and then wishes he hadn't said anything.

Charley has never seen Gabe's eyes so piercing. "Git me outta' this Injun' camp. Tell yer friend my regards. That pretty thing can wait here." Gabe appears weary. His tone somewhat pleading, "I wanna' die alone."

His words send an icy chill through Charley. He stares at Gabe then backs out of the sweat lodge.

Charley talks with Ariana and Little Bear. Several women from the village stand close by. Gabe is on the litter between his two mules. He lays on a fine brain tanned buffalo robe, a gift from Little Bear.

"Your woman will be safe with the women of the village."

Charley makes the friend sign then takes Ariana's hand and they move off alone. Charley embraces her tightly.

"I feel badly for our friend. If it wasn't for me this would not..."

Charley interrupts her, placing his fingers gently across her lips. He kisses her then holds her for a brief time. "No one is to blame. I love you. I'll be back."

Charley rides Red and leads Old Jake. Little Bear rides alongside. Ariana runs and squeezes Gabe's hand then pulls away to watch. Tears stream down her cheeks.

Charley and his Indian friend sign their parting. Charley understands that the Indian does not have a good-bye like the White Man. He looks perplexed when Little Bear hands him some red flannel strips then speaks with a tone of deep respect.

"Wa-Ta-Tanka makes the wind blow. The flying red cloth," he makes the sign of wings beating. "Good medicine."

Charley looks at Little Bear closely then starts to leave. Little Bear motions him. "Medicine good," with a sweeping motion of his right arm he thrusts his thumb into his chest. "Dakota tongue straight."

"I believe you." Charley nods and leads Gabe away. Rusty, loose, neighs then follows behind.

For several days Charley leads his dying friend across the prairie. He is sure that he is being followed but whoever it is, they are not close enough to distinguish. He suspects it is the same Comanches. They've got a grudge to settle and it seems they are bound to fulfill it. They know better then to approach within rifle range. And Charley believes if they do come, it will be on their terms. But when and where he wonders?

Charley halts, cautiously looks around, then dismounts and takes his canteen. He gives Gabe a drink. Gabe doesn't have long and he struggles to talk. "Don't yuh be burying me...in the...ground."

"We are almost there, Ol' Hoss. I am taking you home—Gabe." Charley coughs.

"Injuns will be a comin'. Bury me so the sun...shines on me."

"The sun shinin'..." Charley is bewildered.

Gabe musters his strength. "Don't want no—dirt kicked on me."

Charley is upset. "But, Gabe the wolves will dig..."

"Hellfire, I kilt a bunch—of them." He clutches his wound, "What's the difference? Maybe they can chaw on me—fer a change." He manages a smile. Charley looks at him serious like.

"Don't yuh' fret. I've...done what I want mostly. Turn muh mules loose," Gabe chokes. "They'll go to Kearney."

Charley looks away to clear his throat then speaks softly, "Gabe." Charley waits for Gabe to finish his cough. "You gotta' tell me, Gabe. That Mountain Man... that one that fell in love with the girl...in Taos, that was you, wasn't it?"

Gabe nods. "What happened to her, Gabe?"

Gabe reaches out and clutches Charley's hand. Charley sees anger in Gabe's eyes.

"Dem' greasy Mexicans killed her," he chokes. "Don't know if'n I've got any sons...if'n I do...I'd want 'em to be like...you."

Charley fights back a tear. Gabe coughs. "Don't want no one a...weepin' over me. Get my diary for me...Son."

Charley squeezes Gabe's hand. As he walks away, he wonders if that was their last parting gesture? Charley searches in vain through Gabe's gear. Suddenly the thought dawns on him. He has never seen Gabe write in any diary. He rushes back to Gabe who appears to be dead. Charley stares across the prairie while he fights back the tears.

Suddenly, a blood-curdling war cry snaps Charley around! But he reacts as if he's in a trance. He finds his rifle in his hand and aiming. Charley drops the first Indian he sees dead in his tracks.

Unnoticed by Charley, the Comanches have planned well this time. Three warriors close in behind him. Charley draws his pistol and reaches for Gabe's rifle that is beside Gabe's body.

Charley's look is frightening as Gabe suddenly raises up from the mule litter. Charley's face is white with shock as he dives out of the way of Gabe's line of sight.

Gabe blasts the closest Comanche. The others look as if they've seen something from the spirit world and flee. Gabe's mules stomp and bray loudly.

Charley jumps to his feet and stares at his friend, Gabe is dead. Charley is angry now. He yells and waves Gabe's big rifle. "You're not gettin' my friend."

The Comanches gather in a circle to talk. The older one speaks first. "He will kill us all. Let us stay far back from his big gun. The old man dies. Let us wait for the paleface to bury him."

"We will dig up the old man n' skin him," says the angry one.

"We will urinate on him!" says another.

"We will stop his journey to the Great Beyond." The other warriors shout in agreement and ride around ki...ying.

Charley stares across the Platte River. This is where it had all began, his friendship with Gabe. Charley observes the Comanches, who stay their distance. He then makes a crude raft from the numerous driftwood logs along the bank. He crosses on Red, while Rusty follows behind. Once on the other side, he uses Old Jake and Charley Boy to pull the raft to the island.

Gabe's body lies on the crudely built burial scaffold. Charley has covered him with the buffalo robe. Charley removes the red flannel strips that Little Bear gave him. He takes Gabe's large beaver hat, the sign of the free trapper. Charley smirks as he thinks Gabe was not beholden to anyone. Charley walks to the scaffold. "You taught me a lot...Gabe. I'll never forget you, Ol' Hoss."

The sky begins to blacken. The Comanches look stunned as they watch from the bluffs across the Platte. The angry one motions his arm. "He buries the old man like the Sioux. We cannot urinate on him."

The older Comanche fearfully looks at the blackening sky. "Sioux burial is sacred. The Great Mystery is angry!" Ki...ying he rushes away. The others take a hurried look at the scaffold then the darkening sky and gallop after the old man.

Charley hangs the red strips on the upright poles. He takes Gabe's big beaver hat and lashes it tightly to one of the poles. He bows his head for a quick prayer and then steps back. He looks up where Gabe lays underneath the buffalo robe. "The robe will keep you warm for your journey." He steps forward and touches Gabe's beaver hat. "With a hat like that you're free, Old Friend." He quickly turns and walks away.

The sky continues to blacken and fingers of lightning flash across the bleak plains. Across the river, Charley turns Old Jake and Charley Boy loose. Old Jake, as if to say good-bye, honks loudly then runs. Charley Boy nickers and kicks his heels.

Charley feels it is a parting gesture. He grins as he watches Charley Boy follow Old Jake. Charley, with a shout, races with the mules. After a short distance, he then reins up and gives his quick wave. A violent thunder and lightning storm erupts. Charley rides for a last look at the scaffold.

He thinks to himself, those Comanches won't bother him anymore. They must be clean out of the country by now. The last he saw of them, they were riding like the devil across the prairie. The storm had put the fear of God into them. He'll soon be obliged to find some shelter himself. He reins around and rides like the wind.

Uppermost on his mind, Charley has got to go back for his woman.

10

*T*he ground looks familiar as Charley trots along. It won't be long now. He is anxious to see his woman and he nudges Red into a dead gallop. Ahead he sees the trees along the stream where Little Bear's camp was. But something seems strange. He sees no camp. He should be able to see some teepees. Maybe they've moved downstream, he thinks to himself.

Charley reins up sharply. Concerned, he glasses the area. Along the river two bodies lay on branches in the trees. They are buried the Sioux way. Red flannel flutters in the breeze. Scattered campfire rings, hide strips, broken buffalo bones, and clothes litter the ground.

A cold chill runs up Charley's spine. In his head, strangely he hears Indian drums. He moves cautiously forward, then extremely concerned, he races ahead.

Hawks and Crows squawk and fly up into the trees. Charley stares at the bodies in the branches. He gasps in relief when he sees the warrior trappings hanging from the burial trees. He then anxiously dismounts and examines the ground.

He finds several pieces of bloody Mexican clothes and he follows a trail of blood to the river. He hurries back and examines the clothing. Then he finds a trail of a dozen shod horses. He looks around and finally finds the trail of unshod Indian ponies. He quickly mounts up and follows the Indian trail.

Charley and horses gallop across the prairie. Finally, he spots a large dust cloud ahead. He pulls up and glasses the area. He must be cautious, it could be buffalo, but he hopes that it is Little Bear's people.

He breathes a sigh of relief when he focuses in on Sioux Indians. Charley anxiously scans the movement. He sees women, children, horses pulling travois and warriors on the outside, who police the movement. Indian guards are in front and to the rear for protection.

Charley quickly moves forward. When he gets near enough he signs his intentions. Without alarming the warrior guards, he rides in a circle three times. Little Bear trots from the camp in a hurry. They quickly greet. Both are anxious but Little Bear is calmer. Charley looks troubled and swings to the ground. "My woman, Ariana?"

Little Bear is solemn. "She was taken!"

Charley is dumfounded. "Taken?"

Little Bear points to the south. "Wild men! Kwahadies!"

"Comanches!" Charley snaps.

"Lakota Women dig the wild turnip. Strange men come to the village with Kwahadies. They wear strange clothes."

"Mexicans!" Charley sees anger.

"Use knife." Little Bear quickly runs his right hand across his throat.

Charley stares towards the south. He is very upset.

"The Older men were gone from village. Hunt pte." He signs, buffalo. "Young warriors kill Kwahadies." He holds up two fingers.

Charley nods in agreement and signs. "I found clothes n' blood."

"Kwahadies make Lakota heart bad. We cut them up, throw them in river. Strange men, Kwahadies, bad. Go after women." He grasps his chest. "My heart is sad for you. Lakota call your woman—Rainbow-on-shining-Water."

Charley is upset and anxiously swings into his saddle. "I will go after her."

Little Bear reaches up and grabs the jaw strap on Red. With calming words he speaks. "Kwahadies watch for you."

"I am not afraid."

The Indian raises his right arm, "How coala. You are not a big fool." He points up at Charley. "You must wait!"

Little Bear's calming words have an affect on Charley and he realizes it would be foolish to follow them now. Charley reconsiders. He looks off and then finally answers, "I will wait."

"It is good, Eyomashesha."

Charley nods thankfully but is still upset.

His Indian friend signs and Charley dismounts, they lead their horses. Off to their right the Sioux people continue to move across the plains.

"Where do your people go?" Charley gestures to the moving column of Indians.

"Lakota return to the land of the shining mountains." Charley looks puzzled.

"White Rain Mountain is at this place."

Charley waves his right arm, thumb outstretched into his chest. "I have been to this place. The river the Lakota call, Elk River, is there. The White Man calls it the Yellowstone River. The Crows live on their land. White Rain Mountains. Montana Territory."

On hearing that Charley has been there. The Indian shakes his head, a little angry. "Tashunka Witko calls this place the land of powder water."

"Many of my people, the Wasichus, fear Crazy Horse."

Little Bear is still upset. "Little Thunder's village on Blue Water Creek, White Beard the man the Wasichus call Harney." Little Bear gestures in anger. "He came with the horse soldiers, the walking soldiers, wagon guns! He kill many of my people, women, the little ones."

Charley can only shake his head in sympathy.

"For many days Tashanka Witko found our dead, the helpless, the little ones," He sighs. "Little Thunder signed talk paper."

"Not all Wasichus are like this General Harney. There is much fear among the whites. Crazy Horse, Tashunka Witko, he kill many Wasichus."

Little Bear raises his chest. "Tashunka Witko is a great warrior." He looks serious, nods and makes the war sign. "Uncpapa medicine chief, Tatanka Iyotake goes to this land you call Montana. We will join him." He carefully looks at Charley. "He says the people must stay far away from the Wasichus." He grimaces. "Pentouchers talk paper say the land is ours until the grass grows no more. Until the rivers run no more." He gives Charley a pleading look. "Wasichus leave us alone at this place."

Charley looks away then stares at the ground. He looks up as Little Bear leaps onto his horse's back. He gives the peace sign then Charley watches him ride to his people.

Alone again, he leads his horses and ponders, then talks out loud. "One day..." his horses wiggle their ears. "I love the Indian sound boys. Crazy Horse...Tashunka Witko...Sitting Bull, Tatanka Iyotake"

Red nickers and shakes his head, they stop and Charley rubs and pats them. "Bull buffalo, Ta-Tan-Ka! Old Gabe talked about the White Rain Mountains. We were close." Red paws the dirt while Rusty knickers, twitching his upper lip. "Montana, the West, what'd say we go see it all, boys?"

A serious look comes across Charley's face. He removes his watch. "Rainbow-on-shining-Water."

Red and Rusty nicker while Charley gazes to the south.

Fort Lincoln Dakota Territory—Custer home

Snow covers the ground and it is cold. Charley's horses are packed. George and Tom Custer, Captain Thomas Benton Weir, a close friend of the Custers and Myles Walter Keogh, the big, handsome, rough talking Irishman are outside the Custer home.

"Where are you headed, Charley?"

"Wolf trapping." Charley notices as Libbie Custer watches out the ice covered windows. "Hunting buffalo. Forts along the Missouri always need fresh meat."

Keogh looks right handsome with his huge mustache and goatee. "Below zero, Reynolds. Maybe you ought to wait a spell."

"I'm used to it, Keogh." Charley waves and rides towards the north.

Custer turns and looks towards the house seeing his wife Libbie. He turns back. "God speed, Reynolds. I want you back for the Black Hills Expedition!"

Libbie walks out, putting a shawl around her shoulders. She waves to Charley and hurries over to her husband. She looks concerned. "You let him leave in this cold?"

Custer looks at his wife, surprised. "Army hires him by the week, month or year. My little darl. He's his own man. Done this for years, Libbie."

"Even our officers are forbidden to leave! How can he survive alone?"

Tom speaks up. "Don't worry about Charley, Libbie. He's a survivor. He fares well even when he's alone. That's why the men call him, Lonesome Charley."

Custer nods at his brother. "Indian scouts say the same. They call him, Eyomashesha"

Weir looks puzzled. "E-Yo-Ma-She-Sha.?"

Custer answers, "Sioux word for lonesome."

Libbie breaks a smile. "The name fits. I like him."

Charley rides away across the cold Dakota Plains. As the others watch, Libbie asks, "Why does he go off by himself?"

Her husband answers, "Something inside him...something as old as mankind itself."

Charley finally disappears into the wintry landscape. Libbie's soft voice seems to echo from the snow. "I wonder where he goes?"

Back Along the Missouri

Charley, mounted on Red moves along the river. Rusty is loose and follows behind. The temperature is quite cold. But the sun shines across this barren land and makes it seem warmer than it is.

Red stops when he comes to an old beaver slide. He nickers softly and Rusty joins them. Red turns his head, looking at Charley, ears pointed and moving. Charley laughs. "You boys remember better'n I do. Good boy, Red." Charley eases from the saddle and slides down the frozen bank.

He soon returns with a large beaver. The horses nicker and nuzzle his pockets as he loads the beaver on Rusty's pack. "Nothing for you yet, boys." Charley says, as he mounts up and moves further along the river.

Charley hasn't gone far when Rusty wanders away from the river. Charley watches. Rusty soon stops. He paws at the ground and whickers. Charley rides over. "Rusty, ol' boy. You're gettin' too old to..." Rusty continues to stomp and paw with his hooves, like he's pawing for grass under the snow. "I know you're hungry, ol' boy," then it dawns on Charley. He had set some wolf traps but the snow had covered them.

He jumps from the saddle and kicks and scrapes the frozen snow away. Sure enough, there lies a huge frozen wolf carcass. The wind had drifted the snow over the animal but Charley feels a bit foolish for not having trusted Rusty. "Sorry, Rusty ol' boy." Charley rewards his horses with some oats from his pack and moves on.

He finds several more animals this way. Charley then moves into some sheltered trees. He lights a fire and begins to skin the wolves. He cuts two sticks and uses them to skin the tails of the wolves. "That ought to lighten your load," he says, as he loads the pelts on Rusty, who nuzzles him for some more oats. Charley obliges his horses and moves steadily along the river.

Stopping when he spots an area where the beaver have been. He recalls that he had set a trap here. But with the new snow and the frozen ground it's hard to tell. He senses something is wrong. He notices below on the snow, a blood trail.

He leaves his horses and cautiously follows the trail of blood and animal tracks. He is wearing buffalo hide coverings over his boots for warmth but on icy ground they are slick. Down below him, on the ice covered river bottom, he sees two devil bears eating on a beaver. Without warning, his feet slip out from under him. He drops his rifle into the snow as he slides onto his back and down the steep bank. His rifle clatters past him on the way down. He nearly slides right into the snarling animals. They are hungry and Charley has interrupted their meal. The animals growl, snapping and snarling at him. Huge teeth snap viciously as one sinks its teeth into the beaver and drags it away.

The other, turns on Charley, who quickly rolls over scrambling and kicking, trying to gain his feet, while drawing his pistol at the same time. He fires, stopping the vicious, snarling animal. Charley then aims at the other wolverine that drags the beaver away. It stops to hiss and snap his teeth at him.

The echo of the shot fades and the black powder slowly disappears. Charley struggles to his feet, his eyes darting from animal to animal. He hears his horses nicker, "I'm all right." He breathes a sigh then takes a minute to catch his breath. "That was too close," he mutters.

If anything could be called free the nomadic Plains Indians' way of life was that. The life of the free spirit—they ate when hungry, laughed when happy and moved their home every few days. At times it was a hard life but other times it was good. Those nomadic people had learned to live with nature. Constantly on the move, Thompson's small Indian band has wintered in a fine place. The snow is not too deep and the cottonwood trees give them protection from the winds, food for the horses and warmth from the fires. If anything, the winter has been quite mild, cold at times, but nothing of the severe Dakota winters.

As usual, Charley is first greeted by the curs. Old Patch Eye in the lead. The curs have learned to back off and with a few guttural words from one of the Indian women, they do. But they will still dart in and nip you if you don't stay on guard.

Charley wonders, maybe it is because, that for months he's gone then suddenly he shows up. He's a stranger to the dogs. But good old Thompson always keeps his camp. Charley hates to admit it but he kind of likes Old Patch Eye. It seems like a game to the curs, which one can get there first, and which one can do the most growling and biting.

Charley lays the fresh skinned hides of the two wolverines by the tecpee. Running-creek-Woman glances at him while she works on a colorful bag.

Thompson smiles and waves a greeting. He walks over and inspects Charley's catch. "Fine lookin' hides, Reynolds." Charley nods as they walk to his horses to unload and unsaddle them.

"Ought to have seed the look uv your face the last time yuh left here." Thompson laughs while Charley gives one of his half grins.

"Yeah. A good prank."

"It wern't no prank, Charley."

Charley turns serious. "I have a woman..."

Thompson shakes his head like he can't make out what to think. He helps unload the horses.

Charley carries his saddle inside his teepee. He lays the saddle on its side, always on its side. That way the leather on the skirts won't curl up. He pulls the timepiece from his pocket and stares at the writing on the watch.

The next morning Walks-on-Ice watches as Charley and Thompson ride from the camp. She is not worried. She knows they are going hunting. Sometimes she likes it when her man is gone. That way she and the other Indian women can talk woman talk.

Reynolds and Thompson ride across the snow-covered prairie. For some reasons, known only to Thompson, he jabbers on and on telling Reynolds of his vast knowledge about women and such. He jabbers about what it is like to wake up on a cold, frosty morning, alone; about how Reynolds should get married, the Indian way; on and on he rambles.

"Well, oh Mighty-White-Hunter-Who-Never-Goes-Out-For-Nothing. Yeah," he chuckles. "If only you could of saw yerself. That ugly one would've married you. She'd kept yuh nice n warm under that buffler robe. N' yuh know, Reynolds, ugly is only beholden to yer own self. When they's real bad, I call em' plum Ugg-glee."

Thompson stops talking for a minute while they collect beaver and wolves.

"Yer a waken up on a cold, frosty morning...why, there's hardly nothin' better...cept maybe a stiff drink of whiskey."

They stop to remove a couple of beaver then continue on.

"Yuh know, Running-creek-Woman has eyes fer yuh. She has sure nough taken a liken to you. Yuh ought ta get hitched. She'll sew yer shirts, mend yer moccasins, put up the teepee, take it down, gather the wood, build yer fire, build the sweat lodge n' pack in the buffler chips."

They pick up two wolves, tying them on the saddle. They continue on. Reynolds occasionally gives Thompson a strange look but offers no comment.

"Hardly makes any sense a man travelin by his self. Yeah. YesSree, Ol' Mighty hunter such as you'n. Running-creek-Woman. I'm a thinkin' she'd do jest bout any little task fer her brave n' fearlous, mighty hunter. You know, my woman Walks-on-Ice the onliest reason she's my woman is a smile. You smiled at Running-Creek-Woman."

Finally Reynolds reins up. "You have been jabbering for at least ten miles. I ought not to have smiled at Running-Creek-Woman. Where did you learn so much about Women?"

They ride on in silence, for a moment.

Mistakenly, Reynolds looks a question at Thompson, which is all he needs to continue to babble away.

"I ain't no spring chicken. I learned a lot 'bout women. You smiled at Running-Creek-Woman. You ought not to."

Reynolds gives Thompson a, when is this going to stop, look. Finally, as suddenly as he had started, a hush comes over the snow covered land.

In some trees along the river, Reynolds starts a fire. Thompson gets some pemmican from his pack and gives some to Reynolds.

"Buffler berries 'n' charqui. Eat up. Yuh know, Reynolds, women's troublesome worrisome. Sometimes yuh just can't do without."

Reynolds is amused then quietly. "I don't know much...about women. But you do."

Thompson gives an annoyed look. As they munch the pemmican Thompson grabs a wolf carcass. "I'll have these skun by the time yuh check t'other traps."

Charley chortles, "That word skun, when I hear it, it reminds me of Ol' Gabe." Charley smiles and mimics his mentor. In a deep, gruff voice, "I've skun beavers 'n' buffler woofs. Mor'n any man!"

Thompson looks perplexed but Charley continues his shenanigans. "What'd you say yer' name was, Youngin'?" Charley meekly adds in a very high pitched voice, "Charles Alexander Reynolds," then gruffly states, "Well, I declare, a name like that, you must be some kinda royalty!"

Charley does a curtsy. Thompson is caught up in the humor and mimics Charley. They dance around laughing and stomping their feet in the snow, having a good old time. Thompson laughing heartily falls onto the ground. "Them women would think we wuz plum local" he makes the crazy sign. They have a good laugh and then Charley mounts up and rides from the camp to check their trap line.

Thompson undertakes the task of skinning the animals. He is finishing the last animal when he hears a noise. He wonders if it was Charley but looks around suspiciously. He beholds his rifle beyond reach. Slowly, he stoops to reach out. He hears a hiss and an arrow slams into his buttocks. With a yell he drops to the ground. Scrambling sideways he reaches his rifle and fires a wild one handed shot.

In the brush an indistinct figure notches an arrow. Out of the blue, Reynolds charges Red into the figure, knocking him over. Reynolds leaps from his saddle and shoves his revolver into his face. He is only a boy.

Thompson hobbles over while clutching the arrow in his backside. "Kill that heathen sonofa red-skinned-devil!"

"He's only a youngster." Reynolds replies.

"Youngster, my sainted grandmother. Pop the cap, Charley! What'n samhell is he a doin' way out here, any which way?"

"He's just trying to earn his warrior's feathers." Reynolds takes the boy's weapons and then signs. The disgruntled youngster runs off. Thompson grimaces.

"Let's have a look at that, Ol' Hoss. How in this snow covered landscape did you get hit?" Reynolds begins to chuckle. Thompson glares.

"Yeah. Laugh. I wer reachin' fer my rifle."

Reynolds continues to chuckle. "Walks-on-Ice is gonna enjoy this. Not too deep. I can pull it out 'stead've pushin' it through."

Thompson gives him a look then grits his teeth. Reynolds quickly pulls the arrow without difficulty.

Thompson sighs deeply. "Obliged your father was a croaker."

"It's a good thing that boy wasn't pulling a powerful hunting bow, Hoss." Reynolds chuckles. He heats some water on the fire then pours warm water and baking soda, cleaning the wound. Thompson squirms and moans. Reynolds takes his powder horn and finds some moss. He doctors the wound with gunpowder and tree moss.

Thompson only glares as he gingerly mounts up to leave. Reynolds hands up a bandage for him to sit on in the saddle.

"Sure hope that gunpowder doesn't go off." Reynolds laughs heartily, to Thompson's annoyance. Charley douses the fire. The duo head back to the village.

Reynolds and Thompson ride in and dismount. Thompson limps towards the fire. Ol' Patch Eye stands at a distance watching, but only growls. Thompson gives a slight grin, "Well, I'll be! Ol' Patch Eye has took a liken' tuh me. He knows I'll cook his har' off."

At once, Walks-on-Ice notices that something is wrong with her man. She hurriedly comes over and chatters excitedly to Thompson. He waves her off, "Tiz' not that bad. Ol' Doctor I meant tuh say, Ol' Croaker, Reynolds has taken care of the wound." She looks at the bandage then begins to giggle. Thompson is at first annoyed and waves her off then makes the sign for coffee. Reynolds can hardly keep a straight face.

Thompson again makes the sign for the little hand coffee grinders that the traders bring. "We'd like some hot skulljaw."

Walks-on-Ice has to turn away. She laughs quietly to herself then pours coffee, adding a good measure of brown sugar. She goes into her teepee, returning with a bottle of whiskey. Thompson takes a big swig, gargles and then swallows with a smile. Walks-on-Ice watches him then scowls disgusted at the whiskey.

Walks-on-Ice waves Thompson into their teepee. She smiles at Reynolds as Thompson lifts the flap and steps inside. Outside the teepee Charley can hear their laughter. He chuckles when he hears yelps from Thompson and squeals of joy from Walks-on-Ice as she cleans his wound with the whiskey. Reynolds can hardly contain himself.

Running-creek-Woman watches Reynolds from nearby. She heaves while she tries to hide her laughter. Reynolds finally quits smiling.

Walks-on-Ice comes from the teepee. She sees Reynolds look longingly at the inscription on his watch. She watches Charley from the corner of her eye. She sees him look at his watch again then gaze off into the distance. She wonders about Charley as he goes into his teepee.

Inside the teepee Charley fingers the buffalo hide pad on his saddle while he contemplates. He then steps outside and begins to get his horses ready.

Thompson comes from his teepee carrying a shirt. His wife walks out and joins him. They come to where Charley is packing. Running-creek-Woman shyly stands by her teepee holding something in her hand.

Charley looks off then asks Thompson, "How's the buttocks, Hoss?"

"Don't yuh be laughing. Walks-on-Ice put on another poultice. She really enjoyed that. Peers she approves of yer croaker ways. You've got that look."

Charley looks across the prairie then finally turns back, "There's something I have to do." Thompson glances at Running-creek-Woman then looks at his wife.

"Just hope yuh' don't run into one of them Dakota blizzards."

"There's talk about the Black Hills. When I return I'll be riding with the 7th Horse."

Thompson and his wife speak in Arapaho. "She says, what the Sioux call Paha Sapa, tiz land of the Great Mystery."

Charley sounds irritated. "I understand the Indians believe Paha Sapa is sacred land. Tell her the soldiers pay me money. It is money to buy sugar, coffee, n' beads. We mean no harm to the Sioux."

Thompson again speaks with Walks-on-Ice. Running-creek-Woman hurries over and timidly hands Charley the colorful pouch then gingerly returns to where she had been standing.

Charley is both surprised and pleased. He opens the beautifully decorated pouch of porcupine quills and fine beadwork. He sheepishly looks inside at the thread, needles and buttons. He wonders to himself. She must have gotten all this stuff from the traders. He puts the bag into his saddle pockets and swings onto Red's back.

"While you slept, Running-creek-Woman made the saddle pad and mended your shirt," Thompson blurts out. "She says the buffalo hair saddle pad will soften your journey."

"Running-creek-Woman...my journey, how could she know?"

"She is a woman. How else would she know? She says she has seed you long time past."

Thompson hands Charley the shirt. Charley nods in appreciation. "She's seen me...where?" He looks over at Running-creek-Woman. She shyly looks away.

Walks-on-Ice chatters at Thompson, who looks at Charley, surprised. "On the plains to the south, yuh hunt buffalo. At the Flint, the White Man's Ark-an'-saw River, you come to her people, Little Raven chief."

Charley looks at Running-creek-Woman puzzled. "Tell her I am beholden for her gifts." He quickly waves and rides from the camp.

11

harley has just picked up two prairie chickens that he shot, when he hears the distant whistle of the steamer. That whistle sure sounds lonesome out here on the wide-open spaces, he thinks. He knows that his friend, Grant Marsh, has to stop at the woodcutter's pile. Steamboats need fire wood and lots of it.

He wonders if it is true that the, "killer of the Crows," the Mountain Man, John Johnston cuts and stacks wood for extra money. He thinks it is true. But Johnston would be further up the Missouri in Montana Territory. Then it dawns on Charley, Johnston would have to be somewhere around the White Rain Mountains, home of the Mountain Crows. Then again, he's heard Johnston hunts over on the Mussell Shell. One day, he would like to meet the Mountain Man. Charley hurriedly steps into his stirrup and swings onto the saddle.

Charley waves when he sees Marsh standing on the deck, directing the hands loading the wood. Charley hands Marsh the prairie chickens then loads his horses, handing the reins to one of the deckhands. Grant gives a happy smile. "Glad to have you aboard. What in the world are you doing this far south? You rode quite a spell, Charley." He holds up the chickens. "I'm lookin' forward to supper."

"It's good to see you, Grant. I'm happy you're well."

"Headin' for Yankton, Charley?" Charley shakes his head as one of the Mates yells out. "All ready to push off, Captain."

Grant Marsh looks at Charley. "Keep yer' rifle handy, remember the last time?" He motions Charley to follow then turns and heads for the wheelhouse.

Charley quickly goes to his horses and unsheathes his rifle from the scabbard. As he hurries to the wheel he wonders why Grant had to remind him to get his rifle? Usually his rifle is part of him. He's learned long time past, that a man that gets caught without his rifle doesn't last too long in this harsh land. When he sleeps alone on the prairie, he keeps his rifle between his knees under the covers, a trick that Ol' Gabe taught him. Maybe it's Ariana? And then the smile of that Indian woman flashes before him. The way she moves her lips, there is something about her—

Grant pulls the whistle cord. The wheel slowly grinds and begins to churn. Then with a pounding, splashing noise the steamer moves away from shore. Black smoke emits from the stack and the steamer churns down the Big Muddy.

For hours Charley looks off to the side and behind. He's caught up as he watches the waves churn against the shore at the rear of the steamer. The water rolls out in a V and then splashes against the drift wood, washing new crevices in the rock and sand banks. It is soothing to Charley and he is lost in deep thought until Marsh speaks up, "Thunder rollin', Lonesome Charley." Grant points to a thunderhead in the distant sky.

A violent thunder and lightning storm lashes its fury across the Dakotas. Charley watches in awe. The lightning looks like weird looking fingers flashing across the sky. And then the downpour opened up. The hail pounds the ground relentlessly. The large frozen snowballs tearing the vegetation and literally driving the animals into a frenzy. A man caught horseback better find shelter fast or the hail would sometimes tear the flesh from the animals. And there were times when the lightning killed a man's horse, leaving him afoot in this wild land. Most of the time, these kind of storms last for an hour or two but, sometimes, Charley remembers, they've lasted all day and sometimes all night.

Hours later, the storm has died down somewhat. Grant slows the steamer. "It's too shallow to get you in close, Charley."

Reynolds removes his boots and holding his boots and rifle he is ready to disembark. "I'll make it, Grant." Charley gives his customary quick wave and gently spurs his horse forward. Red leaps from the steamer and makes a large splash as he hits the water. Charley yells as the cold water splashes his back and neck. Rusty splashes in close behind him. Grant chuckles out loud and shouts, "One way to get a bath, Charley."

His horses climb ashore dripping water. Charley dismounts and squeezes the water from his clothes. In this country they'll soon be dry. He checks his rifle and ammunition. His brain tanned, willow smoked, well-oiled, buffalo hide bags and scabbard usually keeps everything dry.

Charley surveys the land. He looks off as the faint whistle comes from the downstream steamer. It is Grant's way of saying, God speed. Keep safe until the next time. He realizes that once again he is alone in this vast country. To Charley the whistle sounds like a lonely good-bye.

The country is dry and desolate as Charley heads to the South. He can't help but think back of the fond memories on finding Old Gabe. It seems ever since the country changed more desert like, that he thinks of Gabe and their ride to bring Ariana. This time, with Gabe gone he'll have to do it alone.

Charley has taught his horses to move at what he calls, a running walk. A pace just like the steady trot of a lobo wolf or what some call a dogtrot. They learned fast and are tough plains wise animals. Red and Rusty can cover long distances. There are times when Charley rides over a hundred miles in a day.

Charley walks his horses down the old streets of Santa Fe. He's heard that this was the oldest town in the entire country. Things still look the same as when he was last here.

Unknown to Charley, a Mexican observes him as he rides to the livery stable. He leaves Rusty there then rides Red out of town. He notices a Mexican ride away but pays him just a casual look. Riders come and go and there is no reason for him to suspect anything. But then his last visit flashes into his mind. He shakes it aside and spurs Red on.

He rides past familiar landmarks and when he sees the unique high mesa with the lone windblown pinion tree he knows he's getting near. He passes between two giant Saguaro Cacti, tops a rise and reins up.

Charley looks at the well-to-do ranch. The estate stretches as far as the eye can see. There must be thousands of spotted long horn cattle grazing, scattered across the sagebrush-covered ground and rolling hill country. Well-bred Spanish horses graze in the nearby pastures. Pinion trees dot the landscape and mesas are scattered here and there. A romantic place, he thinks to himself, this New Mexico Territory.

Charley ties Red and looks around at the courtyard. He notices a Mexican lady busy working. He recognizes her. It is Evita, a maid. Charley walks over.

"Senor. If you look for work." Suddenly, she recognizes Charley and becomes excited. "Ay dios mio. Oh, Senor Charley!" She makes the sign of the cross and hurries into the hacienda.

Ariana's Brazilian, Mexican beauty is obvious. Her aristocratic rearing is plain to any onlooker as she strides from the house. Her flashing eyes look stunned and her full lips are speechless as she and Charley stare at each other.

Finally she cries. "Oh Charley...my Charley!" They move together. Charley embraces her strongly while tears of joy roll down her cheeks.

"Ariana!"

"Oh, Charley. My Charley. I've waited watched for you. I've all but given up." He holds her snugly.

Finally, she takes his arm and leads him to a patio.

Charley smiles at Ariana's mother, Sofia. She smiles warmly in return. Evita brings lemonade and places it on the table. Charley nods in appreciation and sips the lemonade.

Two boys run by kicking an empty tobacco can. Charley chuckles at the boys, who smile and continue their game. "Hush, Boys. Play in the pasture." Ariana scolds. The can lands near Charley. Luis runs over and looks up at Charley who kicks the can across the yard. Luis playfully shouts, "Senor, come play with us." Ariana smiles, "Hush now, Boys. Off with you."

The boys reluctantly kick the can towards the pasture. Charley watches, "Fine boys, Ariana."

"Friends of my cousin, Evita. Do you remember the waterfall?"

"I remember it well...the adobe house."

"Let us go there. I'll ask Evita to fix a basket with...wine." She flashes her eyes and smiles. "You hitch the buggy, please." She squeezes his hand lightly. Charley nods then she goes into the house.

Inside, Sofia smiles at her daughter. "I've never seen you smile so, Ariana." Ariana skips her feet and twirls her skirt in happiness. That is all the answer her mother needs. Evita laughs as she hands Ariana a basket.

"Gracious, Evita." Still smiling, she steps out the door.

Sofia looks at Evita. "I am happy for my daughter. I," she makes the sign of the cross. "Antonio, I just..." her words trail off as the door closes shut.

The buggy moves along the river. Charley has turned Red loose and he follows like a pet dog. Ariana clutches Charley's arm and smiles often. They pass familiar places and then come to the waterfall. They both stare in deep thought as they look at the sparkling pool below the falls. The soothing noise of the water takes them back to a special time. When they splashed each other in the heat of the day, to cool off and when..."Our friend Gabe, I think about him often."

"I'll never forget him. He was one—well, one of a kind, a true friend."

"I will always be grateful. Tell me about leaving Little Bear's camp."

The memories come flooding back, some very hurtful and Charley struggles to tell. "Gabe hung on for several days. He asked me to bury him the Indian way." Charley looks away and stares at the water. "I buried him by his cabin on the river. At the same place where I first went into the mountains with Gabe." Charley clears the lump from his throat. "Gabe told me he didn't know if he had any sons, that he knowed about." Charley cracks a smile. "If"n he did, he wanted em to be like me," he said. Charley chokes and starts the horses off.

Ariana clutches him then puts her arm around Charley. "Oh, Charley. He was shot helping me. Often, I think about it. I feel so badly."

Charley reins up. "Whoa. Whoa, you horses." He looks serious at Ariana. "Gabe lived how he wanted...we die how we live."

Ariana reflects. After a while Charley gets a mischievous grin. "I can see Ol', Gabe looking down from that burial scaffold." Charley gruffly imitates Gabe. "I can hear him say. Yer' learnin', Boy!" Charley moves the reins and they ride on in silence.

Ariana sounds apprehensive when she finally breaks the silence. "I will not forget when Antonio and his hired Comanches came to the camp."

"I should never have left you there. When I returned to the camp, I found two dead bodies."

Ariana becomes angry. "Antonio and his..."

"Scum!" Charley interjects.

"I despise that man! I will never again live with such a cruel devil! If my father would have only realized what a treacherous man he was dealing with."

"Now that we both know, let us not waste our precious time talking about that..."

She interrupts. "My heart could never belong to such a man." Then, as if thinking out loud, she says, "Gabe wanted to die alone. Little Bear, I admired him."

"In the states, our government policies for the Indian is bad. Little Bear's people moved to Dakota Territory. The War Department squabbles with Indian Affairs. The Easterners, mostly what they want, is the land. The Indian is caught in-between and the Army takes the blame."

Ariana points. "I remember so well."

Charley pulls the horses to a halt. He stares at the reddish colored adobe house. He then turns and gently embracing Ariana, he kisses her.

"It seems like forever," she touches her fingers to his lips. "Hold me tight. Kiss me hard, Charley."

Charley kisses her hungrily, his stomach churns and his throat becomes dry.

"In my heart I felt you would come to me. You waited so long."

He coughs trying to clear the dryness, stumbling for words. "His men watched for me. I did not know what happened. I moved from place to place. Oh, so many times, I started to come to you. But I wanted to make a stash." Ariana looks perplexed. Charley realizes she doesn't understand his expression. "Enough money," he adds. "Maybe we could go away? You never answered my letter."

Ariana is surprised. "You did not receive my letter? I mailed it the same day I wrote it." Her eyes flash, rolling upwards. "That despicable..." Her look says it all.

Charley finally moves the buggy while he contemplates her words. He takes her hand, helping her to the ground. They walk hand-in-hand to the adobe shack.

Charley lights a fire in the stove. The sheepherders used it when staying here. The metal stove was small but when blazing, warmed the shack quickly. The dry cottonwood and mesquite logs will have the stove glowing in a few minutes.

Ariana removes the wine from the basket, "Charles," she holds up the bottle. Charley nods and cracks one of his frank expressions. He walks over to her. She hands him the bottle then removes two glasses from the basket.

Charley looks surprised. "I figured we would have to use my Army issue tin cup. Evita packed the basket. How would she..."

Ariana interrupts him with a telling look.

They touch glasses then sit them on the crude table. Charley cuddles her and their lips touch lightly. He holds her tightly, kissing her softly then gently kissing her neck. She squeals and pulls away, handing him his glass and taking hers. Their eyes meet.

Charley takes a sip and sits his glass down. He fumbles in his pocket and removes the gold watch and holds it up for her to see. "You were never far away. Whenever I look at it, I always think of you. If only you knew how many times, how many times I..."

Ariana beams. "I remember when you did not have a timepiece. We fell asleep, I was late returning to the ranch. My Mother was very upset. She would never tell my Father." They laugh.

Charley returns the watch to his pocket. He sits their glasses down and they embrace. "This time, nothing, no one is going to interfere in our going away."

"Oh, my Charley. It has been so long."

Charley clears his throat.

"Tell me." Ariana is anxious.

"It's hard for me to tell you."

She pleads. "What? Tell me."

"I don't understand it myself." Charley takes a deep breath and reaches deep within himself. "It's like I have been in love with you forever. Something always

116

happens. Antonio is bound to cause trouble." Anger shows in Charley's eyes. "You were watching from the window. Antonio and his men...what they said about my mother..."

"I sometimes hope that the lieutenant would not have stopped you. Charley, no one can meddle anymore!"

Meanwhile, the rogue looking Antonio and several of his Mexican henchmen come to the Esteban Ranchero. The Mexican that Charley had seen when he first arrived in Santa Fe, now rides with Antonio.

Angrily Antonio dismounts, yelling to the others, "I will take care of Luis, take the other boy!" Antonio grabs Luis who kicks and screams, biting Antonio. The others grab Luis's friend, who at first yells, then is frightened into silence. Antonio slaps Luis as Sofia and Evita run from the house.

Sofia screams, "Don't do this thing. You are hurting the boy. Luis, he has done nothing! Ay, dios mio!" she makes the sign of the cross. Evita and Sofia try frantically to stop the Mexicans. They are both roughly shoved to the ground. Antonio gestures wildly, threatening them, while the boys are roughly loaded onto the horses.

Two of Sofia's unarmed workers hear the commotion and come running to help. The Mexicans kick them to the ground and shoot both of them in the stomach. The Mexicans laugh and ride off, leaving them to die. Sofia screams bitterly, "Ay, dios mio! No no!"

Several days later, light shines through the window of the adobe shack waking Charley. He will take Ariana home today. He quickly dresses and hurries outside.

Charley checks Red then hitches the horses to the carriage. He is interrupted by the sound of hoof beats. He sees a Mexican rider hurrying to the adobe. Charley cautiously walks around the buggy while tucking his pistol into his belt. The Mexican attempts to communicate in Spanish. "Senorita Fernandez, Don Luis."

Charley doesn't understand and gestures for the Mexican to wait and Charley hurries to the house.

Ariana has been watching and steps outside. "What does he want?"

"It's about your father," Charley says.

Ariana quickly turns to the Mexican and shouts. "Senor! What do you want?"

"Senorita! Don Luis is very ill. I am..."

Ariana cuts him off, turning to Charley. "Father is ill. We must leave at once!"

Charley waves the Mexican off and quickly runs to the wagon. Ariana hurries inside the adobe to grab her things then she runs out the door to the buggy. Charley lends his hand, helping her onto the seat. Charley shouts and the horses race down the dusty desert road. They ride in silence. Charley watches the road for rocks. But their occasional glances at each other shows him that she is very worried. Charley wonders if maybe it might be some kind of a scheme by Antonio to get Ariana away. There is nothing that—

Ariana interrupts his thoughts. "We are almost there. Hurry, Charley!"

Charley reins the horses up but Ariana leaps from the carriage before it comes to a stop at the Esteban Ranchero. She lifts her dress and runs into the house. Charley feels that it is best that he wait outside. It is Ariana's family and he doesn't want to intrude but he's close by if Ariana needs him. He puts the buggy away and then saddles Red and waits.

It seems like a long wait but it has only been a short time when Ariana comes from the house. Charley can tell by her red face and puffy eyes that all is not well. He goes to her. "Ariana! Don Luis is..."

Ariana clutches him firmly. "My Father is very ill. I must go. I will come to the La Fonda when everything is..." she stops talking on seeing Charley's look.

Charley is perplexed but holds her strongly. "I will meet you there. Is there is anything I can do? Name it, I will do it."

"I know, my love."

Charley wipes a tear from her cheek then gives her a squeeze and goes to his horse. He mounts up while she stands watching. They quickly wave and Charley trots off. Tears stream down her face while she watches him, until he rides out of sight.

Ariana turns and hurries back into the house. Her mother and Evita are still very much upset. Her mother walks to Ariana. "Oh, my daughter. It is not your father."

Ariana is shocked. "What is it, Mamacita? You must tell me!"

Sofia looks at Evita then back to her daughter. "Antonio! They came here," she sobs. "He took the boys! He will do them harm."

Ariana shrieks. "Why, oh, why? What does he want?"

"You must send Senor Reynolds away at once. He will not ever let anyone else have you." Sofia's voice is firm.

Evita pleads. "Ariana, you must!"

Ariana walks away then turns to her mother. "Oh Mamacita, I love him. I could never ask..."

Sofia butts in, "You must, my daughter. Antonio has a hundred men, his hired Comanches. He says this time he will not fail. He will make sure the, "Gringo" is dead." Sofia shakes her head in disgust. "I do not like the word. I pray our people should never have learned that word, "gringo" from the soldiers." She puts her arms around Ariana. "My daughter, please. He is ruthless. He will stop at nothing. He will bring harm to the boys! His..." she makes the sign of the cross. "He is despicable! They killed two of the workers!"

"Charley loves me. I do not..."

With a mother's tenderness, Sofia puts her fingers to Ariana's lips. "Oh, my dear, you must think of a way! Your Charley, he loves the adventure, the danger. It will always be so. Antonio will never let anyone else have you. Never, this man!"

Evita who has been standing silently by, joins Sofia and they embrace Ariana, who begins to sob.

Evita drives the carriage as she and Ariana sit silently on the seat. She guides the horses along the dusty Santa Fe street. She pulls to a halt at Esparza Freight and leaving Ariana, she enters the office.

In just a few minutes, Luis and his friend run out the door and climb onto the seat. Ariana is elated and cries and hugs and squeezes the boys tightly. Evita starts the team and reins the horses to the La Fonda Hotel. She writes a note then goes inside.

An hour later Evita reins to a halt at the Adobe shack. Ariana and the two boys sit silently. Although quite young, the usually frolicking boys can tell by Ariana's forlorn look that not all is well yet. They nudge Ariana on hearing hoof beats coming. "He comes," says Luis.

Charley looks apprehensive as he dismounts and ties his horses. He hurries to the buggy. "Ariana! What is it? Is there trouble?"

"Charley, we must talk." Her look is different than any he's ever seen before. He raises his hand to help her down. She turns to the others. "Wait here for me, please." Evita nods with a worried glance at Charley.

Charley hasn't survived many years alone on the plains because of luck. Looks say a lot and Charley suspects that something is wrong. He couldn't put his finger on it before. He turns to Luis and his friend, "One day soon I'll kick the can with you boys." The boys' silence and their serious glances say it all. Charley nods to them then helps Ariana down.

It seems like it takes forever as they walk around to the rear of the Adobe shack. "Your look is hurtful Ariana. Your father, the boys—is it bad?"

Ariana struggles. "You must go, Charley."

"Go?"

She sobs. "It can never be. Our love will never be. We can never be together"

"We talked of going away together!"

She turns away. "My mother—you're roaming the Plains, the adventure, you love the danger. She says that will always be so." Ariana chokes. "It—it's no life," she can't finish. Her hand goes to her mouth. Charley looks away. Finally she flings her arms around him. He embraces her strongly. "Oh, Charley," she sobs. "You must go."

"Do you really want me to?"

"We've had our love, Charley. Now you must find a life without me."

"I will not ride away without you!"

She clings to him then she pulls away. He pulls her back, kissing her hungrily. She finally pulls away.

Charley's look becomes stern. "What is it?"

She can only look at him. Charley sees anger. "It's Antonio—I should have done away with that..." His words trail off.

Ariana blurts out angrily. "You must go! He has a hundred men. His hired Comanches will kill you!"

"Gabe Green always said, "One brave man with a good rifle willin' to stand his ground can hold off a hundred men."

"No! I will not have it! You must go." She cries. "It would be unbearable for me to see you. " She looks away sobbing, unable to finish—quietly she sobs. "Please go. It was not meant to be." She moves slowly towards the buggy.

Charley's stare is hurtful. He feels crushed as he watches her, with great effort, get into the buggy. Then anger flashes into his mind as he mounts his horse.

Charley does not hear Luis's small voice. "Why do you cry, Mamacita?"

"I love him. "

Charley rides over and starts to speak.

"You must go. Find a life without me."

With a last pleading look, Charley spurs away. Ariana sobs then speaks out loud. "Vya con dios, my Charley. I will never forget you." Evita tries to console Ariana.

Charley rides feverishly away but his path is not away from New Mexico Territory.

Antonio's holdings are well guarded. Over one hundred Mexicans and Comanches work at the huge estate. Guards are everywhere even on top of the water tower. Several are near the expensive horses. Others sit mounted near the house.

Esparza Freight wagons come and go. Several Mexicans break horses in a corral. Others herd the cattle on the rangeland. Antonio comes from the house and walks up to two of his henchmen.

One of the Mexicans gestures to Antonio. "He is gone, Senor Delgado. Your Comanches trailed him a full days ride."

"It is well. The bravado of this gringo scum, coming here to make trouble!"

Out of sight of the estate, two Red buckskin horses munch on some grass. Behind a small mesa they are well hidden in some scrub pinion trees.

On top the mesa a rifle lays on some rocks. A half-empty prairie belt lays close by. On a flat rock numerous bullets lay in a neat row. Several spare, full boxes of cartridges lay nearby. A buffalo hunters' crossed stick rifle rest leans upright, with support of several stones.

Steady hands carefully lay a big Remington rifle into the V of the buffalo stick rest. Calculated fingers adjust the yard increment on the sight. A 50 Cal. Caliber shell is inserted into the breech.

Glasses are raised and watch as Antonio waves his arms to brag. "Look what I have. This Gringo! This foolish man could not ever provide for my Ariana in such a manner."

On the small mesa. from further than twenty yards away, the slamming of the action can be heard. Then, the distinct click of the cocked hammer. Anger flashes as steel blue eyes sight down the barrel. A deep breath is taken in—a sigh is heard as half is expelled. "One brave man with a good rifle willin' to stand his ground can hold off a hundred men," rings loud in Charley's ears. A steady finger slowly squeezes the trigger.

In the neighborhood of six hundred yards away, the two Mexicans laugh at Antonio's remark. A blood spot suddenly appears on the forehead of one of the Mexicans. Brain matter and blood splatter Antonio's face. He screams in horror. "Ay, dios mio!Ay, dios mio!" He turns wild-eyed as he hears the delayed echo of a rifle shot. Antonio and the others look around in panic.

Suddenly a blood spot appears on the nearby Mexican. He emits a groan and drops to the ground stone dead. Another delayed shot echoes through the ranch yard. Antonio crawls through the dirt screaming. "Ay, dios mio. Where are they? Where..." He ducks his face when a shot kicks up the dirt near him then ricochets with a whine across the dry land. Antonio's men yell and run for their horses. Others already mounted, ride around frantically trying to figure out where the shots come from. But no one is close by in sight. It is chaos as Comanches and Mexicans, those afoot and mounted run everywhere.

With a cough and spitting dirt, Antonio jumps to his feet and runs.

A Mexican yells. "No one knows where the shots come from!"

"Look for the powder smoke!" shouts another.

Charley's blue eyes are intense as his sights hone in on Antonio. His lips grimace. He squeezes the trigger.

Antonio screams as the 500-grain slug flips him head-over-heels. The delayed shot again echoes. Antonio grabs his leg and scrambles and claws the dirt, frantically crawling for safety.

Several men rush to help the injured man. They quickly drag Antonio behind the water tank. Bullets continue to land everywhere, keeping the men in total disarray. Now that he feels safe behind cover, the white-faced Antonio yells. "It's that slimy, gutless gringo! He hides like the weasel he is."

A Mexican shouts. "No one can find the powder smoke!" Antonio grimaces. "Find him!"

His men ride in every direction.

Charley continues to wreak havoc. He stops for a moment to glass the area. He mutters to himself. "Every step you take you'll think of me." Suddenly a smile comes across his lips. He scans the water tower then quickly loads his rifle. "Might wash some of the scum off," he says out loud.

Shot after shot he fires into the tower. He hones in on the top metal rings. It is terrifying for Antonio and his men below. Wood chips fly, dropping on them, while the lead slugs puncture the tank. Water leaks through the bullet holes, down on top of them.

The two guards on top of the tower can only squat together in fright. 500-grain lead bullets ricochet off the metal rings with a terrifying whine.

The men on the ground are in the same predicament. Every time they start to run, Charley lets a bullet fly into the dirt near them, keeping them pinned down. Suddenly, water begins to gush in several places. At last, a 500-grain slug strikes with a thud then careens off the metal ring. The tank explodes.

Water drenches the men below. Amidst angry, frightened yells and screams of pain, boards and metal drop on the cowering Antonio and his hombre cohorts.

The two guards tumble, screaming to the ground, rolling and moaning in pain. Antonio, now half-crazed with fear and anger, shouts at several of his Mexican and Comanche henchmen. "He will pay dearly. You hombres, go! Bring me Senorita Fernandez! If you have to drag her by the hair! Andaley! Go!"

Charley smiles and then winces in pain, jerking his hand away as he touches the hot barrel of his rifle. He lays it down and runs to get his horses ready. He knows that he has got a hard ride ahead of him. Antonio will send every man available to hunt him down.

He quickly throws his bag on his horse and unties Rusty, leaving him loose to follow behind. He'll have to switch horses but Charley knows it will be an hour or longer before they find his hiding place then his trail to follow. He runs back up the hill for his rifle and prairie belt. He makes a quick survey of the ground. He usually keeps the empty shells but he has no time to gather them now.

He takes a hurried look with his field glasses at the ranch. He sees a dozen or so riders leaving the ranch going in the opposite direction. He wonders why but then hurries to his horses and races away from the ranch.

As Red settles into a running walk, Rusty follows a short distance behind. Charley begins to contemplate the events. He's got a measure of satisfaction out of shooting up Antonio's fine estate. But he's lost the only woman he has ever loved. His thoughts take him back to the adobe shack. He is elated then he flashes back to Antonio's forceful ploy to get him away from Ariana and he again sees anger. Nothing is beyond that man. Nothing!

Swiftly, Charley jerks hard on the reins. Red skids to a halt. Rusty almost running into Red, the stop was so sudden. It suddenly hits him. Those riders leaving the ranch were riding in the direction of Ariana and Evita when they left the adobe shack. It has been several hours but still Charley feels uneasy about those riders. Nothing is beyond that man. Murder included.

Charley reins around, cutting across the rough country. It's the shortest route. It will be hard on the horses but they've been ridden hard before. "Sorry, Ol' boy," Charley urges Red on.

The buck brush as Charley calls it is hard on the horses. Charley has to be careful. There are thorny bushes that will pierce a horse's side or a man's leg. "Com'on, Red. Good, boy." Red's ears perk up.

A half hour later, bruised and scratched, both rider and horses finally emerge onto the road leading to the Esteban Ranch. Charley reins to a stop and quickly changes horses. He leaps into the saddle and trots towards the ranch. He's not sure what he'll face when he gets there but he will just have to take that chance.

Soon he reins Rusty to halt. He listens intently. It sounds like gunshots coming from the ranch. He spurs Rusty ahead and charges towards the gunfire.

Ahead he sees several men shooting at the Esteban house. Gunfire comes from the house. Charley looks puzzled. It must be Ariana or Evita shooting at Antonio's men. Charley dismounts, grabs his rifle and runs to some nearby Pinion trees for cover.

Antonio's men are unaware of Charley. One by one, Charley eliminates three of the men. The others attempt to run away. But now, whomever shoots from the house, they have Antonio's men in a crossfire. Charley fires away and it is brutal. The last of Antonio's men try to flee. Several more are on the ground and appear to be wounded.

Charley watches astonished as Ariana's father, Don Luis, pistol in hand, runs from the house. Charley is startled when this normally peaceful man runs up to one of the wounded men on the ground. Point blank he shoots the man and then kicks him. Don Luis then runs to another man who is crawling, scrambling trying to get away. His efforts are in vain. Don Luis walks up and yells. "You killed my daughter, you slimy pig! You slimy pig, you killed my Ariana!" Don Luis empties his pistol into the man's guts as the man begs for mercy. The man's body twitches for a moment then lays still.

Don Luis falls to his knees sobbing. Evita runs from the house and sobs beside him.

Charley is stunned.

After what seems like a long time, the scene flashes into Charley's mind. He hears Don Luis's words over and over, "You killed my daughter! You killed my Ariana!" Charley hears one, two, maybe three shots. He doesn't remember how many shots Don Luis fired into the helpless man. It is like the shots were fired into Charley's innards. He's never been totally stunned before. His legs feel numb. Rooted to the spot, he just stands there staring at Don Luis and Evita who sob and hold each other, muttering unintelligible.

Finally, Charley is able to understand Don Luis as he sobs. "Ariana is dead. She was trying to save Luis. I ask that you go, please, senor. I am so sorry. Please, go. Ay, dios mio! Ay, dios mi! My beautiful daughter."

Charley is shocked beyond words.

He doesn't know how long he's been standing there. He finally walks to his horses. They seem to sense something is wrong. They nicker softly. Charley mounts up and rides off alone.

It seems like he rides in a daze. He can barely remember switching horses. He's traveled how far, he doesn't even know. And he cares little now if Antonio's men were to catch him. All he knows, is that if they try to kill him, he'll take a bunch of them with him.

Several days later Charley awakes to the nickering of his two horses. He leaps to his feet, realizing that his horses are unsaddled. The saddles and all his gear are on the ground nearby. He looks around for his rifles and finds the Sharps right beside his bedroll. The other is in the scabbard by his saddle.

Strange, he doesn't even remember getting here, much less unsaddling and rolling out his bedroll. And then Ariana flashes into his mind. It doesn't seem real, kind of like he went to sleep and had a bad dream. But, deep down inside him something tells him that it was all so real.

Charley roams the prairie hunting. He often looks at his watch, reading the inscription. "Forever, Ariana," Along the Missouri he traps beaver and wolves. He skins and dries the pelts then moves on. It seems like it's the only way for him to ease his sorrow.

Back at Fort Abraham Lincoln, Tom and George Custer walk across the grounds. They stop and gaze at the wide Missouri below them. "Some country, isn't it? I remember last winter, then the spring thaw. The sounds of the breaking of the ice there is nothin' like it anywhere." Tom says.

Custer's mind is elsewhere. In his brisk manner, George Custer speaks out. "Yeah," while nodding, he looks westward then in an official tone, "Captain, Custer. Have the Indian scouts find Lonesome Charley." George Custer surveys the rolling bluffs and broken land along the river. He then gazes across the prairie almost like he expects to see a rider coming.

"No one has seen him for months, Autie."

"We surely want him along on the Black Hills Expedition. He's on the Plains somewhere, huntin' buffalo. Find him."

Tom smiles. "Maybe he's found himself a woman and is holed up somewhere?"

George Custer cracks a smile. "Charley...no, not Charley Reynolds. He's the one man I'd bet money..."

Tom leaps to the opportunity. "You still owe me five dollars from the last bet." The two brothers shake hands on the bet and Tom hurries off, laughing.

Charley moves to the Painted Canyons of Dakota Territory. He feels he is being followed and looks suspiciously around and waits to see if someone is there. But no one is following.

One day, Charley realizes he has got to get over this. The pain seems to have eased outwardly, but not in his heart. He ponders if anything good could be said about the whole affair with Ariana? He's thankful for one thing. He did not have to see her dead. He did not have to remember her shot up body. At least he can remember his beautiful Ariana the way she really was.

Lately, off and on, Charley has been thinking of his camp keepers, Thompson, Walks-on-Ice and Running-creek-Woman. He contemplates his last time there. It brings to mind their reaction, "The Black Hills" he says out loud. His horses point their ears and give him a curious look. He looks at his horses and then stares across the land. Quietly, he says, "Paha Sapa, The Black Hills."

12

*T*he treaty of 1868 had set aside a 43 000-square-mile reservation for the Sioux Nation a vast area reportedly abundant with fish, game and timber-covered mountains. Uncharted by the White Man, this sacred Indian sanctuary was known as, Paha Sapa—the Black Hills.

General Philip Sheridan had recommended that the Black Hills region be given military protection. Broken treaties and the infiltration of dishonest Indian agents, were apparently the major reasons for the growing number of Indian uprisings. George Armstrong Custer, who had little patience with political matters, was avidly interested in exploring the region. Upon hearing rumors a private party of prospectors was about to strike out into the Black Hills, he quickly alerted General Alfred Terry. According to Custer, the leader of the supposed excursion was the keeper of a bawdy house and the type of individual who would likely further aggravate the already riled Sioux. Custer also made a written proposal to Sheridan, outlining his plans for a responsible and orderly expedition into the Black Hills for the purpose of determining the whereabouts of certain mineral deposits.

Custer's enthusiasm and his propensity for meticulous preparation, lead his superiors to request that George Custer is involved in the military's role in the Black Hills Expedition of 1874. In addition, he was afforded the luxury of appointing some of his favorite people to accompany him; among them were his two brothers, Tom and Boston and Charles Alexander Reynolds, scout and guide.

Fort Abraham Lincoln Dakota Territory—June, 1874

Elizabeth Custer makes a final adjustment to her gown then decides to write in her diary: As a habit, Libbie reads her words over then closes the diary. She straightens her gown and descends the stairs to greet her guests. What a pleasure it is to be entertaining in their new home!

"Autie, do I look presentable?"

The smile says it all. "You are lovely, Libbie," he says, kissing her cheek. "Of course, some of these men remember you on the trail between Yankton and Fort Rice. No matter what, you are surely more presentable now than then!" He laughs.

"Oh, Autie," she cries. "Sometimes I wonder if you ever take me seriously."

"After ten years of marriage? You are not sure?" He brushes some lint from the sleeve of his uniform. "Hurry, dear. Our guests are waiting!"

A number of privileged civilians, who will be accompanying the military command on the Black Hills Expedition, are gathered for a party at the Custer home. Standing near a window is Professor Winchell, State Geologist from Minnesota, who is listening politely to the expedition's engineer officer, Captain William Ludlow who is trying to explain the Army's obligations to the Sioux. George Bird Grinnell, a paleontologist and St. Paul photographer, W. H. Illingworth, are deep in conversation while the Custer brothers are telling some exaggerated military tales to the President's son, Lieutenant Fred Grant.

"This is going to be a wonderful journey," General Forsyth says to George Custer as he enters the foyer.

"I am really looking forward to this, Sandy," Custer replies earnestly. "More than any other campaign, this one has all the ingredients of an unabashed victory."

"You're not expecting any trouble from the Sioux?"

"We've prepared well. This is strictly an exploratory exercise. I believe the Indians know that. Besides, what tribe would attack a military unit of this size? One thousand men strong, fully armed, with .45-caliber Springfield carbines?"

"I think even the Sioux possess the wisdom to refrain from agitating in this case, General."

"I would hope so. Nevertheless, we don't take their threats lightly. They have not been treated well and with all due respect, they have a right to be angry."

Captain Ludlow overhears Custer's words. "If I might interrupt, General... we're taking those three Gatling guns along as an added precaution. That should be enough to keep them at arm's length!"

"Gatling guns are fine in practice skirmishes, when they function properly. It is an impossibility to run down fleet Indian ponies with condemned cavalry horses pulling Gatling guns, Captain."

Ludlow looks at Custer for a moment, mulling his words over, then nods in agreement. "What you're saying, General, is in order to fight Indians, you have to catch them."

"Precisely, Sir."

General Terry arrives an hour later to announce that the expedition is scheduled to be underway the morning of July 2nd. There is great jubilation as the guests join in song, toasting the occasion and their host.

"Play Garry Owen once more!" Custer begs the young man with the accordion. "Come Libbie! Let us dance!"

Several weeks pass and the only sign of Indians are the columns of smoke rising occasionally from the purple desolation of the Paha Sapa. Charley Reynolds is pleased to once again bring good news to the command.

"A right fine morning, Captain," he says to Tom Custer.

"Well if it isn't the Chief Scout of the best cavalry outfit in the country. I'm sure glad you're along, Reynolds. I've been wondering when I was going to see you again," says the good-natured soldier. "What have you been doing all winter, Lonesome?"

"Not a lot."

Tom stares at the scout for a moment, "Reynolds...you speak fewer words than any man I have ever met! What goes on in that head of yours?"

"There just isn't much for a fellow in my position to say."

"This is a pleasant journey, I agree. But that doesn't mean you have to remain silent day after day. Don't you get lonely out there by yourself with no one to talk to?"

"Oh, I talk to people now and then...trappers, hunters and some of the soldiers too. I talk to the Indians sometimes."

"I've heard that. Captain Allison tells me you get along well with the Sioux. Is that true?"

"I suppose you could say that I do. The Lakota people are a good people. It's too bad our Chiefs in Washington can't see it."

The General joins the conversation. "I agree, Reynolds," he says, tipping his hat forward. "I agree. The Indians should be treated with more respect. They are humans after all."

Charley waits for a moment for further comment but hearing none he waves, just as Tom grins and speaks out. "I'll bet you got a woman somewhere, Reynolds."

Charley gets a weighty look then turns away and quickly rides off.

Custer jabs his brother. "You touched a nerve on Charley, Tom. Maybe just maybe..." Custer's words trail off as he watches his scout ride away.

Charley rides ahead to find Bloody Knife. The half Ree and Sioux is Custer's favorite Indian scout among the sixty some scouts hired for this excursion.

Bloody Knife is weary, having ridden half the day from a miner's excavation on a hillside some miles away. The old man with the beard has discovered the shining stones, he tells Charley. The word travels like wildfire and Custer orders camp be made along French Creek. There is excitement in the air—laughter, song and good humor.

Despite orders to his subordinates, that the discovery must remain a secret until officially announced in Washington, Custer can't wait to write to Libbie telling her the news. But, first of all, he must send word to General Sheridan. It suddenly occurs to him that the two closest places from which to send a telegram are Bozeman, Montana and Fort Laramie. He decides on the latter and summons his adjutant.

"Cookie, I need a volunteer to carry a dispatch to Old Bedlam. Right away!"

The soldier is dumfounded. "But, Sir! That's 150 miles...through Sioux country!"

"I know, Lieutenant. That's why I want only one man. One who won't be too easily detected by the Indians—preferably someone who knows the route."

"I'll do my best, Sir."

The adjutant returns within the hour. "I'm sorry, Sir. There are no volunteers. One of Tom's men seems to know the territory but he says it sounds like suicide."

Custer is not surprised by the lack of cooperation, for the route is surely a dangerous one. "I'd go myself, if I weren't under orders to stay with this expedition. Sheridan's got to know about this!"

"If you want my opinion, Sir...the only man really up to the task is, Lonesome Charley."

"I can't afford to send Reynolds. Tom maybe or Jim, but not Reynolds."

"Is that all, Sir?"

"That is all, Lieutenant!" Custer follows the officer outside where several soldiers are gathered around a campfire.

"Lieutenant Cooke tells me no one is willing to volunteer to carry a dispatch to Fort Laramie," Custer growls. "Is that so?"

There is silence until the soft-spoken Reynolds steps forward.

"General, I will go."

"No, Charley," replies Custer, "I can hardly ask you to go. It would be a disservice to the Army."

"Give me the dispatch," Reynolds says in his firm, quiet way, "and I will carry it to Fort Laramie."

"Do you know the route?" Custer asks quietly.

"I've been close, General. I've been nearly all over that country. I can find it. At least I have the advantage of being familiar with these Indians. I can travel by night. I have a good compass and you have seen for yourself how bright the stars are in these northern skies."

Charley's pitch is more than the General can resist. "I might be making a mistake, Reynolds. But Sheridan must get this report and get it quickly. Can you be ready to leave at daybreak?"

"Yes, Sir!"

"Good. We'll ride with you as far as the South Fork of the Cheyenne. From there you'll be on your own. Would it help if the farrier puts Red's shoes on backwards?"

Charley chuckles, "I never would have thought of that trick. Yes! That's a good idea!"

"Thank you, Reynolds. It's a pleasure to have you with us."

"My pleasure, General!" Charley replies, his blue eyes sparkling in the firelight. "Good night, Sir."

In good spirits now, General Custer joins many of the soldiers as they sing, "The Girl I left behind."

"Then to the East we bore away To win a name in story And there where dawns the sun of day There dawn'd our sun of glory: Both blaz'd in noon on Alma's height When in the post assign'd me I shar'd the glory of that fight Sweet girl I left behind me."

The five companies of soldiers arrive at the Cheyenne's South fork some fifty miles south without any trouble from the Indians. Sitting around the campfire, Charley has reloaded his prairie belt and is checking the action on his newly acquired single action .45 Colt pistol. He is surprised that the Sioux seem to be ignoring the 7th, allowing the troops to roam at will across their sacred buttes and hills.

"Don't forget, Lonesome," says James Calhoun, handing the big canvas mailbag to Charley, "there's a letter to Maggie in here."

"That's right," Custer chimes in. "There's one for the Old Lady too! Forty candlelight pages. I'll be upset if she doesn't get it."

Reynolds only smiles. The mailbag is a sight! Calhoun has written comical remarks all over the outside and in big black letters: *Black Hills Express—Protected by the 7th Cavalry!"*

When darkness falls over the camp, the echo of creaking leather announces Lonesome Charley's departure. General Custer's sluggish salute reveals his uneasiness.

"Take care of yourself, Lonesome," he says in an almost inaudible whisper. "God speed."

Reynolds strikes out along a small creek with only a sliver of moonlight to guide him. A feeling of emptiness engulfs him. Had he forgotten something? The uncertainty lingers until dawn but nothing comes to mind. After twenty-four hours on the trail, he spies a safe place to rest on a rocky hillside under a group of pine trees. There's plenty of tall grass for Big Red and a comfortable patch of thick sod near a large outcropping. Too tired to eat, he stretches out on the ground and immediately falls into a deep sleep.

A blazing orange sun is far above the horizon when Charley is awakened by his unsettled horse. Red is snickering, softly stomping his unorthodox shoes into the turf. His ears move back and forth; first one then the other. Charley knows the signs and scurries to his feet. A half mile away, some Indians in full battle dress, are leading their war-ponies. "Lay, Red! Lay!" Charley quickly whispers.

Red's front legs bend and he drops on his haunches and rolls to his side. The sweat begins to run down Charley's back so he removes his coat. He reaches for his canteen and takes a drink. There isn't much left. He can't believe the change in temperature; even the barrel of his rifle is hot to the touch.

Patiently, he strokes Red's neck and whisper's softly; "It's going to be all right, old boy. Soon as those Indians move along we'll find some water."

When the warriors finally disappear, Charley leads his horse to a creekbed. There is only a trickle of water and he has difficulty filling the canteen. He returns to his makeshift camp to wait for the night and the relief of the cool mountain air.

The man and his horse continue their trek in this manner for three days. But each creek has less water and every day the sun seems hotter. Big Red becomes so weak, Charley is afraid to ride him. He pulls Red's shoes to ease his discomfort. When they reach Fort Laramie on the fourth or maybe the fifth day, he doesn't know how long, the lone messenger's wounds attest to the treachery of his journey.

"Good God, have mercy!" cries the guard as Reynolds takes the final painful steps to the garrison gate. "Where have you been, I mean..." The young man stammers, repulsed by the sight before him. "State your name, please."

Unaware that his outward appearance is reflecting his inner pain Charley is surprised by the guard's behavior. He forces a smile and feels his lip split. "Reynolds. I have official dispatches from General Custer of the 7th Cavalry."

"Your mouth is bleeding, Mr. Reynolds. I think you have need of a doctor."

"But I must see that the commander gets these dispatches right away!" Charley protests.

The guard summons the Officer-of-the-Day to take the mail bag to the commander. "Now, the doctor," he says with a tone of persistence.

Charley has no strength for an argument. The post surgeon inspects his mouth and immediately recognizes that his patient is suffering from dehydration.

"You must drink, Mr. Reynolds. Drink until you think your gut is going to explode. Here," he says handing Charley a tin cup of water, "this is a start. Drink slowly at first. There's a jug full over there on the table. Refill the cup from that. I'll be back shortly. I have salt tablets and some salve in my tent that will help heal those cracked lips."

The soothing effect of the water amazes Charley. It feels good on his swollen tongue but the pain is almost unbearable and he has to force the liquid down his throat. He concentrates on the Apache water jar on the table and swallows hard. The jug intrigues him.

"What are you staring at, Reynolds?" asks Dr. Jones, as he re-enters the room.

"Where did that jar come from?"

"New Mexico. My station was near Santa Fe during the war—at Fort Marcy."

Charley takes another sip of water and thanks the doctor for the salve and tablets. "I was at Fort Union."

"Fort Union," Jones replies thoughtfully. "That's where old Colonel Smith was when he got court-martialed. M. Nathan Smith...used to think a lot of himself. Did you know the old buzzard?"

"I knew him. Why was he court-martialed?"

"He was taking graft from a shipping company but the scheme blew up in his face when his partner on the outside got killed."

Charley's big blue eyes brighten. "Do you know the name of his partner?" he asks excitedly.

"Sure. He was an important man in Santa Fe—one of the richest in all of New Mexico the way I hear it. Delgado was his name. Antonio Delgado."

Charley gulps. "Who killed him?"

"Some mysterious fellow named Mendoza. He must have really hated Delgado. He sent a letter and all the records of the freight company to the Secretary of War, sliced Delgado to ribbons in Santa Fe, then left for Mexico. No one has seen him since."

"He finally got what was coming to him," Charley says unconsciously. "Too bad it wasn't sooner." The doctor looks surprised.

"It's hard to believe!" Charley exclaims. "I worked for that outfit when I was there—The Esparza Freight Company. I knew Delgado...better than I knew Colonel Smith...a lot better. I remember that Mendoza chap too."

"Well, if that don't beat all!" Dr. Jones replies. "I guess you know how hot-blooded those Spaniards can get."

Charley nods while he mulls over Jones' words. All at once the hurt, and then Ariana flashes before him. Now it seems everything is gone. Gabe is gone. There is nothing left in New Mexico, except fond memories, fond memories of his once beautiful Ariana.

"You best drink some more water, Reynolds." Charley snaps back to reality as the doctor speaks. "I suggest you stay here for several days and get some rest. This dehydration is not something you should take lightly."

"Thanks, Doctor. I'm looking forward to some sleep."

The swelling in Charley's lips and tongue dissipates overnight but he feels lethargic. The shock of the news of Delgado is fresh in his mind, and his heart throbs incessantly as he recalls fond memories of Ariana. He ponders the possibility of changing his travel plans and riding instead...not possible. He must return to Fort Lincoln. Furthermore, his faithful horse Red is still ailing and needs more rest. Charley waits three more days before riding to Cheyenne to catch the eastbound train. The Quartermaster issues him a voucher for the fare as he leaves, "Old Bedlam."

Once aboard the train, Lonesome Charley realizes he has not fully recuperated. As the dreary scenes whisk monotonously past the window, his thoughts wander back to New Mexico. Slumber follows. He misses several stops and awakens only when he hears the hiss of steam as the little black locomotive pulls up at the North Platte depot. Among the passengers are five new Army recruits, all headed for different posts along the route. They are a noisy bunch of boys chattering excitedly about their future plans with the Army, and how they're going to, "scalp the savages." Charley tries ignoring them. A herd of buffalo grazing some distance from the tracks triggers the memory of his hunt with Cody and the Duke. Suddenly, the disruptive young recruits intercept his daydream.

"You're a braggart!" one shouts.

"No more than you are, Smithers. You ought to go back to Leavenworth for some more training. You didn't learn much."

The argument seems to be getting out of hand, so Charley decides to intervene. "You fellows spend a lot of time at Fort Leavenworth?"

"Yep," four answers chime in harmony.

"Too much time for me," adds Smithers.

"How about Fort Kearney," Charley quizzes the young men. "Have you been there?"

"We've all been there. Guard duty. But I've been there more than these other greenhorns," brags the biggest of the group.

"Did you ever hear of an old man named Trapper Green?"

The boys exchange glances but none offers a reply.

"Did I say something wrong?" Charley presses.

"You mean Trapper Green?" says the big fellow.

"Yeah that's the one!" Charley exclaims.

"Was he a good friend of yours?"

"Well back in Sixty we spent some time together hunting and trapping. I just wondered if you boys had seen or knew of him around the fort? He's...dead now."

They mimic one anther's blank expressions before the spokesman finally replies. "We all knew old Trapper Green. If it's the same one you knew...we heard he died. We heard the story how he died."

"Yeah, he's dead all right," offers one recruit.

"And you must be his friend!" adds another.

"The one that buried him the Indian way, the one we heard about," says the big one.

Charley feels emptiness in the pit of his stomach. "What do you know about Ol' Gabe?"

The big fellow speaks up. "Well, you could hear him coming a half mile or more, yelling and cussing at his mules. Most people stayed at arm's length—never knew when he was going to take a swing at you. But he could tell a good story and most of us liked him a lot."

Charley is visibly saddened. "Have you boys seen his mules, Old Jake and Charley Boy?

The Army had put them into service, one of the young men tells Charley. He thanks them for the information and returns to his seat, and closes his eyes once more. "The good ones don't quit lessin they get kilt by an injun...or they just die." He can hear the old trapper reciting his Mountain Man's philosophy, "One brave man with a good rifle, willin' to stand his ground, can hold off a hundred men."

When Reynolds disembarks onto the platform at Sioux City, reporters who have learned that it was he who had carried news of the Army's gold discovery in the Black Hills, besiege him. In classic Lonesome Charley style he very politely tells them much less than they were hoping to hear. He longs to return to Dakota. There is unfinished business there. Perhaps he'll just roam the desert for a month or two. Obtaining steamer passage with his old, friend Grant Marsh, once again courtesy of the Army, Charley arrives at Fort Abraham Lincoln in late September.

With the winter solstice only weeks away, it's a joyous scene at Fort Lincoln, as the officers and their wives are enjoying one of the few winter activities out of doors. One of the officers from down river has loaned the Custers a magnificent sleigh. The beautifully adorned vehicle, complete with brass bells and a kerosene-fueled foot warmer, is the handwork of a prominent stage builder in Bismarck. Not to be outdone, Fred Grant and Boston have constructed their own sled—two railroad ties attached to a pair of bony mules. Only under constant prodding do the indignant creatures attempt to move the heavy contraption and its jovial passengers through the snowdrifts.

Reynolds slowly approaches the sleighing party.

"Look, Autie," Libbie exclaims. "Charley Reynolds is back."

"Well, what a surprise!" George Custer yells to the shy man on the dun-colored horse. "Reynolds! It's good to have you back. Come along...take a ride with us."

But Charley isn't in the mood. "Just passing through, General. Thought I'd best give my regards and let you know I'm back home. I'll be up at Berthold and Standing Rock for a month or two."

"Good. Stay in touch, Reynolds," Custer says, waving as the sleigh glides through the new-fallen snow.

At the Palunta Wakpa or Grand River Agency Charley comes to sell some skins. Among many Indians milling around is Little Bear. He watches Charley as he rides by. Charley also notices Little Bear and smiles at him and waves the friend sign.

Inside Charley sells his wares. "Where will you be heading?" asks the trader.

"Fort Rice, maybe Stevenson."

"You be careful, Son. Why don't you get yourself a partner?" warns the trader.

Charley waves and turns to leave. The trader reaches under the counter and grabs a newspaper. "Hold on, Charley. I saved this for yuh. Figured you'd stop by someday. Why, you're famous." He hands Charley the newspaper.

Charley opens it and is surprised when he reads in big letters.

"CUSTER'S SCOUT—CHARLEY REYNOLDS...THE MOST DARING AND SUCCESSFUL SCOUT OF THE NORTHWEST. After Carrying Dispatches from Custer through 200 Miles of Indian Country...TELLS A SIOUX CITY JOURNALIST WHAT HE KNOWS ABOUT THE GOLD IN THE BLACK HILLS

Every member of the Expedition Satisfied that the Hills are Rich with Gold and Silver Deposits."

_____The Sioux City Journal is speaking of Charley Reynolds styles him, "the most daring successful and popular scout of the Northwest. Reynolds had just come in from Fort Laramie on his way to Bismarck and was interviewed by a Journal man."

13

*B*uffalo hump ribs roast on the fire. Reynolds sits on his bedroll gazing at the stars. His rifle and pistol lay on the canvas. He takes his watch from his pocket and reads the inscription, "Forever Ariana." He listens to the raucous duet of some coyotes.

Immediately, his horses nicker, Charley seems to be caught up while he studies his watch. The horses nicker again. Quickly, Charley leaps to his feet, picks up his pistol in one hand and grabs his rifle with the other. From the darkness he hears a voice.

"How coala, Eyomashesha!"

Charley gets a heavy look and lays his rifle back down. He recognizes his friend, Little Bear's voice. The Indian had come unannounced and Charley is not sure he's in a mood to visit. But Little Bear is his friend and he must be cordial.

Charley's voice is dull, "How do you do, my friend?" He motions the Indian to his camp. "Come, warm yourself eat."

The Indian rides, up slides off his horse and walks to Charley's fire. He uncoils a 30-foot length of rawhide thong from his waist belt. The thong is tied around his horses' neck. The horses act up a bit, nickering and stomping their hooves. After a while, they settle down while continuing to move their ears and eyeing one another. Little Bear lays the thong on the ground as he sits down.

After the smoking ritual is completed Little Bear speaks.

"Long grass past for many sleeps, my people at the Wakpa Shell Country." He makes a wide sweep of his right arm.

Charley nods in agreement and says, "Your people were going to the land of the powder water."

On hearing the hollow sound of Charley's voice, the Indian observes Charley with a perplexed look. He signs that he is hungry then unsheathes his knife and cuts two pieces of rib. He hands Charley a piece on the end of his knife. He wipes his knife off, placing it back inside the beaded sheath. "Grandmother says, no talk on empty belly." He signs rubbing his stomach. He takes a bite grunting as he eats.

Charley eats but he is subdued. Little Bear notices that Charley often stares into the darkness like he is looking for someone.

"My friend, your heart is on the ground," He places his right hand, fingers compressed and down over his heart, then swings his hand out and downward with the palm now turned up. "Like the eagle that soars high and looks down on the Wasichus's Iron Horse." Charley only looks.

The Indian speaks again. "The Eagle's heart is on ground. He see Iron Horse divide great herds, kill pte. I see White Hunters ride across prairie on Iron Horse, shoot Tatanka and leave to rot.

Charley manages a smirk with a nod. "You have much wisdom, my friend. It is bad. I understand when the eagle sees pte rot, it makes his heart sad."

"Long time past, Kwahadies, Mexicans take your woman," Little Bear makes the question sign. "You look for Rainbow-on-shining-Water?"

Charley solemnly nods then looks into the darkness. "She is far away."

"You find, no?"

Charley feels a deep turmoil as he recalls his ride to Santa Fe. Finally, after a long time he manages to force the words out, "She is dead."

His Indian friend looks away for a long while then says, "Little Bear's heart is on the ground."

After a while Charley turns, "Life goes on."

Little Bear finally gestures to his horse outside the camp. The firelight glistens off the stallion's coal black coat. He holds up first one finger then another, "Two Winters beyond, Absaraka village come. Take pony, Swift Wind." He spreads both hands, holding up all his fingers and two thumbs, "Ten pretty women I would not trade for Swift Wind. After many sleeps I go, see horse, no. I return to village. My father give me Runs-Like-Wind."

Charley admires the magnificent animal. "He is a fine looking animal."

"I always remember Swift Wind. You must find another. Find Indian woman. Indian woman like teepee," he laughs lightly.

Charley finally smiles then looks at the horse and nods that he understands.

"It is like the wind that blows the bad smell of buffalo rot away. The Great Mystery makes the winds blow the smell of sage, ripe chokecherry, the bloom of the rosebuds, smell of rot all gone."

"Not all Wasichus are bad," Charley says.

"Question, you go across prairie to White Rain Mountain place?" nods Little Bear.

With a serious look, Charley nods in return.

"Wasichus kill animals, dig the ground for the yellow stone. Wasichus like floodwaters of river. Tatanka Iyotake says we cannot get rid of the Wasichus."

Charley watches as Little Bear coils the rawhide thong, tucking it into his waist belt and leaps onto his stallion. Charley makes the peace sign. The Indian with only a half smile mimics.

"For many snows the Lakota warriors have fought our enemies the Crow...the Pawnee, the shaved head Osage," then pointing to Charley, then himself. "We all are warriors!"

Charley acknowledges with a nod, "We are different people, it does not mean there must be war!"

Little Bear makes the sign, clutching his heart, "My heart tells me, one day." He makes the sign for the future. "Time in front. The Lakota will fight the White soldiers." He looks solemnly at his friend and points, "You will fight with White soldiers, Char-Lee!"

Charley looks hurt but he somehow feels that Little Bear speaks the truth. Little Bear makes the friendship sign, "We are like friends, growing up together brothers. Eyomashesha." Little Bear kicks his steed and disappears into the night.

Charley stares into the darkness until the black stallion's hoof beats fade away. He ponders their talk, "like friends growing up together brothers." It is full of meaning and he thinks about the wisdom of the Indians. He again considers his feelings for his lost love then contemplates where his next ride will be.

It takes a while for Charley to find the trail but he understands the necessity that the camp moves every so often. He follows the sign of the trailing lodge poles and comes to Thompson's camp.

But something is not right. Even the cur dogs stand at a distance eyeing him. Thompson and Walks-on-Ice watch the mongrel dogs with a surprised look. It is strange but the animals seem to have a sixth sense. The dogs have been known to howl up and down the river for a hundred miles or so, when a human death has occurred in this land of the Dakotas. The dogs sense that something is wrong and they look at Charley and whine. Old Patch Eye watches him closely then gives some mournful yips and trots away.

Walks-on-Ice gives her husband a strange look. She gives off the impression that her Indian wisdom understands the dogs' whining. Thompson and her wave a greeting but Charley only returns a half hearted nod. Running-creek-Woman is bolder. She smiles at him and holds his horse. Charley tries hard not to show his feelings but the others can see that he is not his cheerful self. The three of them help pack his gear into Charley's teepee then leave him alone.

For several days they notice his forlorn look, when often he gazes across the prairie. Other days Charley leaves at dawn, going off alone then returning at dark. Only speaking when forced to then going into his teepee.

At sunrise one morning, Thompson has coffee boiling when Charley comes from his teepee. Thompson hands him a cup. "What's troublin' yuh, Hoss?" Charley takes the coffee then considers the steaming cup of brew.

"Ain't none of my affair. Running-creek-Woman says it is a woman," adds Thompson. Charley manages to crack a half smile.

That is the only sign Thompson needs and he talks on. "The day she was born she has lived with nature. Her father, a big red headed trader, he wuz killed by 'em red rascals. She has faced life, death. She understands life. She is not a big fool."

Charley's eyes brighten a bit, he speaks quietly, "There was a woman I really cared for, like you and Walks-on-Ice."

"The one I mailed the letter tuh?" Charley nods.

"Then go to her."

"It is too late."

"Tiz hardly too late for someone you have strong feelings uv."

"A lot has happened since I was last here." He looks off. "She is dead. She was killed."

Thompson turns away to gather his thoughts. He feels extremely bad for Charley. He contemplates for a long while, then quietly says, "Talk about what yuh feel, tiz the only way. Once it is out, it will ease yer hurt."

Charley grimaces then musters his inner strength. "It happened some months back. The hurt goes then it returns. Then the anger—it's hard to explain. I've seen death during the war, seen many deaths on the plains...this really affects...it seemed when I was coming here...the closer I got to your camp, the worse it got." Charley glances at Thompson's lodge. "Maybe it's because of the women." He shakes his head, bewildered.

"Do yuh s'pose..." Thompson rubs his chin then glances at Reynolds. "I 'onderstand, Charley. Someone close, s'pecially a woman, tiz dear to one's heart." Thompson grabs the pot and pours more coffee then looks at Walks-on-Ice who comes from the teepee carrying a parfleche. "Walks-on-Ice an' I will take the skins to the trade store. Will you come with?"

Charley shakes his head no, "I will stay."

Thompson and his woman get the horses ready to go. Charley helps tie the travois poles on Walks-on-Ice's horse. They then load the skins onto the travois.

Thompson turns to Charley. "Tiz thar' an'thing yuh wants?"

"Yeah, some powder n' lead."

Thompson nods, "Whiskey's in my lodge, Reynolds. Help yer' ownself. Might do yuh well to take a snert. On second thought, drink a whole bottle."

Walks-on-Ice gives her man a serious look then mounts up on her horse that pulls the travois. She gives Charley a sly look then surprises him when she speaks in English. "Running-creek-Woman...what White Man call teepee, she like." Charley looks puzzled as he watches the two of them ride off.

Thompson waits until he is out of earshot of the camp and turns to his wife. "What yuh say to sister? What she say?"

Walks-on-Ice rolls her eyes, smiles and gives her man that crafty Indian look. She then mutters, "Running-creek-Woman is not big fool"

Charley watches them disappear over a rise then goes into his teepee and comes out carrying some gear. The buffalo hide covered wood container holds his buffalo skinning knifes. Charley has mended his shirts and other personal items before. Anyone who lives and travels the plains alone must learn certain skills, besides tracking and hunting. Using his new sewing gift he begins to repair his hide-covered canister. Often he looks about, daydreaming.

Running-creek-Woman comes from her teepee, stokes the fire then busies herself around the camp. She gathers wood and occasionally glances at Reynolds. Not paying close attention Charley manages to poke the end of his finger with the needle. "Ouch," he mutters while he licks his finger. She walks over and signs, uttering some words in Arapaho. She holds her hand out, "Give."

Charley is reluctant and shakes his head. She is insistent and finally, through signs and much jabbering, Charley hands her the canister.

She puts it inside her lodge and then she fills a buffalo paunch with water and hangs it over the fire. She cuts up some buffalo meat and some wild turnips and puts them inside the paunch to cook.

Charley goes to his pack and gets his file for trimming hooves and begins to trim his horses' feet. He trims the frog with his jack knife and inspects their feet closely. Off and on he glances towards the camp. He notices Running-creek-Woman while she cooks and goes in and out of the teepee and visits with the other women.

Charley finishes the final trimming on Red's rear hoof and puts his leg back down. "Good boy, Red. You too, Rusty I'll take you boys closer to the river. It is better grazing there."

Charley leads his horses by the river and turns them loose to graze. He then sits down on a rise of ground and begins to sharpen his knife. He gives an occasional guick look at his horses, who hurry here and there, trying to beat each other to the well watered, rich grass shoots. He chuckles out loud, "You boys have a whole prairie full of grass, no need to fight over it." He knows that after a while that they will settle down and graze without the competition.

Charley looks around when he hears laughter coming from a small pocket of water off from the main river channel. He decides to investigate what all the noise is about. Before he realizes it—there they are in the water—a half dozen Indian women bathing and splashing about.

Charley feels his face flush. The women don't seem to be a bit nervous and only giggle and make shy glances at the White Man that has interrupted their bath. They giggle and laugh and continue to splash around.

In his hurried look Charley can't help but see Running-creek-Woman standing waist deep in the water. She timidly smiles at him then dips her naked body into the water.

Charley is embarrassed and abruptly turns around. Quickly he walks away. He can hear their laughter as he passes his horses. Ears pointed, eyes on him, they seem to wonder suspiciously. "What are you looking at?" he says. They wiggle their ears and then lower their heads to graze.

He sits down scratching his head and wondering. What a fool he must have looked like, standing there, his mouth probably agape. He should have known better. After a while, he leans back on the bank and tries to think of something else, but all that comes to mind is Running-creek-Woman's enticing look. He finally drifts off.

He wakes up suddenly, startled by a noise. Quickly, he rolls aside while drawing his pistol. He moves quickly to his feet, pistol cocked and ready, only to see a startled Running-creek-Woman shriek and drop a bowl full of stew.

"Scared the hades out me!" he yells. But then he sees the frightened look on her face. He tries to amend. "I apologize." He realizes that she might not understand. At once, he holsters his pistol then begins to make sign. "Your moccasins are quiet like the wolf."

She begins to pick up the meat and turnips. She blows and brushes the dirt off then returns the food to the horn bowl. She holds the bowl out to him.

Charley grins and shakes his head then gestures. "I would like you to bring more." She shakes her head disgustedly, walks to a small rise of ground and sits down. Charley is taken a bit but then realizes that she pouts. He recalls back home, his sisters, especially his one sister, if things didn't go right, she sat and pouted. His step mother just let her be. Sooner or later she'll get over it, she said.

Charley walks over to his horses and begins to fuss over them. After a while Running-creek-Woman goes to the fire then returns with a fresh bowl of meat and hands it to him, along with a wooden spoon. Charley looks at the spoon with a puzzled look. He points, "The spoon, where did you get it?"

She manages to tell him, "Your pack," she motions towards camp. Charley sits the bowl down and grasps her hand, shaking it in a gesture of thanks. She doesn't understand and shakes her head. "I am obliged for the stew," Charley says.

She looks at him and slowly raises her right hand. "How."

"No! Not how do you do. I say, thank you." He laughs, she smiles then shakes his hand and signs and utters some Arapaho and English mixture. "You heart on ground...my people sad, they go across prairie find place lift spirit." He looks inquisitive while she chatters in Arapaho and then she goes to the camp.

Charley turns around to get his horses and steps right onto the buffalo horn bowl spilling its contents. He quickly looks towards camp to see if she had seen what happened. Not seeing her, he hurriedly bends down and attempts to brush and blow the dirt from the meat. He then eats while making hurried glances, expecting her to return.

After a while, Charley brings the bowl to camp and gives it to her. And when she smiles, his heart skips a beat. He wonders just what it is about her smile? She signs and speaks, mixing English with the Arapaho tongue. "Question, buffalo good?"

Not even thinking about his words, Charley blurts out, "Tastes just like prairie...buffalo... I mean go-oo-od," he hastily nods and sweeps his right arm from his heart outwards. He smiles while she looks puzzled but finally grins along with him. Charley sheepishly looks away and then his eyes light up in surprise.

Running-creek-Woman's horse is hitched to the travois, her lodge is down, loaded and ready to leave. "This place," she points at herself then Charley. "We all go." He shakes his head, but she is insistent. She again points at him and then to herself, "We go, we all go across prairie."

Charley finally nods. He goes, and bringing his horses to camp, he begins to saddle up Red. She helps pack his gear and leads her horse with the travois as they leave. Charley reins up. He steps down and gets a blanket for Rusty. He motions for her to ride Rusty and holds his hands together for her to step up onto his horse. She waves him aside and nimbly jumps onto Rusty's back. Charley looks surprised, but then figures that if she can get on a horse like that; she can probably ride very well.

They move off along the river. The rolling hills are covered with rich prairie grass standing as tall as the horses' bellies. They travel up and down the undulations that stretch across the land. The gentle prairie wind whips the grass and as far as the eye can see, it looks like oceans of waves on the sea.

Buffalo and antelope graze contentedly. The forever-following buffalo wolves give them a watchful eye. Many of the big wolves are grey, with a few black and white mixed in. There are times when at least fifty of the large predators run in a pack. They trot along near the herds waiting for any sign of weakness of the animals. They especially go after the almost helpless young calves. Charley admires the colors as the sun glistens off the green grass into a yellowish green hue. It is splendid country, wild and untamed.

Running-creek-Woman seems to know where she is going and Charley lags behind enjoying the scenery. He sees her top a rise ahead then disappear. He spurs his horse and Red breaks into a trot. He reins up sharply as he looks around.

Below him is a sequestered valley. The valley teems with bird and animal life. He watches in awe as the Indian woman skillfully unloads her lodge and it seems to arise in minutes.

Off to the side is a sheltered grove of cottonwood trees. Bushes of wild berries and plums line the ravines and gullies that jut out from the river. A small creek meanders through the edge of the valley. He can hear the gurgling sound as it slowly trickles towards its junction with the river.

Charley hobbles his horses, leaving them to graze. He walks the valley, looking around. He thinks to himself she really knows how to select a campsite. He finds a high vantage point.

In the distance he watches grazing buffalo and antelope. His attention is diverted to an eagle that soars high in the sky riding the gentle air currents. Below the eagle and riding the airwaves is a red tailed hawk. Charley is mesmerized as his eyes dart from one to the other of the gentle circling birds. They seem to float along on nothing. He relaxes and stretches onto his back. The cotton white clouds move aimlessly across the big sky. It is so soothing and he is soon lost into deep thoughtfulness.

Charley raises his head up. With a startle he jumps up and looks around! Everything seems to be all right. It seemed like, just a few minutes ago he sat down. He looks over near the teepee and watches as Running-creek-Woman puts the finishing touches on a round shaped lodge. Charley walks down with a look of wonderment on his face.

She points to him then pours some water inside the small lodge and steam issues forth. "Give me your clothes," she speaks and signs.

Charley is embarrassed and reluctant. She comes to him, tugging on his jacket. He pulls away, "Wait! Wait! I will do it."

She quietly laughs to herself while Charley goes into the teepee and finally emerges wrapped only in a blanket. She motions him to enter. Holding tightly onto the blanket he stoops over and then drops to his knees to crawl inside the small opening of the sweat lodge. She jerks the blanket from him when he quickly scurries inside.

She smiles while she heats rocks and pours water on the hot stones creating steam. She gets from her pack some cedar sprigs and throws them onto the hot rocks. The steam and heat gives off a pleasing odor. She lifts her head while she sniffs the aroma of the cedar. "Good," she says out loud.

Meanwhile, inside Charley enjoys the aroma of the cedar and the steam. He's never been in a sweat lodge before but it seems to ease off his inner turmoil. Sweat beads on his body and face. He feels himself captivated and wonders, maybe there is some wisdom to the Indian's belief of their sweat lodges. Not only is it soothing and relaxing, it seems spiritual. The Indians haven't survived for all these centuries without some kind of wisdom.

Running-creek-Woman gets a mischievous smile. Laughing to herself she gets more hot stones from the fire. She continues to pour more and more water onto the hot rocks, until it is so hot inside, that Charley feels he is going to faint. He finally yells and scurries out of the lodge. She giggles when he quickly covers himself with the blanket. She motions for him to a pool in the creek. He bails in the cold water, almost taking his breath away. After the initial shock the plunge from hot to cold actually feels good to his body.

For several days Running-creek-Woman heats rocks goes for water and pours it onto the rocks while Charley crawls in and out of the sweat lodge then plunges into the cold creek. He feels enchanted and his thoughts bounce from Gabe Green to Ariana. Both are gone now and he must cherish their memories. Then always he returns to the lovely Indian woman outside and her smile. He feels the urge to touch, her to kiss her but he is apprehensive, he's not sure of himself. He's puzzled why he is so drawn to her. She seems to know what he is thinking and feeling, even before he does. One thing that weighs heavy on his mind—is—well—he's learned from Thompson that according to their custom, once she enters his lodge they are married. He's already had one case of bad in-laws that supposedly negated his marriage to Ariana. He doesn't want another.

Running-creek-Woman has made Charley's bed inside the lodge. During most of the day, Charley goes to the high vantage point to watch the wild life and to ponder. She sleeps near the fire in a small lodge, wrapped up in a blanket. She had made the shelter like the sweat lodge, of bent willow branches into a dome shape. She covered it with skins and blankets. It is cozy inside as she made the opening towards the fire, which she keeps burning through the night.

One night they have finished eating and they are sitting around the fire. Occasionally, he catches her subtle glances as she looks at him. He recalls how Ariana's beautiful hair used to glisten from the glow of the fire but then he thinks to himself she's dead. I've got to stop wondering about her. Nothing will bring her back.

There are times when he catches a look at Running-creek-Woman. The tint of her dark hair, joined with the auburn strands, fairly glowed from the light of the fire. But there was something about her smile, her lips that intrigued him. She had this little way when she spoke softly, the way she formed her lips. It caused his heart to skip.

Charley stretches and yawns. "I am going to sleep," he signs, laying both hands together on the right side of his face, leaning his head to the right.

Her brown eyes follow him as he stands and walks to his animals. She watches while he checks and makes sure everything is all right. She watches longingly as he goes to the lodge. She catches his look from the corner of his eye. He gives a quick wave to her then lifts the flap and goes inside.

Running-creek-Woman turns and gazes into the darkness as a lone wolf utters a mournful cry across the land. While she rests on her blanket she notices the flap of the teepee move as Charley slyly peaks out. Again she looks around as another wolf joins the others howling up and down the river.

She drifts off to sleep for a short time and then leaps to her feet when the horses whinny. She hurries out and checks to make sure everything is all right then returns to the fire. She watches the flap, thinking that he must have heard the horses. The flap doesn't move and she thinks he's probably sound asleep. She wonders to herself, if she were an Indian she could sneak up and have two fine ponies to brag about. She chuckles out loud, "I am Indian, at least part."

She stoops and tosses several more branches into the fire, keeping them off to the side so they won't burn up too fast. She adds some buffalo chips then wraps the blanket around her and stands near the fire. Dark clouds begin to block out the stars. The air seems to change. A storm is brewing. She looks fearfully at the sky, then views the lodge flap.

Charley is awakened when he hears the horses' subtle nickering. He opens the flap and is surprised to see Running-creek-Woman standing near the opening. She is wrapped in her blanket. He stammers, "The horses...the..."

"Horse safe," she mutters. "You not hear?" Charley looks astonished.

Using sign mixed with English, Running-creek-Woman speaks with difficulty. "Arapaho woman smile come inside man's lodge, she his woman."

Charley looks dumfounded and manages to stutter, "It...it...is not my lodge." Then he quickly thinks, what a foolish reply.

She bends down brushes past him and steps inside. The lodge is cozy, warm from the glowing coals of the fire. His bed of blankets laid on top of a buffalo robe, lays off to the side nice and restful.

Charley stands with a blanket wrapped around him. He is caught off guard and stoops and tosses some buffalo chips and small limbs onto the fire. He nervously fingers his blanket, unsure what to say or do.

She speaks and signs, "Little Raven village chief had many wives. Some say that Sitting Bull has four wives." She fingers the hair from her face and flips her head. The firelight gives a rich auburn glow to her hair and it falls long and straight over her shoulder.

Charley's eyes linger on her hair. He feels his face flush and wonders, if it's the radiance of her hair or the red from his own face, that makes him feel that way.

He questions why is he so disturbed? It is almost like he's afraid. He's been with a woman before, but for some reason he seems to be afraid. Then he thinks to himself, he's not afraid, he's unsure. Unsure he's ready to take up with a woman again. Finally, he begins to get a grip on his emotions.

He looks at her appreciatively. She senses his feelings and smiles when she sees the goose bumps on his arm. She tips her head and puckers her mouth, gesturing with her lips.

Charley takes the hint, "Kiss."

She gleefully smiles, "Kissss."

He gently holds her face in his hands and tenderly touches his lips to hers. She pulls away and smiles that smile.

She shakes her head, "Kissss." In the Indian manner, she takes Charley's face and holds her cheek next to his. He feels her face warm and moist as they stand cheek to cheek. He's never before kissed in the Indian way, but he likes it. Their cheeks together radiates warmth, and sends shivers throughout his body. He can feel the heat from her. After several minutes, he pulls away and smiles tenderly to her.

Charley nods, not sure she will understand, "You have never been kissed, I mean like the whites."

She holds her mouth open, "Kissss," and Charley kisses her softly. She can't get enough of his kisses and for a long time their lips continue to touch. Their cheeks come together in the Indian way. Outside the lodge, the haunting cry of a wolf echoes in the distance.

Several hours later Charley awakens to howling wolves. He sits up and listens. The howls seem to echo across the land from every direction. He looks down at Running-creek-Woman who is fast asleep. The glow from the fire glimmers off the soft skin of her face. Charley smiles as he learns her features. He snuggles close and falls back asleep. Only the glow of the fire remains.

All at once, lightning lights up the inside of the lodge. Violent thunder erupts then rumbles across the heavens, shattering their sleep. Running-creek-Woman shrieks and Charley can feel her tremble as she snuggles close, clutching him. He holds her comfortingly.

"It will be all right," he says as he holds her tightly. After she has calmed somewhat Charley rolls over and throws a couple of ash limbs onto the fire. She had thought of everything and had gathered the wood from the creek bottom and buffalo chips from the prairie. The thunder continues to boom violently and the lightning frequently lights up the inside of the teepee.

He gives her a sheepish look. She looks at him puzzled as he stokes the fire. She watches him closely wondering why he gave her that look.

"In the Indian way, this means we are married." He says with a combination of English and sign.

She slowly enunciates. "Mar-rieed?"

"You know, like Thompson says. It is the Indian way when a woman smiles at you n' enters your lodge—well, she is your woman. In White Man's lingo we are married. That means you get to cook for me, mend my clothes, pack in the buffalo chips. "

She looks at him with a disagreeable eye then is distracted by the thunder. Charley realizes that she doesn't understand everything but says, "I will keep the fire burning. It will be a comfort for you." She looks at him in appreciation and says. "Brother born night of Thunderbird."

He looks at her inquisitively. "Born night. I understand. Your brother was born the night it thundered. Your people call, Thunderbird."

She nods, "Big Thunder."

Charley grasps what she wants to tell him. "Your father named your brother, Big Thunder." She smiles.

"Your father, he must have talked English?"

She nods when she hears the word. She points at him, "Say English I know not all...long time past."

"Question. When I speak in English you understand little? You say it has been a long time since your father spoke English to you."

"Not all understand," she smiles. And Charley can't resist kissing her.

"Sioux killed father." She looks hurt and Charley embraces her. "Your father was killed by the Sioux," She nods.

Then she beams, "I like kiss. My father, my mother, she like kiss."

"Your father used to kiss your mother and she liked it." Running-creek-Woman grins and nods. "Many times, kiss Indian way."

Charley smiles, "I like the Indian way. I like to kiss you." He softly kisses her lips then holds his cheek to hers. She jumps when thunder crashes loud above them. Charley comforts her and then she pulls away. "Old men talk, say Thunderbird angry, goes across prairie...arrows of fire shoot the earth, Thunderbird big!"

Speaking to himself out loud Charley mulls over her words. "Thunderbird go across prairie. Thunder roll across prairie. White men call the land plains, Indian call the land prairie." he nods. "Arrows on fire, the white man's lightning. Thunder rolling across. Thunder rolling on the high plains. Thunderbird big. Something great will happen."

She murmurs in fright then clutches him tightly when the thunder booms loud above them. Charley holds her snugly as the thunder reverberates long and loud across the plains then crescendos with a loud burst. In an audible whisper Charley says, "Thunder rolling across the high plains. Something great will happen."

He looks at her, "Thunderbird go." She returns his look then giggles. "You hear horse, no," shaking her head. He looks dumfounded. "I return to the village," she holds up two fingers, "Two horses. Chief gives me many honors."

Charley nods, "You say you could have stolen my two horses while I slept." He smirks and nods. "When you return to the village you would be honored by your chief." Shaking his head he says, "It's that sweat lodge. That steam...the smell of the cedar makes me sleepy." He then asks, "How do the Arapaho count time?"

She begins to shake his hand. He laughs, "No, not how but how do the Arapahoe count time?" He holds up his hand and then alternates his fingers.

She holds up one finger then two, "one sleep here, two sleeps there."

"I mean count a long time?"

Running-creek-Woman smiles. "Long time past."

Charley chuckles. "You say last summer, last winter."

"Long grass time beyond. One winter beyond." She looks at him inquisitively, and then at the smoke flap as the rains come softly at first, then pelting hard.

Charley throws more wood and buffalo chips on the fire and she snuggles close. She lays her head on his chest and they listen to the rain as it patters and pelts against the buffalo skin lodge. It is a soothing sound.

They lay cheek to cheek and both sleep soundly. Distant scattered thunder rumbles on across the plains.

For the next several days she gives Charley steam baths, cooks for him, walks along the river and goes to his vantage point to meditate with him.

Late one morning, Charley walks to the vantage point alone. He looks around contentedly. He wonders what will happen when he's ready to leave. He watches Running-creek-Woman when she comes from the lodge. She walks towards him then stops and examines the ground. He looks curious when she kneels down on one knee to look. She then walks up and joins him.

"I watched when you looked at the ground."

"Buffalo tracks."

Charley attempts to refresh her memory and teach her more English. "I wish to hunt."

"How." She raises her palm.

He lifts his arms and shrugs his shoulder. "No. Hun-nnt hunn-nt."

Finally she purses her lips. "Hun-nt."

Charley nods then points. "You hunt?"

She shakes her head and points to herself. "Skin buffalo." She gestures to him and then she goes to the horses.

Charley watches with a puzzled look, wondering what she is going to do. She sings a chant while she rides back and forth on the buffalo tracks. She then rides up to Charley. "Pony tracks on buffalo trail. Good sign, heap."

He's not really sure what she means but he nods. She motions him to follow and she leads off following the buffalo tracks.

Charley quickly saddles Red and follows. He watches in awe as she puts on an extraordinary display of riding skills. Bareback she rides into a small herd of buffalo and separates one from the herd. Skillfully she drives the beast towards him. He is so engrossed in watching that he forgets to draw his rifle and shoot. They need fresh meat. She rides over, speaking unintelligible Arapaho. He's glad he can't understand the way she is talking. She lifts her arms and shrugs her shoulders. He looks dumfounded. The buffalo makes its way back to the herd.

"I know. I know! I forgot to shoot."

She watches as he slides from the saddle and grabs his, "big fifty." He lies down on the ground. He sights down the barrel and squeezes the trigger. The animal quivers, falls onto its haunches, then rolls over dead.

She looks at him surprised. He grins and shrugs his shoulders. "Good shot no." She smiles at him with a sheepish look.

He steps into the saddle and they ride to the downed animal. They dismount leaving the horses loose. Charley draws his knife and sticks and bleeds the buffalo. He then begins to remove the hide. He skins the neck hide back far enough to tie on his rope. Then making skillful cuts on the legs he then hooks his rope to Red's saddle horn and pulls the hide to one side. He is careful not to allow dirt to get on the meat.

He then begins to quarter the yearling animal. She impatiently utters and motions Charley to stop. He backs off with a curious look. She unsheathes her large butcher knife and signs for Charley to bring her his hatchet.

Charley gets his hatchet from his war bag that is always on his saddle and hands it to her. She then proceeds to skillfully put on a quick display, of how to cut and butcher a buffalo.

While Charley watches her, he is reminded of his buffalo days, when he trailed the herds for meat and hides on the Republican River in Kansas. He felt he could skin and butcher a buffalo with the best of the buffalo skinners, but watching her, he now believes different. He says to her, "Not fair you have more experience." She grins at him and continues to slice away.

He goes on and on. "Indian women do all the skinning and butchering of the animals. That is, unless the warriors are off hunting by themselves or on a war party. It's just not fair." She pays no heed to him.

While she cuts and chops away, he signs, "I'll go to the camp. I will return in a short time." He points, "I bring lodge poles," he nods and walks away. She watches him curiously. Reynolds stoops to clean the blood from his hands with some grass. Unseen by him a huge rattlesnake slithers away.

When he returns she is finished with the butchering. While he hooks the travois to Rusty, Running-creek-Woman comes over. She smiles and bends to clean her hands on the grass. She hears the unmistakable warning of a rattlesnake. She freezes. She is face-to-face with the coiled rattling viper.

Suddenly she yells out! Her horse screams and runs off! In a flash, Red runs over Rusty following dragging the travois. Red snorts loud and rears, stomping at the ground. Rusty whinnies and paws the dirt.

Charley immediately grasps that a rattlesnake has bitten her. He runs to her as she limps out of the way. "I hate them sonofa-buck-toothed rattlesnakes," he shouts.

He grabs her, lifting her up and carries her to a safe distance. Red, wildly pulverizes the rattler into the dirt.

Charley lays her on the ground. She clenches her teeth trying not to cry. Perspiration forms on her forehead. She jabbers something in Arapaho.

"Lay still!" Charley looks at the bite marks high on her leg just above the leggings. "Easy, lie still," he says as he quickly draws his knife. She grits her teeth when he makes an incision. He quickly sucks on the cut then spits out the poison. He ties a tourniquet above the cut. He can hear Red's occasional outburst as he screams out, stomping the ground.

"I've got to get you to camp," he says as he takes a hurried look at her, then runs to make the travois ready. He carefully loads her and moves off slowly.

It is not long and they reach camp. He lays her inside the lodge and makes her comfortable on the soft buffalo robe and blankets. He removes the tourniquet. "I've got to go for medicine. You lie still."

She looks worried as she mutters, "Med-a-sun."

Charley hurries outside. Quickly, untying the travois, he drops it to the ground. He leaps on Red and whistles for Rusty. "Haaa-ya," he spurs Red into a full gallop and races for Thompson's camp. Thompson has whiskey there and from his father the doctor and the surgeons on the Army expeditions he knows it will help Running-creek-Woman.

The others at Thompson's camp watch curiously as Charley rides up, leaps to the ground, hurries into Thompson's lodge and returns with two bottles of whiskey. He immediately unsaddles Red and flings the saddle on Rusty. He places the whiskey on each side of his saddle pockets and races away.

Inside the lodge Charley examines her badly swollen leg. "You must drink the medicine." He gently tips the bottle to her lips. "Drink. It will help." She gags and spits out. "I know it tastes terrible but you've..." he forces her to take some. "Yuh' gotta drink." He frequently tips the bottle to her lips forcing her to drink.

She spits, gags and throws up. He lets her rest some while he cleans up the mess. Then he grabs one of his canvas bags, dumping out the contents. "My father was a doctor. Medici-nnne-man," He gently forces her to drink more. Her eyes roll she is soon inebriated and delirious. She continues to throw up often, while he holds the bag for her. "Medici-nnne...work goo-ood," he says. He feels sorry for her, she is so sick but there is something about the whiskey in the blood stream, at least that is what he has been told.

He forces her to take more. She glares at the almost empty bottle then looks panicky at the second full bottle on the blanket. She pulls away muttering, "Med-suuun...nooo!" Finally, she throws up again then moans and faints. "I truly feel bad." He covers her with blankets and watches her closely. He feels empathy while she tosses, turns, sweats and mutters.

In the morning he watches her open her eyes. She is still woozy and a bit sick. She manages to smile as he examines her leg. "The swelling is down," he says. He looks at her serious like, "You had me scared. I was afraid the whiskey would kill you before it took effect."

She looks at him, puzzled. She tries to lift up. Her head falls back onto the blanket. She motions outside and Charley grasps that she needs to go outside. He helps her to her feet and she staggers and wobbles then clutches him tightly, but slowly he manages to help her outside.

She pulls free and staggers behind the teepee to throw up. He listens to her gag. His stomach feels a little woozy itself, as he recalls the first time he drank alcohol when he first met Ariana. It's funny, he suddenly feels that he can think about Ariana without feeling that want for something he can't have.

Running-creek-Woman breathes a sigh of relief from the fresh air and Charley helps her sit down. He brings the robe and blankets outside, spreading them on the ground for her to rest on. She looks at Charley with appreciation. "Agency warriors... drink the strange drink that burns," she fingers her throat. "Men drink fire-waader. Beat their women, make strange fight, make sick," she coughs.

"You say at the agencies the warriors drink water that burns the throat, fire water, white man's whiskey. They get drunk, fight and beat their women." He touches her forehead, wiping the perspiration, "That is good you understand. You are learning." She looks curiously.

"You speak more better English." As a second thought, he adds, "And you understand the evils of whiskey. You rest. I will go and bring the buffalo meat."

Charley hurries away with his horses and it is not long until he returns with the butchered meat. Lucky the wolves hadn't found it. They will have to dry some and when they return they will take the rest to Thompson's camp. There is something about the climate in this land that meat will last a long while. That is, if dried and left hanging in the shade where the air can move around it.

He motions towards the sweat lodge. "You go, I will get it ready."

She watches him heat the rocks then place them into the sweat lodge. He goes to the creek for water and when everything is ready he carries her to the lodge. After an hour or so she emerges with a smile.

He looks at her thoughtfully. Charley can tell that she feels much better. Perspiration and water drips from her wet hair and trickles down her body. He can't resist and kisses her.

While Running-creek-Woman goes inside the teepee, he skewers some meat on the green willow sticks. He places them in the ground near the fire, where he can rotate them. When she comes out she is dressed and begins to comb and braid her hair.

"Your hair is beautiful," he says.

"Beau-tee-ful," she shakes her head, puzzled.

"When the light is just right, the red shines gorgeous." Her look tells him that she only partly understands. "Pretty. Very pretty," he gestures.

She moves her lips forming that little half smile. His heart jumps. After she is done with her hair, they eat and enjoy each other. Often she looks at Charley contentedly and smiles.

"It is good," Charley smiles happily in return.

"Good," she nods.

For several days Charley attends her as she goes in and out of the sweat lodge. One day she opens the flap and sticks her head out smiling at him. Her smile turns into a sly look.

Charley looks curious until she motions for him to join her. He chuckles. "There's not enough room for the two of us." She closes the flap then her hand comes out motioning him inside. He laughs heartily while he joins her. Their giggling coaxes Red and Rusty to come over. They stand contentedly by with pointed ears, as they toss their heads, neighing softly.

The next morning the horses are packed and they are ready to leave. Charley signs and asks her, "Wait please."

Her face is somber while she watches him walk to the vantage point. She keeps an eye on him while he takes a look around at the peaceful valley. He sees a red tailed hawk as it dives for a meal and he nods. He then walks down and joins her.

Together they view an eagle high in the sky. Charley looks at her tenderly then squeezes her hand. "I have never known someone that knows me like you do. You are remarkable."

She grasps his meaning and grins. "Re-mark-abe."

He reaches for her face then rubs his cheek on hers. He pulls away and gently runs his fingers around her dimples. She smiles that smile. His heart skips a beat. His eyes brighten. It suddenly dawns on him what there is about her smile. He softly traces his fingers on the little facial lines running to the corner of her mouth. "When you smile like that, it is like you know me, here." He takes her hand and touches his heart. She looks tenderly at him. Her eyes become moist, small tears form and one by one slowly roll down her face. He brushes them away then embraces her tightly. She clings to him with a life like grip. Her look says, she never wants what ever it is that they have, to end.

A few days after they arrive back at Thompson's camp, Thompson and Walks-on-Ice return with their wares. Charley gives them a quick wave. Running-creek-Woman sings happily while she sews blue beads on a piece of white buffalo skin.

Walks-on-Ice smiles while she looks around. She wears that crafty Indian look again when she speaks in Arapaho to Thompson. "Arapaho medicine work good, heap." She looks at Running-creek-Woman then to Charley. Her and Thompson laugh.

"I am going to learn Arapaho one day," Charley says.

Thompson chuckles. "She says Rapahoe medicine work good, heap. Running-creek-Woman is not a big fool." Thompson and his wife again laugh heartily.

Running-creek-Woman looks at them bewildered but smiles. Charley smiles then Thompson gets a serious look and gestures with his head, for Charley to follow him. The others watch while Charley and Thompson walk out of earshot to talk.

Charley looks grave, "Something wrong? Did you get my powder n' lead?"

"Yeah. Yer' gonna' need 'em!" Thompson nods seriously.

Charley looks surprised. "What is it?"

"Ol' sit on yer butt, Sittin' Bull, Crazy Horse many of the Sioux, continue to roam the Yellowstone Country. There have been several cases of settlers, miners, they ain't comin back. When a search was made their hacked up carcasses wuz found."

Charley glances at Thompson, then gives Running-creek-Woman a frank look, and he then walks over and disappears into the lodge. Distant thunder begins to roll.

Running-creek-Woman hurries to the lodge. She pulls the flap open then pauses, momentarily. Her eyes look apprehensive. She watches the darkening sky. The stiff buffalo hide flap clatters in the wind when she closes it behind her.

A few minutes later they emerge. She stands near the flap while Charley goes to his horses and saddles Red. He steps into the saddle. Rusty whinnies furiously and follows as Charley, with a quick wave, rides from the camp.

Walks-on-Ice joins her. The two women sing a soft, Arapaho, brave heart song. They watch as the threesome tops a rise, disappears only to reappear a few minutes later, going up another rise.

Running-creek-Woman stares, as it appears that they stopped for a brief moment. It looks like Charley's arm waved but she's not sure. She looks at Walks-on-Ice who slowly nods. Finally, horses and rider move out of sight over the last rise.

14

Charley eases his horses into a steady, running walk and several days later he sees the familiar Standing Rock Indian Agency sign.

He observes the uproar. The Indians mill around, riding back and forth, drums beat constantly and the soldiers are much on edge. He decides to set up his camp some distance away. Charley feels that it will be much safer to watch and learn the situation and then he'll find his friend, Captain Allison.

That night, Charley goes to the agency. He sees many Indians gathering away from main buildings and the well-traveled road. He cautiously approaches, remaining in the background. A large fire roars and drums beat furiously while wild chants and yells come from the dancers. Charley notices another white man across and behind the circle of Indians.

Unpredictably, Charley notices one of the dancing warriors that look familiar. His face scowls in anger when the warrior displays a white man's trophy a gold watch. Charley has seen enough and leaves in indignation.

After two days of observing the Indians. Charley rolls out his bedroll. With all that he has learned he feels uneasy, but then consoles himself that tomorrow he'll report to Captain Allison. He is still angry about the gold watch and it bothers him tremendously. Soon, Charley is fast asleep.

Charley thrashes about, tossing and turning in a dream. *He looks into the fierce, blood-shot eyes of Sitting Bull. Over and over, "Tatanka Iyotake, Tatanka Iyotake," rings in his head. In the background, Charley watches an Uncpapa scalp dance.*

Hundreds of Sioux Indians watch. A huge log fire is built. Stoic warriors walk out and seat themselves around the fire. The warriors are stripped to breechclouts and moccasins. Scalps hang from their bodies. They sit in silence.

The stoic Sitting Bull struts to the circle of drums. He stares for some time. He then raises the drumstick. Suddenly with a violent thrust of his arm the pounding begins. Other drummers join. The pounding is intense. "Boom, boom...boom, boom."

Charley jumps in his sleep, when unexpectedly, the warriors spring to their feet. Some set up wild shouts, while others yell furiously. Others chant a song of triumph. They shake and display the scalp pole, as they distort their bodies into every kind of shape, reciting brave deeds.

In a foggy background, Charley can see another white man observing the dance. The man is big and wears tall leggings to match his size.

Suddenly Charley recognizes an Uncpapa Indian, Rain-in-the-Face. Charley rolls restlessly as Rain-in-the-Face distorts his body wildly then displays a gold white man's watch. Charley tosses and rolls in anger. He sees the hazy outline of Sitting Bull and Rain-in-the-Face. He hears their vicious chants. Unexpectedly, both wield a tomahawk as they bear down upon him.

Charley wakes up with a yell! He is in a cold sweat and stares at the coals of his fire. He can still see the blood-shot eyes of Sitting Bull. The wild, distorted eyes and face of Rain-in-the-Face. It is cold out and Charley fans the coals of his fire and soon has coffee boiling.

It is early afternoon when Charley rides into the agency. He notices hundreds of Indians milling around. He passes the crude, Standing Rock sign and reins up.

He cautiously looks around, surveying the situation. He sees two white men leaving in a wagon loaded with grain sacks. As they pass he glances suspiciously at the sacks marked, U. S. GOVT. The two men scowl at him and move out towards the river.

Inside the Agency, Charley is greeted by Captain Allison, who in his own words, is on official military business.

"Nice to see you again, Reynolds. We've been concerned about you—Mrs. Custer asks everyone who happens through these parts: "Have you seen Lonesome Charley? She really is worried."

"I owe everyone an apology, Allison. I was gone much longer than I had planned. I'm not very faithful about writing letters, either. But I have already been to Fort Lincoln so the Custer's won't be worried any longer."

"I'm glad to hear that. Are you planning to winter here?"

"I haven't any other plans. But I don't have a permanent residence, if that's what you're asking."

"Well, no need to worry. You're welcome to use my tent any time. I'm away quite often and I'd be happy to share my meager accommodations. Besides, I enjoy your company."

Charley is grateful for the compliment, "And I enjoy yours, too. Thanks for offering your tent."

"It's settled then. Come, I'll buy you a drink."

Once inside the Hatch Trade Store the older mustached trader pours them a drink. At one of the tables the agent, Major Palmer sits with a grubby looking bearded man. Palmer cocks an ear and watches Charley and Allison suspiciously.

The whiskey doesn't taste bad at all. "This is the first in quite a while. Thank you."

"My pleasure. Say, Reynolds do you know Big Leggings Brugier?"

"I remember the name."

Allison grins. "And his face as well, no doubt! He agreed to meet me here today. I hope you'll stay close by. I may need some help."

"I'm always glad to help when help is needed. What kind of trouble are you expecting?"

"I'm not sure...it may be nothing. I'd just feel more at ease knowing you're here with that big buffalo gun of yours."

When Brugier finally makes his appearance he raises his hand, "How... washte."

Charley gets a mischievous look, raises his arm, "How...Wash day Wednesday"

Allison bursts out in laughter, joined by Brugier. "Didn't know you to be such a humorous chap, Reynolds," he continues with bursts of laughter. The big man, Brugier chuckles away. Major Palmer gives them occasional looks of disgust.

Big Leggings Brugier can hardly wait to tell Captain Allison and Reynolds how he overheard an Uncpapa Indian by the name of, Rain-in-the-Face, bragging about two white men he had killed on the Yellowstone River.

Charley looks surprised. He recognizes Brugier as the same man he had seen at the Uncpapas' scalp dance. "You must be referring to John Baliran and Dr. Honsinger," Charley says, a tone of urgency in his voice. "I observed the Uncpapa's scalp dance at Standing Rock. That must have been what they were so excited about."

"You knew Baliran and Honsinger?" Allison asks.

"Yes. I was there. I didn't see who killed them but I saw plenty of sign and observed an Indian watching our camp—before the attack. I arrived in time to chase them to the river. They jumped their horses into the Yellowstone and swam across." He pauses to take a sip. "Two of the soldiers tried to follow them, one of them drowned."

"Could you identify him?"

"I know Rain-in-the-Face. I've seen him here at the Agency many times. Seen him at Berthold. I believe he was who I saw just a while ago."

Allison motions his head and the trio move to another table a short distance away. "I didn't want Palmer to hear," says Allison quietly.

Charley gives a quick glance towards Palmer's table. "It is hard to know who to trust with all the graft n' grain theft." He looks at Brugier then to Allison, whose eyes are demanding. "I noticed a wagon leaving as I rode in—full of grain sacks marked, U. S. GOVT." says Charley sternly.

Big Leggings scowls, "I know. Did you hear the Uncpapa Rain-in-the-Face brag about killing the two civilians?"

Charley's upset, "I didn't hear all but I was convinced when Rain showed off the watch."

Allison observes the two men then glances at Palmer, "General Custer will be angry."

"The men were unarmed! I'm disturbed about it myself." says Charley.

Allison motions his head and Charley and Brugier nod.

Major Palmer's eyes follow them as they walk towards the door. "Another drink, fellows?" the Major surprises them.

Charley shakes his head. Brugier calmly replies, "Too cold out. It's time for me to return to camp." The door clatters shut behind them.

"I'll notify the major that I'm riding to Lincoln right away to give the news to Custer," announces the Captain. "He'll be happy to hear it!"

"I'll ride along with you, Allison." Charley says with enthusiasm. "Safety in numbers, you know."

As the pair prepares to leave Allison cautions Brugier: "Not a word of this to anyone Mr. Brugier. Can we depend on you?"

"Oh yes, Sir!" the rugged looking plainsman replies, his giant hand waving energetically as the Captain and Charley ride off.

Up river at Fort Lincoln Headquarters, General Custer, Captain Dandy and Charley are gathered in secret. Dandy writes an employment voucher for Charley. "You can identify Rain-in-the-Face? The pay is five dollars a day. Not much to lay your life on the line."

Charley shrugs his shoulders with a smile and nonchalantly replies. "We die how we live, Captain." Charley's eyes shift towards George Custer.

"The orders are sealed. Captain Yates is not to open them until you are away from the fort," adds General Custer austerely.

"Agent Palmer is not to be trusted," says Dandy his look moving from Custer to Charley. "If he gets word of this he will tip, off the Sioux!"

Charley nods in understanding, "Tomorrow is ration day."

Dandy looks angry, "Burns my rear end they get their rations during the winter, get the latest arms bullets powder..."

Custer interrupts, "Leave the reservations during the summer. The young bucks raid, kill innocent settlers. And then you have the Eastern sympathizers."

Charley looks away, then back, "Yeah! They know a lot about it sitting on their butts behind some desk back east. It's a bad situation."

"Irks my butt! The War Department orders us to round 'em up. Indian Affairs gives them arms on the pretext that they need them to hunt!" Captain Dandy hands Charley his voucher then continues. "Something goes wrong, the Army takes the blame. Far as I'm concerned they can use their bows n' arrows," he looks at Reynolds. "God speed, Charley."

Custer stands, "Yeah, God speed, Lonesome Charley. Keep an eye peeled for more grain thieves. And be careful Charley."

"I will, Sir. And thank you, Captain Dandy." Charley gives his quick wave and goes out the door.

Under "very secret" orders, Tom Custer and two companies of cavalry are dispatched to ride to the Standing Rock Agency, arrest Rain-in-the-Face and carry him back to the garrison for trial. Custer urges his men to proceed with utmost diligence and the posse is underway within an hour.

It is extremely cold. Several Indians suspiciously watch while Captain Tom Custer, Captain Yates, Lieutenant Harrington, Lonesome Charley Reynolds and one hundred soldiers ride into the agency. They rein up, dismount and set up a picket line. They wait.

Several hours later only a few Indians show up for rations. Captain Yates speaks in a hushed voice to his officers. "Harrington, the Sioux are suspicious. Take your Company and ride out." He leans closer. "Ride back in four hours." Yates turns and loud enough for all to hear, "Lieutenant Harrington! Take your men and go question the Sioux downstream about the killing of white men on the Red River!"

Harrington nods to his first sergeant and he begins to have the men saddle up. The officers synchronize their watches.

Reynolds speaks up, "We've got to handle this right or we'll have one heck of a fight on our hands!"

The others look seriously at Reynolds. "You can identify Rain-in-the-Face," says Harrington.

Tom Custer briskly says, "All you have to do is point him out, Reynolds. We'll have to get him out of there fast!"

Harrington nods then gives a hurried salute. He mounts up and motions his soldiers along. "At the gallop, yahooo."

The others eagerly watch until the hoof beats fade away.

Soon after Harrington is gone, the Indians begin to appear. Before long there are several hundred, all covered with blankets, milling around.

Captain Yates can see the telltale sign of what he suspects are rifles and other weapons protruding from their blankets. The Indians receive their beef rations and the women leave for their village. Many others, mostly warriors, make their way over and then go inside the Hatch Trade Store.

Yates nods to Captain Custer. Tom selects six men. Charley and the others check their arms to make sure they are ready, then follow Tom into the trade store.

Inside as planned, the men casually position themselves strategically. The Indians come and go as they please.

Once inside the sutler's store Charley's role as sleuth begins. It is difficult to see the faces of the blanket-wrapped Indians. He speaks briefly to the sutler than wanders about as if he's lost something on the floor, looking up occasionally for a glimpse of the accused. When the Indian lowers his blanket from his face, Charley recognizes his man. He casually signals Tom who is standing ready just inside the door. Tom approaches from behind and throws his arms around Rain-in-the-Face and pins him to the floor. Charley grabs Rain's rifle and the others quickly tie his arms behind him.

It is a volatile situation. Several Indians step forward. Chief Two Bears is vehement. In Sioux he warns the other Indians. "It was said, we would never allow soldiers to take one of our warriors alive!"

Captain Yates yells to Charley. "What'd he say?"

"Two Bears urges the Sioux to fight. He says they would never again allow soldiers to take their warriors alive!"

"Reynolds! Tell him many Sioux will die! Many soldiers wait outside. Many more are coming, are already on the way!" Yates turns to a soldier, "Orderly! Get agent Palmer here quickly! Ask him to come and explain to the Sioux the reason for the arrest!" Yates then adds, "That snivelin' conniver!"

The orderly hurriedly salutes and heads for the door as he shouts, "That's what I call him!"

Captain Yates turns to Charley as the orderly slams the door behind him. "Reynolds! Tell Two Bears that he has much wisdom. He knows many of his people will die. Tell him we will not leave without Rain-in-the-Face!"

Charley turns to Two Bears and with soothing words of wisdom calms the Chief. Two Bears in turn whirls around, and gestures and speaks to the warriors who rush forward, "Many will die! We must wait!" Two Bears holds his arms outstretched, finally calming the others.

All heads turn as the orderly bursts through the door. "Palmer says that if you want him you know where to find him!"

"He really is a snivelin'..." shouts Yates.

"That's what I told him!" agrees the orderly then excitedly adds, "He surely didn't like it much, Sir!"

For the time being, the Indians back off while the soldiers bind Rain with a long rope and quickly take him out of the building.

The Indians inside follow and many others gather to watch. Charley looks at Tom Custer and both breath a sigh of relief as Lieutenant Harrington and his company of cavalry ride up.

Rain-in-the-Face is strapped to the saddle of a horse. "Move 'em out, boys," Yates quietly orders. Charley rides to the front and the others follow. Looking behind, they see many of the Sioux mount up and follow at a distance.

A bitterly cold wind picks up and Charley raises his collar around his neck. He looks ahead and then reins up, waiting for Captain Yates. "Cannonball River is just ahead, Sir. It wouldn't sur..."

Yates waves Charley off then points ahead. "You're surely right, Reynolds. Look up ahead!"

Charley wheels around to look. Across the river, suddenly many Sioux gather, with still others riding in from the east. Captain Custer rides alongside Charley and Yates. "What do you think?" Yates asks Tom.

The fearless Tom Custer states matter of factly, "Don't dare show any sign of fear—or they'll hit us like flies on a dead dog!"

Yates and Charley can't help but chuckle lightly. Yates nods, "Any suggestions, Reynolds?"

Charley nudges Red forward then turns, "Keep the men ready! I'll parley with them."

Yates shouts, "Draw carbines!Load carbines! At the ready!" Charley kicks his horse into a lope and the others watch while he reins up at the river's edge.

Two Bears, along with several wildly painted warriors ride to the opposite side. Yates and Tom watch as Charley and Two Bears, using signs, parley. Charley then spurs Red into a gallop and reins up.

Yates anxiously asks, "What'd you tell them?"

Charley gets a crafty look, "I told him if his warriors started anything, I'd turn him into a three-eyed corpse with my buffalo gun." Yates and Tom eye each other then Charley adds, "We better move 'em out quick, Captain."

Yates looks surprised but motions the soldiers to follow, "Advance!" and rifles at the ready they move forward. On reaching the river, "skirmishers out." The trained cavalry soldiers know what to do. While one platoon and sergeant stand guard, the others cross. They then stand guard while the other platoon crosses. The Sioux shout angry insults and wave obscene gestures. They've learned these gestures from the white soldiers and civilians at the agencies. As the soldiers gallop past, two platoons form a rear guard. Except for two brief halts for rest and water, the pace is kept up throughout the day.

Finally, the group arrives at Fort Lincoln. Rain-in-the-Face is chained and jailed with a white man. It's the same man that was driving the wagon that Charley watched a few days ago.

General Custer hurriedly walks over to Charley, Yates and his brother Tom.

"What did you really say to Two Bears, Charley?" Yates asks.

"I said that Rain-in-the-Face would receive the same treatment as a white man." General Custer listens while nodding.

Tom pipes up, "That isn't all you said!"

Charley eyes brighten, "Oh, I did tell him that we had no intentions of giving Rain-in-the-Face up."

Charley tips his hat to Yates and Tom, "General," he says to Custer, with a brief salute then rides over to the stables.

Tom shakes his head in disbelief, "Has more guts than a wounded grizzly." The others nod in agreement and watch as Charley comes back over.

Charley coughs, "Life's going to be dull around her for a while—think I'll take myself a Steamboat ride."

General Custer nods in agreement, "You've earned it, Charley. Keep in touch."

Tom scrutinizes Charley with a sly look, "You got a woman holed up somewhere we don't know about, Reynolds?" Charley only smiles, then gives a quick wave and walks towards the barracks. George Custer pokes Tom in the ribs, "Knock it off, you know Charley better'n that."

The press explodes the story on every front page. The 7th Cavalry is praised for its bravery and superior handling of Indian matters. Rain-in-the-Face is jailed for trial and vows to kill Tom Custer, cut out his heart and eat it. The story spreads far and wide fueling the flames of mistrust, anger and revenge.

Reynolds spends the winter months doing what he loves best—hunting and trapping between Forts Berthold, Rice and Lincoln, to satisfy the appetites of hungry soldiers who dine regularly on the wild game he brings. While distancing himself somewhat from all matters political, he stays abreast of Indian movements and is not above eavesdropping now and then, particularly at the Standing Rock Agency, where he spends much of his time.

When Rain-in-the-Face escapes two months after his capture, the press quickly spreads the word, cautioning the likes of Tom Custer to be wary of crazed savages. The fires of discontent are fanned to new heights and even Charley takes the warning seriously. But he knows that the coming season will ease the tension. When the Big Muddy is released from her icy bondage, the Indians will leave their winter haunts and spread onto the plains in search of the pte and Wapiti.

The swishing sounds of Spring, break-up the sight of chunky brown masses surging southward, a signal to start planning for warmer weather. After making the necessary preparations and tending to the needs of his horses, Charley rides out to Fort Abraham Lincoln.

The Quartermaster at Lincoln is the bearer of good news. Two more expeditions on the Yellowstone have been planned and the military has requested the service of, none other than Charles Alexander Reynolds. The shy man accepts the assignment then inquires politely as to the itinerary.

The Quartermaster tells him that they will explore the river from the mouth to the head of navigation, surveying its banks and charting the course as they go. Charley is excited to learn that he'll be traveling on the "Josephine" piloted by his good friend, Captain Grant Marsh. In addition, among the interesting assortment of passengers will be General Forsyth and the President's son, Lieutenant Fred Grant.

Knowing how much the Captain enjoys the fresh game from the northern plains, Charley's baggage includes an antelope, a large mule deer and some prairie chickens. Marsh waves at the lone hunter as the Josephine pulls into berth, her freshly painted ribs leaving a swath of green along the side of the dock. Charley waits for the hundred or more officers and soldiers to board the vessel, before hurrying up the plank to shake the waiting hand of the Captain.

That evening, Captain Marsh invites Reynolds to join him for dinner. The waiter brings a chilled bottle of champagne to the immaculately appointed table with its white linen and shimmering silver. He half-fills one glass and waits for the Captain's comment.

"Fill them up," Marsh orders. "I want to make a toast to my guest."

The young man obeys and with a slight bow disappears in the direction of the galley.

"To one of the nicest gentlemen I've ever had the pleasure of dining with," announces the Captain as he raises his glass, waiting for Charley to do the same. "And...by far the greatest huntsman on the Missouri!"

Charley smiles. Despite his maturity he sometimes still finds a compliment unnerving, "Thank you Grant—and to the best riverboat captain who ever sailed the Big Muddy!"

Marsh empties his glass as the waiter sets two generous portions of braised antelope on the table. "I can hardly wait to dig in. It's been awhile since I've had a meal like this."

Charley sips his champagne and watches as his host tears off a chunk of meat and stuffs it into his mouth. He mutters unintelligibly, chewing with the right side of his jaw, then the left, filling his glass as he does.

"Mmm-mm!" says the Captain, finally wiping his mustache with the big white serviette before downing the champagne. "You're not drinking, Charley. What's the matter—the champagne tainted?"

"It's just fine, Grant. I never have acquired a taste for champagne."

"Well, that's all right, Charley. I understand. Besides, that leaves more for me."

A well-dressed sophisticate at an adjacent table, suddenly interrupts the conversation. "My compliments to the chef, Captain, simply delicious. This meat is exceptionally well prepared—enough to tickle the palate of an epicure!"

Captain Marsh acknowledges the comment with a smile and turns to Charley. "Tickle the paddle of a...what did he say?"

Charley nearly chokes over his companion's humorous remark and comical expression. Then the Captain laughing, twists a probing finger into his ear as though it could no longer be trusted.

"I believe he's enjoying his meal but he's got a strange way of saying it," remarks Charley.

"Well, whatever he said, I surely hope he's enjoying it," Marsh concludes. "I don't understand some of these folks—always putting on airs like they were some kind of royalty. Say, Charley," he continues, "after all the years I've known you—what is it now—five, six years?—I must say, I really enjoy your company."

"It's been enjoyable for me too, Grant, even though it is months between visits. I feel like I've found a home here along the Big Muddy."

Marsh's tongue is looser now after his fourth glass of champagne. When the waiter appears he orders another bottle. "You know, Lonesome, since gold fever struck these parts I feel there are big things going to happen"

Charley looks at Grant inquisitively.

"Well, Charley, the traders have been robbing the Indians blind. Not just the Indians either...the soldiers too!"

Charley listens intently as the Captain rambles on. The waiter clears the table and brings dessert and coffee, just as Marsh finishes the second bottle of champagne.

"Bring us some cognac—and cigars too!" he says brusquely to the waiter, who disappears with great haste. "I've been on the river a long time, Son. I went up and down the Mississippi for years and I don't ever remember hearing so much lying, cheating and stories about government graft. Why those bast..." he pauses knowing Charley's dislike of cussing. "There have been times when I delivered empty corn sacks to the Indians, knowing full well that some crook is going to make a profit. Graft, Charley. That's what's running this country now. From here, right on up to the President."

Stopping to sip his brandy, he notices the intense concentration of Charley's bright, blue eyes. He lowers his voice. "Yep. I mean, Ulysses S. himself! His son Fred is aboard right now. He's a likeable young man but you be careful, Reynolds. I'm not so sure we can trust him, what with all I've heard about his Uncle Orville. I overheard talk about extending the reservation boundaries some time ago, just so Belknap and his cronies can control everything—including the Indians!" He pauses to light a cigar. "Lo and behold, this past March, the boundaries were extended—by Presidential order, no less! Mark my words, Lonesome Charley something big is going to happen."

Grant watches Charley as he looks off, like he is thinking. "What is it, Reynolds?"

"When the Thunderbird is big, something great will happen."

"What in the name of hades does that mean?"

"I was just recalling, it wasn't too long ago during a thunder storm. An Indian friend told me, when the Thunderbird goes across the prairie, shooting arrows of flame at the earth."

Grant interrupts. "You're not turning superstitious on me?"

"No! But you've heard how their beliefs come true. You've heard the Thunder, as it rolls on the high plains."

Grant's eyes roll upwards as he nods. He reaches over and picks up Charley's empty glass.

"Go ahead, Grant. I enjoy a little brandy now and then." Charley takes a sip of the flavorful liqueur, then another. "You know, Grant, I've heard some things myself. I've noticed how the prices have increased at the trader's store at Lincoln. Some items are double what they charge at the General Store in Bismarck. I wish I knew what to do about it, Grant."

"I know how you feel. I get so blasted mad, sometimes I could spit nails!" Marsh exclaims, his eyes flashing angrily.

The alcohol continues to amplify the Captain's emotion and Charley is relieved when the waiter brings more coffee. "It's troubling to all of us, Grant," he says, trying to quiet the mood of the conversation.

"Troubling? It's downright discouraging, Reynolds! Particularly for the soldiers and civilians too...out there risking their necks to protect the interests of these crooked politicians!" Grant's look changes and he chuckles, slurring his words. "Maybe a reservation should be set up for someone besides the Indians," he laughs loudly while Charley chuckles along with him.

"For politicians, Grant." As Charley finishes the last of his coffee a group of men gather on the deck singing, "For He's A Jolly Good Fellow."

"Sounds like they want to celebrate tonight, Lonesome. Shall we join them?"

"Thanks, no. I plan on being in the saddle by five in the morning." They rise from their chairs.

"I understand, Charley," Marsh says, putting his arm around Reynolds' shoulder. "I apologize for spouting off. You're a good listener. I hope you'll keep what you heard tonight under your hat."

"You have my word, Captain," Charley assures him. "Good night, Grant."

As the "Josephine's" crew prepares to shove off the following morning, Reynolds and the Captain once again share a few parting words.

Grant smiles. "I'll be looking forward to seeing you again soon. We can always use more game, you know." Then shaking Charley's hand he adds jokingly: "Try not to bring anything that'll tickle that epicure's paddle."

Charley laughs aloud. "See you soon, Captain!"

"It's been a pleasure, Grant," Charley says with a warm smile

Marsh hollers a last warning, "You tell General Custer hang onto his hair. You do the same, Charley."

15

*T*he Lakota Sioux (a family of three bands the Tetons Santees and Yantons) who had abandoned their original Minnesota homeland in the 18th Century were unfriendly by most accounts. Even the Crow and Arickaree approached the Sioux with caution and Lewis and Clark during their travels made mention of the Lakota's aggressive nature. However, the White Man's increasing violation of Indian rights, eventually led all tribes to search for solutions to their problems. It was the Lakota's reputation that placed them in the position of leading a campaign against further infringements of Indian treaties.

Renewed hostility instigated by Crazy Horse, Sitting Bull and others, represented a threat unequaled by previous skirmishes. An alarmed General Sheridan communicated his observations to President Grant, who turned to the Indian Affairs for a resolution. In an attempt to regain a measure of control the Affairs ruled, that all Indian warriors were to be on their respective reservations by January 31, 1876, and remain there until further notice. In turn, the War Department was informed of the mandate and Secretary of War, William W. Belknap, was notified to be prepared to enforce the order if necessary.

Perhaps, unbeknown of, to President Grant, Belknap himself was being observed; not officially at first, but he certainly was under the close scrutiny of a few important Dakota residents. Rumors abounded. Traderships were sold or exchanged for favors to Belknap cronies, and to protect their lucrative investments, reservation boundaries were arbitrarily extended to envelop several agencies and trader stores. Indian rations often disappeared en route to the reservation. Profiteering on the northern plains was fast becoming a way of life among a few greedy newcomers. The Indians were eager to obtain guns, ammunition and liquor and there were plenty of unscrupulous traders willing to fill their requests.

Standing Rock Indian Agency, Dakota Territory—Fall, 1875

Nipping the last fragile leaves from the sparse, brittle brush, a brisk Autumn breeze issues its first warning of things to come. Inside his quarters, Captain Edward Allison, listens as General Carlin, explains the details of his next mission.

"This Eugene Waldorf fellow is an employee of the Standing Rock Agency," says General Carlin pausing to draw on his oversize cherry wood pipe. "We've got to have those records he's carrying. They're the key that'll blow the lid off this scandal!"

"And where do you think I'll find this, Mr. Waldorf, Sir?"

"I have information that he's headed for Bismarck, come Saturday. He's to deliver the documents to yet another upstanding citizen—the Marshall, of all people!"

"Is there a single individual, who isn't connected in some way, to this disgrace?"

"It gets dirtier every day, Captain. It is a disgrace! If you need help in carrying out this assignment, I suggest you contact Custer. Bismarck natives get a little wild on Saturday night as, you know."

"I wouldn't attempt it alone—not now. There's too much at stake. Besides, the Sioux are restless. I've overheard a lot these past few weeks. I'd like to have the services of Lonesome Charley, if possible. He's someone I can trust in almost any situation—has a way with the Indians and no one can match his marksmanship."

"He's Custer's prize scout, Allison. He might not be willing to part with him."

"Well, no harm in me asking, is there?"

"Certainly not," Carlin says, smiling. "Good luck to you, Captain. I'll be anxious for your return. Good night."

Captain Allison arrives at Fort Lincoln to find his old friend recuperating from a slight fever.

"Are you sure you're up to this, Reynolds?" he asks, after repeating the details relayed to him by Carlin.

"You want me to accompany you into a sporting house?" he asks, hoping he had heard the information incorrectly.

"Yeah, the Red Chimney. You mean to tell me you've never been to the Red Chimney, Charley?"

"No."

"Well if you say so—I reckon there's a first time for everything!"

"I'm not sure I understand, Ed. Why would the City Marshall be conducting business in a bawdy house?"

"This doesn't have anything to do with his official duties, my friend. General Carlin said that the old marshal, who's a keen businessman, thought he wasn't getting his fair share of the profits. He's demanded to see the agent's records and threatened to expose a few important people, if he doesn't get his way. I don't know how Carlin fits into the picture, but he says those records are crucial to an investigation that the Indian Affairs is conducting."

Although Grant Marsh's words of last summer remain clear in his memory, Charley is overwhelmed by the convoluted explanation. "I'm glad you came for em," he says, as he begins to dress. "I haven't been much use to the 7th, the past few days. I'm sure they won't miss me for another."

Reynolds and Allison arrive at the Red Chimney shortly after sundown. Charley recalls the words of his father warning of, "the price a man might pay should he venture into such dens of iniquity." He throws back his shoulders and nervously strokes each side of his mustache as they enter the smoky reception room.

Allison mistakenly interprets the gesture, "don't get excited, Charley. We're here for one reason—and one reason only!"

Charley can't control the blush, which Captain Allison finds quite amusing.

"That's all right, Charley. I was only in a place like this once myself. I learned a lesson I shall never...God save the Queen!" he exclaims suddenly. "I don't believe my eyes. There's that Waldorf fellow, now. He's heading up the stairs. Come on, follow me!"

Allison flies up the stairs, three to a stride, with Charley close at his heels. When they reach the landing, Eugene Waldorf, a large packet tucked under his arm, turns to see what's causing the commotion behind him.

"Mr. Waldorf?" Allison inquires.

"I'm Waldorf," he confirms, his frightened eyes peering over wire-rim spectacles. "What do you want?"

"I want that packet you're carrying."

Allison steps up to the confused young man who raises his arms in surrender. The papers fall to the floor and just as the Captain stoops to retrieve them, a burly red-faced gentleman steps through the doorway at the end of the hall.

"What's taken you so long, Eugene? I've been waiting a half-hour for you. Who are these men?"

"I don't have any idea, Marshall. They want the records I brought for you."

The Marshall doesn't waste time in tackling the problem before him. "You mean, they tried to rob you? Well, you just don't know who to trust these days! I just happen to have an empty room in the guardhouse this evening. You're under arrest you, scoundrels!"

Before the Marshall can draw his weapon from its holster, Charley's arms are around the big man's hulk. His new .45 Schofield pistol-barrel, forms a white ring as it presses into a fleshy sweat-beaded temple. A stunned, Eugene Waldorf, obligingly hands his small Derringer to Captain Allison.

"Who in-the-name-of-the-law, are you bandits? What do you want with a bunch of papers? There's not a thing there would interest you, I swear," the Marshall protests, as Charley ushers him backwards through the open door.

"We'll be the judge of that, Marshall," Allison answers. "But first of all, we're going to make sure you don't get them back."

"Get on your knees!" Charley orders, amazed that he sounds like such a bully.

Once their victims are bound, gagged and securely locked in the room, Reynolds and Allison proudly march down the stairs through the door and into the night.

"Sure you wouldn't like to stay around and celebrate our victory, Reynolds?"

Reynolds answers with a smile, as he steps into Rusty's stirrup and swings into the saddle. His sense of accomplishment, after the excitement, is his own private reward. As they head for home, he listens contentedly as his friend babbles about their gallantry; no doubt the War Department will honor them with medals for such bravery, before two characters as dangerous as Waldorf and the Marshall; for showing such restraint in a battleground as evil as a whorehouse! Allison entertains Charley for the duration, laughing away the hours of an otherwise tedious journey.

He is surprised to see Standing Rock appear on the horizon before sunrise.

A week later Charley rides into the agency leading Rusty. He sees many Lakota Indians. Some are in a drunken state, loitering, complaining bitterly about how badly they are being treated. He sees his friend, Little Bear, and several Lakotas talking with a Government dispersing agent and two other whites. They are looking at some skinny mangy spotted cattle. Little Bear glares at the cattle, he and the Indians gesture madly.

The Government man gestures angrily, "That's the best you're gonna get. Take 'em or leave em!"

Little Bear speaks angrily in Lakota, the white interpreter translating, "He says, they stink! The dogs wouldn't eat them!"

The man glares at the Indian when Charley rides forward, "They have a bad smell. Not even the hungry dogs would eat them. He's right."

Little Bear gestures, talking angrily, while Charley speaks for him, "He says you eat them feed them to your family!"

The government man looks daggers at Charley, "Mind your business. It's none of your affair!"

Charley frowns at the man, "You eat them feed them to your family."

More Indians and Whites gather around. The Government man is still angry, "These Indians are going to have hell to pay! We've already received the ultimatum— all Indians caught off the reservation by January 31, 1876, will be considered hostile!"

A trader in the growing crowd speaks up, "The Indians have a treaty, by whose word?"

The man scowls, "Indian Affairs, War Department, and by President Grant!— that should be well enough!"

"Yeah! And what will the army do with violators?" shouts the White trader.

"The cavalry will round them up. Sheridan says, kill them if necessary!" rebounds the angry Government man.

The white interpreter speaks to the Indians who are bitterly angry. They understand the word, "kill." They gesture angrily leap on their horses and ride off. Little Bear and Charley's eyes meet just briefly. Charley gives a quick wave but looks grave, as he recalls his friend's words. "You will fight with White soldiers, Char-Lee!"

The Lakota Sioux had few allies in the White establishment but they had their own sources of information. They saw no imminent improvements on the horizon— only more restraints, more broken promises, more degradation and less food. The White Man's latest order was more than the last threads of dignity could bear. The year of 1876, was off to a bad start, in spite of plans for the country's Centennial celebration.

While at the agency Charley learns that the Indian Agent is preparing for a visit from Orville Grant, the president's brother and Secretary of War, William

Belknap. When the agent sees Charley is about to leave, he hurries toward him with an unusual request.

"Reynolds, I am expecting some guests," he says, a note of exigency in his voice. "I didn't get much warning, but they sent word they're in need of a guide. There isn't anyone else in these parts with your experience. I'd surely rest easier knowing they're in your hands, certainly if they're wandering out yonder amongst the savages."

"How long will my services be needed?" Charley asks. He is anxious to do some hunting along the Cannonball; perhaps meet or find Little Bear again.

"Only a day or two, I'm sure. They've heard so much about the unrest among the Sioux, I believe they want to get a feeling for the Indians' mood, themselves. Something was said about inspecting the new reservation boundaries too."

Charley's curiosity dictates his decision. He agrees to take the job and starts immediately with preparations.

When the dignitaries arrive—a day late due to inclement weather—Reynolds is surprised to learn that they are accompanied by a trader named Parkin, who follows them around like a faithful dog. Charley tries to strike up a conversation with the man, but Parkin is tight-lipped and offers little information. Charley's nature doesn't permit him to pry. After three days of traveling through icy wind and infrangible, fog Orville grant finally persuades Belknap that they should head for home. Parkin seems relieved.

Charley postpones his trip up the Cannonball again when General George Armstrong Custer summons, him to Fort Lincoln the following day.

"I heard about your romp at the Red Chimney, Reynolds," Custer laughs. "Did you enjoy yourself?"

Charley thinks for a moment before answering; there's only one person who could have told Custer. "I had a wonderful time, Sir—but not nearly as much as Captain Allison. Tying up those crooks was easy. Getting Allison out of there was a difficult task, I assure you."

"Well, is that so? Wait till I see Eddy again!" Custer's grin fades quickly. "I need someone to take a dispatch to Bismarck and one to Standing Rock. Can I depend on you Reynolds?"

"Must be something important," Charley replies.

"Everything is important nowadays, Reynolds. But most important is a letter to my friend Barrett, in New York. If all goes well, I'm going to take some leave. Do I have your permission?"

"If you're asking my permission, you surely must be in need of rest, General" Charley responds in jest. "Permission granted! And yes, I'll carry your dispatches. Is tomorrow morning all right?"

"Fine, Charley. Thank you. Give my regards to Allison—that devil!"

Captain Allison's interpretive skills allow him to learn of Indian movements long before most government officials. The Arickaree who have cowed to the Lakota in the past, are now exhibiting aggressive behavior themselves and suddenly, seem sympathetic to warring Sioux. He relays his observations to his friend, Charley Reynolds.

"Charley, I'm uneasy about this Indian business. The Rees are alarmed. The Lakota don't intend to obey that order; they're still up on the Yellowstone. I don't think any of them are planning to go on the reservation."

"They've been gone all summer," Charley replies. "I'm not sure what to make of it."

"One thing is certain, Reynolds. We can't afford another massacre like the one in Minnesota. The Sioux are not gentlemen warriors!"

"I can't dispute that. I'm going on up to Berthold for a while; do a little trapping and try to find out what's on their minds."

"I hate to see you go, Charley. It's dangerous traveling alone. Is there someone else who'd go with you?"

"No. I prefer to go alone. I'm not used to having a sidekick—only my horses."

"Well, you know best. I'm going to miss your company. Say, I have just finished this book. Why don't you take it along with you. I know you'll enjoy it."

"Thanks, Ed. I never seem to get my fill of good reading material. I'll see you in February."

"So long, Lonesome Charley. See you soon!"

Charley and his two red horses move quickly along. He pulls out his timepiece. And thoughts of Ariana drift into his mind, then quickly flash to Running-creek-Woman. He can see her auburn hair, that—that smile. Abruptly, Charley reins up. "Whoa, Red. Easy, Rusty," their ears wiggle in anticipation as they halt. It is 12 noon in this land of the Dakotas. Charley regards his two companions while he ponders, "Why not, we got time," he spurs Red and away they ride.

Red and Rusty sense something familiar and they pick up the pace. Charley chuckles, "Know where we're going don't ya, boys?"

The barking cur dogs warn the village. Running-creek-Woman drops the white tanned skin she works on. She smiles in delight when she sees Charley ride up. She comes running picking up a branch then holding his horses while he dismounts. She hands him the limb and Charley grins as he notices the advancing, growling, snapping pack of cur dogs. Old Patch Eye makes a bold charge in close, then dashes behind, as Charley swings the club, barely missing. "Nearly got yuh," Charley laughs.

From inside Thompson's lodge comes a familiar voice, "Wack those mangy curs, Charley! We'll have 'em for supper. Hold a celebration!"

Charley swings at the other dogs that yip as they scurry away. They stop to eye him from a safe distance while growling. He chuckles then turns to Running-creek-Woman who gives him a yearning look. He is about to embrace her when he sees Thompson come from his lodge followed by Walks-on-Ice. Charley is shy about embracing her in front of the others.

Thompson and his wife smile and wave but Charley can sense that something is wrong. Running-creek-Woman unsaddles the horses and Charley helps her, turning them loose. Red and Rusty whinny contentedly and race off to reacquaint themselves with the horses of the village.

"Ever eat dog, Charley?" Thompson surprises him when he walks over.

"Can't say as I have, Thompson," Charley looks dumfounded.

"Yuh' knows, the Rapahoes ur' noted for the way they cook their dogs. I heard tell they l'arned the trade from the Cheyennes." Walks-on-Ice looks at Thompson skeptically, while Running-creek-Woman looks at Charley. Thompson rattles on and on, "They don't bother to skin em', kinda like the White man scalding a hog. The difference is, the Rapahoe throw the dogs straight into the fire, burn the har right off of 'em. The young bucks sit around licking their chops, waiting for the feast." he pauses for a breath. "Funny part of it all, when the smell of that burned hair is gone and they jerk that charred carcass off'n the fire, and split that awful looking black mess away, the meat looks good enough to eat—right tasty, too." Charley gives a halfhearted chuckle while he shakes his head.

Walks-on-Ice raises her fingers to her mouth, "shhhuh." She clenches together the fingers of her right hand bringing her hand to her forehead. Holding her hand upward she makes a slow horizontal circle to the left then points at Thompson.

Charley bursts out in laughter. He understands what she says. In between outbreaks of laughter he manages to blurt out, "She says your brain is in a whirl, Thompson."

The others join and they laugh for a spell.

Thompson finally stops laughing his countenance turning grave. "Ol' Sittin' Bull 'n his Uncpapa has moved in close to the agency! The hang-around-the-fort Indians act badly frightened."

Charley chuckles, "I call them sugar-n'-molasses Indians. Last I knew of Tatanka Iyotake, he was out in the Yellowstone country."

Thompson gestures. "He plumb scared the daylights outta' the upriver Indians. They finished thar trade 'n moved down river. The alarm has spread clean up and down the river!"

Charley looks around thoughtfully. "Ol' Sitting Bull hates what he calls, the Wasichus. He refuses the white man's handouts. He hates their spotted cattle. Ol' Bull says even the mongrel dogs won't eat the bacon." Charley starts towards the lodge then turns to Thompson with a serious tone, "First time he's moved in from the Yellowstone country so close!" He glances at Running-creek-Woman who walks away. Charley faces Thompson, "I'm headed up river in a few days, it is possible I'll run in to Ol' Bull."

"Yuh watch yer backside, something has braced up the Uncpapa."

His wife interrupts with an outbreak of half angry Arapahoe. Thompson listens closely then nods in agreement. He looks around then gives his woman a stern eye. She utters another outburst. Thompson looks at Charley. "She says we are worse than the old men of the villages who have nothing to do. They go from teepee to teepee, talk all day with the old women." Thompson points towards Charley's teepee, "Yer woman waits for yuh in the lodge. Walks-on-Ice says we will have time to talk, all day, next day. I've only seen her really angry just once," Walks-on-Ice warns him with an austere glance. "I wouldn't want to get her dander up like that again."

"Neither would I," says, Charley. He turns and quick steps to his lodge. He lifts the flap and stoops inside.

Running-creek-Woman stands with her back to him. He quietly embraces her from behind. He then gently runs his fingers through her hair, admiring the auburn luster.

She sighs then quickly turns to him and holds her cheek to his. Their cheeks are warm, moist and soothing. It is a great comfort for her. After several minutes their lips find each other. They kiss like there are no tomorrows. For several minutes her mouth hungrily absorbs his moist lips. She feels like she could swallow him up. Her exploring tongue finds his and she displays soft sighs of pleasure. She's never kissed like that before. Her moans and sighs are relished.

Charley finally pulls away. Tears of joy slowly trickle down her face. He grabs her and for a long while they cling to each other, cheek to cheek.

Charley reaches down and throws a few branches of ash wood onto the fire. Running-creek-Woman looks at him from the corner of her eye while she begins to pack her possessions into some colorfully painted rawhide parfleches. He inspects the baggage curiously, "The Village will move at sunrise. Winter three moons, me all stay long time, maybe?"

"I should have known," he says. He goes to the opening, pushes away the flap then he turns. "I go talk, I will return shortly."

She gives him a funny look. "You go talk." Charley shakes his head when he sees her grin and he steps outside.

The wind has picked up and there is a chill in the air. He looks at the sky and thinks to himself, it won't be long and the snow is going to fly. Thompson comes from his lodge wearing an old army overcoat. Walks-on-Ice is busy by the fire. Charley notices how mature and comely she looks, wrapped in a bright red blanket. Her white deerskin leggings with the blue trade beads are colorful. The beads and dyed red porcupine quills on the instep of her moccasins, sets her off as the stately woman of the band. She is filled with wisdom and her sharp eyes and ears absorb everything.

"When will you move the village, Thompson?" Charley asks.

"Figur'n tomorrow," he warms his hands over the fire.

Walks-on-Ice looks up, "One cold beyond."

Charley looks at Thompson, "She says last winter was bad."

Thompson glances at his wife, "Yeah. You remember, Charley, last winter there wasn't enough grass along the river. Not nearly enough cottonwood bark for the horses. I should have selected a better place."

His wife speaks up running her hand across her throat making the sign of the Sioux, "Nai Chuntu Wakpa."

Charley agrees with a nod, "She suggests wintering on the river the Sioux call Nai Chuntu Wakpa. The white man's Heart River."

Thompson nods his head, "She might be right, Charley. What say you?"

"There's plenty of grazing, it's close to the forts, the trade store—might be she's got a good suggestion." Walks-on-Ice watches Charley from the corner of her eye then cracks a subtle smile as she looks away.

"Tomorrow it is, then," Thompson utters. "Yuh'll go with us?"

"I will," Charley looks above at the sky.

"Tonight we'll have a good feed fer supper. Walks-on-Ice will cook up one of those curs—maybe Ol Patch Eye."

"You want eat dog, you cook," she scolds.

"Now, now I wer only funnin," Thompson chuckles then looks at Charley. "Skewered buffalo loin, turnips, parched corn and and one patch eyed cur." He grins, "Charley, I've got a bottle of whiskey, some champagne left from one of the traders. I'll uncork." He gets a devious look then says quietly, "We'll all have a little drop of the creature."

"It's cold enough I might just have a shot or two of that coffin varnish myself."

Walks-on-Ice warily observes the two men. Running-creek-Woman walks over to the fire. Her smiling eyes look around. Walks-on-Ice can tell that she is happy that Charley has returned. She speaks in Arapahoe and the two women begin to make preparations for the meal.

Charley gazes up as he notices a few snowflakes fall. The others look above. Small flakes begin to trickle down the wind blowing them in little swirls.

Thompson addresses the others with a worried look. "I surely hope it don't turn into one of those full fledged Dakota blizzards." he says wishfully.

"Don't feel so," Charley says, looking at the smoke and flames of the fire, "unless the wind switches around to the north."

"Well, let's get started then. Won't be long'n it'll be dark. Throw some wood on the fire, I'll uncork the jug, Charley."

"To be cautious I'll picket and hobble the horses tonight, Thompson." Charley glances around. "Looks like the women have gathered 'nough wood."

"We need a rip roar'n fire tonight. I feel in the mood." he grins at the others. "I might jest kick up my heels do a little foot stompin'." Walks-on-Ice gives him a cunning look while she and Running-creek-Woman bring some meat to the fire.

Charley goes to look for the horses. He finds them in a low-lying, saddle like dip in the ground not far away. Standing with their heads down, they've eaten their fill for the time being and are resting. "Maybe I'll just leave you boys, snow's coming on 'n you need your energy for tomorrow." The horses watch him then Charley turns and walks back to the fire.

The two women tend the cooking, making occasional glances at their men. They chatter women talk in Arapahoe. Thompson has uncorked the jug and already drinks out of a tin cup. "Grab yer' cup n' I'll pour you a chug."

Charley brings his cup and Thompson pours him a drink, "Might even get yer woman to have a drink."

"After that wrangle with the rattlesnake, I don't know." Charley answers while he shakes his head. Thompson takes a healthy drink then looks skyward, seeing the snowflakes that fall more frequently.

Charley motions with his head and Running-creek-Woman comes over. He offers her a drink. "You try." she is reluctant and shakes her head. "Just a little," he says, holding out the cup. She takes a sip then spits out the liquor.

Thompson chuckles. "Cut it with some wader, mix the two, half ev this n' half dat."

Charley goes to his canteen and dilutes the strong smelling drink. He then gives her another sip. This time she is able to swallow. She rubs her throat, but then smiles at the men.

Walks-on-Ice takes a sip from Thompson's cup then tends the fire. Thompson watches her, "She's had a nip now and then before Charley. Matter of fact she drank the lion's sha..." Walks-on-Ice interrupts him with a scolding glance.

Thompson breaks out in laughter and begins to dance around. "Hi-yaa, hi-yaaa!" He stops and takes another long swig. "I almost forgot," he hurries into the lodge. A few minutes later he brings out a bottle of champagne, pouring some into another cup. "What could be more fun'ner than dancing around the Dakota plains with a couple of wild Indian women. It'll be a hog killin' time!" He skips his feet, almost falling over. He then continues his antics, grabbing Walks-on-Ice, who is hesitant but joins him.

She nimbly skips and hops about, chanting as she motions for Running-creek-Woman to join her. With near perfect rhythm the two of them dance nimbly around the fire. They stop occasionally to sip the champagne.

Thompson takes another stiff belt and joins the women, hopping first on one leg then the other trying to imitate the women's chant as the three of them dance about.

Charley tips his cup and chuckles at the dancers. He recalls the first time he tried to dance with Ariana. He almost spits out his drink when he, remembers how sick he got. He wonders to himself what would it be like if she was still alive. Running-creek-Woman and Walks-on-Ice interrupt him. They tug on his jacket. The two women then grab him, leading him onto the Dakota dirt.

Thompson yells out, "Cm'on, Charley! Let us show them Indians how to kick up their heels." He stops and takes another drink. He then leaps and yells and hops over by the trio.

At first, Charley is reluctant but then thinks to himself, why not? He grabs Running-creek-Woman and the two of them dance about. She is very sprightly but Charley is quite catty himself. He tries and makes a good attempt of imitating her steps.

Thompson yells and claps, grabbing his woman, doing the white man's do-si-do. He trips and falls into the dirt. Walks-on-Ice helps him up. Thompson takes another drink and hangs onto her while they continue to leap about.

Suddenly Walks-on-Ice shouts out loudly in Arapaho. She holds her arms up. The others come to a stop, looking at her. "Shhh..." she says, making the Indian sign for silence.

The others all turn towards the camp and listen. Almost in perfect harmony the cur dogs howl from the darkness. Some set up deep howls. Others yip, sounding almost like a pack of hungry coyotes. It seems as if every cur in the village is yipping and a yapping. Several young boys and other members of the small camp are standing by, curiously watching them.

Simultaneously Thompson and Charley burst into laughter. "Even the cur dogs laugh at us." Thompson yells, tipping his head skyward and giving off howls and yips himself. The dogs of the village turn silent, then almost as an answer to Thompson, they emit another chorus of howls.

"I can hear Ol Patch eye above them all," Thompson laughs so hard he stumbles and falls onto the ground. The others break into laughter as Charley attempts to help his camp keeper to his feet. But Thompson has had too much to drink and he pushes Charley away. "Ol'—Patch Eye he—he knows he's goin'—get his har burnt on the far..." They all continue to laugh except Thompson, who is dead still in the snow.

Walks-on-Ice speaks in Arapaho then rubs her throat. "Ah, the White man's firewater, too much." Charley, a little tipsy himself, stoops to help Thompson.

Walks-on-Ice pulls him away. "Him sleep, leave him."

"He'll get mighty cold out here tonight."

"Cover with blanket. He'll wake up when he is cold. Wake up too soon, he'll get angry."

Charley nods his head as Walks-on-Ice goes to her lodge and brings a blanket and covers Thompson. He understands that Thompson, like many Whites and Indians that he knows, if awakened too soon, they get angry and most want to fight. It won't hurt him and Charley is sure that when he wakes up from the cold of the night, that'll he come running for the warmth of his teepee.

Running-creek-Woman gets some wood bowls and using a horn spoon scoops up their meal. The three of them sit around the fire eating. The women like the champagne and have a couple of hearty sips. Occasionally, they smile and chuckle loudly. They glance at each other and laugh when Thompson kicks out his feet and makes frequent gasps and slurs in his sleep.

Snow continues to fall lightly. By the time Charley and Running-creek-Woman bid Walks-on-Ice a good rest, a white sheet of snow covers the Dakota prairie.

Charley throws some wood on the fire then walks his woman to the teepee. Then leaving her, he goes out to check the horses. About half way there, feeling a little dizzy, he decides they will be all right and he returns to camp and goes inside the lodge.

Inside, Running-creek-Woman is already snuggled warmly in her blankets. Charley checks the woodpile making sure there is enough then begins to undress. He almost falls as he attempts to remove his boots, finally sitting down to complete the chore. It is a struggle and he ends up kicking his trousers off, leaving them lay where they land. He gingerly crawls under the blankets and snuggles beside his woman.

She shrieks when he rubs his cold hands on her. Charley mutters, "Cold feet, warm heart." She kicks out as he tries to put his cold feet between hers. They both begin to chuckle, ending up in uncontrollable laughter. Finally, she allows him to snuggle close and shortly they both fall fast asleep.

Several hours later Charley awakens with a startle. For some reason he feels uneasy. He gropes around for his clothes. Finding them he quickly dresses, slips on his boots and throws some wood on the still glowing coals. He grabs his rifle and prairie belt on the way out of the teepee.

In the early morning, a three inch blanket of snow has lit up the darkness. Charley straps on his belt as he looks around. He gulps in huge gasps of air while he gets his bearings. The fresh chilled air feels good and helps clear his cloudy brain.

The snow has all but put out the fire, leaving only a few smoldering coals. He eyes a large hump lying near the fire. Dark shadowy figures, slither and dart away. Instantly, Charley reaches for his pistol then remembers that Thompson was laying there when they went to bed. He chuckles out loud when he realizes that during the night Ol Patch Eye and a half-dozen of the curs, looking for warmth, had cuddled on top and around Thompson.

Charley continues to chuckle then he quickly makes his way out to check the horses. He seems uneasy about Red and Rusty and the other village horses. It would be just like some of the agency young bucks to go on a horse stealing foray during the night, especially with the new snow and all.

Charley doesn't see any of the animals and he cautiously walks over to where he had last seen them yesterday. The snow is just deep enough and he finds no tracks. He's not real alarmed because he knows that his horses will seek shelter in a ravine or grove of trees. Anywhere they can find out of the wind, which has died down, and the snow is only coming occasionally now. He decides that maybe he's just uneasy about their talk yesterday. What Thompson had said about the Uncpapa moving close to the agency, he had already known, but never the less, he's still concerned. He decides to return to the lodge.

On the way by the fire he notices Thompson all covered with snow and decides to heap the smoldering coals with wood, lots of it. It will take the chill away when Thompson wakes up.

Inside, he undresses and carefully slides beside Running-creek-Woman's body. She leaps wide awake when he touches her skin. She scoots away holding her body away from him until he begins to feel warm. "You sleep, no?" she asks.

"I don't remember. I woke up feeling queer about something."

She looks at him curiously, "White man's firewater."

"It is all right. Everything is..."

"Outside, I listen you laugh."

Charley chuckles then says, "Let us talk at sunrise."

She gives him a pleasing grin and begins to rub her hands on his chest.

Outside their lodge, Thompson yells loud enough to awake the whole village. "You mangy flea bitten..."

Running-creek-Woman cries out startled. Charley rolls beside her and resting on their elbows, they look towards the racket outside.

They can see the light of the now blazing fire through the skin of the lodge. They laugh on hearing yelps and growls and Thompson cursing. They smile at each other when they hear Walks-on-Ice shout, "Only a White Man would build a fire big enough so you can't get near it to warm yourself," she mutters on. "Indian build small fire then warms himself." They see her shadow as she walks over to Thompson. She continues to chatter away.

Under the blankets Running-creek-Woman laughs. Charley begins to laugh with her while they listen to the noise from outside. Soon the whole village is awake.

As Charley and his woman come from their teepee, Thompson struggles to free himself from the blanket. Walks-on-Ice brushes the snow away while he struggles to one knee, looking around. He starts to laugh, "Last thing I recall," he gets a surprised look, then reaches over and grabs his tin cup filled with snow. He brushes and blows the snow away and lo and behold, there is still a drink left perfectly chilled. He raises the cup up. "To all my friends, I must not have drank much last night," he laments, "I'm still thirsty this morning... n' down de hatch." he downs the drink then utters a deep sigh.

Running-creek-Woman and Walks-on-Ice both frown as they watch Thompson swallow the drink. Charley wonders, as they all chuckle, about how the dogs did not tip over the cup?

Thompson begins to scratch his scalp. Walks-on-Ice smiles, "You sleep with dogs, you wake up with fleas." The others join her in the laughter. "You sleep by yourself."

"You laugh now, but I'll get the last laugh when I skewer them flea bitten mutts onto the fire. Come to think of it, winter's here. They are just about good'n fat. Good 'nough to eat." He struggles to his feet. "Com'on, Patch Eye." He whistles, "Here boy—good doggy."

Charley breaks in, "I hate to bring you bad tidings, but I've got to go find the horses."

"They're not gone stolen by some..."

"With the wind and snow I figure they're holed up in some sheltered pocket close by. If they smelled Indians they'd of warned me."

Thompson chuckles, "We got a whole camp full of Indians. How in burning blazes can the horses know which is which?" he bursts out in laughter.

"Both Red and Rusty can tell," says Charley. "It's puzzling, hard to figure out but it is just like their homing instinct. Nobody knows how, but horses will travel two and three hundred miles to their last camp."

"If something don't waylay them," Thompson nods, then clutches his forehead.

"I'll go find the horses. If we are going to make it to the Nai Chuntu Wakpa today, we'd better start making tracks."

Thompson grabs some of the left over supper and begins to eat. The others start packing their belongings, making preparations to dismantle the lodges. Running-creek-Woman watches Charley as he heads across the snow to look for the horses.

She looks surprised when she sees an Indian riding towards camp. She watches with a concerned look. The Indian, she recognizes him as an Arickaree from along the big river. He talks with Thompson. Thompson points to Charley's footprints in the snow. With a quick wave, the Ree, rides off on Charley's trail.

It is not long and the Indian rides from the camp. Running-creek-Woman and Thompson look serious as Charley leads his horses into the camp. "They were holed up just like I thought," Charley stops. Thompson scrutinizes Charley, waiting for him to tell them about the runner.

Charley looks around, "Nothing real troubling, I won't be going to the winter camp." Running-creek-Woman looks disappointed. "I have to go upriver. When I return I will stay longer." With a frown, Running-creek-Woman turns and begins to pack Charley's gear.

Thompson comes closer, "What is it?"

"The Ree brought a note from the Quartermaster. You were right, Thompson. The Uncpapa are reported to be near the agency."

"How in blue blazes did the Ree find you? Just how did he know where to look?"

"You know yourself, Thompson, the Indians seem to find out. How they do it is beyond me. My guess is that several were sent along the river."

Thompson sneers while he nods. "I'll hold the horses, get your saddles." It is not long and Charley is saddled up Thompson waves a quick wave, "See yuh' at the winter camp, Charley. Watch that Auburn scalp lock." He leaves Charley alone to say good-bye to his woman and goes to help Walks-on-Ice, who looks on with a worried look.

Running-creek-Woman brings a pack for Charley, who ties it on the pack horse. He'll ride Rusty today. Charley shoves his rifle into the scabbard then pulls her around behind the horses. He holds her tightly, touching his cheek to hers. He feels her tremble. "It will be all right. Only a few days will pass 'n I'll return." She is worried. He squeezes her tightly then they kiss, her lips feel cold, "It will be all right."

"Return soon," she gives him a tearful glance then holds the bridle strap while Charley mounts up. She watches as Rusty's and Red's hooves kick up their own trail in the fresh blanket of snow. Charley turns and gives her a quick wave.

Something seems out of place to Charley as he rides up to the Berthold Agency, but he can't put his finger on it. Grant Marsh's words once again come to mind and the scene at the Red Chimney flashes unexpectedly to mind. He ponders the mandate handed down by the President. January 31 is not far off and still the Indians are roaming the plains.

"Good afternoon," he says, introducing himself to the new Agent. "Reynolds—Charles Reynolds. I've recently been to Standing rock. I understand the Sioux have been gone from the reservation all summer—that they're up here, trading with the Rees."

"I'm so glad you've come. There, have a seat," says the middle aged looking man, pointing to a rickety stool by the stove. "My name's Darling by the way, Charles Darling."

"Pleased to make your acquaintance, Mr. Darling," Charley replies, shaking the clammy and trembling hand of the nervous Englishman.

"I do hope you're going to stay awhile, Mr. Reynolds. There's bad blood among the Indians, you know. The Army promised us protection but so far there's been none. I see trouble ahead. Sitting bull has never been seen so close to the Agency before."

Charley's voice is calm. "There are some problems, I know. There's a lot of hatred and mistrust between the Sioux and the Arickara. It's been that way for many years, but I'm not sure if the Army can resolve what you call, bad blood."

"Good God, man! This isn't some lame squaw we're talking about here—this is Sitting Bull and the Uncpapa! I'm frightened, Reynolds and I'm not ashamed to admit it. If those Red devils decide to go on a rampage—well, we don't stand a chance here at the Agency. The trader and I aren't much match for a band of wild savages should they attack us. If we can't depend on the Army, I'd feel a lot safer with one such as yourself to keep an eye on things."

"I came here to do some trapping," Charley tells the nervous man.

Darling's chin drops, his bottom lip quivers. "I would pay you well, Mr. Reynolds. You're the best I know. I'll make it worth your while. Please, Reynolds, I'm begging."

Charley refuses to commit himself, saying he will think it over. That night, Darling's pleas echo in his head; he cannot sleep. Charley reasons to himself, he knows Custer does not want any of the agents to get suspicious. But he could keep an eye on the Indians for General Custer. He could also have time to trap. He dresses and proceeds to the Agent's quarters.

"I've changed my mind, Mr. Darling. I can trap but I'll be keeping an eye on the Sioux—Or wait until later on in the winter. The quality of fur will be better then anyway."

"Oh, thank you, Mr. Reynolds. I shall be indebted to you more than I can ever repay."

"Not one word of this to anyone." Charley cautions Agent Darling, sternly.

"Not a word," Darling breathes a sigh of relief.

Lonesome Charley spends all but the last few weeks of winter at Berthold, watching and listening as the Indians come and go from the Agency. He is certain that trouble is brewing but aside from a few skirmishes, perpetrated by overindulgent whiskey drinkers, Darling's anxieties are put to rest. Reynolds returns to Fort Lincoln in late February.

Walking across the parade grounds one cold March morning, Reynolds, George Custer and his brother, Tom are discussing the corruption of the post traders and its effect on the Indians and soldiers. Custer and his wife Libbie have just returned from leave and spent some time in New York with his friend, Barrett.

"I'm happy to have you back, Reynolds. You're on the payroll. I've instructed the Quartermaster," the General says to Charley. "There'll be plenty to keep you out of trouble these next few months."

Suddenly a messenger approaches. "Sir!" he says to the General.

"Yes, Corporal?"

"I have a message, General," the courier says handing a paper to Custer, "an important message, Sir...from the Sergeant-at-Arms of the House in Washington."

"Thank you, Corporal."

Charley notices Custer's expression turn to gloomy seriousness.

"I hope it isn't bad news, General," Charley says, anxiously waiting to hear the contents of the message.

"Wh—What now? What does it say?" fires Tom Custer.

Custer is not happy, "I knew it!" he shouts. "I've had a feeling. Looks like I'll be leaving the garrison for awhile boys."

"Where? What's it about, Autie?" Tom demands to know.

"I have to go to the Capitol to testify before the Heister Clymer hearing."

"Those crooked, scheming thieves!" Tom shouts, stomping his boot into the hard ground.

"Calm down, Tom. Don't get so riled." Custer pauses, deep in thought, before continuing. "I don't like it, but I knew it was coming. I've had some time thinking it over. I contemplated putting it all in writing, sign it and send it to Washington with Terry. But then I wouldn't be there, to defend my own words, should they start manipulating my testimony. I have to be there—in the flesh—and that's that!"

"As your friend General, I hope you'll be careful of what you say around those politicians," Charley says quietly.

Tom's mood has settled somewhat. "That's good advice, brother. We know how powerful the President's men are, don't we?"

"I know—I'll be careful. You can count on it! I certainly wouldn't want to miss out on the coming campaign."

"No, Sir!" Charley exclaims. "I wouldn't want to miss it myself, General."

"It's hard to say what this expedition will accomplish. But as long as Grant has chosen the 7th to round up all the, "hostiles," then I want to be there to make sure it's handled with precision. I think you both will agree—we can't afford to make any mistakes."

"Not even one!" Tom utters affirmatively.

Charley is not surprised that Custer has been summoned to Washington. Marsh was right; something big was going to happen and this would be the beginning. He tries not to show his concern. "That will be quite an undertaking General. Surely, President Grant wouldn't want it to begin without you."

"He might have a different opinion after the hearings, Charley. By the way, I want you to start doing some more reconnaissance. I need to know how many Indians are off the reservation, where they are and who's in charge of the villages. I'll need to know how much ammunition they've got and—well, you know what I need, Charley. I know I can depend on you. Keep me informed—anything you feel important, wire me! Meanwhile, I best be telling the Old Lady about this and start making some travel plans. Hope to see you both at dinner this evening."

A few weeks later in the stables at Fort Lincoln, Tom Custer is embroiled in a friendly argument with his brother Boston and Captains Keogh and Weir, about the breeding of their respective thoroughbreds. Charley has finished grooming his horses and is inspecting some tack, when a sliver of metal slices up under his thumbnail. Wincing, he sucks hard on the injured thumb to ease the pain.

"I'm going to the saddler's to fetch a new picket pin. This one's broken," he says to the noisy debaters, who barely notice that the quiet man is talking to them. "I'll return shortly."

When Keogh decides the discussion is getting too lively, he gets in the last word before changing the subject. "My mustang, Comanche, can outdo all your fandangled breeds!" he boasts. "Say, I wonder how the General is making out in Washington?"

"He left Washington already," Tom tells the surprised Captain. "Libbie told me just this morning that he's in Chicago. She said he's under house arrest. I warned him not to talk too much!" Tom exclaims.

All at once, Reynolds returns with the latest edition of the Bismarck Tribune. "Listen to this!" he says, reading from the paper with a pitch of excitement. "President Grant has the national hero George Custer arrested."

"Let me see that," Tom demands, grabbing the paper from Reynolds. He begins to read aloud: *"Grant's administration is one scandal after another! Impeachment trial for Secretary War Belknap! Custer is arrested in Chicago after implicating the president's brother in the Post Tradership scandal. The President himself may be involved."* He stops for a breath. "Those conniving..."

"That imbecile," responds Weir. "We've all seen the graft cheating the Indians—empty corn sacks, double prices for the soldiers. Politics!"

Keogh's eyes light up, "Grant and Belknap's crooks! Politics! Grants' own brother has already plead guilty, resigned!"

Tom looks off thinking, "What is going to happen now? What about the campaign?"

"Major Reno is the senior officer, isn't he?" Charley asks the stunned soldiers. "Somehow I can't picture him in charge of the regiment."

Tom finally speaks up. "Senor officer is ALL he is. The Major's Army career is a joke. The only thing to his credit, is the fact that he bought a lot of expensive horses for remounts! I can picture him all right," he sputters, "but I can't imagine me taking orders from him."

"Calm yourself, Tom," Keogh pleads. "We'd better find out from the General before we go making any crazy speculation as to who's in charge of this outfit."

Reynolds concurs and the discussion ends abruptly.

The President's administration is in shambles. General Custer had predicted correctly: Grant does not look favorably on the General's zealous efforts to uncover the scandal that is rocking the very foundation of his presidency. He responds by urging the General of the Army, William Sherman, through Lieutenant General Sheridan, to send to the head of the Department of the Missouri, General Alfred Terry, to take the field as commander of the Expedition of 1876. And who will be in charge of Custer's regiment—none other than Major Marcus Reno.

When Custer finally receives official word that he has been, "excused"' from the campaign, he is very angry. Nonetheless, the flamboyant young commander isn't about to give up easily. He wants to be in charge of the campaign. In his mind there is none other more capable than himself; moreover, few of his superiors would argue that point. Custer, possessing enough sense to pursue his goal quietly and according to protocol, makes good use of the tools of modern communication. For weeks the telegraph offices at Chicago, St. Paul and Washington buzz as Custer's superiors consider the outcome of the campaign without their, "bad boy general." They are reminded more than once, of the $200-a-night fee offered Custer, by a New York firm, to fill several speaking engagements. In addition, publishers who literally begged for the General's stories were sympathetic, and regularly agreed that Custer had every right to be outraged at the punishment handed out by Grant.

After calculating the dangers of allowing his nemesis to roam about the country flapping his jaws, Grant reluctantly revises his original assignments, restoring the persistent George Armstrong Custer to commander of his own regiment.

Meanwhile, out in Dakota Charley comes to Thompson's camp. He is greeted but the others are heavyhearted. Running-creek-Woman looks up from her beadwork on the white buffalo hide. She gives a half smile and helps unpack the horses.

Suddenly Ol Patch Eye darts in behind Charley and not only bites him but also tenaciously hangs on. Surprised by the suddenness, Charley yells and whirls around, kicking his leg. Thompson runs over yelling, kicking out at the dog, "You mangy cur, patch eyed knot head—yer' a goin' on the fire!" Charley kicks again and the dog yelps and scurries for a hiding place.

Thompson hurries back while looking at Charley with a serious look. "You all right?"

"Just a nip, nothing to cry about." Charley begins to laugh.

Thompson gives a halfhearted smile, "Indian runners came. Running-creek-Woman is upset—the whole camp is!" He glances over to where Old Patch Eye disappeared, "Even the curs sense something is astray."

Charley looks around then nods with a serious look. "They find out faster'n our telegraph."

"Blasted politics, Charley! What's gonna' be the outcome?"

Charley only looks then, "They've got rifles, ammunition."

Thompson angrily kicks at the dirt, "I've heard!—There's a call all up and down the Missouri—clean to Fort Robinson 'n the Spotted Tail Agency in Nebraska."

Charley looks over at Running-creek-Woman, "Hundreds, maybe thousands are leavin' the agencies. I have a feeling they'll make a stand!"

Thompson gazes at Charley then walks to his lodge, leaving Charley alone with his thoughts.

Spring has sprung across the land of the Dakotas. It is the grass moon, April, when Charley and Running-creek-Woman, with their belongings come to the sequestered valley. New life buds everywhere and fresh, green undulations of prairie bursts forth. She sets up the lodge while Charley walks up to the vantage point to meditate. She watches him when he takes out his timepiece, staring at it for some time.

After finishing the lodge, she makes sure the camp is in order. Running-creek-Woman goes into the lodge. A few minutes later she emerges, wearing a scarlet blanket draped around her shoulders. She walks up and joins Charley. He stares at her then tries to ease her seriousness, "You look very comely."

She looks perplexed, "Comely?"

"Fine-looking! The color of your hair, the blanket, you look striking. Eight tanned buffalo robes for the blanket." She nods a half smile.

Charley smiles at her then continues to stare off across the prairie. After a long time she quietly speaks, "Councils are held. Runners go to the four winds. The people are divided. Many join Tatanka Iyotake!"

For several minutes Charley collects his words, just when she has something to say, he looks at her. "It is bad. It is troublin'. No one knows the outcome."

She becomes a little angry. "Palefaces! With the crooked tongue of a snake, speak to the people. They lie."

"Politics! Settlers want the land, they want gold," is Charley's answer.

"Pol-a-tic." she enunciates.

"Like your people, the Arapaho, long time past. They argue then split. Become enemies, fight with the Cheyennes then join together, make war on the whites."

She looks away, "I watched you look at the shiny, yellow shell. Your eyes look far away."

Charley is astonished and speaks out loud, almost for his own benefit. "How

180

could you know?" He looks away then surprises even himself, "Do you feel a man can love two women?"

She doesn't understand and looks puzzled, "Lo-ve?"

He reaches over and touches her heart, "How we feel, here."

She raises her arm, "How."

Charley coughs, "Not how. What we feel for each other—like brothers, like sisters, you and Walks-on-Ice—friends growing up together."

She now understands the Indian expression. "Like friends growing up together. Brothers."

"Not quite, almost the same." He nervously clears his throat, "I wish to talk about the other woman."

Running-creek-Woman nods in understanding. The words come hard for Charley. "She meant very much to me—I still carry good feelings in my heart for her." Charley holds his hand near his heart, "She has been gone two snows."

Running-creek-Woman is deeply touched. She gazes above while she gathers her thoughts. "Long time past," she makes the sign for a little girl. "Grandfather traded with men from the great water. Grandfather gave me a shiny, shell necklace."

Charley looks puzzled, "French traders from the Pacific Ocean?"

She is surprised, "You know these people?"

Charley shakes his head, "Show it to me."

"It was lost."

She opens her blanket and holds out a beautiful pearl abalone, Mexican, silver necklace she is wearing. "Grandfather rode three sleeps to find the traders.—I will always remember the shiny, shells on the lost necklace."

He admires the necklace, "This one is beautiful."

She nods, "It is not the lost one."

When Charley finally grasps her meaning, he shakes his head in wonderment at her wisdom. "It was always hard for me to talk about what I feel inside. With you it is easy. You know my heart." He takes her hand and they walk down and go into the lodge.

Several days later Charley walks to the river. He looks troubled as he watches the Big Muddy flow past. Unnoticed by Charley, she watches him. She quickly disappears behind the lodge and vomits. After making sure her face is clean, she walks out and joins him. "Your heart is on the ground," she gestures.

He nods then musters his courage, "I go with the horse soldiers."

She looks at him, upset, "What does this mean?"

"I will guide the Soldier Chief. Like the wolf scouts of your people, like the Sioux."

"Long Hair! The one the Absaraka call, Son Morning Star. He kills many of the Sioux, the Cheyenne. He led the Bluecoats to Black Kettle's village. My people died at the Washita."

"Black Kettle's warriors killed many unarmed settlers. They had White captives. His warriors were trailed to the village." Charley pauses waiting for her reaction. She is quiet. "One of the women cut a White baby boy from his stomach to his neck, then threw him in the snow to die, so the soldiers could not return him to his family. Long Hair, as you call him went against orders. He ordered his soldiers not to kill women and children, only those who shoot at them. Only those who try to bring them harm."

Running-creek-Woman looks away angry then tears well up into her eyes, "Long before the settlers came, the people lived on the land."

"I know what you say. It is hard to know what to do. The soldiers don't make the orders, they just do their job."

"When the warriors leave the camp their women are afraid for them. They sing brave heart songs for courage."

Charley reaches for her, gathering her in his arms. They embrace cheeks for a long time.

Thompson's camp is solemn as Running-creek-Woman and Charley ride in. Charley eyes the fire with a look of surprise. It appears that Thompson has skewered one of the curs on a spit over the fire. Charley looks at Thompson who carries a smirk. "I hope it's not Ol' Parch Eye," Charley says to himself.

Charley and his woman dismount and began unloading the travois. Busy at his task, Charley doesn't notice as Running-creek-Woman disappears behind a lodge to vomit. Walks-on-Ice watches then comes to her with a worried look, "You have the morning sickness." Running-creek-Woman gazes long and hard across the plains. Walks-on-Ice feels her friends' stomach. "Have you told him you carry his child?"

Running-creek-Woman contorts her mouth, shaking her head finally breaking into a blubber. Walks-on-Ice gives her a comforting shoulder, "You must tell."

Running-creek-Woman shakes her head, "He would be troubled."

"You must find a way. You carry his child."

Running-creek-Woman finally begins to compose herself. She looks away while she ponders. Turning back to Walks-on-Ice she sighs, "Talk paper—we send him the talk paper." Walks-on-Ice looks puzzled as she ponders and nods her head.

"Your Thompson can make the white man's mark on the little white book."

"Our people the Arapahoe, our name—we are called Mother of all tribes. You will become his child's mother. You must tell."

Running-creek-Woman shakes her head. Walks-on-Ice senses that Running-creek-Woman is afraid, "I will speak with Thompson about the talk paper."

Running-creek-Woman thoughtfully looks, "Thompson, he show me how to mark talk paper?" Her friend looks relieved and they walk from behind the teepee.

Several days later the others watch as Charley and Running-creek-Woman saddle his horses and get his pack ready.

Thompson hands Charley a diary. Charley looks at it then puts it in the pack. "Don't forget, Charley, write on the talking paper." Thompson smiles at Running-creek-Woman and makes the writing sign. "I will show her how to understand the marks on the talking paper." Running-creek-Woman returns Thompson's smile.

"I will." nods Charley.

Old Patch Eye comes out of nowhere and makes a quick dart for Charley. Thompson kicks out at the cur yelling, "You flea-bitten tick-eatin'—come winter you'll roast on the fire!" Charley scans the empty spit over the fire.

"It wer only a yearling antelope." Thompson chuckles at Charley's surprised look. "You've kinda got used to Old Patch Eye, have you?" He waits for Charley's nod then carries on, "I don't have to tell ya', Charley, hang on to yer' hair. It's the biggest campaign ever. If the government would deal fairly with the tribes, we shouldn't worry so. Army has the feelin' the Indians will scamper back to the reservations."

Charley shakes his head and gives Thompson a serious look. He then goes into the lodge with Running-creek-Woman.

Inside she turns and faces him, "You are happy when you hunt the danger." Charley looks at her kindly. She leans down and from her belongings she lifts an antelope hair robe. When she straightens up, she grimaces in pain and clutches her stomach. Charley looks startled but she holds out a white jacket, handing it to him. He admires the brain tanned, buffalo skin, soft as velvet. He feels it, rubbing his fingers over the fine beadwork.

She touches the colorful beads on the shoulders of the jacket. "Wear it when you hunt buffalo. Pony tracks on the buffalo trail. A good sign, heap."

Charley beams as he studies the shoulder strips. Carefully put together in the shape of hoof prints, are the intricately sewn yellow pony tracks. The tracks follow the little brown patches of beads that symbolize the buffalo. Solid blue beads, symbolizing the Indian's sky, surround the yellow and brown, sun and earth colors. Charley is elated, as he puts it on, he marvels when it fits him perfectly. He looks at her tenderly, "There is something I want to say."

She looks anxious and puts her fingers to his lips, "This lo-ve you say we feel in our hearts," she touches her chest. "My heart feels lo-ve for you." She gives that little half smile.

Charley's heart skips and he embraces her hard, holding her for a long time. He then pulls away but it's difficult for him to talk. "I have to do this. I've been preparing for it for a long time. I'd sooner di..." She begins to speak but he interrupts.

"I have to tell you... The first time ever I laid eyes on you... The first time ever I saw your smile I..."

She blurts out, "Our people are called Mother, of all tribes." She holds her arms across her stomach. A tear slowly trickles down her face.

Charley looks at her tenderly but he is puzzled about what she said. He doesn't grasp what she had tried to tell him. He then embraces her.

Thompson holds the horses while Charley reluctantly steps into the saddle. He quickly waves then rides away. He suddenly pulls up, then reins around and returns.

He tenderly looks at Running-creek-Woman, who stands beside the others. His words are spoken very lovingly, "You are a special woman."

She looks puzzled. Thompson looks at her, "He says you are a special woman."

Tears well up into Running-creek-Woman's eyes. She looks at the tear filled eyes of her sister, Walks-on-Ice. Charley dismounts and motions her over. Running-creek-Woman fairly leaps into his arms. Charley gazes into her eyes, "I forgot something," he tenderly holds her head, placing her cheek to his. For a long time she clutches him. While their cheeks cling together he slowly strokes her hair.

Then abruptly he turns and mounts up.

Thompson notes his wife's glance then looks at Running-creek-Woman, "Charley means to say he loves you."

Charley quickly waves and rides away. The others watch for a while then Thompson goes about his work.

Running-creek-Woman continues to watch. Walks-on-Ice softly asks, "Did you tell him that you carry his child?"

Running-creek-Woman looks down, shaking her head. She then looks back for Charley. The two sisters begin to sing a braveheart song. Finally they are unable to utter the words. Sobbing uncontrollably, in the Indian manner, they embrace each other cheek to cheek.

Charley is out of sight now, having disappeared over the last ridge. Running-creek-Woman feels her stomach as Walks-on-Ice leaves. She stands alone, looking over the land of the Dakotas, wondering when her Charley, father of their unborn child will return.

May 17, 1876, Fort Abraham Lincoln, Dakota Territory

Under the Department of the Missouri's Commander, Brigadier-General Alfred Terry, the heroic 7th Cavalry has been directed to corral the "Hostiles," and return them to their reservations—Destination: Westward to Montana Territory.

A procession two miles in length and designed to outshine the most spectacular of July Fourth parades, moves slowly westward leaving Fort Abraham Lincoln behind in the morning mist. There is music in the air, compliments of the famous 7th Cavalry band, all mounted on their high-stepping gray steeds. They are playing, "The Girl I Left Behind," as General George Armstrong Custer, riding at the head of the column, exchanges loving glances with his beautiful wife Elizabeth. The cavalry, the infantry and the scouts, here as well with her handsome husband James, follow Margaret Custer Calhoun closely. There are pack mules, artillery and too many wagons to count. The colorful Indian scouts dressed in their finest attire are uttering mystical chants of war. It is an awesome sight indeed.

Twelve troops of mounted soldiers, each one easily identified by the color of its mixtures of high-bred, range-bred horses, are led by the blood bays, the grays, while the browns, the blacks, sorrels and bays and last, but not least, the mixed-color troop, complete the roster.

Big Red steps high and proud as he responds to the call of the trumpet. His rider exhibits all the quiet confidence of the man he is reported to be: *The greatest huntsman and scout to ever ride the western plains—Charles Alexander Reynolds!* Dressed in a striking white buffalo skin jacket with modest fringes and colorful Indian beadwork, he leans slightly in the saddle to make sure his light-blue Army trousers are tucked neatly into his tall riding boots. Across the pommel of his McCellan Army saddle rests a cal. 50-70, 1863, Sharps carbine. Strapped around his waist, his prairie belt holds his new .45 caliber, Schofield pistol. His "Big Fifty" long-range Remington, protected by a buffalo-hide scabbard, is tied securely onto the saddle. The beautiful beaded sheath is a parting gift from his friend, Little Bear.

Red suddenly neighs loudly, his head moving from side to side; ears twitching. "Don't be pretending to be all high and mighty, old boy, just because Rusty has to trail along with the beef cattle and spare horse remuda." At the sound of his master's reassuring voice, the big claybank horse immediately settles into an easy gait, as the 7th pushes west on its march across the Land of the Dakota.

Reynolds allows his mind to meander, recalling his experiences on past campaigns and expeditions. The 7th Cavalry was by far the most impressive of all and today, as the sun is breaking through the mist Charley feels a sense of pride and camaraderie such as he's never known before.

Libbie Custer looks behind at the column. She looks in awe at the strange aberration in the sky. She gazes around to see if she was the only one who witnessed the powerful sight. No one else seemed to notice.

Straightening his somewhat rounded shoulders, Charley's serious sapphire eyes mirror the blue beads of his jacket, as they scan the length of the command.

The 7th sets up their camp thirteen miles west of Fort Abraham Lincoln. The soldiers are happy to be on the trail again, although their pay has been withheld until now. When the last tent passes inspection, they converge on the paymaster's wagon like a horde of schoolboys, invading an unattended candy store.

"Don't Push!" one complains to the other behind him.

"It ain't me doing the pushing, private."

"Hush your mouths!" screams the paymaster. "I hate to see grown men acting like a pen full of noisy hogs."

"We just want our money," comes a plea from the back of the pack.

"You ain't got nothing to spend it on," counters the paymaster. "What's the hurry? Custer made sure you whiskey soaks didn't waste your money on rotgut whiskey and whores in Bismark! Ya' ought to be glad."

The man with the money is correct of course; unless there happens to be a poker game in the offing, which there often is. Lonesome Charley watches the young men's moods change quickly, from pushing and poking, to jesting and joking.

"I'll bet you've never played poker!" challenges one confident-looking corporal.

"Yeah—well I heard you lost your shirt the last time you played."

"He lost more than that!" interrupts a sarcastic one.

Soon they are all laughing and plans for the next game are underway. A soldier by the name of Stone notices Charley standing near the wagon.

"Care to join us, Mr. Reynolds?"

Charley smiles. "No thank you," he answers. "You fellows are too swift with those cards. I'm afraid you'd take advantage of a novice such as myself." The Scout explains further that he has a meeting with the General and bids them good night.

After Custer delivers a briefing to his officers and scouts, Charley and the others leave the Custer tent so the General and his wife can spend some quiet time together. Libbie will return to headquarters with Maggie and young Autie Reed's sister, little Emma, in the morning.

Reynolds rolls out his canvas and sitting cross-legged, begins to write in the diary given to him by Walter Gooding the Custodian at Fort Lincoln:

"May 17 1876—Traveled west over high rolling prairie. Camped at Heart River." Then noticing the inscription on the front page he stares thoughtfully at the words contemplating their meaning. *"Charley Reynolds may your shadow never grow less."* A nice compliment he muses, checking his watch. No wonder he's tired!

Before the bugle sounds reveille the enormous camp has begun to stir. When the first whiff of coffee drifts from the cook's tents, the troopers and horse strikers have already watered and grained their officers' mounts. Private John Burkman, Custer's faithful horse striker, and known as the "dog robber," grains Custer's two prized mounts, Dandy and Vic. Suddenly the camp is alive with activity as hungry Horse Soldiers line up for their breakfast at their respective fires.

Not too many minutes later, Chief Trumpeter, Henry Voss, is given the word to sound Boots-and-Saddles and before the final note's echo is heard, Charley has finished brushing and graining his two prized buckskins. He can hear Sergeant-Major William Sharrow and the company's First Sergeants shouting the commands to their companies.

"Get them wind suckers ready, soldiers! Look proud lads, look proud!" urges young Lieutenant Sturgis.

"Move it men," hollers another. "You sure don't want to be last—eatin' everyone else's dust. Move it or you'll get a double ration of Uncle Sam's seed cakes!"

With routine and calculated swiftness bridles are buckled snug; backs of horses are cleaned; as if one motion, 689 blankets and saddles are lifted through the air and settle onto the backs of the horses. Large tin cups rattle, saddle leather creaks, and horses whinny and sigh as girths are cinched tight. Carbines and pistols are checked and rechecked; ammunition is made secure in the pouches. Then comes the familiar decree from Sergeant-Major Sharrow: "To the horse!" The order blares across the Heart River Valley as young men and seasoned veteran cavalrymen alike move quickly to line up at the heads of their horses. They wait, alert for the, "Prepare to mount!" As the order is repeated down the line by each First-Sergeant, every cavalryman grabs his left stirrup. When the final command is uttered... "Mount!"—the nearly seven hundred men swing into their saddles with the precision of a well-made timepiece.

Reynolds has decided to give Big Red a rest today and is mounted on his spirited companion Rusty. Charley can see Custer's flag bearer, Sergeant Hughes, Captain Tom Custer and Lieutenant Cooke all mounted on a slight hillside to the north. Off to the south, some distance away, is the main column of the 7th. Lieutenant Calhoun and his wife Margaret are sharing an embrace; the General and Libbie too. Charley instantly recalls his last embrace with Running-creek-Woman. He can see the paymaster waiting patiently beside his wagon for the women he'll carry back to the garrison. Tom and Cooke amble over from their positions to bid adieu to Maggie, Emma and to the pretty Libbie, whom they lovingly refer to as, the Old Lady. Hesitating as long as possible, Charley finally slaps Rusty's rear and rides toward the group just as the Paymaster is helping the General's wife, Maggie Calhoun and Emma Reed into the wagon.

"Charley!" Libbie cries when she sees him ride up. "I've been looking for you. You'll watch out for the General, won't you?"

"Now Libbie," Charley reassures her with his usual calming tone, "don't you worry." He tips his hat, "Maggie—Emma."

Young Autie Reed, a good-looking 18-year-old with a novel smile, waves from horseback to his sister. He's all smiles and is extremely excited. It's his first jaunt onto the plains with his three uncles.

Charley looks around and watches Captain Benteen and Major Reno both look indifferent as they wait in front of their respective wings. Reno scowls at civilian interpreter, Fred Girard. In Custer's brief absence to testify at the Clymer hearings, Reno was in command of the regiment. He had replaced Girard. But Custer had restored Girard to duty. Major Reno looks at Captain Custer, another of his sore spots. The Major did all he could to harass and put in their so-called place Tom's energetic and fun loving, Company C soldiers. Tom's men have built a strong dislike for the Major.

Captain Frederick Benteen carries a good Civil War record. He is a good soldier but with an immediate dislike for his commander, George Custer. Charley wonders whether Benteen resents that a younger man is over him, or not. From his first meeting with Custer, Benteen has built a strong dislike that festered into a jealous hatred for the man.

Even though Benteen himself fought against his "southern brother'n" as he called them, and Custer fought against the south, southern pride runs deep and this may have had something to do with Benteen's feelings against George Custer. And then there was the Washita affair. Charley wasn't at the Washita, but had heard the tale from several officers who were. Even though Major Elliott took it upon himself to ride off alone and was slaughtered and horribly mutilated, along with fifteen other soldiers, Benteen blamed Custer.

As Charley wonders about the scowl on Benteen's face, he contemplates a verse in the Bible from his younger days. Proverbs, he thinks, "Jealousy is rottenness to the bones." It seems to fit, Charley says to himself. The premature white haired Captain watches in disgust, the delay of the good-byes to the "Custer clan," as he calls them.

The General returns his wife's wave as John Burkman holds onto Vic's halter. Charley contemplates Custer's words to Burkman, "A soldier has to serve two mistresses; while he's loyal to one the other must suffer." He turns to Charley and says soberly, "Let's head west, Lonesome Charley!"

Charley's momentary recollection of Running-creek-Woman's parting words to him triggers a sympathetic response for the controversial commander. "I understand what it's like to say good-bye to someone you love, General."

Custer is taken by the sincerity of his Chief Scout's comment. "I'm obliged Reynolds—Thank you, very much."

As the paymaster's wagon pulls out of sight, Custer spurs his horse then riding toward his flag bearer he yells for all to hear: "For-ward! Yo-oooo!"

Charley whirls Rusty and rides hard for the front. The mood of the men is solemn as the regiment advances briefly into a gallop. The scouts and vedettes ride past the regiment. For sixteen officers and four civilians this is a final good-bye—and good-bye forever for not only them, but for nearly three hundred more hardy soldiers riding behind. It seems out of the ordinary that good-bye forever was at the Heart River. Oh, how many hearts were to be broken. They couldn't know that the muffled sound of hoof beats in the Dakota dust, was echoing their final mark on the soil at the Heart River.

16

U nder threat of impeachment, William Belknap had stepped down from his position in the War Department. Orville Grant, the President's brother, had resigned his position.

Ulysses S. Grant was perhaps disgusted by the misdeeds of his underlings; but the fact that they got caught was inexcusable. Additionally, he was infuriated by the brazen testimony laid before the Clymer committee by one George Armstrong Custer. The young General had implicated a number of other top-ranking military officers, forcing the President to re-evaluate his entire administration. He would like to have punished Custer publicly, but chose instead to hold his tongue, saving his most caustic remarks only for ears he could trust. In fact, he gave the appearance that by ignoring the proverbial thorn in his side, the nuisance would simply disappear. He was wrong, of course.

Washington's climate, on the surface at least, appeared cooler by the time the Expedition of 1876, left Fort Lincoln. However, "Grant's Revenge," as it was termed in the newspapers, remained a popular topic for discussion and provided ample ammunition for Grant's opponent in the upcoming presidential election campaign. But as far as the Indians were concerned, embarrassment of one or two government officials even the President himself, was little solace for past malfeasance. The storm cloud of controversy had spilled over the walls of Washington politics and now hovered over the broad plains of the Indian nation.

It was times like these that a good scout's talents were inestimable. Lonesome Charley Reynolds, probably the most talented of all, was well known to the Army. Brigadier-General Alfred Terry referred to him as, *"the most trustworthy scout on the Missouri,"* and there were others in the private sector who regularly echoed that sentiment. For months, Reynolds had quietly observed the various Indian bands as they moved up and down the Big Muddy and he faithfully relayed his findings to the General. Rumor and speculation mushroomed as travelers in the Montana Territory reported sighting the same bands as far away as the Tongue and Powder rivers and along Mizpah and Pumpkin creeks. And they were seen on the Rosebud too; even along the Big and Little Horn Rivers which flow into the Yellowstone. One thing was certain, in Reynolds' mind though; he knew the massive concentration of Indians couldn't stray far from these major watersheds without jeopardizing the strength of their war ponies. The large herds could not subsist on the trickle of the small creeks and seasonal washes.

Charley's immeasurable worth as a hunter too was a bonus rarely enjoyed by the military. The new men of the 7th Cavalry would soon realize the quiet man's skills— which seasoned veterans such as General George Custer had known and appreciated for years. His wife, Libbie, appreciated and wrote in her diary about Charley.

"Alone this young man with the frank face and big blue eyes would start off into Indian land with only his horses for company when even our officers accustomed as they are to hardships were forbidden to go."

Ten Miles West of the Little Missouri, Dakota Territory, May 31, 1876

A blood-red sun erupts into the sky, its wake oozing across the dry plains of the Sioux Nation. A lightning bolt strikes the ground igniting a small prairie fire. A sleepy herd of buffalo stampedes unexpectedly as their dust and the smoke from the prairie fire blanket the horizon. Several crows, a magpie and some meadowlarks have gathered in the sparse theater of sagebrush to celebrate the dawn—a phenomenal display of orange and crimson haze. Their songs are lost to the winding ravines and rugged draws of the harsh land. The unyielding path of the Little Missouri River parts patches of chokecherry, bulberry and wild plum. Over the centuries, "Little Muddy," has carved a jagged scar—nearly a mile wide in places—on the Dakota landscape. From the tall buttes to the churning waters in the canyons below, this is Little Muddy's legacy—the, "Badlands."

On his way back to camp from a scouting foray, Charley watches a lone horseman riding towards him. He kicks Red out to a dead run, riding directly at the youngster whom he recognizes as Autie Reed. The youngster pulls up and whirls his horse around kicking him, heading for camp. "Whoa up, Reed. Whoa up! It's me, Reynolds."

Reed reins to a stop breathing a sigh of relief as Charley rides over. "What in the devil are you doing out here alone? If the General or Captain Tom finds out."

Reen is excited. "I stole out of camp. Yesterday, when we passed those rocks Uncle Autie pointed out some Rocky Mountain sheep."

Charley shakes his head. "N' you want to take a crack at getting one?"

"Please, Mr. Reynolds? I've never shot one."

"All right, but we have to hurry. Stay behind me."

With Autie Reed helping, Charley hurriedly skins the capes of three Rocky Mountain sheep, ties them on his saddle and looks at the youngster. "When we get close to camp, you'd better sneak back the same way you came. Did the picket guard say it was all right?"

Young Autie beams then gets a surprised look, "How did you know I talked to the guard?"

Charley smiles, "I was your age myself once."

"Thanks, Lonesome Charley." Reed kicks his mount and rides for camp.

"Rider coming in!" yells the guard when he spies Reynolds riding from some distance.

"Yeah. It's Charley and Big Red. I can tell the way he's riding," comments Sergeant-Major Sharrow. He turns and shouts to the guards on the picket line: "Rider coming in! Pass the word...its Lonesome Charley!"

After dismounting, Reynolds unties the heads and capes of the bighorn sheep from the back of his saddle and asks one of the horse strikers to take care of Big Red.

Outside the regimental tent, General Custer is talking to Captains Keogh and Weir and his two brothers Tom and Boston. Captain Thomas Benton Weir had been with the 7th since it's forming on July 28, 1866. He fought with Custer at the battle of the Washita and was, and still is, a faithful friend of Custer and his wife Libbie. He commands Company D.

As Charley approaches, the General speaks up.

"Reynolds—we heard the shots. I figured it was you. I've heard your, "Fifty," and my own too many times to be mistaken."

Thomas Weir nods to Charley, "You've got fresh meat."

Charley nods to Weir and the others then turns to the General. "I could use a couple of hands to get the meat," Charley says with his usual smile He hands one of the sheep capes to George Custer. "This one's yours, Sir. It should make a first-class head mount."

"Are you sure, Lonesome?" Custer asks. "This is one of the finest Rocky Mountain Sheep heads I've ever laid eyes on!" he exclaims, inspecting both horns and the shape of the huge nose. "Are you sure you want me to have this one?" he asks again.

"If you can find room on your wall between that antelope and the white owl," Charley answers grinning proudly.

"For this trophy," Custer says flipping the brim of his hat, "I'll make room! I am surely obliged, Reynolds."

Once the troops commanders relay the orders tents are dismantled, wagons loaded and soldiers mounted smartly upon their high-stepping horses. Proudly leading his outfit, Custer waves as Reynolds takes leave to scout the trail ahead.

After riding for an hour Charley finds himself daydreaming again. It's been a few long days and he feels Red weakening to the challenges of the rugged terrain. He checks his timepiece. He reins his horse around, heading back to give the commander his report.

"Well, Lonesome, what did you find out there in the wilderness?" Custer asks.

"It's rough General. One hill after another."

"Any Indian sign?"

"I found a couple of willow shelters along a stream just beyond that butte over there."

Custer looks in the direction of the scout's outstretched arm. "Is that all?"

"It was a small party. Moved out not long ago." Charley begins to button his jacket. "Is it turning cold?"

"It does feel a bit colder," replies the General, shaking his shoulders and turning his collar up.

"Sure beats the Capitol though, doesn't it?" When Custer reserves comment, Charley drops the subject. "It's going to be hard on the wagons. We may have to build some bridges."

"Yeah Reynolds...it sure is better than being cooped up in Washington."

"I read all about it in the newspapers. If it's true what they say...well the country's being run by a bunch of crooks!"

"It sure seems that way. But now, with Belknap out of way and Orville Grant resigning and pleading guilty, maybe they'll get things straightened out. But you know what really gets my dander up?"

"What's that, Sir?"

"All of us in the Army risking our lives; our families suffering hardships while people in our own government, who should be behind us, they're the ones who are letting us down!"

"They've let the Indians down too. Not only do they overcharge the soldiers, they're really gouging the Indians!"

"I know what you mean, Charley. The Indian is being pushed around, the greedy Whites are taking their land, and now these crooked traders are selling them half-barrels of corn and flour."

"And that's only the half of it," Charley adds. "When I was at the Standing Rock awhile back, the Indians were getting empty barrels and being charged for full ones. The traders were selling the corn and flour elsewhere; charging the government and doubling their profits." Suddenly Charley reins up. "I see a prairie chicken."

The General nods. Reynolds dismounts, grabs his rifle and walks some twenty-five feet before he fires. When he picks up his headless trophy he finds there is not one but two dead birds. Apparently the second victim was behind the first, taking the shot through the neck. He quickly guts the birds, hurries back to his horse and ties them to his saddle.

"Sorry I interrupted, General," the scout says, slightly short of breath as he gets back into the saddle. "But those chickens will be fine eating tonight. You were saying?"

"Actually, I think you interrupted yourself," Custer responds. "Reynolds, I'm amazed. It's hard enough to shoot the head off one bird with a rifle, let alone two in one shot!"

Charley smiles, recalling Tom Custer's earlier remark, "Just got lucky, I reckon!"

When a flock of Canada Geese flies overhead, Custer reins up and looks above. "That reminds me," he begins smiling. "That time in 73 on the Yellowstone, Tom and I were hiding in the brush along the river. Neither of us knew the other was there. A lone goose came flying over; I fired and it dropped—nearly in front of me. When I went over to pick up my catch, there was Tom, claiming the goose was his.

Apparently we both fired at the same time. But you know, Tom. He told everyone it was his shot that hit the bird."

"Did you ever settle it?"

"No! Probably never will." Custer's grin fades. "Say, do you remember when Orville Grant and those others came to Fort Lincoln with that trader? I think his name was Parkin."

"Sure I remember," Charley answers, his eyes squinting as if to refresh his memory. "That Parkin was a mysterious fellow."

"Then Fred Grant went on up the Yellowstone, too. Well that's when a lot of the problems began. When they extended the boundaries of the reservation, that really helped their friends. You know who I..."

Custer stops and raises his glasses. Charley does the same.

"I've never seen so much game, Reynolds!" exclaims the General. "Just look at those antelope, would you. There must be thousands of them!"

Bringing their horses to a halt, the two men quietly dismount and remove their rifles from the scabbards. Then each dropping to one knee, fire almost simultaneously. Their targets likewise, fall instantly. While they bleed and gut the well-nourished antelope the conversation continues.

"You know, I've been thinking about that job offer I had—maybe I should get out of the Army after this campaign. I don't feel I can do a good job as long as this corruption continues to infiltrate the military."

Reynolds is surprised and hesitates before asking, "What job are you talking about General?"

"Some outfit in New York asked if I would like to try lecturing. They offered me a generous fee—very generous!"

"Oh, a civilian job!" Once again Reynolds pauses, pondering the consequences should the General resign.

"Well, Charley?" Custer speaks up. "Don't turn silent on me now, man!"

"I don't know quite what to say about it, Sir. I've never been comfortable giving advice but it seems worthy of consideration. How does Libbie feel?"

"We haven't discussed it much. She gets so upset when she reads about all the scandal in Washington; I try not to talk about it. It just worries her. Maybe I'll mention it again when I get home." He stands and stretches. "I'll go find some men to help me with the meat, Charley. Why don't you ride ahead and find us a campsite for the night? Check with the others scouts too. And keep your eye out for anything suspicious. It's not just the Indians I'm concerned about—there may be some rocks hidden in the water, if you know what I mean."

As the troopers begin pitching the tents, a loud report from the heavens, trumpets the start of an oncoming storm. Thunder rumbles across the Dakota plains and lurid flashes of lightning lights up the sky.

Charley tends his horses. He raises erect and listens intently to the rolling thunder. General Custer walks over. "What do ya' think, Reynolds? Is it a good omen?"

Charley rubs his horse then quietly answers, "Depends on your belief. Indians look for a sign. They believe when the Thunderbird flies across the sky shooting its flaming arrows at the earth, something big will happen." Both men gaze at the stormy sky.

Custer nods, "Thunder rolling on the high plains." Their blue eyes hold for a moment then George Custer quietly replies, "Something great will happen!"

Custer takes another look at the sky then goes to where Tom, Boston and Lieutenant Cooke stand in a group talking. A wall of rain follows the second clap of thunder. Hurriedly, the men carry on unloading the wagons. The rain falls from the darkened sky in sheets, whipped by the cold, razor-sharp wind. For the soldiers it is a struggle to hold the canvas still and when the tempest finally retreats, most are tired and chilled to the bone. As the temperature continues to drop, the remaining drizzle eventually turns to snow. At midnight Custer steps from his tent flap. He looks concerned as the falling snow turns into a whiteout. By morning there are three inches on the ground.

Alarmed at the severity of the weather and realizing the soldiers and animals could use some rest after the storm, General Terry directs the regiment to remain in camp until conditions improve. The men are glad to take it easy and play cards but the camp duties seem to be endless. It is the morning of June 3rd before they get the order to continue. By daylight the blue clad regiment is in the saddle and on the move again.

June 5, 1876

Captain Myles Walter Keogh approaches a circle of men who are awaiting their morning meal.

"Good morning, Captain," comes the greeting from Autie Reed, "not long until we eat, is it, Sir?"

"I hope not, Reed." Keogh replies in his unmistakable brogue. "I'm nearing starving myself. I hope that cook's found something better than that slop he served up yesterday. I could eat a hardy chunk of buffler' meat."

"I seen some buffalo yesterday. Might be there is more around. Maybe Lucky Man Reynolds will bring in some fresh meat. He's out hunting, Captain." Reed grins.

"I surely hope so, Lad. If anyone can find game it most surely will be Reynolds. Mark my word, Laddie Buck. Of all the great huntsmen that this Irishman has cast his eye upon, Ol' Lucky man Reynolds tops the list." replies Keogh.

Behind the group, in front of a large tent, hang two flags—Old Glory and the regimental colors. They are still; there's not a breath of wind. Inside, sitting at a small table, is George Custer.

He takes a pen from the inkwell and begins to write then pauses momentarily, his blue eyes staring deeply into a framed photograph of his pretty dark-haired young lady. The candle flickers to his sigh. He stands and opens the tent flaps for more light and takes a mental inventory of the weapons on his bed—a gun belt, two .45 cal. half-cock English Bulldog pistols snug in their holsters and a Remington sporting rifle, black powder 50-70 caliber with octagon barrel leaning against his cot.

Atop a ridge, above the camp, a lone Indian scout has been quietly surveying the soldiers. The birds scatter as he bellies along in the dust to get a better view. In the distance, faintly at first are sounds of stirring buffalo. A rifle shot cracks the still morning air. The commotion is louder now. Another shot rings out and hoof beats begin to rumble across the hills. The Indian's jaw tightens. He looks to his left; then right. Confused and unable to determine the source of the gunfire, he crawls back to his horse, grabs a handful of mane and swings himself onto its back. Instinctively, the animal gallops away from the noise when he feels the pull of the rawhide thong on his jaw.

The Sergeant-of-the-Guard is alarmed and hurries to the Officer-of-the-Day, Lieutenant Sturgis, who quickly goes to the regimental tent.

"Colonel, Sir! I heard shots over yonder!"

"I heard them, Lieutenant," Custer replies unconcerned. "Sounds like Reynold's 50-70. He knows we need fresh meat."

"You suppose he's rounded up fifty or more buffalo, Sir?"

"Rounded them up, maybe. But he won't be taking more than we need. Have the men stay alert though."

"Aye, Sir."

A poised Charley Reynolds and his favorite buckskin horse, "Big Red," stand on a ridge waiting for the right moment as the buffalo stomp angrily at the turf. He's already killed several from the ridge before they stampeded. He wears his Santa Fe pencil roll hat and the new white jacket from Running-creek-Woman. Suddenly he spurs the well-trained animal and rides after the herd. Dirt and dust fly as hunter and horse ride hard into the herd driving the frenzied beasts in a circle.

"Hi-ya!" Reynolds calls out, as he leans over in his saddle and fires a shot. The 50-70 belches smoke and the buffalo goes down. "Good boy, Red! We got 'em, Red. Good boy!" The horse turns obediently as the rider's knee presses into a rib. Reynolds reloads his single-shot carbine and looks down the barrel as a huge bull comes into range. Flame and seventy grains of black powder belch from the muzzle in a deafening blast and the buffalo skids into the dust. The hunter pulls another brass cartridge from his prairie belt. Balancing skillfully in the saddle, he inserts the round into the chamber with precision and slams the action shut. Instinctively, Big Red lunges forward and separates another buffalo from the herd. Hooves pound, muscles stretch, Red powers ahead, carrying his rider on his ride, moving in for the next kill. "That's it! That's it!" Charley encourages his mount. Reynolds lays his rifle across the pommel of his saddle and squeezes the trigger. The explosion reverberates across the barren land and before the blue-black cloud clears, the 500-grain lead slug has pierced its target. The mighty Tatanka's front legs buckle and it tumbles nose-first into the sand.

Charley quickly slips out of the saddle. He finds a little knoll to rest his rifle on. He drops to the ground prone and continues to fire and load, fire and load. When the last shot echoes across the land, almost evenly spaced across the prairie, are a dozen buffalo. He'll bleed and gut them so they'll cool then get help from the soldiers. The camp will be in high spirits to have fresh meat. He takes a last glance as the stampeding buffalo disappear over a ridge.

Reynolds walks his heavy-lathered horse to cool him down while he goes about his task of bleeding and gutting the buffalo. An eerie stillness lingers over the plain as Reynolds kneels to the task before him. He has just finished the last of the dead buffaloes when Big Red startles him with a nervous snort.

One hundred fifty feet away is a huge black buffalo wolf, his powerful jaws spread, revealing a vicious sneer of white teeth. He has already had his first taste of blood and growls at the man and his horse—the only obstacle between him and a hearty meal of fresh buffalo.

"Not many of you big fellows left. You're a dying breed." Charley says quietly. Quickly Reynolds raises his Sharps and takes aim. A well-placed shot scatters dirt and rocks underneath the wolf's belly. Ki-ying and yelping the frightened, but otherwise unharmed animal, clambers for safety. The hunter reloads and fires a parting shot.

"I'll let you go this time," he says aloud, sympathizing with the scarce hungry buffalo wolf as it disappears over a ridge. He chuckles out loud when he recalls his old mentor Gabe Green's words just before he died. *"Maybe the wuffs can chaw on me... for a change."*

Charley removes his weathered hat and slaps the dirt from his clothes then surveys the plain. He removes his jacket, running his fingers over the beadwork. He cracks a warm smile, "Pony tracks on the buffalo trail. Good sign, heap." As he sheaths his knife his thoughts take him back to his youth and his carefree hunting trips with his older brother. But this ride is different.

For twenty days the regiment has been on the trail having faced everything from searing heat and dust to torrential rain and mud. The mood among the soldiers is somber. There is a general feeling of uneasiness, and even Charley Reynolds privately questions his own apprehension about this latest ride. He recalls sending a wire to the general in Washington advising of the growing unrest among the Indians, namely the Dakota Sioux and Cheyenne. He had warned that the army could expect to find as many as 2000 Indian lodges. From his own observations as a courier between army posts and as a frequent visitor of the various Indian agencies, he knew in his own mind, that the Indians were prepared to fight.

Charley eases into the saddle and begins to ride toward camp. The sky begins to form threatening black clouds. But for now, his blue eyes squint into the mirage of the bright morning sun and once again his thoughts take him back to his childhood.

Red snorts unexpectedly shaking Charley from the luxury of a rare daydream. The handsome animal comes to an abrupt halt and points his sensitive ears to the east.

Reynolds brings his carbine up quickly. It is only the huge buffalo wolf he had scared off earlier. The beast snarls a low growl through a curled upper lip, as if to say, "Go away—you're intruding in my territory."

Charley keeps his distance, guiding Red away from the angry wolf then coaxing the horse to a running walk toward some rocky crags along the river.

"Rider coming in, it's Lonesome Charley." Shouts the guard as Reynolds approaches the cavalry camp. Charley dismounts and leads his horse over to Custer's tent where Custer stands with several of his officers. "I have several buffalo down, Sir n' I need a couple of wagons and some hands, General."

George Custer turns to his brother. "Captain, take Sergeant Finley and several men and the wagons and go help Reynolds bring back the meat. My mouth is starting to water already!"

"Yes, Sir!" Tom says obediently before kidding Charley. "Wagons, likely one will be enough. Some stray Indians probably killed a buffalo and Lonesome Charley run them off before they had a chance to butcher it!"

Reynolds smiles as Keogh's laughter booms above the others. When they turn to leave, Autie Reed and Boston run to catch up with Tom.

"Uncle Tom," cries Autie, "can we go along?"

The Captain waits for the General's nod of approval before he has the teamsters hitch the mules to the wagon.

"Come on, Autie. Hop aboard!" Boston yells, as he jumps onto a wagon seat and grabs the reins from his older brother. "Haya! Com'on, you mules. Giddup!"

Tom, Sergeant Finley and Charley share a little friendly chitchat as they ride easily alongside the wagons. When Boston sees the dead buffalo he halts the mules and jumps down to look at the shaggy hulks. Autie Reed follows, running from animal to animal.

"Look at this, Uncle Tom!" Autie screeches, "I can't believe it! Do you know Uncle—they all look like they're shot in the same spot? Right through the ticker! I don't believe it!"

Tom looks down at the wide-eyed youngster and mutters so only he can hear. "Autie, if you call me Uncle one more time, I'm going to tan your hide!" Then abandoning his stern demeanor he continues: "Yes, Autie I know. Didn't we tell you how lucky your Uncle Charley is?"

Autie blurts out, "You should of seen the lucky shot he made on the sh..." he mutters unintelligible words almost giving away his sneaking away from camp. "Lucky?" Autie repeats quizzically.

"Sure. He's just plain lucky. That's why the Rees call him, "Lucky Man!""

When Sergeant Finley can no longer stifle his laughter, Autie realizes that Tom is putting him on. "I'll get you for that, Uncle Tom," he teases, running as fast as he can, fearful his uncle may retaliate.

The Captain instead turns to the soldiers who are standing idly by the downed bison. "Alright boys, let's get to cuttin'! We've got to haul that meat back to camp. We'll be leaving for the Powder River soon."

The men set to work and in a couple of hours the party is headed for camp with wagonloads of freshly butchered buffalo. The company cooks gather around the party. Custer's cook hurries to greet them.

"I want a few tongues and the humps, Tom. I'm going to fix a feast before we hit the trail!"

After pestering Charley for an hour or more, Autie finally is awarded one of the buffalo heads for his part in helping bring the meat back to camp. Captains Keogh and Weir, Lieutenant Calhoun and Custer's Adjutant, Lieutenant Cooke are standing around the campfire complimenting Charley and the cook for the delicious meal when General Custer breaks in.

"Lieutenant Cooke, we'll be moving out in forty-five minutes. Notify the Wing commanders. First company ready will get the advance as usual."

"Yes, Sir! We'll be ready! How far will we be traveling—twenty miles?"

"Maybe ten, twelve," Custer replies, stopping to make a mental calculation. "We're in rough country. Reynolds, how far do you think we can go before sundown?"

"In this country we'd be lucky to make ten miles, if that."

When everyone has finished eating General Custer confers with General Terry who spends much of his time riding in the wagons. Custer again addresses his Adjutant. "All right, Lieutenant let's get the men rolling. By the way, Reynolds, that buffalo wasn't bad at all...a little on the strong side, maybe."

Reynolds is surprised by the remark until he looks up to see the smirk on the General's face. He had enjoyed the meal as much as everyone else and Charley knows it.

Once the troops commanders relay the orders, tents are dismantled, wagons loaded and soldiers mounted smartly upon their high-stepping horses. Proudly leading his outfit, Custer waves as Reynolds takes leave to scout the trail ahead.

The long column nears the Powder River. More than seven hundred horses and mules paw and pound their hoof prints into the soil leaving a trail of dust clouds two miles back. The 7th Cavalry has arrived in Montana Territory.

Custer joins Reynolds who has ridden ahead and is peering from the bluffs at the river below.

"How does it look, Reynolds?"

"There's a dandy spot over that way," Charley says pointing to a large grassy flat at the water's edge.

"Looks good from here. Let's go see for ourselves."

The campsite is better than they had expected and soon the command arrives and begins the ritual—unloading the wagons and putting up the tents.

"Lieutenant Cooke!" Custer yells to his Adjutant. "Inform Major Reno and Captain Benteen to set up the battalion wings. Have them post the guards and set the picket lines."

"Aye, Sir!"

Several platoons of troopers take their horses to graze in the rich Powder River grass. Others tie their mounts to the ropes that have been strung from wagon-to-wagon to form the picket lines.

Brigadier-General Terry, who seldom rides a horse, is edgy after bumping along in his wagon all day. "Alex!" he screams to his orderly. "Is Custer's tent ready yet?"

"It appears ready, Sir!"

"I didn't ask how it appears. I want to know if it is ready!"

"I'll go and see, Sir...right away, Sir!"

When the nervous servant returns with his confirmation, Terry ambles over to Custer's quarters and walks in. Custer has just started a letter to his wife and does not look up. Terry blows lightly at one of the candles on the table.

"Oh," stammers the startled Custer, jumping to his feet. "Good evening, Sir!"

"Evening," replies the bewhiskered man half-heartedly. "Take your seat. We need to talk. I want to know where the main body of Indians is before we start making our plans. I've sent couriers to Colonel Gibbon. Tomorrow I'll take two companies and go to the mouth of the Powder. I hope Marsh is there with the steamer by now."

"When will you return, Sir?"

"Well, it's about forty miles there and back. I'm not looking forward to two days in the saddle, so you can be sure I'll spend some time resting aboard the steamer," he sighs in a tired way. "When I return I'll have a better idea of how to conduct the scout. I should receive word from Crook by then, if not sooner. In fact, if all is well with Colonel Gibbon, he should be aboard the steamer when I arrive there."

"Yes, Sir. The sooner the better!"

Terry lifts the tent flap and makes his exit without another word.

Forty-eight hours later he revisits Custer's tent. "Well, Colonel, have you learned the whereabouts of the hostiles yet?"

"Sir, after talking to Charley Reynolds I'm certain we'll find them on one of the Yellowstone tributaries. Many suspected they would be along the Little Missouri but as you know we found no sign of them there. Tomorrow when we leave on the scout all streams from the Powder westward will be thoroughly surveyed." Custer waits for Terry's nod before continuing. "With Colonel Gibbon coming down the Yellowstone all the major rivers will have been searched. His command will be scouting Indians along the Rosebud and the other streams on their way to join us."

Terry clears his throat. "I have Colonel Gibbons' report that they have sighted no Indians."

"But, Sir, Lieutenant Bradley and several of Gibbon's Crows say that a big village was spotted on the Tongue River. The village hence had moved over to the Rosebud."

"I can't issue orders on rumors, Custer!" Terry says again, clearing his throat.

"I'll be sending Major Reno in command,, along with the right wing on a scout up the Powder."

"Major Reno?" blurts the surprised Custer. "Major Reno, Sir?"

"I did say, Major Reno. And I would like Reynolds along as one of the scouts. That Reynolds is very capable of the task. I know I can depend on him."

"I can't argue with that, Sir, but Reynolds has a felon on his hand. He really should rest. I be...beg your pardon! Major Reno is a junior officer. Shouldn't I be..."

"My decision has been made," Terry answers firmly. "If there's nothing else, you'll pardon me. I'm tired and need some rest."

Custer salutes and follows the officer out of the tent. For several minutes he stands in the darkness mulling over yet another insult from the Army—the same Army that has been the beneficiary of his dedication and inexhaustible energy for many years. He feels the weight of sorrow pressing against his chest. After a moment of silence he tells his orderly to summon Tom to his tent.

Charley accompanies Tom to Custer's tent. Tom's temper gets the best of him as his brother informs him about Terry's order.

"Just who does he think he is? I can't believe this! He's nothing but an armchair general. Why doesn't he go back to that fancy office in St. Paul and sit his dead butt down on that posh leather chair of his? It would surely fit better there than in a saddle." He pauses for a breath. "Doesn't he realize that we're fighting Indians out here? Real Indians! That sot doesn't stay sober long enough to..."

George Custer finally raises his voice. "Captain! Calm down! It's likely that Terry's taking his orders from higher up."

Tom butts in, "It's Grant's way of getting even for your testimony at the Clymer hearings."

Charley is upset too. "The President would be making a grave mistake ordering Terry—or anyone else for that matter—to deploy incompetent officers just to satisfy his need for vengeance. Those Indians are ready to fight and we shouldn't be expected to lay our lives on the line knowing the man in charge doesn't have any idea what he's up against.

"Bravo, Reynolds! Good God, Charley," an amazed George Custer says clapping his hands. "I don't recall ever hearing you carry on that way. I agree with you but there's not a thing I can do about it."

"You should be the officer leading that scout, General," Charley adds. "If what you say about the President is true..."

Tom butts in, "that means Terry has to know about it."

"This whole business has the smell of a skunk!" Charley says.

"That's right!" exclaims Tom. "A dead skunk! Has Terry assigned the Troops yet?"

The General evades his brother's question and turns to Charley. "Troops B, E, F, I and L troop, the right wing. C Troop will be going too," he adds facing the young captain. "Lieutenant Harrington will be in command of your company."

"You mean to tell me I'm not going with my own Company?" explodes Tom Custer thrashing his arm into the side of the tent and kicking a campstool into the air. "That...that!" he leaves in anger.

"Charley. Will you tell that bad-tempered brother of mine to get his behind back in here?"

Reynolds obliges. He steps out of the tent but Tom is nowhere in sight. Instead, Captains Weir and Keogh have heard the commotion and they are approaching at a fast pace.

The following morning the 10th of June, the Brigadier-General sends his orderly to inform General Custer that the remaining troops, the left wing will be heading out for the Mouth of the Powder River the next day. The camp is buzzing with supposition and speculation as to Terry's reason for choosing Major Reno rather than Custer to lead the scout. But Terry offers no explanation. Reno, a permanent sneer on his face, has little to say.

After a hearty lunch the scouting company mounts up and prepares to ride out. Tom is still wearing a disgusted scowl; he can't help but remember how Major Reno, in Custer's absence, constantly harassed and figured all kinds of ways, as the commander, to payback Tom's Company C soldiers. He tried everything from extra duty and parade ground drill to downright punishment. Charley feels badly that he didn't get a chance to talk to the fiery Captain. Tom had disappeared and instead of searching for him Charley felt obligated to add a notation in his diary before retiring. Charley checks his timepiece; he makes a mental note of the time and day. It is 3 o'clock p. m. June, 10th.

Several hours pass and Reynolds breaks away to look for sign of game. The Powder is only a mile or so away but all he's discovered so far is some old buffalo bones and the outer edges of stretched hide. After a while he trails a large mule deer. Although Charley has heard hundreds of hunters' tales over the years alluding to the abundance of wild game in the region, he is still amazed that there is so much of it—all healthy and ripe for the picking. After following the trail for about two miles he spots the deer standing motionless in a small patch of brush. He dismounts, walks a few feet ahead of Red, and shoots. The animal flinches momentarily before all four legs fold under its dead weight. Another clean shot.

Reynolds notices that the thumb he'd injured before leaving Fort Lincoln has swollen some making it difficult to dress the deer. When the job is finished puss is oozing from the festered thumb. Charley gets a piece of cloth from inside his saddle pockets and makes a bandage. He pours some iodine onto the wound, wrapping the cloth tightly around the painful injury. Then loading the venison onto his horse he begins his ride back toward the troops, still keeping an eye out for more trace of the Indians.

Meanwhile, Custer and Lieutenant Cooke have spotted some antelope grazing down on the river.

"Look at that, Cookie!" he whispers just loud enough for Cooke to hear. "That one at the edge of the grass is mine!"

Quickly slipping out of Vic's saddle he steps about twenty paces to the left, raises his octagon-barreled Remington and fires. His target lunges forward then slumps breast-first to the ground.

"How do you like that," Custer exclaims. "Right through the old ticker! Wait till I tell Reynolds."

A couple of days later Charley shoots another deer. When Charley returns the troops are lounging around camp. He unloads the venison and walks across the grounds to tell the company cooks about it.

"More meat huh, Charley?" asks a soldier.

"Nice fat buck. Ought to be good eating."

"Some of the boys have been wondering—do you ever miss anything you shoot at?" asks another soldier.

"Not unless I want to," Charley replies with a smile.

The soldier jabs a nearby soldier in the ribs. "Must be that Lieutenant Calhoun doesn't often want to hit those antelope. Isn't that so?" The others laugh. "You know, Calhoun found a nice buck one day, Charley. It was just sitting in the grass, missed it with the first shot but that second shot was right on target. Killed it deader than a door nail. When we ran over to fetch his prize the cussed thing was dead. It had been dead for several days—maggots crawling all over it and everything. Killed somethin' already dead. What a shot!"

"I've seen you miss your share too," pipes up a private.

Charley's thumb is throbbing so he steps over to Tom Custer's tent for a shot of whiskey.

"That's a nasty-looking mess Reynolds. Hadn't you better show that to Doc. Porter?"

Charley tells the Captain it's not necessary and bids him so long. He is awakened early the next morning by the frustrations of a strange dream. *In his sights just out of rifle range are thousands of bison, elk and antelope grazing contentedly within a circle of Indians teepees.* When reveille sounds the wake-up call at four a.m. he's anxious to get out of the sack.

On Reno's scout several days pass without incident although the mood of the men is somber, almost listless. Under advise from the officers, Major Reno decides it best that he send the Gatling gun battery back after the gun which is cumbersome and was abandoned.

Meanwhile, on the Yellowstone River at the mouth of the Tongue, soldiers are sitting around a campfire enjoying George Custer's roasted antelope. General Terry is visiting Custer in the latter's tent. He appears worried. "Reno should have returned by now but there's been no word."

"Something must have happened or we would have heard by now," Custer says in a subtle I-warned-you tone.

"What could have possibly happened?" the frustrated Terry demands to know. "The weather surely has been favorable enough."

"There are thousands of Indians out there, General. It wouldn't surprise me at all if they decided to attack."

"The Indians aren't that foolish Custer. They've got their own scouts, as you well know. They must be aware that with Crook approaching from the south and Gibbon from the northwest...well they haven't got a snowballs chance in hell and that's that!"

Disgusted, Custer mutters under his breath: "And Reno no doubt fell in a vat of firewater and is too drunk to stagger home!" He grins impishly at Terry.

"Good night, Colonel!" Terry growls as he turns and steps briskly to his own tent.

Custer adds a final note to Libbie's letter. After extinguishing the candle for some mysterious reason he wonders about the candle flame. Where did the flame go? George Custer ponders deeply while he looks intently out his tent flap into Montana's darkness.

17

*C*razy Horse. The mere mention of the Oglala warrior's name conjured panic and terror in the minds of most Wasichus. White prospectors told endless stories of Crazy Horse's sometimes-violent vigilance along, "The Trail of Thieves." Clutching to the faith bestowed upon him in the form of a polished stone, a red-tailed hawk and his spotted cape, this fearless Indian believed strongly in his Medicine Dream. He was invincible. And he had not forgotten the White Man's intrusion into the sacred Paha Sapa.

Denouncing the Wasichus' "generosity," as nothing more than subterfuge and chicanery, Crazy Horse, like Sitting Bull, refused to acknowledge Indian Affairs and generally ignored the Agency rituals. He felt powerless over the Pentouchers so far away in Washington; but pitted against the Pony Soldiers on Indian Land he was over flowing with confidence. The sight of the Bluecoats marching unrestrained on the western plains only angered him more, stoking his bold spirit to a fever pitch.

When Colonel Joseph J. Reynolds attacked a band of Cheyenne near the fork of the Powder and Little Powder rivers, destroying most of the village, the few remaining survivors were forced to flee into the freezing Montana cold. After three sleeps they arrived fortunately, at the camp of the Oglala and Crazy Horse where they were fed and given warm clothing. It was then, after the two bands held council, the decision was made to move northeast and join the growing numbers who sought the wisdom of Sitting Bull and his Uncpapas. Thus began the Great Gathering of the Indian Tribes.

Indian runners brought word to Sitting Bull: "Many soldiers are coming to fight." All Indians would be prepared. The spring grass sprouted quickly and their war-ponies grew stronger with each new day. Camp circles grew larger and each time the mass moved in search of forage for the animals—three sleeps at one camp, one at the next and four more on No Name Creek, before the month of June had blessed the Land of Montana. Never before had so many assembled at one time. They pushed westward crossing the Powder River and then the Tongue. They would strike south once they reached the Rosebud and soon the day for the Great Medicine Dance of the Uncpapa would arrive.

Heading north from Fort Fetterman with his command, General George Crook, named, "Three Stars," by the Indians, was following the Rosebud on June 16th, when he was spotted by a dozen or so Cheyenne scouts, called wolves. Crook's unit represented the largest third of the War Department's planned three-prong attack, the other two commands being Terry's and Gibbon's. The Cheyenne perceived the approach of the Pale-faced Bluecoats as a huge threat and hurried to take the news to their leaders. Crook on the other hand, was certain that his regiment, over one thousand strong was not in any danger of attack.

Upon hearing of the Army's approach however, Crazy Horse struck immediately, killing nine soldiers and driving the remainder along with many Shoshoni scouts, back to Wyoming's Wild Geese Creek. Some of the victory trophies strangely enough were discarded. The shorthaired scalps of the troopers were unworthy of display in the lodges. Crazy Horse and his warriors rejoined the other bands of Sioux and Cheyenne on Great Medicine, what the White-Man called, Sun Dance Creek. Other bands of Sioux and Cheyenne warriors rejoined their respective camps still on the Rosebud River.

General Crook, perhaps embarrassed by his inability to fend off his opponent's attack, further complicated the War Department's efforts by failing to send word of his setback to either Gibbon or Terry. Crook's failure to warn the other regiments of the Indian's strength was considered a gross disregard by many, especially since at this same time, he had sent out couriers to several different agencies to acquire more Indian scouts. Many reasoned if he could send out couriers to acquire more Indian scouts, then why could he not send couriers to warn Gibbon or Terry or Custer?

As military miscalculations, poor judgment and disobedience continued to pick away at the Army's supposed superiority, the winds of war were gathering speed, churning the turbulent storm clouds that loomed over the Yellowstone River and along Rosebud Creek, pushing them ever nearer to the valley of the Little Big Horn.

At the Mouth of the Tongue River on the Yellowstone, June 17, 1876

George Custer and two of his Arickaree scouts, Red Star and Strikes Two, have detected the remains of an Indian village along the Tongue's eastern bank. From all indications the site has been abandoned for several months. The trio is digging around in some ashes when Strikes Two unearths a half-burned cavalry jacket. Its three brass buttons denote that the owner was a Lieutenant. Not far off, Custer spots a fourth button and down at the river's edge Red Star finds a human skull. Feeling a little uneasy after the discovery, Custer leads his scouts back to his company to pass the news on to Terry.

Meanwhile, Major Reno has finally decided to reveal his whereabouts. When his courier informs Terry that the troops are returning by way of the Rosebud, General Terry sends his personal aide back with an order to hold their position on the Yellowstone until he is instructed otherwise. Gibbon and Major Brisbin in the meantime, are on the north side of the Yellowstone and Custer is proceeding along the south side to join them.

Several days later Custer's command nears the mouth of the Rosebud, they reunite with Major Reno's six companies. On the Yellowstone River two miles below the mouth of the Rosebud, the 7th Cavalry troopers begin making camp on a flat beneath the eerie shadows of a high rocky bluff. Once his tent is ready Custer joins his brother at the campfire. Tom is listening to Charley Reynolds tell Keogh, Weir and Calhoun what Lieutenant Bradley, Gibbon's Chief of Scouts had discovered along the Rosebud.

"Hello brother...good afternoon boys," Custer says as he approaches. "Say, Charley I've been meaning to ask you...how's that thumb of yours?"

"It was healing nicely until yesterday but it's started festering again. I don't like to ask Captain Keogh for more of his sour mash but that's what was helping it heal."

"If you'd drink it, I wouldn't mind giving you a shot once in awhile Charley," Keogh says without sympathy. "It just breaks my heart to watch you soaking your cussed thumb in such fine whiskey."

"Maybe you'd be better off drinking a little less of that fine swill, Keogh!" Weir smiles jokingly at Keogh, as Custer breaks in before the discussion gets out of hand. "Did you find out anything else, Charley?"

"More Indians," Charley answers, managing a weak smile. "Lots of Indians!"

"Somehow I knew that would be your answer."

Captain Weir speaks up. "Mitch Boyer keeps on saying there's Otoe Sioux, Otoe Sioux."

"He's right!" adds Lieutenant Calhoun. "Charley, didn't you say that Bradley said more Indians were joining the further they trailed them up the Rosebud?"

"That's true. They counted close to four hundred campfire rings in one village alone. It must be the same village that Lieutenant Bradley saw on the Tongue about a month ago. The further they rode, the bigger the camps. Boyer knows the Sioux. He fears even more will join."

"I'll speak with you boys later," says Custer as he walks off towards the steamer. He stops to talk to his striker, John Burkman, but is still in earshot of the group.

"It looks like we're in for a hard fight," Keogh remarks. "What about Major Reno, boys? Can we depend on him in a fight?"

Captain Weir shakes his head, "He's untried. I've heard that all he did during the war was take leave and purchase horses for the remount." Weir waits for Tom's reaction

Tom Custer butts in. "Reno should be court-martialed!" he shouts, kicking in disgust at the dusty turf underfoot. "Leading his troops halfway round the country like sightseers...anyone else pulled a stunt like that would be court-martialed!" He turns to the others, slightly calmer. "I wonder what General Terry had to say?"

"Yeah what did Terry say?" Lieutenant Calhoun demands to know, then adding as an afterthought, "I agree. Reno should be court-martialed."

"I've heard that General Terry stated that Reno offered no explanation of his disobedience." Adds Keogh.

"If Terry was to do the right thing," Tom continues, "he'd remove Reno and... and..."

"And replace him with Benteen?" Weir intercepts Tom's thought. "I don't trust that surly complainer either!"

"That would be the last straw! That's the nitwit who accused my brother of abandoning Major Elliot down on the Washita...then he even had the audacity to write to the newspapers, too. It'll be a cold day in Hades when I take orders from that jackass! Keogh's the one who should be in command—not Reno and surely not Benteen!"

"I understand how you feel, Tom," Keogh responds modestly to the praise. "I appreciate your confidence in me but Terry will have the last word. Right, boys?"

When the others remain silent, Charley voices a rare opinion. "Whoever's in command, they'd better know that we're trailing an enormous band of Indians—not just the Sioux but the Cheyenne as well—and I believe they're ready to fight if they have to."

"Tell me, Charley," George Custer says, as he walks back, "What was going through your mind when you wired me in Washington? You must have been as surprised as I was to learn that there may be as many as two thousand lodges."

"Grant Marsh warned me that something big was going to happen. Based on my own observations the information I learned at Berthold, and from listening to conversations at the Standing Rock, I am sure Marsh is right. Captain Allison is always on top of the situation, too. He knows the tongues and signs and he understands much of the talk among the Indians. He agrees that the mood is very tense. There may be more than two thousand lodges by now. Lieutenant Bradley says, and according to Gibbon's scouts, the Indians had already headed up the Rosebud in mid-May."

Custer looks concerned, "General Terry had planned on after Reno's return, for me to take the entire regiment up the Tongue River. Then to cut across to the Rosebud, above the village that Bradley had discovered, and push the Indians back down the Rosebud."

Keogh is firm, "Yeah. That plan would have worked. With Terry and Gibbon's soldiers pushing up the Rosebud we would of had the Sioux trapped between the two columns."

"In rough country they would have been hard pressed to flee across the hills." Charley adds.

"That's all changed now, thanks to Major Reno," remarks Tom Custer. "That dunderhead!"

Custer stares down at the circle of dusty boots and draws a deep breath. "Well, boys, I will acquaint with Terry what he can expect in the way of Indians. As for Reno, there's not much I can do. Terry offered no explanation. Whatever decision he makes it'll be his and his alone."

"Maybe so," Tom adds unhappily, "but it's us who'll have to live by it!"

Just as Custer turns to leave the campfire, General Terry's young orderly rushes forward. "Colonel Custer, Sir. General Terry's compliments. There will be a conference aboard the Far West in one hour."

"Colonel, no less!" mutters Custer under his breath. "My express gratitude, Corporal. I expected as much." Custer turns and walking backward salutes to Charley and the disgruntled officers. "We'll talk later, boys. Remember though...no use crying over spilled milk. A success will sooner return us to our station."

"General, Sir!" Charley hurries forward.

Custer stops, motioning Charley forward.

"The thought just struck me, Sir. Captain Ball n' Lieutenant McClernand rode a long scout along the Big Horn River to the old Fort C. F. Smith. They then cut across to the Little Horn valley and across the Little Horn River. It might be well that we learn all we can about their scout."

"Rightly so, Reynolds. Find out all you can. I've learned a few things from their report. With the fresh Indian trail up the Rosebud I'm sure Terry will send..."Custer rubs his chin then walks towards the steamer, leaving Charley standing alone.

Lieutenant Colonel George Custer, nimble and energetic as usual, strides briskly up the gangway and waits patiently for the slow, aching Colonel Gibbon and an overweight Major Brisbin to board the Far West. General Terry ushers the officers into the ship's crowded dining room, which is being used to store some of the 7th's supplies. Custer is slightly amused at Gibbon's excuse for moving so slowly.

"I've got such a sore rear end from bouncing along on those darn hard wagon seats I can hardly walk!"

"You got piles, Sir?" asks the forward Major Brisbin. "I had them myself once. That's an extremely painful condition. I found an old horse doctor in St. Paul who..."

"Blast it, Brisbin!" shouts Gibbon. "I suppose there are other reasons for having a sore behind."

"Mine gets awful sore sometimes too. Rheumatism!"

Custer can't pass up the chance to get his two-cents worth in. "Sad state of affairs, gentlemen. I understand there's a lot of that going around."

"As long as we're all airing our dirty laundry...it's that cussed blazing heat that gets me down," Terry complains, totally ignoring Custer's jest. "I'm so light-headed at times, I have trouble concentrating on even the simplest of tasks. I'll have to ask my physician, Captain Doc. Williams, if he has a remedy for sunstroke."

Terry sees that Custer is about to make another remark and quickly directs his attention to the business at hand. "I've reviewed the scouting reports; the information each of you has reported and have decided on a plan. It seems almost certain that the Indians will be somewhere on the Little Horn. Grass Lodge Creek and Rotten Grass seem to be their favorite haunts."

"But those creeks are forty or fifty miles up the Little Horn Valley," protests Major Brisbin.

"I only hope one of the columns will find the Indians." Terry eyes the officers. "Step this way, gentlemen. I have a map on the chart table over here."

As Terry explains his strategy the discussion is peppered with the occasional sarcastic remarks of Major Brisbin, who has difficulty concealing his dislike for George Custer. Every time Custer offers a suggestion or imparts some advice, based on his experience, Brisbin counters with his own ideas, discounting the junior commander's credibility. Colonel Gibbon, who feels that it was his scouts who first discovered the Indians, although he made little effort to pursue them, still feels that he should get first crack at the Indians. Whether just an act of bravado in front of the others, he does not make matters any easier and the session drags on into the early evening hours. After listening to Custer's lengthy words, Terry finally summarizes the preliminary plan and asks for comments. Brisbin looses his composure.

"I don't understand, General why you insisted on my presence at this meeting... why don't you just let the Custer Clan handle the Indians on their own if they're so-so good?"

Custer, after putting up with Brisbin's snide remarks and icy stare all afternoon has also reached the boiling point. "The Custer Clan, as you call us is one..."

"Gentlemen! Gentlemen!" Terry yells, his voice breaking. "Let's finish what we started; it's getting late. Major Brisbin, I want you to mark the route as we go over our plan." Handing a blue marking pencil and pins to the blustery officer, he continues. "Colonel Custer, I think that you should proceed up the Rosebud on the trail of the Indians that Major Reno found a few days ago. It looks almost certain the trail will lead to the Little Big Horn."

Gibbon nods as Brisbin pushes a pin clean through the map and into the table.

"I think you, Custer, should still proceed southward, perhaps as far as the headwaters of the Tongue River and then toward the Little Big Horn." The General pauses, noting Custer's consternation. "I feel that you should bear constantly to your left, so as to preclude the possibility of the escape of the Indians to the south or southeast, by passing around your left flank."

Brisbin raises his eyebrows and smirks at Gibbon as Custer interrupts: "But, General Terry, Sir..."

"Yes Colonel. You have a question?"

"Correct me if I'm wrong, Sir but I was of the understanding that General Crook on his way up from Wyoming would be following the Rosebud River. Looking at the map, Sir it seems to me, that my regiment will only be covering the same ground as General Crook. It would be likely that Crook has already covered the headwaters of the Powder and Tongue Rivers. If as we suspect, the Indians are on the Little Horn..." Custer takes a deep breath and continues. "With all due respect, Sir...it will be almost impossible for my command to follow these suggestions and still be in supporting distance of the rest of the command."

Before Terry can respond, Brisbin breaks in, "Excuse me, General Terry, Sir, I feel your plan is well thought out. It seems to me, that my four companies of cavalry should go along. Gibbon's infantry also. I feel General—and I think Colonel Gibbon will agree—that if you and your staff went along in command we would be certain of success." he pauses just long enough to clear his throat and straighten his shoulders. "With all due respect to Lieutenant Colonel Custer...after what happened in Wash..."

"Thank you for your suggestion, Major," Terry cuts in. "I'll give it some thought."

For the first time there is no comment, no argument, no criticism—only the sound of the pins cracking through the brittle paper as Brisbin marks the last leg of the trail. Terry looks curiously at each of the officers and recognizes Custer's frustration. The young commander remains uncomfortably tight-lipped.

"Colonel Custer, unless you see sufficient reason for departing from these orders, I desire that you stick close to my instructions...unless in the meantime you receive further orders, of course." Before adjourning, the General announces that the plan is set. "And Custer, you'll have your regiment ready to ride by 12 noon tomorrow. I'll have my acting assistant Adjutant General, Captain Edward Smith, write out my instructions and he will deliver them to your person. Thank you, gentlemen. That'll be all."

As Terry prepares his papers on the old steamer, he summons his orderly who has been standing by on the deck for most of the day. "Bring a bottle to my quarters, young man. Maybe that'll help with this cussed sunstroke."

An hour or so later, after Custer and Gibbon have left the steamer, Brisbin returns and reiterates his earlier suggestion to General Terry. "You're not going to send, pardon my expression, that wild-ass loudmouth in command are you? Not after President Grant had him arrested in Chicago and all that other scandal!"

"I'm well informed of the President's feeling towards, Custer."

"Sir. With your permission, I would like to offer Custer, Lieutenant Low's Gatling gun battery."

"The guns have already left for the mouth of the Big Horn River," adds Terry with a surprised look.

Brisbin's gets a smug look. "Custer is not aware they've left."

"You have my permission, Major. Keep it quiet, but keep me informed."

Several hours later after offering the Gatling guns to Custer, who agreed to take the guns then refuses, Brisbin approaches Terry on the deck of the steamer.

Terry gives a tired sigh and motions Brisbin inside as lightning flashes and the rain begins. "I'll insist Custer take the Gatling guns along, but you'll be riding with Colonel Gibbon and I..." he catches himself, before revealing too much to the conniving Major Brisbin. "I have other orders for Custer—verbal orders that he'll receive before departing. We have discussed a waiting fight, engaging the enemy, fighting a waiting fight, giving enough time for the other battalions to arrive." Terry takes a deep breath, rubbing his sleeve. "Captain Ball and Lieutenant McClernand have both pointed out that Tullock's Creek is a fair route. Almost on a direct line to the tongue...and I might add, a much shorter route to the valley of the Little Big Horn," Terry's eyes roll in deep thought. "After talking with McClernand and Ball, I have this feeling that we'll find the Indians in the upper reaches of the Little Horn valley."

Major Brisbin gets an excited, devious look, "Ah...I see! Wouldn't that frost that loudmouth Custer's butt, if our column engages the Indians first? Wouldn't that really smite him?" Brisbin eyes Terry while rubbing his chin, "I suppose that would really put him in his place," Brisbin, leaning closer to the General. "Maybe it'll teach him to stop badmouthing the President and his men."

General Terry sees his orderly approaching with a bottle of liquor. "Care to join me for a drink, Major?"

"Yes, Sir. Maybe a few snorts will help my rheumatism."

After Brisbin's offer, Custer boards the Far West. He notices General Terry and the Major sharing a toast. Cloaking his bitter anxiety with a cool smile he approaches, and altogether ignoring Brisbin, says to Terry: "Excuse me, General. At first, I thought it would be prudent to take the Gatling Guns along, but they are already on the way for the mouth of the Big Horn. They would be hard pressed to make it back here in time for our departure tomorrow. A storm rain has already set in. Besides, they are clumsy and so slow moving, they'd only impede our march. Major Reno had a great deal of trouble with the guns on his scout."

Major Brisbin, swallowing a measure of confidence, replies before Terry has digested Custer's statement. "I get the feeling that the Lieutenant Colonel would just as soon be off on his own. Maybe he wants all the glory for himself, General!"

Custer is surprised at the Major's attack but continues to ignore him. He can smell the liquor and realizes that some soldiers get their courage from a bottle.

"All right, Custer," Terry says, as if he too hadn't heard Brisbin's remark. "I see your point. The Gatling guns are very slow; I know that. I'll amend the order... you'll depart as planned without the guns," Terry turns to cough. "You understand, Colonel Custer, whichever battalion or regiment finds the Indians first is going to have to engage in a waiting fight, giving time until the other command has time to arrive." Then, as if he almost forgot Terry adds. "And don't forget Tullock's Creek," he warns.

"I understand that, Sir," Custer responds curtly.

"That's about all you understand, Colonel!" Brisbin blurts out, tipping his glass and emptying it.

Custer finally acknowledges the Major's presence. "At least I can sit a horse, Major. I'd consider myself unfit if I had to rely on a wagon to carry me into battle!" Terry raises an eyebrow in surprise. Satisfied he has adequately defended himself, Custer brushes quickly past the dumb struck officer then stops and turns. "And I surely do not get my courage from a bottle, Major!" Custer walks away then leaves the steamer.

"Why, that irreverent cock of the walk, who does he think he is?" exclaims Brisbin to the weary General.

"I did not appreciate his comment about riding in the wagon, Major. But you asked for it. You've been insulting the man all day long." Terry chuckles, "I'm surprised he didn't throw you overboard." Terry continues to chuckle, finally bursting into laughter, after looking at Brisbin's dismayed look.

The rain has stopped for now, but threatening clouds continue to hover along the Yellowstone. But Charley has seen it rain or hail in one spot while a quarter mile away it was dry. Big Red whinnies contentedly as Charley rubs down his horse's shiny summer coat. "There you are, boy. Ready to ride!" Charley says affectionately to the animal, running the brush one more time through Red's tail. Suddenly the horse's ears peak and Charley turns to see General Custer approaching camp. The deliberate tempo of his step is indicative of his mood, having just left the Far West. Reynolds decides to investigate.

"General?"

Custer lifts the flap of his tent and closes it behind him. Charley has never before seen this officer act so strangely. He walks away from the commander's tent; confused, a little hurt.

Captains Tom Custer, Weir and Keogh are enjoying a drink at Tom's fire when Keogh sees Charley standing outside Custer's tent. "Come along, babbles," Keogh jokingly refers to Tom Custer's two medals of honor from the Civil War. "You too, Thomas Weir. Let's see what Charley is up to."

When Tom opens the tent he is upset. Standing inside George Custer stares at the small stove. Tom has never seen his brother with such a downcast look. "Autie! What happened? What'd those sleazy..."

Charley quietly interrupts grabbing Tom's elbow. "Easy, Tom find out what the General has to say."

"All right, all right, Reynolds." he turns to Charley, "You boys wait outside. I'll find out what happened."

The others walk a short distance away and wait.

In a slightly lower tone they hear Tom ask his brother: "What is it? What happened?"

Custer finally answers. "It's the orders!" he stammers. "And that squirrelly Major Brisbin!"

Outside the tent Captain Weir motions the others to follow, "Ought not to be eavesdropping boys." He leads them out of hearing distance.

After several minutes pass, Tom exits his brother's tent, walking up to the anxiously waiting men. "What about the orders...what are they?" Weir demands to know.

Captain Custer takes a swing at an imaginary enemy. "There's just no way... how under God's green earth Terry expects to succeed with this absurd plan is beyond me. He wants the regiment to ride clean to Wyoming—never mind that Crook's already there—and then ride all the way back down the Little Horn!"

"Are you sure, Captain?" asks a shocked Captain Keogh.

"And that isn't the half of it! That's not so bad!" Tom Custer continues. "That Major Brisbin—that dunderhead who can't even sit a horse—Brisbin actually tried to convince Terry to take Brisbin's four companies of 2nd Cavalry, combine them with the 7th Horse's twelve companies, and then have Terry ride in command of the whole outfit. He even suggested taking the useless, slow, moving Gatling guns."

Captain Keogh butts in. "That blatherskite, Brisbin! That's ridiculous! Ridiculous! Brisbin's cavalry n' Low's battery of Gatling guns departed for the Big Horn hours ago. I can see the handwriting on the wall."

Tom Custer angrily shouts out, "A lard butt that can't sit a horse n' an arm chair general! Been behind a desk fourteen years!"

Thomas Weir breaks in. "It sounds like a setup for failure to me!"

Charley speaks up. "It sure looks that way. I hope Terry realizes what we're up against. We're trailing a lot more Indians than I first estimated. I've said it before... something desperate is going to happen. Those Dakotas n' Cheyenne will fight—I believe they'll fight hard!"

Tom nods his agreement with the lead scout. "That's the first time I've heard you get riled, Reynolds. Charley, several of Gibbon's Indian scouts will ride with us."

"Mitch Boyer understands the Sioux and he knows every inch of this land, even down to the miles," says Charley.

"Yeah, Charley," Keogh laughs. "You're beginning to sound a lot like us rough-talking soldiers."

"One thing, Charley," Tom Custer says, "You know we trust your judgment."

"We all do," Weir adds, slapping Charley's shoulder.

"We all know you're the best, Reynolds. Boyer must be second best." Tom adds.

Reynolds is warmed by the sincerity of the soldiers. "I usually try to keep my personal opinions to myself but I just can't imagine that overweight Major Brisbin trailing Indians. Tom and I have talked to Gibbon's men and I'm sure the rest of you have. They told us that the Major rides in the ambulance wagon most of the time—and the Colonel himself is often riding right there with him!"

"Maybe they think they are a couple of charioteers!" exclaims Captain Weir.

"Yeah. Cavalrymen called, wagon-riding doughboys! They're a couple of pompous jackasses," Keogh remarks, his Irish brogue more prominent than usual. "I suppose they consider themselves a cut above the rest of mankind...riding around in their royal carriage."

Charley and Captain Weir are amused by the Captain's humor but the younger Custer sees only the seriousness of having to deal with two incompetent commanders on such an important campaign.

"It's no joke!" Tom exclaims. "That Gibbon has been sick for days. And the Major never shuts up about his rheumatism."

Weir interrupts, "Rheumatism, my royal behind!"

"Boys!" General Custer says, walking from his tent, raising his arm for silence. "Let's keep our comments to ourselves. No use upsetting the other boys. I've got to talk to Lieutenant Cooke. You men better get some rest. The regiment will leave tomorrow, as soon as Captain Marsh can get the Far West across the river with the rest of the supplies."

Tom Custer is suddenly cheerful. "I don't need a rest. Come on, Myles, Thomas, Charley. Let's go aboard the steamer. I could use a good stiff belt!"

"Good idea, Captain Custer," agrees Thomas Weir.

"I don't think I want any of that coffin varnish," says Charley, "but I'd like a few last words with my friend, Grant Marsh before we leave."

"Well I don't know about you boys, but I could drink the Yellowstone dry!" brags Keogh. "Say, Charley, a few stiff belts might help that thumb of yours to heal. If you don't like the sutler's rotgut, ask Captain Marsh for some of his private stock. I heard he has some real fine whiskey that goes down nice and smooth."

Charley smiles. "Yes, I know. Grant appreciates good liquor. Maybe I'll try some."

"By the way, Charley, it seems I heard your name called at mail call."

Charley looks puzzled, "I wasn't expecting any letter."

"I could have sworn I heard the sergeant call out, Reynolds," Keogh adds.

As the foursome approaches the sutler's station, aboard the steamer Captain Grant Marsh has just come from his quarters. He sees Charley immediately and hurries to greet him.

"Reynolds!" Grant exclaims noticing the painful expression as he accidentally bumps Charley's hand. "Good God, my friend, I'm sorry. What did you do, Charley?"

"Oh, it's just minor, Grant. Nothing to get alarmed about."

"That looks bad!" Captain Marsh beckons Reynolds to follow him and Charley gives a parting wave to the three officers.

Grant waves to the others and yells, "You boys look in need of a little drop of the creature."

"Rightly so, Grant!" Keogh exclaims, while Weir and Tom Custer grin and give Marsh a quick wave.

"Come join us later, Grant." Tom shouts back as they head inside.

"You been killing any more of that game that tickles the paddle, Charley?" asks Marsh as they enter his quarters. "I ran across an Englishman a while back who explained what that remark meant—tickle the palate of an epicure—so now I can say it aloud without getting my tongue twisted."

Charley laughs. "That was a tasty meal, Grant. Is that cook still with you?"

"Oh, he shows up every now and then...when he's broke and sober. He's one heckofuva cook if you keep him away from the bottle. And speaking of that, I want you to have a drink of my finest. Sit down over there, Charley!" he says, as he pours two small glasses full. "Drink up, my friend!"

Marsh downs his portion and sighs happily. "That ought to ease the infection a little," he comments, ignoring Charley's cough and refilling the glasses. "That thumb looks real bad, Lonesome Charley. Perhaps you should have Doc DeWolf or Porter look at it."

Charley takes another swallow of the whiskey. "It'll be fine, Grant. Custer's horse striker, John Burkman claims he can fix me up a poultice."

"Old Nutriment," Marsh mutters, "Eats anything in sight. Scuttlebutt is, even Custer's dogs have to fight him for the scraps. One soldier said he even bit one of the dogs on the lip vying for a chunk of meat." Marsh laughs heartily.

"Dog robber, some of the soldiers call him," Charley chuckles and takes another sip. "It's festered like this before but it's always healed up. I keep knocking it on things. It's my own fault it's not completely healed. I'll just have to take more care while I'm on this ride."

Grant notices that Charley's eyes are not as blue as he had remembered them. "I wouldn't be much of a friend, Charley, if I didn't tell you...you've got a nasty infection and to tell you the truth you look real pale." He takes another sip and continues. "I know you don't want to miss this ride but if you rested, that infection would disappear. You could stay here aboard the steamer with me."

Charley stands; his face flushes. "Captain, I've been preparing for two years for this expedition. I would rather die than miss it!" He tips his glass up and downs the contents in one swallow. "Keogh was right, Marsh," he sputters. "This stuff— whatever it is—seems to help." Marsh grins and fills another glass that Charley downs with one swallow.

Realizing that no amount of talk was going to convince Reynolds to call off his plans to ride with the 7th Cavalry, Marsh motions for Charley to sit again then changes the subject. After the captain consumes most of the bottle's contents the conversation becomes noticeably one-sided and Reynolds catches himself drifting off.

"You'll have to excuse me, Grant," Charley says finally forcing himself to an upright position. His knees feel weak and he's a bit light-headed from the liquor. "I'd better go get some rest. Tomorrow's a busy day."

Marsh rises and puts his arm on Charley's shoulder. "I'm glad you came to see me. We'll have another talk when you return, my friend, after this Indian trouble is over. You hang on to them auburn locks of yers, Lonesome Charley."

"I will, Sir. Thanks for everything. My thumb feels better already."

As Charley walks toward the gangway he can hear the noise coming from the vessel. Many of the officers have been drinking heavily since early evening and their voices are loud and boisterous, their speech slurred. Tom Custer who is playing poker and having obvious difficulty handling the slippery cards beckons Charley to join them. But the scout waves and shakes his head.

Charley decides to take in some fresh air and he leans against the rail. He scans the still threatening dark clouds while listening and making occasional observation of the soldiers. The whiskey has begun to warp the senses of even the sharpest minds of the 7th and Myles Keogh, who rarely discusses his personal life, finds himself confiding to James Calhoun his innermost feelings for a sweetheart in New York.

"She's a wonderful girl, Jim. If anything happens to me...if one of them Red savages cuts out my heart or tears off my hair...you'll take my belongings to her, won't you?"

Calhoun's response is sincere. "At your service, Sir," he says proudly, his chest protruding as if to accept a medal. "If I can't handle it myself I'll ask Lieutenant Carland to help. Did you say she lives in New York?"

"My sister lives in New York," interrupts another officer.

"Yeah that's right, Jim," Keogh says. "Take my things to my sister. She lives in Ireland—not New York."

"Who's in Ireland?" Calhoun asks as the communication begins to break up. "What happened to your sweetheart?"

For whatever reason Keogh seems to lose interest in the conversation and starts singing his favorite Irish melody, "Garry Owen." The men are, for the moment, free of military constrains. Even Captain Benteen, who has had more than his usual ration of liquor, is apparently enjoying the drunken antics of Major Reno and Lieutenant Benny Hodgson, who are singing and dancing to the accompaniment of a discordant Captain Keogh.

Suddenly a loud, "ya-hoo," is heard above the singing. Tom Custer has just won a large sum at the poker table and jumps onto his chair to announce his good fortune. "I'm rich! I'm a winner! All us Custers are winners!"

Benteen flinches at the drunken boast. The mere mention of, "Custer," instantly rekindles his hatred for the famous young general and he shouts above the noise to Lieutenant Godfrey. "George Armstrong Custer is a trumped-up phony! I don't care what they say. Custer abandoned Major Elliott on the Washita River and that's that!"

"What are you whining about now, Benteen?" asks Keogh who is once again aggravated by the officers' constant complaining. "Can't you stop your belly-aching for one night? Good God, man!" Keogh's eyes are flashing wildly. He reaches for another drink.

Under the influence, Bloody Knife, Custer's favorite Indian scout, slurs his words and flashes an angry gesture at Benteen. He then gives a toothy guttural laugh.

Unnoticed by the boisterous, crowd General Custer and his younger brother Boston, have been quietly talking and drinking coffee. Not wanting to interfere, the two Custer brothers can't help but hear most of the conversations. Custer listens to several of the officers singing one of his favorite songs.

"Sweet girl I left behind me."

"The hour was sad I left the maid A ling'ring farewell talking; Her sighs and tears my steps delay'd—I thought her heart was breaking. In hurried words her name I bless'd I breathed the vows that bind me And to my heart in anguish press'd The girl I left behind me."

Custer proudly sings, "Sweet girl I left behind me."

Lieutenant Godfrey, recognizing the potential for physical combat replies quickly to Benteen's comment. "Elliott took it upon himself to leave. He knew the risks!"

"Buffalo dung on a Georgia hog pile!" Benteen shouts back. "I still say the command should have looked for him."

"We did look for him. He was already dead!" Godfrey tries to explain. "You know how many more Indians were downstream, Benteen? Should Custer have risked the whole command to go after someone who was already dead?"

"Well..." Benteen is at a loss for words. "Well, I would have done things different!" he mutters finally. Godfrey who is familiar with Benteen's argumentative tendencies cleverly steers the conversation away from Custer. "If I remember right you've had some brave moments yourself, Captain. Like when you confronted that Indian boy who was bound and determined to kill you."

"Yeah I guess that did take a lot of guts," Benteen replies. A smile of satisfaction broadens his square jaw as he recalls the episode of years ago. "I gave him the peace sign several times but he kept coming. He was only thirteen or fourteen too. I don't know how many times I let him shoot at me before I fired...ten maybe a dozen rounds."

"A dozen rounds?" asks a disbelieving eavesdropper.

"You deserved a medal for that, Captain." adds Godfrey continuing to appease the intoxicated officer.

"I was finally forced to kill the boy. It was either him or me." Benteen stares smugly at the curl of smoke from his pipe.

"That's one great story, Benteen," Major Reno roars. "You've even got me believing that bull crap."

"That's much better'n the horse dung you sling." Benteen glares at Reno then sees George Custer. He staggers over as a hush comes over the steamer. "I don't forget, Coloneeel," he slurs out.

Custer coolly smiles, "And what might that be, Captain Benteen?"

"Major Elliott!" Benteen shouts.

"You cannot regret his death more than I, Captain. He was a fine officer."

Captain Weir staggering, weaves his way over, "Yeah! Aren't you the one who shot the Indian boy, Ceer-nel?"

"Ever since you were appointed captain your bravado irks my rosy, red behind, Weir!"

Keogh saunters over as Weir laughs. Benteen moves forward seemingly ready to take a poke at Weir. Keogh grabs Benteen from behind, twisting his arm. "We are Officers and Gentlemen aren't we, Captain?" Keogh gives an extra tug on Benteen's arm.

"I was only joking!" Benteen slurs. Keogh releases the arm.

George Custer calmly takes a sip of his coffee, "Tell me something, Colonel Benteen. How did you feel after you shot and killed that young Indian boy?"

"I sure didn't feel good about it. I have a son of my own. You know I had no choice!" Benteen snaps.

"But you still pulled the trigger, Colonel...and rightly so. Major Elliott pursued a band of Indians. Those Indians killed him and his men. After he was cut off and surrounded, it was too late." Custer briskly says.

Weir speaks up. "There is not one of us that do not regret his loss."

"That's right, Benteen. And now I have some letters to write. You boys better get some rest. We leave at noon tomorrow. Good evening, gentlemen," Custer politely says then turns on his heels and goes out the door.

The others silently stare.

Keogh's Irish voice breaks the quietness. "Lieutenant Carland, I want you to write out a list of some of my personal effects...if anything happens to me." The others watch as Carland looks hard at Keogh then sits down at one of the tables and begins to write.

Outside a severe thunder and lightning storm lashes its fury across the Montana sky. On the gangplank Bloody Knife staggers about, Grant Marsh helping him. Charley sees the pair and hurries to assist them.

Bloody Knife sits on his butt and mutters something in the Arickaree tongue. "Let him sit for awhile," Grant mutters, "That cold ramp will cool his behind." They chuckle. Then with a sense of quiet anxiety the two friends contemplate the storm.

Charley's thoughts quickly slip back to Running-creek-Woman. He can see that beautiful smile, the way she forms her lips. Lightning flashes above the steamer but Charley can only see that night on the plains inside their teepee. It was the first time they were together. The thunder boomed loud and the lightning lit up the inside of their teepee. She was afraid and he remembers Running-creek-Woman's words about the Thunderbird. *"Something great will happen."*

Grant's anxiety is clear, "It's not a good sign! You know you don't have to go, Charley."

Charley looks startled as Grant's words then Running-creek-Woman's ring in his ears. His eyes brighten as lightning flashes across the sky. "What are you trying to say, Grant?"

"Something big is going to happen!" Grant exclaims, while Bloody Knife mutters again. "What's he muttering about now?"

"He says the Thunderbird is angry. When Thunder rolls on the high plains something great will happen!" Charley again looks above. "He says he is fearful!"

Grant blurts out, "It's the creature in the brown jug, that devilish liquor," he looks at Charley his eyes pleading. "Don't go, Lonesome Charley."

Charley gets a determined look, "I'd sooner die than miss it!"

Keogh has overheard their conversation and staggers over by the two. Boston Custer walks out to help with Bloody Knife as Charley helps him get to his feet. Hail begins to fall while they slowly make their way down the gangplank.

Boston Custer reaches out a supporting arm, "Looks like he's drank his share."

"White man med-a-cine bad," Bloody Knife mutters, causing the others to laugh.

"The thunder is going to roll," Grant yells from above.

Captain Keogh puts his arm around Marsh's shoulder. Marsh senses what Keogh is going to say and joins him. "Let the thunder roll!" The men hurry for cover as the large, walnut sized hail pummels down.

Inside the steamer Major Reno slurs his words, "I'm going back to camp!

Which one of you soldiers is going to help me down the gangplank?"

Several of the younger men offer their assistance and except for a few stragglers, the celebration is all but over.

Inside his tent, George Custer lights a candle and writes a letter to his wife. He stands, yawning and stretching then peaks out his tent flap as the hail pounds off the canvas. He opens the flap and catches a couple of the ice balls in his hand. He surveys the storm with a concerned look.

When the last of the red-eyed soldiers finally staggers into camp it is well after midnight. The downpour has stopped and only a few drops of rain fall from the sky. But like a distant drumbeat echoing through the walls of a canyon, occasional bursts of thunder, rolling on the high plains rumbles across Montana Territory.

Charley Reynolds awakens to the loud laughter as the group passes his tent. He reaches for his watch. Now would be a good time to write that letter to Running-creek-Woman. He lights a candle and begins to write:

June 22 1876
Running-creek-Woman,

All is well here on the Yellowstone. The Ol' Thunderbird is sounding off from the heavens as I write. First came walnut size hail, then buckets of rain fell. Hope all is well at Thompson's camp. Hopefully by now, Thompson has been able to teach you how to understand the white man's talking paper. The trip here was uneventful, wood, grass and water was plentiful at most camps. I was able to hunt often. Killed several Rocky Mountain sheep, several buffaloes and you were right, "Pony tracks on the buffalo trail good sign, heap." The buffalo skin jacket wears well. Tomorrow, when we start up the Rosebud on the trail of the Indians I will be wearing it. Most of the officers believe the Indians will scatter and flee but I believe differently. According to the trail there is Otoe Sioux, meaning heaps of them. I will try and write again in a few days but the steamer and some of the Ree Indian scouts will carry the mail back to Lincoln. Hope all is well with Thompson and all. It gives me great comfort to see your smile. I can see your hair and can almost feel your warm face next to mine. All for now, ~~with to~~ Charley Reynolds.

Charley stops writing and contemplates. He had started to write, Love Charley, but then he scratched it out signing only his name. He doesn't understand everything about his own feelings but he'll have to sort his emotions for the lovely Indian woman out later. Maybe it's because of his uneasiness about this ride? It could be that felon on his hand? Maybe that affects his feelings?

He looks again at the timepiece thinking of Ariana. Maybe it's because in his innermost emotions he's never really gotten over her. Maybe he's really been in love with two women? But how could that be?

After rereading the letter several times, Charley neatly folds it and puts it into an envelope and writes the address.

c/o Thompson Indian trade store
Fort Lincoln, Dakota Territory

Charley looks up and listens as distant thunder rumbles. He stares with a sense of deep anxiety. During the Civil War, Pea Ridge flashes into his mind. He remembers at the crack of dawn, the artillery cannon fire boomed first. As the soldiers waited for the charge the cannon fire rumbled across the battlefield to soften the enemy, then came the charge. But it always seemed that something big happened after the cannon fire. Charley removes the letter from the envelope and writes more.

P. S. Only a few days out of Lincoln we had several severe thunder and lightning storms. A big storm hit earlier. Lightning and hail the size of walnuts pummeled the camp. I can still hear the thunder rumbling across the high plains. One of the lieutenants, who saw the Indian camp twice during the last month, feels it will be the greatest Indian fight to ever take place on the continent.
It seems there is something to your belief, Running-creek-Woman, "something great will happen."

He places the letter in one of the saddle pockets. He cleans his rifle then reloads some extra cartridges. He fills his prairie belt with the 50-70 brass shells and starts to clean his pistol. But suddenly feeling chilled and drowsy, he crawls into the warmth of his bedroll and is asleep within minutes.

It is three hours later when Charley is awakened by Chief Trumpeter Voss's rendition of reveille. He notices the dampness of his bedding—evidence of an overnight fever. Scenes from his dream flicker in and out of his mind. He had dreamed of old Gabe Green. *"Drink some of that brown-jug whiskey, youngin'. It'll heal up that hand quicker 'n any med-sin them quacks is a peddlin'!"* Charley smiles. The whiskey must have helped for his thumb does feel better. He finishes cleaning his pistol and goes to tend to his horses. Just to be on the safe side he'll get Custer's striker, John Burkman, to fix him a poultice.

On the far side of the camp Tom Custer is suffering from a terrible hangover. He has been up much of the night, puking. Myles Keogh, also slow to rise, saunters over to his canteen and takes a long drink of water. His head is pounding.

"I must not've drank much last night," his voice hoarse from singing. "I'm still thirsty!"

"Well you might not have drunk enough but I know I did," admits Tom. "I don't feel much like getting out of the sack and that's going to be a real problem here soon because I gotta go!"

Just within earshot Autie Reed overhears the conversation and can hardly wait to pick on his sickly uncle. Without warning he pounces on Tom's bedroll and starts tickling his ribs. "Come on, Uncle Tom. Time to get out of the sack!"

"Darn you, Reed." Tom protests. "Leave me alone! I gotta go pee!"

Charley laughs as he walks up in time to hear Tom and watch the antics. Nearby, Boston Custer, who is always being picked on by his brothers, relishes seeing Tom getting his just due.

But the young prankster shows no mercy. He fills a cup with water and begins to pour it a trickle at a time on Tom Custer's head. "Come on, Uncle Tom," he teases, "the Indians are attacking us!"

"Indians my—If you don't stop messing with me, boy I'll get a hold of you and I'll pound...oh God, my head!"

"That will teach you to drink more than your share! Here, have a drink of water. It's better for you."

"Okay, Autie give me some. Maybe it'll help." Tom leans forward to the cup in the outstretched hand but just as he's about to take a drink, Reed throws the water in his face and takes off running.

"You'd better run," Keogh warns, laughing heartily and holding his head at the same time.

"And you'd better not come back any too soon," Tom adds, as he staggers for the shelter of a nearby outcropping to relieve himself. Gingerly stepping in his bare feet avoiding the small prickly cactuses.

Autie waits until the hung over Captain returns and lowers his aching body back into the bedroll before sneaking around Tom's blind side with another full cup of water. But his uncle is watching with a half-closed eye and just as the youngster is about to empty the cup, Tom jumps up and grabs his pant leg. The agile Reed slips from his grip and Tom drops back to the ground moaning and groaning, dizzy from the exertion. "Come on, Reed. Lay off," he begs. "Please."

"All right, Tom. I'll quit but you better get yourself together. I hear you'll be riding with Major Reno today."

Tom's expression turns sour. "Who told you that?" he demands to know. "You'd better be funnin! Or there's going to be...to pay!"

Autie Reed sees that Tom is about to lose his temper. "I was only funnin' honest. Don't get angry, Tom please."

"That's nothing to be funnin' about!" the captain replies seriously. "I should've lit into him last night. Maybe I'll do it today."

"I apologize, Tom. Don't get all upset now," Autie pleads, wishing he hadn't gone so far with the teasing.

"What a bunch of misfits! I can't believe some of the officers. Horse trader Reno—grumbling Benteen—ol' rheu-ma-tic-tic Brisbin—sorry bunch of I don't know what."

"Some of the men are complaining. I've heard them," Autie Reed says excitedly. "They say that President Grant wants to get even with Uncle George and he's punishing him—putting him in his place."

"Autie, you'd better stop calling him, "uncle" in front of the men. He doesn't like it any more than I do."

"But you both are my uncles. I don't know why."

"Just never you mind why, boy. Now come along and help me get our gear ready." Tom coughs and groans as he bends to pick up his belongings.

Charley breaks in, "You boys better get ready to ride. Boots and Saddles will sound soon enough." Charley turns and leaves.

Tom Custer watches Reynolds then turns to Reed. "There goes the finest gentlemen you'll ever meet on the plains, Autie."

"I know, he's taken me hunting several times. I like Charley. He's my friend."

Tom returns to the former conversation, "Whatever happens, Autie you stick close to us, you hear? Boston, you do the same. George and I, Calhoun, Weir and Keogh, Charley Reynolds, Smith and Yates and a few more like Charley, like them... we could whip the Sioux nation by ourselves. We don't need the likes of Reno and that grumbling Benteen around. He's just not good for morale. You remember that, Reed!"

"Yessir, Captain," Autie responds with an official salute. "Hey, I'm ready for some grub. Are you?"

Tom Custer pales at the thought of food as the two prepare for the upcoming ride. "You go on and have your breakfast. I'll get something later."

"Boots and saddles," sounds at 11:45 and just before noon the, "prepare to mount," order is echoed from troop to troop. There is excitement in the air once again. Horses are prancing, neighing; saddles creak and tin cups rattle as the nearly seven hundred soldiers take to their mounts. At the head of the regiment a somber Charley Reynolds is aboard Red—not a big horse in comparison with some of the Kentucky bred thoroughbred cavalry horses but a horse with a, big heart, always eager to obey his master's command. As the band begins to play Garry Owen, George Armstrong Custer reins another of his favorite chargers Dandy, out of the column and gallops over toward General Terry, Major Brisbin and Colonel John Gibbon. The music causes the horses to step lively and the men are keenly alert. The General and his staff look pleased as the regiment passes in review and Custer's pride smiles beneath the broad brim of his hat. "Not a sore backed horse in the regiment," Custer smiles at the trio.

"Good luck!" Terry says to Custer.

"Now don't get too greedy...remember there are enough Indians out there for all of us!" Gibbon smiles while Brisbin smirks and gives a halfhearted wave.

"No, I will not," Custer politely tips his hat and Terry, Gibbon and Brisbin watch him ride hard for the head of the column that is already nearing the mouth of the Rosebud River.

"Maybe our plan will work," Brisbin remarks quietly to Terry. "So far, that loudmouth is cooperating."

General Terry does not acknowledge the remark and looks at both officers. "Colonel, Major, shall we head back to the Far West?"

"Yes, Sir, right away, Sir!" The 7th cavalry band strikes up with, *"The Girl I Left Behind Me."* General Terry and the others turn to listen to the regiment as the singing echoes out across the Yellowstone Country.

"The hope of final victory Within my bosom burning Is mingling with sweet thoughts of thee And of my fond returning. But should I ne'er return again Still worth thy love thou' It find me; Dishonor's breath shall never stain The name I'll leave behind me."

George Custer's 7th Cavalry travels twelve miles before making camp. Reynolds has noticed that several more bands of Indians have joined the main trail along the Rosebud. He is not sure whether they are scouting or hunting parties but he alerts Custer and the other officers to be on guard.

To Autie Reed the, "camp order," is simply an excuse to let off a little steam. He overhears several of the soldiers talking about some antelope Curly had reported, not far from their camp. Autie Reed leads his horse from the camp. Reed knows that there are many Ree scouts plus the Crows that come and go all day so it won't appear strange if he leaves for a while.

Curly chews some dried buffalo meat then looks surprised as he watches Autie talk to the picket guard then leave the camp.

In no time at all, Autie is riding hell-bent-for-leather into a herd of antelope. Whooping and hollering the young man runs a straggler until it tires enough to take a shot. He misses.

Then Autie spies a huge pronghorn and takes chase. After a lengthy run he closes in on his prey. He carefully aims and fires; instantly the animal drops. Reed quickly puts his rifle in the cavalry socket attached to the D ring of his saddle. Yelling with excitement Autie spurs his horse toward the fallen antelope but without warning his fast-moving mount stumbles into a prairie-dog hole, crashing hard to the ground and sending the shocked youth head-over-heels through the air. Reed gets his bearings just in time to see his startled gelding regain its balance and run out of sight into a nearby draw. A little shaken, he picks himself up and limps in the direction of his runaway horse.

Like many youths, Reed had not stopped to consider the consequences of his actions. It suddenly occurs to him that Indians may be lurking close by or even in the draw and he shudders at the thought of being attacked. Here he is alone, his horse has run off and with only a knife to defend himself. He remembers the scouts with the command have reported sightings, of Indians. He remembers Charley's words, "When you don't see Indians is when they are usually around."

He feels his stomach tighten, his throat is dry. But he has no choice. Just as he approaches the draw, his horse bolts past him nearly knocking him to the ground. Reed notices the animal's bug-eyed fear and realizes that something else has spooked the poor creature. Suddenly a loud snort echoes from the draw. Autie reels and finds himself no more than one hundred fifty feet from a huge buffalo. There's no mistaking the signs. An outcast run off from the herd, it's a bull on the prowl; bellowing, snorting, pawing, as only they can do. The youngster wastes no time. Running as fast as he can in pursuit of his fleeing horse he feels the ground shake beneath him; the heavy throaty breathing at the back of his neck; the bull is gaining on him. He doubts he can outrun the big buffalo but what else can he do? His legs are beginning to tire.

By chance, Curly has come in search of Reed. Both about the same age, Curly leaving for his scout, heard the shot and had followed Autie. At once, recognizing the danger, he whips his bay stallion to an all-out gallop toward Reed. Then hooves pounding and dirt flying, he clings to his horse's mane with one hand and reaches down to give Autie a hand up. The Indian's agile mount avoids the charge of the cantankerous bull and the two boys ride to safety, the runaway gelding following close behind. For Curly this is a natural experience, as the young Crow warriors have been riding and taking part in Indian horseback games since a very early age.

Autie Reed grins broadly while he bows to the earth to thank his good graces. For a moment, he forgets that Curly does not speak English and rattles away while he points to the heavens. "It was only providence, whatever you want to call it, that brought you here." Curly looks puzzled than mutters a guttural response.

Knowing he is in deep trouble if anyone finds out about this latest escapade, Autie Reed using what little sign language he has learned from the General and Lonesome Charley, convinces Curly to keep it a secret. Before Curly departs to continue his scouting duty with Goes-Ahead, Curly quickly guts and then straps the antelope to Autie's saddle. Reed waves to the young Indian as Curly gallops off to meet Goes-Ahead.

The young hunter, a little bruised and dusty, leads his horse back to camp trying not to attract the attention of the soldiers and least of all his uncles.

"What in the devil!" screeches Captain Tom Custer, when he sees the slain antelope? "Where in all Montana Territory did you get..."

Autie Reed, who thought he was alone, nearly jumps out of his torn britches. "Please, Tom. Don't tell Uncle George."

After pressing the youngster to tell the whole story, Tom can barely keep a straight face. "You're a numskull! You've alarmed the guards! Don't you realize what could happen? There are a thousand Indians out there. They only need to hear one shot and they'd be on us like a swarm of hornets! Don't you ever pull another foolish stunt like that again. And if the General hears you calling him, "uncle," one more time, he's going to send you back to the Yellowstone. Mark my words, Autie my boy, you're treading on thin ice!"

Convinced that the white-faced youngster is truly sorry for his actions, Tom quickly turns and walks away for fear he can no longer contain the belly laugh he's so far concealed.

"What are you grinning about?" Boston asks Tom as the elder brother joins a group of men who have gathered around a fire.

Tom makes Boston and the others promise not to let the story go any further, then goes on to tell them about Reed's hunting trip. In true Custer fashion, each event is stretched beyond the truth, making the story so hilarious that the soldiers are choking with laughter. A curious Captain Benteen stands nearby. The tapping of his empty pipe on the sole of his boot seems to annoy no one but the magpie who has dropped down for a meal of scraps.

Hearing the laughter, George Custer quickly reviews the orders with Adjutant Cooke and sets out to investigate the ruckus. An immediate silence falls over the jovial assemblage as the Commander approaches.

"Well, don't let me interrupt the party," he remarks, a little puzzled by the sudden quiet. "What's all the noise about?"

Tom finally speaks. "We were—that is Ba-Ba, Bos and me," he stammers, "We were telling the boys about the time that father had never seen an alligator—you remember about father and the alligator down south, in Texas?"

Custer smiles. "You mean that time we played a prank on Father...we told him that the dead mule in the river was an alligator?"

"Yeah, that was sure funny!" Tom answers a little nervously. "I can still see him running and hopping from his tent, trying to get his pants on at the same time."

Boston notices Tom is staring at him with a comically hopeless grin. He takes the cue, laughs loudly, nudges the private next to him and soon the group is once again in an uproar. Benteen walks away in disgust as Custer is cleverly drawn in by the ruse.

"Come along, Tom," Custer says, finally, after completing the story about the alligator. "We've got work to do."

Tom follows dutifully. "I sure miss father, Autie," he says with sincerity.

"We'll have to take leave when we get back to Lincoln and go home to Monroe. I'm eager to see how Nevin is doing on the farm."

"Of all us, Nevin was probably the only one who loved farming," Tom concludes as he sees Charley Reynolds walking toward them. "There's Lonesome Charley."

Custer motions to Reynolds. "Good. I need a word with him. Hey, Reynolds," Charley steps over to talk with Custer and his brother.

Custer beckons Lieutenant Cooke over. "Lieutenant, notify the officers to assemble at headquarters at once."

"Aye, Sir."

After his talk with Custer, Charley retires early and is preparing for his scout the following morning hours before the camp begins to stir. He talks with several of the Indian scouts, including Mitch Boyer and Curly. The nomadic Sioux and Cheyenne routinely follow the well-worn Rosebud trail for water and in search of the large antelope and buffalo herds. That fact is well known, but Charley wants to learn more from the Crow Indian scouts.

Curly at seventeen, is the youngest. He is tall and muscular with high cheekbones and distinctly chiseled facial features. The Crows have a distinct way of braiding the hair in front of their ears, the braids hang long and forward over the front of their shoulders, instead of down the back of their neck. Curly's blue-black hair hangs in two long braids, on each side of his neck in this unique style. At the forehead his hair is combed in a roach, upwards in true Crow fashion—a very handsome lad indeed.

Mitch Boyer, the half-breed of French-Sioux descent, has a clever mind and is a valuable asset to the campaign. There are five other members of the Crow tribe and nearly forty Arickaree scouts as well. But the Crows have traveled this land for many years raiding Sioux and Cheyenne camps and stealing their horses and capturing their women or children. Even though Curly is just a youngster he has hunted along the Rosebud on a number of occasions and has accompanied several war and scouting parties too. The Sioux are his enemy and he is eager to help the Army's cause.

Scout on the Rosebud, June 23, 1876

Charley, although impressed with Curly's enthusiasm, listens carefully to the warnings of the others. Then when the dawn breaks he rides out alone several miles ahead of the main column. The other scouts and the vedettes are out; reconnaissance is in force; this is the romantic 7th Cavalry at its best. Still, Charley is uneasy. His mind wanders over past experiences on the Great Plains—vast buffalo grounds of Kansas, Nebraska, Colorado and now on the high plains of Montana Territory. All those years of experience are at work now and Charley is all business when he discovers more sign of the Indians. He removes his watch from its pocket, tries to guess how far behind Custer is, then wonders what would have happened if Ariana were still alive. He fondles the watch for a moment and returns it to the pocket. For three years he has ridden with the 7th Cavalry but never before has he had such a feeling within—a strange feeling he can't explain even to himself. Trying to solve the mystery in his mind brings no relief so he talks to his horse for a while, in hopes that the answers will suddenly come if he speaks loud enough.

Suddenly he notices more Indian sign ahead. The territorial marker, a small piece of red flannel tied to a sun-bleached bone, warns of his trespass on Indian land.

"Whoa up, Red. Easy, Boy." He stares at the signs then his eyes intensely focus on the red flannel. In a blurred vision he sees his brother William and the lance with the trailing red flannel strips. The vision bounces to his friend Little Bear, and then the red flannel on his friend Gabe Green's burial scaffold.

The morning shadows shrink rapidly as the sun reaches mid heaven revealing the naked form of the Rosebud's pristine valley. The lone scout reminds himself that it is right near the Summer Solstice. He again removes his watch from its special pocket and flips it open with his sore thumb. Very sore! It's almost noon. Red's ears turn back in appreciation as Charley pats the horse's neck. The animal will need water soon. Charley's eyes seem extra sensitive to the bright glare. Not until he pulls his hat down for shade does he notice the fresh trace. Everything else he'd seen so far was old. He looks carefully around and then takes Red to the creek for a drink.

Following the trail of scratched and torn topsoil it's apparent that the Indians are pulling several hundred travois; there are too many pony tracks to count. Charley's grip tightens as he makes a mental notation of each new clue. Suddenly Red breaks stride. Charley scans the horizon expecting to see more wild game. Instead, barely visible on a small rise some six hundred yards distant, a mounted Indian is watching him.

Something doesn't seem right. The Indian isn't moving; only watching. Charley finally reaches for his glasses and focuses in on his subject. A polka-dot neckerchief, fur skullcap single feather, along with two stuffed birds clinging to the sides, it's Mitch Boyer. Charley is surprised he hadn't recognized him instantly. His eyes must be getting weak. He signals the Indian to join him and they continue to follow the trail together.

An hour later they come across an abandoned camp. Reynolds dismounts and counts the fire rings.

"What do you make of this, Boyer?"

The guide answers in broken English aided by the occasional sign: "One moon past Loo-tenant Bradley find this village."

"I count almost four hundred rings. The General should know about this right away. Where are they headed, Boyer?"

For whatever reason the Indian seems eager to tell Reynolds all he knows. "When I live with the Sioux, many winter gone, Uncpapa hold Great Medicine Dance. The Rose moon, when the night sun, fills the sky many, many Otoe Indian come. Lakota watch Sitting Bull Uncpapa make good medicine. You know this?"

Charley's eyes are open wide. Almost to himself he speaks. "The night sun fills the sky...the full moon. The roses bloom in all of Montana during June." Charley looks along the creek at the wild roses, their pink blossoms shining in full bloom. "The roses bloom on the Rosebud River, the Rose Moon... when the moon is full...the month of the fat horses." He searches Boyer sternly, "The Wasichus call it Sun Dance."

Mitch Boyer lets a rare smile slip. "Wasichus!" he repeats. "Wasichus have bad medicine!"

Charley returns the smile. "After Medicine Dance, where do the Sioux go?"

Serious again, Boyer appears a little suspicious. "You not know?"

"I don't know, Boyer."

"Sioux follow Lodge Pole Trail to Great Medicine Creek. Then to Greasy Grass Creek. There is much food. Antelope, Pte, Wapiti. Otoe Sioux! Otoe Sioux!"

"The river the Crows call Greasy Grass...the Little Big Horn!" Charley says more to himself than anyone else. "Boyer, before long we must take the news back to General Custer. For now we'll split up. That way we can cover more ground. I'll stay on the trail for a while longer."

"Curly will be along soon," says Boyer and rides off.

As Charley watches Mitch Boyer disappear, he senses his vulnerability alone here in the Land of the Big Sky. Red, his long-time companion, feels his rider rigid in the saddle. The wary animal steps cautiously, ears and eyes alert. Charley's thoughts begin to rotate from present to past as he watches the scarred turf pass beneath him. He daydreams longingly as Running-creek-Woman flashes into his mind. He remembers their last kiss, her smile, how they rubbed cheeks in the Indian way.

Soon the afternoon's first shadows appear. He wonders where Custer is; if things would have been different if Ariana had lived; if the Sioux are watching him; if Allison has raided any more sporting houses; if Sitting Bull is as powerful as the Ree scouts say; what will be the outcome if the Indians are on the Greasy Grass? He glances down at his carbine posed stiffly across the pommel of his saddle. His knuckles are white, reminding him to loosen his grip. It's time to turn back.

Charley snaps to reality and grabs his rifle and dismounts to examine the chopped-up Montana soil. He drops to one knee to get a better look at the fresh lodge pole marks that have joined the trail from the east. He begins to count, when a noise from behind startles him. Whirling in the scratched turf, he quickly levels his Sharps, cocking the hammer at the same time. It's a false alarm; in the distance he, sees a large mule deer bounding away. His heart beating, Reynolds jumps to his feet and reminds himself to be more alert in the future...and less concerned with the feelings that have been haunting him.

Out of the blue, Reynolds sees movement. The Indian scouts evidently had spotted Reynolds some time ago but seem not to be in any hurry to talk to him until they suddenly realize what Charley has found. Using sign and a combination of English and the Crow tongue, the scouts decide that there may be as many as one hundred fifty more Indians, likely Sioux that have joined the main trail. Boyer suggests that the three travel together but Reynolds insists on scouting the western bank of the river before taking the news to Custer.

"I'll ride the west bank for an hour or so and meet you boys later, when the command stops for water."

Curly and Boyer mimic Charley's trademark wave as he rides to the bank of the river.

"Char-Lee brave!" exclaims Curly as the pair rein their ponies to the left and move back along the main trail.

Boyer nods, speaking in the Crow tongue, "Many winters have gone, long time beyond. I have heard the white man's talk about the white scout, Charley. Many say he is Indian friend." He lays his reins across the pommel and makes the sign for great, "It is good to meet such a great one."

The Custer brothers seem to be enjoying the freedom of the trail when Reynolds finally gallops back to the command. Tom and Boston have taken sides against Custer and his Adjutant, Lieutenant Cooke, in an endless argument over the benefits of strong drink, particularly whiskey. Tom is still suffering from his overindulgence the previous night.

"Look at you!" Cooke says to Tom. "You're as sick as a dying dog...and you can sit there and tell me with a straight face that whiskey is good for what ails you?"

"It cleanses the soul," Tom replies with an impish grin.

"Hogwash!" blasts the red-faced Adjutant.

"Hello, Reynolds," Custer says as Charley rides nearer. "You boys finish that argument. I want to talk to my scout. Come, Lonesome Charley let's ride ahead. Tell me what you've seen so far today."

"Two more bands have joined the main trail, General." Charley pauses for the commander's comment.

"Is that all?"

"That's three bands I've discovered so far—just along the Rosebud. There's no telling how many others are coming from the south and east."

"How big are these bands, Charley?"

"The last one I came across, Curly and Boyer helped me count the marks. We figured anywhere from a hundred to a hundred fifty. They're crafty devils, General!"

"In what way?"

"They're following old trails. It's hard to tell what tracks are what—sometimes they're two weeks to a month old, sometimes more. The ground is really scarred bad. I'm sure that one of those trails is the same one Lieutenant Bradley and his scouts found several weeks ago. It's almost impossible to estimate the numbers accurately. I'm troubled that there may be too many Indians."

Custer, who reads Indian sign as well as most veteran scouts, is perplexed by Reynolds' report. "You think the Sioux are headed for the Little Horn, Lonesome?"

"Sir, I've never seen so much sign—anywhere! A blind man could follow the trail. The entire valley along the creek is dug up from their trailing lodge poles. It reminds me of the plowed fields back home in Kansas."

"I'm sure they're headed for the Little Big Horn, Charley. Captain Ball's scout, back in April, did not reveal any fresh Indian sign when they crossed the Little Horn valley. With Crook coming up from the south it is almost certain they'll be somewhere on the Little Horn."

"They don't have too many choices, General."

"There's only one, as far as I can see."

Charley looks firmly at the general. "Trouble is, just whereabouts on the river?" The scout reaches down and tucks a loose latigo saddle strap back through its loop. "Boyer says the Sioux and Cheyenne almost always follow the lodge pole trail to the Greasy Grass after the Great Medicine Dance."

Custer's speech quickens. "Curly told me that they'll follow Great Medicine Creek to the Greasy Grass after the Sun Dance. On the map that stream flows into the Little Big Horn River!"

"The Greasy Grass is the Indian name for the Little Big Horn. They are one and the same river." Charley pauses a full minute pondering the Indian movements he has observed in the past. "Curly and Boyer say the same as the other scouts...there's plenty buffalo and antelope in the valley and no shortage of water. The Crows know the ground well. Sometimes the Sioux will follow the stream as far as the headwaters in the Big Horn Mountains. But they might have other plans. I think they'll do whatever

Sitting Bull and the other chiefs counsel them to do. What if they're in the upper portion of the Little Horn? According to General Terry that is where we can expect to find the Sioux."

For a long while they ride in silence each submerged in his own private thoughts. The music of the plains—the howl of a lone buffalo wolf, the cawing Crows, the chattering magpies, the meadowlark—mingles with the sounds of creaking leather, heavy breathing and the sporadic percussion of iron horseshoes clashing with dust covered rocks.

Custer has been reliving the distressing moments of the conference aboard the Far West and finally speaks up. "I appreciate your loyalty, Charley—not just for your scouting duties but for being a friend as well. Back there on the Yellowstone...well, I was disheartened, to say the least. I've never quite had that feeling before."

Reynolds is surprised at Custer's frankness. Yes, Charley knows the feeling... the bloody scene of his fight with Antonio flashes in front of him...not a friend in the world. He's not sure what to say but suddenly the words come almost voluntarily. "When I was a young boy my uncles built a school; a religious school. That's where I received my early education. There's one passage I learned there from the Good Book. I'll never forget it: "A true companion is loving all the time and is a brother that is born for when there is distress. The book of Proverbs, I believe."

"What do you think that means?"

"Some so-called friends aren't really friends at all. A true companion is a friend who'll always stand beside you, even when times are tough."

"You never cease to amaze me, Charley. You're a true companion. After these three years riding together you're like another brother to me. Libbie said you were the kind of man I could trust. She was right." Custer smiles and reaches down and pats his appreciative horse. "Dandy and Red have served us well, have they not, Reynolds?"

"Yes, Sir. There's been many a time when Red and Rusty have been my only true companions." Charley confesses as he leans forward and rubs Red's ears. "You know, General I've been having some strange feelings about this ride. Nothing I can put my finger on...it just seems to be different from other campaigns."

"I know what you mean. After that thing with the President, what happened back on the Powder and now this ridiculous scheme with Brisbin...and I believe Terry..." Custer raises his voice in exasperation. "It seems like the Army's entire chain of command is turning against me!"

"Ever since Grant became President there's just been one scandal after another. He was a hero during the War; I've heard soldiers all across the country say what a good commander he was."

"He was a fine general," Custer answers emphatically, "One of the best. We fought in many campaigns together. I considered him a friend...maybe not a true companion," he laughs sarcastically, "but a friend, nonetheless."

"What happened? How can one man change so much in such a short time?"

"Turned into an Old Bummer, too much strong drink. Politics, I hate politics!

A man can't even make a friend without owing him or his cronies some kind of favor! I confided in my wife that my doctrine has ever been that a soldier should not meddle in politics."

Reynolds suddenly reins Red to a halt as they cross the fresh Sioux trail Charley had discovered earlier in the day.

"Whoa, Dandy!" Custer orders, then quickly dismounts to inspect the tracks.

The horses are left unfettered to munch on the fertile Montana grass as the quiet scout and his hardy leader kneel to examine the sign more closely. The message is clear to Charley. Months ago when he had wired Custer that they could expect two thousand lodges, that news may not have been taken seriously. Now Charley is certain there are more, maybe hundreds more. It is a serious state of affairs indeed!

Custer stands, his favorite sporting rifle in hand. The fringes on his buckskin pants flutter slightly in the gentle breeze and the sun's devil rays dance on his shiny black cavalry boots as he gazes silently, thoughtfully toward the southern boundaries of Montana's great wilderness. Charley wonders if the General has read the same message.

18

By the hundreds they came—the Cheyenne leading the way followed by, the Brule, the Oglala, the Sans Arc, the Minneconjoux, the Blackfeet and finally, the Uncpapa Sioux who guarded the rear of the large procession. Before the White Man's month of June had neared the full moon there would be thousands. They had come to learn the wisdom of the legendary Uncpapa Chieftain whose name, literally translated was, Tatanka Iyotake, "Buffalo Bull Sitting Down." Or "Buffalo bull sit down.'"

It was the Month of Fat Horses, the ripe chokecherries, when the great camp circles settled on the upper reaches of the Rosebud River. The moon was bright and full, the grass high; the land was thriving with plant life and new generations had joined the animal herds. This was Montana Territory in its entire splendor—disguising the uneasy preamble of what would become one of the most vicious and hideous battles to ever be fought on American soil.

Sitting Bull despised the White Man; that was no secret. But his beliefs differed from that of other tribal leaders. This Medicine Man showed his hatred by ignoring the enemy. Generally refusing to converse with the White race, he more often than not, stayed away from the Indian Agencies and usually would not accept the annuities allotted to his tribe by the federal government. But although he avoided contact with his adversary, Sitting Bull's complaints had been heard as far away as the Capitol itself. His references to the handouts were not complimentary. He disliked the stinking, spotted cattle offered as a substitute for the Indian's hallowed bison. He complained bitterly about the worm-infested flour and the greasy pig meat, the Wasichus called bacon. Even his dogs wouldn't eat it and the fat lay rotting on the plain full of maggots, attracting only the hungriest of buzzards. It seemed to the Indians that the evil White Man was destroying everything.

John Finerty, a newspaper reporter and correspondent, who often accompanies the Army's front lines into battle, had this to say about his first sight of the famed Uncpapa Chief:

"Sitting on his horse his broad face wide jaw, hair parted in the middle like most Sioux and a prominent nose his fierce bloodshot eyes stared solidly for over a minute. I did not have to be told—this was the great Sitting Bull."

The few White Men who had observed the elusive Medicine Man described him similarly. Lonesome Charley Reynolds had seen him several times. Once during the winter of 1875, he had seen Sitting Bull near the Berthold Agency. A peaceful band of Arickaree traders had gathered at the outpost with their abundant supplies of arms, ammunition and commodities such as corn, coffee and sugar. Outnumbered by Sitting Bull and his formidable Uncpapa Sioux, the Arickarees felt threatened and quickly surrendered their goods to the superior clan. News of Sitting Bull's rare appearance near the agency had sounded an alarm up and down the Missouri River. Although not surprised that other hunters and guides feared the Indian, the man's spiritual leadership intrigued Reynolds. It was not only the Uncpapa who had gathered along the Rosebud to learn from Sitting Bull's vision...they had all come. They had all come to witness the most torturous of Indian customs—the Sun Dance.

The Great Medicine Dance on the Rosebud River

"Stay away from the Wasichus! Stay far away from the Wasichus," Sitting Bull had advised the other Sioux and Cheyenne leaders. "Only if they come after us shall we fight!" The Wasichus had followed and now it was time for the Great Medicine Dance of the Uncpapa.

Thousands of Indians from over a half-dozen bands had gathered to take part in the celebration. The Sacred Pole, painted red, blue, green and yellow to symbolize the four directions of the earth, stands prophetically in the early-morning sunlight; its rawhide thongs hanging in limp innocence as preparation gets underway for the annual ritual.

Even the women and children are not spared the gruesome sight as the Chieftain immerses himself into a chant while the young Indian, Jumping Bull, using an awl and a knife, lifts and cuts off skin from the wrist to the shoulder of each arm. One hundred pieces of flesh are sacrificed before he is hoisted into position on the Sacred Pole to await his Medicine Dream. Horrified onlookers watch as the young Indian slashes Sitting Bull's chest. The Indian stares boldly into the sky and utters not a sound, barely wincing as two pieces of bone are skewered through the muscles of his chest and then attached to the rawhide strips dangling from the pole.

Chanting and singing to the Great Mystery, Wakan Tanka, Sitting Bull doesn't seem to notice the blood running down his sides, dripping onto the alkaline dust below, his offering of the scarlet blanket to the Wakan Tanka.

For hours Sitting Bull chants and stares full-face into the blazing summer sun until he is nearly blinded by the searing light. His chanting becomes weaker and after a long time he falls backward suspended from the Sacred Pole, silent, motionless. His leathery bonds stretched taut are still securely fastened to the bloody bones that protrude from his scarred chest. Later, no one could recall just how long, whether days or how many hours, that Sitting Bull hung from the rawhide thongs.

"He is dead!" cries one of the Sioux women finally. "Cut him down. You must cut him down!"

Several members of Sitting Bull's tribe hurry to investigate; but to their amazement the Chief is very much alive.

"The Great Wakan Tanka has spoken, my friends. In my dream I see many soldiers falling into Indian camp...falling to their death. We must fight the Pony Soldiers. And I, Sitting Bull, shall be the last to surrender my rifle!"

Suddenly the huge camp is alive with chanting and singing. Their leader's vision has given them renewed strength and courage—they will fight to the end. "Death to the Bluecoats!" they shout. "Death to the Wasichus!"

June 24, 1876, 5 A. M., 43 Miles South of the Yellowstone

George Armstrong Custer inspects the log as Lieutenant George Wallace, keeping the official itinerary, makes a notation.

Lieutenant Cooke, the Adjutant is there. Charley Reynolds rides over for any last minute instructions.

"Thirty-three miles yesterday, Cookie," Custer says cheerfully. "I'd say that's respectable."

"Yes, Sir," replies the Adjutant. He then fastens his pack to the saddle before Custer orders the forward.

"We should make another thirty miles." Custer says as he draws his Webleys, re-checking their loaded cylinders. "The horses are in fine shape."

"Thanks to this lush forage," Charley reaches and pats the neck of his horse.

"This horse is in greater shape than I've ever seen him." Cooke slaps the hindquarters of his gray charger.

On the bank of the Yellowstone River, not many miles away, General Terry and the Montana Column is preparing to break camp. The stodgy commander waits patiently for the signal that the troops are ready to move then enters the exact time in his diary. The mood of the troopers is calm and confident as they line up in formation. General Terry will continue on as planned.

Custer's scouts come and go all morning, supplying a constant flow of information to keep Custer and his staff well informed. None of their findings have been worrisome however, until Curly appears shortly after noon with his report. Evidently the main Sioux trail has split, something Custer had not anticipated. He immediately orders a halt. The soldiers are told to rest while he confers with his staff.

"Now what," Tom asks after Charley explains that the Sioux trail has divided into two trails; one following the Rosebud and the other along a left branch.

"They're a crafty lot," remarks Custer. "They know that anyone following them will have to split up and that takes time. What do you make of it, Reynolds?"

"Why not send Curly on one trail and Goes-Ahead on the other? For all we know, the two trails may join further south on the Rosebud—or maybe even west on Ash Creek."

Tom grins. "Ash Creek, that's where we ought to send Benteen. Come to think of it," he adds, laughing heartily, "Major Reno should go along too, just in case Benteen loses his royal behind!"

"All right," exclaims Custer trying not to laugh himself, "Captain!"

Tom knows when the Commander of the 7th calls him, "Captain," it's time to quit skylarking. "What creek did you say, Charley?" he asks, winking at the quiet scout.

"Ash Creek," Charley smiles in answer to the devilish officer. "The Sioux call it Great Medicine Creek."

"If it's the one Boyer pointed out," Tom says, suddenly very serious. "They'll likely ambush any companies we send down there!"

"Reynolds, I believe you're right," Custer says with a tone of urgency. "I'll have Curly and Goes-Ahead follow the trails as you suggested." Turning to leave he then pauses, "Crook's cavalry should be close by now. I'll have to inform the others to be on the alert for his scouts—Terry's too. We wouldn't want any of our armies' friendly Indian scouts shot by mistake."

"The scouts are ranging as far as ten or fifteen miles in front of the column. I'll pass the word, General."

"I'll inform Lieutenant Varnum." Custer turns and shouts for his Adjutant. "Lieutenant Cooke!"

The Adjutant, upon hearing the call from several yards away straightens his giant frame from its cross-legged position on the ground and hurries toward Custer. "Yessir!" he replies, nearly out of breath.

"Inform Lieutenants Varnum and Hare to instruct the Indian scouts to be on the alert for Crook's scouts—Terry's too. We wouldn't want any of our armies' friendly Indian scouts shot by mistake. As soon as we move out I want more outriders...two more front and rear!"

"More, Sir?"

"Yes, Lieutenant. The Sioux have split into two parties and the trail is getting fresher every hour. See to it that the flankers are in position also."

"Yes, Sir!"

Lieutenant George Wallace reads over his logbook:

"June 24th – Started 5 a.m.; in about an hour the Crow scouts came in and reported fresh signs of Indians but not in great numbers. We followed the right bank of the Rosebud crossing the first two running tributaries seen."

After nearly four hours' rest the Dakota Column starts to move again. It is 5 o'clock and from Montana's broad clear sky the hot summer sun continues to wring the moisture from the ground below.

Lieutenant Wallace recorded:

"At 5 p.m. the command moved out: crossed to the left bank of the Rosebud; passed through several large camps. The trail was now fresh and the whole valley scratched up by trailing lodgepole."

Stinging alkaline powder, kicked up by the iron-shod horses, irritates the soldiers' eyes and solidifies their perspiration causing their skin to itch and burn. No one is spared the discomfort.

Two of the Crow scouts approach Custer and Mitch Boyer. The wise one, White-man-runs-Him speaks first, Boyer interprets. "Long time past many winters gone, this Crow Indian land. Our enemies the Dakotas now say this land it theirs. The Crows called hills Wolfteeth, the Americans, the White Man call, Wolf Mountain."

Half-yellow-Face speaks up. Boyer again talks for the Crow. "We Up-sah-ro-ku, large beaked bird. We Crows lead soldiers, high butte, see far. Maybe see Sioux." Boyer points off in the distance.

Custer stares towards the hills where Boyer points then nods. Boyer is stolid, "The Dakotas not far ahead."

Custer looks beyond then eyes each of the Crows. "I would like my Crow boys to lead me to the Dakotas, as the Crows call the Sioux. Find the Sioux village."

Boyer nods to the General then waves to the Crows and they ride off speaking and gesturing in the Crow tongue. Custer watches as they, at a fast trot, hurry south up the Rosebud. Custer mounts up and waves the forward. He picks up the pace knowing that the Indians are within thirty miles or so.

It is nearly three hours later when Custer instructs the adjutant to set up camp. Only small fires, using dry wood, are allowed.

Lieutenant Wallace noted in his log book:
"... At 7:45 p.m. we encamped on the right bank."

When the order to camp is finally heard the soldiers drop from their mounts and sprawl out in the bluestem grass near the small stream. It is cooler by the creek but sleep doesn't come easy for Autie Reed. Holding on to his reins for fear his gelding might run again he drifts in and out of consciousness. He can hear some officers talking in the background. "Wolfteeth Mountains. Sitting Bull." But none of it makes sense and he's much too tired to care.

George Custer notices that Major Reno is suffering more than the others and walks up to say a few words—anything to get his mind off the day's heat.

"It's timely you bought that hat, Marcus," Custer says cheerfully, referring to the straw hat Reno had purchased aboard the Far West.

"Yes, Sir!" the Major replies coldly, removing the hat and wiping his forehead with a red handkerchief. "I wish I was back on that steamer now sipping a cool mint julep." Then shaking the sweat from the hat he continues, "Maybe I'd purchase another just like it. This one's nearly soaked through to the brim. It feels like I could burn up."

"Lieutenant Varnum and some of the Rees are out. The Crows are out to. Hopefully they'll locate precisely where the Sioux trail leads." Custer gestures to the camp, "Wood, grass, water Reynolds knows a good campsite."

"I see, Colonel," replies the weary Major. "It's a darn sight better than traveling in this confounded heat!"

Custer sees the pained expression on Reno's face. He tips his hat politely and in his energetic manner hurries away muttering in disgust at the self-pitying officer's complacent attitude.

Custer joins a camp circle as James Calhoun, Tom, Boston, Weir and some others listen to one of Myles Keogh's colorful tales.

"The Cimarron—that's where I named my horse," he continues, after acknowledging George Custer's arrival. "He got hit by an arrow and screamed just like one of those bloody Comanches. That's where he earned his name, Comanche."

Laughing, Tom finally speaks out. "See here, boys, we can listen to the Irishman's tall-tales all night long but boys, you need to get some shut eye. We've a hard day in the saddle tomorrow."

"I want all fires extinguished before darkness sets in," says Custer. The officers take their leave, nodding to the General as they start off to their respective bedrolls.

George Custer finally drops down in the grass for a quick nap. His eyes closed he rests on his elbow, his head in his hand and anticipates the scouts' return from the Sioux trail. What will be their final message?

And Terry's command, Custer mulls over their whereabouts? He must anticipate Terry's Montana Column like his own, is only thirty miles or less from the Little Big Horn. What George Custer is unaware of is, due to unnecessary delays, the Montana Column had only started to disembark across the Yellowstone for their route up Tullock's Creek at 4:00 a.m. this morning. Total distance traveled on the 24th of June, merely four miles.

George Custer on the other hand, even with the support of twelve companies of experienced soldiers, is cautious. He orders more flankers on either side as well as to the front and rear. He doesn't want any surprises.

Suddenly the bivouac is alive with excitement. Autie Reed awakens to the noise and jumps up to join several others around the fire.

"What in..."

Reed finishes for Tom: "What in the devil is it!"

"Hush up and listen," yells, Tom Custer.

In the twilight the silhouettes of two figures are running toward them. "Otoe Sioux! Otoe Sioux! Soldier Chief," they are crying, "Son Morning Star!"

Custer finally recognizes the name given him by the scouts when they reach his fire. It's Curly and Goes-Ahead. Custer calmly eyes the two scouts. The General motions to Reed. "Autie, you go find Bos n' the two of you get some shut eye. I will see you in the morning." Autie Reed looks at his uncles disappointed but he understands that he's not privy to their talk. He obediently saunters away to his bedroll.

Curly raises his right hand. "Otoe!" he exclaims proudly holding a not to old bloodied White-Man scalp up.

Forgetting that the Crows speak or understand little of the White-Man tongue Tom demands, "Where in the devil did you find a scalp? The Sioux ambush some poor fellow?" Tom grabs the scalp to examine it more closely.

"Soldier Chief!" whispers Goes-Ahead, finally getting Custer's attention and handing him a second scalp.

Tom nods then anxiously waits for the General. Understanding the Indians' traditions, Custer turns to his cook. "Give the boys their meal," he says. Custer kneels down and patiently waits for the Crow scouts to eat. Finally he asks calmly using sign talk. "What is it, Curly, my boy?"

Hearing the commotion Charley Reynolds decides to see what is going on at Custer's fire. He is a little surprised when Custer hands him one of the scalps.

"What do you make of that?"

All eyes are on Charley while he examines the matted bloody hair. Reynolds turns to the two scouts and after several minutes of flying hands and excited broken English, mixed with the Crow tongue, he confirms his own suspicions.

"Could only have come from one place," Charley finally says confidently.

"Crook's command?" inquires Tom.

George Custer breaks in. "If I understood them correctly, Reynolds, the two trails did meet...the Dakotas have rejoined in one large camp further up the Rosebud."

Charley nods. "There's much sign of a fight where they found the scalps. They also found White-Man beards. The Sioux tossed the scalps away. Goes-Ahead says the hair is too short—not good enough to hang on the Dakota's scalp pole."

"Not good enough, my royal behind!" Tom barks. "Those red rascals, they are nothin' but a bunch of savage devils!" He pounds a fist into his hand. "How can we be sure they're from Crook's soldiers?"

"None of our men are missing," Charley says patiently. "They found cavalry gear, a damaged McClellan saddle and some brass spurs. It is unlikely Terry's outfit could have made it that far."

Tom chuckles. "That's for sure! Knowing Brisbin and Gibbon, they probably haven't made ten miles yet!" Tom stares off into the surrounding hills. He mulls over what has just taken place. "No wonder a courier from Crook hasn't shown up. That's if he's even sent one? It seems out of the question...the Sioux even with the Cheyenne, could whip General Crook's command? They've got a larger outfit than we do!"

Custer ponders Tom's questions. "Anyone with any trail savvy at all should be able to figure out that something has happened with General Crook. There is no way of knowing for sure. But those scalps, the Sioux joining in one camp." Custer finally motions for quiet.

"I'm asking you to keep this to yourselves." He pauses and signs the message to the two Indian scouts, they respond with a nod. "I don't want to unduly alarm the regiment; we've got enough to think about as it is."

A short while later George Custer finds his trusted scout writing a few words in his diary. "How's the hand, Reynolds. How are you holding up?"

"I'm just fine, General." Charley says with a smile, hiding his infected hand behind the diary. "Yourself?"

"Couldn't be better," Custer replies as always, striving to keep spirits up. "Reynolds, the Crows, Mitch Boyer, say that not too far ahead, maybe two miles, the Sioux trail has turned to the west. They say their customary way across the Chetish or Wolf Mountains is the Lodge pole Trail. They told me about a high butte on the mountain. They say there is a saddle like dip. Many times the Crows have looked far across the hills when fighting the Sioux. With the greatest apprehension I have been mulling over following the trail west. If I should choose to follow, I'd like to be close to the lookout by early morning so I can see for myself just where those Indians are. It is unlikely, but may perhaps be that some bands could split off n' turn down Tulloch's creek."

"Yeah! That might not be a bad idea, General. Wouldn't it be something if they did turn down Tullock's, they'd run smack-dab in to Terry's Montana column. I've never seen so much land torn up by Indian ponies. It's likely we'd be able to see the smoke from their cooking fires whether they're on Tullock's or elsewhere. My own hunch tells me that they are on the Little Horn."

"I believe you're right, Reynolds. George Herendeen who knows this country thinks Tullock's is far too rugged n' there's not enough water to support such a large body of Indians. That means they're somewhere on the Little Horn," Custer says with confidence. "Once we catch them I don't think the warriors will fight...not with their women and children right there in camp. They won't risk them getting caught up in a fight."

Charley interrupts, "Excuse me, Sir. Depends on where along the river they are. If they are in the upper valley like General Terry figured, then what?"

"I've fought these battles before, Charley. When they see us they'll go back to their reservation...just like they always do." he notices Charley's look of surprise. "You're awful quiet, Lonesome Charley."

Reynolds closes the diary and tucks it into his saddlebag. He faces away from Custer and tugs defiantly at the leather strap before fastening it. "You know my feelings, General."

Custer tries to picture in his mind what would happen should the Indians decide to fight. "If they start with their usual hit-and-run tactics they'll find Terry's outfit first. He's got the shortest route. I sure would've done things differently...but no use crying over spilled milk." He pinches the brim of his hat and shifts it slightly forward. "I've got Terry's instructions," he says bitterly. "I'm to keep heading south." Custer notices Charley's expression when he looks away. "What is it, Reynolds?"

"May I speak freely, General?"

"I thought you were," Custer cracks a smile. "You have a right to speak your piece, you know that. Your experience and prudence is of great value. I trust your confidence."

"I'm obliged, General." Charley clears his throat, "What if the Sioux are on the lower part of the Little Horn River? We've just looked at plenty of sign that they've had a fight with General Crook. Whether just a small skirmish or Crook is at a standstill, we don't know. What if the Sioux decide to go after Terry?" Charley says, quietly turning to face Custer again. "It could be a wipe out. Terry and his men don't stand a chance on their own—even with the Gatling guns—which are more trouble than they are worth."

"I have instructions, Charley..."

"What are the instructions, orders, whatever you want to call them, Sir?" Reynolds interrupts, raising his voice enough to surprise even himself.

Custer replies, "It's fixed in my mind—word for word! Terry's instructions leave me some leeway. But it's his final message that nails me to the wall."

"I was under the belief that General Terry had full confidence in you."

"He desires that I conform to his instructions unless I see sufficient reason to depart from them. You see why I'm so irritated don't you? It seems that no matter what I do if something goes wrong they'll hang it on me."

"Sounds like they've got you just where they want you, between the devil and the deep blue sea, as the saying goes. It seems that way, Sir. Terry's legal background is his advantage. It's hard to tell what an order is and what isn't. But just as sure as the sun rises and sets I am convinced...if the Indians go after the Montana column first it's not gonna be pretty. The entire regiment will be in peril, maybe as good as dead!" Charley kicks at the dirt. "Sir. You're well aware that back in April, both Captain Ball and Lieutenant McClernand rode up the Big Horn on a scouting mission. On their ride back to the Yellowstone they cut across the Little Horn Valley and followed the Little Horn River part of the way. They confirm that it's an easy jaunt from where they crossed the valley over the ridge to, and down Tullock's Creek. What if Terry follows Tullock's like he hinted at?"

"He could be at the divide right now. I strongly suspect that he'll see the need to send a courier. I wonder if he will?" Custer gazes off towards the hills. "You're fairly sure the Indians are going to fight aren't you, Reynolds?"

"I have seen Sitting Bull's steely cold eyes. He's not afraid of the White Man's Army and he has a powerful influence over those who've gathered for the Sun Dance. They'll follow his lead. In my heart I feel Sitting Bull will not turn his back this time. I believe they will fight n' will fight hard!" Charley says firmly. He has a worried look as lightning flashes in the far distant darkening sky. "Those Indians are warriors. From the time that they were little they've been trained for war. They've been pushed to their limit!"

Custer has listened to every word. "By the way, Charley...you can't hide that hand from me forever, you know. Keogh's over standing by the fire. Why don't you go ask him for some of his sour mash?"

Charley grins. "I'm not in the mood to listen to Myles belly-ache about giving up his whiskey! I'll be talking to you later, Sir."

Charley finds John Burkman who again fixes him a poultice using hardtack and water then wraps a bandage. "Southern cure from the Carolinas," brags Burkman.

Reynolds carries his saddlebags while he walks slowly toward Rusty. His mind races from one thought to the next. His head is aching now more so than his thumb. Suddenly he hears someone approaching at a brisk pace from behind.

"Reynolds," Custer calls out in a husky whisper, "I need a further word with you."

"What is it, General?" Charley waits for the Commander to catch up. Custer motions him on and they continue on, stopping when they reach Rusty. Anticipating a ride Reynolds throws his saddle on Rusty. He ties his saddlebags on the saddle then faces Custer waiting for him to speak.

"I did not want to unduly alarm the men, but this scalp business, the trail turning west is troubling. I've determined to send Lieutenant Varnum and his party to the mountain. Varnum requested a White Man to talk to and he asked for you. I would like you to ride up there with them." Custer doesn't give Charley time to reply. "By the way, I want you to convey my compliments to the Crow scouts. They've done exceedingly fine work. Tell them when I go to Washington; I'll convince the Big Chiefs to help all the Indians. If I ever get in charge of Indian Affairs, there will be some big changes in policy. They'll be first on my list to help."

"They'll be glad to hear that, General. I'll ride up the mountain with Varnum. I'm interested to take a look myself."

Custer thoughtfully eyes his scout then looks off into the hills. Charley's voice is dead serious, "It wouldn't surprise me one bit to run into Terry's vanguard or his scouts. What I learned from Captain Ball's scout it's only fifty miles or so from the divide down Tullock's to the Yellowstone." Charley rubs his hand while he stares off into the darkness. He pats Rusty, checking the saddle's cinch. "Wouldn't it be something if the Crow taunt left on Ball's scout was to be the place where the Sioux and Cheyenne are gathered?" Charley gives the final jerk on Rusty's cinch.

Custer looks puzzled. "It seems I've missed something, Reynolds."

"Well...you remember we talked about their scout. One of their Crow scouts, Jack Rabbit Bull, left a taunt to the Sioux."

"What kind of taunt?"

"You know, General how the Indians are. Apparently Captain Ball's scouting party crossed a well-watered valley along the Little Horn. Jack Rabbit Bull took a hardtack box made some markings on it and stuffed some green grass inside the cracks. It was a warning to the Sioux that when the long grass time comes, our summer, that they would be cleaned out."

Custer rolls his eyes and frowns in deep thought. "Come to think of it, Reynolds, I overheard Terry talking; Doctor Paulding with Gibbon's soldiers mentioned something about that. I never gave it much thought. You know me, Reynolds. I'm not very much superstitious." Custer turns and shouts for his orderly. The young soldier comes on the run, "Orderly! Remind Lieutenant Cooke to instruct the camp to extinguish all fires. Unnecessary noise will not be tolerated. On the, double quick."

"Yessir!"

Charley eyes Custer with a grave look while he swings into the saddle. He gives his quick wave then stops and turns, "We've been gaining on those Indians all day, General. More are joining every mile! The Dakotas are not more than thirty miles to our front! We could overtake them."

Custer grimly regards his scout while he ponders: *All the signs seem to indicate that the Indians are not in the upper reaches of the Little Big Horn River; they are downstream much closer to the mouth; but what if some bands of the Sioux or the Cheyenne turn north down Tullock's Creek? We've got to be in a position to support the Montana Column; no matter what. We've got to be in position to move in any direction.*

Charley addresses Custer's concerned look, "Terry's soldiers are likely riding straight for trouble. Those scalps the Crows brought in, the trail's sudden turn to the west; should be sufficient reason enough!"

George Custer can't dismiss from his mind the discovery of the scalps. And still Crook's courier has not shown up. He gazes into the darkness; he tries to picture in his mind the taunt left by Jack Rabbit Bull. Should he continue to follow Terry's instructions and go south to the headwaters of the Tongue? But if Reynolds is right Terry should be expected any time coming over the ridge. *"First command to find the Indians if they deem it prudent are at liberty to attack. If the need, be they must fight a waiting fight giving time for the other columns to come up."* The words are engraved in Custer's memory.

Custer looks up at Charley and brusquely speaks, "The Crows say we cannot cross the divide in the day time without the Sioux seeing us. That can only mean one thing. I would have to move into position in the dark to get as close as possible to the divide by early morning." Custer pauses briefly to ponder. "Another thing, Reynolds, the scouts say the butte is only about eight, maybe ten miles away. If the Indians are not on the Little Horn it will be merely a short ride back to the Rosebud." Custer thoughtfully eyes Reynolds then looks off into the hills. "So long, Lonesome Charley. You take care." Custer says soberly, adding as an afterthought, "I expect Crook's courier will be here before you return." With a quick wave Charley rides off leaving Custer alone to mull over his next decision.

Custer thinks about what premise his orders were founded on. Several scouting parties found nothing on the lower part of the Little Horn. All, including General Terry, calculated that the Indians would be on the upper part of the Little Horn Valley. Mainly the headwaters of the Tongue and Rosebud Rivers were discussed. Even Rotten Grass Creek was considered but all on the upper part of the Little Horn. Now suddenly the trail has turned to the West. All signs are that the Sioux and Cheyenne are much lower, possibly near the mouth of the Little Horn. The trail has turned at least 20 to 30 miles lower down than anyone expected. All indications are; the Indians are within thirty miles. It is possible that the 7th will overtake them. Decisions must be made.

He wonders about Reno; the man's been drinking on the sly. But other officers have a nip now and then too. He's seen them drink on other campaigns, also. As long as they do their military duty I won't upset the officers. On the other hand, I will not tolerate overindulgence. He recalls the time while on campaign he had to have General Stanley arrested for overindulgence. I just will not tolerate drunkenness.

And Benteen, why is Benteen so full of hate? He's always been treated with respect. The other officers are as dependable as the day is long, but Benteen? Always grumbling questioning everything, never happy. Decisions must be made but I need, "sufficient reason."

Now that he's had time to think over his discussions with Reynolds, the Crow's scouting report along with his instructions from Terry, it all comes together.

He recalls what Reynolds had tried to tell him. He has had sufficient reason in his hand. Yes literally, when he held that scalp from Crook's command. No couriers from General Crook could mean that his outfit has had a battle with the hostiles and he has been defeated or is at a standstill with his wounded. Not a one of the commanding generals had any inkling that the hostiles could whip 1200 men strong of Crook's command. Those scalps and the Sioux trail's sudden turn to the west...at least 20 miles before expected, decisions, decisions and decisions! He contemplates Reynolds' words. Lonesome Charley has already figured it out.

The last light of day dips behind the Wolfteeth range. George Custer looks up from his contemplating. He watches as Rusty carrying Lonesome Charley disappears into the night shadows of the Chetish Mountains.

"Adjutant, Cooke!"

"Yessir!"

"Have the orderlies notify the officers to assemble at headquarters without further delay!" Cooke salutes and hurries off. Custer reaffirms his hard choice. He has sufficient reason to depart from General Terry's instructions. George Custer has made his decision.

"Pass the word. We're moving out! Pass the word."

June 25, 1876, in the Shadow of the Wolfteeth Mountains

The night is dark with only an occasional small sliver of light from the moon. Using a small candle Lieutenant Wallace again makes a notation in his official logbook:

"Unable to start until near 1 a.m."

Barely visible in the darkness the meandering string of cavalry whispers its way into the uncertainty of Montana's midnight shadows. Squeaky leather, rattling rifles, nervous horses neighing and snorting, the chilling echo of a wolf's wail and the click of iron shoes against the rocky valley floor, the occasional curse of an embarrassed soldier as he stumbles over an unseen obstacle. Every sound relays the message to follow their Commander.

Joining Lieutenant-Colonel Custer at the head of the column, Captain Myles Keogh comes up from the pack train. Captain Weir comes up also. The tension is evident.

"Hear anything from the front, Sir?" Keogh asks, noting that Custer appears to be trembling, perhaps from the cool night air. It seems it has cooled considerably since their last camp.

"Not enough light yet, Keogh." Custer answers, turning his collar down, shivering a little as the cold air chills the perspiration on his neck. "Lieutenant Varnum will send word at once if anything at all can be seen. His scouts are more excited than ever...they've never seen so many Indian trails in these parts."

"Those scouts are good men but they have a habit of stretching the truth," Weir remarks.

"Especially now, they're close to the Sioux...ten can become a thousand at the blink of an eye," adds Keogh.

"You're right, boys," Custer agrees. "None of them count too well and they all tend to exaggerate."

Weir nods, "We're getting closer to the enemy and they're wound up tighter than a drum!" Weir hears something, "Rider coming, Sir." Girard rides up and dismounts.

Custer peers through the murky darkness while Girard leads his horse over.

"I'll ride up to the high hill...have a look for myself. I'll take Fred Girard along, hopefully we'll be able to see something. Will you show me the way Girard?"

"General, I'll go. But might it be better if we wait for first light?" Custer nods.

Girard returns Custer's nod then says, "The Crows say they've been there many times. They can see clean past the river to the bench lands. With all the Crows a lookin' it pears' tuh me we ought to call it the Crow's Nest."

"Bully for you, Girard," replies Custer as they chuckle. "The Crow's Nest it'll be. We'll leave as soon as Lieutenant Varnum sends back his scouting report. In the meantime, we'll keep moving."

Girard looks tired. "If the Captain here would be so kind as to offer me some of his sour mash...kinda takes the chill off."

Keogh grumbles. "I guess I can spare a little," adding a grin. "Medicinal purposes only, of course!"

Girard chuckles at Keogh's good-natured humor. He had expected the usual complaint.

"Captain!" Custer barks as Keogh turns to leave for the pack train. "Lieutenant Mathey informed me which company pack mules had been giving the most problems. Mathey said he did not want to make comparisons but that Companies G and H were less efficient. Mathey said that Lieutenant McIntosh had taken the criticism good naturedly but Benteen had become very angry."

"Sounds just like Benteen?" Keogh says, a little angry.

Custer with a nod of his head agrees, "If the Indians scatter and run we'll need the fastest and the most manageable mules for the pursuit. Keep a sharp eye on the mules, Captain."

Keogh nods then turns back. His Irish brogue is strong, "begging your pardon...n' my French, Sir. I'd like to run those miserable, shave tailed, kinky haired, hard headed stubborn son-of-a-jackass mules from here to "Kingdom Come!"

Custer turns before breaking out in laughter. He knows how troublesome the mules can be. "And by the way, send Adjutant Cooke to me will you, Keogh?" The others continue their laughter while Keogh walks away filling the air with blue oaths.

June 25, 1876. It is 4:13 a.m. when sunrise splinters over Montana Territory. George Custer's command is halted in a sheltered ravine while he waits for word from the Crow's Nest. The men eat hardtack and bacon, drink coffee and rest.

Lieutenant Wallace recorded:

"While waiting here a scout came back from Lieutenant Varnum who had been sent out the night before. In a note to Gen. Custer, Lieutenant Varnum stated that he could see the smoke of the village about 20 miles away on the Little Big Horn. The scout pointed out the butte from which the village could be seen...about 8 miles ahead."

It is close to 8: a.m. when the Ree scouts bring Lieutenant Varnum's report to Custer. After Cooke receives orders to inform Major Reno of the amended itinerary, Girard and Custer and three Ree scouts take leave of the command and ride out for the Crow's Nest.

The terrain is a gradual rise, hilly with scattered patches of sagebrush and numerous stands of stunted cedar and scrub pine. Large rocks can pose a threat to man and beast alike. Dismounting from time to time to lead their horses in the gloomy shadows of the ravines, the plainsmen travel without saying much. All is quiet around them until a large mule deer, startled by their intrusion, bounds gracefully across their path. Custer raises his rifle and takes aim. Then smiling at Girard he slowly lowers his prized Remington and the duo continue their journey without speaking a word.

As their horses begin the climb along the steep ridge to the outlook, their heavy breathing is prominent now, as the pace slows their muscles flex with each upward thrust. Suddenly Girard spots a rattlesnake only six feet ahead of them. Custer and Girard rein up instantly when the rattler waves the warning. The sound of shuffling hooves sends a muffled echo across the mountain peaks as the men shepherd their animals away from the unpredictable reptile. Girard points his rifle in the direction of the snake.

Girard finally speaks, "I kill him," he says to Custer, indicating that the rattler would make a fine meal.

"Just leave him be, Girard," Custer whispers gruffly, reaching into his jacket pocket for some dried meat. "Here...chaw on this."

Meanwhile, White-man-runs-Him has heard the disturbance and motions for them to climb to the summit. Custer leaves Girard with the Ree Indians who are standing guard over the horses while he hikes to the vantage point.

Sheltered Ravine, Wolf Mountains, Montana Territory, June 25, 1876, 10:00 a.m. Return From the Crow's Nest

At the cleverly concealed encampment Charley leaves the scrub pine tree. He leads Rusty to the spare horses for a well-earned rest. Then mounting his frisky reserve he and Big Red ride away from the soldiers for some peace and quiet. Finding a shady spot behind a bush, he stretches out for a well-deserved nap, leaving his horse to chomp on the succulent grass nearby.

George Custer meanwhile, talks with a nervous-looking Sergeant Curtis. "What's that you say, Sergeant?" Custer is asking, as Cooke, Keogh and Tom look on.

"Captain Keogh has just informed me of a matter of some importance, General," Cooke states urgently before Curtis can answer.

"Well, Captain, what is it?" inquires the Commander.

"One of the hardtack boxes fell off," Tom blurts out interrupting.

Keogh clears his throat, his Irish brogue is strong, "One of the hardtack boxes come off the mule during the night march, Sir. Sergeant Curtis here was dispatched on the back trail to find it. He found it all right."

"I'm not too concerned about one hardtack box. It wasn't ammunition?" Custer sternly eyes Keogh then his brother.

Tom chips in, "We made certain there was no ammunition boxes missing. It was hard to tell in the dark but to be on the safe side Keogh sent..."

"But begging your pardon, Sir," Keogh continues parting his mustache from his upper lip. "When the Sergeant and his detachment found the box they also found three Indians. They shot one but the others ran off."

Cooke try's to inject some humor. "They ate half the crackers, too!"

"S-s-s son-of-a-devil!" Custer stammers.

Noting Custer's anger Cooke tries to appease. "Curtis assures me they only ate a few..."

Custer eyes his Adjutant with a serious stare. "It means the Sioux likely know our position. You killed one, Curtis—what about the other two?"

"It's a serious matter indeed, General," remarks Keogh, ignoring Custer's question. "And it's possible the Indians know where we are, but I think the Sergeant did his best under the circumstances."

"Of all the cussed misfortune!" mutters Custer. "I had planned on keeping the regiment hidden today...moving after dark again then surprising them in the morning. If those Indians disclose our position to any of the chiefs, we're in for one hell of a battle, men—all over a box of dried hardtack!"

Keogh continues to talk with Custer as he swings to the ground and turns Comanche over to his striker. "Curtis is very upset with himself, Sir. One really can't blame him for doing what he thought was right. The men are on pins and needles again not knowing what is going to happen next."

"Anything else?" Custer looks at Tom.

"One of the White scouts, Herendeen that we picked up at the Yellowstone, says he found fresh tracks nearby. Boyer says he saw several Sioux on the ridge, he suspects they're heading to warn the village"

Keogh looks angry. Tom yells. "The Sioux know exactly where we're at!"

"I believe you're right, Tom." Keogh nods.

George Custer looks again to Keogh, "I don't blame Curtis, Captain. It can't be helped now. I'll talk with you boys later. I want to have a word with..." General Custer looks around, "Burkman, John!"

"Yessir, General!"

"Bring Vic up will ya', John?" Custer then grins at Burkman knowing how temperamental he can be, "Please." The illiterate private dashes off quickly bringing Custer's prancing warhorse.

Without summoning his Adjutant, Custer rides bareback through the camp informing all the company commanders of the revised schedule. Hushed voices elevate in excitement as the news they all had anticipated is now a reality. The word whispers through the regiment from man to man.

Charley relives his jaunt to the Crow's Nest. *He remembers the scouts' words, "Otoe Sioux! Otoe Sioux!" White-man-runs-Him urges the others to come and look.*

Charley recognizes the smoky haze without the aid of glasses. According to Custer's map the camp must be at least twelve, maybe fifteen miles away. Custer made the correct decision. He had sent them to the Crow's Nest and now their suspicions were confirmed. The huge Indian camp was there below them in the lower valley of the Little Big Horn.

"Would you look at that? Just look at that, Charley! I've never seen so much smoke—not even at the Washita!"

Charley marvels at the magnified image. His naked-eye view was impressive but this surprises him more. "You don't suppose the Sioux are trying to throw up a smoke screen?"

"Nothing would surprise me now, Reynolds."

"Boyer says he could see horses—so many they looked like worms crawling. I don't see any—Well, I'll be...Lieutenant. Every Indian Cayuse on the Great Plain must be on those flat hills!"

Charley and the Crow scouts wait patiently as Varnum scans the panorama. The mirage-like aspects of the morning sun, which has already begun to warm the air, soon will camouflage the huge camp in the valley below. They remain silent until he lowers the glasses.

"I have trouble making out anything." Varnum comments at last. "Boyer n' the Crows must have good eyes, Charley."

Charley gives Varnum a puzzled look. "My friend Hard Rope had a powerful eye too. I remember him spotting a spike elk out of a herd of fifty or so bedded down in some sagebrush. No one else, except myself, out of our party could see the spike antlers not even with glasses—but one of the men rode down and spooked the herd and sure enough the spike stood up and ran off."

"Must be something in their diet—something us Wasichus don't eat on a regular basis—like rattlesnake!" Varnum turns and winks at Boyer and the Crows.

The scouts know that Charley is making mental notations while the enemy is still visible. "I don't know what it is, Lieutenant," Charley replies. "Most of the Indians I know all have keen eyesight."

Fred Girard pants his way to the lookout. He scans the valley to the distant horizon...nothing. Gradually he focuses on a thick, blue-gray cloud. He shifts slightly to the left then back again. The cloud is hovering over the entire valley. "Look there! That moving black mass! That's gotta be their pony herd."

At the rest spot Charley raises his head to look at Big Red then gazes around. Seeing everything is all right he mulls over in his mind the past events.

He weighs what the next day will bring. He contemplates Custer's fighting tactics. Will they sneak in during the night? Will they hit the Indian village when they are most vulnerable? Will Custer attack at the crack of dawn with the sun at their back? It is hard to picture a better situation of forcing the Indians to lay down their arms. Another thing, Custer will have time today to send a courier to General Terry to inform him of the location of the village. If the Dakotas flee up the Little Horn Valley, Custer can ride back to the Rosebud, head upstream and cut off their retreat. It is hard to figure out a better position to be in.

He recalls when the 7th had departed three days ago from the Yellowstone River. Some expected the Indians might turn down Tullock's Creek. Others believed that the Sioux would almost certainly be found on the Little Big Horn but on its upper reaches. At the time the orders were given many including General Terry and his staff, expected the Indians to be on Rotten Grass Creek or the headwaters of the Tongue or the Rosebud rivers. But now the Sioux and Cheyenne were in the one place no one even considered.

Charley wonders about the 7th Cavalry's supporting Montana Column. Of all places to be, those Indians are squarely in position to strike Terry's column. Either on a direct collision course with Terry coming up the Little Big Horn, or just a few miles jaunt over to Tullock's Creek to attack. Charley questions where and how far Terry's column has come. At only 20 miles a day Terry's Montana soldiers should be showing anytime.

Charley remembers his conversation with George Custer.

"That's why we've got to surprise them, Charley."

Reynolds suddenly recalls the scalps. "But you haven't heard from Crook yet have you? What about Terry?"

"Reynolds, can you imagine what would happen if we continue south now? Good God man, we'd be lolling around the headwaters of the Tongue and the Sioux would be marching up and down the Little Horn valley with three more scalps on their poles—Terry's, Gibbon's and Brisbin's!"

"To tell you the truth, General, with the short route Terry has up Tullock's Creek I was a little afraid he would be ahead of us. He can't be that far away. It doesn't take much figuring. They don't stand a chance on their own."

After retrospectively examining the Far West conference in his mind, the flustered Commander confides to his scout: "Reynolds, the Army has been my life; you know that. If I were in charge of this expedition there'd be no question what to do. I thought it was my military duty to testify at the Clymer Hearing; it was a moral obligation. But I've been given the bum's rush ever since I got back to Fort Lincoln.

Now I'm forced to take orders from a man who'd rather be playing toy soldiers on a leather-top, desk propped up in an overstuffed chair. Darn those crooked politicians. There isn't an honest one among them! They've ruined the military!"

"Beg your pardon, Sir," Charley interrupts. "But I can't be blaming only the politicians for this mess we're in. How about the War Department—old Belknap and his cronies; and all those traders up and down the Missouri making fortunes selling Indian corn and the like? And worst of all, a substantial number of military personnel are up to their belt buckles in all this scandal too. Selling the Indians empty sacks of Government corn and getting paid double. You know as well as I do that those corn kernels are spread from the Rocky Mountains all the way through the Army chain of command, right up to, and including the President!"

Custer doesn't have to be reminded that graft and corruption have defamed military honor. "Thanks for listening to me spout off, Charley." He pauses, smiling inwardly. "I should learn to keep my mouth shut and take my own advice once in awhile!"

"Advice, Sir?" Charley inquires.

"You know that old saying, Charley...no use crying over spilled milk. But we've got to do something. As I think back to the War, the element of surprise was crucial. Many battles were won by catching the enemy off guard." He stops, removes his hat, and looks up at the sun.

"What are your plans, Sir?" Charley asks.

"I've already instructed the regiment to move up and stay hidden in the ravine of the dry creekbed nearby. I'll keep them out-of-sight today then move tomorrow." He looks up at the sky again, "Any suggestions, Reynolds?"

"Don't forget the Sioux trail that split yesterday then reunited several miles to the south," Charley gestures. "There's a possibility they'd do it again, General."

"What are you getting at, Charley?"

"It seems likely that we trailed through one of the larger camps in the dark last night."

Custer is deep in thought. "Several of the men picked up souvenirs they stumbled over last night. Those scalps the Crows brought to camp." He frowns, turns away and walks briskly to a tree some twenty feet away.

While Reynolds waits for Custer to return he checks his hand. His thumb is oozing again. He checks the soiled dressing and applies another makeshift bandage complements of the Army.

Custer eventually returns showing renewed spirit and a look of unshakable determination. "Reynolds. General Terry mentioned a waiting fight. For all we know he could be in the Little Horn valley right now. And maybe, just maybe, Crook can't be that far away either. If the situation is prudent I plan on dividing the regiment into four battalions. I'll send Major Reno and Captain Benteen each with three companies, the advance will lead the attack and the other battalions can provide the reserve."

"Benteen and Reno, Sir?," Charley interrupts again. "What about Captain Keogh?"

"Major Reno and Captains Benteen, Keogh and Yates are the senior officers. Captain Keogh is as fearless as they come. I'll have his troop with me."

Reynolds shakes his head. "I'm just not sure. I'm not sure."

"Reynolds, in the late war my Michigan Cavalry came out the victor in countless battles. Many were won by sending in a smaller force to occupy the enemy in front. That obliges the enemy to contend with the movements of the force in their front. The enemy is so caught up in the battle they are unaware of what is coming. Without warning I would then sweep in from the rear with a larger force. And that's not all. The reserve would strike with a flank attack n' it wasn't long and the battle was over. If the Indians decide to fight, the advance will engage them up front then my five troops will hit them with a rear or flank attack. The reserve can hit them at any vulnerable spot that they see fit. I know you're not a military man, Charley but you spent time in the war, you've been on several campaigns."

Reynolds forms a picture in his mind. He has no doubt...the Indians are going to fight. "It just might work if Benteen and Reno are up to the task."

"Fo-for-heaven sakes, Reynolds." Custer had started to swear but then remembered his promise to Libbie not to swear. "It's routine cavalry battle tactics. They both know it as well as saddling their horses."

Charley breaks in, "Reno has not fought Indians before, General! You know yourself how frightening, how terrifying it is to see warriors riding hell-bent-for-leather screaming, ki-yiiing, shooting, stirring up dust...arrows landing all around sticking in their chest, their eyes, face, whatever!" Charley gets a stern look, "Old Gabe Green first told me when Indians see strangers coming and they don't know if they are friend or foe they'll charge right at them screaming and yelling! Most men who are not friends and don't know Indian tactics will turn and high tail it runnin' like a scalded dog! The Indians know the instant they flee that they are an enemy. Only those few brave men will stand and face them."

"Turn your back on Indians and run is to invite sure death!"

Charley nods in agreement. "Every soldier has a picture of the horrible torture they'll put you through if they catch you alive." Charley fingers the poke around his neck.

Custer looks at the buckskin pouch inquisitively. "I know it's unnerving to the bravest. But you can't show fear to Indians. I've noticed it before but what's in the pouch, Charley, your charm bag?"

"Two bullets."

"Two?" Custer is curious.

"Gabe Green was an old plainsman and friend who taught me a lot. When I was just eighteen I went into the mountains with him. I can almost hear Gabe's gruff voice when he tossed me that poke. "Kill the meanest cut-throated, red skinned Injun with the first bullet. Save the last bullet for yerself!"

Custer eyes Charley with an intense look for a while, "We'll have to really be on guard for Terry's scouts and we need to know if the Rees and the other Crow scouts have found anything new. We better get moving."

"One thing is certain, General. If we go down in that valley we must make sure there are not more Indians upstream! You know that they will spread their camp circles for three or four miles along the rivers, sometimes maybe more."

"Reynolds! You are beginning to think like a military man. You remind me of myself never leaving anything to chance." Custer turns to leave then stops, "One other thing, under the state of affairs we are in the best possible position." Charley eyes the General curiously. "If the need be we can move in any direction. North down Tullock's creek or back south up the Rosebud."

"You're right about that, General. We are in a position to see and if there is an attack on the Montana Column we can move in any direction."

After reliving his jaunt to the Crow's Nest, at his shady rest spot Charley Reynolds has fallen asleep. The last word he had received was an attack the next morning. With the infection on his hand he needs the rest. But restful sleep does not come. The Thunderbird dream plays through his mind. Charley rolls and thrashes about on the ground. *A giant black bird soars high in the sky. Running-creek-Woman's words ring loud in his head, "Thunderbird big. Something great will happen. Something great will happen."*

The strange creature dives closer then hovers above him. Its huge wings flutter vigorously. Its pinions generate a thunderous noise. Charley laughs out loud. It suddenly dawns on him that the wings make the thunder. He hears the resonance echo through the Wolf Mountains. Charley's feet kick out. The bird's talons shoot bluish red arrows of fire at him. His body jerks and quivers as he tries to avoid the flaming missiles. Suddenly screeching shrilly, the enormous bird swoops down at him. The fearful raptors' long sharp talons spread in a vicious menacing manner. He raises his arms to ward off the huge predator. The birds' shrill shriek is terrifying. Charley yells out. His cry and the birds' screech mingle, echoing through the Wolf Mountains.

"H-e-y, M-i-s-t-e-r Reynolds. Hey, Mr. Reynolds!" Autie Reed, shouts.

Reynolds awakens startled. He is not sure how long he's been asleep when Autie Reed and a half-dozen trooper friends walk over with their horses.

"Hey, Mr. Rey—We heard you saw a big village down at the Little Big Horn. What did you see? How many Indians are there?"

The quiet scout looks around. He wipes the cold sweat from his face as scenes of the Thunderbird drifts in and out of his thoughts. He is careful not to alarm the young men. "Yeah, Autie," he finally says quite casually, "I'd say there's quite a few Indians down in that valley. But don't you worry none, we can handle 'em. We'll stay here the rest of the day. The Montana Column should be up any time."

"I heard a couple of the officers talking. They said Terry's men have a much shorter way than we do."

"Any minute now, Autie they could be riding up."

"We heard we're going to ride to the attack today—right away!" exclaims Private Moore.

"Where'd you hear a thing like that?" Charley asks, thinking the boys are about to pull a prank on him.

"One of the hardtack boxes fell off during the night," bursts out Reed. "When the Sergeant found it there was Indians!"

Charley begins to recall Custer talking with his officers. He vaguely remembers hearing officers' call. Reynolds realizes they're serious. He jumps to his feet and straightens his clothes.

"I heard one of the officers say Custer didn't see any Indians." The young soldier then adds, "Even with glasses."

"You nitwit!" chimes another. "Not even the Indian scouts with their hawk eyes can see Indians fifteen miles away."

Reed breaks in, "It's only twelve miles."

"Can't see Indians at twelve miles anyway," retaliates the soldier.

"Captain Benteen says Custer saw no Camp," remarks another.

"What does Benteen know anyhow? All he does is gripe."

"But Girard says that's a mistake. Custer thought Charley was looking at the tops of the white buttes."

"I heard Lieutenant Godrey say that the village is bigger than any the General's ever seen before," says another wide-eyed private to Charley. "It is bigger than the one at Washita!"

An enormous tough-looking corporal called, Irish, whose name erases any doubt about his ancestry, bellows his confidence in the 7th Cavalry. "Nothing to worry about lads. The 7th Horse can whip any bunch of Indians anywhere!"

"If the Irish are as tough as they al-vays talking," comments a soldier of obvious German descent, "Vee can vip the whole Sioux Nation!" He smiles at the scowling Irishman. "Vot I mean to say, if the Irish are tough as the Germans vee can vip all the Indians in Montana!"

Reynolds senses the start of a never-ending argument and is glad to see Keogh approaching and hurries over to him. "Autie Reed says we're goin' in!"

Keogh looks serious as he nods, "The General says we'll attack without further delay!" Keogh glances away then clears his throat, "Lieutenant Wallace thinks Custer will be killed!"

"What are you tryin' to say, Captain?"

"If they decide to fight instead of runnin', you're a civilian, your job is done." On hearing the commotion of some unruly horses behind, Keogh pauses to look then swings back to Reynolds. "None of us would think less of you if you just rode on outta' here."

"I've never showed the white feather!" Charley's reply is uncompromising.

"Back on the Far West I left a copy of my will with Lieutenant Carland and a list of some personal effects."

"I don't have much to leave," Charley states.

The Captain, with an uncommon shake of the scout's hand, bids him adieu. Bewildered by the gesture, Charley is unable to respond to the somber-looking officer. He feels his insides draw taut as Keogh walks away.

Charley gets a strange feeling. He looks around. Maybe it's the sudden change, the Sioux trail turning to the west...those scalps. Maybe it's the coming change of orders. Perhaps it's just the felon on his hand that bothers him. And maybe, just maybe it's that darned Ol' Thunderbird dream.

"Boys, I need to lighten my saddle some," he says at last. "Anybody need a shirt? And I won't be needing these," he adds, emptying his saddlebags and spreading his gear out onto the ground. "I've got a sewing kit someone can have." And thoughts of Running-creek-Woman flickers before him. Charley recalls the day she shyly handed the beaded sewing pouch to him. He stares off while her beautiful smile sticks in his mind. Charley quickly picks up the beaded sewing pouch. He gestures for them to help themselves. The young troopers are reluctant to accept Charley's belongings.

"I'm not superstitious or anything," Irish declares, "but I ain't taking none of it. I bet Mr. Reynolds seen something from the lookout he ain't talking about. Is that so, Mr. Reynolds?"

Lonesome Charley doesn't answer. "Come on boys. I can't pack all this. It'll slow me down."

Two of the soldiers begin sorting through the heap on the ground but Autie Reed and the others follow the young Irishman's lead and return to their troops.

Reynolds takes leave of the boys and rides to the spare horses. He calls for Rusty who trots toward him immediately when he recognizes the familiar kissing sound of his master's lips. Dismounting, Charley picks up an Army oat bag that is almost full. He sees more oat bags on the ground here and there. "Soldiers must have thrown them away. It'll lighten their load going into battle. Lucky for you," he pats Rusty's neck and is rewarded with a friendly lick. He gives his horses a couple of handfuls of oats. He rubs between Red's ears then Rusty's. The animals are obviously happy to see Charley and appear to listen as the scout's thoughts suddenly overflow.

"If I get out of this alive we'll go back to see my nephew, Charles Edwin. I bet he's a fine young fellow by now. It'll be good to see Will and Jemima too. How did I end up here in Montana? I wanted to see the west...the White Rain Mountains. Well, there they are, boys," Charley points south towards, what the White-Man call the, Big Horn Mountains. "Wasn't I headed for the Far West?" Oscar and Mildred suddenly come to mind; then Trapper Green. "It's your entire fault Gabe! Maybe I would have become a doctor in Oregon...and raised a family," *He recalls the shack on the Platte river; hunting his first buffalo; the warrior drawing his bow and the sudden blast of Green's big rifle. He remembers the dead Pawnee full of arrows. His whole upper body that he could see head, and face even the very top of his head, was all painted red.* "Now ya' know why they're called Redskins!" Gabe bellows.

"Saved my hide and I never really...spent enough time with the old man. Went off to be a soldier instead. Then got tangled up with one of those Mexican girls you warned me about...Ariana." Rusty's ears flatten as the pitch of Charley's voice alters. "You remember her too don't you, old boy? Yeah, I had the good luck to find someone else's Mexican girl, Antonio...that no-good crook!" It's Red's ears that twitch this time. "I wonder if she were still..." Then thoughts of Running-creek-Woman flash before him...the night they were married the Indian way. The first time they really got to know each other. The thunderstorm, the huge black bird in his dream.

"Reynolds!" calls George Custer who is just a stone's throw away. "Charley!" he yells again riding closer when he fails to get a response. "Reynolds, are you all right?"

The scout finally recognizes the call and whirls around so fast his hat falls to the ground. "Sorry, General," Reynolds apologizes bending to pick up the hat, "I must have been daydreaming again."

Custer notices Charley's sallowness.

"Just thinking about someone," Charley anticipates Custer's look.

Quietly the General asks, "You think of her often?"

Charley nods.

"She must be special."

Charley bites his lower lip while nodding up and down. Then out of the clear blue, "Do you think a man can love two women?"

Custer looks puzzled. Finally, he nods in agreement.

"Is that thumb bothering you again?" he asks, swinging from atop his tall thoroughbred and jumping to the ground.

Charley shakes his head. "No, Sir. Everything is fine. I was also thinking about my family back in Kansas."

"You know, Charley, your job is done. You don't have to go down in that valley. You can stay back with the pack train. You don't have to ride in with..."

Charley cheerfully interrupts, "I haven't seen the Little Big Horn, this part of the west." His look sends a message to George Custer that no amount of persuading is going to deter him.

"Reynolds," Custer continues solemnly, updating his scout on the findings regarding the hardtack box "Sergeant Curtis isn't sure if that Indian they killed this morning was from the big camp or not. I don't expect that there is any way of telling where those three might have come from?"

Reynolds shakes his head. "General, there's so much Indian sign around here it's impossible to recognize the trails any longer. We could go back and try to follow their tracks but it would probably be a waste of time."

"I don't know that we have a lot of time to spare."

"Not much time at all if they know where we are."

"And if they do the surprise is over. They'll descend on Terry like flies on a dead carcass!" Custer exclaims excitedly then smiles when he notices Charley's amused expression.

"We surely wouldn't want them to hit us in this rough ground," Charley looks up at the approaching soldiers.

Captain Keogh, Tom Custer and Lieutenant Cooke have spotted the General talking to Reynolds and are hurrying to join the pair. Major Reno and Captain Benteen hurry over while Lieutenant Godfrey, Captain Weir and other officers gather. With a nod to the officers, Reynolds walks out of earshot leaving the officers to have their talk.

"General, we've been wondering," Cooke manages to say before the Commander interrupts.

"I've determined to go ahead, men," he says, pausing with a nervous cough just long enough to collect his thoughts. "I believe it is prudent to send a battalion to the high bluffs to the left of the dry creek to see what can be seen. Charley Reynolds' trusted opinion is that after the Sioux branched off to the east yesterday, sending a battalion in that direction is necessary. Their movement will be as rapid as the terrain will allow." Custer pauses for comment.

"I agree, Sir." Keogh comments as Cooke nods in agreement.

"We must know precisely if there are any camps upstream in the Little Horn valley," Custer continues.

Benteen nods but says nothing.

Custer gestures to the officers. "I say again, their movement is to be swift. I want nothing to impede the rapidity of their march. They'll need no scouts, no surgeons. The reconnaissance is to be of quick duration."

Adjutant Cooke breaks in, "Sir. If I understand correctly, the reason for sending the detachment to the left is to see if there are Indians upstream?"

"You remember the Washita, Cookie." The lieutenant glances quickly at Benteen whose eyes get an instant glare. Custer pauses only briefly, "After our attack, how many camps were spread out along the river?" As an afterthought Custer adds, "If we can catch them all together we can whip them." Cooke nods along with the others, while Benteen remains tip lipped then asks,

"And if the detachment runs into Indians, are they at liberty to attack?"

"Colonel Benteen, they will have authority to pitch into anything but will send back word at once!" Custer barks.

Weir speaks up, "And are to alert the command immediately, if any camps or smoke is in the valley towards the Big Horn Mountains."

"Smoke?" Reno speaks up with a confounded look.

"Yeah. You know, Indians light fires, fires give off smoke." Although well meant, Weir's words come off a bit sarcastic.

"I didn't ask for your smart aleck." Reno glares at him while several of the officers smile to themselves.

"My apologies, Major!" Weir cuts in, "My words were not intended..."

Custer interrupts, "Right, Major," he then continues. "I'll assign the companies later. We must know if there are more Indians upstream."

Tom Custer, who so far hasn't said a word, has a doubtful look while he glances at Benteen then to the General. Tom Custer knows as well as all the others that Benteen and Reno are the senior officers and will lead the supporting companies.

Custer glances briefly at Tom dismissing his younger brother's skepticism. "Lieutenant Varnum is searching for something to eat. He will take the scouts with him." The General looks for any reaction from his officers but only Tom is shaking his head.

"Gentlemen," Custer pauses. He looks around to the men who have no more comments. "Meanwhile, Tom, Myles, Cooke, Major Reno, Captain Benteen," he turns to the others. "Gentlemen, I want you to get your soldiers ready without further delay! You know the routine. First company commander to report his company is ready will have the honored position of the advance."

The officers mount up. Charley watches as they trot obediently toward the column. He strides back to Custer. "Where will I be riding, Sir?" He doesn't hear a reply. "General!"

"Lonesome Charley, for the time being," Custer finally answers, "the scouts will ride to the front, Mitch Boyer and the Crow scouts and the Rees with Lieutenants Varnum and Hare."

With his familiar wave Reynolds bids the commander farewell and leisurely walks away. Charley listens as one familiar voice can be heard above them all. Benteen is already complaining to Captain Weir about the orders, among other things. The volume is increasing steadily and now Charley can hear every word.

"What's that blabbermouth up to now?" Benteen loudly spouts off when he notices Custer riding past.

"Shh-shh!" Thomas Weir warns. "For Pete's sakes!"

Benteen imprudently shows his lack of concern. "He's been riding around in circles for two days. He never shuts up. He's a blithering idiot! When does the man sleep for crying out loud? Does he have any idea what he's doing?"

"I reckon he doesn't need much sleep," Weir glares at Benteen. "And he wouldn't be here if he didn't know what he was doing. After testifying in Washington most of the officers thought he'd be court-martialed but the President knew he'd be more valuable on this campaign."

Benteen laughs. "Valuable! Hah! My royal behind!" he grumbles. "He's out here in no-man's-land because the President is trying to get rid of him. Grant is afraid he'd be roaming the country shooting off his big mouth."

"Yeah! You're dead on with that thought, Benteen. The President certainly didn't want George Custer to reveal everything and who all was involved!"

Charley finally tires of the nonsensical discussion and begins to groom his horse. In the distance, George Custer's order is loud and clear.

"Lieutenant Cooke. Let's get ready to move 'em out!"

Charley hears a soft voice calling, "Reynolds, Charley Reynolds," he looks around and sees Doctor Porter approaching. The Doctor holds something in his hand. "Charley! Darn it all I've been trying to catch up with you since we left the Yellowstone."

"Doc, my thumb's all right."

"It's not your thumb Charley. I've been carrying this around for two days." He hands Charley a letter. "When I did remember I had this for you, you were out scouting the whole night. My apologies, my friend."

"Not to worry, Doc, can't be anything important." Charley glances down at the address. "Why it's from my friend and camp keeper, Thompson." He smiles, "I didn't expect to hear anything, figured we'd be headed home before a letter would even get here. Thanks, Doc." Charley nods and walks away opening the envelope. He's got to hurry, the regiment will be moving out any minute.

Charlee A. Reynolds, Ol' Mighty White Hunter Who Never Goes Out Fer Nothin'. G-greetin' from Kamp on Big Muddy.

Hope all is well. Running-creek-Woman is anxious fer yer safe return. Walks-on-Ice and me two. She did want to tell you A head of tyme of yer goin to Dakota. She was afraid to tell yerself that she carrys yer child.

Charley stares at the words on the paper in disbelief. He is stunned by the news. After a while a big smile slowly spreads across his face. He rereads the words over and over again, hoping that he read correctly. Charley beams, looking around for someone to tell. He sees the doctor standing nearby, "Doc! Doctor Porter. Hey, Doc, come quickly." As the Doc hurries over Charley finishes reading the letter.

"She knowded that you wanted to go with Custer's cavalree. She did not wish it would upset you cause you might not wanta go. She feels that she should have told you. Now she feels that her man should know when he is gonna to be a father. All goes well at the kamp. She has love fer her Charley. All for now I'll sign off with Running-creek-Woman. p.s. She is no longer afraid of the Thunderbird. She says that the, 'Something Great,' is the child that she will bear. Writ tuh us."

"What is it? Something wrong, Charley?"

Charley gets a broad grin, "Hey, Doc, I'm gonna' to be a father!" Charley is delighted.

"Father! Father of wh..." Porter looks totally flabbergasted. "I...pardon me, Charley, I was not aware that you had someone. Custer, none of the men were aware."

"She's the sweetest thing since brown sugar in black coffee."

Doc Porter can't help but smile along with Charley. "Congratulations are in order," Porter extends his arm; Charley clutches his hand, shaking the Doctor's vigorously. "Careful, Charley." the Doc winces with pain. "I might need these fingers for surgical work someday."

"I apologize, Doc." Charley releases his iron like grip.

"Who is the special woman?"

"She is special too, Doc. She's an Indian, Arapahoe, at least part. She got some white blood too, Norwegian."

Porter looks over to the command then cracks a smile. "So that's where you been going off to all those months."

"You know how most of the men are with breeds. She's an Indian, hey squaw man. You know how it goes."

"Most of the time they're just funnin'. It makes no matter now, if she's a good woman that's all that counts."

"I just want to tell you, Doc. My father was a doctor. I have a lot of admiration for you not carrying any rifle or pistol, for helping the sick and wounded."

"It's nothing, Reynolds, but I'm obliged, Charley." Porter notices the command getting ready to pull out. The doctor wheels and heads for his horse. "We must mount up, Charley."

"Keep this to yourself, Doc. Please?" Charley hurries to mount up thinking to himself. "So that's it. It's no small wonder she told me before I left, Arapahoe, her tribal name means, "Mother of all tribes. She was trying to tell me she was going to be a mother. I wish I had known."

19

HARPERS WEEKLY. March 18 1876 Destructive tornadoes swept over Missouri Illinois and Indiana on the night of the 27th ult. In St. Charles Missouri buildings were blown down and several lives were lost.

Generals Crook and Custer at the head of 2000 men have left Forts Laramie and Lincoln to compel Sitting Bull and his braves to remain on their reservation.

*L*ike a raging tornado the whirlwind of corruption and mistrust continues to stir the confusion, frustration and hatred among America's Indians. Shifting from the nation's Capitol to the so-called Great American Desert, the storm had vented its fury over Kansas, Oklahoma and Texas, ripping through Colorado, Nebraska, and Dakota Territory. On June 25, 1876, the vicarious black cloud loomed perilously over Montana's vast landscape. The, "hostiles," were angry! Indeed there was Thunder Rolling on the High Plains.

President Grant had sent his best soldiers to Montana but George Armstrong Custer, whose flamboyance often overshadowed his remarkable military career, perhaps was the best of all. But manipulative politicians did not understand Indian heritage and culture nor did they care to learn about it. They constantly tested Custer's skills on the battlefield. His last mission at the valley of the Little Big Horn was to say the least misguided.

Riders in the Sky

Elizabeth Bacon Custer, the lovely dark-haired wife of the, "boy general," had stood by her husband through twelve happy years of marriage. Her husband's regiment left Fort Abraham Lincoln May 17, 1876. She wrote in her memoirs about that day:

"From the hour of breaking camp before the sun was up a mist had enveloped everything. Soon the bright sun began to penetrate this veil and dispel the haze and a scene of wonder and beauty appeared. As the sun broke through the mist a mirage appeared which took up about half of the line of cavalry and thenceforth for a little distance it marched equally plain to the sight on the earth and in the sky."

Did Libbie Custer have a premonition of things to come? She claimed in later years that she did indeed. Riding in the heavenly image were W.W. Cooke, Robert Hughes, William H. Sharrow, Henry Voss, Henry Dallans, James McDonald; Autie Reed, a nephew by marriage and her brother-in-law, James Calhoun and Boston and Thomas Ward Custer. Among the others were George W. Yates, Edwin Bobo, H.

M. Harrington, Algernon E. Smith, James Butler, James E. Porter, J. J. Crittenden, Daniel McIntosh, Edward Botzer, George Lee, Myles Walter Keogh, Thomas B. Weir, Winfield S. Edgerly, Marcus Reno, Frederick Benteen; and riding at the head of the column with her husband, George Armstrong Custer, his noble scout the, "brave and silent Charley Reynolds."

There were many other fine officers and enlisted men who rode with the 7th Cavalry that day but none of them could have envisioned the blood bath that awaited them in Montana Territory. None but Elizabeth Bacon Custer had seen the, "Riders in the Sky."

Nearing the Noon Hour, June 25, 1876, Destination Valley of the Little Big Horn

As the Dakota column prepares to move on, carbines and carbine straps are made ready; the ammunition is checked; 45 Colt revolvers are inspected and re inspected; troop dispersements and pack train adjustments are complete. Captain McDougall and Company B will have the rear guard of the pack train. Lieutenant Mathey will conduct the pack train escort with six soldiers and one noncom from the other companies. Thirty-one officers, 637 enlisted men, six civilian packers, one colored interpreter, four white scouts and forty odd Ree and Crow scouts wait for the Soldier Chief to give the order of the day.

Lieutenant Godfrey among several other officers certainly does not like the way Captain Benteen finagles the honored position of advance. After seeing to nothing in his company, Benteen then reports first to Adjutant Cooke. Godfrey studies Captain Benteen sternly.

"Ver...Very well, Captain Benteen you may have the advance." Custer stammers. Reining Vic to the right, it is 11:45 when George Custer allows Captain Benteen to lead the regiment westward up the divide.

After setting too fast a pace to Benteen's dislike, George Custer assumed the lead of the regiment. Before 12:00 noon the command crosses the divide between the Rosebud and the Little Big Horn rivers.

Descent into the valley of the Shadow of Death

Charley looks out across the grass and sagebrush covered hills towards the far western sky. Lightning flashes. He attempts to shake his bad feeling. Then again he reasons, lightning in the Montana sky happens all the time. He considers again about that something great and now he knows. He's the father of a child. His thoughts wander to the valley ahead. Then suddenly like the fire arrows of Running-creek-Woman's Thunderbird vision, something else strikes him. Their descent into the valley of the shadow of death...or is it in the valley of deep shadow? Charley Reynolds nods his head as he mulls over the Bible verse he learned a long time past from the 23 Psalm.

About one mile over the divide at 12:05 Custer raises his right arm to signal a halt. Charley Reynolds pulls on the reins and listens while Adjutant Cooke and Custer rein aside to talk. "Captain Benteen will have the advance with D, H and K companies. He'll head left on a scout to see if there are any Indians upstream. Instruct Benteen to send a courier if he sees any Indians. If not, he's to return to the main trail at once. Benteen's ride is to be rapid and of short duration."

Cooke repeats part of Custer's order back, "Major Reno will have A, G and M companies."

Custer nods. The energetic Commander instructs his Adjutant to order Benteen to begin his scout. Lieutenant Cooke gallops quickly to Captain Frederick Benteen.

"Captain Benteen. The General's compliments, Sir," Cooke says with an official air. "You have the advance. You will take your battalion, Companies H, D, and K on a scout to the left of the main trail. The General directs you to proceed to a line of bluffs over a mile away."

"He's not a General, Lieutenant Cooke," Benteen retorts. "He's merely a Colonel!"

Cooke is angered by the officer's sardonic and ill-timed remark. He stares icily into Benteen's eyes. "Keep your mean-spirited comments to yourself, Captain!"

"Colonel to you, Lieutenant." Benteen glares at the bewhiskered Lieutenant who completes the order, his every word spoken with concise clarity.

"The General," Cooke continues with sarcastic emphasis, "also directs you to send an officer with six enlisted men in advance, have them ride rapidly. They are to ride to the top of the bluffs to see if there are any Indians upstream. Your battalion is to follow the movement of the detachment as rapidly as possible. That will be all, Captain. Move your battalion out, at once!"

Benteen half-heartedly returns Cooke's salute before motioning his battalion to follow him left of the trail, towards the bluffs. Benteen gives a quick wave to Reno as he rides past speaking briefly to the Major.

"Muster up, men!" Reno orders. "Get them horses in line. Company commanders assign horse holders. Count off by fours!" It is twelve minutes after noon when Major Reno is leading his three troops along the left bank of the waterless creekbed, called Sundance Creek by the Sioux, Ashwood Creek by the Crows. At times Major Reno's Battalion parallels Custer's five companies who are on the right bank of the creek. From time to time, depending on the terrain, a distance of up to five hundred yards separates the two battalions. At the front of Custer's column, Charley Reynolds views the movement with intensity, always alert, watching listening.

After traveling only fifteen minutes, Custer who is riding a quarter-mile in front with Keogh and Cooke, reins his mount to a stop and addresses his Adjutant. "Cookie that line of bluffs over there, he points to his left. "I was unable to see those bluffs from the Crow's Nest. It does not appear that Benteen can see anything from those bluffs."

Keogh and Cooke steer their horses closer to get a better look. After looking at the terrain Custer points out the high bluffs. He then instructs Cooke to have Trumpeter Voss deliver a message to Benteen.

"The Trumpeter, Sir?" Cooke responds in surprise.

"Lieutenant. We've got to know as soon as possible if there are Indians upstream. Have Voss instruct Benteen that if he finds nothing at the first line of bluffs, he has authority to go on to the second line of bluffs...but remind him to hurry with all due haste! If he sees Indians send back word at once! He's to use discretion then return to the main trail the command is following."

"Aye, Sir. I'll instruct the Trumpeter promptly!" he replies reining his big gray charger in search of Henry Voss.

Fred Girard and Reynolds have discovered fresh horse trace only a mile or so ahead of the column and Charley decides it is important enough to tell George Custer about the find.

"We must stay on guard for anything unexpected. I've sent orders for Benteen to take this route. If he gets to this point here," he continues, pointing to the bluffs off to their left, "he should be able to see the valley. I've instructed Lieutenants Varnum n' Hare to warn the scouts to be wary of any Indian trails branching off the main trail. We must not be caught off guard with an ambuscade."

Reynolds and Keogh again look at the bluffs and hills for reference points before nodding in agreement.

"Reynolds," Custer adds after noticing the wrap on Charley's hand. "If that hand is going to hinder you I will have the surgeon take a look at it."

"It's just fine, General, just fine. I'll go find Bloody Knife."

"Good, Reynolds. I want a word with the scouts before we move much farther."

Believing that Custer is finished Charley spurs Red off, Custer shouts, "The horses are going to need water soon. We've got a hard ride ahead." Charley reins up sharply turning back to the General who briskly continues. "Find out from the Crows n' Boyer about water. There's got to be water somewhere along this dry creekbed. If nothing else we'll water at the Little Horn."

"I've already seen to that, Sir."

Custer's look of surprise turns into a smile. "I had almost forgot why the 7th Horse requested your services as guide, Reynolds."

Charley cracks a sheepish smile, "The Crows say there is a small creek ahead that branches into the main creek we are following. Boyer says about a mile or so from the river the creek branches in on the right bank. He says it usually has water in it." Charley rides slowly away waiting for more instructions. Hearing none he spurs off down the dry creek.

Twenty minutes later, once again, Custer summons his Adjutant. "Lieutenant Cooke, have Sergeant Major Sharrow direct Captain Benteen as follows: If he sees nothing from the second line of bluffs tell him to go on to the valley and if he sees nothing there go on to the next valley. If he is to be absent longer than expected notify headquarters by courier and in case he should find any traces of Indians, at once notify the command. Tell him to use discretion so as not to be left behind. Once he is satisfied that it is useless to go farther in that direction, join the main trail."

Cooke dashes to the column. "Sergeant, Major!" he calls out.

"I'm right here, Sir," Sharrow says as he trots up from behind.

"Custer wants you to deliver a message to Benteen."

"I don't understand?" replies Sharrow perplexed. "Shouldn't I have one of the orderlies deliver the message?"

Cooke's stern response is augmented by a fixed glare. "No, Sergeant Major! The commander wants you to ride to Captain Benteen."

"Yes, Sir." Sharrow straightens up in the saddle.

Cooke pauses then coughs, sure now that he has Sharrow's attention. "The message to Benteen is this: Custer directs you Captain Benteen, If you see nothing from the second line of bluffs go on to the valley and if you see nothing there go on to the next valley. If you are to be absent longer than expected notify Custer by courier and in case you find any traces of Indians at once notify Custer. Use discretion so as not to be left behind. Once you are satisfied that it is useless to go farther in that direction join the main trail."

"Are there any questions, Sergeant Major?"

"I have only one, Sir. Knowing Benteen he'll want to know which valley."

"You tell that bickering complaining…" Cooke shouts so loud that his horse dances sideways. "Whoa, whoa," correcting the excited animal. "I hope just this once Benteen can obey an order without grumbling!" Then reasoning to himself it might be too much to ask, he continues looking Sharrow straight in the eye.

Sharrow is disturbed by Cooke's growing aggravation. Finally he breaks in. "I understand. Will that be all, Sir?"

"So there are no blunders, Sergeant, repeat the message, please."

William H. Sharrow rattles off the order as if he'd said it a thousand times but before he rides away, Cooke adds a final few words, lowering his voice and smiling.

"You know yourself, Sergeant that Benteen is a top notch soldier if he would just stop his never-ending bickering. And by the way, Benteen should know without being told but remind him to be quick! Custer talked about sending Major Reno to attack the camp. That means Benteen's battalion needs to come in hot haste. That is all, Sergeant Major," Cooke assures him with a smile. "On the double quick, Sergeant!"

Meanwhile up ahead and still following along Sundance Creek the column moves at the jump. Ahead of the column, Charley Reynolds rides at the gallop. He reins up sharply. "Whoa Red! Whoa!" while he scans the chopped up soil below him.

Big Red skids to a halt, chomping at the bit and snorting. "Easy, boy, easy!" Charley looks down at the countless Indian pony tracks that have crossed here. He quickly looks around as several of the Ree scouts ride over on some nearby bluffs. Charley then looks at the well-worn trail below him. For a short distance he follows the wide path to the south. The trail looks a week old, maybe a little older, he believes. He comes opposite of the branch of the creek bed that joins from the south. There is an opening in the trees and the trail crosses the dry bed of the creek. Charley turns quickly when he hears the pounding hoof beats of the fast approaching column.

Custer reins to a quick halt.

Charley points out the crossing to the General. "There's been a huge bunch of unshod Indian ponies that crossed here."

Custer eyes the cut up Indian horse trail then looks around. He sees a teepee partially hidden by some ash trees, standing by itself, along the dry creek bed. Once again he stares down at the chopped up crossing then gazes off to the south. "It appears to me that Captain Benteen will strike this same trail upstream. He should be able to see where the trail leads."

Custer trots off waving the column on. As a matter of habit he takes stock of the landscape. Towards the bottom of the creek bed to the west the valley is widening out onto a level plain. It is right close to three miles from the river when Custer slows to a walk. Reynolds' alert eyes quickly spot a teepee downstream near a small hill. Off to the side is another teepee that looks partially wrecked. Reynolds points to what looks like horsemen.

"You're right, Reynolds, one bunch." Suddenly Custer is distracted by the Ree scouts. Downstream he notices two teepees, one standing below a small knoll and another partially wrecked. He quickly searches the hills to the south for any sign of Benteen or his trail dust.

"Better order Reno over, Lieutenant Cooke just to be on the safe side!" Custer doesn't wait for Cooke to respond, he waves his arm to Major Reno, beckoning him over. Reno is looking away and does not see Custer wave. The General finally gets Reno's attention by waving his hat for him to bring his three companies across the creek. In the meantime, an orderly dispatched by Lieutenant Cooke is already galloping hard to give Reno the message.

Ree scouts from Varnum's assistant, Lieutenant Hare, ride up. One of them hands Custer the "talking paper." Custer hurriedly reads the note.

"I could see Indians from a high hill. The Indians seem to be running away. Herendeen says we must hurry to catch them. Lieutenant Hare."

Custer pockets the note and asks Red Bear: "How big is the camp?"

"He says there are many lodges!" Fred Girard interprets for the wide-eyed Ree Indians.

"Do not tremble because of the Sioux," the Soldier Chief attempts to give confidence to the Rees. "Today you will gather many great honors, take many of your enemies' ponies. The Dakotas will run in fear of the Arickaras!"

Girard interprets for Boy Chief who signs his own observation. "He says there are many Sioux ponies."

"Tell them to go straight for the Dakotas' pony herd! I want them to round up all the Sioux horses." Brusquely, Custer says, impatiently waiting for Girard to translate before he continues his interrogation. "How big is the village?"

Charley reports that Varnum had sent word through one of the Rees that he could not see the entire village for the trees and the bends in the river. "Any sign of Captain Benteen's battalion?" Custer fires. "Some of the Rees scouts could see trail dust to the south indicating riders." Charley says calmly, quietly.

"Don't you ever get wound up, Reynolds?" Custer asks, as he wipes the sweat from his brow.

"By and by, there's plenty of time for that, Sir."

About two miles from the Little Horn River, several more Arickaree scouts have come upon the vacated Indian village. Below the high bluffs to the north of the creek, a lone teepee stands near a small hill. Several hundred yards away is another partly disbanded lodge. The Rees know by the drawings and the shape of the lodge that it belongs to their hated enemies, the Dakotas. Excited by the prospect of being the first of their band to destroy Sioux property, the overzealous scouts strike the buffalo hide structure, counting coup and slashing at the primitive structure with their knives. They then look astonished and point ahead of the column at a small band of Sioux moving slowly away towards the river. Custer barely slows down.

"Lieutenant, Cook. Have Captain Yates order a detail to investigate that teepee." Cook acknowledges with a brief salute and quickly rides over to Yates. A five man Company, F detail, hurriedly swings to the ground. Sergeant John Wilkinson pulls the flap open and looks inside the lodge. "There's a dead Indian in here." Wilkinson shouts. "He's laid out on a makeshift platform."

Custer overhears Sergeant Wilkinson and whirls Vic around. "Burn the Lodge," Custer's voice echoes out from the hills and bluffs above the Sioux burial teepee.

Captain Yates instructs the soldiers to set the teepee afire.

Meanwhile, Fred Girard spurs his horse to the top of the knoll above the lone, Sioux burial lodge. He can see clean to and across the Little Big Horn River. He sees the Indians and horses stirring up dust in the Little Horn valley. The same Indians that Reynolds had spotted before. Excitedly Girard speaks out loud, "There goes some Indians. It looks to be about three miles away!" At the same time he sees Indians directly ahead of the column. He hollers and waves his hat, "Here are your Indians, General...runnin' like devils!"

Custer's Ree scouts are leery of the Sioux riding slowly ahead of the column, seemly unconcerned about the soldiers behind. Shouting and riding into a dry ravine beyond the teepee the Rees refuse to go ahead. Lieutenant Hare urges the Rees to go ahead but they refuse to move.

"I ordered you to go straight for the Dakotas' village," Custer shouts at the Rees. "You were instructed to go straight for the Sioux ponies, capture many! You have disobeyed me. Move aside and let the soldiers pass. If any man of you is not brave I will take away his weapons and make a woman of him."

While the Rees laugh and have their own brisk talk, Fred Girard quickly rides down and explains to the Rees, who then ride off towards the Sioux. Custer smiles, he knows the Indians well and his taunt, although making them angry, has worked.

Hearing the commotion Myles Keogh, Tom Custer, and Charley Reynolds rush over to Custer.

"What is it?" Tom cries as he brings his horse alongside his brother.

"Take a look for yourself, Tom," Custer says pointing ahead to the Indians.

As the thick column of black smoke rises from the burning buffalo hide lodge they gaze toward the Little Horn. Above the Indians in their sightline three miles away, a huge dust cloud is forming on the other side of the river above the valley.

Keogh and Tom cover their faces trying to get a closer look at the body inside the burning teepee. But the smoke from the burning hides is thicker now and they are forced to turn away from the smoldering structure. They ride back over near Custer and Charley who continue to fix their eyes on the huge dust cloud in the Little Horn valley. The General motions the column on. "What do you make of that, Reynolds?"

"It's difficult to know for certain, General. Those Indian horses are stirring up plenty of dust. Has to be coming from the huge pony herd we saw from the Crow's Nest."

"They must be fleeing then," remarks Keogh, who fails to get a comment from the others.

"Do you think it's a trick, Reynolds?" Custer asks.

"Anything is likely. Those Indians dead ahead don't seem to be too concerned."

"The herd boys will run the horses back and forth before they drive them into camp, for no other reason, other than to create a diversion," remarks Custer.

Keogh gets a serious look. "Don't want another Fetterman affair."

Reynolds quietly gazes at the Indians ahead of the column. "It's been said that William J. had boasted, that with 80 men he would ride through the whole Sioux Nation."

Keogh responds. Yeah! And Crazy Horse n' the Sioux made short work of Fetterman and his 80 men."

George Custer quickly ponders their situation. He is well aware of the Fetterman massacre. "Not a single one of em' lived to tell the tale." He looks over at Reno and his column riding parallel about ten yards away. Custer points to the Indians moving slowly ahead of the column then shouts. "Major Reno. Lead out. Follow those Indians! Try n' bring them to battle. You'll be supported by the whole outfit."

Reno waves his battalion on and moves ahead. Custer and the others cautiously follow a short distance behind. George Custer is not about to let the Sioux draw him into any kind of an ambuscade.

Reno has not proceeded very far when the Indians disappear into the trees lining the creek. They then reappear riding up the bluffs to the north. Custer immediately orders Cooke to send an orderly to recall Major Reno.

Armed with the inconclusive information provided by the Ree Indians,

266

Reynolds and Custer rejoin Tom and Keogh, just as Lieutenant Cooke rides up. A bit over a mile from the river Custer pats Vic's neck, rubbing between his ears. "The horses need water badly!"

Charley smiles, "I remind you, General" Charley points at the wide sweeping tree line less than a quarter mile to their front, "The north branch of the creek is straight ahead!"

And Lieutenant Varnum hurries down from some hills to the south to make his report to Custer. Tom Custer sees the lieutenant and interrupts. "Rider coming this way, it's Lieutenant Varnum."

Custer motions for the others to follow and the plainsmen gallop toward the approaching scout. Varnum reins up a little excited, "General! About an hour ago I could see the village from the high bluffs."

Custer interrupts, "What did you see?"

"I guess you can see about all I can of the situation," adds Varnum.

"I don't know. What can you see?" asks the General."

Varnum excitedly gasps for breath, "The whole valley in front is full of Indians. And you can see them when you take that rise," Varnum points to the right front.

"Any sign of Benteen?" Custer asks earnestly.

"I believe I saw something on the high bluffs but I could not distinguish it for sure. It appeared to be some horsemen n' dust then they disappeared." Varnum points to the south.

"All right, Lieutenant! Very well, we'll push on!"

Varnum spurs off as Custer speaks to Reynolds. "Those bluffs ahead that Varnum pointed out, I must learn as much as possible of the character of the ground. Boyer n' the Crows say, there is a coulee that leads down from the bluffs to a crossing at the river." Charley nods in agreement.

"Well, boys, perhaps it's time we gave 'em one of our diversions," Custer says to the others pushing his hat off his brow and straightening his posture. Custer's order to Cooke leaves no doubt as to his plan. "Lieutenant Cooke, order Major Reno to go down and cross the river. Tell him to move at whatever pace he deems prudent. Attack the village. He'll have the support of the whole outfit." Cooke eyes Custer patiently while he pauses, looking to the back trail for any sign of Captain Benteen's battalion. "Tell him that I will go down to the other end and drive them. I will have Benteen hurry up and join in the attack."

Then responding to the Irishman's concerned expression he continues. "Captain Keogh, you ride with Lieutenant Cooke. Go with Major Reno to the river. Make sure the crossing goes well. Report back to me at once."

Keogh is curious about Benteen's progress since he had taken the advance. "Any word from Captain Benteen's advance movements?"

"Not yet! He can't be too far away. Lieutenant Varnum believed he could see horsemen on the high bluffs to the south. We cannot waste valuable time to wait.

Lieutenant Hare sent a note saying the Indians were on the run and we must hurry to catch them. Voss returned an hour or so earlier. And Sharrow returned not long ago. The Sergeant Major says Benteen can't be that far away, two miles at the very most."

Custer turns back to Keogh, "Myles, you and Cooke return immediately. Review the situation at the river. Anything that takes place, I must know," Custer pauses while he looks downstream. "We'll water at the creek over there." Custer points ahead to the tree line of the north branch of the stream. "Major Reno will water at the river. You and Cooke rendezvous over there by the creek or on those bluffs directly above."

"Yessir!" Keogh replies gruffly, spurring Comanche to an instant gallop. Custer pauses looking at Reno's soldiers. Custer's orderly rides alongside of Reno, giving the Major the same order.

"Take the scouts with you," Custer shouts over to Major Reno.

Reynolds looks down at his saddle pommel switching his reins from one hand to the other and then back again. "Sir, I'd much rather ride with your personal command."

George Custer is moved by his loyal friend's remark. "Reynolds, you know how I feel. I'd rather have you with my troops but my concern is for the entire command. You know the scouts always ride in with the advance. Besides, your knowledge of the Indians is needed most. Reno has never fought Indians before, Charley. I'm depending on you and the others who have fought Indians and know their tactics, to keep an eye on things. I think you understand, don't you?"

"I suppose I should consider it a compliment, General," Charley replies forcing a smile. "I realize it's an honor for the scouts to ride in with the advance battalion to attack. I'm just uneasy about Reno's lack of experience."

"Reynolds, if we catch the warriors in the village with their women and children it'll be all over. This is not like the winter on the Washita with the cold and snow. This is the long grass time as you call it, and we can run them down quickly. We'll simply engage them long enough then chase them out of the valley. Their women, children, the old men, will flee to a safe haven and then we'll have them. Likely they'll lay down their arms right there...and agree to return to the reservation. Another thing there'll be no risk for them to lay an ambuscade for the Montana Column."

Reynolds is surprised at Custer's confident attitude. "Both Reno and Benteen have got to hit them at the right time," he reminds the Commander.

"Both know what to do..."Custer answers almost angrily. "They both know Terry's orders...whichever column finds the Indians first engages in a waiting fight, holding them at bay until the other columns arrive." Custer looks out almost as if he expects Terry to ride up. "Doesn't that seem straight-forward to you, Reynolds? I don't expect we'll have to fight a waiting fight. Those Indians are not going to risk their women and children in camp."

"Yeah, you're right, General. They usually fight just long enough to give the village time to scatter. I shouldn't worry so."

"Lonesome Charley," Custer says, turning to face Reynolds, "Remind Bloody Knife to stir the rest of the Rees to round up all the Sioux horses they can. The Sioux and Cheyenne can't flee without something to ride. It'll mean a lot to Bloody Knife to act as chief."

Charley cracks a sly, grin thinking about the news he'd received just over an hour ago.

"What is it, Reynolds?" Custer is brisk.

"I was just thinking, General. I'm going to be a...well...well I'll tell you later. It's nothin' that can't wait." Charley grins. "Consider it done, General I'll inform Bloody Knife. Keep in mind, those Indians directly in our front. Don't want them decoying you into some kind of trap," Charley warns, waving cheerfully as he whirls Big Red around and heads to join Reno's battalion.

"No I won't. You be careful, Lonesome Charley. Godspeed," warns Custer quietly but Reynolds does not hear. For a moment George Custer watches after Reynolds. He couldn't know that his spoken words would be his final farewell to the most trusted scout and guide on the plains and his loyal friend.

Major Reno crosses to the left bank of the dry creek bed and trots ahead for the Little Big Horn River. Lieutenant Cooke and Captain Keogh ride past the Major.

Cooke pokes a barb at the Major. "Myles Keogh is going in with the Advance. And I am going too."

Reno only smirks then looks straight ahead. "Hold them horses in men. There are plenty of Indians for us all ahead," Reno shouts.

Earlier, on Benteen's off-trail scout, from some high bluffs, Lieutenant Gibson looks far up the valley of the Little Big Horn with his field glasses. He has an unmistakable view yet he sees no sign of Indians. He waves his hat signaling Benteen and his soldiers below, "No Indians in the upper valley of the Little Big Horn." Benteen immediately gives the order to return to the main trail. His column executes a right oblique and follows along a dry creek bed.

Charley Reynolds rides on an angle; almost due west then notices a marshy bog with pools of water. Below the bog is a small creek that has water in it. "Boyer was right, Red," speaking out loud to his horse. He glances quickly to his right at the trees lining the north branch of the creek. Red is thirsty but in the cavalry Charley knows that if at all possible all soldiers water their horses together. Red stretches his neck pulling the reins. Charley lets him take a healthy drink then pulls him up. He notices near the wide sweeping bend of the branch that joins the main creek from the north, is a partially torn apart teepee.

"The Indians must have left in a hurry." he reminds himself. Then he casts wary eyes above the tree line of the creek. Going up the bluffs northward are a sizable band of Indians, at least fifty or more. Good thing Custer stayed behind Reno. He'll take care of those Indians when he charges up those bluffs, he thinks. Then out loud he asks, "huh Red?" Big Red responds by cocking his ears, waiting for a command from his master.

Charley sees an opening in the trees of the dry creek bed just south of the morass area. He reins Red to the left. Lieutenant DeRudio from Company A rides up canteen in hand. The officer shouts. "Need to fill my canteen." Charley checks his horse, "River's only a mile or so straight ahead Lieutenant."

"River's probably high from the snow. I can't stand river water that tastes like mud anyhow. I'll take fresh creek water any day."

Charley gives a nod and quickly points to the Indians to the north. "Com'on, Red," he rides on to catch Reno.

George Custer reins up at the north branch of the small creek. There is water. "All right, boys! Ten-minute water call. Sergeant Major Sharrow! Pass the word to the Company commanders."

The officers quickly hurry to their companies. "Water call!" they shout.

Custer dismounts. His horse striker takes the reins and leads Vic into the low bottom of the small stream. His flag bearer does the same.

The company commanders order the sergeants to spread the column along the creek. The men line up to drink, stretching the line out for several hundred yards. Several of Custer's orderlies lead their horses into the small stream.

They quickly look up as Custer shouts. "Don't let them horses drink too much! Don't want any horses going to battle with belly cramps." Custer motions his striker who pulls Vic from the water then let's him lower his neck for another drink. "Hughes, Let's you and I take a quick ride."

Custer's flag bearer nods then hurriedly salutes. "Yes, Sir."

Reno's command advances along as ordered. Their pace alternates between a trot and a gallop keeping the animals as fresh as possible. The flankers are out and the scouts are in position. Holding his carbine in his hand attempting to emulate Custer's expert horsemanship, Major Reno loses his balance almost falling from the saddle. Reno shouts to Doctor Porter who rides past. "You want this blasted thing, Doc?"

Porter shakes his head no. Angrily Reno stuffs his carbine back into the cavalry socket.

Charley Reynolds notices more Indians off to the left riding slowly over some bluffs. He watches as Lieutenant Hare and Reno's orderly, Private Davern, ride towards the Indians and attempt to get a shot. The cunning Indians stay just out of carbine range. Might be those Indians are some kind of a decoy Charley thinks. He wonders about those Indians riding up the bluffs in front of Custer's five companies? They are a crafty bunch.

Reynolds keeps his eyes peeled ever searching for danger. Straight ahead to the west meanders the high water of the river. The Indians call the river the Greasy Grass. To the White Man the stream is known as the Little Big Horn.

270

20

At the flowing together of Sun Dance or Ash wood creek with the Little Big Horn, the river flows in a northwesterly direction. The advance scouts are the first to give the waters a run through. Charley and Big Red plunge into the river followed by the other scouts.

"Keep 'em horses in line lads. Hold your positions, troopers," echo the sergeants' commands as finally the cavalry comes up. The water becomes alive while the plains-hardy chargers rush, one after the other into the river, pausing to drink while their riders fill canteens then scrambling in the belly deep water to the far bank to drink themselves.

Many of the soldiers follow Charley's lead. After watering Red and himself he dismounts, recinches his saddle girth, inspects his carbine and makes sure his pistol is ready for action. As a matter of habit Charley grabs the bullet poke around his neck. He fingers the soft leather and feels the two cartridges inside. Sergeant Miles O'Hara watches as the quiet scout removes the bandage from his festered thumb, discarding it before he eases into Big Red's saddle. Charley's eye is on Major Reno who has turned away from the soldiers to take another drink of whiskey.

Stuffing the flask into an inside pocket, Reno reins his horse in a half-circle. "Muster up men!" he yells. "Get them horses in line. Companies A and M will lead the attack. Lieutenant McIntosh will hold Company G in reserve."

About the same, time satisfied that Reno's battalion is fixed firmly, Cooke quickly eyes Major Reno then reins his mount towards the bank. Apprehensively, Reno turns to watch Cooke and Keogh while they ride out of the water and start back to Custer's unit.

Reynolds rides to the edge of the timber for a quick look down the Little Horn valley. Indians, young warriors charge their horses, dragging brush, stirring up dust across the flat valley floor. A mile or so away, off to his left, are level hills or table lands. To his right, on the eastside of the river, are bluffs that stand over three hundred feet above the valley. The valley looks to be a mile or so across and lies between flat hills to the west and the Little Big Horn to the east. The river winds along in a northerly direction below the bluffs. The valley appears to be somewhat level and looks to be well-suited for a mounted charge.

On the east side of the river, from the top of a knoll Fred Girard has been keeping watch down the valley. "Girard! Fred Girard!" An anxious sergeant shouts and waves. At the same time a couple of the Ree scouts also wave and shout at Girard. Girard spurs his horse to meet the anxious noncom.

"Those Indians are not running! They are coming up the valley!" The sergeant takes a deep breath. "Custer ought to know!"

Girard nods, "I saw them myself."

The Sergeant entreats Girard. "If the General is aware of what's in front of Major Reno n' he deems it prudent might be he will send more soldiers with Reno?"

"Benteen should be up soon. He can't be more'n ten or fifteen minutes away." I could see their dust on the back trail. Girard earnestly replies.

Girard quickly spurs his mount down from the knoll and into the water over to Major Reno, "Marcus, Marcus Reno. Those Indians are not running...they're comin' up the valley. Peers tuh' me like they're standing to fight!"

Major Reno doesn't look up. His eyes remain fixed on the splashing water. He cares little for the interpreter. Besides he is still brooding over Custer's reinstatement of Girard back at Fort Lincoln.

"All right major. Have it your way. Custer ought to be informed!" Girard spurs hard out of the water.

Lieutenant Cooke and Captain Keogh hurry along on their way back to Custer but suddenly an excited Fred Girard is galloping up from behind, waving his arm and shouting.

"Lieutenant Cooke, Captain Keogh," he blurts, "The Sioux are not running they're coming up the valley to fight!"

Keogh and Cooke look at each other then eye Girard. "We're obliged, Girard," Cooke says calmly.

Girard gives a nervous cough.

"Anything else?" Cooke nods.

"The sergeant back there suggested if the General believes it is prudent that he might be inclined to send another company with Major Reno. It's not my affair to meddle."

Cooke waves him off. The two officers smile at the interpreter. "All right Girard. Return to your command. We'll inform the General immediately." Cooke says while he reins around,

The dirt flies as the three steeds respond to the spurs carrying Girard back to Reno's attacking command and Keogh and Cooke back to Custer.

Major Reno, several times more is informed by the scouts, of the growing number of Indians coming up the valley. As his apprehension grows he finally decides and sends two messengers, one after the other to Custer.

Behind Custer and Reno, Captain Benteen moves at a fast walk on his way to the main trail. On the left bank of the dry creek he reins to a halt. He carefully scrutinizes a trail of fresh horse tracks. There can be no doubt that it is a cavalry trail. Iron shod hooves of cavalry horses clearly define their way. Not far up the creek he can see the pack train. Benteen notices thick black smoke further down the creek. He wonders to himself if Custer has struck the camp? But there are no gunshots to indicate a fight. Unaware that Major Reno had followed the left bank and Custer followed the right bank of the creek, Captain Benteen follows along Major Reno's trail. Benteen's battalion hurries along. Ahead he sees the cause of the smoke, a burning teepee. In a short while Benteen reins up at the burning buffalo hide teepee. He dismounts and looks at the dead warrior on the scaffold.

Roughly two miles ahead of Benteen, from a vantage point on the bluffs above the Little Big Horn River, Custer and his flag bearer Sergeant Hughes gaze at the dust in the Little Horn valley. Custer looks to his left at Reno's soldiers crossing the river. He can see Reynolds and Big Red along the tree line forward of the main column.

"There rides one of the most trustworthy scouts to ever sit a horse for the 7th Cavalry, Hughes," Custer comments pointing west of the ever-growing dust cloud. "I have ridden with and have employed those of superior qualities, and good ol' common sense, the best on the plains!"

"Yessir," Hughes agrees. "He's a real gentleman too. It's odd he never got hitched. What about those Indians in front of Major Reno, Sir?"

Custer hardly pays heed as he smiles recalling Charley's reminiscences of the pretty lady from Santa Fe

"For some time now Tom has been having fits. He is suspicious that Reynolds has an Indian woman," exclaims the sergeant.

The commander whirls Vic around to face Hughes. "Sergeant, I will tell you about Charley's love life another time." Custer quickly turns for a last look over the valley, "Those Indians in Reno's front will try n' bluff him. They're few in number. Not enough to do much harm. They'll stay far, just far enough away, just out of rifle range."

Hughes anxiously nods looking around. He points to their back trail at a dust cloud. Dust and smoke roil up near the burning teepee maybe two miles away.

"That'll be Benteen. Right on time Hughes," Custer scans the creek bottom beyond the smoke. "The train must be close behind."

"Might be it is hidden behind the trees along the creek, Sir."

"They better, well they better come in hot haste!" Custer takes a quick glance towards the northeast. "To tell the truth, I was a little worried. Reynolds figured Terry would be here by now! Everything is falling into place!" Custer starts to leave, "Com'on Hughes!"

"The surgeon Henry Porter says Charley's going to be a father," Hughes blurts out.

Suddenly Custer reins up sharply, "Whoa Vic! Whoa! Wh-what did you just say, Sergeant?"

Hughes is excited, "Doctor Porter says Charley is going to be a father."

George Custer's shocked look says it all. He fires a barrage of hurried questions stammering, "He-he what! Ho-how? How could that be? A father, with whom?"

"Porter says he's been seeing some pretty little Indian gal."

Custer's blue eyes slowly turn into a kind look. He cracks a sheepish grin. "Why that son-of-a-doctor. Charley Reynolds a father? Tom was right." He gives the Sergeant a stern look, "Don't you breath a word of this to Tom. I already owe him five dollars."

"Not one word, Sir."

George Custer and Hughes rein to the right and hurry as fast as they can down the bluffs to meet the column. The Commander's personal battle, flag flapping noisily as his blaze-faced sorrel and the Sergeant's black steed dash toward the battalion. The column moves along at a fast walk. As soon as they join the column, Custer reins north for their ride up the bluffs. No sooner has Custer reined around, when a messenger from Reno quickly rides up shouting

"Major Reno's compliments, Sir... The Indians are in strong force in front of Major Reno!"

Custer eyes the messenger in deep thought as Cooke waits for Custer's nod then waves the soldier to the rear.

"Join the column, McIhargey."

No sooner has the messenger joined the ranks when another courier rides hard shouting out, "Major Reno's compliments. The Indians are not running! They are bold in front of..."

Adjutant Cooke tries to calm the excited messenger, "Easy soldier, take a breath."

"The Indians are not runnin' like everybody thought. They're standing bold."

Cooke eyes Custer.

"All right, Mitchell, well done. Join the ranks," says the General. Custer briefly watches the soldier then turns to the adjutant, "Send word to Major Reno, at once."

Cooke quickly turns, "Orderly," he yells. A private rapidly spurs forward saluting. The General and his Adjutant rein off to the side. The private listens intently to their talk.

"Tell Reno to fight dismounted," Custer is brusque, "Crowd them in the rear. We'll soon be with him!"

Cooke quickly halts and scribbles the message handing it to the soldier. Private Goldin gives a hurried salute and speeds off riding hard to overtake Reno's command. Custer and his five companies proceed northwards up the bluffs along the Little Big Horn River.

At the river crossing, Reynolds routinely removes his watch and reads the time. The hands are nearing 2 p.m. While he pockets his timepiece, he watches Private Goldin ride up and hand Major Reno a piece of paper. Charley keeps his eyes on the Major as Reno reads the message. Charley is surprised when the Major stuffs it in his jacket without any expression. It must be important coming from Custer, Charley reasons, then spurs Red off down the valley with the other scouts.

"At the trot! March!" Major Reno stutters through his whiskey breath. When the column reaches a trot Reno trips over his tongue as he again yells, "At the gallop. Ch-Charaaage—Ch-Charaaage!" The soldiers nearest to Reno give the major an odd look.

Reno's soldiers follow the northward direction of the Little Big Horn River.

The turf along the Greasy Grass is so close-cropped from the invasion of thousands of Indian war-ponies over the past few days that small areas of the valley floor have been reduced to patches of chalky white ash. Captain French orders M Company, Sergeant Ryan along with a detachment of soldiers, to guard the right flank and check out the trees and brush along the river.

Like thunder echoing through the canyons of the Wolfteeth Mountains on a stormy night, three companies of soldiers and over forty scouts press onward, watching for the first lightning bolt. There is an intensity that only a cavalry charge can bring to the soldiers as they shift restlessly in their creaking saddles, their sweat-beaded brows furrowing in uncertain anticipation. They are surrounded by the songs of the cavalry charge—the ring of picket pins and brass; the rattle of the 45-70 carbines in stiff leather sockets; tin cups clanging and finally the rumble of galloping hooves as one hundred and fifty odd horses respond to the battle cry.

Some distance behind Captain Benteen's battalion, a lone horseman rides hard to the front. Boston Custer has just acquired a fresh pony from the pack train's spare horse remuda. Boston urges his mount along. "Com'on, boy!" He spurs his horse, "Com'on!"

Riding hard up the eastern bluffs above the river Custer shouts, "Lieutenant Cooke! I want a bold front! Form the companies in a column of four, front into line." Cooke quickly relays the order to the sergeant major.

At once Sharrow shouts. "By Companies. Form fours! March! Front into line. March!" The company sergeants echo the sergeant major down the line. Without halting the companies form into a line of five columns of four abreast.

Custer waves them on as he shouts. "At the trot! Forwarrd you Chargers! Forwarrd!"

Simultaneously, with Reno's charge down the Little Big Horn Valley, Custer's five companies ride as hard as the terrain will allow. Custer alters the pace as they move up the sloping hills. The sound of 225 horses' hooves pounding the turf echoes like rolling thunder across the hills. Two miles ahead of Benteen, Custer's five companies appear as a black mass of horses as they thunder up the bluffs.

At the Lone Sioux burial lodge Benteen mounts up and orders the forward. Many in Benteen's column fail to look or are not in position to see. Only those in the front of the column have an occasion to see Custer's column. Those behind can only see the dust of the column and the company in front of them. Some at the head of the column see the black mass but wonder quietly to themselves what part of the regiment they've just seen. A couple of hundred yards in front of his own battalion, Benteen gives no indication of seeing anything out of the ordinary.

For the time being Benteen picks up the pace. His column rides at a slow trot. A little over one mile from the burning teepee he waves a halt. Benteen shouts, "Watering call!" Captain Benteen's unit stops to water his thirsty horses at the same morass that Charley Reynolds had ridden by on his way to the river.

Lieutenant Godfrey pulls aside writing in his memorandum book. He looks up as his good friend, Captain Weir rides over. "It's nearly two o'clock, Thomas. We made good time. The horses are thirsty, they can use a breather."

"Right, Lieutenant." Weir turns to his solders and shouts, "Lieutenant Edgerly! See to it that Sergeant Martin takes charge of the watering. Wouldn't want any horses bogged down in this marsh. They'd only slow us down!"

"Yes, Sir, Captain Weir!"

Up on the bluffs, Custer waves the command to a slower pace when he catches sight of the Indian teepees below him in the valley. Turning to his brother he shouts, "Captain Custer, send a message to Captain McDougal n' the train!" Tom Custer nods; he has heard his brother's urgent tone too many times to be mistaken. Tom listens closely to the General.

"Orderly!" Tom calls out. A flagging horse and rider stumbles forward. "Your horse is spent, Finkle. Fall back in line." Tom quickly eyes the column of soldiers. "Sergeant Knipe!"

Knipe spurs forward, "Yes, Sir, Captain!"

"Go back to McDougall ride as fast as you can order McDougall to follow Custer with the pack train and to hurry up." Tom is brisk and precise. "Tell McDougall if any of the packs get loose cut them unless they are ammunition and let them go; do not stop to tighten them! Tell Benteen to come on quick—a big Indian camp!"

"All right, Sir!"

"Repeat the message, Sergeant!"

Knipe rattles back the message word for word.

"Double quick time, Sergeant," Captain Custer barks.

At the front of the column, Custer's men yell and shout, breaking into wild disorder. Knipe whirls his horse around. He takes time for a last hurried look when Custer yells.

"Hold your horses boys; there are Indians enough down there for all of us."

Little did Daniel Knipe realize that those shouted words would be the last he would ever hear from General Custer. Sergeant Knipe spurs to a gallop. He takes a long look up the creek they've just followed. He sees dust roiling up. Just over two and one-half miles on their back trail the dust from the pack mules and the smoke from the smoldering teepee roils up in a little cloud. Sergeant Knipe keeps a cautious eye on the terrain as he guides his horse towards the north branch of the creek, heading back to the place they had just watered.

No sooner has Knipe disappeared down the bluffs when the five man detail from F Company catches up with Custer's column. Sergeant John Vickory reins his horse to the front of the column. The Sergeant gives a hurried salute to Adjutant Cooke, "Captain Benteen should be up soon, Sir!"

"He can't be that far Sergeant!" Custer shouts reining Vic around. "A short time ago I could see horsemen by the burning lodge."

"He's halted at a water hole." The sergeant says in a matter of fact tone.

"How far back is he?" Cooke snaps.

"He's right below the hill, just above the north branch on the main creek, Sir! He can't be more'n a mile and a half." Vickory points below to the tree line at the north branch of the creek.

"All right, Sergeant. Report back to Captain Yates." The sergeant salutes while Custer reins Vic around.

A few minutes later, Custer along with Lieutenant Cooke find a better look at the Indian village. They rein to a halt. Custer sighs while Cooke sighs and whistles. At once Custer studies the valley. The teepees stretch out for at least two miles. But a high bluff to the north obstructs their sight of the valley further to the north and thoughts of the Washita flash into Custer's mind. He realizes that they can't see all. "It's big all right, Cookie, it's big. There are likely more around the bend. We've got them all together this time!" Custer confidently says.

Down in the valley Reynolds rides cautiously. He watches and listens for signs of danger. As the mounted soldiers near the Indian village he hears Major Reno's familiar roar over the first sporadic echoes of gunfire.

"Prepare to fight on foot!" Reno yells to his subordinates. "Prepare to fight on foot! There are too many blasted Indians to our front. Davern, I said dismount and form a skirmish line. Whoa up, you troopers!" Much to his aggravation his confused horse, not the troopers begins dancing to the rapid commands. "Trumpeter! Where is... for the love of Pete, where in is my trumpeter?"

"I'm right here," hollers the trumpeter.

"Stay where I can see you." yells Reno.

"I've been right here all the time."

"Another word out of you n' I'll have you for insubordination," slurs Major Reno.

"Sorry, Sir I was only..." He stops short when Reno gives him the mean eye.

The horse holders finally hear the Major's pleas and begin to relay the message. "Dismount! Fight on foot! Horse holders hold your horses together!"

Every fourth man stays mounted to lead the horses away. Sergeants yell out. "Link 'em up men, get those straps hooked men! Quickstep now! Skirmishers out! Quickstep march! Move it!"

Reynolds and the other scouts rein up. Red is snorted and hot for the charge. "Whoa, Red. Easy boy, easy!" He at once takes in his surroundings. Towards the river, beyond Fred Girard, Reynolds scans the high bluffs across the river. The bluffs appear to stand two or three hundred feet above the valley floor. All of a sudden mounted soldiers trot by on the bluffs. "There goes the Gray Horse Company," Reynolds says aloud. "Boy, those gray horses stick out like a sore thumb!" Almost coincidentally he sees the puss oozing from under his thumbnail. He wipes it on his pants then gazes back toward the bluffs as the gray horses disappear from sight. The way they were riding they must have ridden down a ravine he believes. "Won't be long n' Custer will be with us." He yells to Girard.

Major Reno orders his adjutant, 2nd Lieutenant Benny Hodgson, a close friend, to form a skirmish line. Lieutenant Hodgson quickly rides over to a spot pointing out a line. "Skirmishers out!"

From east to west, at around fifteen foot intervals, the soldiers quickly form a line in the valley. "Move it now. Don't waste ammo. Hold your fire until they come in range."

Girard shouts over to Charley. "What is Reno doing? A skirmish line now? What the..."

Charley's answer is interrupted when two mounted soldiers speed past, their horses galloping directly toward the Indian village.

"Whoa up!" Girard yells to the riders. "Didn't you hear? Form a skirmish line!"

Charley tries to help. "Saw the reins soldier," he shouts. "Bring his head around. Saw the reins!"

But the soldiers can't hear above the noise and their lathered up horses race on. Less than fifty feet away, Lieutenant Varnum gives a long look at where the gray horses had passed by on the bluffs. On Reynolds' shout he wheels about. He too yells at the soldiers but his words also are lost in the dust and swirling wind of the charging steeds. The stampeding animals disappear into the crowd of dusty warriors in front of them.

On the skirmish line the company officers take their places behind their companies. Sweat drips from the men. The whites of their eyes are lined with red, the result of constant irritation from a potent mixture of salty perspiration and alkali dust.

"Don't waste your ammunition, boys. Let em' come close then blaze away." Captain French encourages the men.

"You soldiers that can't hit the broadside of a barn aim for the horses," laughs McIntosh. "Send them Injun Cayuses back riderless."

"I can't believe this," Girard says to Reynolds. "I can't believe what Reno is doing!"

"Fred, you took a message to Cooke n' Keogh that the Sioux were standing to fight. Knowing Custer's quick reasoning he likely sent an order to Reno. I watched one of the soldiers ride up and hand Reno a paper."

Girard looks at Charley in disbelief. "Nice of Reno to inform us. What in Hades does he have a bugler for? Those poor souls didn't hear any such order...it is too late for them. I just hope this works or it might be too late for all of us!"

"It'll work," Charley says calmly as he rides closer to Girard. "If the skirmish line holds the warriors will stay their distance. They're no more anxious to take a bullet than you or I. You know, Fred, I believe those two soldiers were probably racing with the other soldiers as to who would be the first into the Indian village, the first to strike a blow. In their dead run to the village they probably didn't hear the word to dismount."

"You're right, Reynolds. I guess we'll have to hold 'em off then," he says swinging down from the saddle and tying his horse.

Charley dismounts, too and leads Red to a stand of bulberry bushes on the outside of a grove of cottonwood trees. "Good boy, Red," he whispers tying the reins to a sturdy branch. Somewhat reluctantly he leaves the big animal. His Sharps carbine in hand he scurries to a brushy cover nearby.

Three or four hundred yards away, behind a stifling curtain of noonday heat and dust, the nomadic Plains Indians guard the edge of their camp, firing randomly at an enemy that is yet out-of-range. Warning of the impeding danger spreads and the helpless ones begin to flee the village. The chants and shouts of those bravest warriors and chiefs at once bring about a swell of courage. The warriors take up their weapons to defend their people, their land and their honor.

"Brave up! Brave up!" The resounding cry is heard over and over again. More and more warriors catch their mounts, joining up with the others.

Hardy war-ponies continue to kick up dirt and dust, impairing the view of the intruders. Unaware that the soldiers are forming a skirmish line, the village dwellers are fearful of a run through their camp circles. Their vivid recollections of past invasions dance in their minds. Bluecoats crashing into camp without warning; charging steeds ripping through teepees; iron shoes stomping through their camp. Panic-stricken women running for their lives, small children and babies crying for their mothers, and old men moaning as they witness the horrid destruction—hopelessly paralyzed by the agony. But Sitting Bull, Tanka Iyotake's Medicine Dream is fresh in their memories and the warriors are roused to renewed vengeance. They will fight as never before.

Out of the blue, two of the soldiers that disappeared into the crowd of dusty warriors in front of them, come tearing back to the line. Reynolds watches with a pleased look of surprise.

To the rear, at the morass, the casual mood here is in sharp contrast to that of the other two battalions. Whether unknowing or uncaring, Captain Frederick Benteen, seems oblivious to the fact that others' lives may depend on his haste to respond to orders—orders that have been arriving on a regular basis from Lieutenant Colonel Custer. When the sound of Major Reno's first scattered gunfire echoes through the draws, the soldiers begin to show their concern.

"Rider coming," shouts one of the soldiers.

Captain Weir and his second in command, Lieutenant Eagerly, both look up as the sound of hoof beats comes from the rear. A lone rider gallops along. Not too far behind the approaching horseman trot the straggling mules of the pack train. Riding alongside, stirring up plenty of dust, are Lieutenant Mathey and his eighty-four soldiers of the pack train escort. Bringing up the rear is Captain McDougall's B Company, the rear guard.

"Why, it's the General's brother," Captain Weir says, as he gazes at his lieutenant. He then looks back to the approaching Boston Custer.

"I take it the "Bos" doesn't want to be left behind, Captain," the lieutenant says. He smiles and waves at the younger Custer brother as several pack mules flounder into the bog.

Weir points up on the bluffs where the mounted soldiers had disappeared a few minutes ago. Boston gives a cheerful salutation and shouts something unintelligible.

Weir and his lieutenant both acknowledge and return Boston's salutation.

Captain Weir shouts, "Tell the General to save some for us."

Boston does not hear the words and spurs onward.

The two officers watch Boston as he disappears into the trees along the north branch of the creek. After a few minutes Boston reappears on the other side. He reins right and spurs his horse northward up the bluffs to catch his brothers.

While Captain Weir, Edgerly and others stand watching a small herd of horses breaks over the top of the bluffs running all out coming towards them.

Ki-ying Ree Indians are close behind driving them. It seems some of the Ree scouts are heeding Custer's caution to roundup or chase off Sioux horses. Ahead of the Ree Indians a lone horseman races towards the north branch of the creek.

"Must be a messenger from Custer," Weir gazes at the rider. "Could be for us or the pack train?"

Crossing the north fork several hundred yards to the north, the oncoming rider anxiously waves his hat and spurs his lathered horse. Behind Knipe, the Ree Indians and their captured Sioux ponies thunder by, headed for the pack train up the creek. Benteen turns and eyes the horseman rushing toward him. He leisurely takes a drink from his canteen then mounts his horse.

Benteen rides northward to meet the messenger. Knipe reins up hard, quickly saluting. Without uttering the routine officers' courtesy, Knipe loudly rattles off, "They want you up there as quick as you can get there. They have struck a big Indian camp!" Knipe whirls his horse to the left.

"Whoa up, Sergeant, where in the devil are you going?" shouts Benteen.

Knipe quickly turns back yelling, "The pack train, Sir! Custer wants me to hurry up the munitions. He wants the ammunition quick!"

"I have nothing to do with that!" Benteen shouts as Knipe spurs off towards the pack train. Several more mules hurry by Knipe then stagger into the morass sinking up to their bellies in the mud. Riding behind, their soldier escort is yelling and cursing in their attempt to catch up with the thirsty mules.

Hardly paying any attention to the mules, Benteen watches Knipe then walks his horse back to the watering soldiers. The firing from the valley continues echoing up the creek. Finally Captain Thomas Weir hurries over to Lieutenant Godfrey, calling out his nickname. "God the firing is getting heavier." Weir looks sternly at the lieutenant while Godfrey eyes Benteen then turns his ear towards the firing.

As Weir walks back to his D Company soldiers, he glares over at Captain Benteen. Weir's boys, as he calls them, keep an eye on him then look over at Benteen as if to say, what are we waiting for? The soldiers talk among themselves wondering why they are not moving to the sound of the guns.

Captain Weir turns quickly as the firing becomes heavier but no move is made. He watches as Benteen's horse raises its head, water dripping from its muzzle. Its nose and ears pointed towards the barrage of gunshots. It neighs loudly. Other horses impatiently join the ruckus.

Weir wonders, what will it take to wake up the dead then mutters to himself, "What worthy intention could there be for the delay?"

Precious minutes pass by. Benteen gives no indication that he hears the firing. Suddenly more scattered gunshots ring out, coming from Reno's soldiers in the Little Big Horn Valley. Startled horses and soldiers are diverted from the water but Benteen pays scant attention.

After waiting for some time, Reno's firing is getting heavier. Captain Weir again hurries over to Godfrey. "I'm fast losing my forbearance! We ought to go over there! Benteen's inaction is enough to tick me off, Lieutenant!"

"I know, Captain. I don't know what he's waiting for!"

Weir stomps off, going back to his own company. He walks up to lieutenant Edgerly. "We ought to hurry up!"

The lieutenant worriedly looks around then nods, "I know, Captain. I don't understand why he's delaying?"

Weir stares towards the Little Horn Valley where Reno's firing continues to reverberate up the creek. After waiting a few more minutes he hurries back over to Godfrey and K Company.

"Lieutenant, Godfrey! I urge you to go with me to Captain Benteen. We ought to be going to the sound of the firing! Go with me, God! You know that Benteen has not one bit of anxiety about showing his dislike towards Custer. If the two of us go he'll have to move!"

"He acts like he can't hear the firing!"

"Buffalo dung, Lieutenant! You hear the firing!"

"I'm hard of hearing and I can hear the shots plainly, Captain!"

"Then go with me!"

Godfrey looks up as more shots echo over the water. "I'm only a Lieutenant, Captain Weir. He'd probably tell me to mind my own business!"

In the Little Big Horn Valley, having moved to an old buffalo wallow, Reynolds calmly and accurately fires shot after shot from his prostrate position. He barely flinches when unannounced, Fred Girard dives to the ground beside him.

"Hello, Lonesome Charley. Hope you don't mind some company?"

"Looks like we've got plenty of company, Fred," Charley looks at Girard as he reloads his .50 caliber Sharps carbine.

Girard reaches into his jacket, removes a flask of whiskey and tips it to his lips. He downs a mouthful with one swallow then offers the flask to Reynolds, who shakes his head no. "You ought to have a couple of swigs, Charley. Isn't that thumb bothering you?"

"Nothing's bothering me at the moment except those Indians." he answers convincingly, raising his Schofield .45 and firing three successive shots to keep at bay some dare devil warriors who dash in too close.

"Reynolds, we're in trouble. I can feel it. Reno's been drinking since last night." Girard pauses for Charley's comment but there is none. He takes another drink.

"I guess he's like me...needs a shot of the creature now and then. Better have a swig, Charley?"

Reynolds examines his thumb and reaches for the flask.

Lieutenant Varnum slides to the ground beside them. "Just in time, I gather." Varnum smiles.

Girard laughs. "Lieutenant. You're more anxious about the whiskey than those Indians."

"It could be our last drink." Varnum taunts with a smile.

Girard waits for Charley to take a swig. "Only one Fred," Charley says nodding. Charley takes a swallow then pours some on his thumb.

"Don't waste that good whiskey, Reynolds," says Varnum with a sheepish grin.

Reynolds hands the flask to Varnum who takes a big swallow then waves his thanks as he runs off towards the horses. Charley and Girard watch Varnum.

Girard looks back. "You know, Reynolds, Benteen should be here soon. I saw Voss and Sharrow return after delivering the orders."

"So far Custer's plan is working. The Indians seem to be staying their ground," Charley says, turning to look at the back trail. "Yeah. Benteen can't be more than two miles behind at the most."

Girard looks straight ahead at some galloping Indians. "I don't know Benteen too good but for some reason, I don't put much stock in him. From what I know, he's always got something to say."

Charley watches the troopers, almost evenly spaced on the skirmish line, spread out several hundred yards across the valley. "The line has got to hold fast at all costs!"

Girard guzzles another drink then notices one of the Ree scouts huddled on the ground nearby. Announcing his departure in three short words he dashes toward the trees where his horse is tied.

Once again Charley is alone. The crack-crack of the 45-70s echoes from the skirmish line as the firing picks up; the smell of black-powder permeates the still air. Lead slugs fly through the trees into the village, ricocheting off lodge poles; some striking limbs, others piercing human flesh.

Reynolds sees another buffalo wallow a short distance away. It looks deeper and may be a better position. He mulls moving over for a moment then darts off. Arrows hiss close by as he scampers to the wallow, diving into the dirt. Unseen by him, a large rattlesnake crawls away.

Reynolds peers up over the edge of the dirt. White-eyed he freezes. He is face to face with the coiled rattler. Already riled at Reynolds' invasion the slimy creatures' tongue darts in and out. Its tail quivers spasmodically, keeping its large rattle waving, warning its prey of danger. Beads of sweat form on Charley's brow dripping into his eyes. It appears that he has no way out. It is weird but he can only think about other soldiers, who in all likelihood, are probably experiencing the same unannounced terror of rattlesnakes as he is.

He would rather take an arrow or a bullet than to get bit in the face by a despicable rattlesnake. He can think of only one thing to do. At a snail's pace, cautiously Reynolds drops his chin into the dirt. Carefully he reaches for his hat. Unexpectedly, through the din of battle pounding hoof beats approach. Reynolds remains dead still, even though the pounding hooves sound as if they are coming right at him. Suddenly a couple of loose horses stampede almost over the top of him. Their stomping hooves just miss trampling him by inches as they tear by, one on one side, and one on the other. The angry snake strikes out missing its fast moving target by a hair's breadth. The hostile but frightened reptile slithers away.

Reynolds breathes a sigh of relief and utters a quick prayer of thanks for the stampeding horses. Angrily he keeps an eye on the hated reptile. He quickly aims his carbine to blast the slimy creature but more approaching hoof beats warns him of danger. He reels just in time to drop a charging warrior. Another riderless steed races by, grazing his shoulder, knocking Charley sprawling to the ground. Unhurt, he quickly jumps to his feet, picking up his Sharps carbine. Everywhere he looks is dust and racing ponies, many of them riderless.

Across the Little Big Horn, George Custer looks down from the eastern bluffs. "Didn't I tell you, Boyer," Custer exclaims. "The line is in place and the Sioux are so all fired wound up on keeping Reno out of their camp they'll never know until it's too late! We'll strike from the rear Benteen will hit them..." Custer's words trail off. He waves Boyer and Curly to follow and they dash to the command waiting below them.

In a coulee that is lined with stunted cedar trees, Custer's news is received with a great deal more enthusiasm. Whistling and ky-ing the lighthearted soldiers wave their hats in the air but the celebration is short-lived.

"We don't have a lot of time, boys," Custer shouts impatiently above the commotion. He looks over his shoulder speaking to his orderly. "Trumpeter!"

"Yessir!" Private Martini moves closer.

In his quick manner Custer gives him the order, "Trumpeter, go back on our trail ride as fast as you can to Captain Benteen and give him this message. Tell him to hurry come quick. It's a big village. Don't stop for anything. Bring the ammunition packs. Be quick! Inform him that I want the ammunition mules from the pack train."

Martini mumbles, unable to hide his Italian accent even with such a short reply. "A-a-m-m-unition mules, bring pack-a-train, pack-a-train?"

Custer shakes his head bewildered then brusquely. "For Heaven sakes, Private! I want only the ammunition packs!" He then quietly adds, "Not the entire pack train."

Martini reins his horse and starts to ride away but Martini is stopped short by Lieutenant Cooke's frantic wave.

"Orderly!" shouts the giant of a man sitting tall in his saddle. Cooke hurriedly turns to Custer. "Sir, I'll write the message. We cannot risk any blunders."

"Right, Cooke," Custer agrees with his Adjutant then barks, "We've got a hard fight ahead. We'll need Benteen, McDougall and all the munitions downstream, Lieutenant!"

"Aye, Sir!" Cooke wheels towards Martini. "Just being prudent, it's for our own well being, Martini—all of us!" While Cooke begins to scribble the order, Custer trots over to talk with Captain Keogh.

Cooke hurriedly writes, *"Benteen come on—big village—be quick—bring packs."* The Adjutant quickly signs, *"W. W. Cooke,"* then looks at Martini sternly. Cooke then writes a Post Script. *"P. S. Bring Pack,"* Martini spurs his horse hard up the coulee.

Custer quickly barks out more orders, "Keogh! Keep the battalion in ready. Yates. Direct the flankers n' outriders to ride the high ground. Don't want any ambushes in this rough terrain! Direct them to report to headquarters the instant Benteen's battalion comes in sight!" Custer looks up the coulee, "Cooke and I will ride back to the bluffs for another look."

Custer looks around like he's leaving something out. Then, with an appreciative look he turns to Mitch Boyer. "Boyer, you n' the Crows have made my heart glad. You have done everything I have asked. You have led me to the camp of the Dakotas. And now you are all free. I requested your service to lead me to the Sioux. The Dakotas have been killing white people and now it is time for the soldiers to fight the Dakotas. You have no duty to fight."

Boyer nods courteously then follows with a subtle warning. "The army has startled the camp with the women and children. You have stirred up a hive of the yellow-fly-that-bites. The Dakotas will fight like the crazy dog warriors of the Cheyenne."

Boyer nudges his pony, riding over to Curly and the other Crow scouts. After a brief talk, three of the Crows return up the coulee to the bluffs overlooking the valley. Boyer looks at Curly, "We go watch the soldiers fight a while." Curly follows the older scout. They begin their ride up the coulee's western bank.

For a moment, Custer watches them while he mulls over Boyer's words of warning.

Martini spurs his horse up the coulee. He hears gunfire; he looks around and sees Indians at a distance, shouting, shooting and waving blankets. His horse gives its final lunges and comes out of the coulee onto the bluffs edge. Martini takes a quick glance to his right at Reno's fighting in the bottom. Suddenly he checks his horse. Boston Custer rides by and shouts.

"Where's the General?"

"He's just back of that ridge," waves Martini.

"Your horse is limping!" Boston Custer yells, and spurs on down the coulee.

In the Little Big Horn Valley in the heat of the fight, Lonesome Charley Reynolds ignores his festering thumb. With nerves of steel each shot is fired with confidence and precision. He is acutely aware of his surroundings, hearing and seeing every movement. When the shooting slows, he instinctively surveys the battle arena, his weapon ready. He notices the reason for the lull. None of the officers are on the line and several troopers have made a run for the trees nearby leaving gaps in the skirmish line.

"What in blue blazes are they doing?" the doctor shouts to Reynolds. "Where in the Sam hell is Reno?" Charley keeps Dr. Porter covered as more soldiers continue to desert the line. The gunfire dies down. Charley looks on in disbelief when eight or ten more soldiers pull away from the line and head into the trees. When a dozen more run, the line collapses.

Suddenly chaos is all around. A swarm of screaming Indians, their lathered ponies pushed to the limit, is charging across the valley. Reynolds looks over at Dr. Porter.

"All the officers are off the line!" Porter yells. "The men have run into the woods!"

Charley quickly looks around, "Looks like Reno pulled the line over to that bench over there and into the woods!"

In the cedar tree lined coulee, Custer whirls as Reno's gunshots can be heard coming from the valley. Custer waves Cooke to follow, "Let us ride, Cookie!" Custer then quickly turns to Keogh. "Captain! Keep em' moving slowly."

"Aye, Sir!" barks Keogh.

On the valley floor Charley sees movement on the bluffs above and across the river. Two riders are off to the left, farther north of where he first saw the gray horses. It could not have been over ten minutes ago. Looks like Custer n' Cooke, he believes. He then sees two more riders coming up behind Custer, "Boyer probably n' Curly," he says out loud. Charley senses some relief knowing that the commander is aware of the battle below. He reloads again and continues his fire.

On the bluffs overhead, Custer and the others view the unsettling situation. "Wh-Wh, What! What in the devil?" Custer mourns spitting trail dust from his mouth. "No more than fifteen minutes could have passed! Where in..."

Boyer interrupts pointing. "The Dakotas keep their distance."

"You're right, Boyer. The Sioux have too much wisdom to attack from an open plain into those woods. Reno must hold his position, give us time to make a crossing. We'll hit them with a rear attack! They won't know what..."

Custer does not finish. He glances at his tall Adjutant who has a worried look. "I know Reno can't hear me but someone might see me wave." Custer reins around looking below at the woods. "Reno needs all the encouragement he can get!" Custer yells as loud as he can. "We've got 'em now, boys. We've got 'em right where we want 'em!" Custer removes his hat and waves it jubilantly as Curly and Boyer look on.

A couple of hundred feet below in the coulee with the cedar trees, the soldiers hear Custer's yell and respond by tossing their hats and cheering.

Custer wipes his brow and replaces his hat then in his quick manner, "Boyer, I am proud of the Crows. But now it is time for the soldiers to fight the Dakotas. Perhaps I will see you another time."

Mitch Boyer nods understandingly. He and Curly quickly shake Custer's hand then Custer spurs Vic, and Cooke following, they gallop toward the column. The duo skids to a halt as they approach the soldiers.

At the water hole, suddenly Benteen's first sergeant yells out, "Rider coming!" All eyes look to the north. Along the creek where Benteen met the first messenger, another horseman rides their way. The lone soldier waves his hat.

"Another messenger," Benteen grumbles. He mounts up and ambles over. Captain Weir swings into the saddle and follows.

"Cap-a-ton Cap-a-ton!" the rider stutters in broken Italian. "Colonel Benteen! I've been looking all around for you!" Martini is excited and almost out of breath. "Custer said to hu..."

"What's the matter with your horse, Private?" Benteen interrupts while he eyes the blood on Martini's horses' flank

"I don't know, Sir. He's been limping badly! General Custer said..."

Again Benteen interrupts, "Why, he's been hit by a bullet! You're lucky it was him and not you."

Martini blurts out handing the paper to the Captain, "I have an urgent message from General Custer!"

Benteen reads the paper tucking it into his jacket pocket then barking. "What's been done?"

"They've abandoned the village. The women and children have skedaddled from the village. Running to the north! They've skedaddled."

"All right, soldier we'll get you another horse. Fall in with your company."

Benteen briefly turns to watch Martini as he joins the soldiers behind. "Soldiers are killing Indians right n' left! The're skeddaddling!"

Benteen reins left, when Captain Weir rides forward Benteen hands him the order. Weir reads it and without comment gives it back to the Commander.

"Any remarks or suggestions, Captain?" asks Benteen sarcastically as he crumples the paper and stuffs it into his jacket pocket.

"For God's sake, Benteen! We've been hearing gunfire up ahead for better'n twenty minutes. We've received how many orders to hurry, come quick! It doesn't take an academic to figure out!"

Benteen angrily interrupts, "My, what big words you use, Captain. Fits your smart-alec nature, big words, big blowhard!" Benteen puffs, obviously beginning to lose his composure. "I should have known better than to ask your meager opinion!"

"This means blood, Benteen. You do what you want, Captain Benteen, Sir!" Weir says through clenched teeth, his knuckles turning white as he clutches the pommel of his saddle. "You may be in command of this battalion but we've just received a written order from General Custer. I'm taking my troop and moving to the sound of the guns!"

"You keep your troops in line Captain or you'll have to face the music!" Warns Benteen as Weir hurriedly spurs his horse back to his company. "I'll have your royal behind, Captain!" Benteen shouts after him.

In the Little Big Horn Valley, pausing to reload, Reynolds scans his surroundings once more. His eyes fix on a young corporal, on the bench of the dry riverbed, where the soldiers have gone after pulling the line. The bank is an ideal position, akin to a rifle-pit. An officer is trying to convince the soldier beside him that Reno is going to charge. Arguing vehemently, the soldier shouts and points towards the clearing in the trees. Charley adjusts his angle of vision and focuses on the cottonwoods lining the clearing. The doubts he had harbored for so long rush to mind as he watches Major Reno.

Deeply troubled, Reynolds hurriedly motions Lieutenant Varnum to come over. Varnum fires a shot then hurries over, "What is it, Reynolds?"

"Something is wide of the mark. Major Reno looks awful scared. I've seen that kind of look before. There's no tellin' what he'll do. Something must be done, at once." Varnum looks over at Reno.

"I'm only a Lieutenant, Reynolds. He'd tell me to mind my..."

"Something must be...what about, Captain French? Something..."

Without a word Varnum hurries off towards the clearing where some soldiers are gathering.

In the small clearing Marcus Reno nervously reins his horse to a halt. Less than two companies of his mounted battalion wait nearby. The remainder of his soldiers, mainly G Company, are scattered helter-skelter in the woods, most of them on foot. Reno has withdrawn to the safety of a cottonwood grove to take a drink. Reynolds watches him as the nervous Major appears to suck the last dregs from his flask.

Waving his arms while he runs, Lieutenant Varnum yells, "For God's sake, men," he pleads. "Get down n' fight! Don't leave the line! We can fight for God's sake! Get down!"

Charley contemplates the line pulling apart. He wonders if the Commander realizes the immensity of his mistake, when the second tragedy unfolds before him.

Bloody Knife, Custer's favorite Indian scout has found Reno's hiding place. But the half Sioux, Arickaree scout's look of dismay is suddenly whisked from his face when a single bullet explodes into his head, splattering blood, flesh, skull, bone and brain matter in every direction.

Only one hundred feet away another soldier tumbles from the saddle. "Oh my God, I've got it!" He cries out.

Reynolds sees an unarmed Dr. Porter running to attend the fallen trooper, the only casualty since Sergeant O'Hara was hit on the skirmish line, and the two soldiers had been swallowed up in the melee during the initial attack on the village.

An already panicked Major Reno, his own face now covered with gore, appears to go into total shock. Without consideration of the consequences, he begins screaming confusing, conflicting orders. "Dismount!" he screeches. Then reeling around in his saddle he yells the next decree: "Mount! Dismount!" Whipping his horse as if to lead a charge, he further exasperates his troops, "We've got to get out of here!"

Nearby, a half dozen circling Indians sidetracks Reynolds. Still entrenched in the buffalo wallow, Charley Reynolds, relying on past experience, continues firing at the warriors. Unless attempting a brave show of fearlessness, he knows the Indians will not needlessly throw their lives away. They will not ride into the line of fire. Brave and fearless yes; foolish they are not. They have had too many fights with the White man. They know and respect the cavalry's strength.

"Charge! We are going to charge." Yell some of Reno's confused soldiers. Without warning, Reno's horse leaps frantically ahead when the Major's spurs gouge his flank. Only those close to him are fortunate enough to hear the word.

Lieutenant Varnum yells trying to stop the bewildered soldiers, "For God's sake, men," he pleads. "Don't leave the line! We can fight, for God's sake! Stand and fight, men. We can whip the whole Sioux nation. Don't leave the line!"

Feverishly Reno whips and spurs his bug-eyed mount leading the panicky rout. They ride away leaving many of their brother cavalrymen in the valley below, seriously outnumbered by the enemy. It's every man for himself—an all out run—for parts unknown.

Varnum jumps into the saddle and his fast-moving thoroughbred steed races to catch Reno. "For God's sake, men," he pleads. "Don't run! We can fight, for God's sake! Stand and fight, men. Don't run!"

"Hold your tongue, Varnum!" Reno fires back. "I'm in command here!"

The so-called charge is the farthest thing from a charge. The Indians attacking from their right, finally force the stampede to turn. Instead of making it to their first crossing, Major Reno and company are forced to the river.

Incredibly, as the tide over a sandy shoal, the wave of blue clad riders appears to roll backwards. Driven by the angry storm of Sioux and Cheyenne warriors, mounted on their sturdy war-ponies, Reno's unit scatters like pebbles on a beach.

As if possessed, the Indians whip and kick their horses into a frenzy. It appears nothing now will stop them. Many of the cavalrymen are overtaken without ever drawing their revolvers. Reynolds watches, helpless and shocked, as five Cheyenne ride up behind an equal number of soldiers, clubbing and stabbing them, counting coup with their lances then jerking the carbine straps over the heads of their victims, shooting them with their own weapons. And to ensure complete victory, one warrior leans low and armed with a vicious-looking stone club, proceeds to bash the skull of his fallen enemy.

Left behind in the stampede, Doctor Porter, fraught with fear, shouts to Reynolds: "Reno showed the white feather. He just took off abandoned, everybody! They're scared out Reynolds. What do we do now?"

Charley raises his carbine and a passing warrior drops in front of the doctor. Charley tries to explain but his words are drowned in the tumultuous ocean of pounding hooves and screaming war cries.

At the water hole, Captain Weir hurries back to his own troop. After waiting awhile and the firing below Reno's flight in the bottom becomes very heavy, Weir rushes again over to Godfrey in great agitation, shouting, "It's been almost thirty minutes! I am going anyhow!"

Captain Weir runs back to his troop yelling, "Lieutenant, Edgerly," The lieutenant immediately grasps what his Captain's intentions are and mounts D Company following Captain Weir on the trail.

Benteen glares at Weir as he rides off then shouts, "I'll have your backside! You bravado riding son-of-a-dirty-devil."

Without looking back, Captain Thomas Benton Weir and forty-nine other men ride towards the sound of the guns. Several minutes after Captain Weir has marched some distance Benteen mounts up Companies H and K and resumes his march. How disastrous that Benteen's angry, lackadaisical attitude would have such a devastating effect on Custer and some 200 men and that because of Benteen's hostility, valuable life saving minutes have been ticking away on the clock.

High on the eastern bluffs above the Little Big Horn, Mitch Boyer and Curly stare in disbelief at the stampeding blue-coated buffalo below them. Flabbergasted they fix their eyes on Major Reno and the pandemonium in the valley.

"Soldiers run," Boyer says in Crow, shaking Curly's shoulder. "Look Curly, like buffalo in a stampede!"

"They bad scared," remarks the young Crow scout, his dark eyes shining with anxiety. "Like black-tail, long-leg jumping rabbit, the soldiers run."

"They're scared out! Dakotas will fight harder now—like crazy dog warriors of the Cheyenne. The Uncpapa, the Oglala will kill the White soldiers like helpless buffalo calves following their mothers!" Boyer adds breathlessly. "Curly, we go. Long Hair must be warned! Soldier Chief is riding into certain death. Without the whiskey Major to hold the Dakotas, there is nothing for the soldiers', only butchery. The Dakotas, the Cheyenne will clean them all out. We go. Make big talk, Soldier Chief."

Then with an extreme act of loyalty, without any hesitation of the danger he is choosing, Boyer reins his horse around then quickly turns to his companion. "Curly, you are a warrior. But you are young n' the soldier fighting is not the Indian way. You go to your village, your family."

"We tell Long Hair Soldier Chief." Curly unswervingly refuses to leave Boyer.

From the highest bluff above the valley floor, Boyer rides hard down the crest of the north ridge. The young Crow, Curly, faithfully follows the older wiser scout. At the edge of the ridge they rein their horses to a skidding halt. A half-mile or more below them is a broad coulee that the Indians call, Medicine Tail Coulee. It runs to the river just north of west for about two miles. Boyer and Curly excitedly wave their arms at Custer who leads his soldiers down the dry coulee for his planned attack on the village across the river.

Thinking it is good news, Tom and George Custer wave their hats and the soldiers cheer.

Boyer looks at Curly puzzled, "Hurry, hurry we must let the Soldier Chief know. We all ride fast before he attacks the village at the crossing!" Boyer points towards the river.

"Bad scared," Curly mutters over and over. "Bad scared, run like scared dog!"

"Sioux will kill all the soldiers, like buffalo," Boyer yells to the younger scout. "Like buffalo hunt!"

Boyer and Curly whip their mounts into as fast a gait as the terrain will allow. At times, reaching break neck speed, as they hurry downhill on a treeless slope to tell the Soldier Chief about the turmoil.

The scouts get there at Medicine Tail Coulee in the nick of time. Boyer's horse slides to a halt as he begins to deliver his report to Custer. "Soldiers run away scared. Turn tail and run!"

"Like long-legs jack rabbit!" Curly adds excitedly.

"Wh-wh-what! Run? Where did they run?"

"Soldiers run," Boyer continues gesturing at Curly. "We watch a while. We all keep good eye on soldier boys. Watch the whiskey Major's horse. Soldiers follow Whiskey Major into the trees. Start shoot, stay only short time. Soldiers run helter-skelter from the trees. High tail it across prairie!"

"Wh-wh-where did they run to, for God's sake?" Custer stammers, his eyes wide with astonishment. "What about the line?"

"Soldiers scatter like stampeding buffalo. Otoe Sioux force soldiers across river, skedaddle up the hills on our same side." Boyer adds.

Curly is signing to Boyer and muttering something about, "Whiskey major," and, "god dogs."

"What's that he says?" Custer asks brusquely.

Boyer gives a quick reply. "Curly says, the trembling one with the little bird heart, the soldier chief with the firewater, quick...running from god dogs on his tail like the long-legs jack rabbit."

George Custer is flabbergasted by the incredible news. "Captain Benteen's battalion. Benteen should have been here by now," he says in frustration to himself. "Boyer, did you see Captain Benteen's soldiers?"

The scout looks puzzled. "No soldiers come to the valley! See dust above bluff. Maybe so Benteen, maybe not," Boyer gestures. "Long way to where Whiskey Major, first cross river."

"On the bluffs above the crossing," Custer snaps.

"We all see dust, same time soldiers in valley run to the bluffs." Boyer and Curly both nod.

"Maybe so Benteen, maybe not," Boyer repeats.

"They must hurry the munitions forward or we'll all be in peril." Custer states quietly. Anticipating the coming action, Cooke notifies the company commanders who ride forward from the command. Lieutenants Smith, Calhoun, and Harrington, ride over. Captains Keogh and Yates approach the headquarters staff. Reining his claybank gelding, Comanche to a halt, the handsome and likable Irish dragoon offers a fiery reply to Custer's latest news.

"High tailed it. Pulled the skirmish line?" Keogh fills the air with blue oaths.

Custer continues with the story. "Boyer says the soldiers disappeared into the trees along the river then stampeded to the bluffs above the river."

"The scouts?" barks Keogh. "What about Girard and Bloody Knife. Herendeen? Did they see Charley Reynolds?"

"Otoe Sioux," Boyer says soberly. "Like buffalo hunt. Otoe Sioux all around the Bluecoats. Little bunches of soldiers hide in woods."

"Any sign of Reynolds?" Custer asks the scout hopefully. But the answer is the same. "Lonesome Charley!" Then quietly as if speaking to himself, "He's going to be a father. If only I'd have known. I would have insisted he stay back with the packs." The others look puzzled. Custer shouts. "I should have..."

Keogh interrupts. Fight and fire shine in his eyes. "That bickering complaining sonof..." he stops short.

"The two of them," Cooke adds, shaking his head in disgust and fire comes into Cooke's eyes, "If Benteen had come up like he should have, there would have been no need to send Major Reno as the advance. At least Benteen has fought those blasted infernal redskins. He will fight. That is, if he ever gets here."

Custer looks back towards the head of Medicine Tail Coulee as if expecting Benteen and his troops to come riding down any moment. He turns to the Irishman. "The detail from F Company and Bos, both said he's only two miles or so behind. Boyer saw dust that indicated soldiers on the bluffs way upstream where Major Reno first made a crossing."

Keogh looks up towards the high ridges, "That's no more than a mile n' a half or two miles back...a lousy ten minute ride. He must be taking his own sweet time. What in God's name could be the cussed delay?"

Custer glances at Cooke then Keogh who speaks up, "We can't turn back now. Otoe Sioux, Otoe Sioux, right Boyer?" The scout bows his head and Keogh answers. "I recall Boyer saying that there were too many Dakotas; that the 7th had nothing left to do except turn-tail and run back to Fort Lincoln. Do you remember that, General?"

Custer looks thoughtfully at his officers and then at the scouts. "We can't go back now the Sioux would hunt us down. To show fear to the Sioux is like signing your death warrant. Like Boyer says, it would be a buffalo hunt. The Dakotas would have us!"

Boyer looks up and nods his agreement. Cooke and Keogh do the same. "Buffalo hunt!" Curly grunts.

"I believe we have only one choice, General," Keogh says at last. "If we turn back, the Sioux will believe they have us on the run. They know the terrain better than we do. General Terry should be here soon."

"But if we attack the village now," Cooke says, wondering aloud. "We'll all be in peril. Without Reno's men to keep them busy...not a mother's son of us would ride outta' there alive!"

"We'd all be slaughtered," Keogh adds quietly. "It's anyone's guess what Benteen is up too!" shouts Keogh, the tips of his long handlebar mustache quivering nervously. "That bickering, complaining son-of-a-shave tailed mule." His face flushes as he rattles off enough expletives to fill a gunnysack. "If we get out of this mess alive someone is going to suffer. Benteen and I are going to have a private talk in the stables, just the bloody two of us."

"There's no doubt in my mind which one of you will come out on the short end of that stick. I'll take bets on the winner!" Cooke laughs.

The light-hearted moment is soon quieted. A serious George Custer learns from the Boyer that another coulee, on the opposite side of the ridges they've been following, eventually leads to the Little Horn River. And a high ridge to the east, crosses above the head of the coulee.

"Captain Yates. Have the five man detail move out at once to the high ridges above." Custer points to the ridge directly north. "Duly inform the sergeant that the moment—the moment they see Benteen or McDougall's soldiers, at once signal or report to headquarters!"

Captain Yates quickly rides over to Lieutenant Reily and gives him the order then returns.

Cooke, Keogh and Curly wait in patient silence as Custer waves Boyer along and rides down the coulee talking to Boyer. The half-breed scout gestures and signs while he points out the terrain to Custer then watches while Custer ponders alone.

Captain Tom Custer rides down to his brother. Custer sternly surveys his younger sibling, "From the high point above there appears to be a small valley at the river. Boyer says there is a desirable crossing."

Tom looks down the coulee as Cooke and Keogh join them, "The Sioux will cross there."

For a brief moment Custer eyes his brother then with a serious tone. "North of the little valley is a high bluff. Our due course of action must take advantage of the bluff. The crossing ought to be covered!"

Keogh speaks up, "It may be prudent to engage a diversionary action to buy some time for Captain Benteen n' the munitions to get here!"

Suddenly a ruckus occurs in the column. Boston Custer has just come up. He hurries to the front passing company after company, row after row of anticipating soldiers, down the length of the entire column.

Lieutenant Cooke yells out to George Custer:

"Whoa up, Sir! Bos has just arrived! He'll be able to tell us how soon Benteen will effect a junction."

George Custer rides back, a look of surprise that turns to quiet concern, hastily beckons Boston over briskly firing questions. "Bos, did Knipe reach McDougall?"

Boston is excited. "I-I passed a..."

Colonel Custer stammers, "Ho-how far is Benteen? Where in the devil is he?"

Boston is calmer now. "I rode right past him on the trail. He was watering his horses at a morass."

Custer is astonished. "He's still watering? Sergeant Vickory has already reported that Benteen was watering when his detail passed." Custer reins sharply around then turns back. "You and young Autie fall in with Calhoun! Stay out of the action until it is prudent."

Boston anxiously gestures, "Autie. I talked with Captain McDougall when I swapped over my horse. Neither Captains Benteen nor McDougall is in any danger. Neither are Mathey n' the train. There were no Indians anywhere back there. Captain Benteen's battalion looked at ease."

Custer looks disgusted. He then reforms the battle strategy in his mind. After a few minutes he confers with his staff. Custer points towards the river, "At the bottom of the coulee is a crossing! Boyer seems to recollect there may be another crossing further north. It's imperative to try n' hold, at the very least, to cover those crossings!" He pauses. "Boys, I don't know where Terry is either. Reynolds figured he would be here by now but..."

"What if General Terry's been delayed?" Cooke interrupts.

"I see no reason for any delay, Lieutenant. If he's run into trouble surely he'd send a courier," reasons Custer, stopping to wipe the sweat from under his hat. While thinking it over he rechecks his .45 cal. bulldog pistols. He reaches behind his saddle, untying his white deerskin jacket putting, it on. The others know the sign for impending action and do likewise.

Tom Custer looks closely at his brother, "If we stay down here we'll all be wiped out!"

Boyer understands the Soldier Chief's concern and mutters to Curly who nods with excitement. Keogh reaffirms the consequences to Cooke as Custer turns away again to collect his thoughts. Yates and the other company commanders gather close by.

The 7th cavalry commander barks at last. "Captain Yates, have the Gray Horse troop go down to, but not cross the river—have the platoons form lines on the ridge above and below—skirmishers out! They'll have to find a suitable spot to cut across below the ridge. Endeavor to formulate a diversion at the river—establish a maneuver as if we're crossing at the ford."

Cooke nods, "The crossing has got to be covered! You'll want holding actions, Sir?"

Custer nods in agreement then points towards the river. "There is a small valley on our side of the river. The high hill north of the valley looks to be a suitable spot to send a detail of riflemen. Select five of the best sharpshooters. Have them positioned on that bluff. They can pour a heavy fire onto any Indians that dare come across the river. On the bluffs above the river position, select a detail of ten men in support of the Sharpshooters, to cover the crossing to the north. They'll also be in position to help protect your flank. Keogh and I, along with C, L and I Companies will head north. Our desire at the river is to lure the Sioux across. That should relieve any soldiers left in the valley. When the others come up, those savages will be vulnerable for a flank and rear attack by Major Reno and Captain Benteen n' the others." Custer gestures to the high ridge above them to the north.

Cooke nods, hurriedly writing in his note pad.

"Up there on that high ridge, Cookie, we'll be able to keep an eye on things."

Captain Custer breaks in, "The moment those Indians see soldiers near the crossings, every red-visaged, demon Indian in the valley is going to swarm across!"

Keogh shakes his head chuckling, "Red-visaged, demon Indians? You some kinda' academic? That's exactly what we want, Tom!"

Custer can't help but chuckle at Tom's surprised look.

Keogh looks at Tom. "How 'bout red rascals, Captain?"

Tom grins.

Cooke looks puzzled then serious. "If there are too many Indians at the river Yates n' Smith cannot hold..."

"If that happens they will withdraw. If and when that happens we can draw the Sioux into our own trap. We'll have the Sioux hemmed in between our forces."

"It'll work! Not only that, it will relieve the pressure on Reno and any soldiers left in the valley!" Tom seems surer of the plan.

"More bluecoats are coming?" Boyer asks Keogh.

Keogh points to some ridges towards the north. "Terry's Montana Column must be just over the ridge, Boyer," Keogh says hopefully.

Custer looks first at Curly then Boyer. "You have risked your life to warn me of Reno's folly. I say again your work is finished. There is still time for you to leave. There will be no danger with the train."

Boyer looks deeply into Custer's eyes, "Wherever you ride, I will ride." Curly grunts and nods in accord.

Custer raises his hand for quiet while he looks around at the officers, "Any remarks or suggestions?"

Captain Yates nods his understanding of their objectives.

"Lieutenant Cooke! Let us move out!" Custer whirls Vic around and beckons the others to follow him. And then the image is gone. His words trail off, lost in the roiling dust creaking saddle leather, rattle of carbines and tin coffee cups, pounding hooves and the scream of war horses going to battle. Custer is gone at the head of the column.

In the Little Big Horn Valley at river level meanwhile, the Indians clearly have the upper hand, whooping and screaming as they chase the straggling cavalrymen, remnants of Reno's soldiers. Lonesome Charley's survivalist instinct appears as a routine adjustment. Shot after shot he fires. The "big fifty" Sharps carbine has become a part of him. While he reloads his Sharps he keeps his Schofield tucked in his belt for quick action in case the warriors might attempt to rush him. He hardly notices the felon on his hand. With one hand kicking open the breech, while the other grabs another cartridge from the belt loops, he shoves the shell into the chamber, while he simultaneously slams the action and cocks the hammer.

Thundering across the valley a striking warrior Black Face, rides a dreadfully fierce black steed. He carries a trade musket. A huge stone war club hangs from his saddle. He whips his horse, riding hard. Another wildly painted warrior carrying a coup stick with fluttering red flannel strips, rides hard and joins him.

"Reno's ran off n' left us to our own fate!" A terrified soldier screams when he spots Reynolds and Dr. Porter.

"Get down!" Charley yells to the soldier who has failed to see the warrior approaching from his blind side.

But the young boy doesn't hear the warning. "Reno's deserted us! That yellow-livered..." he shouts as the dull thud of a long Sioux shaft slams into him. Clutching the hideous wound in his chest, with his last breath, he attempts to utter yet another curse to his errant commander. "You're a dirty no good chicken..."

"Oh my God! I'm hit! I'm hit!" yells another wounded soldier as he falls from the saddle.

Porter scrambles to his feet in an attempt to reach the wounded soldier. He is suddenly surrounded by a horde of Indians. He stumbles, falling beside his patient and miraculously avoids a barrage of arrows and bullets.

"Them no good!" mumbles the wounded soldier. "Them no good...why don't they..." he gasps.

As the harbinger of death hovers menacingly in the smoke-filled valley, Lonesome Charley rises to his feet. He's got to reach his horse. Every move, every step, every breath is calculated according to past experience, hanging him on the thin line between life and death. All at once he sees five Sioux closing fast on Dr. Porter. Firing and screaming as loud as he can, he eliminates the closest attacker. "Look out, Porter!" he yells the warning. "They're right behind you!" Without turning Doctor Porter drags the wounded man into some bushes. Indians, some on foot, some on horseback, close quickly. Shadowed figures on foot dart in behind Porter.

In a nearby patch of woods a mounted figure moves through the shadows of the trees. It is hard to distinguish him through the leaves. He is only a vague shadow amongst the dark cottonwood trees and bulberry bushes. The shadowed figure looks intently at Reynolds. He peers out from the leaves. All of a sudden he whips his steed into a furious charge.

The dark figure metamorphoses to a screaming, hideously painted rider, Black Face. Black covers his forehead forming a "V" from the top of his nose to his jaw. Red pigment circles his eyes. His black steed is painted with red lightning streaks on its front and rear quarters. He whips his horse, riding all out.

Reynolds sees Indians closing around Porter. He fires his carbine. A warrior drops. Charley quickly reloads. He shouts. "Porter!" Reynolds shoots the closest attacker with his carbine then yanks his pistol and fires, tumbling another brave to the ground. He again shouts. "Look out, Doc! They're right behind." Charley feels a ripping pain as if he's been hit by a huge rock. The force of the impact throws him to the ground causing him to lose his rifle and his hat. He struggles to rise. His head collapses.

Just a stone's throw away Black Face sneers as he lowers his smoking musket then utters a scream while waving his musket in victory.

Charley again attempts to lift his head but can't muster his strength. In a haunting vision Reynolds sees Running-creek-Woman's image, her face, her auburn hair. They rub cheeks. Reynolds' head turns. He grits his teeth. His cold fury and adrenaline kick in. He breaks open his Schofield revolver against his leg, ejecting empty shells then reloads his pistol as he struggles to his feet. He raises his pistol and fires two shots keeping the warriors at bay from Porter. Several fleeing soldiers momentarily sidetrack the Indians.

Reynolds wipes blood from his shoulder. Now he is more determined. Once more he warns Porter. "We've got to get out of here," he yells, firing his pistol at the warriors holding them at bay. At the same time, he moves backwards toward big Red. "Run for the timber, Porter! Run!"

While three more fleeing soldiers momentarily sidetrack the Indians, Charley manages to reclaim his carbine. Painfully he reloads. A warrior bears down on him. Reynolds ducks an arrow that hisses close by. He raises his carbine and fires. Indian pony and rider crash to the ground near Red.

Porter leaves the wounded soldier and makes his way towards a bulberry thicket nearby. Several Indians pursue him. Reynolds reloads his carbine. He fires from the hip. An Indian drops. Porter reaches the brush. At the same time, a barrage of arrows cut through leaves and twigs ricocheting and careening off branches all around him.

Two fleeing soldiers stop to drag the wounded soldier that Porter had just left, into some thick brush. They leave him a canteen then flee through the trees. "Don't leave me, for God's sake, don't leave me," the soldier wails.

A panicky young soldier riding by finally gets his skittish horse momentarily under control. He fearfully hollers to Reynolds. "Major Reno pulled foot n' run like a scalded dog! You better get out of..." the soldier's horse bolts. "Whoa! Whoa!" He tugs on the reins but his horse is unmanageable. The young soldier yells over his shoulder to Charley. "I'll send someone back for..."

In a hurried glance Charley sees the young soldier's horse peel out on a beeline towards the river. Charley whirls around and shouts to Porter. "Run for the timber, Porter! Run!"

Porter shouts back, "You go, Charley. Save yourself. You've got a child to think of now! My horse is..."

"I'm not leaving you, Doc!"

Oozing blood on his lapel confirms Charley's suspicions; he has taken a bullet to the shoulder. A vicious looking Sioux rides by. His face is painted a hideous black and red.

"Run, Porter! Run!" The painful chore of reloading is accomplished just in time to squelch the attack of a bloodthirsty Cheyenne brave. Black powder belches from his trusty Sharps War-pony and rider crash in a cloud of dust. Porter dashes through some brush, several Indians following in hot pursuit.

"Get your horse n' get out of here!" Charley screams. He fires several shots with his pistol at some warriors who thunder by chasing a young soldier. His shots scatter the Indians enough for the young soldier to make it to the river.

Dr. Porter's blooded thoroughbred spooked and snorted, is near delirium and refuses to stand still long enough for him to mount. The horse bolts dragging Porter along, barely hanging onto the saddle, his feet bouncing and dragging on the ground. A Sioux warrior races in whirling a stone war club. In a last desperate attempt, Porter manages to thrust himself halfway into the saddle.

Charley reloads his Sharps and blasts the Sioux from the hip giving Porter time to get away.

Porter's horse dashes for parts unknown. In sheer fright the doctor hangs on for dear life. For nearly a mile the stampeding steed races alongside numerous Sioux and Cheyenne war-ponies. Incredibly the charging Indians pay no attention to the rider. Finally, the frightened animal swings towards the river where other cavalry horses are stampeding. Then without breaking pace the doctor's speeding mount plunges off the six-foot high steep bank landing with a tremendous splash in the belly deep water. The terrified steed emerges on the far bank with Porter still clinging on. The spooked horse charges up the bluffs where Reno and his followers have taken refuge. Porter falls from his saddle, hitting the ground with a groan, knocking the wind out of him. A group of confused men gathers around.

"Are we glad to see you, Doc!" An emotional soldier cries, clinging to the torn sleeve of his blood-soaked jacket. "You're the only surgeon left!"

"Doc. DeWolf was killed coming up the hill. The wounded need help!" shouts another.

Gasping for breath, tears well up in the doctor's eyes. He tries to speak but the words don't come. A nearby private offers to give the doctor a hand up. Porter shakes his head no as he tries to catch his breath.

One of Reynolds' admirers, the young soldier who yelled at Charley, runs forward when he recognizes Porter. "Where's Lonesome Charley, Doc!" He asks impatiently. "I saw him down there in the bottom near you. He's all right, ain't he?"

"What about Girard? Half of G Company's soldiers are missing." Someone else shouts.

Another soldier yells out, "Charley made it out didn't he?"

Dr. Porter, his voice quivering, begins to recount the heroic standoff. "He just stood there...brave and fearless like no one I've ever seen firing shot after shot."

"Didn't he follow you?" asks the inquiring soldier offering his red bandanna to the doctor.

"I don't know. I don't know. I couldn't get near enough to help. He just stood out there all alone firing one shot after another, holding those madmen away long enough for me to get on my half-crazed horse. Then he told me to get out of there." He pauses to wipe the dampened dirt from his face. "Reno left the line without telling anyone. Not one word of warning! No blasted bugle...nothing! If it wasn't for

Lonesome Charley I'd be dead, probably hacked to death. He saved my life. That's when he took the bullet."

"He's dead then," says the heavy-hearted private.

"Last I saw of him he was shooting and trying to get his horse. I doubt if he could get out of there alive," Porter says the furor now showing through his tears. "Reno's responsible for this. Where in the devil is that wretched coward?" he shouts, jumping to his feet snorting like a raging bull.

"Benteen has just come up. Reno's bug eyed and half drunk. He's over pleading with Benteen to stay and help." offers a sergeant from Weir's Company D.

"I'm not much for fighting but let me at him." the doctor blurts. "And Benteen where has that jackass been?"

"I'll tell you where he's been," says the sympathetic sergeant. "Captain Weir and our Company D ran them Indians off the bluffs, just in the nick of time to save Reno's butt, while that nincompoop Benteen was lollygagging on the back trail." The unflattering remarks spark a flurry of heated exchanges as the men from both battalions vent their frustration and resentment over the lack of leadership.

"I thought Benteen was supposed to be here supporting Reno," Porter says, a little calmer now. "Wasn't that Custer's order?"

An agitated Captain Weir has been listening. He steps forward and turns to the group of soldiers surrounding the doctor. "How many orders do you need to support your own regiment?" he states. "But Frederick was taking his own sweet time getting here. Isn't that so, Captain Benteen?"

"You insolent dunderhead!" Benteen screeches. "You're under my command, Weir, and don't you forget it!"

"What command?" Weir asks throwing his arms out in a gesture of surrender. "Look at these men, Captain, fighting amongst themselves. This isn't the Seventh Cavalry as I've known it." He spits into the dust. "And just where on God's green earth is Reno? Looking for another flask of whiskey I'll bet!"

"You're good with the bottle yourself, Captain Weir!" shouts Benteen.

Weir waves his arm in disgust. "Yeah! And you're not so bad with the brown jug either, Captain. I might drink after a fight! Not during it."

As Captain Weir and Captain Benteen come ever closer to blows many of the soldiers begin to take up sides. Sadly, the Dakota column's so-called advance, crumbles under the weight of its own ineptitude as the disorder worsens.

Meanwhile, within striking distance and as yet not engaged, Custer, alongside Captain Keogh and headquarters lead C, F, I and L companies up a dry ravine. From Medicine Tail Coulee the ravine starts out northward then curves around in an easterly direction. It divides the first and second ridge north of Medicine Tail Coulee. Almost at once Custer dispatches F Company to another ridge, immediately to his left or north. Custer along with headquarters and C Company scramble up to the top of the ridge adjacent to Medicine Tail Coulee. At the General's direction, Captain Tom Custer orders the company into platoons for a bold show of force. From the top of the ridge they can see to the river and watch to the south for their expected support. Anticipating the coming support, Custer positions the soldiers in the ready for a surprise flank and rear attack on the Indians when Captain Benteen or Major Reno's supporting companies arrive. Custer's location is ideal.

Captain Keogh, with the remainder of the battalion, continues on up the dry ravine towards the east then swings north to a high ridge a mile and one-half east of the river. Benteen, Reno and Custer's soldiers are within two miles of each other.

Above Custer, suddenly the five man detail from Company F, along with a number of other soldiers eagerly call out. "There, to the south. I see soldiers. They're on those bluffs." Only minutes ago, Reno has finally stopped his stampede and for the time being, has found a safe refuge. Custer, Tom, Cooke and others, quickly turn around in time to see the soldiers arrive on the bluffs to the south.

Custer's confidence grows. "That'll be Captain Benteen. He may gripe a lot but he's a fighter!" Custer's eyes light up while Tom and Cooke both gain confidence.

Confidently, Custer scans the field, his eyes and ears missing nothing. His intellect always analyzing his coming moves. "Yates will hold his position at the river as long as it's prudent. I can order him to withdraw at my beckon. With Yates withdrawal those Indians will cross the river and swarm up the ravines like flies on a dead dog. Once they do, Reno, Benteen n' McDougall, will strike them. We'll hit them from the rear. The flankers can blaze away." Custer takes a hurried glance to their back trail. "McDougall and Mathey will be here shortly with the munitions!" Tom and Cooke have a quick look at each other then look down the ridge.

"We'll give em' a lesson they won't soon forget, General." Tom Custer strokes his goatee.

"Mr. Henry Voss, stay close," Custer shouts. "I anticipate I'll be sending you with a message to Yates. The Gray Horse Soldiers will keep their holding action across those lower ridges." The General looks at his brother Tom. "Captain Custer! Keep the soldier with the fastest horse ready. I'll be sending a message to General Terry."

"That'll be Short, Nathan Short, General. Terry must be just over one of those ridges! They ought to be able to hear the gun shots." Tom points northeastward.

Custer looks confidently at Cooke, who looks a little skeptical. "You figure that Captain Yates will draw the Indians across the river? When the Indians go after Yates' retreating soldiers, Benteen and Reno's battalions will strike them at a vulnerable spot, hopefully from the rear."

Custer smiles at his adjutant. "Like drawing bees to honey, Cookie. No difference."

Cooke nervously clears the dryness from his throat. "It just might work...if the others come up?" Cooke mutters to himself.

The men silently beam with renewed confidence as their eyes shift from one to the other, finally watching their leader, waiting for orders.

George Custer lifts his Remington rifle as he beams confidence. "Those flankers n' sharpshooters will make quick work of them. The Dakotas, the Cheyenne won't stand a chance. We'll scatter em' like dust in a Kansas wind storm."

Not too many minutes later, Custer notifies Captain Keogh by bugle. Keogh moves his forces down off the high ridge. He spreads out his formation. With the two platoons each, along with those below, Companies E and F, there are seven groups in a wide bold front. The General is vying for time. The two Company F platoons are in a holding action on the ridge to the north of Custer. Those with Custer on the top of the ridge, opposite the mouth of the cedar tree lined coulee, anxiously watch and wait for Benteen, McDougall and the reserve ammunition.

Lieutenant Cooke rides up alongside Custer. "Sir, General Terry's vanguard should be coming up at any time."

Custer doesn't hide his anxiety. "I don't know what could be keeping him?"

Cooke is disturbed too. "If Terry doesn't come up, Sir, what then? Do we have a strategy?"

Custer barely starts to speak when Tom Custer and his Lieutenant yell as one, pointing to the Company F detail above them.

"Look up there!" shouts Tom Custer.

The five-man detail is waving their hats and gesturing.

Above them, seemingly out of nowhere, ride two bands of Cheyenne Indians from two different directions. Around three hundred yards to the northeast, it is hard to tell just how many there are.

Totally unexpected Tom Custer declares. "Where in the devil did..."

Custer quickly shouts. "Throw some lead! Can't have them flanking us now... blaze away!"

At once, Captain Custer shouts, "By Companies! Ready, aim, fire!" Over a hundred 45-70 carbines belch out lead flame and smoke. "Fire when ready. Give it to em." Tom orders. The cavalrymen load and fire as the Indians return a barrage.

Tom Custer hurries over to his brother. "What in sam hell?" More firing from the Indians abruptly distracts him. Arrows whiz to the ground close by. "Never expected this, brother," Tom says.

George Custer only takes a quick look as he blasts an Indian who makes a brave move to the front. The big Remington is a lethal weapon in his hands. "We have no choice but to throw lead," Custer says to Tom, as he reloads. "The others will soon be up with the munitions and the reinforcements."

"Yeah! When?" Tom frowns. "Captain Yates's is gonna need support before long."

"We've got to dislodge those Indians from behind those ridges. Voss. Sound the rally for Captain Keogh," says Custer bluntly. Henry Voss quickly turns to the north sounding the rally.

Tom takes a hurried glance down the ridge towards the river then fires at the Indians above them.

Simultaneously, with Custer's action on some lower ridges on the north side of Medicine Tail Coulee and above the river, the Gray Horse Company's 2nd platoon has climbed the steep bank out of the coulee and has formed two skirmish lines, one mounted and one dismounted. The dismounted soldiers' led horses safely behind the crest of the ridge. There is a steady skirmish fire as the Indians, hidden in the ravines and gullies, skirmish with the soldiers.

E Company's 1st platoon is making a feint near the river. Company F will soon be along to support Company E. Unwisely, young Lieutenant Sturgis attempts to make a bold show at the river. While he charges forward, he fires his pistol. Briefly, he halts on the bank of the river then charges boldly forward into the water. Without warning a barrage of gunshots belches out from the brush across the river. Powder smoke clouds the air. Sturgis groans as he falls off his horse splashing into the water, his foot hanging up in the stirrup. Before any of his soldiers have time to react, his horse stampedes straight for the Indian camp dragging the lieutenant like a rag doll, his body plowing a furrow in the water. The last the E company soldiers see, is Sturgis's horse race out of the water up the bank then disappearing into the trees.

Lieutenant Sturgis's lifeless body lies in the grass, just outside the Indian camp, where it had come loose from the stirrup. That night, the hostiles burn his body in a huge bonfire. His bloody underwear will be found in the Indian camp by some of the soldiers after the battle.

Even though there has only been a light skirmish, the ruse at the mouth of Medicine Tail Coulee has paid off. The warriors who spotted the mounted soldiers from the Cheyenne camp downstream from the river crossing, are under the impression that the entire 7th Cavalry is riding into their encampment. The old men along with the women and children have fled from the village to the western hills. Custer's bold front has caused many of the warriors to hold back, confused as to what path to take. They line the western bank in case the soldiers charge into to their camp across the river from the east.

But something else is happening. More Indians are now streaming to fight Custer's battalion from a different quarter. Captain Keogh has quickly brought I Company down the ridge. He leads Comanche over to the General. "I believe Captain Yates is going to need some kind of supporting action." For a brief moment Custer ignores the captain.

"Captain Keogh. I had planned on making our fight on this particular part of the field. But those Indians have put our plan in peril. The high ridge is ideal for the other battalions to make a junction. Those Indians up there have changed all that. In order to gain a success we must alter our plan." Custer turns and shouts. "Orderly!" A young private quickly moves over. "Lieutenant Cooke. Direct the orderly to take a message to Captain Yates. Instruct him to execute a slow withdrawal up the north coulee. Tell him we'll rendezvous at headquarters, below the head of the gorge, about a mile from the river. We'll soon be with him." Custer says brusquely.

All eyes briefly watch the orderly spur down the ridge as Tom steps up. He angrily looks around. "There'd be no need to withdraw Captain Yates if Benteen n' the others would come up! How many orders does it take? What could possibly be the delay? He is going to endanger our entire battle strategy!"

"Those Indians came out of nowhere. There's no use in crying over spilled milk. We'll have to execute another maneuver," George Custer says as Tom Custer interrupts him by pointing.

There is a brief solemn silence, when below them the young messenger screams as several arrows slice into him. He grasps the saddle; desperately trying to hang on then tumbles from his horse head first into the dirt. Custer gives Tom a worried look then shouts to Chief Trumpeter Henry Voss. "Trumpeter! Sound the rally!" At once the notes blare across the ridges as Voss blows the rally.

Meanwhile scores of Indians are showing up from the south. The same direction that Custer expected Benteen and Reno to come from. Not only are the Indians up above them but now they are streaming up from the south and from below towards the river. The fight is hot and heavy.

For at least thirty minutes or more the skirmish rages aggressively but with only a few casualties on both sides. Anxious to end the matter, Custer orders Keogh to have the battalion fire by volleys. The Indians have no answer for the heavy fire. The second volley sends them scurrying in retreat back in to the hills.

With a look of quiet anxiety, George Custer scans the field. Finally, he instructs Lieutenant Cooke to write a message. Cooke hurriedly pulls aside and begins to write. The others continue to fire at some warriors, who for now, keep their distance.

In the Field on Little Big Horn
12 to 15 miles from its mouth
June 25

General Terry:
Have struck a big Indian camp on the Little Big Horn, I am in a most terrible engagement with the hostile Indians. Major Reno's battalion (three Co's.) charged at about 2 p.m. but drew back to the hills. I will engage in a delaying fight waiting for the Montana Column along with (Benteen & Reno each with three Co's.) and the munitions (McDougall one Co. rear guard Mathey 84 men escort) to arrive. The field is on the lower river below the mouth of a dry creek the Crow's call Ash creek. Come Quick!

By command of Lieutenant Colonel Custer
W.W. Cooke
Adjutant 7ᵗʰ Cavalry

P.S. Come Quick.

Cooke quickly hands the message to Tom Custer. Tom immediately dispatches

Nathan Short to ride to General Terry. Custer realizes that he can't wait much longer as Captain Yates will need some kind of supporting action.

Below Custer on the rim of the north coulee that runs up to the high ridge, Yates has heard the rally at the battalion and his soldiers execute a slow but orderly retreat up the north rim of the coulee. The soldiers continue a light skirmish action with the Cheyenne and a few Sioux.

Custer looks around with a hint of expectancy. "The others should be here directly. Once Benteen and Reno strike those warriors moving up below, we'll have them."

"And if this does not work, Sir? We can still fight a delaying action."

"You're right, Keogh. I don't think we'll need to look down below, Captain," General Custer points. "Those Indians are doing exactly as I figured they would."

"They're coming across in a swarm, Sir. What about the Sharpshooters?" Keogh nervously looks to their back trail for signs of Benteen's soldiers. "They ought to be able to hear our gunfire."

North of the mouth of Medicine Tail Coulee, on the high bluff above the river the five man sharpshooter detail and the ten flankers had been keeping a lively fire on any Indians crossings the river, holding the bulk of the warriors from coming across. But now they are in a fierce struggle with more Indians from a different direction. Their bluff position is ideal except for one thing. The Indians that had first crossed the river in advance of Custer's arrival, had fled into the coulees and ravines to the north of Medicine Tail. Unknown to Custer, the Sioux and Cheyenne have returned and now have the soldiers cut off from the rest of the battalion. Without back up they are in a no win situation.

Briefly Custer contemplates their predicament and the reinforcements. What can possibly be the delay? Had Benteen and Reno showed up, it is likely that the soldiers could have held their position. "Curse all the luck! We're going to have to throw some lead and drive those Indians back on Yates' flank and rear, Captain. Com'on, lets ride." Custer trots off then shouts behind, "Keogh, have the company trumpeters blow the charge. If nothing else, the other battalions can't help but hear the bugles!"

"Mr. Voss! Trumpeters! By Companies! Sound the charge!" Immediately, Voss signals the company trumpeters and the bugles blare across the ridges, ravines and coulees echoing across the waters of the Little Big Horn.

From the high East Ridge, Custer's brother-in-law, James Calhoun leading L Company rides down the rim of the north coulee for the rendezvous. Custer waves the companies along the ridge, riding for the assembly point with Yates and the others. The Indians swarm behind Yates' soldiers as they move up the slope of the large coulee.

"Captain, Keogh! Fire when ready!" Custer shouts as he raises his 50-70 Remington from the pommel of his saddle. "Blaze away, Captain!"

Keogh barks out the commands in rapid secession, "Companies. By files! By the left flank! Front into line! Advance carbines!" The three companies of mounted veterans wheel their horses to the left, facing down the ridge, cocking their carbines. "Ready! Aim! Fire!" comes the command and nearly one hundred fifty black powder cartridges explode with precision, killing several Indians and driving the others to seek safety behind the ravines and into the gullies. "Fire!" And another volley blasts down the coulee, reverberating across the waters of the Little Big Horn, along the bluffs and trees and can easily be heard two miles away on the bluffs where Reno fled. "Fire!" Yells Keogh and another volley rips into the Indians, its wake echoing down the coulee and along the bluffs.

At this same time, on the hills where Major Reno's battalion took refuge, obscenities and arguments are on the increase. Frightened and confused, groups of officers and enlisted men alike stand by helplessly as Reno and Benteen stand by idly. The soldiers pass the blame onto someone else's shoulders.

"Major Reno ran like a coward, Sir!" shouts a young corporal who decides Benteen is the least evil of the two Commanders. "He just pulled up and ran...left my bunkies down there to fight it out! Not even a bugle call!"

"Sergeant O'Hara was the only one who got it before Reno pulled the line," says a corporal. "He was still alive."

A sergeant stares over at Reno with a shocked look, "Still alive?"

"Still alive n' they left him?" shouts another.

"I heard O'Hara scream when the men took off. "For God's sake don't leave me!"

"I'll never forget it. Them Indians will butcher him to..."

"Shut up, Corporal!" a nearby sergeant screams. "You don't know what you are..."

Major Reno cocks an angry ear while looking at each of his subordinate officers, "Adjutant Cooke informed me that the whole outfit would support us! Where were they? Where in the devil was our support?"

"You pulled foot before Custer could have possibly been in position. You didn't hold fast for a scant twenty minutes!" Porter yells.

Captain Weir gives Benteen an icy stare. "Maybe you should ask Captain Benteen, Major."

"Why you hog, wallowing, imbecile blabber mouth! You're a whiskey soak tuh boot." Benteen squeals. "I've had enough of your smart aleck remarks, Captain. One more word out of you and I'll personally kick the stuffing out of you! You mule headed jackass."

But the angry Commander acts differently when a dozen soldiers walk over to listen.

Suddenly over the shouting, Lieutenant Varnum hears the sound of heavy gunfire. "Listen up men! Listen up! That's Custer! Those are volleys. Listen!"

The distinct crash, crash of heavy gunfire echoes off the waters of the river, resounds off the bluffs, trees and bushes lining the river and is easily heard on the hill.

"Hear that, Wallace! And that!"

"Custer is giving it to them!" says Lieutenant Wallace. "And how!"

"Custer's in a hot fight. He's really giving it to them!" Varnum shouts.

"The General is pouring it on," Benteen's first sergeant yells excitedly.

"Custer is whipping the Indians. He's giving it to them for all he's worth," cries a private.

"We ought to be over there." another soldier shouts.

"Buffalo dung!" sputters Benteen, cupping his hand over the bowl of his pipe.

"You boys are hearing things," adds Reno. The whiskey-drinking officer wipes his sweaty forehead with his bloody handkerchief. Then without warning, he pulls his revolver from its holster and empties it towards the valley a thousand yards away. "You stinking Red devils!" He screams.

The men are shocked at the Major's loss of control but are immediately distracted by the sound of more gunfire. There's no mistaking the heavy, "crash-crash," of the volleys exploding from at least a hundred odd carbines and rifles—the 45-55s, the 45-70s and one 50-70 Remington Rolling Block rifle.

"Listen up! Sounds like bugles. Listen! I can hear the faint sound of bugles. That's General Custer!" shouts a soldier. The others strain their ears listening, towards the north.

"Trumpets are for cavalry, bugles are for the infantry," spouts a young soldier. He receives a glare from the others.

Weir darts angry looks at Major Reno and Captain Benteen. "We ought to be over there! I'm asking your permission to join General Custer, Sir."

Benteen is fed up with Weir's persistence. "Permission denied!" he says with finality.

"Well, I'm going anyhow!"

"The devil if you are!" Benteen shouts back.

Reno moves closer, "I-I remind you both," he stammers. "I am the senior officer here. I am in command!"

Weir coughs almost to the point of choking. "Command! What command? Begging the Major's pardon, Benteen's battalion is a separate detachment. The Captain there has a direct written ord..."

"I am the senior officer here!" Reno abruptly interrupts Captain Weir.

Benteen stares in disgust at the unkempt Commander and turns his back as Weir walks over to his horse and mounts up. "I must remind you once again, Captain Benteen," Weir says, reining his horse around and signaling his men to follow, "You have a written order from General Custer. I read it myself."

"I've two loaded pistols on my pommel, Captain. I'll...I'll shoot where you are," Benteen mutters to himself then adds out loud, "If you try to leave. Do you hear me?"

Turning in his saddle, Thomas Weir pushes his hat to the back of his head revealing the defiant creases of his suntanned face. "I'm sure you will do whatever fits your fancy, Captain Benteen." Weir adds sarcastically. "It would be just like you to ignore the Indians. I wouldn't put it past you one bit to shoot me in the back. But I'm going anyhow!"

"Are you hard of hearing?" Reno screams. "I am in command here! Captain Weir! I order you to dismount your company!"

"You're calling me hard of hearing?" Weir shouts with disgust at Reno, pointing downstream to where Custer's firing can still be heard echoing through the hills.

Benteen has drawn his revolver but Weir urges his horse forward. Following behind him is his entire company. Major Reno once again screams for a halt.

"Do you expect them to listen to you, Major?" a flustered Dr. Porter yells. "You run off n' left us alone down there to fight on our own, for God's sake. What kind of Commander deserts his men? Not even a retreat from the trumpeter."

"That was a charge, Sir."

Porter chokes, totally baffled by Major Reno's bizarre comment. Taking a moment to recover, he spits phlegm on the ground, then stutters. "Ch-ch charge? I've never heard it called such a thing!"

The others are left speechless. They look at each other dismayed at Reno calling his terror stricken stampede a charge. Some turn their backs to the Major in disgust.

Reno turns indignantly to Benteen. "If you'd shown up when you were supposed to..."

When Benteen shifts toward Major Reno, the cocked revolver still in his hand, the Major decides to hold his tongue. But Dr. Porter's vivid recollection of his recent escape from the hostiles rekindles his anger.

"You're a coward, Marcus!" the doctor shouts sternly. "You don't deserve any respect from these men. It's your fault the bodies of their friends and brothers are strewn across the valley." His voice trembles as he recalls his last glimpse of Lonesome Charley. "Poor Charley Reynolds. His own father was a doctor. Charley was one of the finest men to ride with the 7th. And you run off like a scalded dog and left them down there to die. No apprehension at all for the wounded!"

Reno angrily fires back. "One of the privates said that you left a wounded man down there yourself."

"What would you have me do? Stay there until I was hacked to death? Reno, You..." He lunges toward the Major with all the fury of an agitated mother bear.

Responding to the inevitable clash, a sergeant steps in front of Reno and grabs Surgeon Porter. "Restrain him get a hold of him, boys!" he yells. Several soldiers grab the distraught doctor. In the course of restraining him, they stumble and fall to the ground in a heap.

For his own reason Benteen re-holsters his weapon as one of the officers utters a plea. "Men, officers. It's too late to undo what has already been done. Officers! Gentlemen, I beg of you there must be some return to order or we'll all perish."

"Here comes Lieutenant Hare." Suddenly, all eyes turn when a soldier yells.

Panting as if he'd just run a long foot race with Adjutant Cooke, Lieutenant Hare excitedly hollers as he reins to a skidding halt. "McDougall n' the train are close behind. They'll soon be up!" Not far behind Hare, two civilian packers hurry two of the ammunition mules up the hills, one packer leading the other, whipping the mules along.

A lieutenant shouts, "Now we can go to Custer!"

Major Reno makes a feeble attempt to restore some resemblance of order. "Now that the ammunition has arrived we can avenge the loss of our brother officers."

Not only have they already wasted precious time, but oddly enough there is delay after delay. Major Reno wastes valuable time to hike down to the river to search for his dead friend and adjutant, Lieutenant Benny Hodgson. And before that, he waited for the delayed pack train to arrive to get the shovels. Afterwards, when they finally moved out to go to Custer, they halted and waited for the dismounted men who were deserted in the woods, to climb up the bluffs. Precious life saving time, ticking away, ticking away into oblivion. Time wasted that will soon result in the annihilation of George Custer and five brave companies of the Seventh Horse.

Meanwhile, from the valley floor, scattered shots continue to echo up the bluffs. The Sioux and Cheyenne are reluctant to make a bold charge on Reynolds, knowing that a few of them will be snuffed out. They keep a safe distance between themselves and Charley. He is flat on the ground and continues to load and fire. Shot after shot belches from his Sharps as the Indians continue to ride around stirring up dust and feinting to ride him down.

Not far away, just across the river, a few of the Ree and two of the Crow scouts are engaged in a deadly duel. The scouts are holed up in a grove of trees and have the advantage. Whenever the hostile warriors dare ride in close they are blasted from their fleet ponies. Even though two of the Crows are wounded, this battle within a battle, lasts well over an hour. These Crow and Ree Indians will live to talk about the fight at the Little Big Horn. For many years they demonstrate that those with ammunition, willing to stick it out, could survive that deadly Sunday.

Charley eyes his almost empty prairie belt. He's got to do something before long. He had seen Benteen's battalion arrive on the hill and for some time he had entertained hopes of fresh reinforcements coming down the hill to renew the fight in the valley. Too, he had hoped that Custer would charge through the camp from the north. But with Major Reno's pulling foot and stampeding to the hills, now he believes that no one is coming. He notices Girard, a hundred yards or so away, disappears into the trees. Charley looks around for other soldiers but sees none. Maybe it is time he makes a break for it.

Charley's horse remains calm waiting for his master's command. Untying his faithful companion, Reynolds manages with great difficulty to get into the saddle. He has lost the strength of his hand and his Sharps carbine clatters to the ground. Painfully he jerks the bullet poke from around his neck. He struggles to remove the two brass .45 cal. Schofield cartridges and with great effort loads them into the empty chambers of his revolver. Oddly, he hears a voice in his head, the voice of his old mentor, Gabriel Green. *"Kill the meanest cut-throated, red skinned Injun with the first bullet. Save the last bullet for yerself!"*

For a long moment Charley stares at his pistol. He has barely spun the cylinder in place when he looks up to see three, maybe four or five Indians. They are all around him now.

A hundred yards or so away, Fred Girard hollers to warn Charley. "Get down off your horse. You're an easy mark! Get down, Charley!"

But Reynolds does not hear Girard's pleas. Girard ducks into the underbrush and joins up with other abandoned soldiers when several Indians ride close by.

Nearby, a wildly painted warrior with the coup stick joins Black Face who has his eyes on Reynolds. They separate, then charge from opposite directions. Around and around the warriors circle Reynolds, shrieking loudly, trying to confuse him. It is a buffalo hunt for the warriors mounted on their fastest war-ponies. Reynolds turns this way and that way, trying to keep them in view. The amount of dust is incredible and visibility drops. Drifting dust opens up glimpses here and there. Soon everything looks hazy. Reynolds barely hangs in the saddle. He now looks like the helpless buffalo calves on the early summer hunts, easy prey.

Black Face agilely leans from his horse and picks up Reynolds' hat. Arrogantly, he dons it while he circles his horse around. Around and around they go again, shrieking.

Black Face and Wildly-Painted Warrior rein to a stop. Black Face whirls a huge stone war club. Shrieking incessantly they urge their horses into a ferocious charge.

Hooves pound, the ground shakes, dust flies. Neck and neck the warriors race all out to see who will be the first to count coup on this helpless enemy. Closer and closer they come. Reynolds grits his teeth, he shakes his head to clear his vision. He clutches his watch in his left hand. He spurs Red. In sheer desperation he raises his pistol and fires his last two shots!

Black Face flies head-over-heels hitting the ground with a thud. The warrior at close range is blown backwards from his horse, throwing the coup stick. In slow motion Charley sees his hat drift slowly to the ground. The coup stick appears to twirl through the air for an eternity. Finally, the heavy iron point skewers the coup stick into the ground. The red flannel strips shudder on impact.

Charley hears what sounds like the thunderous roar of the Thunderbirds' flapping wings. But it's Indian' gunshots and pounding hooves. Bullets fly through the air from every direction. The gunfire is deafening now. Charley knows that once on the ground he is doomed. He manages to pull himself up but is slumped in the saddle, his vision blurred as he bounces recklessly to Big Red's erratic gait. A murky scene of charging warriors and fleeing soldiers passes before him. Then something peculiar happens, as if in a desert mirage Little Bear rides by on his coal-black stallion. Reynolds shudders, gazing into the dusty haze to get a better glimpse of his elusive friend. But as quick as he appeared, Little Bear has vanished.

Reynolds feels his knees weaken. He clutches the watch from Ariana tightly in his left hand. In a whirling sensation of sickening dizziness the whole battlefield seems to tumble before him in a never ending blur—the wide smoke-filled sky above; the dusty blood-splattered ash below. The thunderous roar of whipped ponies and whooping warriors, suddenly is nothing more than a hypnotic buzz—the whimpering and moaning of the wounded and dying—Ariana's beautiful face flashes before him as the red flannel flutters through the dust. The aberration of red flannel transforms into Running-creek-Woman's auburn hair, her smile appears then fades. Charley grips his revolver as he feels his hip collide with the turf beneath him. One of the bead strips from his jacket tears apart, little blue beads flashing across his eyes, hitting him in the face. He tries to shake his foot loose but his ankle is twisted in the stirrup.

Fred Girard looks out from the underbrush in time to witness Charley's struggle. But Girard is powerless to lend a hand. If he attempts to do anything, he will only give his position away to the Indians. "No, Charley. No. You should have got down," he says mournfully, quietly, more to himself than anyone else.

Reynolds begs Big Red to stop. Ears pointed the horse slows when he hears the mournful plea. Sensing trouble, the faithful animal instinctively comes to a halt and turns to look at his master, now covered with blood and dust.

"Whoa, Red. Easy, boy," Reynolds whispers, struggling to untangle his leg.

Suddenly a lone shot rips through Montana's raggedness, its echo bouncing off the distant bluffs. Big Red screams his last. As the dead weight comes to rest on Charley's legs, trapping him hopelessly under the horse's hindquarters, Lonesome Charley sees the gold watch dangling from his hand. Fond memories bring relief to his aching body as he clutches the timepiece to his chest. Then lifting his Schofield .45 skyward he aims at an Indian who is holding a stone hatchet above his head. He squeezes the trigger...twice, three times. Each impotent click rings in his ears as the hammer falls on another empty chamber.

From the corner of his eye Charley can see a Sioux warrior running toward him now. A ray of sunlight pierces the smoky haze and bounces off the razor-sharp edge of his ax blade as the Indian comes closer. Suddenly there is a swarm all around him, ripping at his clothes, jerking his prairie belt and pistol, emptying his pockets, prodding and kicking him. He tightens his grip on the watch as the Indians quickly strip Red's saddle and load up their newfound possessions. They're in a hurry, Charley hears them say. Many more Wasichus will die. His face feels warm and his last aberration is Running-creek-Woman's warm cheek against his. Then something strange happens. Charley hears the wails of a newborn baby, and then his life's force is gone. Charley Reynolds is dead.

Plodding along the trail of fallen Bluecoats left by their brave fighting men, a number of Sioux women are muttering amongst themselves as they methodically strip and mutilate the bodies, tending to the task as if it were a regular occurrence. An occasional moan or scream interrupts the ritual as they poke, prod and kick the living as well as the dead, moving from one fallen enemy to the next in search of weapons, ammunition and anything else that appeals to their curiosity.

From yards away, as he rides with a dozen Sioux and Cheyenne warriors, Little Bear notices one of his tribesmen kneeling over a dead horse. Something is strangely familiar to him—the color—the color of red clay. Pulling on the rawhide war bridle of his favorite stallion, Run-Like-The-Wind, he tells the others to go on without him. He trots over to the slain horse, carefully looks at the color of the mane and the nose. Then, slipping his leg over the back of his black steed, he leaps to the ground. There is no need to look any closer. The body beneath the horse is that of his friend, Char-Lee Lo-onesome.

"Eyomashesha. He is friend," Little Bear speaks to the other Indian. "I know this White hunter from the buffalo prairie." He points to the east and tells the young warrior he can leave.

Jumping onto his pony with ease, the young warrior shouts to Little Bear. "Hoka hey! Hoka hey! A good day to die!" Then with a crack of his pony whip, war pony and rider thunder off to join the others.

Little Bear stares at the body for a time, a feeling of sadness in his heart. "If only the Wasichus would not force us to live on the reservations where our people starve...with only their spotted cattle and no buffalo to hunt. They corral us like animals. Don't they understand, Char-Lee? We are people too! Time in front, my friend perhaps one day all Indians and Whites can live, no war."

At that moment an unexplained silence falls over the valley. Little Bear hears a faint ticking sound. He crouches near Charley's body. The noise is louder now. Out of the blue, a scene from his past flashes into his memory. It was three snows, long time past, during the Snow Moon on the Ingan Wak Pa when he visited Char-Lee's buffalo camp. Yes, he remembers the shiny gold box and the ticking that had startled him at first.

With great care, Little Bear pries the clenched fingers from around the timepiece and holds it up to his ear. He recalls the quiet scout's smile; how funny Char-Lee thought it was that he was frightened by the noise. The shiny box meant so much to him.

"Hurry, hurry!" shout some warriors as they ride past Little Bear. "You're not going to stay with the women and children! Hurry. Let the old men stay with the helpless ones. Hoka Hey! Hoka hey!"

Hesitating for a moment, Little Bear stoops and cuts the beaded strip from Charley's jacket. He then leaps onto his black stallion and rides to join the noisy group. Run-Like-The-Wind's hooves pound the soil relentlessly; his black mane drifts backwards as he runs all out toward the river crossing. Little Bear, stripped to only his breech-clout, has a blanket wrapped around his legs, his war-bow and quiver slung low on his back. In one hand he grips the rawhide jaw rope; a captured soldier Springfield 45-70 carbine is in the other.

Like his mount, his black hair loosened from its braids, flutters freely behind him in the wind. Plunging into the icy waters of the Little Big Horn River, horse and rider race to catch the other Sioux and Cheyenne war horses as they head up the coulees and ravines in search of the enemy, all the while shouting the cadent war chant.

"Hoka hey! Hoka hey!" they repeat over and over again. "A good day to die! A good day to die!"

21

George Custer has executed a successful reuniting of his battalion just below a knoll at the south end of the hogback ridge. Here, while the companies remain in battle formation, he has a hurried conference with his officers. The Sioux and Cheyenne are still keeping their distance while seeking any chance to close in. Word has quickly spread amongst the Sioux and Cheyenne that upstream another group of cavalry have joined the soldiers that they chased across the river to the bluffs. They are still apprehensive that more soldiers are coming. The Indians are not yet ready to sacrifice all.

As of this time, Custer only has a few casualties. Mitch Boyer has been wounded in the leg and has lost his horse. However, there is still full time and hope amongst Custer's soldiers for relief. Even though there appears to be an ideal knoll at the north end of the ridge, he will be further away from his supporting seven companies and the reserve ammunition. With a strong belief that the reinforcements will still come up, Custer's strategy is to move further north.

Boyer, the French-breed Sioux scout, is upset at the plan. He boldly speaks out as Custer is repeating the last minute instructions to his brother.

"General!" Boyer shouts, pointing, "If you go over there, we'll be ambushed! Hundreds of the Dakotas, the Cheyenne go into hiding behind the cut banks. Not a Mother's son of us will come out alive!"

"We've got to find a place to make a stand where the others will come up and relieve us. Reno n' Benteen have seven companies with them." Custer says respectfully.

"The Dakotas are many, Otoe. The Dakotas hide in the ravines and draws. You cannot see how many! They'll soon be on all sides!" Boyer insists on using the Sioux word, Otoe. Most of the soldiers including, the Custer brothers, understand that the word means, heaps of them.

"He may be right!" Tom Custer agrees. "We really don't know how many there are, brother."

"Boyer has a strong heart, he is a great warrior among many but he has no understanding of cavalry movements, Tom." Custer says abruptly, then turns to the scout. "We've got to be in position to pin down the Sioux when attacking the coming reinforcements. You ought to know, Boyer, the Sioux must be worried, too. They fight while looking over their shoulders. They've seen the other soldiers as well!"

"Soldiers scared out, not come! Soldiers not come at Medicine Tail crossing. Soldiers scared out not, come here."

Tom interjects, "If anything, they're going to save their own butts!"

"Otoe, many Dakotas, the Cheyenne hide behind the ridges. I know the Dakotas. I know how the Dakotas fight." Boyer insists.

"I want to set up a perimeter all around on the high points, wait for the others to relieve us. Anything else, Tom?" Custer fires. He has made his decision.

"We'll execute the movement" says Tom.

Boyer angrily kicks the dust, "I say again, they're scared out!" He limps over to Curly who holds a horse he had caught when one of the soldier casualties occurred. Boyer points over the ridge toward the head of the north coulee that they have just passed. "Curly, you are young. You know little about fighting. Get out of here. Go to No hip Terry! Ride north! Even though I am wounded I go with the soldiers. I have been shot before. If the others do not come, we'll all be cleaned out anyway! General Custer believes the others will come and relieve us. I believe they're scared out!" he says, realizing it may be his final ride.

Over an hour later a long range sniping action ensues along the hog back ridge. Custer is in a safe holding position. From the north end of the ridge, George Custer and several officers urgently look to their back trail. They glass the high point, where earlier Custer, Cooke and the scouts had viewed the large village down in the valley. Three miles away they can see silhouettes of mounted soldiers on the high ridges. At long last, reinforcements are on the way.

What Custer doesn't know, is that the company of soldiers is only Captain Weir and his loyal soldiers. Neither can he see the approaching Indians, on foot now, creeping ever closer from the valley below. The Indians are hidden behind knolls and ridges, out of sight in the tall grass and sagebrush. They use every sort of cover available.

On seeing the approaching soldiers, the Commander scans the area below him. He feels the need to set up a corridor. Custer is concerned for the safe arrival of the reinforcements. As he examines the area below him towards the river, he sees a likely area. In order to facilitate the expected arrival of the reinforcements he immediately orders the Gray Horse Company and his brother Tom's C Company, under Lieutenant Harrington, to ride down the slope to the south.

Followed by those who have vowed to bring death to the Wasichus, a Cheyenne war chief and his following, are hiding behind a lower ridge as Companies E and C start down the hill. Upon seeing the first sign of the Bluecoats the chieftain is taken aback and the Indians scatter and flee away. But nothing happens and the Chief comes back. He's shocked that the enemy's numbers are so few but he is even more astonished when the soldiers come to a halt.

"Look! The soldiers on the gray horses...they stand on the ground like the walking soldiers." The chief waves the warriors to return. Hundreds of them hurry back. "Come on! We can kill them all," he proclaims, stoking the courage of the scantily clad warriors. "We will kill them all! The Everywhere Spirit has got them. Come on! We can kill them all."

A great cry arises when the warriors rush the soldiers. Those that are mounted whip each other's horses as they tear out in a frenzy! Those on foot give a loud shout as they swing their war clubs and rain down arrows into the horses and soldiers.

The fighting is hard. The superb guide and scout, half-breed Mitch Boyer and the acting assistant surgeon, G.W. Lord, are killed in the onslaught. After the battle, twenty-eight soldiers' bodies will be found in a deep ravine. Their flesh so badly decomposed that the burial party could only shovel dirt on top of them from above.

To the Indians the battle seems swift—a glorious game with the odds stacked highly in their favor. To the men of Custer's battalion—his companions, his lifelong friends, his own kin—the over three hours of combat is an eternity. Like a churning whirlpool, the bronze skinned horde swirls around the severely outnumbered soldiers—shooting, screaming, stabbing and finally crushing their very souls.

The forty some officers and soldiers on the hill must know that time is running out for them. But there is still a faint glimmer of hope. There is still time for reinforcements to come. On the knoll where George Custer halted to make his stand, fighting General Terry's waiting fight, Custer shouts out a desperate order to Lieutenant Cooke. "Form a circle! Shoot the horses!" Cooke quickly directs the soldiers. At this time, Custer's horse Vic is north of the knoll. Other soldiers are reluctant to shoot their life line, their companions. "It's our only hope, that's an order," shouts Cooke. "The General says shoot the horses." After a moment, Cooke mutters out loud, "It's our only hope."

There are a number of dead horses in a half moon circle. Dead soldiers lay draped over their horses and lay all around on the ground. Above this circle, at the top of the knoll are five dead horses and seven soldiers. The soldiers fire desperately. Most of them will die as brave men. Some will save a last bullet for themselves.

Below, at the half moon circle of dead horses, the fighting will end hard. George Custer, Captains Custer and Myles Keogh among others, are barricaded behind dead horses. George Custer has a brief conference with Tom then rifle in hand, he hurries over to the north side of the ridge to where his reserve soldiers are holding the led horses.

Tom fires a shot then ducks down. He looks over at Keogh. "The General still believes Captain Benteen will come." Tom hollers, as he tries to ease the tension of their seemingly hopeless state of affairs.

"You believe they'll come Tom?" Keogh says, while he shoves cartridges into the cylinder of his colt.

Tom shakes his head in the negative. "He's always the idealist. He said to me, could be they are cut off."

"Yeah." Keogh raises his arm over the dead horse and fires a couple of shots at several Indians running by below them, "n' I don't like Irish whiskey."

Tom gives a half smile. "I laughed...then I told him, scared off maybe! How n' blue blazes could they be cut off? Every Indian in Dakota Territory is around us."

Both men laugh nervously.

Lieutenant Cooke chimes in from above. "Bet five dollars they don't come!"

Tom grins. "Autie still owes me five...come to think of it, ten now after I found out about Charley. Might even be fifteen? I wonder how Charley fared down in the valley?"

Cooke fires at an Indian that jumps up from the grass fifty feet below. "With Major Reno runnin' out on his soldiers, if I know Charley Reynolds, he'll go down swinging!"

"You can bet your boots on Charley going down shooting. I wouldn't want to be one of those red-visaged Dakotas ridin' near Charley's trusty Sharps." Keogh pauses, waiting for an answer. None comes. "Hey, boys doesn't a battle cancel all bets?" Keogh quips.

"Darn it all. You're right, Keogh." Tom mutters. "There goes my ten dollars."

"You'd better collect before long." Keogh grimaces, realizing that he shouldn't have said it and starts to apologize. "My apologies..."

"No apologies needed, Captain." Tom fires another shot then quickly reloads. "I wonder what they're mad about? They were fine at the dance last night." Tom chuckles.

"Yeah, Ol' Sittin' Bulls' Sun Dance!" Keogh gives Tom a serious gaze then quietly laughs.

Tom looks above them. He watches Lieutenant Cooke reload his pistol from behind a dead horse. Close by, the handsome 2nd Lieutenant, Van W. Reily, wounded and semi-conscious, slowly crawls around clutching his pistol. 1st Lieutenant Algernon Smith lies on the ground dying of wounds he received while leading E Company in the onslaught several hundred yards below. Smith along with several others barely made it back to the hill. He fell off his horse and the others dragged him behind the dead horses that were shot for the barricade. Other soldiers from C Company are scattered helter skelter about the field.

Tom's eyes closely follow his brother, mounted on Vic. George Custer leads two platoons in a fierce charge on the Indians that approach from the northwest. Vic's white forelegs gleaming in the sunlight as the gallant horse carries his master forward. Charge after charge Custer carries out, keeping the Indians in apprehension. Custer reins his gallant horse around the knoll towards the east, charging more Indians. The Indians scatter in every direction but then return when the charge ends. Before leaving, Custer had left the senior officer Captain Keogh in command. Custer had said that he was going to execute a maneuver to catch the attention of the reinforcements that are on the high hills two or three miles away.

Minutes later, Tom apprehensively listens to the spasmodic bursts then the steady gunfire coming from over the ridge. Several minutes later, a barrage of shots rings out. Tom dashes to the top of the knoll. Towards the east the dust and smoke is thick. The men with Custer scatter in all directions only to be shot or dragged off their mounts by hidden warriors. Those that are killed outright are the privileged ones.

Like a mirage emerging out of the dust and powder smoke, George Custer rides furiously up the slope. Another barrage of shots sounds off from the surrounding hillsides. Clouds of powder smoke emanate from the grass, sagebrush and hidden draws and ravines of the landscape. Tom watches in horror as his brother suddenly slumps over in the saddle. Tom runs franticly to reach his brother. He fires his pistol while he runs, killing a warrior and thinning out the Indian horde. A distant shot rings out, powder smoke emanates from the grass on a nearby ridge top. Custer's warhorse, Vic, or Victory, the proud winner of seven races screams his last. Custer's prized gelding hits the ground, his strong legs stretched out still in racing form. Tom reaches out to his brother, barely grabbing him as he tumbles from the saddle.

Keogh and Cooke rush to help. Cooke directs the soldiers barricaded behind the dead horses at the top to provide a withering cover fire. Tom and Keogh drag their fallen comrade behind a dead horse at the barricade.

Through a hole in his left breast, his life's' blood oozes from the wound of the flamboyant Commander of the famous 7th Cavalry. The seeping blood colors splotches of crimson on General Custer's white deerskin jacket.

Tom Custer rests his brother's head in his lap. "It'll be all right, Autie. We're gonna make..."

Even though his eyes are distant the General's strength and staying power is incredible. He grits his teeth attempting to lift his head. Gingerly, Custer tugs on Tom's sleeve. Tom leans closer. Keogh stoops down. "Tom...'n I...will stay with... wounded...Keogh...Try n' break thro..." He coughs while Tom holds his handkerchief over the wound. "Break...through...Benteen. Don't know why...they're not..." he coughs holding his chest.

Lieutenant Cooke slides to the ground with a troubled look. He fires a couple of shots to let the Indians know that there is still a restful place in the, "happy hunting ground," for any brave Indian soul that gets too close.

Captain Keogh gives a worried look at Tom and Cooke then quietly states, "It'll be our last chance!" With a quick wave he darts for his led horses motioning his men to follow. "Trumpeter!" he yells.

In a sheltered pocket north of the ridge, Keogh mounts remnants of F, L and his own Company I, nearly one hundred soldiers. "We've got to break through to the other detachments. Do anything to draw their attention. That means that some of us are going to be exposed on the high ridges so they can see us!"

Lieutenant Calhoun, Custer's brother-in-law and commander of Company L shouts, "That'll be us, Captain!" Before Keogh can respond, Calhoun turns and waves his men to follow south along the ridge. "Company L! Form twos! By the right flank! Fooor Waaard!"

"Whoa up, Lieutenant! We ought to keep the companies together!" Keogh's words are lost in the noise of pounding hooves and gunfire.

Keogh watches in dismay as a few hundred yards along the ridge, Calhoun's soldiers are struck from behind by hordes of warriors hidden in the ravines and behind the ridges. Cunningly the warriors had let the column pass by then struck hard from the rear. "They've got Calhoun flanked! Trumpeter! Sound the charge!" Keogh shouts.

Instantly, the bugle sounds and Keogh's soldiers gallop down the backside of the long hogback ridge to assist Calhoun and draw attention to the watching soldiers on the high point.

A long time later, suddenly an onslaught of shots comes from behind the ridge where Keogh and his hundred men have ridden. The battle rages fierce, especially on a knoll towards the south. Keogh's men will later be found dead, scattered around him on the lower part of the ridge. Keogh's dead trumpeter lays straddled across Keogh's body, his sergeant close by. Lieutenant Calhoun and his dead soldiers would be found, not far away, on a knoll southeast of Custer Hill.

On the hill below the half-moon circle of dead horses, shot by the General and his soldiers for a barricade—Autie Reed and Boston Custer are killed with a barrage of gunshots and arrows. Tom Custer watches, powerless to help. Hard to see figures crawl, ever closer, inching their way up through the grass and sagebrush covered hill.

George Custer slowly raises his head from the ground. Shadowy figures dart here and there. With an uncomprehending gaze the General looks around. Painfully, he aims his bulldog pistol. Click is followed by click-clack-clunk as he slowly cocks the hammer. Empty. Custer grimaces a rictus grin. At close range, a figure points a rifle, casting an eerie shadow on the blood soaked ground. A loud shot rings out. Custer's head slams into the ground, a bullet through his temple.

The Sioux and Cheyenne Indians have accomplished what no one man or regiments of men could do in four years of fighting in the Civil War. The flamboyant commander, leader of the famous 7th U.S. Cavalry, George Armstrong Custer is dead.

In what the Indians call, time in front, the White Man's future, many Indians would come forth to claim that they had fired the fatal shot, although no one would ever know which Indian fired the killing shot.

A two-time Medal of Honor winner in the Civil War, George Custer's younger brother, Tom, will fight as few men have ever fought before. Tom knows it is all over. He sorrowfully looks around. He coldly raises his rifle. A raw-boned warrior rushes in and grabs it. Tom desperately holds on.

Several more warriors swing their rifles as clubs, hitting both Tom and their warrior friend, a relative of the Hunkapapa medicine man, Sitting Bull. Amidst the dust, yells and grunts, the fierce struggle goes on and on. They grapple in a life and death struggle. After what seems like an eternity, Tom wrenches the rifle away. He points it at the warrior and pulls the trigger. The click from the empty rifle sounds as loud as if it was a cold frosty morning. In sheer desperation, Tom grabs the rifle by the barrel and swings it at the warrior. The warrior ducks. But Tom swings so hard that he loses his grip on the piece and the rifle flies out of his hands, hitting another warrior twenty feet away. The warrior bends over in pain as the butt end of the rifle thuds into his stomach.

Tom attempts to kick his opponent in the crotch. He punches the warrior then grabs his braids pulling him close biting him on the nose. The warrior screams hideously, when Tom Custer attempts to bite his nose off. The other warriors are finally able to help their friend and stab, beat and punch Tom to the ground. They continue to pummel him to a bloody pulp.

They jerk off his buckskin jacket and rip off his clothes. On stripping off his cotton undergarments they notice the "goddess of liberty" tattoo on Tom's arm. They are so angry thinking that he is the Soldier Chief of the army, they hack and brutally mutilate his body. Finally, they disembowel him. Three days later, soldiers who first discovered the dead can only identify Thomas Ward Custer by his initials T.W.C. as part of the tattoo on his arm.

Wounded and semi-conscious, an officer, Lieutenant Van W. Reily's eyes are glazed over. Pistol in hand, his large mustache quivering, he attempts to raise himself up but only has the strength to lean on one arm. Several warriors suspiciously look on at a man that seems to have come back from the dead. Finally, one of the Sioux grabs the pistol out of his hand and fires it at his head. According to the Indians, he would be the last soldier to die.

Barely three miles away on the highest point above the Little Big Horn, a swaggering Captain Benteen, truant Major Reno and nearly seven companies of veteran soldiers have been in position to witness the blood bath. Although too far away to distinguish closely the action, many know that Custer is fighting the Indians. Others turn a deaf ear and a blind eye. While the Sioux and Cheyenne warriors rush to snuff out a few stragglers the surviving 7th Cavalry looks on in dismay, as old men and women descend like vultures on their fallen comrades. The battlefield turns into swirling cloud. Dust and black powder clouds nearly block out the sun.

Beyond the river toward the bench lands, the late afternoon sun is beginning to set in the western sky; long shadows stretch eerily across the Valley of the Little Big Horn. Towards the south, echoes of shots from Major Reno's surviving soldiers and Sioux and Cheyenne riflemen, continue to be heard coming from the bluffs.

Slowly, instinctively stepping over battle debris, a coal black stallion carries his master to the top of a ridge—the place where three brothers had fought their last fight.

Little Bear views the remains of five dead cavalry horses. Their carcasses are beginning to bloat, casting a circle of ghostly silhouettes across their riders' lifeless forms. The air is hot; there is a putrid odor all around and it is difficult to breathe. A giant cloud of black powder and alkaline dust is compounded by smoke from the Indian fires set along the banks of the Greasy Grass. Gradually, the murk begins to drift skyward revealing yet more death and destruction in the valley below. The mournful whinnies of Myles Keogh's wounded Claybank horse, Comanche, can be heard. In answer, Run-Like-The-Wind, whinnies mournfully and Little Bear feels heaviness in his heart recalling his friend's undignified doom. In a gesture to the Great One, Little Bear holds the gold timepiece up to the heavens. With a voice like thunder he speaks.

"Ah Char-Lee...Char-Lee Lo-onesome! Eyomashesha! The White Man's time-in-a-box. I wonder if it knows, today is the time of the Sioux. I wonder, Char-

Lee, if the pentouchers with the talk paper will stop their lies. Only then will come the time for the Wasichus, Char-Lee. I will keep your time-in-a-box my friend. I will wait for the tick-tick to bring the time when we can live with the White Man. No war."

Little Bear studies the shoulder strip he had removed from Charley's jacket, the beaded gift from Running-creek-Woman. "Pony tracks on the buffalo trail," sadly, he shakes his head, "No more." Solemnly he speaks his last words, "Like friends, growing up together, brothers—Eyomashesha!"

The handsome warrior gently nudges his black stallion and the pair moves down the ridge to the bluffs overlooking the river and valley. Little Bear hears commotion from the valley. He watches as four raw, lean, young Indian runners, wearing only breechclouts, mounted on sleek, fast war ponies watch Sitting Bull. Tatanka Iyotake gestures to the four corners of the earth. The young runners kick hard and race off to carry the news of their great victory to the four winds.

As the blood-red sun melts, onto the horizon, a smoky afterglow lingers on the fringes of Montana's battle scorched plains along the Little Big Horn River—for today at least, the land of the Sioux.

Hoof beats pound relentlessly across Montana, Wyoming and Dakota Territory. As fast as a lightning bolt can strike the ground, word telegraphs from village to village. Like a wildfire on a windy day, friendly Indian runners ride into Fort Abraham Lincoln. Apprehensively, Libbie Custer watches out her window as the Indians gesture and talk. She has had a feeling of uncontrollable anxiety and now she feels, in her heart, that something terribly bad has happened. She senses that her companion of twelve years is gone. As if to say, "Goodbye Forever," the misty "riders in the sky" of her vision appears before her.

A few miles down the Missouri River Indian runners race into Thompson's camp gesturing and talking worried talk. Strangely, the cur dogs sense something is in the wind and begin a mournful howl. Old Patch Eye tips his head backwards, his jaws open wide forming a low and long mournful plea.

Walks-on-Ice and Running-creek-Woman watch Thompson with a disquieting look. Running-creek-Woman clutches her belly feeling for the unborn child in her womb. Tears well up in her eyes and she begins a keening, wailing Arapaho dirge. Walks-on-Ice sobs and joins her. The two sisters hold each other. Cheek to cheek together they sob.

The valley of the shadow of death is silent now. Nearly three hundred bodies lay strewn across the dusty hills and valley floor along the Little Big Horn River. The bodies of those brave men will turn black and bloat in the hot sun for nearly three days before receiving a scant burial, a scene of sickening ghastly horror.

Before that memorable day of June 25, 1876, will end the Thunderbird has begun to show its face. A deep rumble reverberates through Montana's wild mountainous country. Ominous black clouds gather over the White Rain Mountains. Rain starts to fall. The giant black bird swoops across the darkening sky then down over the Wolf Mountains. Lurid fingers of lightning shoot from its talons. Flaming arrows touch the earth then career silently into oblivion. Dark clouds mingle and collide. Thunder crescendos then rumbles along the hills, echoing off the river and across the valley floor, invading the deathly silence of those slain. An occasional breeze subdues the smell of death with a whiff of wild chokecherries and buffalo berries.

The lifeless carcasses of Big Red and his master, Charley Reynolds, lay in the grass. The Sioux lance leans over seemingly about to fall. Its red flannel strips flutter a quiet warning. The surest shooting rifle on the plains lies silent in the grass where it fell. In their haste to pillage the bodies the warriors failed to see this prized plunder. It would merit the highest honor in any warrior's lodge. Never again will the Great-White-Hunter-Who-Never-Goes-Out-For-Nothing and his two red horses be seen riding across the Great Plains. The greatest plainsman of them all Charley Reynolds, is quiet. It seems his soft, gentle voice will remain quiet forever.

The distant thunder is beginning to fade now leaving the valley silent. It is a haunting silence. Only the occasional rumble of Thunder Rolling on the High Plains disturbs the peace.

Epilogue

C harles Alexander Reynolds was born on March 20, 1842 in Warren County Illinois. His family was quite religious and Charley was well-educated. He left home at the age of 18 for the Far West. Amongst his contemporaries he was considered a superb scout, guide, huntsman, and a gentleman.

"Without any sort of doubt," wrote E. W. Howe in 1931, "Charley Reynolds was a more efficient mountain and plains man than Buffalo Bill; probably neither Kit Carson nor Jim Bridger was as efficient. So far as I am able to judge, Charley Reynolds was the best all-round shot in the history of the West. This reputation came from such men of experience as General George Crook, familiar with arms from youth at West Point to generalship in the Civil War, and in the Indian wars. He was himself a hunter; he once told me that when a young lieutenant at frontier posts, he was often detailed to supply meat. This is the real test, and General Crook said Charley Reynolds could get more game with fewer shots than any other man of all those he knew in his long experience with scouts, guides, trappers and soldiers. When Lonesome Charley's dead body was found across the river from where Custer made his last stand, fifty-eight empty cartridge shells surrounded him."

An eyewitness account of Charley Reynolds, during the time when Major Reno, without warning lead a panic-stricken rout to parts unknown.

"...Gerard and Reynolds reached the brow of the hill only a minute or two after Culbertson had left it. Although this had now become a very dangerous spot they loitered here until A and M went out, Reynolds remaining mounted in spite of Gerard's suggestion that he ought to dismount in order to lessen the chances of being hit. At the moment the troops left the two were some distance apart and Indians got in between them. Reynolds then started out to overtake the troops, apparently by going along the farther side of the line of timber, which we know now contained a good many Indians. The impression left by Gerard's account is that he did not get very far before he was hit. In falling he lost his rifle and as he struck the ground was dragged some, how far we are not told. The headstone for Reynolds now stands over 200 yards west by north from the point where, according to Gerard, he was hit. Gerard's account seems, in this particular, to agree with an account by Dr. Porter in possession of Mr. Dustin. In this account Dr. Porter said that while he was attending a wounded trooper (Private Henry Klotzbucher, as the context shows) Reynolds called to him that the Indians were firing directly at him and was killed an instant later. The only difference between the two accounts is that, according to Gerard, Reynolds was mounted and riding to overtake the troops, however, that in timing the two accounts tally to a dot Klotzbucher was hit in the volley that killed Bloody Knife, a minute or two before "A" and "M" went out on the gallop...."

—Charles Kuhlman's *Legend in History*

Author's Notes

Many of the events of the fight at the Little Big Horn are based on certain known facts and actual happenings. Careful examination of firsthand accounts and the testimony at the Reno Court of Inquiry form an integral part of what really happened on that fateful day.

Although we will never have or learn all of the facts about the Custer fight, for those willing to do their research there are a number of truths that are available. Keep in mind that bigotry, culture and background contribute to a lack of understanding. And every last one of us has a limited view as we cannot discern motives or intentions.

In order to understand the historical truth of events that day of June 25, 1876, much time and effort is involved. It usually requires many years of research and countless hours of on-the-field study. In a serious study of the fight at the Little Big Horn one must piece together, as you would a jigsaw puzzle, the many confusing and sometimes seemingly contradictory accounts. Once the outside pieces are in place the other pieces start to fit more easily.

The abandonment or desertion (desert means to forsake or leave especially, when most needed), of George Custer's five companies of 7th Cavalry is a well-known fact to many avid researchers of western history. In addition it was a well-known fact to many of the soldiers who survived the battle. But Esprit de corps is a strong inducement to remain silent. Even though they may not have known every detail of what was going on these seven companies still were under orders and military rules to move to the sound of the guns.

As well, there seems to be a wide spread belief that all of Custer's regiment died at the Little Big Horn. Of the five companies that went with Custer, all or approximately 212 men perished. According to General Terry's letter to General Crook on July 9, 1876, of the entire regiment of twelve companies two hundred and sixty-eight officers, men and civilians were killed and fifty-two wounded. Thus a large number of soldiers and scouts, both Indian and White of the remaining seven companies survived.

Not far from where Charley Reynolds body was found just across the river at least four of the Ree and two of the Crow Indian scouts had been engaged in a deadly duel. The scouts were holed up in a grove of trees. Whenever one of the hostile warriors dared to ride in close they were blasted from their fleet ponies. Even though two of the Crows were wounded in the battle within a battle, the fight lasted well over an hour. Because the Crows and Ree scouts stood their ground they had lived to tell their part about the fight at the Little Big Horn. For many years later they proved that as long as one had ammunition that those willing to stick it out and fight could survive that deadly Sunday. Thus, we have a most telling case in point for Major Reno.

Accordingly, it was very plausible for others to survive had it not been for two crucial happenings. Those two happenings will become known as you read on.

Time and distance

A most important facet of the fight and a most critical one is the timing of events. The crafty Lyman Gilbert, Major Reno's lawyer at the Court of Inquiry on January 13, 1879, saw this importance:

> "The question of time and distance about which such differing evidence has been given is not in my mind of great importance except as it determines the relation of one command to another. And this relation and position can as the court has no doubt already observed be fixed independently of watches."

But was this, "relation and position," as the court supposedly had already observed, "be fixed independently of watches?" In other words, what battalion was where and when in relation to the other battalions?

Consider briefly, the regiments' 12 mile journey to the Little Big Horn on the day of battle. Almost all of the officers and soldiers either testified or made out reports that along those 12 miles there was a lone teepee and a water hole. Since that day the teepee or Sioux burial lodge has been known as, "the lone teepee." The water hole back then was often called a morass. Once we know the correct locations of those two prominent landmarks, "the lone teepee," and the morass, we can gauge the participants' testimony in relation to time and distance to or from those landmarks. Understandably, once we know the correct sites, those locations never change. They are fixed landmarks the same as Custer Hill, or Reno Hill. Thus we have a time factor.

Once we know the locations of those well-known landmarks we can eliminate preposterous sayings such as Captain Benteen and Major Reno's testimonies.

Captain Benteen stated:

> "I think it was 7 miles from the burning tepee to the morass. I am convinced that when the order brought by Martin reached me Gen. Custer and his whole command were dead."

Major Reno stated:

> "I believe that when I came out of the timber Custer's command was dead."

It seems that Reno and Benteen convinced the court of their faulty reasoning. Supposedly Custer was already dead so what difference would their delay matter? The facts bear out that George Custer's battalion had as yet not even engaged the Indians at this time. So how did the disaster happen?

What would have been the outcome had Reno kept his soldiers in the timber? He would have held the bulk of the Indians at bay providing Custer the opening to strike their rear or flank. General Miles who fully examined the ground had the following to say about Reno's position:

"… A strong position that had formerly been the bed of a river, or behind what is known as a "cut bank," where he dismounted his command; his horses being thereby furnished a safe shelter in the brush and timber in the rear of his line of troops. His men occupied an excellent position, where they were completely covered behind what was to all intents and purposes a natural rifle-pit, and from which they could fire and easily enfilade the Indian village. If he had held this position it would have been of the greatest advantage and might have had a decisive effect upon the final result."

Consider the first major blunder. Major Reno had fled the valley without warning his soldiers. He abandoned every soldier and scout that was not close to him, including Charley Reynolds. Not one trumpet call was sounded. And during their blind run to parts unknown, only one of those veteran officers made any kind of an attempt to execute any sort of a routine, rear-guard action.

Civilian scout/interpreter Fred Girard rode with the 7th Horse that day. Girard did not have to worry about repercussions from the army. Girard fought down in the valley. He was there when Major Reno pulled foot and ran. This eye-witness said the following about Reno's stampede:

"The Indians picked off the troops at will; it was a rout not a charge. All the men were shot in the back. Benteen and his command came up and the demoralization of Reno's men affected his own men and no attempt was made to go to Custer's aid."

And when those panic stricken men arrived on the hill, Court Recorder Jesse Lee recorded:

"It is but natural however that almost every officer and soldier who survived that disastrous move from the timber to the hill would in his own mind by imperceptible degrees ultimately arrive at a conclusion that after all it was the best thing to do-and results which could not be foreseen at the time may have been taken into consideration to excuse or palliate. Esprit de corps is a strong inducement to participants to do this not withstanding they may have no responsibility in the matter."

Court Recorder Lieutenant Jesse Lee's answers to the court at Reno's Court of Inquiry are crucial for understanding Custer's demise. Finally, when all is said and done, time and distance means lives saved or lives lost. In this case its result was the complete annihilation of five companies of Custer's 7th Cavalry. Lieutenant Jesse Lee likely said it best at Major Reno's Court of Inquiry. Consider blunder number two.
Lieutenant Lee had written:

"It is an undisputed fact that Gen. Custer received no support whatever from the seven companies of his regiment which remained on the hill under Maj.

Reno's command. It seems that there was indecision and tardiness and that the move that was made downstream was not begun by Maj. Reno's orders until after the pack train had arrived. Two pack mules were sent for each carrying 2000 rounds of ammunition and none was issued. Lieutenant Wallace testified that he saw one box opened and men helping themselves. So it appears that Maj. Reno's command was not so badly in need of ammunition after all."

Only one of the seven companies, D Company made any kind of an attempt to engage the Indians. A general officer of that time period, General Nelson Miles, was quite familiar with Indian fighting having fought in the Indian Wars himself. General Miles had a remarkable record. He was in command when both Geronimo and Chief Joseph surrendered. He knew Custer and his officers well. General Miles had the following to say about Company D's attempt to go to Custer and the others lack of support:

> "That may have been a time when one troop under a gallant officer might not have been able to go where seven troops could and ought to have gone."

Only Captain Weir's Company D attempted any kind of movement to assist Custer. After hours of confusion and delay eventually all of the seven remaining companies were corralled by the Indians. Hence they were compelled to defend themselves. Most of those men survived. Thus, providing more evidence that it was possible to fight at the Little Big Horn and live to tell your story.

An in depth study reveals that much of history's timing of events is nearly two hours off. The evidence demonstrates had those officers in command moved their soldiers immediately to Custer when they arrived on Reno Hill, they likely would have prevented the whole disaster. Even delaying one half hour to two hours they still ought to have saved some of Custer's soldiers. Reliable evidence shows that Custer or some of his men were still fighting until 6:00 p.m., perhaps even later. Custer's battle lasted at least 3 hours which means that the seven supporting companies listened to his gunfire, throughout that time and only one company out of the seven made any kind of real effort to go to Custer's aid.

General Nelson Miles wrote:

> "It is not expected, that five troops could have whipped that body of Indians, neither is it believed that that body of Indians could have whipped twelve troops of the Seventh Cavalry under Custer's command, or if his orders had been properly executed. The fact that after Custer's five troops had been annihilated, the Indians who came back and engaged the seven troops were repulsed and they failed to dislodge these troops, is proof that the force was amply strong, if it had only acted in full concert."

Miles then went on to say:

> "No commander of troops can expect to win victories with seven-twelfths of his command remaining out of the engagement but when within earshot of the firing."

Just two years after the battle General Nelson Miles rode the battlefield with twenty-five Sioux and Cheyenne Indians who fought there. And we have to ask why? Why would General Miles go to all that difficulty to ride the same ground that Major Reno and Captain Benteen had to cover and time his ride by the watch? What would prompt General Miles to even consider such an investigation?

Evidently General Miles had some very strong and sound reasons to undergo such a task. Could it have been likely that Nelson Miles might have conversed with several of the surviving soldiers or officers of Custer's command on the 1877 campaign against the Nez Perce? Or is it likely that Miles talked with Custer's surviving soldiers when he was in command of establishing Fort Keogh in July of 1876, only a few days after the battle? With all the talk after the fight it seems highly probable that surviving soldiers would be more than ready to tell all that they knew especially to a veteran general, active in the army at that time. Is it possible that General Miles believed that Custer had received no support from the remaining seven companies?

Miles gives us some insight into his possible reasons for his lengthy ride (at least 300 miles there and back) to examine the battlefield. Miles wrote:

> "It was a terrible affair, almost a national disaster; and there were some most remarkable features connected with it. The loss of two hundred and sixty-two men under such circumstances would have caused a very searching investigation in almost any country, and it is strange that there has never been any judicious and impartial investigation of all the causes that led to that disaster."

After his full examination of the battlefield General Miles wrote:

> "At a smart trot or gallop as a cavalryman goes into action fifteen minutes would have brought the whole command into the engagement. This we proved on that same ground by the actual test of moving our horses over it and timing them by the watch."

Again we repeat what General miles wrote above:

> "No commander of troops can expect to win victories with seven-twelfths of his command remaining out of the engagement but when within earshot of the firing."

Why would General Nelson Miles have ridden the same route—the very ground— that Major Reno and Captain Benteen had to travel to reach Custer? And furthermore, why would he have timed his ride by the watch if he had not believed that those two senior officers had the time to lead their battalions to Custer's relief? The evidence is powerfully clear that Miles suspected from the beginning that Major Reno and Captain Benteen had been close enough and had the time to support Custer.

That leads to another question. Why was nothing done by the army?

Why did the army not follow up with an investigation of the death of over 265 of its men? Perhaps the following is the answers: With President Grant still smarting over George Custer's testimony at the Heister Clymer hearings, it doesn't appear likely that the President would have allowed Generals Sherman or Sheridan to proceed with any kind of an investigation, especially with the President's public hostility towards George Custer. Furthermore, it is not too difficult to imagine what a slam it would have been for the Seventh Cavalry to have had the truth revealed to the public in 1876. What a huge black mark or pall would have been cast on the most Romanticized regiment on the plains less than ten years after its infancy. Even now the Custer conflict is still one of the most written about subjects in American History, perhaps the world.

In a Nut Shell, the Custer Fight

*O*n June 21, 1876, the steamboat, Far West lay in the waters of the Yellowstone River moored tightly along the bank. That afternoon, General Terry's conference with his commanding officers took place aboard the steamer. The conference was held to settle on a plan regarding the Indians and which column, the Dakota, or the Montana column would go in pursuit of the Indians.

The Indians were first discovered on the Tongue River in the latter days of May by Lieutenant James Bradley who commanded the mounted detachment and Indian scouts with the Montana Column. Major Reno's scout from June 10th to the 17th had trailed those same Indians south up the Rosebud River.

The historical evidence verifies that most, if not all of the commanding lieutenants of the expedition had expected the Indians, mostly Sioux and Cheyenne, to be on the upper portion of the Little Big Horn River. The, *"general impression,"* was as Custer said in his letter on June 22 to the *New York Herald* that the Indians would be on the headwaters of the Rosebud and Little Big Horn.

The Dakota column was selected to follow the Indian trail south up the Rosebud. General Terry himself would accompany Colonel John Gibbon's Montana column. The Far West would transport Terry, Gibbon and Major Brisbin up the Yellowstone near the mouth of the Big Horn River. At that point, the Montana Column and its supplies would be transferred to the south bank of the Yellowstone. That column would move south with hopes of cooperating with the Dakota Column provided the Indians were found. General Terry had written to Sheridan that the first column to strike the Indians there *"might be a waiting fight."* In other words, the column that made the first contact with the enemy might have to fight a holding action, to create or make available enough time for the other column or columns to get there. Days before the battle, Lieutenant Bradley, who evidently got his information from General Terry, wrote, in his diary that whichever column found the Indians first, was at liberty to attack.

Before departure, Custer received a hand written letter of instructions from General Terry. At 12:00 noon, June, 22, Custer's regiment, twelve companies of the 7th U.S. Cavalry started on the trail of the Indians. The further south they followed the trail, the wider it became. On June 24 the trail kept getting fresher and fresher, especially so towards evening. Lieutenant George Wallace who kept the official itinerary recorded that they had passed through several large camps and the valley was marked up from the numerous trailing lodge poles. To the scouts the sign indicated that the Indians were not over thirty miles ahead. The 7th could overtake them. Two miles below the mouth of Davis Creek[1] George Custer's regiment halted to make camp. The Little Big Horn River was across the divide to the west, about 24 miles away.

There are those who accuse Custer of rushing into battle exhausting his men and horses. But when we know and examine the hard facts, we find that Custer's mileage was actually less than 30 miles a day as spoken by General Terry's letter. The following should squelch any lingering doubt and false accusations that Custer rushed to battle.

As previously stated, General Nelson Miles actually conducted a full examination of the battlefield just two years after the fight. With him he had 25 Sioux and Cheyenne that had participated in the battle. He conducted many firsthand interviews with numerous soldiers and enemy Indians who fought in the battle. Miles wrote:

> "A general impression has gone abroad and to some extent prevails throughout the country to-day, prejudicial to General Custer. He has been accused of, "disobeying orders," and it has been said that, "he had made a forced march," that, "he was too impatient," that, "he was rash," and various other charges have been made, equally groundless and equally unjust, and all started and promoted by his enemies."

Those words of General Miles, "equally groundless and equally unjust," might sound a little harsh to historians today who have accused Custer of rushing into battle. However, they might want to look closely at the written record. The day before battle, during the 24th, there were several long periods of rest that lasted for hours. Darkness had already set in when Custer was informed by his Crow Indian scouts, who had been scouting to the front that the Indian trail had unexpectedly turned west.

Some accuse Custer of immediately turning west on the Indian trail claiming that he had somehow planned ahead and schemed to do this all along. Of course, they say, this move was to garnish all the glory for Custer. Careful examinations of the miles traveled and the eye witness accounts show otherwise. It was only after Custer had learned that there were indications that the Indians might be camped on the lower portion of the Little Big Horn River instead of the upper portion of the river, that Custer made his decision to turn west. Undeniably, there is absolutely no way that Custer could have known ahead of time that the trail was not going to continue south along the Rosebud and then turn towards the valley of the Little Big Horn at its upper reaches. The fact that the Indians were within thirty miles indicated they were on the lower portions of the river. This suspected location of the Indian village on the lower river was the one place that the army had not even considered.

Unknown to the Montana Column and its leaders, General Terry and Colonel John Gibbon, they were all in a most precarious position. One of the largest Indian villages ever assembled stood only a day's ride to their front. Lest we forget, those same Indians eight days before, had ridden in the neighborhood of thirty-five miles during the night to attack General Crook's outfit of over a thousand men strong. The Montana Column made up of cavalry and infantry, some three hundred and ten odd soldiers according to General Terry's figure,[2] could be headed straight for trouble. Not only that, Colonel Gibbon was sick aboard the Far West, leaving command to General Terry who basically was an armchair General. As a lawyer, he had spent most of his career behind a desk. With the information George Custer had at the time, he evidently grasped the gravity of the situation as he was not an armchair General.

In addition, Custer was informed by his Crow scouts, who for many years had traveled this country often and knew this land well, that he could not cross the divide that separates Rosebud Creek with the Little Big Horn River during the daylight without his command being discovered by the Sioux or their Cheyenne allies. As well, firsthand evidence substantiates that Custer's plan had been to remain in hiding the next day on June twenty-fifth. Custer would move into position in the dark hours of early morning of the twenty-sixth of June. Another thing, no one knew for certain whether some bands might split off to the north and follow Tullock's Creek.

One other important factor that many fail to consider is Custer's camp; the mere fact that Custer had the regiment set up camp at the present-day town of Busby, Montana, is proof alone that Custer had planned on staying the night there. Anyone who has packed a mule or horse and set up camp can attest to the fact that it is a labor intensive happening. Just think about feeding and watering well over seven hundred horses and mules, saddling those same horses and packing up 160 mules with pack saddles, the heavy ammunition and hardtack boxes, and who knows what else? Furthermore, Custer had no way of knowing what information his scouts would bring him from the front. The facts verify that it was after at least 9:00 p.m. when George Custer finally made his decision to follow the Indian trail west. In addition, many accusers have never even considered the question, what if the Indian camp was not on the Little Big Horn? You see, if the Indian camp was not on the lower reaches of the Little Big Horn, Custer could have easily turned the regiment around, rode back to the Rosebud and resumed his ride up the Rosebud.

Thus, the 7th Horse made a night ride of about seven miles up Davis Creek towards the top of the divide. Custer halted to conceal the regiment. After daylight and only after receiving word from Lieutenant Varnum that the village was insight, did Custer leave to go to the high butte, (the Crow's Nest) to see for himself just exactly where the Indian village was located.

Meanwhile, even though Major Reno was the senior officer it seems that Tom Custer moved the command up the trail a few miles. The 7th was concealed in a sheltered canyon to spend the day of the 25th in hiding. Since leaving the camp on the Rosebud the regiment's total distance, including the night ride, was under eleven miles.

After Custer's return from the Crow's Nest and only after he had had been informed that several different sightings of Indians had occurred, did he decide to attack. Without doubt, these sightings led him to believe that his command had been discovered by the overly aggressive Indians. As we have learned, those same Sioux and Cheyenne Indians had swarmed to attack General Crook eight days earlier on the upper Rosebud Creek.

Several things must have been running through Custer's mind. He had to weigh the chance that if he did nothing or if he had continued south up the Rosebud, the Indians would flee and scatter to the four winds and the army would have to hunt them down again. There was also the risk that the Indians would race to attack his command in this rough terrain. Bear in mind, Custer had been informed by the Crow's that a large village had stood just up the Rosebud from their last camp at Busby. There were signs in that camp that a battle had taken place.[3] It appears logical that any commander who possessed that kind of information would reason; there was a good possibility that the Terry, Gibbon column was marching straight into a hornet's nest or the yellow fly that bites, as the Indians aptly called the yellow jacket. The evidence reveals that Custer must attack at once. Keep in mind, that it was only after these several events happened that Custer decided to attack.

Consequently, the 7th regiment passed over the divide before noon. At 12:05 p.m. George Custer halted his command and formed four battalions. Earlier that morning while at the Crow's Nest the Crow's, George Custer, Mitch Boyer, the half French and Sioux scout, Charley Reynolds, scout and guide and Fred Girard, the interpreter for the Arickara scouts (Rees) had pinpointed the location of the village.

Leaving nothing to chance, Captain Benteen's three companies were sent on a scout to some hills to the left of the main trail to see if there were any more Indians or their camps upstream in the valley of the Little Big Horn. On previous campaigns George Custer had very nearly learned the hard way that the Indian villages could be spread out for miles along the rivers or creeks. Benteen's scout was to be rapid and of short duration. Once Captain Benteen had ascertained that there were no Indians upstream his orders stipulated that he was to return to the main trail at once.

Benteen's battalion was the first to leave. Custer and Major Reno's battalions would follow the dry creek bed (now called Reno Creek) which led to the Little Big Horn River and the Indian village.

Reno's battalion of three companies followed the left bank of the creek bed while Custer's battalion of five companies followed the right bank. Lieutenant Mathey's eighty-four man pack train escort along with Captain McDougall's Company B, whose duty that day was the rear guard, the pack train and the spare horses of the remuda followed around twenty minutes behind on Custer's trail along the right bank. Custer and Reno followed the path of the creek bed which ran—first in a northerly direction then curved around in a westerly direction. At various times, depending on the terrain, up to five hundred yards separated the two battalions.

The lower portion of the dry stream has a south and north branch. (See map) On the lower segment there were two prominent landmarks—a lone teepee and a watering hole or morass, as it was called. But what makes those two locations prominent? Almost all of the participants talked, testified or wrote about—a lone teepee and a morass or watering hole. Captain Benteen wrote about both a burning lodge and the morass in his official report dated July 4, 1876.

Major Reno only wrote about a standing teepee in his official report dated July 5, 1876, and did not mention a morass. In fact, not a one of Major Reno's battalion even made mention of the morass. There is a good reason for this. Why? Nary had a one of Reno's men watered at the morass smack-dab along the main trail. Reno's battalion reined sharply left before the morass hence, none of the Reno battalion saw the morass or water hole.

Accurate locations of these two landmarks are crucial to precisely measure distance and time. In many cases these two locations are our only means to measure which battalion was where and when in the regiment's twelve mile ride to battle. In addition, the eyewitness testimony can be fit onto the land itself and their accounts can authenticate what battalions were where and at what time?

Over the years writers have had one big problem with placement of the teepee and the morass and there is good reason for the confusion. Contrary to popular belief among many, the lone teepee came first then the morass came afterwards on the seventh's line of march. In other words, the morass was west of the lone teepee. Once we place the lone teepee and the morass (or water hole) in their proper places, many events on that day of June 25, 1876, come sharply into focus. One truth discovered, leads to other truths verified.

As Custer and Reno's battalions moved down Reno Creek valley, ahead of Custer a lone teepee stood below a knoll. At least two more were scattered here and there. Custer proceeded with caution. In the neighborhood of three miles from the river and one mile above an abandoned Indian camp, Major Reno's battalion was ordered to join Custer's. Reno crossed over from the left bank of the creek to merge with Custer's battalion. The two battalions then traveled alongside each other for a few minutes. At very close to two miles from the river the battalions reached the lone teepee. Among several others, including Charley Reynolds, Fred Girard rode up on a knoll a short distance from the lone teepee. From the position and height of the knoll Girard could clearly see large portions of the Little Big Horn Valley. He could see dust and Indians seemingly running away. About the same time, a small band of Indians was seen not far to their front. "Here are your Indians running like devils," hollered Girard from the top of the knoll. Soon, Custer ordered Reno to try and bring the Indians ahead of the column to battle and he would support him. Custer would no doubt be wary of an ambuscade thus, he cautiously stayed behind Reno to provide quick support. But the Indians soon disappeared among the trees along the creek.

Previous to this, Lieutenant Hare had been on that same knoll as Girard. He had sent a note to Custer that the Indians were seen running away in the valley of the Little Big Horn. All the indications led them to believe the Indians were about three miles distance and fleeing. It was then that Custer instructed Adjutant Cooke to order Major Reno to go down and cross the river and attack the Indian village in the Little Big Horn Valley. Custer would move his battalion down river on the bluffs to the north and attack as the maneuvering force while Reno kept the Indians occupied in his front.

One thing that should be pointed out here is, even though many officers after the battle claimed that Custer had no plan, their military service tells a different story. How so? Almost all of Custer's officers were veteran officers of the Civil War and had served in the west since 1866. Most of the officers had been with the seventh cavalry for years. They were veteran officers quite familiar with Custer's tactics. Without a doubt, Custer's strategy was clear to most, if not all the officers.

Private Taylor had stated:

"So why was it not good tactics to fall back from the vicinity of the river, drawing the Indians away from their village and Reno, and giving Benteen a chance to strike them on their flank or rear?"

If a mere private, who was not privy to the officer's confidential talk, understood Custer's tactics should not the officers who commanded those very maneuvers have known? Without a doubt they did. Custer's maneuvers amounted to a classic battle plan. To say that Custer did not have a plan was just another trumped up distraction after the battle to keep the public from learning what really happened. Actually to say that Custer did not have a plan doesn't say much for the officers of the Seventh Cavalry. Most of those same officers were at the Washita and participated in Custer's tactics. To say that Custer did not have a plan, is like saying that the veteran officers of the seventh cavalry did not understand cavalry maneuvers. So then the question could be asked; Why or what were they doing in the U.S. Cavalry? Not to be left out, Captain Benteen was expected to join in the combined action. We'll soon find out just how close behind Custer, Captain Benteen's battalion really was.

On the main Reno Creek, around a quarter mile above the junction of the north fork and just around the bend from the morass, Custer and Reno's battalions separated to move into position for the attack. Reno's battalion reined sharply left and crossed the dry bed of Reno Creek. Reno's battalion trotted three-quarters of a mile and watered at the Little Big Horn River. Custer continued his path straight ahead for a few hundred yards and halted to water his men and horses at the north fork of Reno Creek. But where was Captain Benteen's battalion?

Some would have us believe that Benteen was four miles distance and nearly sixty minutes behind. Not hardly. A good comparison of Custer's route with Benteen's route on his scout, show almost identical miles traveled with only one difference. Benteen's route was more rugged but this was only so for Lieutenant Gibson, who was the officer selected, along with six enlisted soldiers, to ride to the top of the high bluffs to see if Indians could be seen, while Benteen and the others waited below. About the time that George Custer's battalion was approaching the north fork of Reno Creek to water, Captain Benteen's battalion had returned from those hills to the south. Benteen had already struck Reno's trail on the left bank of the creek and was either approaching or at the place where Custer and Reno had merged, three miles from the river. Captain Benteen's battalion was only fifteen minutes or less, and no more than two miles behind Custer and Reno. The only thing is though, Benteen's battalion was around the bend of those double looped bends of Reno Creek, out of sight of Custer's battalion. That picture would soon change.

Custer' hard ride up the bluffs, simultaneously with Reno's charge in the valley—Custer's route to the land area of Medicine Tail Coulees

After watering at the north fork, Custer's battalion charged northward up the bluffs at the same time that Major Reno's battalion charged down the Little Big Horn Valley to attack the Indians. At some point on the bluffs it is evident that Custer saw Benteen on his back trail. This is a stunning surprise to many writers, but let us briefly mull over what actually happened on those bluffs. Sergeant Daniel Knipe, from Tom Custer's C Company, was sent to the rear with an urgent message to both Captains McDougall and Benteen to hurry it up. We note the urgency of the message when we read that McDougall was instructed that if any of the packs, except the ammunition packs, come loose that he was not to take time to tie them but to cut them off and leave them.

Sergeant Knipe left Custer from this same area of the bluffs. His firsthand testimony states that he had looked back and could see the dust of the pack train. Knipe would have been looking down hill in a southeasterly direction or up Reno Creek valley. The same valley they had just rode down. The smoke from the burning teepee and the dust from 160 mules would have been easily visible. That dust was about two and three quarters miles away. This is the actual measurement from Reno Hill. In his own words, Captain Benteen stated that he was one mile ahead of the pack train. If one thinks about it, that places him less than two miles away, moving towards Custer on the bluffs.

According to Lieutenant Wallace three companies of cavalry in formation, in a column of two's, would have measured one hundred and fifty to two hundred yards long. Benteen's battalion of three companies, measuring one hundred and fifty to two hundred yards long, mounted on galloping horses, all on a wide open Montana prairie, would stand out like a full moon in the night sky. Can you see the picture?

Another thing, one of Captain Yates duties likely was to assign details as outriders (vedettes) to reconnoiter. One of his F Company details was assigned to inspect the lone teepee. That five man detail surely had been the soldiers who set fire to the lone teepee. We don't know how long that took as there were two or three other teepees with dead bodies in them from the fight on the Rosebud with General Crook's command. The detail had to ride hard to catch up with the battalion as Custer kept moving, stopping only to water. The detail more than likely stopped to water at the same place (north fork) that Custer watered. They rejoined the command while moving up those same bluffs. The F Company sergeant would have immediately reported exactly where Benteen was located.

At this time, Benteen would have been out of sight from anyone on the bluffs as he was below the hill in the trees along Reno Creek. The bluffs or hills that lead up to Reno Hill shield a large portion of the North Fork below the hill. Another thing, Sergeant Knipe stated that he had met McDougall four miles from the Indian camp and that he had met Captain Benteen half way between McDougall and the Indian camp. The Indian Camp was a half mile ahead of where Knipe left the bluffs and Custer. That leaves Benteen only two miles from the camp. The North Fork is one and one-half miles from Reno Hill and Benteen was watering his horses only two or three hundred yards above that. Knipe's half way or two miles estimate to reach Benteen is dead on.

After reporting to Custer, the F Company detail, or details were sent ahead to continue to reconnoiter. On the bluffs, at a point overlooking the river, Custer halted to view the huge village spread out for three miles below him in the valley. Custer then led his command along the west side of a high hill, now named, Sharpshooter Ridge,[4] reined right and rode down a coulee lined with cedar trees nowadays called Cedar Coulee where another halt was ordered. Custer, Cooke and others made a quick ride to the edge of the bluffs overlooking the river then returned to Cedar Coulee. Custer then released the Crow Indian scouts from their duties. Too, he dispatched Private Martini with an urgent message to Captain Benteen who was at the morass watering his horses, still only about fifteen minutes behind Custer and Reno. It is important to understand that Custer, at this particular time wanted only the ammunition mules and not the entire pack train. His veteran officers should have grasped this and eventually did. While on Reno Hill after much delay, Reno and Benteen talked it over and sent Lieutenant Hare to the rear to immediately bring up the ammunition mules.

For reasons known only to Captain Benteen, he would delay at the morass, dawdling away precious time. Sergeant Daniel Knipe, after delivering his message had just left the silver haired Captain at the watering hole. Totally unaware of Benteen's delay, the Custer battalion continued down Cedar Coulee to its mouth. The General reined left entering Medicine Tail Coulee. About this time, near the head of Cedar Coulee, Private Martini and Boston Custer riding in opposite directions had passed each other.

Not too many minutes later, Custer's maneuvering force was on its way towards the river to begin the attack in support of Major Reno's battalion. To the rear, at the morass, Benteen would still be in the same area when Private Martini meets him. Keep in mind that Martini had left Custer nearly twenty minutes after Knipe. At the very least, thirty precious life saving minutes had ticked away on the clock. At the time Custer was moving down the coulee to begin his attack at the river, suddenly two of the scouts signaled him from one of the high ridges near Weir Point. Custer and his brother Tom waved their hats in return. Mitch Boyer[5] and Curly rode furiously down the North Slope to meet him.

Thinking they were bringing good news, Custer again halted his column. The weighty news that Curly and Boyer brought was totally unexpected. The two scouts informed Custer that Major Reno's battalion had fled to the hills on the same side of the river as the Custer battalion. This was shocking news. Without Reno's soldiers to hold the Indians' attention in their front, George Custer's whole battle plan was in serious jeopardy. He must now change his entire strategy because of this.

There is no doubt, from the messages sent and Custer's actions that his plan was to reunite the entire regiment downstream. Custer would delay for a few extra minutes to allow time for Reno to regroup. This would also allow time for the rest of his regiment to come up including the precious reserve ammunition. During the halt, Boston Custer joined the column.[6] Boston would have the newest information from the rear. Indisputably, Boston would inform the General as to any pertinent fresh information, especially concerning the locations of Benteen's battalion, Mathey's escort, McDougall's rear guard and the pack train.

After this, and verifying that his plan had dramatically changed, Custer dispatched Company E, known as the Gray Horse Company, on a maneuver towards the river. While Custer and his other four companies turned up the north branch of Medicine Tail Coulee, Company F was dispatched to a high bluff (lower Blummer

Ridge) just north of their route. While Captain Keogh's companies continued on up the coulee, eventually arriving at the High East Ridge.

At the same time, Custer with headquarters and possibly Tom Custer's C Company, turned up the slope riding two hundred feet or so to the top of Luce Ridge. From this ridge Custer would be in position to monitor the action at the river and most important on the list, they would watch for the expected arrival of the other supporting companies, along with the vital ammunition carried by the pack mules. Lo and behold, there was some good news for Custer, or was it? It is evident that Custer himself either saw Benteen or was informed by one of the F Company details on the lookout on one of the ridges that Benteen's battalion had joined with Major Reno on the bluffs.

At this time, less than two and one quarter miles ride separated Custer from Reno and Benteen's seven companies.[7] Even though Custer had seen Benteen earlier from the bluffs above the north fork and expected Benteen's arrival, this was extremely good news. The Seventh might not pull off a victory (at this time Custer was well aware of the large camp) but perhaps they could scatter the large camp or they could fight a waiting fight (holding the Indians at bay) giving time for the expected Montana Column to arrive. Custer, who always fought aggressively would talk his strategy over with Captain Tom Custer on his staff, Adjutant Cooke, and Mitch Boyer. It is reported that Boyer knew this land well even down to the miles. Custer's opening skirmishes begin in this area.

At times it is hard to figure Custer's exact strategy and how the companies or battalions were made up. Without any doubt, there was fighting on Luce and Blummer ridges and some fighting near the river. Apart from Custer, both E and F Companies would split up, making four platoons in all. Those two companies were part of Captain Yates' battalion. They obviously would support each other along with the remaining companies. This was a combined action that the whole 7th regiment was expected to participate in and was militarily obligated to execute.

Eyewitness Indian accounts and artifacts, along with dead bodies, confirm that Custer had moved his command in a bold show of force, splitting his command into seven groups. This bold move confirms that at least two companies, likely E and F were split into platoons. Custer was maneuvering and skirmishing, holding the Indians at bay, keeping them in suspense, buying some time for the rest of his command to join in the fighting.

Near the river above a cutback to the north of Medicine Tail Coulee's mouth, Custer had also sent a detail to a high bluff, likely through Captain Yates. Also, ten or more flankers were dispatched to a nearby hill position to support the others and to provide a withering covering fire at any Indians crossing the river and attempting to ride up the ravines and gullies. Clearly Custer expected Captain Benteen, McDougall, and Major Reno along with remaining seven companies to strike the Indians from the south. This would hem the Indians moving up the draws and coulees in between the two forces. Without a doubt, George Custer intended on making his fight in the land area of Medicine Tail and Deep Coulees that contained an ideal crossing at the river. Beyond a shadow of a doubt, all of Custer's coming maneuvers were executed with the belief that the other seven companies of the regiment would join in the combined actions.

An unexpected attack by a party of Cheyenne Indians opened Custer's battle. This skirmish, unknown by many researchers, occurred on what are now called Luce and Nye-Cartwright or Blummer Ridges. Out of the blue, not only was this a complete surprise attack, the Indians appeared from the least expected direction, from above, and not from below where the bulk of the warriors were coming from.

In addition, numerous bunches of Indians that had treed Reno on the hill were now streaming to fight Custer from the south. Totally unforeseen, those particular Indians were coming from the very direction that Custer expected his supporting seven companies to come from. What a shock! With no support in sight those two attacks, seemingly out of nowhere eventually compelled Custer to move to Last Stand Hill away from his expected support. Had Custer's supporting battalions come, this attack by the Indians would have only amounted to a temporary diversion and would not have been crucial. General Miles interviewed 25 Indians on the spot who fought in the battle. Miles had written about this part of the fighting: *"As the Indians tell the story, this was a stand-off fight—give and take."* And when Custer moved further north the Indians also told Miles about the fighting later on Custer ridge: *"Here for some time it was an even contest."*

Militarily wise, Custer's moves were well executed. The General, a man who never left anything to chance, had thought about everything. Well, not quite. His plan ought to have worked except for one thing that he never expected. George Custer did not have any inkling that the others would not support him.

General Custer's horse striker survived the fight at the Little Big Horn. He was assigned duties with the pack train. Sometimes referred to as dog robber, as he ate the table scraps, thus depriving Custer's dogs of them. Private John Burkman, according to today's standard, was illiterate. But his description of Custer's fight is the only one of its kind, and quite stunning. Dog robber, John Burkman, hit the nail on the head when he stated about Custer:

"He knowed he was leadin' his men into a helluva big fight but he didn't figger then that they'd be left to fight and die alone just two miles further on, up on top the hill."

Notes

1. From the high divide west of the Rosebud, Davis Creek trails down in a northeastwardly direction ending at Rosebud Creek. At times, Rosebud Creek was called Rosebud River.
2. Some muster rolls tally from a low of 356 to a high of 377 soldiers and officers.
3. On June 24th Custer had cautioned his Crow scouts to be on the lookout for Generals Terry or Crook's friendly Indian scouts. Custer did not want his scouts to mistake the other commands' friendly Indian scouts for the enemy and perhaps some be shot by error. This information implies that Custer must have evidently believed that Crook or Terry's column would be, or could be in the area, otherwise why the caution to his Crow scouts? Too, Custer's Crow scouts had brought evidence that Crook's command had been in a fight with the Indians. On the evening of the 24th Custer's Crow scouts brought him scalps and white man beards that they had picked up from one of the Sioux camps along the Rosebud. That evidence is convincing that Custer had knowledge of Crook's fight before he decided to turn west on the trail. This may have been running through Custer's mind, reasoning that if he stayed in hiding on the 25th then moved into position on the morning of the 26th it would allow more time for the Wyoming and the Montana column to participate in the combined action.
4. It is highly likely that Custer would have dispatched a detail to this high ridge to look for Benteen's battalion or for other tactical reasons.
5. This may well be the sole reason why Mitch Boyer died with Custer. How so? Consider the following. While at the halt in Cedar Coulee Custer released the Crow scouts. They were not required to fight. They had led him to the Sioux and now they were free to go. The other Crows survived the fight as they left Custer at Cedar coulee. Mitch Boyer and Curly also left the halt, but chose to ride up on Weir Point or close by to watch the fighting. Not too many minutes later they witnessed Reno's panic rout to the hills. This was a shocking event and a matter of the utmost urgency. It is the author's belief that Mitch Boyer the loyal man that he was, took it upon himself to inform Custer of the gravity of the situation. Boyer and Curly hurriedly rode to the bluff's edge and signaled Custer below them in Medicine Tail Coulee. Curly could not speak English, but Boyer could speak English well, having been with different traders and scouting, guiding and hunting parties for years. Perhaps Boyer felt it too urgent a matter for the seventeen year old Curly to be left to try and explain this on his own. After informing Custer those two scouts decided to stay with the command. Curly eventually would leave before the serious fighting took place; Boyer stayed on only to lose his life in a ravine down the slope from Last Stand Hill.
6. Boston Custer, the General and Captain Tom Custer's younger brother was assigned duties as a civilian forger with the pack train. Boston was affectionately referred to by his brothers, George and Thomas as, "Bos." As Custer and Reno's battalion moved down Reno Creek at the lone teepee only two miles from the river a band of Indians was seen directly ahead of the column. Custer ordered Major Reno to, "Try and bring them to

battle" but the Indians disappeared, likely in the trees along the creek. In next to no time, Custer's Indian and White scouts informed him that dust and even more Indians were seen in the Little Big Horn Valley and that they were running away. No doubt Charley Reynolds was one of the scouts. It was then that General Custer made his decision to begin the attack on the village in the Little Big Horn Valley. Around this particular time and unnoticed by many, Boston Custer rode back to the rear of the pack train. He talked with Captain McDougall, unsaddled his horse, caught and saddled a fresh mount then high-tailed it for the front to join his brothers. Many writers, including some historians, have never satisfactorily answered, how was it possible for Boston Custer to join his brothers before George Custer's battalion was ever engaged and yet Benteen, who was closer to Custer's command than Boston, supposedly did not have time to join Custer? Eye witness accounts bear out that Boston Custer was behind Captain Benteen's battalion and passed Benteen's battalion ahead of him at the morass or water hole as he rode to join his brothers. How was it possible for, "Bos" to do this and yet purportedly there was not enough time for Benteen, or Reno, or McDougall to provide support for Custer? How was it possible for Boston Custer to pass Benteen at the morass then ride past Private Martini at the head of Cedar Coulee? (See map) Keep in mind that Private Martini had just left Custer in Cedar Coulee only a few minutes before. Martini was carrying an urgent message to the rear to Captain Benteen. Accurate placement of the lone teepee and the morass or water hole helps immeasurability to understand this scenario. Many writers egregiously place the lone teepee four and one-half miles up Reno Creek or even further up the creek. More so than the lone teepee, writers mistakenly place the morass four and one-half miles to six and one-half miles up the creek when the morass was much closer to the river. As you will see by the map and the accurate placement of the lone teepee and the morass the unexplainable questions of Boston Custer's ride are readily answered. After passing Benteen at the water hole only three-quarters of a mile from the Little Big Horn River Boston Custer had only a two mile jaunt to reach the head of Cedar Coulee. On a fresh horse Boston had likely around a fifteen minute gallop to his rendezvous with Private Martini at the head of Cedar Coulee. After that, Boston would have reached Custer's column in ten minutes or less joining them during their halt in Medicine Tail Coulee. At this time only a few Indians on the east side of the river were aware of Custer's presence. Custer's battalion was yet to be engaged.

7. The following may have sealed Custer's doom. It is the author's belief that had Custer not seen or learned that Benteen had united with Reno on the bluffs that Custer may have turned his column around and rejoined the others on what is now called Reno Hill. At this time, there were obvious tactical reasons not to continue his charge into the Indian Village. That might come later when he had reunited the whole command. There is another possibility. Custer's actions or what he did do prove that he had decided to make his fight in the land area of Medicine Tail and Deep Coulees. Once he was surprised by the Indians from the high ridges above Medicine Tail Coulee and those Indians streaming to his position from the south and his subordinates did not come, Custer was forced to fight a holding action on Last Stand Hill. But even at that, the others did not come.

Hill from which the Crow
Scouts viewed the large
Indian village in the valley
of the Little Big Horn

Custer's Regiment

*V*iew is looking northward. Less than a quarter mile beyond the metal shed or north of the tree line is Reno Creek. The creek was called Sun Dance by the Sioux, Ash wood or Ash creek by the Crows. At its headwaters the creek starts out northward then curves around and meanders for the most part in a westerly direction. On its lower portion the creek has two main branches a south and a north branch. The Sioux and Cheyenne Indian trail led west along the north side of the dry creek bed. Around a third of a mile above the north branch the Indian trail crossed over to the left bank then led to the Little Big Horn River. At different times Custer's command passed along this area. Along this trail on the lower two miles of the creek there were two important landmarks, a lone teepee and a water hole or morass as it was called back then. Almost all the participants gave testimony in relation to either the lone teepee or the morass or both of these landmarks. As the 7th Cavalry arrived at the lone teepee first on their line of march down Reno Creek it is important to view the locations in sequence. Lieutenants Varnum and Hare along with the Crows and some Ree Indian scouts arrived in this area first. Although there are a number of hills from which the valley can be seen from the high rocky tree covered bluff is where the author believes that Curly and the Crow Indian scouts viewed the valley of the Little Big Horn. The hill offered easy access from the trail. The Crow's could see signs of a large Indian encampment, smoke and dust, Indians riding here and there stirring up dust and the herd boys driving a huge pony herd. To the left and below the Crow scouts along the north side of Sundance Creek (Reno Creek) was the remains of a recently abandoned Indian camp. According to several Indian and soldier accounts there were at least two teepees (likely three) spread out over a large area. The lodges held dead Indians killed at the Rosebud fight eight days before. Sometime after the Crow's viewed the large village in the Little Horn valley Custer and Reno's battalions came up.

Gerard's Knoll, The Lone Teepee stood below the knoll in this area

*M*any of the eyewitnesses who passed through the abandoned Indian village stated that one teepee in particular stood about two miles from the river below a hill or knoll. Inside the teepee was a single dead Indian on a burial scaffold. (The arrow marks the knoll below which stood the lone teepee). When Custer and Major Reno's battalions arrived on the scene several incidents took place. From the knoll above the lone teepee interpreter Fred Girard saw Indians about three miles away in the valley of the Little Big Horn. About the same time he saw Indians not far ahead of the column. Girard waved his hat and hollered. "Here are your Indians running like devils." Ahead of the 7th horse rode forty or fifty Indians seemingly unafraid. Girard said: "Custer hallooed over to Reno beckoning him with his fingers and told him you will take your battalion and try and bring them to battle and I will support you." For one hundred and thirty-three years those spoken words to Reno that were directed to the Indians in their immediate front would cause an untold number of writers to confuse Custer's orders. What was said, who said them and at what location were they said? Once the Indians were spotted ahead of the column and in the valley Custer evidently believed that his surprise attack was over. "Burn the lodge," ordered George Custer and the teepee was set on fire by a five man detail from Captain Yates' Company F. And the two battalions moved on. Prudently Custer kept his battalion behind Reno's as a caution that the Indians might attempt to lead them into some kind of ambush. But the Indians soon disappeared among some trees then were seen going up the bluffs above the north fork. Whatever those Indians were up to it was then that Custer had adjutant Cooke issue an attack order on the village in the valley to Major Reno. Custer would deal with those Indians in his front when he rode up the bluffs. The separation of the Custer and Reno battalions took place about one third of a mile east of the north fork junction. As Reno reined sharply left Custer again yelled "Take the scouts with you."After the battle Major Reno used Custer's words above ("I will support you.") to attempt to prove that Custer's support would come from the rear when from the very onset Custer's, attack the village order delivered by Cooke, stated that Custer would go down to the other end (north end) of the village and drive them. The mere fact that Custer continued on in his same line of march to the north fork of the creek demonstrates that his support for Reno was not going to come from behind. Reno understood this from his orders as well as the fact that the Custer battalion did not follow him from behind.

*A*t the flowing together of the north fork and the main Reno Creek, Paul Pryor caught this large snake when we slid down the steep bank to examine the creek bottom. The picture was taken at the exact junction of the north fork. Fortunately this was not a rattlesnake but it certainly got our blood pumping faster. It is likely that some of the soldiers in the Little Big Horn Valley fight faced some gut wrenching encounters with rattlesnakes as they kneeled or lay in the grass. The Little Big Horn River is about three quarters of a mile to the west from the north fork junction. According to several soldiers besides Martini and Knipe, Captain Benteen's battalion watered at a morass on the main Reno Creek only two or three hundred yards (east) above the north fork junction. Benteen was much closer to Custer's battalion than almost all writers of Custeriana have supposed. Benteen's battalion was at the very most only two miles in the rear which measures out to be an easy ten-fifteen minute ride behind Custer. Once we identify where the two prominent landmarks were located in June of 1876, we will be able to see that Captain Benteen's battalion arrived on the bluffs (Reno Hill at least an hour and twenty minutes ahead of histories egregious time. Captain Benteen was on Reno Hill in time to provide the needed support to the Custer battalion. Benteen for whatever reasons along with the other companies, left Custer in the lurch.

*W*hat a morass area looks like. This is not where Custer or Benteen watered. Looking in a southerly direction on the north fork of Reno Creek the picture was taken in June of 1990. Notice the lush green grass where the water from the morass once stood. Note also the low bottom of the creek and the large gully of the creek bottom. Observe too how deep the bottom is. This is likely the reason why Captain Benteen only two miles behind Custer could not see Custer's battalion as it watered along the north fork. Custer's soldiers were hidden from Benteen's view in the low bottom of the creek and by two fringes of trees that jutted out into the valley from the north branch. According to Sergeant Daniel Knipe and Private John Martini, the two messengers sent to the rear to Benteen from Custer, they both met Captain Benteen after they crossed the north branch of the stream within two or three hundred yards (east) of the north fork junction. This substantiates Captain Benteen when he stated that he was on the bluffs above the river in time to witness Major Reno's rout. Some confused matters when they claimed that Benteen's battalion halted at a morass first then after watering he passed the lone teepee. As Sergeant Knipe stated in truth Benteen was watering his horses about a mile west of the lone teepee. In other words on their route down Reno Creek Benteen passed the lone teepee first then came to the morass or water hole. Sergeant Daniel Knipe and Private John Martini, the two soldiers who carried messages to the rear, were the only soldiers who rode past the area of the morass three different times. Those two soldiers were not apt to forget where they met Captain Benteen. For those who do not know, the morass was so close to the main trail that the pack mules floundered into the bog as they made their way west along the trail. Much of the testimony actually states that the morass was on the main trail.

North Fork

At different times, Custer' entire
regiment passed through this area

*T*he view is the tree line of the north fork. Notice the level terrain on the approach to
the north fork of Reno Creek. Except for the missing tall native grasses and sage
brush this is how it might have looked to George Custer. Custer's Battalion rode through
this area. Benteen's battalion along with Lieutenant Mathey, Captain McDougall, and the
pack train came later. About one third of a mile above the north fork junction the main
Indian trail turned left and crossed the dry bed of Reno Creek. According to Lt. Wallace the
official topographical officer and acting engineer Major Reno's battalion reined left on the
Indian trail. Custer continued on and watered at the north fork creek below the tree line.
Reno's battalion turning left helps to understand why not a single one of Reno's soldiers
including the Major himself wrote or testified about the morass. This seems perplexing
because at the same time many of Reno's soldiers wrote or testified that they saw teepees
including the lone teepee. Major Reno wrote about a single teepee in his official report.
Once we have a clear view of what order those two prominent landmarks were located, it
becomes abundantly clear why none of Reno's men saw the morass and failed to mention it
in their testimony or writings. Major Reno's battalion had already reined sharply left before
reaching the morass. Hence none of Reno's men saw the morass or water hole.

*P*icture shows a different view of the north fork of Reno Creek. Note the mostly flat terrain. Custer likely rode right through this site. The morass where Benteen watered is to the left of this picture on the main Reno Creek. Both Knipe and Martini met Captain Benteen likely to the left of the above view or perhaps somewhere in this very view.

*A*t different times Custer's entire regiment passed through this area. Around 600 yards to the northwest from the house is the north fork junction. The morass is no more than 200-300 yards east from the North Fork Junction on Reno Creek proper. Reno's battalion reigning sharply left separated his battalion from Custer's. Reno's battalion likely rode through the area of the rancher's house and outbuildings on the way to the river to begin the attack. The Custer battalion continued ahead for a quarter mile or so where he stopped to water his men and horses on the north fork of the creek. A close up view of the north fork tree line reveals why Captain Benteen, only two miles behind, was unable to see the Custer Battalion until Custer left his watering. Once Custer charged northward up the bluffs his battalion would have been clearly visible to anyone coming behind. The first soldier messenger sent from Custer on his way back to Benteen, Sergeant Knipe, among others, stated that after he crossed the north fork for the second time, now riding east, he looked over south and saw Captain Benteen. He stated that he had seen Benteen watering his horses on the main Reno Creek. The second messenger, Private Martini moved off from Custer nearly twenty minutes after Knipe. After Martini crossed the north fork for the second time he stated that he met Benteen within a couple hundred yards. Evidently the morass extended over a large area. It was just around a bend of the creek (west) from where Reno split from Custer. Evidently, Custer rode past the morass but watered on the north fork. Whether he saw it or not is anyone's guess. Once we place the morass where it truly was located on June 25, 1876, we see that many writers' placement is over four miles off. This measures out to wasted time by Captain Benteen. Many would claim that this time was well-spent on Benteen's off trail scout. But the facts bear out that the time wasted was not wasted on Captain Benteen's off-trail scout but was time squandered at the morass and much, much more time wasted on Reno Hill which ultimately led to the destruction of Custer's five companies.

Little Bighorn River runs in a northerly direction, from left to right below the bluffs.

After watering at the North Fork, Custer charged up these bluffs. Among the high points are Reno Hill, Sharpshooter and Weir point.

North Fork

*O*n his return from his scouting mission on the high bluffs south of Reno Creek, Army Chief of Scouts, Lieutenant Varnum, rejoined Custer as the column moved down Reno Creek. Custer asked Varnum what he could see. Varnum said that the whole valley (Little Big Horn) was full of Indians and that Custer could see them from that rise to their front. The rise to the front (north) was the bluffs lining the east side of the Little Big Horn. (Arrow) The highest peaks on the bluffs are what are now called Reno Hill, Sharpshooter and Weir Point or Ridge. In addition and most important, Lt. Varnum an hour or more before Reno separated, stated that he had seen the Indians in the valley. On several different occasions, Varnum reported his findings to his commander. So, we see that Custer did not ride to battle blind as many would claim. Custer would charge up those bluffs at a thunderous pace to view the village. His course was straight towards Sharpshooter Ridge. We can readily see that five companies of cavalry going up those bluffs would clearly be visible two, three or even four miles away from Reno Creek's valley. Custer and his men would have been exposed on treeless bluffs for at least ten to fifteen minutes. Too, going to the actual ground shows that Reno could not expect Custer to support him from behind, because of the fact that Custer was aware of where the village was located long before his order to Reno. Another thing, if Custer was going to follow Reno, Fred Girard, who went to the river with Reno, would simply have waited for Custer to come to the river instead of galloping back to catch Cooke and Keogh to inform them that the Indians were strong in front of Reno. Clearly, Custer had planned on going up those bluffs before he formulated his attack order for Major Reno. In addition, as Reno's battalion charged down the valley on their attack on the village simultaneously, Custer's battalion charged up the eastern bluffs above the river. Many of the soldiers of both battalions could see each other. Without a doubt, Reno positively knew that Custer's support was not going to come from behind.

Below is double looped bends of Reno Creek. Gerard's knoll stands opposite or north of the western loop. Lone Teepee stood below not far from the dry creek bed.

"We moved down through a small valley and around the foot of the bluff. When we got as far as that we could look down this little valley and see objects ahead of us. We could not tell whether they were Indians or buffaloes. At this point I understand that Custer gave the command to Reno to overtake those Indians and he would support him. ... " This view verifies Sergeant Ryan's above words: Here again the "support him" was directed to the Indians in their immediate front. In addition, by looking at a map or going to the ground itself we can see that the creek curves around, hence "around the foot of the bluff" exactly as Sergeant Ryan had stated. The picture was taken from the gravel road that runs along the south side of present day Reno Creek. The view is looking up the creek in somewhat of a northeasterly direction. This distant view shows Reno Creek's wide open valley. Clearly shows that from the bluffs above the Little Big Horn River and looking up Reno Creek why Custer or anyone of his officers or men could not help but see Captain Benteen's battalion on their back trail or vice versa. The sightline from the most northerly point of Reno Hill is less than two and one-half miles to where the lone teepee stood on a wide open plain. Unmistakably, with glasses Benteen's battalion would have been visible from farther away even four miles or more.

A part of the Crow Indian's yearly re-enactment on the large flat at the mouth of Medicine Tail Coulee. This view is looking towards the west side of the Little Big Horn River from Medicine Tail Coulee. This is the coulee that Custer started down to attack the Indian village when he learned from Curly and Mitch Boyer that Major Reno had fled to the bluffs. This forced Custer to change his entire battle plan.

*P*icture shows Last Stand Hill at the Crow Indian's yearly re-enactment. Note how large the horses appear. The bluff or hill is to the north of the mouth of Medicine Tail Coulee. The hill was of prime importance to George Custer. On June 27, 1876, five of Custer's dead soldiers were found on the east side of the bluff near the top. The author believes that those bodies were soldiers from a five man detail that was sent there to assist other soldiers to cover the vital river crossings. According to the eye-witness Curly, Custer also sent a number of flankers 10-15 near the bluff position. Those men along with the five man detail were dispatched by Custer (likely through Captain Yates) to cover two ideal river crossings, one to the north and one to the south. The five man detail likely was made up of sharpshooters chosen by Custer and Adjutant Cooke. In the 1870s Plains Indian warfare, it is hard to visualize someone foolhardy enough to ride within range of this bluff with crack shot soldiers shooting down at you from a concealed position above. Custer's moves are understandable when we believe the eyewitness that Custer had learned that Major Reno had fled to the hills some two miles upstream and that Custer himself either saw or was informed that Captain Benteen had joined up with Major Reno. Custer's moves undoubtedly were executed with the belief that the other seven companies would make haste to the sounds of the guns. Had Custer maintained his safe holding actions on the high points he would have lasted as long as his ammunition held out. Exactly as the "no shows" Major Reno and Captain Benteen did until Colonel Gibbon and General Terry's forces arrived to relieve them on the 27th of June. The physical evidence along with the eyewitnesses clearly demonstrates that George Custer had full intentions of making his fight in the land area of Medicine Tail and Deep Coulees, along with the cut bank and this hill overlooking the river. With his natural ability to make quick accurate decisions it is very probable that George Custer viewed the river crossings as the most vital part of the field. Custer was only forced to move to Last Stand Hill when seven twelfths of his regiment did not show up as part of the combined action.

*T*he author mounted on one of Shawn Realbird's prized quarter horses in the Little Big Horn Valley. Shawn lives here with his family. The river is directly behind at the tree line. Notice the steep bluffs above the river. To the left the bluffs slope down ending just south of the mouth of Medicine Tail Coulee. To the right the bluffs lead up to Weir Ridges which are not shown. According to the Cheyenne warrior Wooden Leg, the Minneconjou and Arrows All Gone camp circles were in this area.

*L*ooking southward we see a different view of the Little Big Horn Valley. In the background to the left are the bluffs or hills that line the right (east) bank of the river. These are the bluffs that Custer rode up and across after he crossed the north fork of Reno Creek. The tree line in the background is not along the river but extends out from the river in the valley somewhere near where Sitting Bull and the Uncpapa Sioux were camped.

*C*row Indian, Shawn Realbird a rodeo Cowboy and a member of the Crow tribe. Shawn, and his family live not far from the mouth of Medicine Tail Coulee. Kindly Shawn and his father Chuck Realbird made arrangements and took me riding. A couple other Crows along with some young Crow Indian boys rode along with the party. Most of the Crow Indians that I've seen ride are expert riders even at a very young age. It certainly was an exhilarating ride to say the least. The horses easily carried us across the river at Medicine Tail crossing as the water was only up to their bellies. Then we rode up and over Weir Ridges. After that we trailed down through Cedar Coulee to Medicine Tail Coulee, Custer's route. We finished up by riding down Medicine Tail Coulee across the large flat and back across the Little Big Horn River. There unquestionably is a different perspective when you sit on the back of a horse and attempt to visualize the Crow Indian scouts or the Sioux and Cheyenne warriors and soldiers as they rode into the extraordinary confrontation on June 25, 1876.

*T*he author on a Montana mustang called Tornado getting ready to make a charge in the ABC miniseries "Son of the Morning Star." The author was one of the White Scouts. The movie was filmed in Montana.

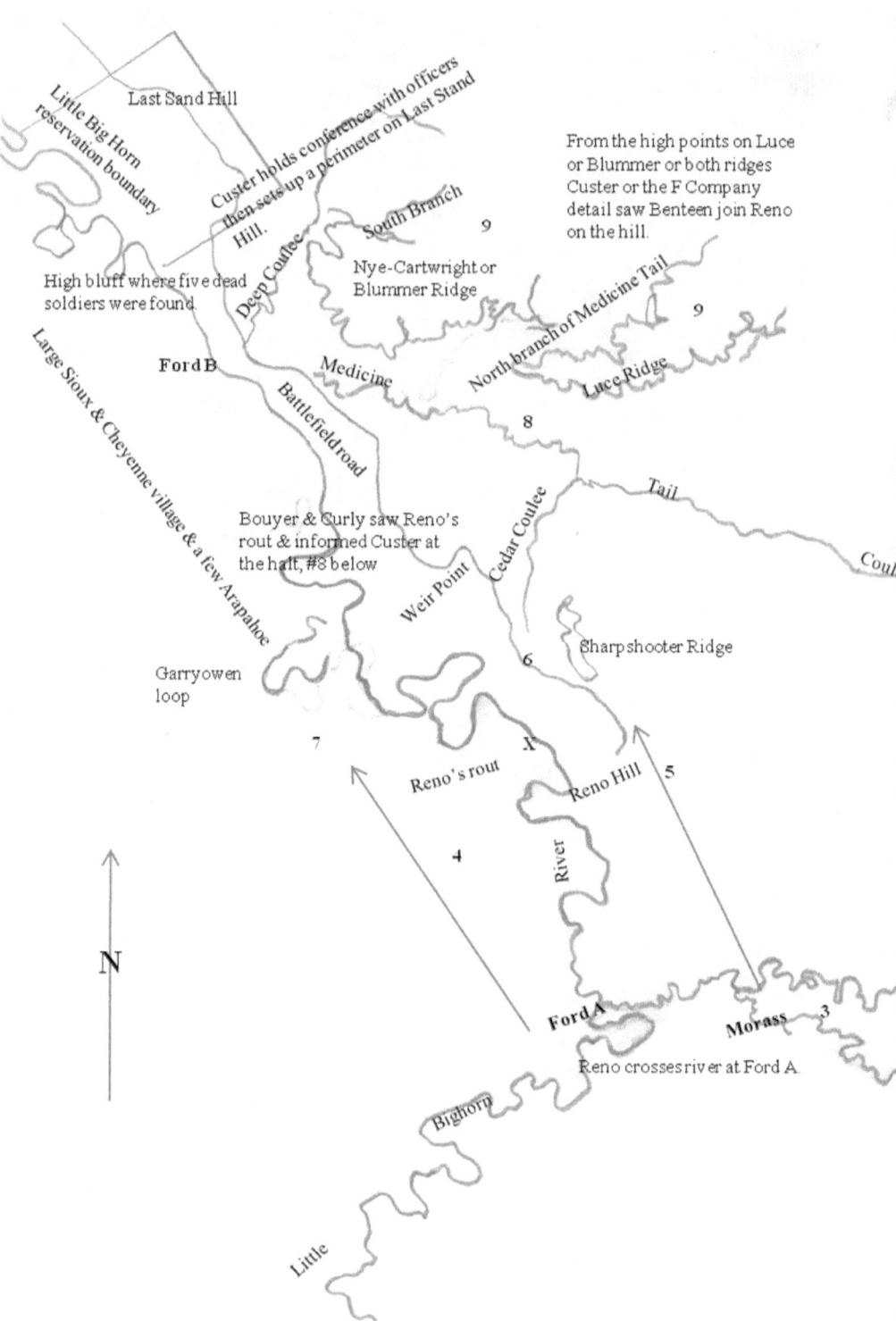

Last Sand Hill

Little Big Horn reservation boundary

Custer holds conference with officers then sets up a perimeter on Last Stand Hill.

From the high points on Luce or Blummer or both ridges Custer or the F Company detail saw Benteen join Reno on the hill.

South Branch

9

Nye-Cartwright or Blummer Ridge

Deep Coulee

High bluff where five dead soldiers were found.

North branch of Medicine Tail

9

Luce Ridge

Ford B

Medicine

Battlefield road

8

Large Sioux & Cheyenne village & a few Arapahoe

Tail

Coule

Cedar Coulee

Bouyer & Curly saw Reno's rout & informed Custer at the halt, #8 below

Weir Point

Sharpshooter Ridge

6

Garryowen loop

7

X

Reno Hill

5

Reno's rout

4

River

N

Ford A

Morass

3

Reno crosses river at Ford A.

Bighorn

Little

Map legend on following page.

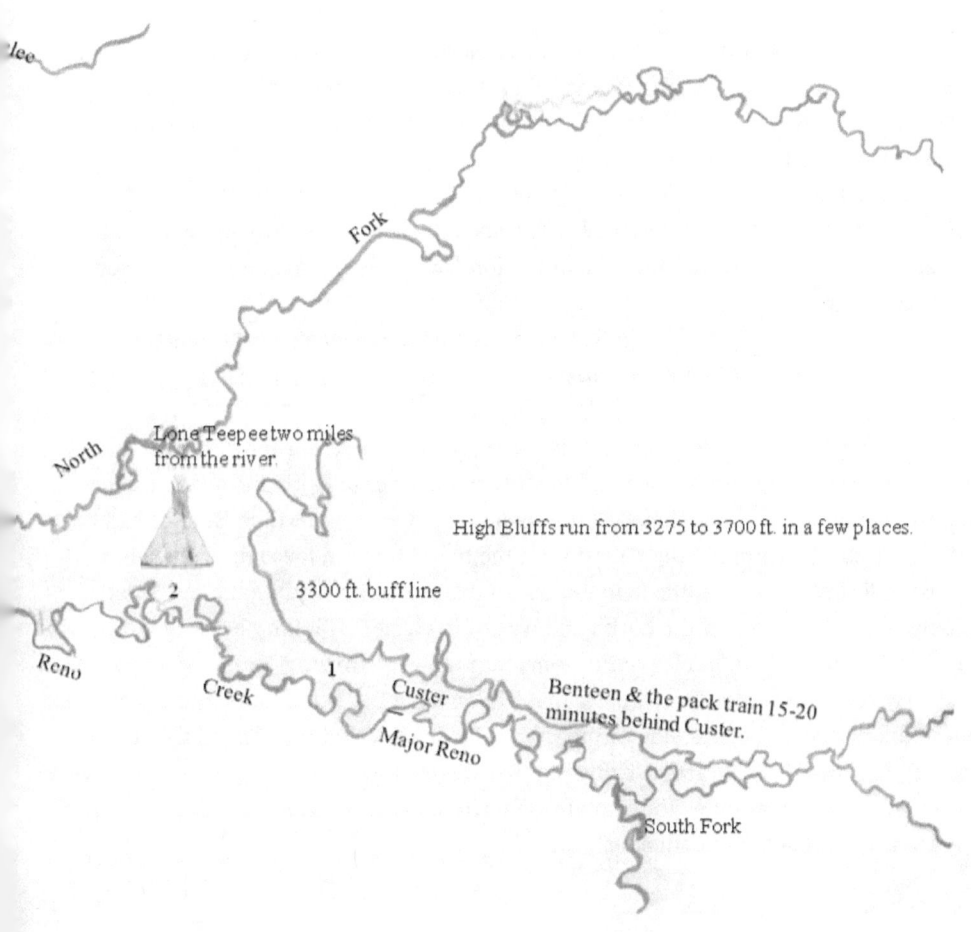

lee

Fork

North

Lone Teepee two miles from the river.

High Bluffs run from 3275 to 3700 ft. in a few places.

3300 ft. buff line

2

Reno

1

Creek

Custer

Major Reno

Benteen & the pack train 15-20 minutes behind Custer.

South Fork

Map Legend

1. Custer's battalion followed the main Indian trail west along the right bank of Reno Creek. Somewhat parallel to Custer, Reno's battalion followed the left bank. Custer and Reno merged around three miles from the river and one mile above an abandoned Indian camp. After returning to the main trail from his scout to the south Benteen's battalion the rear guard and pack train followed along the main trail 15-20 minutes behind Custer.

2. Custer and Reno arrived at Gerard's Knoll and the Lone Teepee. Indians were spotted ahead of the column. The two battalions continued on for a few minutes. Reno received his attack orders.

3. Custer and Reno separate. Custer continues straight ahead and waters at the North Fork of Reno Creek. Reno reins sharply left and waters at the Little Big Horn River at Ford A.

4. Reno charged northward, down the Little Big Horn Valley. After around two miles Reno halted and formed a skirmish line some distance from the Indian village.

5. Simultaneously with Reno's charge, Custer made a hard ride up the bluffs where he halted to view the Indian village below.

6. Custer turned down Cedar Coulee. While in Cedar Coulee, after a brief halt and a quick jaunt to the bluff edge Custer sent Trumpeter, Private Martini with an urgent message to Benteen. Private Martini and Boston Custer riding in opposite directions passed each other near the head of Cedar Coulee.

7. After fighting for 20 minutes or so Reno led his soldiers in a panic rout to the bluffs now called Reno Hill. When he reached the top of the hill he was joined by Captain Benteen's battalion, Custer as yet to be engaged.

8. Upon leaving Cedar Coulee, Custer's battalion, the maneuvering force, reined left and entered Medicine Tail Coulee on his route to the river to begin his attack on the Indians in support of Major Reno. At this same time, Curly and Mitch Bouyer had been watching Reno's fighting in the valley from the high bluffs on the right bank. They witnessed Reno's panic stampede to get out of there. Bouyer leading the two scouts quickly rode to the edge of the bluffs and waved to Custer. Thinking it was good news, Custer halted his battalion. He would soon learn the very worst of bad news. Bouyer and Curly rode down to inform Custer that Major Reno had pulled foot and led a panic rout to the bluffs on the east side of the river. This unexpected rout forced Custer to change his entire battle strategy. Knowing that Benteen was only 15 minutes to the rear Custer waited a few minutes for Captain Benteen to come up. Curly confirmed Custer's halt. Benteen did not come quick as ordered.

9. The physical and the eyewitness's testimony clearly demonstrate that Custer was making his fight in the land area of Medicine Tail and Deep Coulees. This area included the vital river crossing and the cut bank bluff, north of the large flat at the river. Custer's fight began on Luce and Blummer or Nye-Cartwright ridges. It is beyond question that Custer had wanted to rally the entire regiment downstream. Reno's panic rout along with Benteen's failure to obey Custer's written order, and the lost time contributed in large measure to the extreme confidence and boldness of the Indians. Eventually with no supporting companies showing up Custer was forced to set up a perimeter on the high points in the area of Last Stand Hill. But still, Custer received no support from the seven remaining companies. Not one iota. Some sat on the bluffs, the commanding officers in total fear, apprehension, confusion, panic and whatever else you want to call it. Those men were under military obligation to move. Both Captains McDougall and Benteen had orders to move to Custer. When all is said and done, Custer's five companies were left in the lurch, deserted, abandoned, forsaken, ditched, cast off.

www.ingramcontent.com/pod-product-compliance
Lightning Source LLC
Chambersburg PA
CBHW020422030726
47495CB00006B/1620